SAS
STORIES OF
HEROES VI

JAY GARNET
SHAUN CLARKE
DAVID MONNERY

BLITZ EDITIONS

This edition published in 1995

Published by Blitz Editions
an imprint of Bookmart Limited
Registered Number 2372865
Trading at Bookmart Limited
Desford Road, Enderby
Leicester, LE9 5AD

Copyright © 1995 by 22 Books

The moral right of the author has been asserted

ISBN 1 85605304 0

Typeset by Hewer Text Composition Services, Edinburgh
Printed in Great Britain by Cox and Wyman Limited, Reading

SOLDIER Q: SAS

KIDNAP THE EMPEROR!

SOLDIER Q: SAS

KIDNAP THE EMPEROR!

Jay Garnet

Prologue

Addis Ababa, Ethiopia.
'Haile Selassie, former Emperor of Ethiopia,
who was deposed in a military coup last year,
died in his sleep here yesterday aged 83. A
statement by Ethiopian radio said he died of
an illness after a prostate gland operation two
months ago. He was found dead by attendants
yesterday.'

The Times, 28 August 1975

April 1976

North and east of Addis Ababa lies one of the hot-
test places on earth. Known as the Afar or Danakil
Depression, after two local tribes, it points like an
arrowhead tempered by the desert sun southwards
from the Red Sea towards the narrow gash of
Africa's Rift Valley.

For hundreds of square miles the plain is unbroken but for scanty bushes whose images shimmer
above the scorched ground. Occasionally here and
there a gazelle browses, wandering between meagre
thorn bushes across rock or sand streaked with
sulphur from the once volcanic crust.

Even in this appalling wilderness, far from the

temperate and beautiful highlands more often associated with Ethiopia, there are inhabitants. Most
are herders who wander the scattered water-holes.
But some make a precarious living trading slabs
of salt levered from the desert floor – some five
million years ago the depression was a shallow inlet
of the Red Sea and its retreat left salty deposits that
still cake the desert with blinding white. Camels
transport the blocks to highland towns.

Soon after dawn on the morning of 19 April, a
caravan of ten camels, groaning under grey slabs of
salt done up in protective matting, set off from their
camp along unpaved tracks towards the highlands.
There were three drovers – two teenagers and
their father, a bearded forty-five-year-old whose
features seemed parched into premature old age
by the desert sun. His name was Berhanu, not
that it was known to anyone much beyond his
immediate family.

Yet before the week was out it would be known,
briefly, to a number of the Marxists who had
seized power from the Emperor Haile Selassie
eighteen months previously, and most importantly
to Lieutenant-Colonel Mengistu Haile Mariam,
then number two in the government but in effect
already the country's implacably ruthless leader.
A record of Berhanu's name may still exist in a
Secret Police file in 10 Duke of Harar Street,
Addis Ababa, along with a brief description of
what Berhanu experienced that day.

The caravan had just rounded a knoll of rock. It was approaching midday. Despite a gusty breeze, the heat was appalling – 120 degrees in the shade. Berhanu, as usual at this time, called a halt, spat dust from his lips, and pointed off the road to a small group of doum-palms that would provide shade. He knew the place well. So did the camels. Nearby there was a dip that would hold brackish water.

With the camels couched, the three sought relief from the heat in the shade of the trees. The two boys dozed. It was then that Berhanu noticed, in the trembling haze two or three hundred yards away, a group of circling vultures. He would not have looked twice except that the object of their attention was still moving.

And it was not an animal.

He stared, in an attempt to make sense of the shifting image, and realized he was looking at a piece of cloth being seized and shaken by the oven-hot gusts. Unwillingly he rose, and approached it. As he came nearer, he saw that the cloth was a cloak, and that the cloak seemed to be concealing a body. It had not been there all that long, for the vultures had not yet begun to feed. They retreated at his approach, awaiting a later chance.

The body was tiny, almost childlike, though the cloth – which he now saw was a cloak of good material – would hardly have been worn by a child.

Berhanu paused nervously. Few people came to this spot. It was up to him to identify the corpse, for he would no doubt have to inform some grieving family of their loss. He walked over to the bundle, squatted down and laid the flapping cloak flat along the body, which was lying on its face. He put a hand on the right shoulder, and rolled the body towards him on to its back.

The sight made Berhanu exhale as if he had been punched in the stomach. His eyes opened wide, in shock, like those of a frightened horse. For the face before him, sunken, emaciated, was that of his Emperor, Haile Selassie, the Power of Trinity, Conquering Lion of Judah, Elect of God, King of Kings of Ethiopia. Berhanu had known little of Ethiopia's steady collapse into poverty, of the reasons for the growing unrest against the Emperor, of the brutalities of the revolution. To him, Selassie was the country's father. As a child he had honoured the Emperor's icon-like image on coins and medals inherited from his ancestors. And eight months previously he had ritually mourned the Emperor's death.

Berhanu felt panic rising in him. He fell to his knees, partly in adulation before the semi-divine countenance, and partly in a prayer for guidance. He began to keen softly, rocking backwards and forwards. Then abruptly he stopped. Questions formed. The presence of the corpse at this spot seemed miraculous. It must have been preserved, uncorrupted, for the best part of a year, and then somehow, for reasons he could not even guess at, transported here. Preserved where? Was he alone in seeing it? Was there some plot afoot upon which he had stumbled? Should he bury the body? Keep silent or report its presence?

Mere respect dictated that the body, even if divinely incorruptible, should be protected. Then, since others might already know of his presence here, he would show his innocence by making a report. Perhaps there would even be a reward.

Slowly, in the quivering heat, Berhanu gathered rocks and piled them in reverence over the body. Then he walked back, still trembling. He woke his sons, told them what he had seen and done, cursed them for unbelievers until they believed him, and hurried them on their way westwards.

Three days later, he delivered his consignment of salt, which would be sold in the local market for an Ethiopian dollar a slab. He collected his money, and went off with his sons to the local police chief.

The policeman was sceptical, and at first dismissed Berhanu as a madman. Then he became nervous – for peculiar things had been happening in this remote part of Tigré province over the past two years – and made a telephone call to his superiors in Addis.

From there, the bare bones of the report – that deep in the Danakil a local herder named Berhanu had found a corpse resembling the former Emperor

– went from department to department. At each stage a bureaucrat decided the report was too wild to be taken seriously; and at each stage the same men decided in turn that they would not be the ones to say so. Within three hours the *éminence grise* of the revolution, Mengistu Haile Mariam, knew of it. He also knew, for reaons that will become apparent, that the report had to be true.

For the sake of the revolution, both the report and the evidence for its existence had to be eradicated. Mengistu at once issued a rebuke to every department involved, stating the report was clearly a fake, an error that should never have been taken seriously.

Secondly, he ordered the cairn to be visited and the contents destroyed. The following morning, a helicopter containing a senior army officer and two privates flew to the spot. The two privates unloaded a flame-thrower, and incinerated the cairn. The team had specific orders not to look beneath the stones, and never knew the purpose of their strange mission.

Thirdly, Mengistu ordered the disappearance of Berhanu and his sons. The police in Tigré had become used to such orders, and asked no questions. The three were found, fed, flattered, transported to a nearby army base with promises of money for their excellent work, and never heard of again. A cousin made enquiries a week later, but was met with bland expressions of sympathy.

The explanation for the presence of the Emperor's body in the desert in a remote corner of his country eight months after his death had been officially announced might therefore have remained hidden for ever.

There was, as Mengistu himself well knew, a possible risk. One other man knew the truth. But Mengistu had reason to think that he too was dead, a victim of the desert.

The existence of this book proves him wrong.

1

[faint text from previous/show-through page, partially legible]

Thursday 18 March 1976

The airport of Salisbury, Rhodesia, was a meagre affair: two terminals, hangars, a few acres of tarmac. Just about right for a country whose white population was about equal to that of Lewisham in size and sophistication, pondered Michael Rourke, as he waited disconsolately for his connection to Jo'burg.

Still, those who had inherited Cecil Rhodes's imperial mantle hadn't done so badly. Across the field stood a flight of four FGA9s, obsolete by years compared with the sophisticated beauties of the USA, Russia, Europe and the Middle East, but quite good enough at present to control the forested borderlands of Mozambique. And on the ground, Rhodesia had good fighting men, white and black, a tough army, more than a match for the guerrillas. But no match for the real enemy, the politicians who were busy cutting the ground from under the whites.

Rourke sank on to his pack, snapped open a tin of lager and sucked at it morosely. He had been in and out of the field for twelve years since first joining the SAS from the Green Jackets: Rhodesia on unofficial loan, for the last two years; before that, Oman; before that, Aden. In between, back to the Green Jackets.

The money here had not been great. But he'd kept fit and active, and indulged his addiction to adrenalin without serious mishap. At thirty-four his 160lb frame was as lean and hard as it had been ten years earlier.

But now he had had enough of this place. He was tired: tired of choppers, tired of the bush. The only bush he was interested in right now belonged to Lucy Seymour, who hid her assets beneath a virginal white coat in a chemist's down the Mile End Road.

The last little jaunt had decided him.

There had been five of them set down in Mozambique by a South African Alouette III Astazou. His group – an American, another Briton and two white Rhodesians – were landed at dusk in a clearing in Tete, tasked to check out a report that terrorists – 'ters', as the Rhodesian authorities sneeringly called them – were establishing a new camp near a village somewhere in the area. Their plan was to make their way by night across ten miles of bush, to be picked up the next morning. Four of them, including the radio operator, were all lightly armed with British Sterling L2A3 sub-machine-guns. One of the Rhodesians carried an L7 light machine-gun in case of real trouble.

Rourke anticipated no action at all. The information was too sparse. Any contact would be pure luck. All they would do, he guessed, was establish that the country along their line of march was clear.

But things hadn't gone quite as he thought they would. They had moved a mile away from the landing zone and treated themselves to a drink from their flasks, then moved on cautiously. It was slow work, edging through the bush guided between shadow and deeper shadow by starlight alone. Though they could scarcely be heard from more than twenty yards away, their progress seemed to them riotous in the silent air – a cacophony of rustling fatigues, grating packs, the dull chink and rattle of weaponry. To penetrate their cocoon of noise, they stopped every five minutes and listened for sounds borne on the night air. Towards dawn, when they were perhaps a mile from their pick-up point, Rourke ordered a rest among some bushes.

They were eating, with an occasional whispered comment, when Rourke heard footsteps approaching. He peered through the foliage and in the soft light of the coming dawn saw a figure, apparently alone. The figure carried a rifle.

He signalled for two others, the American and the Briton, to position themselves either side of him, and as the black came to within thirty feet of

their position he called out: 'All right. Far enough.'
The figure froze.

Rourke didn't want to shoot. It would make too
much noise.

'Do as we tell you and you won't be hurt. Put your
gun on the ground and back away. Then you'll be
free to go.'

That way, they would be clear long before the
guerrilla could fetch help, even if there were others
nearby.

Of course, there was no way of telling whether
the black had understood or not. They never did
know. Unaccountably, the shadowy shape loaded
the gun, clicking the bolt into place. It was the
suicidal action of a rank amateur.

Without waiting to see whether the weapon was
going to be used, the three men, following their
training and instinct, opened fire together. Three
streams of bullets, perhaps 150 rounds in all, sliced
across the figure, which tumbled backwards into
the grass.

In the silence that followed, Rourke realized that
the victim was not dead. There was a moan.

The noise of the shooting would have carried
over a mile in the still air. He paused only for a
moment.

'Wait one,' he said.

He walked towards the stricken guerrilla. It was
a girl. She had been all but severed across the
stomach. He caught a glimpse of her face. She was

perhaps fifteen or sixteen, a mere messenger, probably with no experience of warfare, little training and no English. He shot her through the head.

He would have been happy to make it his war; he would have been happy to risk his life for a country that wasn't his; but he was not happy to lose. The place was going to the blacks anyway. So when they offered to extend his contract, when they showed him the telex from Hereford agreeing that he could stay on if he wished, he told them: thanks, but no thanks. There was no point being here any more.

Now he was going home, for a month's R and R, during which time he fully intended to rediscover a long-forgotten world, the one that lay beneath Lucy's white coat.

The clock on the Royal Exchange in the heart of the City of London struck twelve. Two hundred yards away, in a quiet courtyard off Lombard Street, equidistant from the Royal Exchange and the Stock Exchange, Sir Charles Cromer stood in his fifth-floor office, staring out of the window. Beyond the end of the courtyard, on the other side of Lombard Street, a new Crédit Lyonnais building, still pristine white, was nearing completion. To right and left of it, and away down other streets, stood financial offices of legendary eminence, bulwarks of international finance defining what was still a medieval maze of narrow streets.

Cromer, wearing a well-tailored three-piece grey suit and his customary Old Etonian tie, was a stocky figure, his bulk still heavily muscled. One of the bulldog breed, he liked to think. He stuck out his lower lip in thought and turned to walk slowly round his office.

As City offices went, it was an unusual place, reflecting the wealth and good taste of his father and grandfather. It also expressed a certain cold simplicity. The floor was of polished wood. To one side of the ornate Victorian marble fireplace were two sofas of button-backed Moroccan leather. They had been made for Cromer's grandfather a century ago. The sofas faced each other across a rectangular glass table. On the wall, above the table, beneath its own light, was a Modigliani, an early portrait dating from 1908. In the grate stood Cromer's pride and joy, a Greek jug, a black-figure amphora of the sixth century BC. The fireplace was now its showcase, intricately wired against attempted theft. The vase could be shown off with two spotlights set in the corners of the wall opposite. Cromer's desk, backing on to the window, was of a superb cherrywood, again inherited from his grandfather.

Cromer walked to the eight-foot double doors that led to the outer office and flicked the switch to spotlight the vase, in preparation for his next appointment. It was causing him some concern. The name of the man, Yufru, was unknown to him. But his nationality was enough to gain him immediate access. He was an Ethiopian, and the appointment had been made by him from the Embassy.

Cromer was used to dealing with Ethiopians. He was, as his father for thirty years had been before him, agent for the financial affairs of the Ethiopian royal family, and was in large measure responsible for the former Emperor's stupendous wealth. Now that Selassie was dead, Cromer still had regular contact with the family. He had been forced to explain several times to hopeful children, grandchildren, nephews and nieces why it was not possible to release the substantial sums they claimed as their heritage. No will had been made, no instructions received. Funds could only be released against the Emperor's specific orders. In the event, the bank would of course administer the fortune, but was otherwise powerless to help . . .

So it wasn't the nationality that disturbed Cromer. It was the man's political background. Yufru came from the Embassy and hence, apparently, from the Marxist government that had destroyed Selassie. He guessed, therefore, that Yufru would have instructions to seek access to the Imperial fortune.

It was certainly a fortune worth having, as Cromer had known since childhood, for the connections between Selassie and Cromer's Bank went back over fifty years.

The story was an odd one, of considerable

interest to historians of City affairs. Cromer's
Bank had become a subsidiary of Rothschild's,
the greatest bank of the day, in 1890. The link
between Cromer's Bank and the Ethiopian royal
family was established in 1924, when Ras Tafari,
the future Haile Selassie, then Regent and heir to the
throne, arrived in London, thus becoming the first
Ethiopian ruler to travel abroad since the Queen
of Sheba – whom Selassie claimed as his direct
ancestor – visited Solomon.

Ras Tafari had several aims. Politically, he
intended to drag his medieval country into the
twentieth century. But his major concerns were
personal and financial. As heir to the throne, he
had access to wealth on a scale few can now truly
comprehend, and he needed a safer home for it
than the Imperial Treasure Houses in Addis Ababa
and Axum.

Ethiopia's output of gold has never been known
for sure, but was probably several tens of thousands
of ounces annually – in the nineteenth century
at least. Ethiopia's mines, whose very location
was a state secret, had for centuries been under
direct Imperial control. Traditionally, the Emperor
received one-third of the product, but the distinction
between the state's funds and Imperial funds was
somewhat academic. When Ras Tafari, resourceful,
ambitious, wary of his rival princes, became heir, he
inherited a quantity of gold estimated at some ten
million ounces. He brought with him to London

five million of those ounces – over 100 tons. By 1975 that gold was worth $800 million.

In London, Ras Tafari, who at that time spoke little English, discovered that the world's most reputable bank, Rothschild's, had a subsidiary named after a Cromer. By chance, the name meant a good deal to Selassie, for the Earl of Cromer, Evelyn Baring, had been governor general of the Sudan, Ethiopia's neighbour, in the early years of the century. It was of course pure coincidence, for Cromer the man had no connection with Cromer the title. Nevertheless, it clinched matters. Selassie placed most of his wealth in the hands of Sir Charles Cromer II, who had inherited the bank in 1911.

When Ras Tafari became Emperor in 1930 as Haile Selassie, the hoard was growing at the rate of 100,000 ounces per year. In 1935, when the Italians invaded, gold production ceased. The invasion drove Selassie into exile in Bath. There he chose to live in austerity to underline his role as the plucky victim of Fascist aggression. But he still kept a sharp eye on his deposits.

After his triumphant return, with British help, in 1941, gold production resumed. The British exchange agreements for 1944 and 1945 show that some 8000 ounces per month were exported from Ethiopia. A good deal more left unofficially. One estimate places Ethiopia's – or Selassie's – gold exports for 1941–74 at 200,000 ounces per annum.

This hoard was increased in the 1940s by a currency reform that removed from circulation in Ethiopia several million of the local coins, Maria Theresa silver dollars (which in the 1970s were still accepted as legal currency in remote parts of Ethiopia and elsewhere in the Middle East). Most of the coins were transferred abroad and placed in the Emperor's accounts. In 1975 Maria Theresa dollars had a market value of US$3.75 each.

In the 1950s, on the advice of young Charles Cromer himself, now heir to his aged father, Selassie's wealth was diversified. Investments were made on Wall Street and in a number of American companies, a policy intensified by Charles Cromer III after he took over in 1955, at the age of thirty-one.

By the mid-1970s Selassie's total wealth exceeded $2500 million.

Sir Charles knew that the fortune was secure, and that, with Selassie dead, his bank in particular, and those of his colleagues in Switzerland and New York, could continue to profit from the rising value of the gold indefinitely. The new government must know that there was no pressure that could be brought to bear to prise open the Emperor's coffers.

Why then, the visit?

There came a gentle buzz over the intercom.

Cromer leaned over, flicked a switch and said gently: 'Yes, Miss Yates?'

17

'Mr Yufru is here to see you, Sir Charles.'

'Excellent, excellent.' Cromer always took care to ensure that a new visitor, forming his first impressions, heard a tone that was soft, cultured and with just a hint of flattery. 'Please show Mr Yufru straight in.'

Six miles east of the City, in the suburban sprawl of east London, in one of a terrace of drab, two-up, two-down houses, two men sat at a table in a front room, the curtains drawn.

On the table stood an opened loaf of white sliced bread, some Cheddar, margarine, a jar of pickled onions and four cans of Guinness. One of the men was slim, jaunty, with a fizz of blond, curly hair and steady blue eyes. His name was Peter Halloran. He was wearing jeans, a pair of ancient track shoes and a denim jacket. In the corner stood his rucksack, into which was tucked an anorak. The other man, Frank Ridger, was older, with short, greying, curly hair, a bulbous nose and a hangdog mouth. He wore dungarees over a dirty check shirt.

They had been talking for an hour, since the surreptitious arrival of Halloran, who was now speaking. He dominated the conversation in a bantering Irish brogue, reciting the events of his life – the impatience at the poverty and dullness of village life in County Down, the decision to volunteer, the obsession with fitness, the love of danger, the successful application to join the

SAS, anti-terrorist work in Aden in the mid-1960s and Oman (1971–4), and finally the return to Northern Ireland. It was all told with bravado and a surface glitter of which the older man was beginning to tire.

'Jesus, Frank,' the young man was saying, 'the Irish frighten me to death sometimes. I was in Mulligan's Bar in Dundalk, a quiet corner, me and a pint and a fellow named McHenry. I says to him there's a job. That's all I said. No details. I was getting to that, but not a bit of it – he didn't ask who, or what, or how much, or how do I get away? You know what he said? 'When do I get the gun?' That's all he cared about. He didn't even care which *side* – MI5, the Provos, the Officials, the Garda. I liked that.'

'Well, Peter,' said Ridger. He spoke slowly. 'Did you do the job?'

'We did. You should've seen the papers. "IRA seize half a million in bank raid."'

'But,' said Ridger, draining his can, 'I thought you said you were paid by the Brits?'

'That's right,' said Halloran. He was enjoying playing the older man along, stoking his curiosity.

'The British paid you to rob a British bank?'

'That's right.'

'Were you back in favour or what?'

'After what happened in Oman? No way.'

'What did you do?'

'There was a girl.'

'Oh?'

'How was I to know who she was? I was on my way home for a couple of months' break. End of a contract. We had to get out or we'd have raped the camels. The lads, Mike Rourke among them, decided on a nice meal at the Sultan's new hotel, the Al Falajh. She was – what? Nineteen. Old enough. I tell you, Frank – shall I tell you, my son?'

Ridger grinned.

Halloran first saw her in the entrance hall. Lovely place, the Al Falajh. Velvet all over the shop. Like walking into an upmarket strip club. She was saying goodnight to Daddy, a visiting businessman, Halloran assumed. 'Go on then,' Rourke had said, seeing the direction of his glance. He slipped into the lift behind her. She was wearing a blouse, short-sleeved and loose, so that as she stood facing away from him, raising her slim arm to push the lift button, he could see that she was wearing a silk bra, and that it was quite unnecessary for her to wear a bra at all. He felt she should know this, and at once appointed himself her fashion adviser.

'Excuse me, miss, but I believe we have met.' He paused as she turned, with a half smile, eager to be polite.

He saw a tiny puzzle cloud her brow.

'Last night,' he said.

She frowned. 'I was . . .'

'In a fantasy,' he interrupted. It was corny, but it worked. By then she had been staring at him

20

for seconds, and didn't know how to cut him. She smiled. Her name was Amanda Price-Whyckham.

'Eager as sin, she was,' Halloran went on. A most receptive student, was Amanda P.-W. The only thing she knew was la-di-da. Never had a bit of rough, let alone a bit of Irish rough. So when Halloran admired the view as the light poured through the hotel window, and through her skirt, and suggested that simplicity was the thing – perhaps the necklace off, then the stockings, she agreed she looked better and better the less she wore. 'Until there she was, naked, and willing.' Halloran finished. 'My knees and elbows were raw by three in the morning.'

He smiled and took a swig of beer.

'I don't know how Daddy found out,' Halloran continued after a pause. 'Turned out he was a colonel on a visit for the MoD to see about some arms for the Omanis. You know, the famous Irish sheikhs – the O'Mahoneys?'

Ridger acknowledged the joke with a nod and a lugubrious smile.

'So Daddy had me out of there. The SAS didn't want me back, and I'd had enough of regular service. Used up half my salary to buy myself out. So it was back to pulling pints. Until the Brits approached me, unofficial like. Could I help discredit the Provos? Five hundred a month, in cash, for three months to see how it went. That was when my mind turned to banks. It was easy

– home ground, see, because we used to plan raids with the regiment. Just *plan* mind. Now it was for real. I got a taste for it. Next I know, the Garda's got me on file, and asks my controller in Belfast to have me arrested. He explains it nicely. They couldn't exactly come clean. So they do the decent thing: put out a warrant for me, but warn me first. Decent! You help your fucking country, and they fuck you.'

'You could tell.'

'I wouldn't survive to tell, Frank. As the bastard captain said, I'm OK if I lie low. In a year, two years, when the heat's off, I can live again.'

'I have the afternoon shift,' said Frank, avoiding his gaze, and standing up. 'I'll be back about nine.'

'We'll have a few drinks.'

As the door closed, Halloran reached for another can of Guinness. He had no intention of waiting even a week, let alone a year, to live again.

Yufru was clearly at ease in the cold opulence of Sir Charles Cromer's office. He was slim, with the aquiline good looks of many Ethiopians. He carried a grey cashmere overcoat, which he handed to Miss Yates, and wore a matching grey suit, tailored light-blue shirt and plain dark-blue tie.

Though Cromer never knew his background, Yufru had been living in exile since 1960. At that time he had been a major, a product of the élitist military academy at Harar. He had been one of a group of four officers who had determined to break the monolithic, self-seeking power of the monarchy and attempted to seize power while the Emperor was on a state visit to Brazil. The attempt was a disaster: the rebel officers, themselves arrogant and remote, never established how much support they would have, either within the army or outside it.

In the event, they had none. They took the entire cabinet hostage, shot most of them in an attempt to force the army into co-operation, and when they saw failure staring them in the face, scattered. Two killed themselves. Their corpses were strung up on a gallows in the centre of Addis. A third was captured and hanged. The fourth was Yufru. He drove over the border into Kenya, where he had been wise enough to bank his income, and surfaced a year later in London. Now, after a decade in business, mainly handling African art and supervising the investment of his profits, he had volunteered his services to the revolutionary government, seeking some revenge on the Imperial family and rightly guessing that his experience of the capitalist system might be of use.

He stood and looked round with admiration. Then, as Cromer invited him with a gesture to sit, he began to speak in suave tones that were the consequence of service with the British in 1941–5.

As Cromer knew, Ethiopia was a poor country. He, Yufru, had been lucky, of course, but the time had come for all of them to pull together. They faced the consequences of a terrible famine. The figures quoted in the West were not inaccurate – perhaps half a million would eventually die of starvation. Much, of course, was due to the inhumanity of the Emperor. He was remote, cut off in his palaces. The revolutionary government had attempted to reverse these disasters, but there was a limit imposed by a lack of funds and internal opposition.

'These are difficult times politically,' Yufru sighed. He was the ideal apologist for his thuggish masters. Cromer had met the type before – intelligent, educated, smooth, serving themselves by serving the hand that paid them. 'We have enemies within who will soon be persuaded to see the necessity of change. We have foolish rebels in Eritrea who may seek to dismember our country. Somalia wishes to tear from us the Ogaden, an integral part of our country.

'All this demands a number of extremely expensive operations. As you are no doubt aware, the Somalis are well equipped with Soviet arms. My government has not as yet found favour with the Soviets. If we are to be secure – and I suggest that it is in the interests of the West that the Horn of Africa remains stable – we need good, modern arms. The only possible source at present is the West. We do not wish to be a debtor nation. We would like to buy.

'For that, to put matters bluntly, we need hard cash.'

Cromer nodded. He had guessed correctly.

'The money for such purposes exists. It was stolen by Haile Selassie from our people and removed from the country, as you have good cause to know. I am sure you will respect the fact that the Emperor's fortune is officially government property and that the people of Ethiopia, the originators of that wealth, should be considered the true heirs of the Emperor. They should receive the benefits of their labours.'

'Administered, of course, by your government,' Cromer put in.

'Of course,' Yufru replied easily, untouched by the banker's irony. 'They are the representatives of the people.'

Cromer was in his element. He knew his ground and he knew it to be rock-solid. He could afford to be magnanimous.

'Mr Yufru,' he began after a pause, 'morally your arguments are impeccable. I understand the fervour with which your government is determined to right historic wrongs . . .' – both of them were aware of what the fervour entailed: hundreds of corpses, 'enemies of the revolution', stinking on the streets of Addis – 'and we would naturally be willing to help in any way. But insofar as the Emperor's personal funds are concerned, there is really nothing we can do. Our instructions are clear and binding . . .'

'I too know the instructions,' Yufru broke in icily. 'My father was with the Emperor in '24. That is, in part, why I am here. You must have written instructions, signed by the Emperor, and sealed with the Imperial seal, on notepaper prepared by your bank, itself watermarked, again with the Imperial seal.'

Cromer acknowledged Yufru's assertion with a slow nod.

'Indeed, and those arrangements still stand. I have to tell you that the last such communication received by this bank was dated July 1974. Neither I nor my associates have received any further communication. We cannot take any action unilaterally. And, as the world knows, the Emperor is now dead, and it seems that the deposits must be frozen . . .' – the banker spread his hands in a gesture of resigned sympathy – 'in perpetuity.'

There was a long pause. Yufru clearly had something else to say. Cromer waited, still confident.

'Sir Charles,' Yufru said, more carefully now, 'we have much work to do to regularize the Imperial records. The business of fifty years, you understand . . . It may be that the Emperor has left among his papers further instructions, perhaps written in the course of the revolution itself. And he was alive, you will remember, for a year after the revolution. It is conceivable that other papers relating to his finances will emerge. I take it that there would be no question that your bank and your associated banks would accept such instructions, if properly authenticated?'

The sly little bastard – he's got something up his sleeve, thought Cromer. It may be . . . it is conceivable . . . if, if, if. There was no 'if' about it. Something solid lay behind the question.

To gain time he said: 'I will have to check my own arrangements and those of my colleagues . . . there is something about outdated instructions which slips my mind. Anyway,' he hastened on, 'the instructions have always involved either new deposits or the transfer of funds and the buying of metals or stock. In what way would you have an interest in transmitting such information?'

Yufru replied, evenly: 'We would like to be correct. We would merely like to be aware of your reactions if such papers were found and if we decided to pursue the matter.'

'It seems an unlikely contingency, Mr Yufru. The Emperor has, after all, been dead six months.'

'We are, of course, talking hypothetically, Sir Charles. We simply wish to be prepared.' He rose, and removed a speck from his jacket. 'Now, I must leave you to consider my question. May I thank you for your excellent coffee and your advice. Until next time, then.'

Puzzled, Sir Charles showed Yufru to the door. He was not a little apprehensive. There was something afoot. Yufru's bosses were not noted for their philanthropy. They would have no interest in passing on instructions that might increase the Emperor's funds.

It made no sense.

But by tonight, it damn well would.

'No calls, Miss Yates,' he said abruptly into the intercom. 'And bring me the correspondence files for Lion . . . Yes, all of them. The whole damn filing cabinet.'

That evening, Sir Charles sat alone till late. A set of files lay on his desk. Against the wall stood the cabinet of files relating to Selassie. He again reviewed his thoughts on Yufru's visit. He had to assume that there was something behind it. The only idea that made any sense was that there was some scheme to wrest Selassie's money from the banks concerned. It couldn't be done by halves. If they had access – with forged papers, say – then he had to assume that the whole lot was at risk.

And what a risk. He let his mind explore that possibility. Two thousand million dollars' worth of gold from three countries for a start. If he were instructed, as it were by the Emperor himself, to sell every last ounce, it would be a severe blow to the liquidity of his own bank and those of his partners in Zurich and New York. With capital withdrawn, loans would have to be curtailed, profits lost. When and if it became known who was selling, reputations would suffer and rumours spread. Confidence would be lost.

Even if there weren't panic withdrawals, future deposits would be withheld. The effects would echo down the years and along the corridors of financial power, spreading chaos. With that much gold unloaded all at once, the price would tumble. And not only would he fail to realize the true market value, but he would become a pariah within Rothschild's and in the international banking community. Cromer's, renowned for its discretion, would be front-page news.

And that was just the gold. There would be the winding-up of a score of companies, the withdrawal of the cash balances, in sterling, Swiss francs and dollars.

Good God, he would be a liability. *Eased out.*

He poured himself a whisky and returned to his desk, forcing himself to consider the worst. In what circumstances might such a disaster occur?

What if Yufru produced documents bearing the Emperor's signature, ordering his estate to be handed over to Mengistu's bunch? With any luck they would be forgeries and easily spotted. On the other hand, they might be genuine, dating from before the Emperor's death. But that was surely beyond the bounds of possibility. It would belie everything he knew about the man — ruthless, uncompromising, implacably opposed to any diminution of his authority.

But what if they had got at him, with drugs,

or torture or solitary confinement? Now that was a possibility. Cromer would gamble his life on it that Selassie had signed nothing to prejudice his personal fortune before he was overthrown. But he might have done afterwards, if forced. He had after all been in confinement for about a year.

Now he had faced the implications, however, he saw that he could forestall the very possibility Yufru had mentioned. He checked one of the files before him again. Yes, no documents signed by the Emperor would be acceptable after such a delay. Anyone receiving written orders more than two weeks old had to check back on the current validity of those orders before acting upon them. The device was a sensible precaution in the days when couriers were less reliable than now, and communications less rapid. The action outlined in that particular clause had never been taken, and the clause never revoked. There it still stood, Cromer's bastion against hypothetical catastrophe.

Cromer relaxed. But before long he began to feel resentful that he had wasted an evening on such a remote eventuality. He downed his whisky, turned off his lights, strolled over to the lift and descended to the basement, where the Daimler awaited him, his chauffeur dozing gently at the wheel. He was at his London home by midnight.

Friday 19 March

'So you see, Mr Yufru, how my colleagues and I feel.'

Cromer had summoned Yufru for a further meeting earlier that morning.

'After such a lapse of time and given the uncertainty of the political situation, we could not be certain that the documents would represent the Emperor's lasting and final wishes. We would be required to seek additional confirmation, at source, before taking action. And the source, of course, is no longer with us.'

'I see, Sir Charles. You would not, however, doubt the validity of the Emperor's signature and seal?'

'No, indeed. That we can authenticate.'

'You would merely doubt the validity of his wishes, given the age of the documents?'

'That is correct.'

'I see. In that case, I am sure such a problem will never arise.'

Cromer nodded. The whole ridiculous, explosive scheme – if it had ever existed outside his own racing imagination – had been scotched. And apparently with no complications.

To hear Yufru talk, one would think the whole thing was indeed a mere hypothesis. Yufru remained affable, passed some complimentary comments about Cromer's taste, and left, in relaxed mood.

The banker remained at his desk, deep in thought.

31

He had no immediate appointments before lunch with a broker at 12.30, and he had the nagging feeling that he had missed something. There were surely only two possibilities. Mengistu's bunch might have forged, or considered forging, documents. Or they might have the genuine article, however obtained. In either case, the date would precede Selassie's death and they would now know that the date alone would automatically make the orders unacceptable. The fortune would remain for ever out of their reach.

Yufru had failed. Or had he? He didn't seem like a man who had failed – not angry, or depressed, or fearful at reporting what might be a serious setback to the hopes of his masters. No: it was more as if he had merely ruled out just one course of action.

What other course remained open? What had he, Cromer, said that allowed the Ethiopians any freedom of action? The only positive statement he had made was that the orders, if they followed procedure, would be accepted as genuine documents, even if outdated.

Under what circumstances would the orders be accepted both as genuine and binding? If the date was recent, of course, but then ... If the date was recent ... in that case the Emperor would have to be ... Dear God!

Cromer sat bolt upright, staring, unseeing, across the room. He had experienced what has been called the Eureka effect: a revelation based on the most tenuous evidence, but of such power that the conclusion is undeniable.

The Emperor must still be alive.

Cromer sat horrified at his own realization. He had no real doubts about his conclusion. It was the only theory that made sense out of Yufru's approach. But he had to be certain that there was nothing to contradict it.

From the cabinet, against the wall, he slid out a file marked 'Clippings – Death'. There, neatly tabbed into a loose-leaf folder, were a number of reports of Selassie's death, announced on 28 August 1975 as having occurred the previous day, in his sleep, aged eighty-three.

According to the official government hand-out: 'The Emperor complained of feeling unwell the previous night (26 August) but a doctor could not be obtained and a servant found him dead the next morning.'

Although he had been kept under close arrest in the compound in the Menelik Palace, there was no suggestion that he had been ailing. True, he had had a prostate operation two months before, but he had recovered well. One English doctor who treated him at that time, a professor from Queen Mary's Hospital, London, was quoted as saying he had 'never seen a patient of that age take the operation better'.

There had never been any further details. No

family member was allowed to see the body. There was no post-mortem. The burial, supposedly on 29 August, was secret. There was no funeral service. The Emperor had, to all intents and purposes, simply vanished.

Not unnaturally, a number of people, in particular Selassie's family, found the official account totally unacceptable. It reeked of duplicity. However disruptive the revolution, there were scores of doctors in Addis Ababa. Rumours began to circulate that Selassie had been smothered, murdered to ease the task of the revolution, for all the while he was known to be alive, large sections of the population would continue to regard him, even worship him, as the true ruler of the country. As *The Times* said when reporting the family's opinion in June 1976: 'The Emperor's sudden death has always caused suspicion, if only because of the complete absence of medical or legal authority for the way he died.'

And so the matter rested. Until now. No wonder there had been no medical or legal authority for the way he died, mused Cromer. But the family had jumped to the wrong conclusion.

'Sir Charles,' it was Miss Yates's voice on the intercom. 'Will you be lunching with Sir Geoffrey after all?'

'Ah, Miss Yates, thank you. Yes. Tell him I'm on my way. Be there in ten minutes.'

He stopped at the desk on his way out.

'What appointments are there this afternoon?' he asked.

'You have a meeting with Mr Squires at two o'clock about the Shah's most recent deposits. And of course the usual gold committee meeting at five.'

The Shah could wait. 'Cancel Jeremy. I need the early afternoon clear.'

He glanced out of the window. It looked like rain. He took one of the two silk umbrellas from beside Valerie's desk and left for lunch.

2

Those who had met Sir Charles Cromer over the past twenty years knew him only as a calculating financier, who seemed to live for his bank, seeking a release in his work from a stultifying home life. In point of fact, he was a closet gangster, utterly amoral, and with more than a dash of sadism in him. This aspect of his character had long been suppressed by his intelligence, his social standing and the eminence of the professional role he had inherited.

Only twice in his life had Cromer truly expressed himself. The first time was at school, at Eton. There, as fag and junior, he had borne the crushing humiliations imposed upon him by his seniors, knowing that he too would one day inherit their power. His resilience and forbearance were well rewarded. He became a games player of some eminence, playing scrum-half for the school and for Hereford Schoolboys with a legendary fearlessness. He also became Head of House. In this capacity he had cause, about once a week, to dispense discipline in the sternest public school traditions. Sometimes he would preside, with awful formality, over the ritual humiliation of some unfortunate junior who would be beaten in the prefects' common room. Meanwhile the prefects themselves read idly, disdainfully refusing to acknowledge the presence of the abhorrent object of Cromer's displeasure. Sometimes, for a lesser offence, the beating would be administered in his own study. Both occasions gave him joy.

It was at a House beating in his own study that he once allowed his nature to get the better of him. The boy concerned had dared question the validity of his decision. The insolence of the suggestion drove the eighteen-year-old Cromer into a cold and dedicated anger. The beating he then delivered, with the full weight of his body, drew blood beneath the younger boy's trousers. When examined by a doctor, marks were even found on the victim's groin, where the cane had whipped around the side of his buttock and hip.

The traditions of the school demanded complete stoicism. Even after such a caning, the boy would have been expected to shake hands with his persecutor, then continue life as normal. He might bear the stigmata for weeks, but he would say nothing, nor would anybody else.

This time, however, there was a comeback. The boy's father was a Jewish textile manufacturer determined to buy the trappings of English culture for his offspring. The boy himself was less certain that he needed them. Cromer's actions decided him: he telephoned his father, who appeared the following day, pulled his son out of school and obtained a doctor's report. Copies of the report were passed to the headmaster, the housemaster, Cromer's parents and his own solicitor. It was only with the greatest skill that a public scandal was averted. Cromer himself, who was amazed to find that he was considered to have done something amiss, was severely reprimanded. It changed his attitude not at all. But it did teach him that, if he wished to indulge in such activities, he would have to cloak them in a veneer of respectability.

The only other time that Cromer was able to let himself go was in Berlin immediately after the war. He had been too young to see any active service. The war was over just as he finished his training. As a newly commissioned second lieutenant, he flew into Tempelhof airport in Berlin in July 1945, the first time the victorious Russians had allowed the Western allies into the former German capital. Berlin was still a charnel house, a wilderness of buildings torn apart, squares and streets littered with rubble, a population half-starved. Cromer rapidly saw that he had been presented with a unique opportunity. The occupying troops were the élite, buying goods, labour and sex with money, cigarettes, food, luxury goods. Marks were worth nothing; sterling and dollars were like gold.

For the first year, when the Germans were still regarded as the enemy and the Russians as friends,

Cromer was in his element. He transferred in his own cash and bought for derisory sums anything of value he could lay his hands on. It was amazing that so much had survived the war unscathed – Meissen china, Steinway and Bechstein grand pianos, hallmarked silver, exquisitely embroidered linen, nineteenth-century military paraphernalia by the ton, even a Rolls-Royce Silver Ghost. He hired a warehouse near Tempelhof and had it sealed off. For two years, he packed in his treasures. He was by no means the only one to take advantage of the Berliners in this way, though in the scale of his operations he was practically unique.

In early 1948 Cromer, now a captain, was given as administrative assistant a teenage second lieutenant, Richard Collins. For Cromer, this turned out to be a providential appointment. As well as fulfilling his normal duties, organizing patrols and the distribution of food, Collins was soon recruited after hours to supervise the stowing of Cromer's latest acquisitions. It was not a demanding job – a couple of evenings a week at most – but it was regular, and he was promised a share of the proceeds.

One evening in May, when Collins was closing up for the night, a task he had been taught to do surreptitiously, he heard a crash around the corner. He ran to the side of the building and was in time to see a bottle, flaming at one end, sail through the newly made hole in one of the windows. A Molotov cocktail.

Collins knew it would be caught by the wire-mesh netting inside the window and guessed it would do little damage. Hardly pausing, he sprinted into the rubble-strewn shadows from which the bottle had come, in time to see a slight figure vanishing round the next street corner. Collins was young, fit and well fed, and the teenage fire-bug, weakened by years of malnutrition, had no chance of escape. Collins sprinted up from behind and pushed him hard in the shoulders. The German took off forwards into a heap of rubble, hit it head on and collapsed into the bricks like a sack of potatoes. Collins hauled him over, and found his head dreadfully gashed and his neck broken.

Collins heaved the body across the unlit street and into a bombed building. He then ran back to the warehouse, retrieved the guttering, still unbroken bottle of petrol from the wire grill, stamped out the cloth, poured the contents down a drain, slung the bottle away into the roadside rubble, listened to see if the crash and the noise of running feet would bring a patrol, and then, reassured, went off to find Cromer.

Cromer knew what he owed Collins. He used his own jeep to pick up the body, and by three o'clock in the morning the German had become just another unidentified corpse in a small canal.

There had been some mention of German resentment against profiteering, but this was the first direct evidence Cromer had had of it. He saw that the time had come to stop.

Within a couple of months, Berlin was blockaded by the Russians and the airlift was under way. Planes loaded with food and fuel from the West were landing at Tempelhof every three minutes and taking off again, empty. Except that some were not empty. It took Cromer only two weeks to organize the shipment of his complete stock in twin-engine Dakotas, first to Fassberg, then on to England, to a hangar on a Midlands service aerodrome. A year later, demobbed, Cromer organized two massive auctions that netted him £150,000. In Berlin his outlay had been just £17,000. Not bad for a twenty-four-year-old with no business experience and no more than a small allowance from the business he was destined to take over.

Now Cromer the racketeer was about to resurface.

After lunch Cromer returned temporarily to his hermit-like existence. His staff did not find his behaviour peculiar; there had been crises demanding his personal attention before. He made two telephone calls. The first was to Oswald Kupferbach in Zurich, to an office in the Crédit Suisse, 8 Paradeplatz – one of the few banks in Switzerland which have special telephone and telex lines solely for dealing in gold bullion.

'Oswald? *Wie geht's dir*? . . . Yes, a long time. We

have to meet as soon as possible . . . I'm afraid so.
Something has come up over here. It's about Lion
. . . Yes, it's serious, but not over the phone. You
have to be here . . . I can only say that it concerns all
our futures very closely . . . Ideally, this weekend?
Sunday evening for Monday morning? That would
be perfect . . . You and Jerry . . . I'll have a car for
you and a hotel. I'll telex the details.'

The next call was to New York, to a small bank
off Wall Street that had specialities comparable
to Cromer's — though little gold, of course, and
more stock-exchange dealings — and a relationship with the Morgan Guaranty Trust Company
similar to Cromer's with Rothschild's. He spoke
to Jerry Lodge.

'Jerry? Charlie. It's about Lion . . .'

The call had a similar pattern to the previous
one — prevarication from the other end, further
persuasion by Cromer, mention of mutual futures at
stake and, finally, a meeting arranged for Monday
morning.

In an elegant courtyard of Cotswold-stone farm
buildings, some seventy miles north-west of London,
Richard Collins raised an arm in a perfunctory farewell to a customer driving off in a Land Rover. A
routine morning's work. One down, twenty-five to
go, a job lot from Leyland.

A lot of people envied Dicky Collins. He looked
the very epitome of the well-to-do countryman in

his tweed jackets, twill trousers, Barbour coats. His Range Rover had a Blaupunkt tape deck, still something of a rarity in the mid-1970s. The farmhouse, with its courtyard and outbuildings, was surrounded by ten acres of woodland and meadow. It was an ideal base for his business, which was mainly selling army-surplus vehicles. In one of the stone barns, converted into a full working garage, there were five Second World War jeeps in various stages of repair, a khaki truck that had last seen action in the Western desert, and several 1930s motorbikes, still with side-cars.

The business turned over quarter of a million. He took £25,000, more than enough in those days. He was forty-eight, fit, successful, unmarried, and bored out of his bloody mind.

For almost ten years he had worked at his bloody Land Rovers and jeeps and trucks, ever since he finished in Aden and Charlie Cromer had given him a £100,000 loan to buy his first 100 vehicles – in exchange for sixty per cent of the equity. Both had judged well. It was a good business, doing the rounds of the War Department auctions. Now things were drying up, prices were rising. Any old jeep you could have got for £100 ten years before now fetched £2000 and up. It was a specialist field, and Collins knew it well. Once he had loved it. The sweet purr of a newly restored engine reminded him of the real thing.

After Aden, he was happy to settle. Hell of a

time. Fuzzies fighting for a stump of a country
and an oven of a city. Chap needed two gallons of
water a day just to stay alive. No point to it all in
the end, with Britain pulling out. Not like Borneo
– that had been a proper show, all the training put
to good use.

Now he was sick of it. Country life could never
deliver that sort of kick. Money? It was good, but it
would never be enough to excite him. The place was
mortgaged to the hilt, the taxman was a sadist, and
even if he sold, Charlie Cromer would take most of
the profits.

Boredom, that was Collins's problem. There was
old Molly to do the house. The business ran itself
these days, what with Caroline coming in two
days a week to keep the VAT man at bay. Stan
knew all about a car's innards and could fix
anything over twenty years old as good as new.
Collins had other interests, of course, but keeping
up with publications on international terrorism
and his thrice-weekly clay-pigeon practices hardly
compared with jungle warfare for thrills. There
were parties, there were girls for the asking, but
he wasn't about to marry again. What had once
been a comfortable country nest had become a
padded cell.

'Major,' Stan called from the garage. 'Phone.'

Collins nodded. He walked through the garage, edging his way past a skeletal jeep to the
phone.

'Dicky? Charlie Cromer. Got a proposition for you.'

Monday 22 March

That morning, Sir Charles Cromer, Oswald Kupfer-bach and Jerry Lodge were together in Cromer's office. The Swiss and the American sat facing each other on the Moroccan leather sofas beneath the Modigliani. Both had been chosen for their present jobs only after an interview with Cromer, who had judged them right for his needs: astute, experienced, hard. Kupferbach, fifty-two, with rimless glasses, had practised discretion for so long he never seemed to have any emotions at all. Professionally, he didn't. His one passion was personal: he was an expert in the ecology of mountains above the tree line. Lodge – his grandparents were Poles from the city of Lodz – was quite a contrast: bluff, rotund, reassuring. He found it easy to ensure he was underestimated by rivals.

Between the two on the glass-topped table was newly made coffee and orange juice. Sir Charles was standing, coffee cup in hand, having just outlined the approaches made to him by Yufru.

He concluded by saying: 'So you see, gentle-men, why we had to meet: I have the strongest possible reasons for believing that the Emperor is not dead. I further believe that unless we move rapidly and in concert, we shall shortly be

45

presented with documents bearing the Emperor's signature demanding the release of his fortune to the revolutionary government of Mengistu Haile Mariam.

'This would be a financial blow that we, as individual bankers, should not have to endure. Indeed, the sums in gold alone are so vast that their release would devastate the world's gold markets. While the short-term implications for our respective economies are not pleasant, the implications for our banks and ourselves as individuals are horrendous.'

The Swiss was thoughtful, the American wide-eyed, caricaturing disbelief.

'Oh, come on, Charlie,' he said, 'that's got to be the most outrageous proposition I've ever heard. What are you on? I mean, my God.'

Kupferbach broke in: 'No, no, Jerry. It is not so foolish. It fits in. There have been a number of approaches in Zurich for loans. They need the money. But their propositions are unrealistic. The World Bank might consider a loan for fighting the famine, but, of course, it would be administered by World Bank officials. They don't want that.'

Lodge paused. 'OK, OK,' he said at last, 'let's follow it through. Suppose the old boy is still alive. Suppose he signs the papers. Don't you think we could persuade the Ethiopians to leave the gold with us? After all, they have to place it somewhere, don't they? We arrange a loan for them based on the reserves. They buy their arms and fight their goddam wars, and everyone's happy. Hey?'

'It's possible,' Cromer said slowly, 'but it doesn't look like a safe bet to me. You think Mengistu would pay interest, and if he did, do you think his successors would? Would you invest in a Marxist without any experience of international finance who came to power and preserves power through violence?'

'I agree. But what do you think would happen if we received these documents and simply ignored them?' replied Kupferbach.

'Whadya mean, Ozzie?' said Lodge. 'We just don't do as we're told? We say we're not going to hand over the funds? We tell the Ethiopians to go stuff their asses?'

'In brief, *meine Herren*, yes.'

'If all this is true,' said Cromer, 'that thought must have already crossed their minds. In their position, what would your answer be?'

'Right,' Lodge said, jutting his lower jaw and biting his top lip. 'Jesus, if I was them, I'd make one hell of a storm. Major banks refusing to honour their obligations? Yeah, they could really have a go at us. International Court at The Hague, questions in the UN, pressure on other African countries to make holes in Rothschild and Morgan Guaranty investments in the Third World. We'd come out of it with more than egg on our faces.'

'Of course,' added Cromer, 'to do that, they'd

have to reveal that Selassie was still alive. It would make them look pretty damn stupid.'

'Yes, but they have less to lose.' It was Kupferbach again, a clear thinker with a coolness that more than matched Cromer's. 'Mengistu could write off the previous announcement of the Emperor's death as a necessity imposed by the revolution. The publicity would be bad for them, but could be catastrophic for us.'

Cromer looked at the two of them in turn.

'Gentlemen,' he said, 'I have been thinking of nothing else for the last two days. I have rehearsed these arguments many times in my own mind. If the Emperor signs those papers we are lost.' He paused. 'We are left with no choice – we have to assume the Emperor is still alive, and we have to get to him before he signs anything.'

Cromer's two colleagues looked at him expectantly.

'What the hell are you suggesting?' said Lodge.

'We have to do the decent thing. We have to kidnap the Emperor.'

They stared at him.

Lodge shook his head in disbelief and went on shaking it, perhaps at the very suggestion, or perhaps at the impossibility of achieving it.

'Jerry, Oswald: don't fight it. It's the only answer. It's either that or immediate retirement. I don't know about you two but I have a very real future in front of me. The Emperor has none. Getting him out, we win all ways. We save him, and we save his fortune – and ours.'

'You goddam English,' said Lodge. 'You think you can still act like you had an Empire. Where I come from, the CIA do that sort of thing, not the goddam bankers . . .' He trailed off, still shaking his head.

Kupferbach seemed to be way ahead of him. 'I see, Charles. You have been doing much preparation for this meeting. May I ask, therefore, why you needed to include us?'

'For the first step, Oswald, the first step. Getting to Selassie. I think I know how to do it. We still have one card to play. Supposing he is still alive, supposing the Ethiopians make him sign the documents, supposing they are dated for just two days before we receive them, I still do not believe we would have to comply. We could argue that the signature must have been produced under duress, since it is clearly contrary to everything the Emperor has expressed in the past. I think we could make such a refusal stand up in a court of law. Of course, it would not do to let things go on that far. As you say, Oswald, the publicity would be catastrophic. But likewise, they would not get their money.

'I think we can pre-empt a crisis. We tell them that signature under duress would not be acceptable, quoting UN Human Rights legislation. I also think I could suggest a way around the difficulty: I will propose that the signature be made in the presence either of the bankers concerned or of their duly appointed representatives, in a situation in which the Emperor could be seen – for that particular day, at least – to be in good health and not the object of undue pressure, physical or psychological.

'That, gentlemen, is how we gain access.'

'Hold on there a tiny minute,' broke in Lodge, 'you're losing me. You mean this has to be done for real? We have to go and meet the Emperor?'

'Well, not we necessarily, but yes, there has to be a meeting between our people and the Emperor. And there are, of course, a number of other implications. The Emperor will have to be in a fit state to hold such a meeting. But then, presumably, he has to be in a fit state to sign the documents at all, so it shouldn't be too much of a problem to produce him in a reasonable state of health.

'A further implication – and this is where I need you – is that the documents for signature have to be genuine. Only in that way can we guarantee access. We have to see what the Ethiopians want from Selassie, and we have to agree to them in advance. And Selassie will agree.'

'Yeah?' said Lodge, sceptically. 'Tell me why.'

'One good reason – only with our co-operation can he assure the financial future of his family abroad. I've already had the family on my back several times. It is clear that, in a year or two, they will not be able to support themselves in the manner to which they have become accustomed. There are several children and countless grandchildren. All will need financial help, which they will not receive unless Selassie signs what will become, in effect, his last will and testament, one that must also be agreed with the Ethiopian government and ourselves. Everything must be prepared in secret, but as if it was for real.

'Thereafter, our duty to ourselves is clear: we cannot allow Selassie actually to sign the papers.'

Collins arrived in London early on Monday evening, parked his Range Rover in a garage off Berkeley Square and strolled round to Brown's hotel in Dover Street. He just had time for a bath, and a whisky and water in his room, when the internal phone went to announce the arrival in reception of Charlie Cromer.

The two dined at the Vendôme, where sole may be had in twenty-four different styles. It took Cromer two courses and most of a very dry Chablis to bring Collins up to date.

'And now,' he said over coffee, 'before I make you any propositions, I want to know how you're fixed. How's the business?'

'You've seen the books, even if you don't remember them. The profits are there. But there's a problem with the management.'

'Fire him.'

'It's *me*, Charlie. It was a joke.' Cromer shrugged

an apology. 'I'm bored. I've been thinking about getting out, taking off somewhere for a year.'

'Not a woman, is it?'

'No. I have to keep my nose clean around home – get a reputation for dipping your wick and business can suffer.'

'So do I take it my call was timely?'

'Indeed.'

'Good. You can see what I need: a team of hit men, as our American friends say. We'll have to work out the details together, but, for a start, we need two more like you, men who like danger, who like a challenge, cool and experienced.'

'What are you offering in return?'

'To you? Freedom. I'll arrange a purchaser for the company and turn any profits over to you. I would imagine you will come out of it with, say, £100,000 in cash. In addition, $100,000 to be deposited in your name in New York and a similar sum to be placed in a numbered account in Switzerland.'

'That sounds generous.'

'Fair. I have colleagues who are interested in the successful outcome of this particular operation.'

Collins had decided to take up the offer in any case. 'Yes. I'm on. I still have a few contacts in the Regiment. I can think of a couple of chaps who may be interested.'

'There's another thing,' said Cromer. 'You will all have to act the part of bankers. For obvious reasons, I can't go. Wish I could.'

'No, you don't, Charlie. It's far too risky.'

'You'll be handing me a white feather next.'

'For *us*, Charlie. Kidnapping an Emperor is quite enough for one job. Spare us looking after you.'

Tuesday 23 March
Back in the Oxfordshire countryside, Collins had only a few routine matters to attend to. He had to confirm a couple of sales, vet a US Army jeep that would eventually fetch at least £3500, and say 'yes' with a willing smile when the village's up-and-coming young equestrienne, Caroline Sinclair, wanted some poles for a jump. But most of his attention was given to tracking down Halloran and Rourke.

It took several calls and several hours to get to Halloran. He learned of Halloran's rapid exit from the SAS, and of his re-emergence in Ireland. A contact in Military Intelligence, Belfast, looked up the files. Halloran had blown it: he was never to be used again. For them, Halloran had turned out more dangerous than an unexploded bomb. There had been reprimands for taking him on in the first place. A couple of his Irish contacts were also on file.

'What's this for, old boy?' the voice at the end of the line asked. 'Nothing too fishy, I hope?'

Collins knew what this meant. 'Nothing to do

with the Specials, the Army, the UDA, the IRA or the SAS. Something far, far away.'

'Good. In that case, you better move fast. The Yard knows he's in London. Looks like the Garda tipped them the wink. Could be a bit embarrassing for us if they handle it wrong. Do what you can.'

Collins made three more calls, this time to the Republic – one to a bar in Dundalk and one to each of the contacts on MI's file. At each number he left a message that an old friend was trying to contact Pete Halloran with an offer of work. He left his number.

At lunch-time, the phone rang. A call-box: the pips cut off as the money went in. A voice heavily muffled through a handkerchief asked for Collins's identity. Then: 'It's about Halloran.'

'I'll make it short,' said Collins. 'Tell Pete the Yard are on to him and that I may have an offer. Tell him to move quickly.'

'I'll let him know.'

The phone clicked off. It could have been Halloran, probably was, but he had to be allowed to handle things his own way.

An hour later, Halloran himself called.

'Is that you, sir? I had the message. What's the offer?'

'Good to hear you, Peter. Nothing definite yet. But I want you to stay out of trouble and be ready for a show. Not here – a long way away. You can come up here as soon as you like. You'll be quite safe.'

He had assumed Halloran, on the run, tense, perhaps bored with remaining hidden, would jump at it. He did.

'But what's this about the Yard?'

'Just a report that your name has been passed over. Are you sure your tracks are covered? Maybe nothing in it, but just look after yourself, will you? Phone again tomorrow at this time. Perhaps I'll have more.'

The second set of calls was simpler. From the SAS in Herefordshire to the Selous Scouts in Rhodesia was an easy link. He had no direct contact there, but didn't need one. He was told Rourke was on his way home. The call also elicited the address of Rourke's family – a suburban house in Sevenoaks, Kent. Rourke senior was still a working man, a British Rail traffic supervisor. Mrs Rourke answered. Oh yes, Michael was on his way home. Why, he might be in London at that very moment. No, they didn't know where. He liked his independence, did Michael. They hoped he would be down in the morning, but anyway he was certain to call. How nice of the major. Michael would be pleased to re-establish an old link. No, they didn't think he had any immediate plans. Yes, she would pass on the message.

Rourke phoned that afternoon within an hour of Halloran. He was still at Heathrow, just arrived from Jo'burg.

'Can't tell you yet, Michael,' said Collins, in

response to Rourke's first question. 'But it looks like a bit of the old times. Lots of action, one-month contract. Can you be free?'

There was a pause. 'I'm interested.'

Again, Collins made a provisional arrangement. Rourke would be back in contact later that evening.

Collins's final call that afternoon, shortly before four o'clock, was to Cromer.

'Charlie. Just wanted to say the package we were lining up the other day looks good. The other two partners are very interested. We're ready when you give us the word.'

'Thanks, Dicky. I have a meeting later which should clarify things. I'll be in contact tonight.'

3

At five o'clock, with the business of the day cleared from his desk, Cromer prepared himself for Yufru's arrival. Valerie Yates was briefed to leave when she saw him. Cromer did not want the possibility of any eavesdropping, intentional or otherwise.

He had planned for himself the role he liked best – magnanimous, controlled, polite, manipulative. He did not wish to be overtly aggressive and thus risk forcing Yufru into a corner. If he had guessed correctly, it should be a delicate, but not difficult matter to persuade him that the two of them should be working together.

'Mr Yufru, Sir Charles,' came Valerie's voice over the intercom.

'Very good, Miss Yates, ask him to come in, and perhaps you could bring in some tea before you go . . . ah, Mr Yufru, I am sorry to impose upon your precious time. Shall we?' And he indicated the sofas.

'It is my pleasure, Sir Charles. Perhaps it is I that owe you an apology. I had no intention of involving you in such an extended intellectual exercise,' said Yufru, as he relaxed back into the ancient polished leather. He crossed his right leg over his left and set the crease of his grey trousers exactly over the kneecap.

'Your idea interested me,' Cromer said, 'so much so that I began to treat it less as an intellectual exercise and more as a practical possibility.'

Yufru's hands came to rest in his lap. He gave no hint of concern.

Cromer continued: 'That way, I can be sure that my response will be complete and therefore as helpful as possible. It is because I think I now finally have a realistic answer to your question that I wish to speak to you.'

Valerie knocked at the door and brought in a tray bearing two neat little porcelain cups, teapot, sugar bowl, teaspoons, milk jug and lemon. Yufru was now utterly still, his face expressionless, his attention riveted on Cromer. As Valerie set down the tray on the table between the two men he said smoothly: 'By all means let us cover all eventualities, Sir Charles.'

Cromer waited until Valerie had closed the door and resumed: 'In our previous conversation, Mr Yufru, we discussed the possibility of my bank being presented with documents signed by the Emperor several months ago. I said an outdated signature would not be acceptable. I think I should tell you that the date alone would not be our only reason for our refusal to comply with instructions.

'We are speaking of documents signed by the Emperor after his deposition. It is well known that he was not a free man. We have no reason to think he was badly treated; but equally we must assume, for our client's sake, that instructions not in his direct interest might have been the product of coercion. In other words, in the circumstances you outlined, we would have a justifiable fear that he might have been forced to append his signature to documents not of his own devising. I fear, therefore, that we could not accept the Emperor's instructions as both authentic and valid. The date, you see, would be irrelevant if the Emperor was a prisoner at the time of his signature.'

Yufru had begun to breathe a little quicker, the only sign of tension other than his unnatural stillness.

'Are you in all seriousness telling me, Sir Charles, that a bank of your standing, with all its international connections, would refuse to honour the authenticated instructions of one of its most important clients?'

'In law, the definition of the word "instructions" becomes somewhat equivocal in these circumstances. I am told that such a document would have the same status as evidence produced under torture. I mean no direct comparison, of course, but the possibility of signature under duress would, I assure you, render the instructions null.'

'In English law, perhaps. But have you considered

what the International Court at The Hague would have to say about all this?'

Cromer smiled. 'I understand that the International Court can deal only with disputes between nations, that is, between governments. It has nothing to say on disputes between individuals, companies or other organizations. Those are dealt with under the laws of the countries concerned. In this instance, the possibility of signature under duress would invalidate any documents under English, Swiss or American law.'

Yufru's eyes had opened wider. His mood had changed to one of incredulous anger.

'You are claiming that the Emperor's fortune can never, in any circumstances, be returned to its rightful owners. I find that an attitude of the greatest immorality. It will be seen by my superiors as a most cynical expression of capitalist imperialism.'

Cromer had touched the nerve he had been probing for. Yufru's anger was a sign that Cromer's speculations had been in some way correct. Yet the anger was assertive. It revealed neither fear nor surprise. Either he was an extremely accomplished politician or, as Cromer had guessed, he had still another card to play: the threat of exposure to a wave of hysterical anti-Western propaganda. It was time to pre-empt any such possibility, and retain Yufru's goodwill.

'I fail to make myself clear, Mr Yufru. My

apologies. I did not say "in any circumstances". I can imagine circumstances in which this problem might be solved in a way favourable to both of us. Perhaps the time has come to consider them . . . Your tea?'

The tea was another small piece in Cromer's game. The ritual of hospitality offered reassurance and a distraction from confrontation.

'But,' continued Cromer, 'the exercise will demand utter honesty on both sides.'

Yufru sipped, his tension dissipating, relieved that there still seemed a way forward, yet wary of Cromer's mention of honesty.

He said: 'Please go on.'

'Very well. I want to suggest to you another . . . hypothesis. I will follow it with a suggestion that should relieve you of your difficulty. I have thought long and carefully about this. It will take a little time. I would ask you not to make any reaction until I have finished.'

Cromer stood up and began to walk slowly round the room. He did not wish to seem to be addressing Yufru directly. He became discursive, donnish.

He asked Yufru to suppose, for the sake of argument, that the Emperor was still alive, and that his mission had been to discover the circumstances in which any documents the Emperor might sign in the future would be accepted by Cromer's Bank and its associates. Yufru would, of course, attempt to disguise the fact of the Emperor's survival. He would hope that Cromer would give an assurance that documents several months old would suffice. In that case, no doubt Yufru would have produced such papers. Likewise, if Cromer had demanded a recent signature, duly signed documents would have appeared, with some plausible explanation.

'What extraordinary assumptions,' commented Yufru.

'I agree. But it is my duty to consider the possibility of such a deception, and it would be wrong of me not to devise ways to prevent such a trick succeeding. In this odd game, I believe I have now succeeded.'

Yufru waited, impassively.

'What now?' continued Cromer. 'Perhaps I should say "checkmate". But that would, I believe, be short-sighted. My assumptions may be wrong. You may have alternative strategies. And, besides, it would run counter to our own banking traditions.

'Let us try another approach, and ask: in these circumstances, would your attempted duplicity be really necessary? I think not. We are by reputation honest and discreet. We would not wish to keep from you, against natural justice, money that I concede is yours. Nor would we wish to reveal to our profession, let alone the world at large, that we have paid over to you such a sum of money. Supposing the Emperor to be still alive, it would certainly be in our interests, as well as yours, to conceal the fact.

'Now, let me move on to my conclusion. As you must have already guessed, I no longer think that this is a mere intellectual exercise. I believe the Emperor is still alive. I believe you have attempted to trick us, and failed. But I also assert our community of interest. That being so, there is I believe, a way forward.

'My suggestion is as follows: that we arrange between us the necessary documents; that duly appointed representatives of the banks meet the Emperor discreetly, in circumstances that would allow us all to see that no undue pressure was, at that time, being exerted; and that thereupon all parties freely sign the documents, transferring the Emperor's fortune, or most of it, to your government.

'Now perhaps I may have your comments?'

The banker sat down again, and looked across at Yufru, who did not yet look up. Yufru poured himself another cup of tea. No sugar, no milk. He rose, walked with his cup to the window and stared down at the twilit street, a river of moving lights, silent beyond the double glazing.

'One question, Sir Charles,' he said at last, 'what, as the Americans say, would be in it for you?'

'We have a reputation to uphold. We do not like publicity. Any public dispute, as I am sure you are aware, would be bad for us, and unless we come to some arrangement you would be in a position to accuse us publicly of duplicity. Besides, once the funds are transferred to you, your country will have to keep the money somewhere. Given our past record, I am sure you will agree that Cromer's is the bank best qualified to administer it on your government's behalf. I would like to think that we shall not be losing by the transaction.'

'I see.'

Then, suddenly decisive, Yufru swung round. Cromer sat back, apparently relaxed.

'Sir Charles, the time has come to talk frankly. I am, as you know, an unofficial envoy of my government. The Ambassador here is aware of our intent to have the Emperor's fortune returned, but has not been informed of my specific role. Officially I am there to vet visa applications. In fact I report directly to the First Vice-President, Lieutenant-Colonel Mengistu Haile Mariam, by whom I am empowered to use whatever methods I can to acquire the Emperor's fortune.

'You tell me that you yourself, or your representatives, must see the Emperor sign in order to accept his signature. Very well, I confirm your guess. The Emperor is still alive. He is, of course, under house arrest, and he is no longer in Addis. If he were, rumours of his survival would be sure to leak out. He is in his birthplace, Harar, in the mountains 200 miles to the east of Addis, with a few chosen family members, in utter isolation. The palace is his own, a citadel, but it is a prison now rather than a home. There is no contact between the guards and the family. Food, drink, laundry, all is left, as it were, on the doorstep.

'The only one to go to and fro is the President's doctor. He has confirmed that the Emperor is still in remarkable health for his years. He has recovered well from his prostate operation. How long will he remain fit? We do not know. He has nothing to live for. But, as you realize, we have much to keep him alive for. There is a certain urgency. But he has so far refused to discuss the transfer of his money, fortunately for both of us as it turns out.

'You say it is in your interests to effect a discreet solution to this problem. It is certainly in ours. Sir Charles, your proposal is . . . very helpful. I must take further advice. Perhaps we could meet, say, tomorrow morning?'

Rourke meanwhile had written himself a nice little sub-plot. He could do with a bit of R and R, but he also knew that there would be no chance of freelance earnings like this once he was back with the Regiment. Whatever Collins was offering, he wanted. So he would call, as planned, and he would go, if asked. That left him with one night for Lucy. He had planned to call her from his parents, when he had been re-civilized by baths, aftershave and good cooking, but these were exceptional times.

'Luce?'

Good that she had answered. She didn't like him

calling the shop, because it meant grief from the Patels, who owned the place.

'Michael bloody Rourke. Where are you, you bad boy?'

'Airport. You free tonight?'

'What do you think? I keep myself free just on the off chance? No, I ain't.'

He heard the banter in her tone, and played along.

'Look, Luce, it's an emergency. I think I'll be out of here again tomorrow. I came all this way just to see you.'

'Oh, sure. Look, I can't talk now. There's people here.'

'What time?'

'I told you: I can't.'

Oh, shit. She sounded serious.

'Why not?'

'Listen. I get off at six. Meet me then. I'll explain. Got to go.'

'It's almost six now! I'll never – Luce? Shit!'

She had hung up. Meet her where? The shop? Her place – wherever that was?

He took a bus into town, rode east on the tube, and walked down the road, past the laundrette and the Moti Mahal and the arcade games, to the shop. It was closed. He banged on the door without any real hope, and slung his pack down with a sigh of disgust.

The curtains behind the wire mesh parted. Lucy

looked out at him briefly. He couldn't read her expression. He saw nothing of her but a mass of black curls and a pair of dark eyes. 'What kept you?' came her muffled voice.

'I . . .'

'Never mind,' she said, as she came out and slammed the door behind her. She was angry.

'What's up?' he asked.

'You think you can swan in any time from anywhere, blow in my ear, and I'll follow you anywhere.'

'I wrote,' he said, slinging his pack on his shoulder. 'Come on, Luce, I'll buy you a drink.'

'Look, there's something I have to explain.'

He stared at her. This was not good.

She glanced round. 'But not here.'

'I thought we could go to the hotel.'

'You really are a bastard,' she said, expressionless. 'You know that?'

'It's all your fault.'

She smiled, sadly, and said with a hint of irony: 'It's nice of you to say so.'

'I mean it. You made me want you.'

'I know what you mean, you daft bugger. You don't have to explain.' She looked at him. 'Go to the hotel. I'll find you there.'

'What are you going to do?'

'Never you mind.'

'OK. Don't be long. I'll get something in for supper.'

She left the alley and walked quickly down the street without turning back.

He picked up his pack, and walked fast in the opposite direction. It was a mile to the Floral Court, where they had first made love before he went to Rhodesia. It had few rivals in this part of east London, because there was not much call for a hotel. Its main source of income was the bar, all bare boards and Victorian mirrors, which supported a hard-drinking darts team and several bar-billiards fanatics. The rooms were merely a way for Pat Sargeant to cash in on the building she had inherited from her father. Now in her fifties, she had never married, and was thus one of those rare creatures, an independent woman. She was short, sturdy, immensely hard-working and she made people laugh. The reason she worked so hard and kept so fit and remained happy, in the midst of fumes and garbage and graffiti, was that she could escape whenever she wanted to a cottage near Maidstone, on a farm where she had been a hop-picker as a kid. Some weekends, and for two weeks in the summer, she would vanish, closing the place up. In autumn, she would drape the bar in hop-bines to remind her of the country and her childhood. Originally the place had been called the George. It was she who had renamed it Floral Court.

When Rourke entered, Pat was behind the bar, a fizz of grey hair and huge glasses, serving a pint to one of the half-dozen customers. She glanced up, smiled a welcome, then frowned, remembering. He stood waiting, until she came across to him. She stared quizzically, saying nothing.

'No,' she said, at last. 'Brain's going. It's that disease that makes you forget. Put me out of my misery.'

'Rourke.'

'Yes. Michael. Got you. You were off to Australia.'

'Africa.'

'Well, same sort of area. And you had a pretty girl.'

'Lucy.'

'That's the one. Dark hair, nice bum. Still around, is she?'

'Pat, I need the room again. Is it free?'

'It could be. It depends.'

'On?'

'On whether you intend to use it for its designated purpose.'

'Which is?' he asked, smiling.

'You tell me. You get the right answer, you get the room.'

'Oh, come on. She'll be here in a minute. I need a bath.'

'Ah, now we get to it. Young man ...' She wagged a finger at him, frowning. 'I know your sort. You want to sully my nice clean room with filthy behaviour, you want to indulge your gross carnal habits in an orgy of unmitigated lust.'

'Well, yes.'

'With Lucy?'

He nodded.

She cracked a smile, and flicked a glass, making it ring. 'Ding! That is the right answer. Twenty-five a night, and you make your own coffee. Get on up. Remember the way?'

The room was as it had been. One of those high, old-fashioned double beds with slatted wooden ends, a Victorian grate of intricately stamped metal, bedside tables with ornate doilies, two ancient bulbous armchairs and a low round table, wardrobe, sink, mirror, kettle, coffee jar. It seemed as if no one had been in the room since he and Lucy were there five months previously.

He slung his pack in the wardrobe, pulled out a fresh if crumpled T-shirt, ran himself a bath in the bathroom next door, shaved, made a coffee, and lay on the bed. All the while, his mind was racing ahead. Lucy was different. She had always been sharp, but never like this: angry, distracted, secretive. He could think of reasons, and didn't like to take any of them seriously. All he wanted was her. No point in forcing a row.

He was beginning to wonder whether she was really coming, whether she had sent him ahead just to get rid of him – and what then? Would he go to her house? Was she still living at home? – when he heard footsteps on the stairs.

She came in, and watched deadpan as he stood

up and came to her. She had changed out of her working jeans into a skirt. She was still wearing the same sweater. He took her hand.

'Luce? What's the matter, beauty?'

'Don't "beauty" me. You can't . . .' She stopped short, and he heard a catch in her voice. 'Look.' Her voice was softer, almost pleading. 'I can't.'

He stood looking at her blankly. 'What?'

She hardened again, and when she spoke her voice rose in anger. 'You were away so long. I didn't know where you were, when you were coming back. You bastard. You *bastard*.' She hit him on the chest. He caught her hand as it came down a second time.

'Hey,' he said gently, holding her. 'Come on now.'

And whether she fell into his arms or whether he took her neither could tell, but suddenly she was there, and his face was in her neck, and she was crying against him. 'Hey,' he said again, and kissed her neck, then her ear, her hair, her damp cheek, and finally her mouth. They kissed as they had kissed the night before they parted, five months before, deep and full. His hand was under her sweater, sliding from the waist of her jeans on to her bare back. No bra, as ever. His hand went right up her back to the nape of her neck, holding her head against his shoulder.

'Oh, Mike,' she said. 'Oh, Mike.'

The urgency of her response and the switchback

changes of signal – the rejection, the anger, the tension, the desire – told him all he needed to know.

He said, still holding her: 'There's another bloke.'

'Yes.'

He knew her well enough to understand everything all at once. She wasn't in love with this other guy, because if she had been she would never have agreed to see him. But she was in deep enough to be frightened, deep enough to be concerned that she shouldn't be seen with Rourke. He was only back for a day or two, then he'd be gone, for God knew how long, and she had a life to live, and what was she supposed to do?

None of this she needed to say. What mattered to him most was that she still wanted him. Because he wanted her, right now, so much that this other bloke really didn't exist. He belonged to yesterday and tomorrow. Today it was the two of them, and nothing else.

She pulled back. 'I can't stay,' she said.

'Lucy, don't do this to me. I love you.'

'You said that before. Then you went away, and you'll go away again, and I have to stay here and look after Mum and work and . . .'

'Don't talk. Get undressed.'

'No! Mike! I'm meant to be out for a walk. Out for a walk!' she repeated bitterly. 'I never go out for walks. I'll have some explaining to do.'

She didn't want to tell him all the truth – his

name, what he did, why she was so frightened of
him – because she knew he didn't want to know,
and he knew she knew.

He drew her to him again, and felt her melt into
him, felt the pressure of her stomach, groin and
thighs. Again his hand slipped up her back. She
shuddered as they kissed.

He locked his arm behind her back, and lifted her
towards the bed, still kissing her. She made one last
attempt to restrain herself, and him, by not lying
back. Instead, she sat. But her legs were apart, and
to keep on the same level as her, he knelt.

It was merely a ritual delay. They both knew
that now.

'Mike, I have to be careful.'

'I know, my darling.'

'I don't want anyone to know I'm here.'

'They won't.'

Bastard. Liar. His senses were full of her, and
right then he would have said anything to get her
into bed.

And she wanted to believe. As his hand went
beneath her skirt, feeling for the top of her knickers
– she was wearing the underwear he had always
admired, the silk ones with pretty decorative edges
– she raised herself so that he could slip them off.

There was a tradition to their lovemaking, well
enough established to thrill them both with the
knowledge of what was coming next. First, she had
to come, somehow, it didn't matter how, against his

73

thigh, against his stomach – she was so wrapped in the power of her desire she didn't care how. This time, he gave her his mouth, kneeling, while she leant back, her back thrusting up from the edge of the bed. He drew her deep into him, working with lips and tongue until he felt her quiver and relax.

Only then did he rise, lift her languid body into bed, slide off her sweater, and at last undress himself.

This next chapter in their lovemaking was also not extended. She was too ready to come again, and he was far too aroused for delay. It didn't matter, because they both knew – whatever she had said earlier – that there would be at least one, perhaps two later opportunities that night.

At some point, while recovering, her hair strewn across his chest and her thigh tight around his waist, he dozed off.

'Hey,' she said digging him in the ribs. 'You said you were going to get supper.'

'I forgot,' he said.

'Bastard,' she said, with a smile. 'I'm hungry.'

'Well, eat,' he said.

Her smile broadened. 'OK. Here I come,' and he felt her lips work their way down his hard, flat stomach.

4

Not far away late that night, while Rourke and Lucy lay cupped like spoons asleep, Peter Halloran and Frank Ridger were walking down an alley near Ridger's rented house. Halloran had bought Ridger a drink. A few days ago, this would have been surprising. But Halloran had taken to going out now and then, and not merely to counteract the boredom. Like a predator, he wanted to know his territory. It was during such a prowl that he had phoned Collins and received the tip-off. Never one to take a chance, he had at once assumed the worst, and had acted accordingly. Ridger had been happy to pull on his old overcoat and go along with his volatile, talkative house guest.

'Come along this way,' said Halloran, looking down a darkened alley, 'we've not been down here.'

'There ain't nothing down there.'

'Further along there is,' replied Halloran. 'A club. I was out walking earlier and noticed it. Perhaps we'll get a last drink.'

At the end of the street there was a call-box, the one Halloran had used to contact Collins.

A few yards away was an abandoned building site, surrounded by a wire-mesh fence, leaning, battered and in places flattened by local kids. It was a mournful place. A year ago the square had been a block of decaying slum houses. In two years' time, no doubt, there would be council flats that would soon be equally tawdry. But at the moment the place looked like a bomb-site. The few street-lights cast long shadows behind the piles of rubble, disguising pits and puddles.

Halfway down the alley, Halloran said: 'Well, Frank, you have been the soul of hospitality. But I'm afraid it's time to be moving along.'

With only the briefest of pauses, Ridger said: 'Oh? Why's that, then?'

'Itchy feet. I get the strange feeling I'm being watched.'

'That's silly, that is. Why, no one knows you're here.'

'I get the funny impression they do. I can tell, you see. Eyes in the back of my head. Comes from years of action. Take today: I just got an overwhelming sense of people closing in. Eyes' – his arm swung expressively – 'everywhere. How do you explain that?' And his right arm came up to rest on the older man's shoulder.

'Well . . . I can't explain why you should feel that way, can I? Anyway you've no need to worry. You're safe here.'

'Now, Frank, don't tell me you'd not rather I

was gone. Not much social life with me here, is there? You have friends. You've been calling a few. I know, you see.'

Ridger's shoulders tensed under Halloran's hand.

'Holy Mother, how do you ... ? You've been watching me ... Well, what does it matter? I can have friends, can't I?'

'Of course you can. But it makes me nervous. Now, who was it you were calling on your way home today?'

'Just a pal. We arranged ... a drink for Saturday.'

'Oh, yes. I'd like to meet him, too. I'm getting lonely as hell, you know. What's his name?'

'Come on, Peter, what do you need his name for?'

'And number. Let's arrange a threesome.' They were nearing the end of the darkened street, ten yards short of the phone box, its single light-bulb casting a pale glow on the damp pavement. 'We'll call him from here.'

'Oh, no, Peter. We can't do that.'

Ridger's prevarication turned Halloran's suspicions into blinding certainty.

'I think I know why not.' And with that, Halloran's left arm came round and slammed the air out of Ridger's lungs. The older man doubled up. Halloran hauled him vertical against the wall, grabbed a handful of hair, forced his head back and stared into his face. Ridger, open-mouthed, dumb, struggled to fill the collapsed tissue under his ribs.

'You see, I have reason to believe your friend was no friend of mine. How much do you get paid for shopping me? Hundred quid? Is that the going rate round here' – Halloran began to bang Ridger's head against the wall on each emphatic word – 'for a – wild – boy – like – me?'

Ridger began to recover his voice.

'Christ . . . oh, Christ . . . I never told . . . I swear . . . let me be.'

Halloran saw that Ridger was near to collapse. It was time for another tack, for there was more to Halloran than pure violence.

He relaxed his grip on Ridger's hair, and set both his hands on Ridger's shoulders, supporting him. His brow furrowed, as if in displeasure. He would have made a good interrogator.

'Look, I don't blame you, Frank. We all work for money. But I've got to know, see. Self-defence. If I don't know, I have to guess, and that's when people get hurt needlessly. If I know, I can plan. So tell me . . . Quiet now.'

A young man approached down the street, a labourer in denim jacket and jeans, his gait showing him to be the worse for a few pints. Halloran held Ridger's shoulder more lightly.

As the stranger disappeared round the corner, Halloran continued in a low, persuasive voice: 'They'll never know you helped me. I'll just vanish.

Come on, come on now. Jesus, aren't we from the same lovely island? I'm frightened, can't you see? I don't like hitting friends.'

He relaxed his grip. Ridger was breathing more easily.

'Let's talk now, Frank. Come along over this way, where it's quiet and nobody can hear us.' And he took Ridger by the arm and began to lead him past the call-box, across the road to the darkness of the building site.

'I'll avoid the lights, if you don't mind,' he remarked, and gave an abrupt laugh. As they stepped over part of the flattened fence, Halloran produced a torch from the pocket of his anorak to guide them.

Ridger, his voice trembling with shock, but apparently reassured, said: 'All right, then. The coppers were on at me at work, me and a few others. Somebody had tipped them off about you. They know I'm a linkman. They were going to run me in. I want to be out of it. I'm too old for this business. Oh, Jesus. Peter, let me be. Let me be. I don't know what they'll do.'

They were picking their way slowly across the waste ground, the piles of rubble silhouetted against the distant street lamps.

'They won't be doing nothing to you, friend,' Halloran told him solicitously. 'I'll make sure they don't. Let's see if we can find a drink, then. Watch this hole, now.'

They came level with a shadowy pit dug to test the subsoil months earlier.

Halloran's right hand moved again across Ridger's shoulders, as if to guide him. As it did so, the left hand came up to the other shoulder. It held a three-foot length of thin rope with a small weight at the end. The rope swung before Ridger was aware. The weight smacked into Halloran's right hand as the noose snapped taut around Ridger's neck.

His death was silent. His face screamed, but no sound came. Blood and air were locked off in an instant. Halloran applied pressure by crossing his arms. It took Ridger thirty seconds to become unconscious and another two minutes to die, on his knees, forced down and then supported by Halloran's iron grip.

When it was over, Halloran rolled the body into the hole and threw bricks down on it until it was covered with rubble. He checked his work with his torch, tossed some more bricks in and checked again. There was no sign of the body.

He then replaced the rope in his pocket and headed over the rubble-strewn square towards a workmen's hut. To one side of it was a hod for gravel and stones once used in the making of a path across the mud. In the hod he had left his few belongings – his rucksack, containing a few rough clothes. He couldn't risk going back to Ridger's house.

But as if to prove himself right, he approached it

and waited in the shadows a hundred yards away. Near the house was a parked car, side-lights on, with two men in it. After ten minutes, as a few late-night drinkers ambled past and the house remained dark, Halloran saw, by the light of the street lamp, the driver's hand come up towards his face. Halloran, recognizing the action of a man speaking into a microphone, knew the men to be police.

He nodded grimly, muttered: 'Wait on, you bastards,' and headed away.

He walked for twenty minutes, hopped on a bus and went into Leytonstone tube station, to cross town for the anonymity of Earls Court.

As far as the waiting Special Branch men were concerned, both Irishmen had vanished completely. A search of Ridger's house was later to reveal fingerprints, but no further clues. Ridger's body was found only two months later, when work started again on the site.

Halloran broke his journey at Paddington and went into a call-box to contact Collins. It was approaching midnight.

'Pity you're late, Peter,' said Collins, 'but not to worry. We're on, at least so far. Where are you now?'

'Paddington, Major, but I won't be here over-night. I took your warning. I reckon it saved me a turn inside. But I have to drop out of sight soon, for a long, long time.'

'That'll suit us all. There's a train around midday. If you catch it, you should see Michael Rourke. He's our number three. A good team, don't you think?'

Wednesday 24 March

Yufru arrived at Cromer's office at 10.30 a.m.

'Sir Charles,' he said as he sipped a coffee, 'I had a most interesting evening. Mengistu is in agreement that the money must be released at all costs. There must be no risks, no delays. We are to work together to draw up suitable documents and make arrangements for their signature by the Emperor, yourselves and the Ethiopian government.'

'Congratulations, Mr Yufru. It's good to know we are moving in the same direction. Now, to come straight to the point, I have noted a number of matters that should be included in any memorandum of agreement between us. I suggest that we discuss them and that I then draft a first version of the memorandum which will be circulated to my colleagues, to your government and to the Emperor. When I have the comments on that draft, I hope we shall be able to draw up a final version acceptable to us all.

'I warn you, it will be a bulky document. But most of the space will be taken up with specifications of the Emperor's accounts and investments. In addition to these, he owns a number of companies in Europe, America and Africa. These will be the subject of a separate schedule, because they will have to be sold off if the investments are to be realized in full. Such things take time – as much as a year, I'm afraid. But the bulk of the funds is in currencies of various denominations, in gold and in Maria Theresa dollars. It should be possible to place, say, seventy-five per cent of the amounts involved to your account within a week of signature and a further ten per cent within a month.'

Yufru was taking notes in silence. Cromer reached the heart of the matter: the circumstances in which the signature would have to take place. The meeting would have to be on neutral territory. Was there any possibility of flying the Emperor to Switzerland? Mr Yufru looked up, smiled and spread his hands.

'My dear Sir Charles,' he said condescendingly, 'would you, in our position, take such a risk?'

Cromer raised his hands, as if to say: point taken.

'We were thinking,' Yufru continued, 'that we could fly you to Harar. A fascinating medieval fortress, but we also have facilities for tourism there. And, of course, the Emperor would not have to be moved.'

It was Cromer's turn to smile. 'Now, Mr Yufru, you must understand that we cannot possibly meet the Emperor in his place of imprisonment. I am sure that in such circumstances we too might feel . . . under pressure.'

The bargaining continued for an hour. Cromer suggested a number of African countries: Nigeria, Egypt, Zaïre. Yufru mentioned places in Ethiopia with the necessary tight security. Eventually Cromer said: 'Mr Yufru, there is one place that can satisfy both our criteria: an embassy in Addis Ababa, if possible the Swiss. It is the custom, is it not, for such places to be contained within their own compounds? You could provide all the security needed up to the moment the Emperor arrives. Thereafter he is on foreign soil. Your guards will be excluded. In the embassy of a neutral country we can see that no pressure is exerted. I feel that would be entirely acceptable to us.'

'Except that once again the Emperor is outside our control,' countered Yufru. 'It is possible to seek asylum in a foreign embassy.' He recalled the case of the Hungarian, Cardinal Mindszenty, who sought refuge in the American Embassy in Budapest after the Hungarian uprising in 1956. He remained there safely for fifteen years.

'Yes, I see,' said Cromer. 'You will want some assurances from the embassy concerned that they will allow appropriate measures to be taken. What have you in mind?'

'For such details I will again have to consult Addis Ababa.'

'Very well. But there is another problem that you hinted at earlier. How would the Emperor arrive?'

'I mentioned the problem of delivery within Ethiopia to the President last night. It is a relatively simple matter wherever the meeting takes place. There is only one way for top officials to travel efficiently in Ethiopia – by air. In this case, the distance is not particularly great. The Emperor would not, of course, be brought in by plane. The final stage from the airport to the embassy would require police escorts, a darkened car, the clearing of streets – all unacceptable and unnecessary. No, he would be brought in by helicopter.'

It was now 12.45. Both men needed a break. Cromer suggested that each should spend the weekend preparing a detailed proposal of the personnel to be involved and the scheduling. It would have to be in the form of a first exchange of ideas, for he feared nothing could be finalized until well into the following week. Only then could they begin the business of drafting a working agreement.

At that moment, Halloran and Rourke were approaching Oxford. The train was only a few minutes behind schedule. Collins, briefed to meet the 1.15 to Banbury, wouldn't have to wait long.

The two men had met at the ticket barrier at Paddington. Each knew the other was involved. There was a quiet satisfaction that they were on the move together again.

Rourke said: 'Peter, you mick. What have we let ourselves in for?'

'I'm no mind-reader, Michael. The major's not told me a thing. But I'll buy you a drink while we talk about it.'

They sipped Holsten lagers in the buffet car and tried to guess. Must be a small do ... didn't say anything about weapons ... Ireland? South America? Middle East? Don't fancy tangling with the Israelis ... and anywhere in that part you have identity problems ... Cyprus? West Africa? Surely not back to Rhodesia ... wait a minute: Uganda. You think someone is trying to get at Big Daddy Amin? Now that would be something. But where's the money in that? Who'd be paying the bills?'

Despite their experience, they were no nearer a solution when Collins picked them up at Banbury station in his Range Rover.

'Good to see you again,' he said. 'Hop in and we'll have a jolly weekend huntin', shootin' and fishin'. You can pretend to be country squires for a couple of days. How does that suit you?'

The three of them had a light lunch, during which Collins explained as much as he could. It would be an undercover show, probably without weapons, in a foreign country, to kidnap a senior political element. There would be few if any guards. Neutral territory – in an embassy. There wouldn't be any problems about the job itself.

'The problem,' Collins concluded over coffee, 'will be to escape.'

Having whetted their appetite for the adventure,

Collins was as good as his word. He offered them a choice of double-barrel twelve-bore Browning D5s, lent them some wellingtons, and led them out into the field behind the farm to introduce them to clay-pigeon shooting. It was a perfect day for it. The air was sparkling clear and the woods that fringed the field were tinged with the green of budding leaves.

Collins was proud of his layout. The trap, which looked like a solid box from the firing mark, actually contained an automatic release mechanism that fired the saucer-shaped clay discs, or 'birds', at the sound of a human voice. It was programmed not to respond to the report of a gun. Collins had demonstrated twice, and the other two had also tried their hands.

'I shout "Pull!" because that's what one shouts in a normally operated trap,' explained Collins, 'but any shout would do. Now, watch again . . . Pull!'

A disc zinged out in front of him. His gun came up smoothly, he fired and the disc shattered into a black smudge. He lowered his gun and ejected the spent cartridge.

'OK, Michael. Now remember: swing, don't aim. And shoot in front of the bird. It's moving at thirty miles an hour. OK. Stance. Lean forward . . .'

'Fuck!' shouted Rourke. A disc flew out. Rourke lifted the gun, fired and missed.

'Lost,' said Collins with a grin. 'Serves you right.'

'I was right there,' Rourke replied. 'I'll try again in a moment. Now, Major, you have to tell us more. It's totally unfair. All this is fun, but it doesn't help us.'

'I've told you all I can. You'll know more when we get the go-ahead.'

Thursday 25 March

Cromer rose early, as usual. His life was one of very few indulgences, and even fewer human contacts. His marriage, never one of passion, had sunk back to one of mere convenience: a house, well run, a place to entertain necessary guests and an occasional shoot. His real world was the City. He wanted it to be that way, for he had for years harboured an ambition that could be satisfied only through the City, an ambition to exercise unfettered power and feel the zing of individual achievement.

He was not happy with his professional status. The gratitude towards Rothschild's that had been second nature to his grandfather and father had ebbed away. He saw only the framework that constrained him, the galling need to explain and justify his actions in monthly partners' meetings. His father had appreciated that it was just such controls that kept Cromer's stable. But Sir Charles didn't like it. He wanted independence, his own bank, the freedom his grandfather had once had. If he made a break, as he intended to someday, he would need to keep his present customers and win others. To do so, he would need to prove an unswerving, even ruthless, dedication to his clients' funds.

Here, perhaps, was the opportunity he needed.

To lose Selassie's fortune would not only be costly for the bank and a blow to his colleagues; it would show him to be a political turncoat. Who in Africa or the Middle East would trust him with future profits – from oil, perhaps, or metals – if the mere hint of political difficulty was seen to be enough to separate a rich client from his deposits? But if he was known to have preserved those deposits in the face of intense pressure – that would provide him with a name worth having!

Ambition was one motive. Another, equally powerful at this moment, was the sheer thrill of the thing. There had been too little excitement over the last twenty years. He had few interests outside business. He had no mistress. Indeed, he'd never had one. Years ago, when he had first bought the house, there had been the occasional sexual skirmish, but now desire itself had become a rarity. It was not women he loved, but gold, about which he knew a great deal, and about which he would talk with passion.

He was in good company, for the love of gold has gripped all civilizations. Its lure seems illogical: how odd, after all, to dig metal from a hole in the earth, to bury it again in another hole beneath a bank. Yet, because of its rarity, it remains the epitome of wealth, the symbol of perfection, the ultimate medium of exchange between nations, the individual's final bastion against ruin.

Indeed so hard won is gold, so expensive in cash and human life, that in all history a mere 100,000 tons have been mined, eighty per cent of that amount this century. Yet gold is so dense that all the world's supply, the bars of the world's banks and the bullion merchants, the plates and bowls of the ancient Scythians, the Aztec decorations that Cortés plundered, the world's gold coins – the doubloons, dinars, rials, mohurs, dollars, sertums, reis, levas, francs, pesos, ducats, pesetas, guilders, all of the 776 types of gold coin known to dealers – the wedding rings hoarded by Vietnamese peasants, the chocolate-sized tola bars smuggled from Dubai into India, the medals hung around the necks of Arabian women, the whole lot would, if melted together, form a cube the size of a large house, sixty feet per side.

It was part of all this – the wealth, the power, the traditions, the sheer magic of the metal – that was now at stake. Cromer, in his brown silk dressing-gown and leather slippers, brewed coffee and browsed through *The Times*. He shaved and dressed in his habitual suit, and at a few minutes past eight he sat down at his desk to list his objectives.

He needed the financial aspects to be as open as possible, for copies of everything would have to go to Yufru and thence to Addis – a vital link in the chain of confidence with which he needed to surround the scheme. He would have to call Kupferbach at home in Zurich and at the same time ask him about the possible use of the Swiss Embassy. That he could do immediately. This afternoon, Lodge in Greenwich, Connecticut. He needed to confirm to them that everything was moving and warn them about the coming telex requesting an authorized assessment of the Emperor's holdings. The computerized details would have to be retrieved, printed, copied, formally set out, signed and couriered over.

Then there was Collins, and the other two. He needed to approve their accommodation in London, provide their covers, give them information and cash, go over their ideas.

He was preparing to leave when the phone rang. It was Collins.

At a hotel near Portland Place, in a suite on the fourth floor, looking out on the Langham Hotel, that rambling, still bomb-scarred colony of the BBC, Cromer pushed a bottle of whisky towards Rourke and Halloran, on the sofa opposite. Both men were wearing dark roll-neck sweaters, under their jackets, as if they were in uniform. Cromer sat in an armchair. To his left, in a second armchair, sat Collins in tweed trousers and a corduroy jacket. Coats lay on the bed.

'Please, gentlemen, help yourselves,' Cromer said, 'my apologies for offering such anonymous hospitality.' He took in the hotel room with a sweep of his arm. 'We shall be working closely together soon enough, I hope, if all goes well. Until we're certain of that, I prefer to separate my own personal and professional life from this business as much as possible. I'm sure you understand. Now, since it is essential you waste no time in beginning your plans, let me give you the details I have so far. My name is Charles Cromer and I'm an old friend of Dicky . . .'

He spoke for over half an hour, outlining what had happened and what he needed done. He didn't specify the sums involved, but he described Yufru's role, the banking arrangements, his own central position, the fact of Selassie's survival, the need for his removal, the need to prevent the Emperor signing anything, his own plan to gain access to Selassie, the Emperor's arrival by helicopter under tight security, the apparent acceptance of the suggestions so far.

'Gentlemen,' he finished, 'there are countless details still to clarify, but I have to suggest certain conditions to the Ethiopians. To do so, I must know your requirements as soon as possible.'

Halloran poured himself a slug of whisky, and glanced at Rourke. Collins spoke first.

'Don't expect answers right away, Charlie. It's a tricky operation. Not the normal run of things at all. We're used to . . .'

'Stop, Dicky, stop,' broke in Cromer, raising his hands. 'Let's first look at the problem in general terms. What I want to know is, whether we should be proceeding at all. Is it, in theory, possible?'

He was certain Collins would say yes. But the other two had just learned the true scope of the proposal.

Halloran spoke. 'First things first. Getting in, now. I'd like a little reassurance that it wouldn't be all up to us.'

'I hope that won't be too hard. The problem should really be mine,' Cromer answered. 'To the Ethiopians, you are my advisers. You will not be required to say anything much, but must be prepared to look and act the part of bankers. No problem for you, Dicky. As for you other two, neither of you looks too extreme. I thought of crediting you to my Swiss and American counterparts, but there is a chance you'll meet Yufru, so you'll have to be juniors of my own bank. As for your actual arrival, you'll be part of an official delegation. I have no idea how you'll be treated. They may want to hush up your presence. Or you may be passed off as another visiting delegation. Or you may get an official reception. From your point of view, it won't matter. The point is, they will believe you to be bankers and will treat you accordingly, with every courtesy.'

'Passports?' asked Halloran.

'You should have fake identities.'

'You can fix it?'

'No. That's part of your job. I'll do whatever is necessary: money, documentation. Any insoluble problems?'

Collins answered this time: 'We've not done it before but we can find out.'

Again Rourke and Halloran glanced at each other. They both nodded.

Cromer pressed home his advantage. 'It's getting out that'll be the problem. You'll be in hostile country, with an old man on your hands. So let me give you some figures that I hope will make it all worthwhile. My offer is this: £100,000 for each of you.'

Halloran rounded his lips.

'In three stages,' Cromer continued. 'Ten thousand as an advance, payable now. That is, of course, inclusive of the £1000 I guaranteed for you to make yourselves available in the first place. A further £20,000 upon the successful completion of the planning. And the balance upon your return. I would naturally be willing to arrange payment in any currency in the country of your choice. I should remind you that we have excellent contacts in Switzerland.'

*　　*　　*

After Cromer had gone, Collins placed an order for a supper of fillet steak all round. Then, while he was in the bathroom, Rourke and Halloran agreed the money was good, and that there was a fair chance of success.

Collins made way for Halloran to relieve himself and poured himself a whisky. When Halloran returned, Collins said: 'Let's start at the beginning. I think we can act our part as bankers.'

'Any micks in the City?' asked Rourke with a smile.

'Or fucking barrow-boys?' countered Halloran

'Not all City people are public school,' said Collins. 'Besides, you won't have to speak much, and I hardly think the Ethiopians will be fussy about accents. You will have to acquire a certain deference to me, which will be hard for you two. Your job, I imagine, will be to handle the documents, of which there are likely to be a fair number. Any problems there?'

Halloran said: 'I want to get something straight. Where are we going to work? I don't much like the idea of being in London.'

'Indeed,' said Collins, 'we all have an interest in keeping you hidden.'

Rourke agreed. 'We're going to need equipment, phones, plans, maps. We need your house. We can't work out of a hotel.'

'OK. Let's move on, then. Assume we can get there. How do we actually do the job? It has to be done rapidly and silently. There will be others – officials, government people both with Selassie and outside, but probably not many. For one thing, they won't want to attract attention to the operation by having a mass of people. For another, we can make it one of our conditions – a matching delegation, perhaps. After all, the whole point of the op is to see that no undue pressure is being placed on the old man. So let's say three of us, three of them, and Selassie, all together in one room. Where do we go from there?'

Halloran leapt in: 'We have silenced pistols. We take them out. Simple.'

Rourke grinned. 'Peter, you bloody mick!'

Halloran shrugged. 'OK, it's impossible. Just tell me why, clever Dick, and I'll forget it.'

'You think we would risk carrying hardware with us? What if they search us at the airport? Might be routine. Fine lot of bankers we'd look then, eh? Blimey, no wonder they wanted you out of Ireland. You'd sink the bloody place all by yourself, you would.'

Halloran took the rebuke in good humour. 'All right, all right. Knives then,' he said.

They each pondered the implications.

'Messy,' said Collins, 'and not so quick in a group. You have to get to each one individually. Anything could go wrong. And we might not even reach Selassie before someone got out of the room.'

'Right,' said Rourke, 'and they're not all that quiet. I remember once in Rhodesia, one of our guys had to take out a guard. He was dead in ten seconds but the noises – grunts, groans, enough to wake the dead, let alone the living! Guards outside, embassy staff, we don't want them joining the party. Anyone screams, that's it.'

He paused, then said: 'What I reckon is, we need another room. Separate them out and then a bit of close-quarter combat.'

'Ah, now you're talking,' Halloran broke in quickly. 'The old silencer.' And from beneath his sweater round his neck he pulled the rope with which he had strangled Ridger. 'No noise at all. A little slow, but effective.'

Collins grimaced: 'That's what you used the other night?'

'It is.'

Collins turned to Rourke: 'Michael, have you ever . . .?'

'No. But I've done enough karate to see us through this job.'

'All right, then,' said Collins, 'I keep in training too. It sounds a possibility.'

The other two nodded.

'Not bad odds,' said Rourke, 'if we get it set up right.'

Collins poured himself another whisky and fetched some ice from the fridge. The other two remained silent as he continued: 'Let's get to the real problem: the escape. If it doesn't seem feasible in theory we have to stop right here. I've been thinking of some possibilities. Fortunately, someone else has done a similar job just recently. I looked out some of my cuttings. It may be helpful to review it . . .'

'Carlos,' broke in Rourke. Collins smiled. Halloran looked blank.

'Peter, you should read more,' said Collins. 'You might learn something. That raid on the OPEC HQ in Vienna three months ago, remember? It offers a few parallels with our own little job . . .'

And for ten minutes he summarized the operation.

Four days before Christmas 1975, eleven ministers of the world's oil-rich nations and over fifty staff were in conference at the headquarters of the Organization of Petroleum Exporting Countries, a white-fronted building on Vienna's Ringstrasse, the tree-lined boulevard that circles the inner city. Carlos, the *nom de guerre* of a twenty-six-year-old Venezuelan terrorist named Ilich Ramírez Sánchez, and five others entered the building, killed three men, stormed the conference room on the third floor, and held all those present at gunpoint. Meanwhile, a British Special Branch officer had phoned a warning to the city's police HQ. Eight Austrian riot squad commandos arrived soon afterwards, to be driven off by bursts of fire from the watching terrorists.

Carlos was in full control. That afternoon and

throughout the night he issued his demands: the broadcast of a rambling statement in support of world revolution, the provision of a bus to take them to the airport, and a DC8 to fly them to any destination he named. The plan – as Sheikh Yamani, Saudi Arabia's Oil Minister and a prime target, later revealed – was to take hostages, depart and then shoot Yamani and the Iranian Oil Minister, Dr Jamshid Amouzegar, the representatives of the two most right-wing of the OPEC countries.

The Austrian Chancellor, Bruno Kreisky, gave Carlos precisely what he wanted. The plane left as planned for Algiers to release all the hostages except Yamani and Amouzegar, and then flew on to Tripoli, Libya. At this point the operation ran out of steam because Carlos failed to receive delivery of the longer-range Boeing 707 that he needed to get him to his final sanctuary, Baghdad. Instead, he ordered the DC9 to return to Algiers, where he eventually surrendered the two remaining hostages. In return – and presumably as a reward for successfully disrupting the work of the OPEC capitalists – he received a million pounds, supplied almost certainly by the eccentric Libyan leader Colonel Gaddafi, patron of world revolution. Carlos and his fellow-terrorists were allowed to go free by the Algerians.

'There are several things of importance for us in this affair,' concluded Collins. 'The main point is that the team got in and out successfully. How?

By knowing intimately in advance the ground plan of the building. By knowing the strength of the opposition. And by having hostages of such value that their demands were met instantly. As a result, they were then in a position to kill their two prime hostages with impunity, although as it happened Carlos decided not to.'

'Hostages,' pondered Halloran.

'Wouldn't work,' said Rourke, after only the briefest of pauses. 'Selassie wouldn't count. He's only worth something to the Ethiopians if he's in their hands. If we're going to take him away, they'll be better off with us all dead. None of the others would matter that much, either. We wouldn't even get out of the embassy.'

Collins nodded. 'Agreed. That's a non-starter, then. So how do we get out?'

Again it was Rourke who spoke. 'The helicopter. If that's really part of their arrangements.'

'A real genius you are!' said Halloran, wrapping an arm around Rourke's shoulder.

'You can fly?' asked Collins, looking at Rourke.

'Course. I went through the Army Air Corps for the Green Jackets in the early '60s, before the SAS.'

'Good. That makes two of us. I did a civilian course not too many years back. How about you, Peter?'

'Not one of my many talents. But with you two aces, I shan't worry.'

'It's not quite that easy,' Collins pointed out. 'We have to know the type of machine, and then make sure we can fly it.'

Gradually, as the theory of the operation became clearer, other practical questions began to emerge. Collins again pointed out the lessons of Carlos's success. They would need detailed information on the building, the personnel, the timing, the positioning of guards, the type of helicopter, the flight path after take-off. And they would need additional help – a helicopter would not have a range of more than 300 miles. They would either have to refuel or arrange reliable alternative transport. Failure on that point had curtailed Carlos's plan.

At the end of another hour all three had agreed that the scheme sounded possible in theory. That was all they needed to know. The money was good, but that was not the deciding factor. The real lure was the thrill of the thing.

When Cromer returned, he listened to the conclusions and nodded at Collins's last words: 'There's one thing we'll need – details of the building. If it is the Swiss Embassy, we have to know soon, and then get plans of the place.'

'I'll do what I can,' said Cromer. 'I'll be in touch tomorrow evening.'

5

Friday 26 March

Cromer arrived at his office at 8.30. He had an hour to himself, and wished to be completely clear about what he would need to propose. One task would be a formal telex to both New York and Zurich requesting a schedule of the Emperor's holdings, with delivery by courier, at the weekend. But most important, he would have to prepare a letter to Selassie, persuading him to sign the transfer. He looked at the notes he had scrawled the previous day. From them, he would be able to dictate a first draft to Valerie Yates.

As usual, Valerie arrived at 9.15. At twenty-nine she already had the formal, ageless look of the top personal assistant. She always wore a suit, her light hair loose, but never more than shoulder length, with a touch of lipstick that she was at pains to renew several times a day. She was, in a word, impeccable. She knew her role and played it well.

She was only mildly dismayed at her boss's presence. Sometimes, if he had been in the country, she had that time to herself, a few minutes to prepare her desk for the day. The veneer of efficiency carefully polished was part of the framework of her professional life, itself utterly apart from the other world of her private life. She had never shown a flicker of emotion to any member of the bank. She knew that suited Sir Charles. It certainly suited her.

She prepared coffee, took the tray through, and offered a cup to Cromer, who accepted it with: 'Ten minutes, Miss Yates, please,' scarcely glancing up from his notes. She received the mail from one of the two delivery boys, opened it and set it in the leather folder stamped with the bank's seal. Then she checked her own stationery and knocked again on Cromer's door. He began to speak as soon as she sat down.

'Miss Yates, I shall need your help this week as I have never needed it before. The matter, as you will see, is of extreme delicacy. If anything leaks out, even within the company, we shall all suffer. We shall need a separate cabinet for the files and the correspondence.'

'Very well, Sir Charles.'

'You will see the nature of the problem as we go along. The first letter is to Emperor Haile Selassie.' Valerie glanced up. 'No, he is not dead, Miss Yates. He is very much alive, and we are about to persuade him to sign certain documents which will make over most of his fortune to the present government. Hence Mr Yufru's visits.

'The first major hurdle is the Emperor himself. After I have dictated the letter, look out all the usual forms of address – Conquering Lion of Judah, Elect of God, King of Kings – the whole thing. He's still a client even if he doesn't rule the place.'

He waited until Valerie had settled herself and then dictated the letter he had prepared:

'Your Highness,

'It is with overwhelming joy that I have learned of Your Highness's survival throughout these last months. I understand that your circumstances are much changed, for which I offer my condolences. With the respect that we have always shown Your Highness, I would like to make a proposal concerning your affairs.

'As you are no doubt aware, the Provisional Military Administrative Council claims your assets as its own. We can confirm that under the laws of the countries in which the deposits are made, no transfer is possible without your free, written consent. This you have wisely withheld.

'But I would like to bring to Your Highness's attention a further consideration. There are numerous members of your family abroad, many of whom would, in happier circumstances, inherit a certain share of your wealth. Should you die intestate, without leaving a will that we can authenticate as valid, the family, by your own orders, receives nothing.

'I do not believe this to represent your own original intentions. Considering therefore,

– that your assets may in future be blocked in perpetuity unless you take the actions necessary to release them;

– that your family would in these circumstances be destitute;

– that the present government, through whom I must act as the *de facto* power in your country, would not countenance a direct transfer of all assets to your family;

'I make the following proposition:

'That I and my colleagues draw up the necessary documents to transfer an agreed sum to your family and an agreed sum to the present government.

'These documents having been drawn up and approved by Your Highness and the present government, I will authorize a small delegation to witness the signature on neutral territory yet to be decided and in circumstances in which Your Highness would be seen to be free of all pressure.

'I beg you to consider for your family's sake, as well as your nation's, the multiplicity of benefits that would flow from such an action, one that would reflect the greatness of your lineage.

'If Your Highness agrees in principle to this suggestion, I will make detailed proposals as soon as possible.'

Cromer paused. He was pleased with his words. The implication was strong that his last imperial act would be a generous one that would redound to Selassie's credit – and thus to the discredit of Mengistu. The fact that such ringing phrases were designed to accomplish the precise opposite of their stated intentions gave Cromer a tingle of satisfaction.

He then dictated a telex to be sent to New York and Zurich, all very formal, with copies to Yufru:

'Gentlemen, in my capacity as agent for our client known as Lion and under the terms of that agency, I request you to provide me with an inventory of Lion's assets held by you. This should be in two categories: floating assets (cash balances, gold deposits, securities) and fixed assets (those companies of which Lion has whole or part ownership). Please assess all assets at their current market value, in dollars, as of today's rates. I request that such information be delivered to me by standard courier by Thursday next week, together with a summary of information as yet unavailable, if any.'

Lodge and Kupferbach would be amused by the formal pomposity of the request. But Yufru and his bosses should be impressed. He told Valerie to put the telex out at once, keeping two copies, making the tapes herself and bringing them back upstairs with her. Of course, he had no control over what happened to the print-outs at the other end, but they were unlikely to go further and no one in London would know they had been sent.

The two items had taken half an hour to dictate. It was 10.15. Yufru should arrive shortly.

'Thank you, Miss Yates. And more coffee, I think.'

Yufru arrived promptly. The two men could now dispense with the intellectual skirmishing that had characterized their previous meetings. Valerie closed the door, and Yufru sat down at once in his usual place and poured himself a coffee. Cromer sat down opposite.

'Basically, Sir Charles,' began Yufru, 'your proposals are acceptable. The Provisional Military Administrative Council agreed that a banking delegation should witness Selassie's signature in Addis Ababa on neutral territory. Your suggestion of the Swiss Embassy is a good one. The Russian compound would be ideal from our point of view, but the Russians would not take kindly to your inevitable request for the removal of all troops on the day in question. Neither the British nor the American Embassy would be acceptable to us; they are too large and we feel the problems of security would be unnecessarily magnified. As for the African countries . . . although we are still host to the OAU I am afraid that some of our African friends are neither as friendly nor as conscientious as we should like.'

Yufru went on to explain the advantages of the Swiss Embassy. It was set in its own compound, like many of the major embassies, and also stood apart from the city centre. Given the fact that Switzerland was a major depository for the Emperor's funds, it made good sense to hold the meeting there.

'Excellent,' replied Cromer. 'I should imagine my Swiss colleagues can easily establish good contacts with the embassy in Addis. Now: your conditions.'

'We have three. One is that the telephones and telexes must be cut off during the time of the Emperor's presence in the embassy. The reason for this request is obvious: the Emperor would otherwise be given his only possible opportunity to re-establish links with the outside world.

'The other two conditions demand more positive Swiss co-operation. The signing must take place on a Sunday, so that there will be no staff on the premises. And we must provide an official presence of some kind, to ensure that the Emperor's timetable is adhered to. A defection within the embassy would be a severe embarrassment. Now, Sir Charles, you will no doubt have some further points.'

'The size of the delegation, Mr Yufru. I suggest that your delegation should match my own. I shall send a senior aide and two juniors. The bureaucratic procedure alone is considerable. My senior aide will be an expert on the Emperor's liquid assets, in particular his gold holdings. One of the two juniors will be supervising our arrangements with lawyers and company matters. The second will be there simply to ensure the various documents are correctly presented and collated. It would be diplomatic to arrange for two people to sit opposite us with Selassie. That, I feel, would be a balance of forces.'

'Not quite, Sir Charles. The Emperor can hardly be said to be on our side. Three of you should be matched by three of us.'

'Very well,' said Cromer, with a magnanimous sweep of his right hand.

'And we will, of course, provide additional guards to ensure the sealing of the embassy. The compound gates will be locked, and the two-man helicopter crew should be able to take on that particular role.'

Cromer needed to probe for information as deeply as possible without arousing suspicion.

'So we shall expect one helicopter with . . . six people including the Emperor? All coming from Harar?'

'No, no, Sir Charles. The three who will accompany the Emperor will be government members and will be in Addis already. One will be the interpreter. The other two will arrive separately by car. Is it important?'

'I suppose not, except that it seems you hold all the cards. Let's look on the black side. What if the Emperor raises insuperable problems? What guarantee have we of the diplomatic immunity normally assured by an embassy? It seems to me we could have more . . .'

'Oh, come, Sir Charles, you surely don't imagine

that we would kidnap you all or shoot you. My government needs the money. If there were problems, we should, of course, make communications available to you. And you are at liberty to inform your embassy of your presence in Addis, though naturally not the reason for your presence. Our only interest is in arranging for a successful conclusion to the mission, for your rapid return and for the Emperor's . . . removal.'

Cromer nodded slowly. The conditions seemed acceptable, in line with the previous night's discussion. The timing, the transport, the setting, the personnel had virtually been decided.

As Yufru was agreeing to check the details with Addis, Valerie entered with a draft of Cromer's letter to the Emperor. She handed it and a copy to Cromer, together with a copy of his telex to Zurich and New York. Cromer thanked her as she left and glanced through the letter.

'Good,' he said, 'not yet perfect, but good enough for you to have a copy, Mr Yufru. Would you read this carefully over the next few hours and call me with any changes you think necessary? Then I will prepare a formal copy for delivery, via yourself, to the Emperor.'

'It can be in his hands within a day,' said Yufru, as he stood up to go. 'We shall talk again later.'

After he had gone Cromer recalled Yufru's mention of the Emperor's 'removal'. His pause before the word spoke volumes. The Emperor was doomed. The longer he remained alive, the greater the risk of embarrassment to the military regime. Even if he survived to sign, therefore, he would be killed by the Ethiopians, to be buried no doubt in an unmarked grave without honours – exactly the death announced by the military regime nine months earlier.

After lunch, Cromer had just three more calls to make. The first was to Zurich. He spoke to Kupferbach, explaining the business about the Swiss Embassy, the Ethiopian stipulation about cutting the building off during the time of Selassie's visit, and the need for a Sunday meeting.

'We need a diplomatic link, Oswald,' concluded Cromer. 'Contact at the highest level. Do you think you can go to the top?'

'Charles, I shall arrange an appointment with both the Foreign Minister and the Finance Minister. We cannot afford to fail. Therefore I have to tell them about Selassie. That is the only thing that will open those doors and guarantee secrecy and speed.'

'That is what I thought, Oswald. But there is more. To organize this properly, we need plans of the place. We have to know exactly, to the nearest foot, about doors and hallways and the size of the enclosure. Tell them we have to have this information to guarantee our own security before we agree terms. Tell them that it is the only way we can prevent a massive transfer of funds out of Switzerland to the Ethiopians. Tell them anything you damn well like, but get those plans!'

Monday 29 March

Cromer was in early. Company work was beginning to suffer. There were letters to clients, the gold committee, analysis of stock-market trends with Jeremy Squires and young Sackville-Jones – things that should not be delayed any longer if he was to keep on top. As it was, anyone who came into his office noticed the filing cabinet against the wall. He could sense the curiosity. Here lay the explanation for the Chairman's unaccustomed remoteness. The mystery should not be allowed to deepen.

When Valerie arrived, dressed strikingly well in a dark-green skirt and matching jacket over a white blouse, Cromer told her to confirm the usual two meetings – one at 11.30, the other at three o'clock – to organize the removal of the filing cabinet back to storage and to arrange lunch upstairs with Jeremy. Squires had virtually become his deputy over the past five years. The two men scarcely knew each other socially. Squires was fifteen years Cromer's junior, but he was so damn good. Uniquely, Cromer had taken to calling him by his Christian name. Now he needed him to bring things up to date. He went on to scribble some memos, mostly probing the actions and opinions of his staff. Each combined a specialist knowledge – mining, metals, chemicals, foods – with a concern for the funds of particular clients. It had proved a useful system, building a fine combination of personal interest, expertise and general ability.

Yufru called at 11.45, when Cromer was in his first meeting, and again at 12.30, just as he was finishing.

'Sir Charles, your letter is much admired,' he said. 'A most persuasive document. We would like to transmit it at once to Selassie. When can you finalize it?'

That day, Collins, Rourke and Halloran worked out the practicalities of their plan. In the morning, Rourke took the Range Rover into Oxford and bought maps from Parker's in Broad Street. He also picked up as many handbooks on arms and weapons as he could find in Blackwells, including Jane's *All The World's Aircraft*.

Collins had his business to run and was out for the morning.

To stave off boredom, Halloran took one of Collins's twelve-bores into the spring woods. He was gone for a couple of hours.

About midday, he strolled back over the fields bearing a brace of pheasant, the gun broken across his arm.

'We're all right for supper, then,' he remarked

lightly to Collins, who was washing his hands at the kitchen sink.

To his surprise Collins, who had not noticed the absence of the gun, exploded.

'You silly bugger!' he said, snatching a hand towel from a hook beside the sink. 'Did anyone see you? Sam? Molly?'

'No, I don't think so . . . What's up, would you tell me that?'

'You've never shot pheasant before, have you?'

'So?'

'Well, you don't know the bloody rules. They're protected birds. You can't just go out and shoot them any time.'

'Poor little darlings,' said Halloran, sarcastic and self-righteous. 'Fuck me, Major, here we are planning to knock off an Emperor and you're worrying about a few pheasants.'

Collins took a breath.

'Look, it's the close season now. You can only shoot pheasant between 30 September and 2 February, inclusive. Everyone knows that around here. If anyone sees you with pheasant, likely as not they'll have the law round. They're breeding. It spoils next year's shoot. And you without even a game licence! They'd be all over you, Halloran, all over you. And then all over us, OK?'

Halloran licked his lips. 'Jesus.'

Collins shook his head, returned the towel to

its hook, and, seeing that he had made his point, softened.

'Well, it'll probably be all right. But I don't want Molly to get a whiff of them, and that goes for bones and feathers. So we can't eat them.'

He opened a drawer by the sink and took out a plastic disposal bag.

'Here, put them in this and bury them in the woods. You'll find a spade in the lean-to. There'll be a beer waiting for you when you get back.'

That afternoon, the three men spent a couple of hours going through books and maps. The maps allowed them to look at the options for their exit. Northwards lay Eritrea, rebellious but distant, and risky. It would mean setting up fuel dumps inside Ethiopia. A non-starter. Westwards: Sudan. Horrendous deserts, political instability, even further from an easy flight home. Eastwards: desert, crossed by a railway line. Nothing there but 'camp-sites and sheepfolds'. The border that way was closer – 300 miles from Addis – but again, who the hell was going to organize fuel dumps inside Ethiopia, let alone dumps dotted across a hideous wilderness like that? There was only one serious option: south, into Kenya.

Jane's provided a mass of information, but Collins chose to phone around his military contacts to confirm it. This time, the SAS connection would be of no use. Even if he'd still been with the Regiment, this was the sort of enquiry for which he would have disguised his position.

He introduced himself for the company, saying he was preparing a report on the possible market in old aircraft in Africa. Contact led to contact, as if he was a journalist, through the Foreign Office, Army and RAF. Eventually he spoke to an officer who had been seconded to Selassie in the early 1970s and who knew the makes and numbers.

The Ethiopians had some 70,000 men under arms, and were planning a People's Militia of 150,000 as a reserve. They were aiming high, and ready to pay. Though they still had ancient Canberra B2 bombers and Second World War Dakotas as transporters, their fighter squadron was led by supersonic Northrop F5s. The helicopters were of two types: fifteen American Bell UH-IHs and the almost identical Agusta AB 205s (which are the Bells made under licence in Italy), a widely used general-purpose helicopter that carries anything up to a dozen passengers to a range of 300 miles; and a few French Alouette III Astazous, which carry six people up to 375 miles.

The next step was to devise a plan to gain access to the makers concerned. As with all weapons of war there was a market – buyers, sellers and middlemen. Collins's business would make an ideal cover. He was known as a dealer to numerous auctioneers via the Home Office and his credentials were valid. The French make should not present a problem, but it was possible that he would have to go through a US dealer to reach the American helicopters. It might be expensive to gain access, let alone arrange for tuition.

Collins arrived at Cromer's town house that evening shortly before 9 p.m. As he swirled a Courvoisier around his brandy glass, he explained the plan.

'So to get out, yes, we use the helicopter. The problem was the make. Now I know they have two types. There's a strong possibility they will use an American Bell. They got a few as part of a deal with the USA four years ago. There is even a chance they'll use French Alouettes. We don't want to trust to luck. Two of us – Rourke and myself – have flying licences, but we don't want to be wondering where the starter button is when the Ethiopians come at us. We want to retrain with both makes. We can use the company as cover. I'll say I'm thinking of extending into military aircraft. I'll go to the RAF, the US Army, or the suppliers. Give me a few days – I think I should be able to arrange the flights.

'But it may cost money. We have to cut corners. I may even have to put a deposit on one or both of them. So I need your authority to spend anything up to £50,000, which I certainly don't have in the company. It may not happen, but I need the freedom.'

Cromer sipped his brandy and nodded. The

costs were rising: £300,000 for Collins and his associates. Expenses to date: about £5000. Now, possibly £50,000 for the helicopters. Total so far: heading up towards half a million, and some way to go yet. He had no intention of spending anything like that much if he could help it, but to say so would be out of the question. Collins, Rourke and Halloran had to be confident they would return, at least in theory, otherwise they would never go.

'OK, Dicky,' said Cromer, 'go on.'

'Next problem: we plan to head for Kenya. It's English-speaking with good contacts back here, both vital as soon as we get over the border. We can assume the helicopter will have enough fuel to take Selassie back to Harar. But it's unlikely to have enough to get to the Kenyan border. We need a dump of fuel in Ethiopia. It will mean hiring a plane or helicopter in Nairobi and getting the stuff 100 miles or so over the border and hiding it. It may take a few days of Rourke's time and might cost another £3000 or so. He'll need to draw cash in Nairobi.'

'Again, OK.'

Collins knew he was taking a slight risk. Cromer might decide to back out. But, while driving down, he had become increasingly certain this wouldn't happen. Cromer was in too deep. Besides, far better that he had time now to decide on a strategy, than be shocked into a panic reaction later when plans were fully laid.

As it happened, Cromer had in the meantime devoted more thought to the problem than Collins. He had needed Collins's confirmation before developing his own plans further.

'Christ knows what the Ethiopians will do when they realize what's happened,' Collins concluded. 'Shouldn't like to be in your shoes.'

Cromer paused.

'It's all right, Dicky. I have every hope that they will swallow their anger. It will certainly be in their interests to do so. After all, we shall then be in a very favourable position to offer them a generous loan at remarkably advantageous rates of interest.'

Collins smiled. 'You always were a sly bastard, Charlie.'

Tuesday 30 March
Collins began early to trace the machines he needed.

His first call to the Army Air Corps, at Middle Wallop, Wiltshire, brought both good news and bad. The good news was that the unit of 180 men whose job it was to turn out pilots for the Army could indeed lay its hands on an Alouette if needed (although the Army mostly used Gazelles). The bad news was that his former SAS status meant damn all.

Sorry, old boy, but the old boy network had all gone now. All very carefully accounted. These were expensive machines. More than the job's worth to slip outsiders into a retraining programme. A week? Good God, the minimum for retraining was two months. 'Besides,' the voice on the line concluded cheerily. 'There's the age factor. I'll bet you chaps wouldn't even get past the medical. Not that you'd notice in Civvy Street, but if you've seen active service you're probably half deaf. Even if you pass it'll take you sixty hours to requalify.'

Collins tried another tack. Anything for sale?

'Not a hope. The price of things nowadays, we repair everything. Some of the machines we have here are twenty, twenty-five years old. You'd have to buy new, straight from the French.'

Frustrated, Collins decided to try the American helicopters. A call to the Defence Attaché at the US Embassy led him back to the Army Air Corps, to an American exchange officer who proved a model of co-operation. The UH-IH had been used extensively in Vietnam as a combat troop carrier. They didn't carry many men, usually less than a dozen-man squad in 'Nam's hot, low-density air. But what the hell, at $250,000 they had been cheaper than the Chinooks, which held thirty-three. Boy, you get one of those hit by an RPG, and your costs really go through the roof. So, sure, the UHs were useful for 'ash-and-trash' work, food, medivac – all that stuff. But mostly for search-and-destroy missions – couple of pilots, crew chief who doubled as door-gunner, second door-gunner, couple of M60s.

Handy little machines. Still use them at home for replacing crews at remote Minutemen missile-control centres.

'Here? Hell no, sir, we don't have any here. They're not licensed in this country. You'd have to go Stateside for one of those babies. You want to retrain? You could, I guess, at Fort Rucker, Alabama. But it would take you twenty-five hours' flying time. That'll take you, oh, twenty days minimum. That's without avionics training. Took me nine months to get out of that place . . . Buying, sure that'd be your best bet. Contact Bell Textron, they have a training base at Fort Worth, Texas, and they sell the whole deal: chopper, training programme, equipment, the lot. That's what the Iranians go for . . . Sure, sir, glad to be of service.'

Two dead ends. What about civil aviation schools? Surely they had machines? He called the AAC again.

'Well,' said the major to whom he had spoken a few minutes before. 'You might try Mark Winterton over at Kidlington. He's in the helicopter business. Perhaps he can help.'

He might have guessed: you phone the world, and then find what you want on your doorstep. And an individual. Must be better than an organization.

Winterton ran a helicopter hire business. Film, tanker crews, race meetings, he told Collins, anything that needs helicopters. Collins explained his problem, and Winterton rose to the challenge with zest.

Alouettes? Oh yes, quite common in civilian use. Used a good deal as camera platforms for film-making. Did Collins see *The Longest Day*, or *The Blue Max* or *The Battle of Britain*? Remember that terrific shot in *The Longest Day* after landing, which goes on for ever as some of our chaps fight their way along a canal side? Winterton had helped shoot it from an Alouette. And then, at last, the words Collins had been waiting to hear: 'Yes, I could get you into one.'

Collins detailed his requirements yet again and ended by saying: 'I know the rules. But don't they get bent?'

'Of course, all the time,' Winterton told him. 'Twenty-five hours is ideal for retraining. But it's your money. If you want a crash course, you could cut a few corners and fit the whole thing into a few days. That suit you? Fine. Leave it with me. I'll be back to you. Oh, yes, the cost may shock you: £200 per hour.'

The Bells were still a problem. Did he know anything about them?

'Funny thing about the Bells,' went on Winterton, who clearly enjoyed revealing his knowledge and experience. 'At the height of the Vietnam war, they were made under licence in Taiwan – not too reliably. When the Yanks went home they threw a few hundred into the seas. Literally tossed them overboard. But the Chinese went on building them anyway for a bit, and some of them finished up in pretty odd places. Rhodesia got some. Anyway, I think you'd have to go to the States for them, unless they sell them on the continent.'

Well, some progress. He'd try Bell direct in the afternoon.

At five o'clock, when the businesses in Texas would be well into their day, Collins called Bell in Fort Worth. To his relief there would be no point in a trip to the States. A drawling voice from the Training Programmes department told him that Bell itself trained only on the purchase of an aircraft. Sure, the military trained its personnel, but there would be a real problem getting in on that as a civilian. And that applied anywhere – no point going to Germany, for instance, where the Bundeswehr, the Luftwaffe and the Border Control all had military versions of Bells.

'But you know we have a commercial version of the UH-IH? It's designation is 205A-1, but if you find yourself a 205 or 206 you won't have any problem with a UH-IH . . . Yeah, sure we export them, that's our business . . . Yeah, I have a book here. We don't have anyone in England, but, why, we have half a dozen companies in Europe take Bell 205s.'

Collins scribbled down a list of names in Norway, Sweden, Holland and Austria. Holland: that should be possible.

'Yeah. I guess so. That's a commercial airline. They have retraining programmes of their own . . . Why, no trouble at all. Glad to be of service, sir.'

By the time the call ended, it was nearing six. Holland was one hour ahead. They'd be closed.

There was one further call a few minutes later: Winterton confirming he could offer a rapid retraining flight on an Alouette at Kidlington in the week beginning 12 April. Yes, he could pack twenty hours into two days. Gruelling, but possible, if Collins could meet the price: £7000 including tuition, helicopter hire and insurance. Fuel would be extra – perhaps another £500.

The Dutch company, Schreyver Airways, was as amenable to Collins's suggestion as Winterton had been. They were based at The Hague, had several 205s, and were happy to provide a one-day conversion course, for twice the price. They needed telexed confirmation and a ten per cent deposit, but otherwise no problems.

With his own plans all but laid for the helicopter training course, Collins turned his mind to another problem: Halloran. At that moment, he and Rourke were again studying the maps Rourke had picked up in Oxford. But Rourke could set up the fuel dumps on his own – he would be reliable enough, and space in the aircraft would be at a premium. Halloran would be left kicking his heels, with no real purpose over the next few days. It wasn't a good prospect. As the episode with the pheasants had shown, he was not totally reliable, except when he went into action. But there was no alternative. Better out here, in the depths of the country, where Collins could keep an eye on him, than sitting in some hotel room in London.

6

Wednesday 31 March

Yufru called Cromer to arrange a meeting for midday. He was excited: he had had a reply from the Emperor. When he arrived, he set his briefcase on the glass-topped table, threw himself into his now accustomed sofa and spread his arms along its rich leather back.

'Sir Charles, this is high drama indeed. Let me tell you. Your letter arrived yesterday afternoon. I had a car waiting with my courier in it. I thought of taking the letter myself, but . . . anyway, he travelled via Paris and took an overnight flight to Addis via Rome, arriving early this morning . . .'

'Mr Yufru, the letter,' interrupted Cromer.

'Ah, yes. The Emperor dictated a reply in Amharic. I am told he seemed to be his old self, still quite capable of decisive thinking when necessary. At eighty-five! Remarkable . . .'

'The letter!'

'Ah, yes. It was helicoptered to Addis, translated into English, and telexed back to me. A triumph, Sir Charles.' He unclicked the briefcase and handed over the folded sheet. Sir Charles sat back and read the four paragraphs.

'Sir Charles Cromer,

'Your letter has brought Us joy, and We have thought well on it. Our time is near and though Our Kingdom has been torn from Us by atheists, We are Father still to Our country and to Our family. Patiently enduring and making the faith We have in God the basis of all, We believe Our family must one day assume Our burdens, when the present times of difficulty are over. Their destiny is clear, and it is Our duty to ensure their return. To this end, they must live as Kings and Princes. A man cannot be loved as a Prince and live as a beggar. Therefore, We have decided to bestow upon Our sons and daughters the blessings that were once Ours.

'Sir Charles, We take note of your advice, as We once took note of your father's. This cannot be without the compliance of the present government. So be it.

'We therefore order you to prepare the documents necessary and to submit them for Our approval. God grant Us life until we meet, for We stand at the doors of death!'

Cromer let out a brief sigh of satisfaction, smiled briefly and laid the letter on the sofa beside him.

'You have succeeded, Sir Charles, where we have failed. You have our gratitude.'

'Spare me your thanks, Mr Yufru. We have much work to do. I must write again to the Emperor stating how exactly I suggest we dispose of his assets. We will then prepare a memorandum, including the Emperor's assets, that will act as a basis for the agreement. That document in its turn must be drawn up ready for signature by myself, my colleagues, your government, and by the Emperor. Yes, Mr Yufru, we still have much to do.'

'And I will wait. The only matter I must deal with rapidly is your delegation's entry visas. These are, of course, mere formalities. I will simply need from you application forms, filled in, in duplicate, with passport photos.'

Cromer felt a sudden qualm.

'But I take it you do not require the actual passports? My staff are busy, and may need to travel elsewhere before coming to Addis.'

'Well, in the circumstances, Sir Charles, the visas can be issued separately from the passports.'

The letter Cromer dictated to Valerie that afternoon he had carefully planned the previous evening. He modified it only slightly to take account of Selassie's response. Otherwise he preserved what was, in its way, a masterpiece of diplomacy, appealing both to the Emperor and the government.

He briefly reviewed Selassie's wealth and promised the details as soon as they were available. He was, he said, not concerned with actual quantities at present, though he guessed the total amount to be released exceeded $2000 million. He suggested a three-way division: eighty per cent to the government, fifteen per cent to Selassie's family and five per cent to the special account set aside for His Highness in case his situation should change. He concluded with a justification for this distribution, which was bound at first sight to seem to favour a government intent on wasting billions on wars, bribes and lavish buildings.

'Your Highness,

'You say you wish your family to live in comfort. But I beg you to consider that several hundred million dollars is enough for any family to live on, however great their previous expectations.

'I beg you furthermore to consider your country. Your countrymen are surely as much your family as your own offspring. If your wealth is to be distributed, should not your nation receive the predominant share?'

The five per cent special fund was a good touch; it was designed to suggest that, in exchange for his signature, the Emperor might be allowed to spend his days in comfortable exile. Cromer dictated a covering note to Yufru explaining his thinking, adding that if his government sought more than an eighty per cent share, Selassie might refuse the whole deal.

That afternoon he received two phone calls. The first was from Kupferbach in Zurich to say that the Swiss Foreign Office was not in principle against the use of the Swiss Embassy in Addis on a matter of such supreme national importance. Kupferbach said he was attending a meeting in the ministry on Monday to explain personally that this would be the least the country could do, since it meant retaining in Switzerland several hundred million dollars.

The second call was from Collins, to say that he would take Rourke to Heathrow for his flight to Nairobi the following afternoon.

Thursday 1 April

During the course of the morning, two couriers arrived with deliveries for Cromer: one from New York, the other from Zurich. It was surprising to him that there were men prepared to spend their lives in aeroplanes, but it was a godsend at times like this. Each package contained a portfolio of several pages: Selassie's holdings. His own bank's statement also lay before him.

New York's was by far the most complex of the three. It had been on Cromer's father's advice in 1948 that Selassie had begun diversifying his wealth, placing a good deal of it on the other side of the Atlantic. It had been an astute move. Gold from Zurich, at that time selling for $35 an ounce, had been used to buy a spread of stocks amounting to $100 million over ten years. In the following two decades, those stocks, carefully nurtured by Lodge's people, had grown along with the American economy at an average of between five and ten per cent per year and now totalled almost $1000 million. Cromer was always copied on purchases and sales, but he'd never seen the portfolio summarized and assessed in this way.

Then there were companies in which the Emperor was a sleeping partner: a property company in Dallas, a clothing manufacturer in New Jersey, an art gallery in New York – eleven in all, reflecting a passing passion or advice taken or favour given. To liquidate the arrangements would be difficult – perhaps disastrous for the companies concerned and certainly expensive in legal fees.

There was also the gold held directly by the Federal Reserve Bank of New York at Liberty Street. It represented a 100-ton shipment that arrived from London and Zurich in 1939, when Europe was preparing for war. Now, with gold standing at $173 an ounce, it was worth just over $800 million – which was, noted Cromer, a considerably less substantial increase proportionately than the increase in the value of the stocks.

The Zurich statement was simpler. Much of it confirmed what he already knew, for the Swiss gold, though shown to the Emperor's credit in Zurich, had in fact been left in the London vaults, simply out of convenience. This was not an unusual situation. As often with gold (like that from South Africa) it had been transported under arrangements of proven security for many decades and it was simpler to keep it in London, even if it was to be

131

credited in Switzerland. The Swiss banks simply paid a handling and rental charge. A considerable sum had, however, been air-freighted directly to Zurich in recent years. Finally, Zurich also held the Maria Theresa dollars, air-freighted there in the 1940s.

From all three centres there were details of currency accounts which were held for immediate settlements – for cars, works of art, horses, furniture, clothing, anything the Emperor had needed from abroad for himself or his family.

Cromer jotted down the main figures, and tapped them into a calculator.

The grand total was just short of $3000 million.

Friday 2 April

Rourke arrived in Nairobi that morning after an eight-hour flight. He took a rattling cab from Embakasi International Airport, through the capital – spacious, if strangely lifeless after London – to the Hilton, a twenty-storey cylinder that towers over the glass and concrete of central Nairobi on the corner of Mama Ngina Street and Government Road.

Exhausted from a night of fitful napping, he nevertheless began a series of calls to track down a company that flew helicopters. He spoke to two wildlife groups and a film unit, none of whom could or would help; his fourth attempt, after three-quarters of an hour, struck lucky.

The company was called Autoflight and they had a number of planes for hire. He said he wanted helicopters, as soon as possible, to take some equipment north 'to the Ethiopian border'. Yes, said a male voice claiming to belong to an individual named Swain, yes, in theory they could do it; and yes, they could even do it immediately if given a good reason, by which Rourke understood them to mean a lot of money. He suggested a more detailed discussion and was invited to the offices at Nairobi's general aviation airport, Wilson Airfield.

His cab found the place after twenty minutes, back out towards Embakasi. There, in a concrete hut beside a couple of hangars emblazoned with the company's name, he found a man and a woman. Chris Swain was in his mid-forties and dressed in a short-sleeved shirt that hung loosely over his blue slacks. He wore sneakers. He was small, with startling blue eyes and a clipped dark beard. Though Rourke never knew his background, he had in fact been a schoolmaster in England before coming to Africa one summer fifteen year earlier. He had taken a temporary job with Autoflight and never returned home. He learned flying, loved it, eventually took over the business and built it up to its present level: two fixed-wings and two helicopters. Most of his business came from tourists and wildlife management people, contract work with game parks and companies wanting to get people across East Africa in a hurry. One of the monoplanes was out now, and so was one of the helicopters.

'Rourke?' he said matter of factly, 'Swain. How do you do. My wife, Judy, Mr Rourke.'

Judy, originally Judith, was of German extraction. She also wore slacks. She was taller than her husband, and ten years younger, with a mass of blonde curls. Like him, she gave the impression of directness, of physical hardness. She too flew. Her parents had been born in German East Africa, and when she was twenty had made a sentimental journey to show her the place. In Dar es Salaam she had met Chris, been fascinated by his driving intensity and his neat good looks, and had run away with him.

Rourke put his proposition straight, without giving any explanation: he wanted to place enough fuel somewhere up by Lake Chamo, to get either a Bell UH-IH or an Alouette from there back down to Nairobi. He also wanted to be shown a route that was impossible to lose.

Swain raised his eyebrows.

'Ethiopia,' he said. 'I take it you don't wish to apply for a visa and flying permissions? No, I thought not. Well, that simplifies things ... Alouettes I know. Or a Bell UH-IH? They're the 205-As, commercial designation? Good, tough machines. We have JetRangers.'

He sniffed, sat down and pulled out some

grubby maps from under a pile of papers on his desk.

'The filing system,' he said, 'we're flyers here. Try to keep things in order, but the work keeps getting in the way . . . Ah, Chamo.'

He checked some distances with a pencil. 'Yes, quite a way. Five hundred miles. You know the range of your machines? Yes, a touch over three hundred. OK, let's see what's involved.'

It turned out that a great deal was involved. Assuming their helicopter was empty at Chamo, Rourke, Collins and Halloran would need access to a minimum of 350 US gallons of fuel; nine forty-five-gallon drums to be on the safe side. Neither the Bell nor the Alouette held that much in its tank, so they would have to establish two, perhaps three dumps *en route*.

Next, where to place the fuel and how to get it there. Swain's JetRangers couldn't do it all. They would have to have a truck, and use a JetRanger as well. Swain started scribbling on a bit of paper, cross-correlating weights, distances and fuel consumption. Eventually he concluded: 'Shame you need to have a clear route. You could just follow the radio beacons. You simply dial in the frequencies and the aircraft homes in on its ADF – automatic direction-finder.'

'Yeah. I remember.'

'OK, then. How about coming straight down, across country?'

Swain slid a finger across the map south from Lake Chamo.

'What's the country like?'

'Terrible. Featureless. Lava and sand. But you could follow the beacons, then the Nairobi–Addis Highway. It's metalled from somewhere inside the Ethiopian border.'

'But not all the way?'

'No . . .'

'Don't like the sound of it. Besides, I might not be the pilot. The Rift Valley route looks easy.'

'It is. Longer, but you can't get lost. Lakes. Volcanoes. Clear as anything. Now let's see where we make the dumps.'

It turned out that the truck Swain said he could use – a four-wheel-drive Bedford belonging to a local safari company – would have to set out with twenty drums. It would drop seven drums at the Kampi ya Samaki ('Camp of Fish') airstrip at Lake Baringo, then head north 200 miles to the eastern shores of Lake Rudolf, to a desolate headland of lava hills called Kobi Fora. There it would leave fifteen drums.

Following a day later with Rourke, the JetRanger would refuel at Lake Baringo, and again at Kobi Fora, where it would also pick up four drums and ferry them up to Chamo.

'Not that you'll need all four,' said Swain, 'but it's useful to have a reserve.'

Having made its drop, the JetRanger would

then head south again, refuelling *en route*. When Rourke, Collins and Halloran came south in their turn . . .

'How do we find our way?' Rourke interrupted.

'You follow the Rift.'

'I mean when we leave Addis.'

'It's as easy down from Addis as it is north of here. Look at the map. There are lakes all the way and the walls on either side guide you like a tunnel. You won't even need the beacon at Arba Minch . . . Anyway, when you come south, you will have two dumps. You'll see them both on the way tomorrow. Back here the day after, and home on the overnight flight. OK?'

'Sounds good – if you can get the truck.'

'Shouldn't be a problem. There's lots of trucks and labour. We need two drivers and a camp boy. I've got the fuel. But I may have to offer extra for immediate action.'

'Sure.'

'Right. I'll let you know if there're any problems. But we've done this sort of thing before. Survey work, we say. That covers a multitude of sins . . . You'll be flying with my other pilot, young chap called Bob Hudson. He knows all about the Rift. The only thing that'll stop you is the price.'

He did more sums. Nine hundred gallons of fuel at seven Kenyan shillings per gallon. The truck, plus three men. The JetRanger for two days, plus pilot, at £200 per hour. Total: just short of £4000.

In cash.

Rourke sighed. He didn't have the cash and he wasn't authorized to draw that much anyway. He could phone Collins, who could phone Cromer, who could authorize a bank draft. Swain accepted that idea.

'If anything goes wrong,' Swain concluded, 'I'll bloody well fly back up to Chamo and put a bullet through your bloody drums myself.'

He then relented a little and over a beer and sandwiches told Rourke something about Hudson, a young geologist whose passion for the Rift Valley and for photography had led him to the Swains. He had taken a civilian flying course in England and found that the only way he could indulge his consuming interests was by hiring himself out as a pilot.

'He won't be in today,' said Swain. 'But he'll have to come in tomorrow to get things ready. He knows the place better than I do. He can explain all you'll need to remember.'

That afternoon, Rourke returned, drawn with tiredness and heat, to the sanctuary of his air-conditioned hotel room to make his calls, to have a bath, and to sleep.

Selassie's reply, duly translated as before, arrived on Cromer's desk that morning. The Emperor was apparently resigned to the dissipation of his fortune, and had accepted without question Cromer's suggestions. His only stipulation was the release from house arrest of a number of relatives. To this, the Ethiopians had apparently agreed.

Cromer thought the time might be right for a turn of the screw. There must be no backtracking now by the Ethiopians. He wanted to wind up their expectations at once and irreversibly. Before he began the arduous task of drafting the memorandum detailing the division of the imperial spoils he called Yufru.

'Mr Yufru,' began Cromer, 'I have before me both the Emperor's favourable reply to my proposals and an assessment of his holdings worldwide. It may be of interest for you to know that, all being well, your government is likely to be richer very shortly by over $2000 million.'

There was a long silence, then Yufru said: 'Sir Charles, I will inform the powers that be. I should like you to know that if this transaction is completed successfully, Ethiopia will be eternally in your debt. It may quite literally save the country from disaster. Moreover it may well be that with such a sum we shall buy what we need and keep ourselves independent, clear of the clutches of the Soviet Union. Your actions, Sir Charles, will change the course of African history.'

'Oh, come, Mr Yufru, no need for that,' Cromer said, deprecating, magnanimous. 'I shall now draw up the memorandum of transfer and will contact you later.'

The memorandum of transfer. It sounded suitably formal and imposing as a title for the document he then began to draft. It was an intricate piece of work, summarizing how the sums were to be realized: the sale of the gold on the open market, the sale of the shares, the liquidation of the company holdings. There were clauses on the transfer of the sums to local branches of the Bank of Ethiopia, the legal problems likely to be encountered with the companies, the question of taxation, the involvement of the Bank of England and Federal Reserve, both of whom would need to be informed – a myriad of details designed to create the impression of a masterly balance between the conflicting demands of haste and realism, all the convincing detail of a document designed to be nothing but a perfect smokescreen.

After three hours Cromer began to edit his work, cutting here, adding there, swinging paragraphs into a more logical sequence. That afternoon – after dealing with a few urgent letters – he began to dictate a draft of the memorandum, a 3000-word statement that would act as the basis for comments, firstly from Zurich and New York, secondly from Addis and thirdly (possibly) from Selassie himself.

Saturday 3 April

Before take-off from Nairobi, the twenty-six-year-old pilot, Bob Hudson, briefed Rourke about the geography of the Rift Valley. He turned out to be effusive, even over-effusive, about his subject. He had a kinked nose (the result of a rugger injury), and a habit of pulling his top lip back from his teeth when embarrassed. His hearty public-school accent grated constantly on Rourke.

'Look at the map, here,' Hudson said. 'Here's the Rift just outside Nairobi. The walls go up northwards on either side here and here. They spread out as they go past Lake Rudolf, which is where we're heading, and then together again, up through Ethiopia. But the centre's always marked by lakes and volcanoes. Funny place. You know why?'

Rourke gave him no encouragement. Undeterred, Hudson put his hands together in a position as if for prayer, except tilted over, and as he talked they fell apart to dramatize his words. 'The whole of East Africa and Arabia is being torn apart, sort of unzipped, along the line of the Rift. As the sides pulled apart, the middle bit fell. All sorts of things seep up from below – lava and soda mainly – so the landscapes are often all twisted and the lakes are white and salty-looking with soda deposits round the edge. You'll see. Sometime, millions of years hence, this place will be on another continent and over there, westwards, the other side of those hills, there'll be a new strip of ocean. Fabulous thought, isn't it?'

'Uh huh,' said Rourke, unmoved. 'How do I recognize . . .?'

'Well, first you'll see the edge of the Rift . . .' said Hudson, and went on to brief Rourke in rather more detail with the aid of the map. It took half an hour. They were ready to leave shortly after nine o'clock.

The JetRanger was standing on a concrete square thirty yards away from the shed. They climbed in, with Rourke in the second pilot's seat, and fixed seat belts and headsets.

Hudson said: 'Here, take the map. You'll see the way.' He made his take-off checks and pushed the starter button to ignite the turbine.

The helicopter thumped into life, hauled itself slowly aloft towards the haze that precedes the Kenyan rains, and bent away north and west, swinging over Uhuru Park and out above the dual carriageway of Uhuru Avenue. Rourke gave the broad streets and well-spaced buildings not a second glance, straining forward instead to familiarize himself with the geography of the place, which he would have to recall well enough to bring Collins and Halloran on their flight from Addis Ababa.

As the machine picked up its cruising speed of 130 m.p.h., the town fell away behind them. Buildings and roads gave way to patchwork patterns of banana and vegetable plantations, which were in their turn replaced by forest. Suddenly, after fifteen minutes, the ground rose slightly and then dropped away over 2000 feet to savannah and grasslands.

'The Rift!' said Hudson. Then, as he swung north to follow the line of the hills, he pointed out to the left. There, blue and hazy some twenty miles away on the other side of the Rift, was the Mau Escarpment.

Beating northwards, Hudson shouted out the landmarks. Longonot, its dormant one-mile-wide crater blanketed with forest. Lake Naivasha, its fresh water teeming with birds and fish. Lake Nakuru, with its red and white swirls of flamingos. On Nakuru's shores, almost invisible in the yellow grasses, a herd of zebra scattered, spooked by the noise of the helicopter.

Half an hour later, 'Baringo!' said Hudson. 'Lots of crocs!'

He set the JetRanger down on the edge of the strip by the single hangar. There was no one else there. The drums awaited them. Hudson removed a toggle-pump from the rear compartment. The two of them manhandled two drums, weighing 300lb apiece, over to the helicopter, and pumped in their contents, an operation that with the fast-action pump took less than fifteen minutes. They were airborne again within half an hour of landing.

Now there would be a longer gap as the Rift walls fell away almost to invisibility on either side, and the grasses died back to form a parched and desolate landscape of sparse scrub over volcanic rock.

'Heading due north!' said Hudson, pointing at the compass. 'Hit Rudolf one hour after Baringo. Keep an eye on speed and time.'

After that he said little until Lake Rudolf appeared as a narrow sliver ahead. It was at that moment an extraordinary green, the result of algae blooming in its acrid waters, a regular phenomenon that had given the lake its nickname, the Jade Sea. Hudson swung along the lake's eastern edge, up the coast along a pile of crumpled volcanic hills and over a lava plain until a collection of huts rolled towards them. A dusty airstrip ran alongside the huts. A truck was parked nearby.

Hudson put the helicopter down by a shack and as the engine died away an emaciated black came out, wearing tattered trousers and a dirty shirt. A few goats wandered the barren hills, tearing at the scanty plants. Rourke grimaced at the heat and the drabness.

Hudson noticed his expression. 'Bit rough, you think? Not a bit, old boy. This man has class. You should see the others. Stark naked. Probably out fishing.'

They had meanwhile been joined by three other blacks, likewise dressed in open shirts and filthy trousers. They were the crew of the truck. Hudson spoke to them in Swahili. They wandered back to the truck and began to unload the drums. Once again, Rourke and Hudson refuelled. Then from the rear of the truck appeared a net.

Hudson shouted. After another few minutes, the cargo net was established alongside the JetRanger, wrapped around four drums. While Hudson pulled out a line and hook from beneath the aircraft, and proceeded to attach the hook to the top of the net, Rourke surveyed the grim landscape. The place looked as if it had been newly fired in some giant kiln. Towards the lakeside, a few gnarled trees scrabbled for a toe-hold on the lava, bent all about with the effort of growth. Here and there, tussocks of dry grass provided the only other relief from the rocks, grey sand and lava dust. In the distance, hazy behind little whirls of dust whipped up by the hot wind, precipitous crags plunged down to the water's edge. Hudson looked up, wiped his brow and followed Rourke's gaze.

'Barren as hell. And largely because of those damn animals.' He pointed to the goats. 'They pull everything up by the roots. Anyway, walk around if you like. Watch out for snakes. I had a mamba in my rucksack once.'

It was midday and fearfully hot. The wind had risen and was battering their shirts against their bodies. Hudson signalled Rourke into the JetRanger, and said: 'Drink?'

Rourke hadn't appreciated just how dehydrated he'd become and downed a pint of water without pausing. Hudson had sandwiches. The two of them ate.

'Jesus,' Rourke said, 'what a bloody place.'

'Beautiful, often, actually,' said Hudson, 'and very important. Not long ago, Richard Leakey found a fossilized human skull about three million . . . oh, forget it. Sorry,' he said, seeing Rourke glance at his watch. 'All right. Let me have another drink and we'll move.'

Before take-off, in the helicopter, Hudson opened the map again to show Rourke the final leg of their outward journey. At the tip of Lake Rudolf, another 100 miles north, they would swing east over Lake Stephanie, then up towards the Ethiopian section of the Rift, and their destination, Lake Chamo.

'Won't we be spotted?'

'Possibly. Probably. But there's nothing to worry about. There are one or two civilian airstrips, but no military bases. No one's going to follow us. Where we land, there are no roads and damn few people. We take care, of course. We won't be there more than an hour or so.'

They prepared for departure. This time Hudson took the machine up slowly, edged it across above the cargo net, and when he was directly above, continued to ascend slowly until the line went taut and he saw his cargo was safely aloft.

They headed north along the shoreline over the appalling landscape. Then Hudson swung away eastwards.

'The border!' he said after half an hour. Below, Rourke could see a line created by bush-clearance. That was all there was to it. Where there was no vegetation, there was no line. An open border.

North and east of Lake Rudolf, the ground rolled up into rocky hills in which lay a sheet of water: Lake Stephanie, so shallow that it varies from a puddle to a swamp to a ten-mile lake from month to month, depending on the rainfall. Flamingos. Zebra drumming in herds over the open areas. Green sedge marshes where a river from the north evaporated. Mud flats. Rolling grasslands leading to uplands. Then finally, Lake Chamo, twenty miles long, and to the north just visible beyond a forested hump of hills, its sister, Lake Abaya.

Hudson set the helicopter down on the southern shores of the lake back from the pebbly waterside, near a defile made by a stream running down from high ground to the east. As the machine settled beside its cargo, the slapping rotors swished into silence and the scattering of low trees that marked the defile became still. Below them and to their right, reeds and rushes marked the confluence of stream and lake. The reeds were swaying and the sound of splashing came up to them.

'Hippo!' said Hudson, happily.

He had chosen the spot well. He unhooked the cargo net, and the two of them rolled the drums a few yards uphill to a group of thorn bushes. From ten yards away, they couldn't be seen.

147

Rourke looked around. A marabou stork strutted from the shallows, black wing-tips meeting over its back like a gowned professor. Yes, the spot was identifiable enough. The southern shore was a sweep about ten miles long. Much of it was a repetition of reeds and pebbles, but to their right, beyond the defile, a river came into the lake. Rourke took the pad and a pencil, strolled a couple of hundred yards towards it and made a quick sketch of the geography.

As he strolled back, Hudson called: 'Hey, come on!' and then, as he got closer: 'It's 3.30! We want to get back before nightfall. Besides, if anyone saw us come down, someone, somewhere is going to talk. We don't want visitors to find us still around.'

'I thought you said no one lived here.'

'Well, the lake is fished. And there are herders.'

He offered Rourke a drink from his water-flask and they prepared for take-off.

'Oh, one last thing,' said Hudson, 'getting down here I told you it's 250 miles. You'll be OK, if you just come south between the escarpments. That's the southern tip of them,' he said, pointing to hills to the west. 'The lakes will guide you. Now, let's get out of here.'

Kupferbach woke Cromer with a call to his home at 7.10 a.m.

'Charles? I am sorry to call you at this hour,

but I wanted you to know that I have seen our Foreign Minister last night. Are you awake? Shall I call back later?'

'No, Oswald, tell me now.'

'Very well. He will inform the Embassy in Addis that the building must be cleared on Sunday 11 April. The Ambassador alone will know why. You must provide details of what else is required – conference facilities, seating plan, food, papers, and so on. He will be there to hand over the building to your people. Then he will drive away.'

'Finally, I asked for plans. We are a most efficient people, Charles. In the Foreign Office, they have plans of all our embassies, all around the world. It is necessary to have such details in case of the need to escape or to withstand a siege. He has ordered the plans to be copied. They will be with me on Monday.'

Monday 5 April

Collins started selling off his stock. When Stan asked him about it, he said: 'Profits are getting squeezed, Stan. We'll just cut down on costs for a month or two until we see how things shape up.'

Cromer phoned Collins, informed him that the plans had arrived and told him to get down the following day. Collins had, in his turn, told Cromer that Rourke had made the fuel drop and that he would pick him up at Heathrow the following morning, on his way into town.

Tuesday 6 April

When Collins and Halloran met Rourke early the following morning, they found him in remarkably good shape. He had slept for most of the overnight flight and was largely recovered from his gruelling experience.

At first he said little, but driving into London he told the story at some length.

'I've no doubts about getting south from Chamo,'

he finished. 'You could do it simply enough without any preparation. You were right about the Rift: it is easy to follow. We just have to make sure we recognize Chamo when we approach from the north. I've made a sketch of where the fuel is.'

'Confident?' asked Collins.

'No trouble,' Rourke replied with a grin. 'Once we get to Chamo, our troubles will be over.'

In town, Collins told Rourke and Halloran to book a room in the Hilton as an HQ, while he saw Cromer.

He was with Cromer in his office at nine o'clock, even before Valerie had arrived. Cromer told him of the statements of the Emperor's holdings, the memorandum, the agreement of the Swiss to use the embassy and finally indicated the plans on the table between them.

Collins reached for the large envelope Cromer pushed across to him, and slid out the contents. Inside were four blueprint sheets, specifications for the Swiss Embassy in Addis Ababa: cellar, two floors and an overall scheme of the building in its compound. Each room was numbered and the numbers keyed to a list reproduced on the side on each sheet. Underneath the list was a scale.

'Perfect,' said Collins.

'We'll have copies made and you can study them. Let me know if there are any problems. Now, there are other reasons for you to be here. One is to

151

start the business of accreditation. I'm going to
need photographs of you three for visas. For those
you won't need passports. But to travel you will.
Can you arrange false passports for the others in
a hurry?'

'Well, false passports are arranged often enough
in the SAS, but I doubt if I can get them that way.
Maybe we'll have to buy them.'

'How much?'

'No idea. A thousand pounds each? I daren't even
guess. And the time element is tricky. Paper, inks,
Christ knows what. I've no underworld contacts.
Perhaps Halloran can help. You want me to
call him?'

Outside, a desk drawer slammed. Valerie had
arrived.

Cromer said: 'No, not now. Speak to him later.
The other thing is that later this afternoon I'll
have the first draft of the document on which the
transaction will officially be based. You should all
have one. You'll have to know it well. You are
to be a gold expert, Dicky. I'll look out some of
the background to Selassie's gold dealing over the
years and copy them for you.'

'OK.'

'One more thing. Yufru is coming in to collect
his copy of the memorandum today. Just a brief
visit. I'd like you to meet him, but only in passing. We won't get into any long conversations
and anyway, your role will be quite deferential.

Any technical questions you can leave me to answer.'

'But I don't have an identity yet.'

'I thought I would introduce you as my deputy, name of Jeremy Squires. He's a bit younger than you, but if Yufru thinks to check up, he'll find that Squires's qualifications are perfect. I don't want any more deception in the office than that, or something's going to leak out. But I do want to keep Yufru's confidence in us at a high level. He's due at five. Come back then.'

Collins was with Rourke and Halloran half an hour later.

'One more thing,' he added, after briefing them. 'Do either of you know any way of getting forged passports?'

'Jesus,' said Halloran, 'a bit late for that. I assumed Cromer had that under control. Diplomatic status or some such.'

'Well, no. Sorry.'

'Forged passports ... I've tried for that. It could solve a lot of my problems. New identity, no links with the past. Fuckin' business it is, in this civilized country. You have to be in Istanbul. Even there, it's a risk. Fifteen hundred quid is the going rate and there's no way you can check on die-stamps and paper quality, the things the immigration people here pick up on. Forget the forgeries, I say. It's easier to do it legal, that's what I was told, if you're British.'

'Legally?' said Collins. 'I'd better check up on that.'

He glanced at his watch. A quarter to one.

The three men ate in the hotel in order to lunch at Cromer's expense, before the next meeting.

There were a number of tasks still to be fitted in.

First, passport photos. That was solved with a visit to the shopping arcade beneath the hotel. Then came what they assumed would be the major problem of false identities. This turned out to be not as difficult as Collins feared. He called the Passport Office and said he was a Jewish businessman who needed to travel to North Africa. Was there any legal way to avoid being identified by his real name?

The reply was a revelation: 'Well, we don't wish to encourage deception, but lots of people need more than one passport, sometimes in different names. There's no great mystery. We're in the business of issuing passports, after all. If you fulfil the statutory requirements, you get the passport.'

'And the requirements are?'

'A visa application, two photos, details of previous passport. And new name, if different from the old.'

'A new name?'

'Well, most people think you can acquire a new

name only by a deed poll. No, you can do it far more simply, with a Statutory Declaration provided by a solicitor and sworn before a Commissioner of Oaths. The cost is £1.50, £2, no more. Why, sir, you could, in case of need, change your name and have a new passport all within two hours.'

It was as easy as it sounded. Collins called Cromer and obtained the name of a West End solicitor. On his way over to Cromer, Collins called in to the solicitor's office and was shown a copy of the standard change-of-name declaration, comic in its legalistic lack of punctuation and repetitiveness.

They could all get new names and new passports entirely legally, tomorrow.

Collins arrived back at Cromer's office shortly before five o'clock. Cromer's door was open, the outer office was empty.

'Charlie,' he said loudly.

Cromer called him in, told him to close the door and waved him to a sofa. 'Sent my secretary home,' he said. 'I didn't want her overhearing me talking about you as Jeremy Squires. Do you have anything?'

Collins told him about new passports, and handed over the photos for the visas.

'Here, take a look through this,' Cromer went on. 'Take three copies.'

On the table was a pile of half a dozen folders,

each containing a score of photocopied pages: Cromer's memorandum and a three-page balance sheet of the Emperor's holdings.

'If the Emperor ever got to sign this, we'd all be ruined. It's the gold you should know about, almost £2000 million worth. There are a few personal fortunes worth more – the Shah's, the Hunt family in Texas, Howard Hughes – but none so concentrated now in the hands of one man, and none so easily assessed. You can imagine what would happen if we had to . . .'

The phone interrupted him. 'Excellent,' he said, answering. 'Ask him to come up, would you, Jim?' Then, as he put down the phone: 'Yufru. Get introduced and then make yourself scarce.'

Yufru, urbane as ever, bearing a wafer-thin briefcase, raised a supercilious eyebrow at Collins's presence when he strolled over from the lift.

'Ah, Mr Yufru. Let me introduce you to the senior member of my team, Jeremy Squires. Mr Squires is considered the expert in the Emperor's gold shares . . . Mr Squires, Mr Yufru, a representative of the Ethiopian government, and the vital link in all our negotiations.'

The two men shook hands. Yufru placed his case on Cromer's desk and clicked it open.

'Sir Charles, Mr Squires, I have four visa application forms I would like filled in. A mere formality. Simply return them to me, with pictures.'

Cromer glanced at the simple, cyclostyled sheets.

Name, date of birth, profession, passport number. Straightforward enough.

'You don't need our passports?'

'No. I will simply have the correct stamps and signatures added, and return the forms to you.'

He glanced down at the folders held by Collins.

'Yes, Mr Yufru,' said Cromer, 'this is the treaty, and the statement of the holdings. The first draft, a document for discussion over the next few days. Er . . . Mr Squires?'

Collins took the cue.

'Yes, indeed, Sir Charles. I look forward to working with you, Mr Yufru. A challenge, a marvellous experience, I'm sure. Till later then.'

Collins left, surprised to find his heart racing at the success of this simple piece of deception.

Tuesday 6 April

Collins, Rourke and Halloran followed through the rigmarole of acquiring new passports. First, more photographs. Next, a brief appointment with the same solicitor to fill in the Statutory Declaration. Then to a second solicitor, a Commissioner of Oaths – 'Yes, we have to send you next door, gentlemen, to avoid the possibility of fraud' – to swear to the truth of the document.

'You realize, of course, gentlemen,' said the solicitor, who was clearly used to the notion of people changing names, 'that should you for any reason wish in the future to be known once more by your previous name, you simply go through this little procedure again.'

Then to the Passport Office in Petty France to fill out application forms in their new names: Jeremy Squires, David Sackville-Jones, George Smithson. Collins gave Cromer as a reference, and spun a story about business needs – immediate action – leaving the next day – sensitive area – must have passports as soon as possible.

As they waited for Collins to return, Rourke said: 'You realize, Pete, the change will be on record? The police will get around to checking passport applications sooner or later.'

'But I'll be long gone, old son, won't I?'

'Hope so. Just thought I'd remind you.'

Collins walked back to them.

'They'll be ready at three. Let's sink a pint.'

Wednesday 7 April

After an early breakfast, Collins and Rourke drove down towards Oxford for the first day of their training on the Alouette.

Kidlington Airport, which lies off the road linking Woodstock and Oxford, is used for private planes, for training in both fixed-wings and helicopters, and for sales. It was raining lightly as Collins guided the Range Rover between the scattering of offices, lecture rooms, workshops, and hangars to the building that housed Winterton's outfit. They found him with his feet on the table, browsing through sales pamphlets. He was a solid six-footer dressed in a blue Guernsey sweater and jeans.

Over coffee, Winterton probed Collins and Rourke for their flying experience over the last few years.

Rourke had a good head start: during his service in Oman he had flown a Scout and a Bell 47. He had behind him some 500 hours of flying experience, a good deal of it in windy and mountainous conditions in the Arabian peninsula. Flying the Alouette would present him with no great problem – five hours' experience should be enough – but with some intensive training on start-up procedures.

Collins's needs were greater. He had his Private Pilot's Licence and had fulfilled his statutory five hours of flying annually to keep his PPL current, but his experience was limited to piston engines. The Alouette was a turbine.

'At your age,' said Winterton rather unkindly, 'we have a problem with the fatigue factor. It's like playing the piano, learning a new machine. If you've never converted, just imagine the problems – external checks, internal checks, starting procedures for cold and hot engines, warm-up, ground checks, pre-take-off checks, after take-off checks – well, you probably remember what it was like. Anyway, 120 or more points to bear in mind, and that's without avionics training and emergency procedures . . . OK, OK' – he saw Collins's impatient expression – 'just reminding you that there's a limit to what I can force into you in one day. Mr Rourke – Michael – you'll come out all right. But, Major, I'd advise you not to fly unless you have to. You'll have the very, very basics . . . yes, enough to fly, but no more.'

Winterton's warnings turned to incredulity when Collins told him the other two complexities: they wanted to prepare for a rapid take-off at 8000 feet near the equator.

'Oh, my God, Major. The air's less dense by about a third at that height. And if it's hot, that's more difficult still. And you want a rapid take-off? You know in a turbine you can burn out an engine instantaneously if you get the balance between fuel and air wrong . . . Well, gentlemen, we have our work cut out. But I warn you it will be tough, with no guarantees. You're still game? OK, let's make a start. First I'll introduce you to the machine . . .'

He took them outside, through the slanting rain, to an Alouette standing on its cement square at the edge of the airfield.

'You won't remember anything in detail at this stage, but I'll just give you a feel of the problem,' he said over their shoulders as the two men settled into the dual-control pilots' seats, and clicked their belt-and-shoulder harness into place. 'Cyclic controls, throttle, collective pitch, pedals . . .'

So began a day of the most intensive training

either man had ever experienced. Some of the time they were together on the ground, mainly learning to drill into themselves a sequence of checks that would cover the essential instruments in the minimum time. Rourke went up first, with Winterton sitting in beside him. For Collins, who was not to fly until later, the day became a timeless round of rote learning, until, at dusk, he was able to take the controls.

As they drove back exhausted, both knew that however far they fell short of a formal qualification, they would at least be able to get away from the embassy at short notice. What appalled them – and Collins in particular – was that within a few days they would have to repeat similarly demanding procedures with a totally different machine.

Back in the Hilton that evening, Collins and Rourke came to Halloran's room. Collins opened his brief-case, and produced the plans of the embassy, placing the ground-floor sheet on the coffee-table alongside the overall view of the compound.

'Distances. Doorways. Entrances. It looks clear enough. First thing: I think we stick to the ground floor. It makes for a quicker getaway, and Selassie might not be too good at stairs. That leaves only one real possibility. The left-hand rooms are out: they all seem set aside for routine embassy business: secretaries, visas, stuff like that. But here on the right is the main ambassadorial office, linked to some other large room. Doors all round. This is where we set things up . . .'

The three talked on, working out the details of the kidnapping. The conference to be held in the front office. The back office to be arranged for more informal discussions. Cromer could add the details – seating, refreshments, stationery – when he contacted Switzerland. The important thing was the geography of the place, and the order of events.

'You're right, Michael,' said Collins. 'We separate them, one at a time if possible, into the next-door room. I'll have to work out some way to break the conference, to get us in there in the first place. But it shouldn't be hard. I'll talk to Cromer about it tomorrow and we'll spot some weak link in the document. You'll have to leave the stage management to me. Then, Peter, we'll let you take over.'

Halloran smiled. 'One at a time. No problem at all.'

'We ought to make sure there are a few solid pieces of furniture,' Rourke suggested. 'A sofa or two. We don't want bodies lying around in full view.' Collins rubbed his eyes to clear the pricking tiredness. It was after 2.30 a.m.

'Couldn't really be better,' he said. 'A ten-foot wall, heavy gates. We may have trouble with the guards, especially if they're inside the gates. But if we're quiet, even that might not be a problem. Then, after it's over, we grab the old man and head for the helicopter, and hope we can get the damn thing airborne before the guards realize what's going on.' He yawned. 'God. Look at the time. We have to sleep, otherwise Michael and I won't be good for anything in The Hague.'

Collins then went through the plan again, step by step, minute by minute, and each man built the scene in his mind's eye as he talked.

Friday 9 April

If Collins and Rourke had later been asked to recall any details of their day in Holland, they would scarcely have been able to do so. They had taken an afternoon shuttle the previous day from Heathrow to The Hague. Exhausted from their near-sleepless night, they had booked into an airport hotel and after a rapid supper of cold meat and salad, collapsed into bed. Neither could have placed on a map the airfield to which their cab took them in the morning. Their attention, from the first five minutes of their arrival, was directed towards the machine on which they were to train, under the tuition of a dour Dutchman with too many teeth.

The Bell 205-A, like the Alouette, is a turbine, but it is a much bigger machine. In America and Europe, it usually carries up to fifteen people with its twin-bladed rotor. (In the tropics and at altitude – in lower-density air – it carries less.) Collins's brief in-flight experience in the Alouette was of some use, but the major problem was the total unfamiliarity of the instrument layout. On the mastery of this depended the speed of their departure in Addis. Twenty times over the next two days, both men fought to reduce the time of their take-off without ruining the engine.

Their instructor, Piet Osterhuis, was at first less than a perfect teacher. Collins had not told him the purpose of the training. The realization that he could not complete his job to his satisfaction and the feeling that information was being kept from him exasperated him. Only after the following conversation, on the afternoon of the first day, did his mood improve.

'I have no eye-dee, no eye-dee at all what you want to do this for. To take off in two minutes, one minute, I don't know? It matters so much? You have men chasing you with machine-guns?'

Collins, strapped into the pilot's seat, set a finger and thumb against the bridge of his nose in a gesture of exhaustion and suffering patience. He glanced round at Rourke in the seat behind, then with sudden decision leant across to the trainer and muttered conspiratorially: 'Yes. We are from British Military Intelligence. Please do not ask us more. We are depending on your training to save our lives.'

The change wrought by this piece of melodrama was instantaneous. From then on, Osterhuis used every minute to good effect, until, with much reduced checks, both Collins and Rourke were sure of being able to take off in less than a minute.

Saturday 10 April

Yufru had already arrived at the bank, impeccable as usual, with his slim briefcase, which he at once opened. He slipped four sheets of paper – the visas – on to Cromer's desk and accepted an orange juice, while Cromer poured himself his usual whisky.

Cromer had his glass raised in a toast to continued success when the phone rang. It was the weekend porter announcing Cromer's guests.

Within two minutes, Collins, Rourke and Halloran, all dapper in dark suits, with briefcases stamped with the Cromer seal, stepped out of the lift.

'Ah, Jeremy,' said Cromer. 'Mr Sackville-Jones, Mr Smithson, allow me to introduce Mr Yufru.'

'Indeed, gentlemen, a pleasure,' said Yufru, shaking hands with each in turn. 'Mr Squires, good to see you again.'

Then, as Cromer offered drinks, Yufru went on: 'I will not detain you. I have only a few things I wish to say. Firstly, I owe a debt of thanks to you all, and in particular to you, Sir Charles. You gentlemen are certainly very lucky in your employer.'

The three smiled and nodded.

'And the next thing is to reassure you about your visit. You will be honoured guests of our government at the Addis Ababa Hilton. A car and interpreter will be placed at your disposal. But there will be no official functions to attend. My government do not wish to emphasize your presence. Finally, it remains for me to wish you good luck. Perhaps we may meet again when your mission is accomplished.'

Collins, Rourke and Halloran had not said a word. Yufru, wrapped up in the significance of the occasion, merely shook hands with them all again and left. Cromer accompanied him downstairs. When he returned, he found his three colleagues relaxed and laughing in sudden relief.

'Holy Mother,' said Halloran. 'I may look like a banker but I feel a fucking idiot!'

'Pete, you are a fucking idiot,' said Rourke. 'A suit is no disguise. The buggers will suss you right away.'

Halloran frowned. 'Really? Major?'

'Don't worry,' grinned Cromer. 'You look just fine. Any of you need a job when this is over, just give me a call.'

8

The afternoon flight to Addis Ababa, with its stops in Paris and Rome, was uneventful.

The plane touched down at the Ethiopian capital's Bole Airport, an unexceptional collection of glass and concrete, at 6.05. As the engines were still dying, a black Mercedes pulled away from the line of cars in the lee of the main building and swung round beneath the wing to the steps that were being trundled into position. An announcement asked all passengers to remain seated. As the 'No Smoking' sign went off, an air hostess began to show the passengers off the plane.

Collins led the other two down the steps to the sleek Mercedes waiting on the tarmac. A uniformed driver sat at the wheel. Standing nervously by the back door was a small, neat man, grey-suited in the international uniform of bureaucracy. His top lip was pulled back in a nervous smile that revealed a keyboard of glistening teeth. He stepped forward to shake Collins's hand in welcome.

'Asfud,' he said. Rourke felt his small, bony hand twitching with nervousness. Asfud shook hands with the other three members of the delegation, repeating his name at each self-introduction, and adding: 'Interpreter. English, Amharic, French, Italian. London, Paris, New York, Rome.'

Rourke wondered how a man so apparently terrified of life could have acquired that width of experience, or having acquired it, why he should remain so terrified. Perhaps it was an indication of the gravity of this particular meeting.

The Englishmen sank back into the cavernous rear seats of the Mercedes. Asfud climbed into the passenger seat. The car purred away towards an exit in the wire fence surrounding the airport, its progress monitored by two Ethiopian policemen who stood ready to close the gate behind them.

Addis Ababa was an odd mixture of modern splendour and long-established squalor. It was founded by Selassie's uncle, the Emperor Menelik, in 1892. At that time Addis Ababa, which means 'New Flower', was merely the latest in a series of temporary encampments that had each served as the capital until the surrounding woods were exhausted and there was no more fuel for cooking. But Addis turned out to be different. Its setting is delightful. It lies at 8000 feet, amid mountains that grow daisies, lilies and orchids, and its climate is moderate. Menelik, unwilling to move again, planted fast-growing eucalyptus trees for fuel, and the place endured. Soon, the Emperor built himself a palace, a two-storey whitewashed house, the only brick building in Ethiopia at that time. Other permanent buildings followed: workshops, barracks, offices, a chapel, a den for the palace lions.

Since then, much of the medieval squalor had remained unchanged: drainage was still almost non-existent in the outskirts, and there were always more beggars per square mile than anywhere else on earth. But at least this city of 800,000 had acquired a veneer of modernity. Hotels, hospitals, office blocks, shops, the houses of the rich, and the spanking headquarters of the Organization of African Unity, stood within a short walk of earth-floor hovels and tin-roofed huts. Menelik's eucalyptus trees, with their blue-green leaves, were everywhere, offering cover to the jackals and occasional hyena that crept into the city at night. Fiat taxis tooted at likely fares, and women watched over wayside stalls of onions, garlic, pepper and other spices. Everywhere – especially since the 1974 famine – there were beggars: pathetic, mangy huddles of rag, bone and flesh.

Into this once Imperial capital swept the Mercedes. It was a mere ten-minute drive from the airport to the Hilton, a four-square, nine-storey, grey and brown box lying in a fifteen-acre site of rough grass and scattered eucalyptus trees, complete with pool, tennis court and a children's playground. An oasis of civilization in a garbage-heap of a city. There, they were handed keys by a smiling, tail-coated manager.

In exchange, Rourke noted with some horror, they were asked to hand over their passports. This was standard procedure, explained the smiling manager, for unfortunately Addis still had its thieves. The passports would be kept in the hotel's safety-deposit box until their departure.

Their rooms were on the fourth floor, in line down the corridor. There was a distant view over the outskirts towards the towering western highlands that, along with the deserts to the north and east, have helped preserve Ethiopia's independence from lasting conquest.

Asfud informed the men, before they went into their rooms to unpack, that they were guests of the Ethiopian government and would not be required to pay for anything during their one-day stay, and requested them to enjoy the facilities of the hotel and to sleep well in preparation for the conference the next day. He would, he said, return with their car at ten the following morning.

For the next few hours, during which time the men retired to their rooms, showered and dined, scarcely a word was spoken. They agreed there was nothing to be done about the passports. A protest would merely invite suspicion. Otherwise, they were a little army before battle, each man alone with his own thoughts.

Sunday 11 April
But for the lurid colours of the décor, they might have been in any international hotel anywhere. Without needing to be reminded, all three of them ate well and drank a gallon. There was no knowing when they would eat and drink again.

Halloran in particular was remote, his usual flow of superficial banter dammed up behind slightly lowered eyelids. He seemed drugged, robot-like.

At 10.12, the car awaited them.

There were no more words. Each man took his briefcase. In silence, they took the lift down to the lobby, where Asfud hovered uncertainly, and walked out with him to the Mercedes standing in the forecourt.

The Swiss Embassy was a ten-minute drive from the centre, to the north-east, one of the more graceful and spacious areas on the edge of the city, within a mile of the American, Russian, British and German embassies. There was no single diplomatic sector in Addis, though some embassies – mostly African ones – were grouped together near the centre. Like almost all except the smallest and most central embassies, the Swiss Embassy stood behind a fifteen-foot compound wall, topped with barbed wire. It consisted of one main, two-storey building and three smaller ones: a gatekeeper's lodge, a second small bungalow that acted as a guest-house, and a triple garage.

The Mercedes was unremarked in the town.

171

The inhabitants were used to attendant hordes of OAU officials in chauffeur-driven limousines. The Mercedes stopped briefly outside the embassy's double iron gates, allowing time for the gate-keeper to identify car and driver, and then swept grandly through. In the recess of the forecourt, on their right stood another, smaller Mercedes – the Ambassador's – the Swiss chauffeur dozing in the driver's seat.

Two wide steps led up from the paved forecourt beneath a pseudo-classical portico: the building was constructed to a Swiss design when Switzerland first established relations with Ethiopia in 1926. On the steps stood a tall, dignified man of perhaps fifty-five: the Ambassador, formally dressed in dark suit, white shirt and grey tie. He looked the career diplomat *par excellence*: tanned, steel-grey hair, half-glasses. He was alone. The car stopped. Asfud came round to open the door for Collins, who stepped out on to the tarmac, already warm beneath a clear sky. The Ambassador advanced and shook him by the hand, then said, with the merest hint of an accent: 'Morges, Georg Morges. Won't you come with me?'

He led the way up the steps, stopped briefly until the other three were ready to follow on, then continued through an entrance hall, with stairs sweeping up to the first floor, and turned right, through ornate double doors with fluted, gold-coloured knobs and with bolts top and bottom, into what was clearly his own office, airy, spacious and lit by two casement windows. Both were closed; the embassy was air-conditioned. On a sideboard stood an assortment of drinks: juices, cola, tonic water, an ice bucket. There was no alcohol – out of deference, the Ambassador explained, to the Imperial dislike of it. There was also coffee on an electric heater.

The office, normally furnished with an ambassadorial desk, a low table and armchairs, was dominated now by a large conference table surrounded by eight solid, leather-covered armchairs, three along each side and one at each end. Each place was laid with a pad, several pens and glasses of water.

Morges was cool. At his age, and with his experience, he disliked having to hand over his embassy. It would have been interesting, and more fitting, to have been asked to chair the meeting, about which he had been fully briefed. But Zurich had been adamant.

'I believe you will find the arrangements to your approval. You will see that I have placed your delegation along that side. The Emperor should sit at the head of the table. The senior member of the Provisional Military Administrative Council will be seated at the other end. The three other Ethiopian delegates are along this side. This is as you requested. It is as well to have matters properly arranged for such delicate meetings.' The Ambassador allowed himself a brief, cold smile. 'Now, here is the anteroom . . .'

He walked to a second set of doors and swung them open to reveal another, similar office – normally his own conference room – more comfortably furnished with chairs and sofas.

'If either side should need private discussions . . . Now, perhaps you will wish to arrange your documents and take refreshments. Your opposite numbers should arrive shortly. Then the Emperor's helicopter. But my instructions are to leave the embassy at your disposal. I shall return later when the Emperor has left.'

Collins took on his role of leading delegate. 'Herr Morges, everything seems excellent, excellent. We owe your country, and you personally, a debt of thanks.'

Clearly that was all that was necessary. Morges nodded formally, without smiling, said merely 'Gentlemen' and left the building, walking round the side to his Mercedes, which swept him out through the gates. The gatekeeper allowed the gates to remain open. Their own Mercedes reversed round to take the spot vacated by the Ambassador's car.

An uncertain silence fell. The three Britons stared down at the table. Asfud was as nervous as a gazelle. He glanced from Collins to the others and then at the refreshments table.

'Ah, Mr Asfud, please help yourself,' said Collins. 'Gentlemen, shall we?'

Each man named a choice: coffee for Collins,

Coca-Cola for the other two. In addition, each of
them downed another two glasses of water.

Rourke noticed a movement. He nodded towards
the courtyard, where a Daimler was gliding in
through the open gates. It contained three Ethiopians
who would (with Asfud) make up the full delegation
of four. The leader was a minister, Tedema, and
with him were two aides, middle-aged financial
specialists who had made a detailed analysis of
the memorandum of transfer in both English
and Amharic. All three were dressed formally in
European-style dark suits. The gates were rolled
shut and the Daimler stopped by the steps. The
three passengers got out and the car reversed
back through ninety degrees to park beside the
English delegation's Mercedes, leaving the forecourt clear again.

The three men came straight out of the glare of
the sun and in through the door as Collins moved
toward them from the conference room. Tedema
extended his hand.

He was a tall, thin man and remarkably young,
in his early thirties. He was clearly enjoying himself
in the exercise of his authority, as well he might,
believing himself about to supervise the official
receipt of some $2000 million.

'Mr Squires. How good to meet you.' He held on
to Collins's hand as he spoke, a gesture common
to many African countries, but one that Westerners
often take for overt homosexuality, to their own

embarrassment. His accent was too much of a perfection. Sandhurst, perhaps? Oxford?

Collins said: 'Mr Tedema, I am delighted everything seems ready. My own staff . . .' – he introduced each in turn, then went on: 'We have just established the seating plan as arranged from London.' He explained the arrangements, with the Ethiopian nodding rapidly.

'Good, good,' Tedema said. 'Let us be seated.'

Briefcases were placed on the table, documents removed from them and chairs pulled back.

At that moment, as they were sitting down, there came the distant sound of a helicopter. It was half a mile away and coming in low, with the deep thud of twin-bladed rotors. In seconds, the helicopter was over the parking lot, twenty feet up, above the spot where their Mercedes had first stopped half an hour before. Dust scudded away to either side, fogging the window. Collins walked away, back to the door, and through to the lobby. The others followed.

He waited until he heard the engine cut out and the rotors begin to slow. Then he opened the door warily and stepped out into the dying breeze. The helicopter stood some forty feet away. Its rotors swished to a standstill.

Through the reflections on the glass panels Rourke could see a man – no, two – at the controls, freeing themselves from their belts. The one on the far side opened the door, jumped down and ran towards the main gates. He was an officer and was wearing light army fatigues with a sleeveless jacket over a short-sleeved khaki shirt. He carried a light 9mm Uzi machine-pistol and a walkie-talkie.

Halfway to the gates, he stopped and signalled to the two chauffeurs with his weapon. The drivers left their cars and walked rapidly across the tarmac. The three men then hurried over to the gate. The officer waved his weapon urgently at the gatekeeper, who let them through, then followed, pulling the gates to behind him. The officer signalled the three civilians out of sight behind the wall and took up a position immediately outside the gates, at their very centre. Rourke was disconcerted to see one of the drivers emerge from the gatehouse with a rifle of some kind.

The nearside door of the helicopter opened to reveal the second pilot, also in officer's uniform. He stepped down, then turned, opened the rear door and unfolded some steps.

Collins had scarcely noticed the slight figure sitting behind the pilots' seats, in the centre of the aircraft. Through the glass of the door, he had seemed a mere shadow.

Now the shadow moved. It was indeed the Emperor.

The hook-nose and beard were silhouetted against the window beyond. He was in a seat placed in the middle of the rear section, which had been stripped of other seats for the purpose. The figure rose slowly, stooping and slight, and came to the steps. The officer, staring upwards, shielding his eyes from the noonday sun, held up a hand. The old man reached out and stepped down, three steps in all, to the tarmac. The officer moved back, in obvious deference.

The Emperor stood for a moment, his hand free again, staring down, as if in thought, or waiting for his eyes to adapt to the glare.

The officer took a couple of paces back to the helicopter, reached in and took out a walkie-talkie. He spoke into it briefly, looking up towards his colleague at the gate. Number two waved. Yes, the radio link was working fine.

Rourke's gaze focused again on the Emperor. There was no hint of grandeur in his dress. He wore a black cloak tied at the neck, over a grey jacket done up Mao-fashion and matching trousers. His shoes were plain black leather. In stature, too, the figure was merely that of a very old man, shrunken, emaciated, five foot two in height perhaps, no more. He was a wraith, the spirit of a former age.

Yet almost at once his bearing clothed him in regality. Fifty years of near-absolute rule were too ingrained for easy eradication. His hair and beard, wiry and grizzled, framed a bony little patrician face. The eyes, penetrating and compelling, rose. The shoulders came back and the old man walked forward. Collins had read that Ethiopians had once prostrated themselves at the mere passing of

Selassie's green Rolls-Royce. Now he understood why. The old man radiated an authority that was almost tangible.

'No protocol,' said Tedema, as if sensing Selassie's impact on the foreigners. 'He is nothing now.'

The Emperor, flanked by the second pilot, whose machine-pistol remained in the helicopter, slowly mounted the two steps. The party of British and Ethiopians fell back to either side to allow his passage.

With the officer solicitously at his side, Selassie proceeded into the hallway and turned through the open doors into the conference room. As the two entered, Collins moved alongside the Emperor and indicated the place at the head of the table. Without even glancing round the room, Selassie stood at the table head. The officer moved his chair out. The Emperor stepped into position, his chair was lifted in, and he sat, his hands on the arms of the chair, impassive, staring down the table while the others moved round to their own positions.

Asfud had reached the limits of nervousness, his eyes darting from Collins, to Tedema, to the Emperor, and then as if to retreat from the tension these sights loaded upon him, to the swirls of plaster decoration round the top of the walls.

The Emperor suddenly leaned sideways to Asfud as the final chair scraped its way into position. He said something in Amharic, so quietly no one else could hear. Asfud dropped his gaze in a gesture of submission and thanks, and from that moment on seemed calmer, strengthened by an infusion of imperial sympathy.

With everyone in their places, the officer, who had been standing behind the Emperor's chair, placed the walkie-talkie on the table by Tedema and indicated the on-off switch. Tedema nodded. The officer flicked the switch to demonstrate. The device emitted a little beep and a light flashed briefly on and off. Again Tedema nodded. The officer walked rapidly out without a word, leaving the room in silence.

Through the window Rourke saw him reach into the helicopter, lift out his weapon and walk towards the gates. He turned round to look out of the other window. The man slipped through the gate to join his colleague, to form a discreet guard outside the embassy.

Rourke ran a check. Weapons outside the gate: one Uzi, one rifle of unknown make, maybe a pistol or two. Weapons to hand: nil. Opposition: four inside, four outside, with a radio link. Outlook: dodgy.

Tedema, meanwhile, had begun a speech. Asfud was leaning forward to translate into the Emperor's ear.

'. . . as quickly as we can. I am here on behalf of the Provisional Military Administrative Council to sign with you and with the former Emperor the document before us. It is an historic moment for us.

There must be no error. I suggest, therefore, that you read your English version clause by clause. I shall read the Amharic version. We shall then sign both versions. There should be no disparity. The translation has been checked already. The reading may take an hour, an hour and a half. But we shall all have confidence in the memorandum at the end. Is that agreeable?'

The Emperor nodded. Rourke and Halloran were merely watchful.

Collins cleared his throat and began to read, pausing at the end of each clause so that Tedema could follow on with the relevant section in Amharic.

He read on until he came to the clause relating to the release of various grandchildren still under house arrest. This was the moment Collins had chosen to start the real business of the meeting. He paused, coughed, and looked round.

'Minister, Your Highness, I believe there is a further consideration to be, ah, considered in that preceding clause. It relates to the mechanism of payment to the members of the royal family abroad. I would like a brief recess to speak with, er, with my staff first, and then with the Emperor.'

Tedema stared.

The Emperor, his eyes closed in concentration, listened intently to Asfud's murmured translation.

'I think,' responded Tedema coldly, 'that we have done quite enough for the family. We owe them nothing. Yet they are to lead the lives of relatively wealthy people. I fail to see your point.'

'Let me explain,' said Collins. 'The family are to receive fifteen per cent of the total share. I should imagine that there might be some justifiable concern that the family's funds might be spent in areas that would not be wholly, how shall we say, to your country's interests?'

For five seconds Tedema made no response. Then he nodded slowly.

'Ah: subversion,' he said.

'Exactly. It seems to me that it might be possible to spread the payments over a longer period.'

Silence.

'A good point.' Tedema nodded again. 'Your obvious self-interest might after all work to our mutual advantage.'

All this while, Rourke had been merely watchful, waiting for Collins to give the sign for action. Now the moment had come, his senses suddenly focused. He had never been so close to action without a weapon, never been dependent on a colleague. He felt naked. What if they saw through him? Reached for the walkie-talkie? Ran for the door, shouted for the guards?

'Very well.' Tedema's words sent a surge of adrenalin through Rourke. 'You wish to recess? I think we can accept that.'

While Asfud muttered in the Emperor's ear,

Collins deliberately pushed back his chair and selected a few of his papers. 'Shall we?' he suggested, with a casual smile to Halloran and Rourke. They both nodded, and followed him into the ante-room. Collins eased the door closed behind them, and moved away, across the room.

'OK,' he said, in a voice hardly more than a whisper. 'We let them be for a few minutes.' He glanced at his watch, then looked around, as if seeking inspiration from the room. Through one window, the two parked cars were half visible. To the left, stood the guest-house, shuttered and silent. The other window gave out on to nothing but the compound wall.

Collins nodded briefly towards the other door, which led out into the entrance hall. 'Do we have an alternative exit?'

'Not if they've got any sense,' said Rourke. With three swift strides, he was at the door, gingerly pressing down the handle. Then with a shake of his head, he returned. 'Rock-solid.'

They stood in silence. Halloran carefully undid a button of his shirt, reached inside, and pulled out his thin strand of rope. He wrapped it round his hands, then moved into position behind the door.

Collins looked at his watch again. 'Two minutes. Let's give them another one.'

'I hope you know your lines,' Rourke muttered. The idea of relying on words at a time like this unnerved him. He was glad Collins had the job.

'Act One is fine,' said Collins with a taut smile. 'It's the finale I need help with.'

He looked at his watch again, stepped forward and opened the doors, concealing Halloran. Collins coughed deferentially. 'We have a suggestion, Mr Tedema,' he said. 'But before proposing the matter formally we need to go through the wording with Mr Asfud. Mr Asfud, would you be so kind?'

With a nod from Tedema, the little man walked with his usual smile towards the ante-room. Collins backed away, leading him on. As Asfud came through the doors, Rourke closed them, leaving Tedema standing, smiling, his back towards Halloran, who stepped silently foward, the rope taut between his hands.

Asfud, who had clearly been expecting an invitation to sit down, opened his mouth and drew breath to speak. At that moment, Halloran's rope came round his throat, and, as if in a cold fury, the Irishman snapped his arms into a cross behind his head. The rope bit into the Ethiopian's skin. In silence, his eyes bulging, his mouth open, his hands scrabbling at his constricted throat, he sank towards death, as surely as on a gallows, suspended from Halloran's bent arms.

Even before the body relaxed, Halloran used the noose to haul his victim behind the door, where he laid him out. Asfud's feet drummed a soft, brief salvo on the floor, and a stain spread down his trousers.

'Good one, Peter,' breathed Rourke. Outwardly, he was calm, but it was the first time he had seen murder done in quite so cold a manner. He was at once hypnotized by the drama of death and exhilarated that it had been accomplished in such silence.

Halloran, still locking the noose around Asfud's neck, glanced round, assessing how visible the body would be when the next victim entered. He rolled up his eyes and grimaced as if to apologize for his own foolishness, and then dragged the corpse behind the sofa. At last, he seemed satisfied. He removed the noose, nodded at Collins, gave a small smile to Rourke and resumed his position behind the door.

'OK,' Collins said. 'Next.'

He adjusted his face to form an urbane smile, opened the door, and stepped across the threshold. 'Mr Tedema,' he said, with no trace of nervousness in his voice. 'Mr Asfud has no real problem with the language.' He glanced behind him, to one side, as if meeting Asfud's eye. 'We would like your comments before we place the changes before the Emperor.'

Tedema sighed. 'Will this take long?'

'Oh, no. A minute or two.'

For a moment, Rourke thought Tedema was

going to object, because he muttered something in Amharic to his colleague and then to the Emperor. 'Very well,' Tedema said, turning to Collins. 'I suppose I had better come.'

The operation was as straightforward as the previous one. The door closed, and Tedema had time only to look around puzzled and begin a question: 'Where is . . .?' when the rope was round his throat, and he, a taller man than Asfud, was on his knees quivering in Halloran's iron grip.

For another minute, the four men formed a silent, fixed tableau, the only motion being from Tedema's fluttering hands. Rourke watched, intrigued by the sight of an intelligent, supercilious, self-confident individual turning into a useless bundle of flesh and bone at Halloran's feet.

'Now what?' Halloran asked, as he dragged Tedema's corpse over to lie beside Asfud. He slid the noose clear, and slipped it into a jacket pocket.

'Two down, two to go,' Collins said.

Rourke was surprised to hear his own voice. 'We can't pull the same trick again.'

'What?' said Collins, already on his way to the door.

'Too risky. If they suspect . . . if one of them shouts out . . . if the last one switches on the walkie-talkie . . . the guards at the gate can see into that room.'

Collins paused and turned. 'You're right, Michael.'

He spoke with his usual ice-cool tone. 'Not the same trick. We have to do this bit all at once. It's three against three. Peter and I will deal with the other two. Michael, you take the Emperor.'

'But the guards can see.'

'Only if they're looking. We have to move together, get into position behind each of them, then in unison get them against the wall, out of sight.'

All three waited, playing the scene in their minds. None of them doubted their ability to kill. The Emperor himself was a rag doll, easy to lift.

'Remember,' said Collins as if reading Rourke's mind. 'Treat the old man carefully. No use us arriving back with damaged goods.'

'Tell me again,' said Rourke. 'We rescue the young ones and kill the old one, right? Or is it the other way around?'

Collins shot him a wry smile, and glanced again at his watch.

There was only one question: could they preserve the element of surprise? Again, it was Rourke who put it into words. 'Who does what exactly?'

'Let's get on with it, for Christ's sake.' Halloran's voice was a whisper, but it rasped with urgency.

'Wait.' Collins's expression was calm. 'We can afford the time. We're still bankers. We've been talking business in here. When we go in, they'll be expecting the other two to be right behind us. We'll have maybe five, ten seconds' grace before one of them flips. In that time, we have to be behind each of them without arousing suspicion. I know . . .'

He moved to the table and picked up the papers.

'We've all been studying these, OK?' He broke open the binding on the cover, and divided the bundle into three. 'One for each of them,' he said.

Halloran opened his eyes wide. 'What's it supposed to be?'

'Draft revisions. In longhand.' Collins caught the sceptical gazes of the other two. 'I know it's dumb. But it's good enough to get us into position. Any better ideas?'

Silence. Rourke shrugged.

'OK. Back in character. Let's go.'

Collins stepped forward, depressed the ornate door handle, and opened the door. Rourke saw him smile broadly, ready to greet the two Ethiopians at the table.

'Mr Tedema . . .' he began firmly, then broke off.

The two remaining Ethiopian officials were not at the table. The Emperor sat, with his back to the doorway, as before. But the two aides were at the window, smoking, staring out towards the main gates. And one was holding the walkie-talkie. Clearly, he had just been using it. Rourke could see straight over their shoulders. There were the two pilots, backed by the two chauffeurs, standing idly, in full view, staring towards the Embassy. One of them raised a hand in acknowledgement, and the aide did the same, his cigarette languidly resting between his fingers.

He turned, and graced Collins with a grin. 'Wonderful toys they have nowadays,' he said.

Collins's smile froze. After the briefest of pauses, he said in the same bold voice: 'Gentlemen, we have a solution. If you would take your places?'

Rourke and Halloran moved into position behind Collins, both seeing instantly that if either of the two men showed a hint of suspicion, if there was any danger of waving at the guards or calling for help through the walkie-talkie, they would have to move together, fast.

The man with the walkie-talkie stood smiling, waiting. He glanced at the room behind Collins.

Collins turned and addressed the empty room. 'Mr Asfud, Mr Tedema, thank you. We are waiting.' He turned back to the aides. 'They are finishing the translation. Meanwhile we have the original. Allow me.'

And he moved decisively towards the table, extending his papers ready to put them down for the aide. Halloran was right behind him, making for the man's seat. Rourke moved into position behind the Emperor.

'Ah, yes. Of course.' The aide slowly placed the cigarette between his lips, and switched off the walkie-talkie. He walked to the table, placed the radio on it, and sat down. He picked up the papers.

The other aide had moved across the room and just sat down, with Collins behind him when a puzzled expression crossed the first man's face.

'I don't understand. What is it you wish me to read?'

Halloran stood back a foot, and reached into his jacket pocket, feeling for his rope as if for a pen.

'Oh,' said Collins. 'How foolish. The wrong page. Please turn over.'

The aide did so. Halloran's hand came unnoticed out of his pocket.

There was no need for any word.

Collins raised his arm, turned sideways into position, and brought the edge of his hand down in a vicious backhand chop into the neck of the man in front of him. He would have felt nothing. His head snapped backwards. Even if the nerves running down his spinal column remained intact, the shock was enough to snuff out consciousness for hours. He slumped forward, clouting his nose on the table, probably breaking it, releasing a stream of blood.

At the same time, Halloran garrotted the other aide. This, of course, was certain, but it took longer, and proved noisier than the previous two murders. The man's knees came up sharply beneath the table, and his body jerked the chair about as if it were electrified.

All this occurred far more quickly than it takes to tell. And meanwhile Rourke's task was to secure the prize, the Emperor himself. Rourke had been so absorbed by what the other two were about to do that he had given no thought to what it would feel like to grab the old man.

Silence was the first requirement. Restraint next. Those two alone would have been easy: a hand over the face, an arm round the shoulders. But there was no point in silencing and pinioning Selassie, only to find he had the Emperor trapped in his high-backed chair. Before making a move, he had to be aware of longer-term needs: mobility and safety.

The answer was automatic. Even as the first man crashed on to the table and the second began to fling himself back and forth to escape Halloran's noose, Rourke slipped his hands over the chair back and under Selassie's arms, scooping him up as if he had been no more than a tailor's dummy. As he lifted the Emperor, he thrust his left hand clear and clamped a hand over the old man's mouth.

Swinging him away from the chair, and back against the wall out of sight of the guards on the gate, he held his burden firmly clear of the floor. He was light, no more than 100lb. And he had no time to do more than utter a few muted grunts. But he was not quite the rag doll Rourke had been expecting. There was still a surprising amount of strength in the wiry little arms and shoulders.

The sight before the Emperor was, of course, something of a stimulus. The two government men before him were dead or dying. The two others had vanished. True, they were enemies, and in other circumstances he would have had them executed anyway. But right now, there was no telling what the mad Englishmen would do next. All he knew was that they were killers. For all he could tell, he was next. So he panicked, and struggled, his tiny feet kicking out at Rourke's shins, his arms flailing.

Rourke was suddenly at a loss. Their lives depended on getting clear, quickly, with Selassie. That meant subduing Selassie. But not hurting him. Keeping the Emperor's head held tight against his own chest, Rourke changed grips, locking his free arm right around the Emperor's body and both his arms.

'Keep still!' muttered Rourke in the old man's ear. 'We've come to save you!'

Collins was watching Halloran, who still held the aide round the neck. The man was almost dead, but Halloran was not yet ready to let him go. At Rourke's words, Collins looked up, to see Selassie twitching in Rourke's arms.

'Wiry little bugger,' said Rourke. 'I don't know what to do with him.'

Collins put up his hands in a gesture of appeasement, and spoke directly to the Emperor.'

'Listen, sir, Your Majesty.'

Selassie swung his head from side to side in a vain effort to escape from Rourke's iron grip. His eyes were wide, and breath wheezed through his nostrils. He made muffled little noises – 'mm . . . mm' – behind Rourke's hand.

'Christ, listen! We are here to rescue you! Just do as you are told and everything will be all right!'

Something seemed to get through. Selassie stared at him, and the struggling ceased. Rourke relaxed his grip as much as he dared.

'OK,' said Collins. 'That's better. Listen: we have been sent by Sir Charles Cromer. We are not bankers, we are soldiers. He wants to rescue you. We are going to put you in that helicopter, and get you out of the country. Then you will be safe. OK?'

Selassie stared, and did not struggle. Rourke gingerly relaxed further. Halloran had left his victim, and was standing watching, his right hand idly putting away his garrotte. Collins glanced round to make sure they were all out of sight of the guards.

'You understand?' said Collins. Still the Emperor stared.

'Let's move,' Halloran said impatiently.

'We need him,' Collins muttered. 'And we need him to go quietly.'

At that moment, a sound intruded. It was a small electronic beep. Instantly, all four were transfixed. On the table, beside the slack body of one of the aides, the walkie-talkie had come to life. Its little light glowed. A metallic voice came through, speaking in Amharic.

'Kill it!' Halloran said.

'Sh,' whispered Collins. 'The circuit's open.'

The voice ceased. Then it came again, more insistently.

Rourke whispered: 'They'll be wanting to speak to Tedema.'

Collins looked at Selassie. 'Speak to them,' he said, whispering tensely in Selassie's ear. 'Just tell them everything is OK.'

Selassie stared.

'We have to trust him,' said Collins. 'Let him go.'

Gingerly, as if he were handling an unexploded bomb, Rourke released the old man.

As Rourke's hand came free from Selassie's mouth, there was a few seconds' silence. Then the walkie-talkie squawked again.

Selassie yelled one word, a high-pitched shriek, struggled clear of Rourke's arm, and made for the door.

He had taken no more than two paces when all three of them reacted. Rourke and Halloran grabbed him, and then, just as he opened his mouth to shout something else, Collins brought a fist down on the scrawny neck. The old man collapsed on to Rourke's arm.

'Jesus, major. You said to be careful with him.'

'We're not going to get him out if he's shouting his mouth off. Hold him until we see what damage he's done.'

'What the fuck did he say?' asked Halloran.

'God knows,' muttered Collins. 'But it's time to go. With or without his co-operation. Look.'

Across the courtyard, the gate was swinging open. The pilot with the machine-pistol was coming to check up on what he and his mate had heard: a puzzling shout for help in Amharic.

'We could do with his weapon,' Rourke said.

Collins nodded, and signed Halloran to take up a position behind the main doors. Then he glanced at the offending walkie-talkie on the table, still with its light on. He walked over to it, leaned across the dead aide, and lifted the handset. He threw a switch. The light blinked off.

There was a shout from the gate. Halfway across the courtyard, the pilot stopped. His mate yelled something.

'They know something's up,' Collins said.

Seconds later the pilot had disappeared from sight, having reached the building.

Rourke caught Collins's eye, then glanced down at his burden. Collins nodded towards a spot on the floor to one side of the door. Gently, Rourke laid the unconscious Emperor on the floor. A thought flashed across his mind: strange creatures, humans – to be so careful with one individual, while preparing to use extreme violence against another.

They heard the main door open, then close again with a click.

Silence, broken, to the open-mouthed astonishment of Rourke and Halloran, by Collins remarking in a conversational tone: 'Well, I guess the silly bastard's waiting to see if we killed off his bosses.' He paused and glanced at Rourke. 'Am I crazy? Not yet. The sod with the gun the other side of this door is waiting to see what the hell is going on in here. And the one thing he'll be expecting to hear is someone talking. Well, I'm fulfilling his expectations for him, and I just hope he doesn't speak English.'

Rourke cleared his throat. 'Oh, yes, I quite agree, sir. Very steamy weather for the time of year.'

'That's it. Let's just keep talking then, while we make quite certain that our reception is ready. Mr Halloran, would you do the honours?'

The handle of the door went down. Halloran's hand already held the rope. The door opened a crack. Collins stepped across, and pulled it open further, with a ready smile for the wary pilot, careful not to allow the man much of a view into the room, and then turned slightly as if addressing an unseen audience: 'I wonder if it's OK to allow our friend in here?' He nodded in feigned acknowledgement of an instruction, stood back, and beckoned.

As the pilot appeared round the door, Rourke just had time to see an expression of horror cross his face at the sight that met his eyes – two bodies at the table, the Emperor lying apparently dead on the floor – when Halloran's noose went round his neck. The gun fell, swinging by its shoulder band. The pilot's hands locked on to the rope, his fingers seeking a hold. He was strong, this one, and he had had some training. Finding no finger-hold to release the garrotte, he brought his bent arms sharply back to elbow Halloran in the ribs. The Irishman kept his grip.

Rourke and Collins had expected this death to be as silent and as easy as before. This time, though, the pilot was more than a match for Halloran. His neck was still brutally constricted, but now his legs kicked backwards, and his body began to thrash, not in a death throe, but in retaliation.

'Rourke!' Collins's voice snapped him back to conscious thought. 'His arms!'

It took the three of them to complete the death, with Collins and Rourke gripping the pilot's arms, and forcing him to his knees, while Halloran, grim-faced and sweating, wrung life from the weakening body.

When it was over, they stood back and surveyed the mess of the conference room.

'You be nursemaid,' said Collins to Rourke. 'We'll back you.'

While Collins detached the gun from the dead pilot, and Halloran went through the man's pockets, Rourke again lifted the delicate body of the Emperor. He paused briefly to feel the pulse.

Yes, there it was. He looked up at Collins. 'OK, sir. He's a bundle of bones, but he's alive.'

'Let's get the hell out.'

Halloran had found only a pocket knife. Muttering in disgust, he stood up and checked the window.

The gate was closed. The guards – the second pilot and the two chauffeurs – were watching the Embassy curiously. The driver with the rifle was standing with his weapon at the ready.

'And two pistols,' said Halloran. 'At that distance, not a problem.'

Collins ran a rapid check on the pilot's gun. 'It's a Williams carbine,' he said. 'Haven't handled one of these in years.' The semi-automatic rifle had a full magazine. He flicked off the safety-catch and settled the weapon into the crook of his arm. 'Peter, go for the chopper. Check if there's a weapon in there. Michael, you follow him. Sling the old man in, and strap him in. We don't want him recovering consciousness and trying to throw himself out. I'll get their heads down, and then start her up. That'll be our weakest moment. Peter, if you haven't found anything else, you'll have to take over this thing' – he slapped the carbine – 'until take-off.'

The two men nodded.

'OK. Go!'

Halloran ducked through the door, leaving it wide for Rourke. At the main door, Halloran opened it, allowing Collins to speed past him.

Collins ran into the middle of the courtyard, sank to one knee and fired at the gate.

Behind him the two men ran for the Bell. Rourke caught a glimpse of the three men at the gate, with spurts of dust flying around their feet. One was flat on the ground – dead? – another beginning to force the gate open, and the third beginning to aim his rifle. Clearly they weren't ordinary chauffeurs and pilots, but trained soldiers, able to respond even when taken by surprise.

Then Rourke was at the chopper. Halloran was already inside.

'Shit!' No weapon, but there was a box of ammunition. He whipped out a magazine, turned, hauled Rourke up the steps with his spare hand, and jumped down to take over from Collins. Rourke was concentrating on dumping the unconscious Emperor into a seat, and then dragging safety straps around the frail old man. Even as he clicked them closed, he was dimly aware of more bursts of fire from Collins, and another noise: incoming fire, cracking into the chopper.

Through the noise, Halloran yelled: 'The major's hit! Michael! Get started!'

Rourke looked out. Collins was down, a bullet in the knee. He was dragging himself towards the helicopter, while Halloran jumped out and, crouching low, seized the weapon and fired a burst at the gates. Most of a mag was gone, but it did the trick. There was no one to be seen: keeping their heads down.

The gun died, out of ammo.

A figure appeared round the gate's side column, aimed a rifle and fired.

The spare magazine was on the ground beside Halloran, who squatted and snapped off the old magazine.

'Goddam it!' Collins, hit again. The shoulder this time. He rolled over, and began an agonized, snake-like wriggle towards the helicopter.

Meanwhile Halloran had smacked the new magazine into place, aimed and fired. Bullets puffed off concrete, zinged off metal, sent dust scudding up the road from around the gate.

Rourke was in the pilot's seat. How long had this been going on? Seemed like an eternity of slo-mo action, long enough for all of Addis to know there was trouble, long enough for the whole fucking army to mobilize . . .

Rourke addressed the controls. He threw switches.

Fuel boost.

Mixture.

Throttle.

Ignition.

No time for any other checks. No time for the seat belt.

The rotors began to swing above him, the whine of the turbines building, building, until it blotted out the noise of gunfire ten yards away.

Ahead, the gates were open now. Someone would be on a telephone, surely, asking for back-up. The body he had seen lying in the road was gone. So maybe they hadn't taken a casualty after all. So there were still three out there, with just Halloran holding them back.

And now Halloran's second magazine was empty. He turned, leapt into the helicopter, grabbed another mag, and then jumped out again to cover Collins's gasping progress. The wounded man was five yards from the chopper . . .

Halloran slapped in the new mag . . . four yards . . . Halloran aimed, fired . . . three.

The Bell's turbines had reached full, deafening power. Rourke stared down at Collins, unable to do anything for him. The down-draught tore at the major's hair. His banker's suit was a mess of torn material and blood. He mouthed words through the noise and his own pain. Rourke shook his head, unable to read his lips. Behind him Halloran was still firing.

Rourke heard the rattle of Halloran's fire stop, saw the gun-smoke die. Halloran glanced down at Collins, hesitated for a second, then decided. He tossed the weapon into the helicopter's open door, stooped, got an arm under Collins, jerked him to his feet. Collins was sinking now, his eyes beginning to roll, blood loss and pain sapping his consciousness.

The chopper was ready. Halloran yelled something into the major's ear. It was useless. The older man sank beneath him. Halloran went down too, supporting him.

At that moment, Collins jerked. Rourke looked up. The bastard with the rifle was at the gate. A cool one, that – to fire accurately at a time like this. Now he had hit Collins a third time.

Rourke saw him aim again, at Rourke himself this time, the deliberate, controlled action of a professional, and fire. It all happened too fast for him to react. A little hole appeared like magic in the windshield, prettily framed in a filigree of shattered Perspex. It seemed to Rourke he could see straight through it, and clean up the barrel of the marksman's rifle. How the bullet had missed him, he couldn't understand. He felt wet on his hand, saw blood. He was hit. But he hadn't felt the impact. No pain. He felt his shoulder, then his face, followed the trail of blood with his hand. His *ear*, his right ear was bleeding. Even then, with the helicopter trembling to be gone and the turbines whining and the wind roaring, Rourke thought: Jesus, that guy is good.

He looked down again. Halloran was dragging Collins towards the door. He tried to lift the wounded man. In films, it looks easy. In real life, to lift an unconscious man is almost impossible. It's not the weight. It's the distribution of the weight. There's no way to get at the centre of gravity or keep the burden rigid, as Halloran well knew. For a few seconds, he wrestled uselessly, then he turned, and waved an arm violently at Rourke: Take her up!

Rourke pushed the control lever. Above him,

the angle of the blades changed, biting into the air, hauling the machine into the air. He glanced behind him, in time to see Halloran leap on to the skid just as it left the ground, and grip the surround of the open door for support. Beneath him lay Collins's body – it had to be the body, for the last shot had caught the major in the side of the head.

But which way? Not up. Away, to the right, as quickly as possible out of range. He turned the stick, too hard. The machine swung round and tilted, no longer gaining height. Ahead was the compound wall, fifteen feet high. He wasn't going to make it. He righted the machine, it clawed for height: ten feet, twelve . . .

At that moment, Rourke looked back to check that Halloran was safe. What he saw plunged him into further horror.

As the chopper righted itself, Halloran lost his grip, screamed, fell backwards, then, as if by a miracle, seized hold of the skid. For a second he hung there. He was still hanging when the helicopter cleared the wall, no more than a foot or two above the barbed wire. The wire tore him off the skid like a fly hitting a spider's web.

Rourke hoped he died instantly.

He swung his gaze back to what lay below and ahead: roads, houses, the suburbs of Addis.

Rourke risked one more glance behind. The embassy was receding. He could see it all now, the main building, the garage, the gatekeeper's house, the two parked cars, Collins's body in the middle of the courtyard, and the marksman standing beside it, pointing at the receding helicopter. He didn't fire. There was no point now. The machine, with its strange burden, was already out of range.

9

Rourke, his once immaculate suit covered with dust, hugged the contours. The lower he flew, the fewer people would be able to see him, and the better chance he had. Not for long, of course: Ethiopian Air Force planes would soon be out looking for him. No need to make it easy for them.

Sweat seeped down from his armpits, soaking his business shirt. He grabbed his tie – fuck's sake, a *tie*, in these circumstances! – and yanked it off.

Where to for the best?

Less than 200 miles south lay the first stop on his escape route: Lake Chamo, with its hidden store of fuel. But wait one. What if Collins and Halloran were still alive? He wondered briefly if there was any chance they would divulge the escape route, then dismissed the thought.

Below him unfolded the outer fringes of Addis, a few brick houses, wood-and-tin shanties, a decaying factory or two, then only scrub, rocky outcrops and a dusty road. He glanced at the compass. He was heading north.

He could afford to hold course for another

minute. Anything to sow a little confusion in the opposition. Air speed: 110 m.p.h. Fuel: almost full – 300 miles' worth, give or take.

Rourke felt the adrenalin begin to leave him. He took a swig from the flask of water dangling from the instrument panel, and wondered if there was any possible alternative to heading south.

There was none. He had no idea of the country, except what he had seen on the map. North: Eritrea – a breakaway province who would no doubt love to get their hands on the Emperor, if only for propaganda purposes. But too far. He wouldn't get halfway. East: desert. West: mountains. That was it.

Besides, it wasn't just himself he had to consider. He stole a glance at the Emperor, still unconscious in the seat behind.

OK. Half a minute more, and he would make his move. He planned his course of action: to head back the way he had come, but further west along the cliffs and folds that scarred the highlands, hoping they would hide him from the radars and eyes of anyone on the lookout for him.

He checked his fuel again – and stared in horror. The gauge had dropped sharply. Now, suddenly, after flying for – what? no more than five minutes – it read three-quarters full. Even as he watched it, the needle edged down a point.

How the hell could this be happening? At once he knew the answer: the marksman.

There had been other shots, not all of them at the three men. At least one of them had come at him. He touched his ear. It was caked with blood. Nothing serious: a nick. Some blood, no pain. Perhaps the shot hadn't been for him at all. That was why it had missed. Perhaps the man had been aiming at the fuel tank, or a fuel line. Or perhaps there had been other shots Rourke hadn't been aware of, a ricochet. Whatever, the fuel was leaking away.

Instantly, he reassessed his situation. He couldn't make his fuel dump on Lake Chamo. If he tried, he might not even get much beyond the populated highlands. If he was spotted, he would just be a sitting duck. He'd be caught, probably killed, the Emperor recaptured and killed, the whole enterprise in tatters.

There had to be another way.

North, after all, to Eritrea? It was too far by hundreds of miles for him to fly the distance, but – his mind spun a fantasy – perhaps land near a road, hijack a vehicle – he had the carbine Halloran had thrown in the back – and then maybe he would be able to smuggle Selassie into hiding, find a telephone, call London, fix up funds, get them to send a plane. After all, he had possession of one of the most valuable political prizes in the world. Surely, they – the government – the Foreign Office – Cromer – *someone* – would want to see the two of them safely out.

Too much wishful thinking, he decided. Start

again. He was heading north-east, to avoid populated areas. Go with that. What was in this direction, east? He remembered the maps he'd seen in Collins's house, in Chris Swain's office, in the plane flying north to make his fuel dumps. Yes, the Horn of Africa: Djibouti.

If he remembered right, Djibouti – the border anyway – was only about 300 miles from Addis. Now that was a more realistic possibility. They spoke French there, didn't they? Once over the border, he would be able to improvise something through diplomatic channels. He would keep the SAS's name out of it, but after all, he had Selassie.

Selassie was the key. He would be coming round shortly, and Rourke had to have him on his side. Surely to God he knew some English, enough for Rourke to explain what was happening, enough maybe to get some help from the old man. Once he understood he owed the Britons his life, surely he would be happy to help.

'Hey!' he shouted above the whine and throb of the engine. 'Sir! Your Highness!'

Still looking ahead, he found he could reach back far enough to shake the figure behind him. Selassie seemed to have slumped forward in his harness. His head lolled. Rourke felt for his shoulder, and gave him a shove.

Then he looked back. An arm fell clear. It swung and juddered in time with the beat of the rotors.

He reached a second time, and pushed the old man's head. It fell back. The eyes were open.

A new, different panic gripped him. The vacant eyes, the limpness, face slack, chest unmoving . . . The Emperor was not unconscious. He was dead.

Flying time: half an hour, and falling.

Rourke's face creased in an agony of frustration. Below him the shadow of the helicopter chased over grey, dusty soil, scrub and thorn bushes.

The true ghastliness of his situation hit him. He had been contracted to save the Emperor from a murderous regime. Instead, the mission, even in its success, had accomplished precisely the opposite. Moreover, Selassie's fortune had not been saved for the West. Now it would be locked away in perpetuity, and the sole beneficiary would the fucking bankers who had got him into this mess in the first place. To cap it all, a successful escape had now taken him from the frying-pan into the fire – literally, by the looks of the landscape below.

Flying time: fifteen minutes.

A herd of gazelle scampered off to one side below him. In the distance he saw a vehicle, spewing dust behind it as it bumped along.

'Shit!'

The one thing he had to ensure now was invisibility. Hah! He gave a bitter laugh. Him – invisible! He was dressed in a grey suit flying over a wilderness where they spoke Christ knows what and spent their time castrating foreigners, piloting a damaged chopper where there was no other plane for hundreds of miles, running out of fuel, about to land in a furnace of a place, without water, and – if he did come across someone who might offer help to such a surreal creature – to cap it all he was carrying the one man whose face would be instantly recognizable to absolutely the entire population.

The body. His mind focused on the only thing he could do to improve his chances. He had to get rid of the body.

He veered away from hills on his left, out over desert.

The 'fuel low' warning light flicked on.

Do it now!

Rourke pulled back on the stick and slowed his progress over the desert. He checked the horizons, liquid in the heat. No sign of human life. The only movement was a gliding bird, a vulture probably, riding the thermal from some baking rock over a mile away. He dropped down, aiming for a gravel patch near a few low thorn bushes.

The skids touched the sand, the rotors whirled to a standstill, the dust of the landing scudded away and settled. Rourke opened the pilot's door and climbed out. The heat smote him, rising up as if from an open oven. He looked at his watch: 2 p.m. At least the sun was sinking. It could only get cooler from now on.

Standing on the desert floor, he at last removed his crumpled and stained jacket. There was no relief. But at least the heat would dry the sweat from his shirt.

He turned to the rear door, still locked open, and reached for the straps holding the tiny corpse. The skin was wrinkled like stained parchment. Nothing in this sack of a body to indicate imperial greatness. He clicked the belt open, and the body slowly keeled sideways, on to Rourke's outstretched left arm. He brought his right arm up, took the Emperor round the chest and slid him out, on to the ground. He left him lying on his face, laid the cloak along his back, and weighted the edge of the cloak with pebbles to stop it blowing about.

He stood back, and checked. There was nothing but a scattering of thorn bushes, some sparse palms a few hundred yards away, and off to the west, the trembling ghost-images of mountains emerging from the haze.

For a second, he considered covering the whole body with stones, but he had been out of the chopper for five minutes already, and every second meant less fuel and more danger. What was the point in building a grave? It would turn a temporary thing – the vultures would do their work in a few days – into something lasting, which might eventually draw attention.

He climbed swiftly back into the Bell, and punched the starter button. Ten minutes of flying time left – twenty miles at most. He wondered briefly if he had made the right decision. Perhaps

after all he should head west, towards the hills, find
a road and transport . . .

No. People meant danger. He would have hundreds of miles to go in hostile territory. Better trust
to his survival instincts in the desert and get over
the nearest border.

The dust roared away from his rotors, covering
the little corpse, but also dragging the cloak free
of the pebbles and setting it flapping madly. The
helicopter rose, the ground vanished briefly in
a haze of blowing dust. When it cleared, the
chopper was thirty feet up, and as Rourke tilted
away eastward, he saw that the body was nothing
but an insignificant smear.

Keeping low, he flew on, over nothing but the
same featureless flow of dust, rock and scrub.
Nothing here to make him choose one place
over another. He recalled the forbidding notes
on the Operational Navigational Chart: 'limits of
available vegetation information' . . . 'insufficient
data for contour lines' . . .

Any towns? None that he could recall. But wait:
that phrase on the chart – 'numerous camp-sites and
sheepfolds' – gave him hope. If there were people,
there would be food, water, clothing, and perhaps
some means of transport: donkeys, horses, camels,
something.

Something somewhere, perhaps, but not here, not
in this hell-hole, not in time. If he didn't land right
now, he would end up in a heap of wreckage. As

he pulled the stick up, bringing the chopper to a shuddering hover, he saw, fifty yards ahead, a track, hardly more than an absence of scrub and rock, but enough to outline a course used for some human purpose: going somewhere, driving animals.

It was enough. Fuck it, he had no choice.

He drifted off to one side and came down in a shallow defile, probably a watercourse – if it ever rained. He sat there for a moment after the whap-whap of the rotors died away and the turbine ceased its whine, feeling the heat and the silence. He was below the level of the track, invisible unless someone came to the lip of the defile. He could afford a minute or two to gather his thoughts.

The water-canister swung idly from the instrument panel. He drained it, and wanted more. In this heat you had to have those eight pints a day just to keep going, and he didn't give much for his chances of topping up over the next few hours.

He climbed out to piss – there went another valuable pint – then retrieved first the carbine, then a clip of ammunition from the case, and finally his jacket from the floor. He sat down in the shade of the chopper and checked the weapon. He had handled a Williams carbine in training, when they had to try out every foreign weapon the SAS could get their hands on.

He knew the story: Williams was a moonshiner doing time in a US prison – this was in the 1940s – and to pass the time he designed a new gun action

in his head. It was an original conception, allowing
for a very short, quick and reliable return. Later,
he actually started to make the damn thing in
the prison workshop. The authorities slapped him
down, of course, but someone had spotted what
he was up to, and acquired the patent. Colt put
the gun into production, and soon there were four
million of them arming the US forces. They lasted
through until the A3 16 replaced it in the early
1970s, at which point the Williams carbines were
unloaded on to the open market, some of them
filtering through to Third World countries.

Rourke reloaded, then folded the jacket into a
pillow and lay down on it to plan his next step.

He took stock.

Business suit, one, banking executive, for the use
of.

Hand-made leather shoes: one pair.

Tie: one. Particularly useful, that. A chap should
always have a nice striped silk tie when stranded in
the desert with a downed helicopter.

Water: nil.

Food: nil. But come to think of it, he didn't
mind, yet. Christ, was it only that morning he had
breakfasted so lavishly in the Hilton? His mind
told him that it was centuries ago, in some other
universe. His stomach told him otherwise. That was
something to be grateful for.

Fuel: nil.

Prospects: terrible.

Sense of humour: very, very low.

There were, however, a couple of pluses. Weapons: one. Ammo: as much as he could carry.

Sometime, someone would come looking for him from the skies. If they sent a plane within two miles of his landing-site, the Bell would stand out like a prick in a nunnery. He wondered whether he should try to camouflage or destroy it. Camouflage? With the amount of vegetation round there? Forget it. Burn the thing out? And release a smoke signal that would bring the Ethiopian cavalry over the hill? Besides, burn it with what?

Sod it. Just get out. If he stayed here, he would simply dehydrate and be dead in two days.

Except it was still mid-afternoon, and the sun was hammering down, and it was just plain daft to move during the day. He knew the rules. This had to be 120 in the shade. He guessed he had a litre's worth of liquid in him. If he moved at night and lay up in shade during the day, he might survive through the next day, and ought to be able to walk about twenty-five miles, max. So unless he wanted to commit suicide, or he heard a plane, he would stay right where he was until nightfall.

His mind played with memories of desert survival training. Watch birds: circling birds might indicate the presence of water. Camels shit near wells, so if you see mounds of camel shit, watch out for a dried-up water-hole and get ready to dig . . . A voice sounded in his head, some officer who had come to lecture them on the delights of the American barrel-cactus ... must look out for cactuses ... cactuses ...

He woke with a jump.

It was dark, and wonderfully cool. The Bell loomed over him, a shadow against a starry sky. A glow low in the sky told him there was a moon. He blinked, lay still, looked and listened. Something had woken him. Behind him – he could see it clearly outlined as he twisted round on an elbow – was the dark line that marked the edge of his little world. He might have been alone in the universe.

But he wasn't. He heard a shuffling sound, and a sort of panting from close by, above him. He rose quickly, grabbed his jacket and weapon, and ducked down the other side of the helicopter.

Over the edge of the defile a head appeared.

It was a goat, nibbling at a low thorn bush.

Rourke watched. In his experience, animals seldom went off too far on their own. Where there was one goat, there could be others, and where there was a herd, there would be a herdsman.

The goat retreated. There was no further sound.

Rourke waited, straining his ears, waiting for his eyes to gain full night vision. If there was anyone nearby, there was no hint of movement. He needed information. Slowly, he stepped around the chopper, then walked carefully up the gentle fifty-foot slope of the little valley. A crescent moon, low in the sky, came into view, dimly lighting the desert landscape.

There was the goat, browsing by itself a dozen yards away. Odd that it was on its own.

Then he saw a pinpoint of light, flickering – a fire – perhaps a hundred, two hundred yards away. Hard to tell the distance in those conditions.

He sat down again, and thought through his options. He needed food, water and clothing. If there was any walking to do, it would be good to have something comfortable to walk in – these thin-soled shoes would give him hell after a few miles. The camp-site might offer all these things.

If he could get them without revealing himself, so much the better. Of course, he could go in gun blazing, take out however many people were there, and go on his way. But he could not bring himself to regard an Ethiopian peasant as his enemy. Anyway, discretion would serve him better. God knows how far the sound of gunfire would carry on still desert air, and it wouldn't take an Ethiopian Sherlock Holmes to draw conclusions from a pile of corpses and an abandoned helicopter.

He put on his jacket – it was getting cooler by the minute, and if this little op took more than a couple of hours he would need warmth. Besides, it provided a way to carry extra ammunition, just as a precaution. He walked gingerly back down to the Bell, reached into the box of clips, and slipped two of them into the two inside breast pockets

– enough for some security if he didn't make it back to the chopper. Finally, he retrieved his empty water bottle.

He set out towards the distant glow, picking his way between the moonlit bushes. His leather soles scrunched noisily on the desert floor, but there was nothing but the goat within earshot. Still, in response to his training, he stopped every ten paces to listen.

Then, in the middle distance, perhaps 150 yards away, there was a figure, small and stooping: the herdsman. Rourke squatted down, and watched. The man seemed to be casting about. Looking for his bloody goat, probably. Anyway, he had – Rourke hoped – left his camp-site unguarded. The herdsman was moving away from him. Rourke walked as rapidly as he dared towards the fire.

As he approached he saw that the camp was closer than he thought. The fire, which was burning low, had clearly been used for cooking. Moreover, it was not just a chance camp. The moon glinted off the tin roof of a shack, from the other side of which, Rourke could now see, a fence ran, forming an animal pen. Against this darker shadow, the fire glowed. He stopped again to listen, and could now hear the soft rustle of moving animals. More goats.

Then a sickening groan. Rourke grimaced. To anyone who had never heard it, the noise would have sounded like a soul in torment. Rourke, though, knew the sound of old: it was a camel, over by the fire by the sound of it.

He hated camels. The most disgusting sight he had ever seen was an Arab slobbering in tears over a camel caught in the belly by a 66mm anti-tank rocket. It was hard to know which he found the most revolting: the camel's wounds or the beast's slimy green death-spittle.

The place seemed deserted. As a precaution, Rourke removed his shoes, inserted them into the side-pockets of his jacket, and padded in his socks – fucking socks! in the desert! – slowly up to the wall of the shack. There was a door, made of loose wattle. He stood for perhaps five minutes listening. Nothing, not even a snore. The herdsman out in the desert behind him must be alone.

He gave the door a push with the barrel of his weapon. It opened.

Inside was a table, hardly visible in the faint glow of moonlight that came through the small, unglazed window and the half-open door. On the table were a variety of objects: the remains of a meal, Rourke discovered, when he placed his water bottle down and explored with his free hand. His gentle touch revealed a few pieces of fatty meat and some *injera*, chapatti-like unleavened bread, hard, gritty and bitter, but perfectly edible.

Rourke was chewing when he heard slight noises from outside, a foot kicking a stone, a cough, a nose being cleared. He moved against the wall behind the door, deeper into the shadows, pulling his dark jacket well across his shirt, and folding the lapel up over his face. He heard the noise of a piece of fence being moved, a slap, a protest from a goat – the same one, no doubt, that he had seen earlier, now retrieved by its owner.

What now? Rourke already had two possible scenarios. The first involved the herdsman settling down by his fire, leaving Rourke to finish his meal, collect whatever might be useful from inside the hut, and be on his way.

The second scenario had the herdsman entering the hut. So when the door swung open, Rourke was ready.

A figure entered, dressed baggily in a *shamma*, the toga-like shawl that is part of the national dress of Ethiopia. He was a middle-aged man, Rourke guessed. He walked straight across the room, mumbling to himself, picked a large leather water-container out of the shadows – good to know that was there – took a long draught, and replaced the container.

He turned. Perhaps he caught a glimpse of Rourke's bottle on the table. But he had no time to react, for at that moment the side of Rourke's fist caught him just below the right ear. He went down like a marionette with its strings cut. It had been a delicate hit. Rourke checked the herdsman's breathing and pulse to make sure he was still alive.

It took perhaps two minutes for Rourke to strip off the man's sandals, baggy cotton trousers and *shamma*. He changed out of his own clothes, carefully setting on the table his two ammunition clips and the machine-pistol, then bundled the clothes together for later burial: no point in leaving more clues than necessary. He dressed in the loose peasant clothing, discovering to his amusement that the trousers were held up by a belt made of elastic braces.

Then, prowling the hut, he finished the rest of the bread and drained a brackish litre from the leather flagon. Most of the rest he used to fill his own bottle.

'Thanks, mate,' he said, to the unconscious man naked on the floor, taking up his bundle in one hand and his weapon in the other. The clips he inserted into the improvised waistband of his trousers, and left.

Outside, he looked around at the moonlit desert. What now? And where? He could head east by the stars – there, low on the horizon, was the Plough, its two right-hand stars pointing at Polaris, true north. But he had no idea how far the border was. Two days' walk? Or two weeks'?

There was no getting away from it: the sensible thing was to use the effing camel. He went over to it. Beside it was a blanket and a saddle. Another blanket lay on the ground. The camel was couched, reins in place, looking at him with disdain.

'I don't like this any more than you,' Rourke muttered.

He tossed the blanket and saddle over the camel's hump, forced the saddle strap through behind its front legs, and tightened it. He climbed aboard. With a dreadful lurch, the beast rose. He shook the reins, and was off.

With luck, the man would assume he had been robbed by a *shifta*, or bandit, and simply not bother to report the loss. He would be on his way in the morning, probably with his remaining blanket as clothing. By the time Addis traced the chopper and arrived here, the herdsman would be far away. At worst, he would see the helicopter, and make a report. By then Rourke would be long gone.

10

Monday 12 April

Eight hours later, Rourke was twenty-five miles further east, and the worse for it. The only time he had broken his journey was to scrabble a shallow hole to bury the suit and shoes. If there was a trick to riding a camel he had never cracked it. In Oman, he could never relax into the trancelike state achieved by his Arab squaddies. Now, as the hidden sun began to threaten the eastern horizon, he was sore with the chafing of the saddle at the base of his spine and the pommel between his thighs, and horribly tired. The early exhilaration – the sense of freedom, the cool of the night, the hard glitter of the stars, the monochrome expanse of the empty desert (he had seen not a living thing all night) – all that had evaporated after a couple of hours. That was when the aches had started, and his mind had begun to dwell on the immediate past.

He had lost a colleague and a mate. He relived the pain he had seen written on Collins's face, saw again Halloran's doomed attempt to save his boss. Dicky wasn't always a bundle of laughs, and Peter had his faults, but when it came to it, they had fought well together. Quite like the old days for a few minutes. Could he have done more? He replayed the murders in the embassy, the ridiculous attempt to win Selassie's support, Collins's well-intentioned but fatal blow.

No, he couldn't see too much to reproach himself for. They had walked the knife-edge that always divided success from failure, and luck – as often in warfare – had pushed them off the wrong side. Now it was up to him to survive, to make some sense of deaths that would otherwise be meaningless. He – and the story – had to be their memorial. Who dares wins. For Rourke, as for every SAS man, that remained the guiding principle.

But, for the present, just to survive he had to find a place to lie up through the day. The camel seemed in fine fettle after eight hours, but he had no way of knowing how long it would go if he tried to ride through the day. Camels were odd creatures. Once, in Oman, he and his men had come across an oasis where two of the beasts lay in the shade, motionless. His guide explained they were dying. They had become fatally exhausted. They had been made to travel too far, too fast, without enough food, until their legs started to give way. Eventually, their owners would have been unable to make them rise, and had simply left them to die, too weak to eat or drink yet surrounded by food and water. Perhaps another day of walking would reduce this creature to a useless lump. He was surprised to find he cared. The animal had carried him for eight hours, lugubrious but uncomplaining. If he was ever human in some previous incarnation, he was surely a butler.

More to the point, though, he himself would not survive the day. He was already in need of water. Two hours in the full sunlight would turn him into biltong.

He looked around in the strengthening light. He became aware of how very obvious he would be if anyone happened to see him, a lone figure in the middle of a gently rolling plain of sand, rock and gravel. Herdsmen might accost him, brigands assault him, a military helicopter or light plane swoop down to question him, if not spot him immediately for what he was.

He urged the camel up a rise, and cast about for anything that might offer shade. To the west, the desert lay in deep purple shadow; to the east, the dim light already made the ground grey. Off to the south-east, another ridge attracted him. Perhaps a ridge would lead to a dip, and a dip might offer – what? A rock shelter? A tree?

'Come on, Jeeves.'

He slapped the reins and the camel swayed forward. It moaned as it broke into a stiff-legged run, forcing Rourke to lean back to keep his balance. The edge of the sun appeared almost ahead, bathing the desert in a golden light and casting vast long shadows from tiny contours and shrunken thorn bushes. For the first time, as the camel slowed at the bottom of the ridge, Rourke was struck by the beauty of the wilderness around him.

He came to the next ridge, climbed it and looked down. It didn't look promising. It was perhaps twenty feet deep. The only steep slope faced the rising sun, and would shortly turn into a suntrap. The bottom still lay in shadow, and seemed to offer nothing except a single scrawny bush.

He scanned the horizon again, and was now surprised to see something which must have been there all along, but now stood out sharply: mountains, their angular peaks spotlit by the sun. Suddenly, he knew where he was. These were the mountains that funnelled down into the Rift Valley. If he could only follow them, they would lead him south-west, and then south, and take him directly to the only other spot he knew in this stricken land: Lake Chamo, where he had been only a few days before, laying up fuel for the escape.

Well, that was then. The world was different now. Even if he could have covered those 200 miles, it would be of no use. He was better off with Jeeves, a half-empty water bottle and a thorn bush.

He urged the camel down the slope to the bush, where the creature nibbled at a branch.

'Hey, that's my house,' said Rourke, hauling Jeeves's head up.

The bush was only waist-high, and had no leaves.

It would offer no shelter from the heat. But there was a foot of space between the gravel floor and its lowest branches. Rourke saw that he would be able to use it as a support for his blanket.

He dismounted, carefully and painfully, then took off the saddle and blanket, leaving Jeeves standing. He spread one end of the blanket across the bush, and was gratified to find that the thorns hooked neatly into the material. The other end he held to the ground, fixing it firmly with rocks, gravel and sand. He had a makeshift but effective tent, in the best traditions of the SAS.

The very thought of lying down and sleeping seemed to sap the last of his energy. He took a long draught from the bottle, leaving a pint of the warm liquid to refresh him when he awoke, and prepared for sleep.

But what to do with Jeeves? He would need the camel that night, but he didn't like the idea of him standing about all day right over the little camp. He led Jeeves 100 yards along the defile, pulled the reins down and tied them to two rocks. It wasn't much, but there was no time now to come up with a better solution. Jeeves collapsed on to his knees, and started rumbling, bringing up some ancient meal to re-chew. If he was like the camels Rourke knew in Oman, he would keep this up for several hours, and happily rest there until nightfall.

Then Rourke walked back, his feet in shadow, his head already feeling the heat of the rising sun, to his shelter, put the carbine down on his jacket in case of trouble, took the two spare magazines from beneath his belt, shuffled himself carefully under the low, sloping blanket, and slept.

When he woke, the light was dying. His only memory of the day was a succulent dream of Lucy, welcoming him to her, she offering her breasts. Then things had become very mixed up, because she had been talking to an old man, who was both Selassie and his father, and he had told the figure to go away, but the figure had pointed a gun at him, and he had woken to the sun shooting little rays through the material of the blanket above him. He reached out a hand and touched a rock. It was still burning. The blanket had done its job well, protecting him from direct light, allowing him to sleep right through the heat of the day.

As the sun went down and the shadows lengthened across the floor of the defile, he allowed himself a few minutes of luxury to plan his next step. He was almost out of water. By dawn he would be thirsty. He had no food. Another eight hours, and he would be hungry too. But he couldn't suppress a feeling of confidence. As the chart had indicated, there really were 'camp-sites and sheepfolds' scattered across the wilderness. Sometime over the next few hours he would come across a track, and the track would lead on eastwards, and he would find a source of food and water.

As he dragged himself out from under his blanket, and walked up the defile towards the shadowy far end of the defile, where Jeeves was waiting for him, he was already wondering about the border, already planning his arrival at the British consulate in Djibouti, already improvising an unlikely dialogue with a tall public-school chap wearing a Guards tie who lived in a white-painted house complete with flag-pole, and always observed the Queen's birthday . . .

Except that the camel had gone.

He swung round. No sign. He ran up the slope, stared into the deepening twilight, even yelled 'Jeeves!' then shut up, for his voice would carry half a mile in the still air. He cast about, looking for tracks, and found them after ten minutes. They led away westwards. He presumed camels had a good sense of direction, and Jeeves would have known the area. He was off back to his master, or to a well, leaving Rourke quietly muttering 'Fuck' over and over again as he came to terms with the magnitude of his loss.

After cursing himself for his complacency – he must have been closer to collapse than he knew the previous night to have left the camel out there like that – his training took over, and he became coldly rational.

It was at least night. He could walk without immediate fear of dehydration. He would be able to cover ten, maybe twenty, miles. The hills he had seen were over *there* – he oriented himself by the glow of the setting sun – so if he headed due east, he would eventually find a track, a camp-site, a herd, a well, *something*. All he had to carry was his blanket, bottle and gun.

Really, he told himself, it was not much worse than Test Week during SAS Selection. If he could carry a heavy bergen thirty-five miles up and down the Brecon Beacons, he could make twenty miles on the level. If he could come through a bit of 'beasting' – like watching a truck drive away from an RV just as he arrived after a ten-mile run fully laden – he certainly had no need to let an AWOL camel get to him.

It was dark, and the cooling air was sucking the heat from the desert floor. He gathered his gear, and started walking.

When walking, running or marching, by far the most important item of equipment is footwear. A blister is not as bad as the runs – and God knew what that goatherd's bread was made of or what sort of camel filth had been swimming in his water supply – but it can be the death of you. A blister grows, spreads, bursts, making every step agony, wasting time, sapping energy.

Within five minutes Rourke knew he was in for it. The herdsman's sandals were mere strips of leather bound up with material. There was no way they could protect Rourke's soft feet. He felt raw spots developing on each side and where the material chafed his uppers. It was inviting pain, and perhaps infection, to wear them at all.

Now he was barefoot, picking his way across sharp rocks and gravel and desiccated twigs of thorn bushes as carefully as if he were negotiating a bed of nails. His progress was slowed from the punishing 4 m.p.h. he had planned to a meagre one or two. He was, in effect, a cripple, and after eight hours of skinning his soles on this barbed-wire surface, he would be one in fact.

He stopped, and held his head in his hands, creasing his eyes in anguish.

'Fuck!' he yelled, hoping now that someone was there in the void. 'Fuck! Fuck! Fuck!'

Even as he bellowed his frustration, he knew what lay ahead. The options were few. He would stagger on, in hope. If he found help, he survived. If he didn't find help, he had eight hours of hobbling misery followed by a slow and agonizing death from thirst. He could hole up for another day, but eventually, sometime in the next forty-eight hours, the desert would claim him. He knew because he'd seen it: the raging thirst, the cracked lips, the hallucinations, the collapse, then death.

The one thing he would not do was sit and moan.

He stepped forward gingerly, and grimaced as he trod on a pebble. Some of the men used to keep their feet hard, just in case, by going barefoot for weeks at a time on leave. It took about six months to harden your feet, and even then you had to be young – younger than Rourke was.

He was about to step forward again when, on the still night air, a sound came to him. It was a distant rumble that he immediately assumed was thunder. That made no sense. The night was clear, and rain about as likely as a pregnant Pope. Besides, the noise was continuous: a steady . . . not so much a rumble now as a . . .

It was in fact a perfectly ordinary sound, one he had heard so often he had instantly dismissed it as an impossibility. Then, once he had identified it, he became fearful that the extraordinary experiences of the last two days had flipped his mind. He waited, half expecting the sound simply to vanish, and leave him with the fearful certainty that he was hallucinating.

Now came confirmation: a low, distant whistle.

It was a train.

He stood, incredulous. No doubt now. The slow clack-clack of wheels across old-fashioned links, the steady roar of a diesel engine.

Suddenly, he knew it *had* to be a train. He saw again the map at their first briefing session. So much had happened since, he had wiped it from his memory. When they had been considering the best way out, they had thought about going east. Collins had pointed out the desert, the border, the impossibility of setting up dumps there, and the railway, heading down from the highlands, out eastwards along the northern wall of the Rift – the mountains he had seen the previous evening – and then north to the border, and Djibouti.

The noise was beginning to die.

'Hey!' he shouted, and began hobbling like a lunatic towards the sound, grimacing and grunting at each pace, at each sharp pebble that etched itself into his tortured feet.

Then, blessedly, it was sand and smooth rock. He sprinted, then stopped to check his direction. There came the noise – the distant rumble, the soft, seductive toot – further away now. He ran again, ran until the breath tearing in and out of his lungs drowned out all other noise.

His right foot hit something – a root? Even as he fell, he was aware of the damage to his toe. His arms flew out as he fell, with agonizing force, on to something extremely hard. His shins and forearms were skinned, his ribs assaulted as if by a metal bar.

He lay, writhing, splayed across metal and wood.

He had found the railway line.

'Oh, Christ,' he moaned, rolling over, sitting up, eyes shut in pain, winded, not knowing which part of his body to tend first: feet, arms, legs or ribs.

Gradually, his universe opened out. Shock and pain gave way to concern. He was sitting up in the middle of the track. To either side, the rails ran off into darkness, glinting in the light of the stars and a crescent moon hanging low in the sky. If he hadn't been in such a hurry, he would have seen the damn thing from twenty yards away. Idiot. Another mistake.

The train, of course, was gone.

A number of thoughts careered through Rourke's mind. How often did trains run along this God-forsaken line? One a day? A week? A month? No: the track looked in good nick. It was shiny, the result of regular use. But this was not exactly Clapham Junction. It was a single track. That meant the trains had passing places, widely scattered. The trains had hundreds of miles to travel. If they had to wait for each other, the timing could only be approximate. It was hard to imagine how they could arrange for more than about one a day.

And he had just missed it.

He looked longingly down the track.

Another thought penetrated the fog of laboured breathing and pain. He had been running towards the track, with the mountains ahead of him, and the train had vanished to his right, towards the highlands, towards Addis. He was staring west, not east. For his purposes, it had been going the wrong way. That meant, perhaps, there would be another one coming the other way.

Soon? Or in twenty-four hours?

One thing was certain: when it came, if it came, he had to get aboard it.

He took stock. He was standing barefoot in a

stony desert, dressed in a filthy robe, carrying a blanket, a gun and an empty water bottle. That was all. Survival training hadn't prepared him for anything quite so basic. In survival exercises, you usually have something going for you – matches, a mirror, a Swiss Army knife, a candle, a razor – that can lever some advantage from your surroundings.

His only tool was his gun, and that was no help in survival. He had already been in two minds about carrying the thing with him at all. When you're weak, every extra ounce is a burden. But he knew he had to keep it. He could use it to shoot an animal for food. In extreme circumstances, he would have shot Jeeves, torn him apart with his bare hands, and chewed his raw meat like a jackal. If it came to it, he would eat a vulture or a snake. And later perhaps, if he survived, if he got out of this mess, and found himself back among people, a weapon might come in very handy indeed.

He sat by the edge of the track, occasionally standing to experiment with his damaged body. There was nothing seriously amiss. Plans formed, dissipated, reformed. He wondered about using the gun to hold up the train. Too risky. There was no guarantee the driver would stop, and he would have advertised his presence to no effect.

Find a slope when the train might be travelling slower, and leap aboard? Wild West stuff was all very well in the movies, but the train would have to be travelling very slowly, not much more than 10 m.p.h.

Stop it, then. He could have done with Jeeves. Stand him over the track, shoot him, block the train with a dead camel. Or with rocks.

What if the train was guarded? Ethiopia was falling apart. Anything of value, even passengers, might warrant protection. Anything odd, like an obstacle on the line, would be bound to arouse suspicion. He saw himself hobbling out from behind a thorn bush to board the stationary train, only to be confronted by a dozen soldiers.

Now he was beginning to formulate the problem in real terms. How to slow, or stop, the train without arousing suspicion?

He squatted, grabbed the blanket, knelt on it, and explored the tracks with his hands. There was no rail-bed. The sleepers were laid right on the desert floor. The track was narrow, he noticed, several inches narrower than the standard gauge back home. He felt the rails. They were still hot from the day.

Heat.

A fire.

Wooden sleepers! Set fire to a sleeper! Surely a driver would slow as he approached a fire, if only to ensure that the train could proceed safely. Perhaps from a distance it wouldn't arouse all that much suspicion – curiosity maybe, caution, but fires were natural: a bit of glass, a spark would do it.

So he would see it and slow down. But how far away would the fire be seen from? Rourke glanced down the line. At night, a fire would show up for miles.

A thought struck him. The last train had been travelling at night. Perhaps the trains *only* travelled at night. During the day, the carriages would turn into ovens and it would be hard to keep ancient diesel engines cool. Why risk turning a relatively easy journey across a flat and featureless landscape into a death-trap, with a broken-down engine and passengers dying of heat stroke? Wouldn't engineers, passengers and railway officials all agree that this should be a night-time service?

If so, he had no time to waste. The train had, say, 150 miles of desert to cover during the night. It would putter along at – what? 20–30 m.p.h.? That sounded about right for an African train running along a narrow-gauge track without firm foundations. So he was talking about a five- to eight-hour journey. It made sense.

Dawn was at six. It was now 11.06. Jesus! Get moving! But how? He had no matches, no lighter, no fuel.

Fuel wouldn't be a problem. There were enough thorn bushes around to make a fire, a small fire any-way, but he could hardly spend the night hauling armfuls of thorny twigs in from the desert. Besides, it would be tinder dry. Get the timing wrong, and the fire would burn out before the train ever got to it. OK. A small fire, to be lit when he heard the train.

And finally: ignition. The old boy scout stand-by – rubbing sticks together – was a non-starter. As a new recruit, he had seen fire made by hand, on his jungle survival course in Belize. The Indian who did it had a softwood base into which he twirled a fire-stick to build friction, and eventually produce a spark. But both sticks were kept as carefully as matches, and they were far less convenient. The only purpose of the sticks was to teach survival techniques to people who would never use them. Even the Indian didn't need them. 'So that's the way you do it, at home?' Rourke had asked admiringly, through the Army interpreter. The old Indian had given him a withering look, and produced a disposable lighter from his shorts. 'You live like the ancestors if you wish,' he said. 'Not me.'

As Rourke stepped gingerly from bush to bush, breaking off twigs, he realized that he was carrying the only means of starting a fire: his ammunition and the Williams.

Contrary to popular belief, it is not possible to start a fire simply by firing a bullet into tinder. The bullet may be heated by the explosion and the friction of its passage down the barrel, but it never approaches the temperature needed to start a fire. You can even fire a bullet safely into petrol without risk of doing so.

Rourke knew what to do. His only problem was that he had never done it. And since he could only start the fire when the train was approaching, he would have just one chance.

With an armful of thorn bush twigs, he picked his way back to the track, to the blanket he left lying beside it, and piled the twigs over a sleeper.

Then he set to work on the first bullet. He placed it slantwise between a sleeper and the rail, and pressed against it with his thumb. It gave slightly. He turned it, and pressed again. When the lead felt loose in its casing he pulled it out like an old tooth. Carefully, he tipped the powder into a little heap on the sleeper beneath his pile of twigs. Then he did the same thing to three more bullets. That gave him enough powder for a good flare, more than enough to make the twigs blaze up.

The last bullet would demand more careful handling. Once he had removed the lead, he put the cartridge down, making sure none of the powder tipped out. Then he teased a few strands of wool from his *shamma* and shredded them into a soft fluff. Choosing a couple of the thinnest twigs, he broke them and ground them into the palm of one hand with the heel of the other. The powdered wool and wood would be his tinder.

It was at this moment that he heard a sound. He paused, and listened. Silence.

Then he heard it again, and this time it did not fade away: the distant rumble of metal wheels.

With redoubled concentration, he transferred the tinder into the open-ended cartridge, then, as the rumble increased in volume, he blocked the end firmly with more strands of wool, and carefully replaced the cartridge in the breech of the rifle. He rammed the breech closed, and slipped off the safety-catch.

The principle of what he was planning was sound enough. He would place the muzzle against his little heap of gunpowder, then pull the trigger. When it exploded, the gunpowder in the cartridge would set the tinder alight as it travelled down the barrel. The speed and power of the explosion, unconstrained by the bullet, would dissipate quickly, emerging as a puff of smoke with hardly the force of a thunderflash, a grenade simulation. On leaving the barrel, the tinder would scatter into the gunpowder, and – if everything went right – blast it into flame. In theory.

In practice, the blast, small as it would be, might well simply puff the gunpowder away and scatter the twigs. Far from creating a fire, he might simply blow it to bits.

The train was perhaps half a mile away. At 20 m.p.h. that gave him one and a half minutes. He heard the rumble separate itself out into the clack-clack of wheels over rail joints, the clank of carriage-hooks, the throaty roar of a diesel engine.

To enclose the blast from the end of the barrel,

Rourke needed a pad of some sort. He tore hard at the edge of the blanket. It did not give.

A minute.

He ripped at the *shamma*. Again, no good.

'A pad, a pad, a pad,' he muttered, and wiped sweat out of his eyes.

My hand, he thought, I could use my hand. But he pushed the idea away, not willing yet to risk a burn, or worse.

He tried the blanket again, heaving at it in a fury of frustration. It would not tear.

Half a minute.

There was only one thing for it.

He placed the muzzle of the gun on the sleeper, positioning it by feel against the heap of gunpowder. He inserted his right thumb into the trigger. His left hand he cupped over both the muzzle and the gunpowder, making a combustion chamber.

No time for further thought. If he thought any more, he might not do it.

He pulled the trigger.

There was a sharp crack, a flash from beneath his left hand, and then sudden, searing pain. Involuntarily he snatched his hand away and smacked it against his chest.

As he had hoped, it was all over so fast that the burning tinder had had no time to burn him badly. But his hand had been there long enough to do the job. The gunpowder had not scattered, and the tinder had fallen back into it. He watched in fascinated apprehension for the longest second of his life. Then with a swoosh and a burst of fire, the gunpowder came to life.

He leaped up, still holding the gun, grabbed the blanket, and ran back some thirty yards over the desert, the sudden surge of adrenalin driving out any consciousness of painful feet.

Behind him, the mass of dry twigs blazed up, casting a lurid light across the surrounding desert. Rourke threw himself down, below the level of the scattered bushes. In daylight, he would have been easily visible. But he knew he would well hidden by the night, as long as he kept low enough to stop the moon picking up any of his contours.

The fire leaped and crackled, joined now by the sound of the approaching train. He couldn't see it yet, but it must be only 100 yards away. There was no way the driver could miss seeing the fire.

The sound came on, but with no screech of brakes or alteration of rhythm. And then there, a solid block of shadow, its green front flickering in the firelight, was the train itself, rocking on its narrow footing.

When it was a mere ten feet from the fire, there came a yell from the cab, the slam of metal on metal, the groan and shriek of brakes. It hit the fire with its wheels locked, scattering the twigs in a cascade of sparks, and sliding to a stop a few yards past Rourke's position.

In the dim moonlight, all was silent for a few seconds. He couldn't see yet – his eyes were still readjusting to the gloom – but clearly the driver had climbed down. He shouted something. Another man joined him. They appeared as two shadows out of the bulk of the train, walking back to examine the line.

Now Rourke could see more details of the train itself. It was a dinky little thing, with a diesel engine at the front, two freight-cars and a passenger carriage. He had imagined that perhaps it was like one of the old trains in Westerns, with a veranda stuck on the back, handy for grabbing hold of when you were running after it. No such luck. Doors all round, but no rear deck.

The two crewmen – shadows edged by moonlight – were now wandering about behind the train, kicking at rails and, Rourke imagined, the debris of the fire. The driver must have been half asleep. He could have had no clear idea what he had hit, or whether the line or his train was damaged. But it wouldn't take them long to find out.

One of the men shouted. Then a dishevelled figure emerged from the passenger carriage, with a small torch. Its small beam danced about along the carriage side, then down over the tracks towards the first two. All three squatted down. They had found Rourke's makeshift hearth.

Rourke wondered about sneaking up to the front of the train while the three had their attention on the ground. But there was no telling when they might stand, look around them and wonder who or what had made the fire, and if he was up and moving he would be only too clearly visible.

He could lie there, and hope they would simply wander off along the other side of the train. Possible, if they were checking it. On the other hand, they might split up, make separate circuits, in which case he would be in view of one of them all the time.

There was one old trick that might attract them away.

He felt around for a stone, checked the men – they were still squatting over the scorched sleeper, talking in low voices – stood, threw the stone as hard and as far as he could beyond the train, and ducked down again, flattening himself on the desert floor.

Rourke did not even hear the stone land. One of the men stood up. But his attention was still on the track. The conversation continued in a murmur of low voices.

Shit. Next time, the risk would be greater. He felt for a larger stone, keeping his eye on the men through the low filigree of branches. The one standing was half turned away.

Rourke rose to a squat, stood and hurled the stone with all his strength in a flat trajectory a few yards clear of the end of the train. This time, he heard it as it bounced once and scudded across gravel.

The men turned sharply. One said something, and walked towards the source of the noise. He vanished the other side of the train, leaving the other two watching.

Rourke waited in an agony of suspense. If the third man was going to return, best run now, best to risk the run with only two men visible. But if the other two joined the first man, then he would be able to reach the train with virtually no risk at all.

He took up the gun, stood, took a pace. Number two changed position. Rourke went to ground.

There came a shout from the other side of the train. Number two and three walked in that direction. Their shadows merged with that of the train.

Now!

In a flurry of sand and gravel and little sharp stones kicked up by his bare feet, Rourke, swerving round thorn bushes, covered the thirty yards in about ten seconds.

Then he was by the front of the train, squatting down, holding the gun across a knee clear of the ground, and gulping in air as slowly as possible, to suppress the noise of breathing.

He looked through the train's wheels. There, faintly, he could see three pairs of legs, and heard the murmur of talk. There was some minor disagreement going on, probably over the meaning of these strange events: first an inexplicable fire, now an inexplicable thump. One voice was assertive, another noncommittal, another wheedling – two officers perhaps discussing what was happening, against a driver worried about staying on time.

The legs moved towards the front of the train. Rourke moved along the track in the opposite direction, losing sight of the legs for a few seconds. He squatted down and looked through the wheels again. The three men were by the engine now, clearly coming right round the front of the train.

He reached up to try the door of a freight-car. It felt locked. He couldn't risk jerking it – it would make too much noise – and tiptoed on to the other one. Same thing. Christ, if they came round the corner now they would see him. No time to reach the last carriage.

He inserted himself in the gap between the second freight-car and the rear carriage. There were buffers. He ducked underneath, and squatted down again, with the buffers above one shoulder and the carriage-link – two heavy-duty hooks joined by a chain – above the other. He held the Williams vertically between his knees. The two spare magazines still firmly beneath his belt pressed painfully into his stomach.

Stupidly, he was facing the wrong way. He twisted his head, and forced it low. He had been just in time. Two pairs of legs were moving towards him. The driver had apparently climbed back into his cab. They would be moving off within the minute.

The two men went right by him. For a second as they went past, he could see them clearly picked out by moonlight. They were wearing military uniform. The one he could see most clearly was the worse for wear, with his jacket undone. He must have been rudely awakened by the shrieking brakes and sudden stop.

Rourke saw them stop at a door, heard them open it and get in. He looked up. Just above his head, above the chain-link connection between the cars, was a door. It gave on to a little platform that acted as a walkway between linked carriages. To reach the door, he would have to grab the platform, climb on the chain . . . No. Stupid. It would take him straight into the arms of the officers, and God knows who else inside.

From the engine came the whine of a starter motor, followed almost at once by the roar of the diesel. With a hiss and a clunk, the brakes disengaged.

The train was about to roll away above him, leaving him sitting once again in the middle of the track, in the middle of nowhere. He had to climb right now.

He stood in his narrow space, reached for the little walkway beneath the door to act as a hand-hold, and slung a leg over the chain – just as the engine engaged.

With a crash, the chain snapped taut beneath his thigh, lifting him clear of the ground, and nipping flesh agonizingly between two links. He yelped, and almost lost the carbine as he reached up with his right hand to seek another handhold. For a second, he hung as the links ground away at his trapped skin. Then the train lurched, and the chain bent again, enough to release him before it again took up the strain.

The train picked up speed. He worked himself into a safer perch, his feet dangling almost on to the sleepers flicking past below, his left hand still gripping the platform, his right hand holding the carbine.

Now, for the first time, he noticed, on the far side of the door above him, a slim ladder bolted on to the carriage. He could get on the roof. But it was not easy. He was astride the chain (though he didn't like the thought of what might happen if it bent and snapped taut again. Lucy would be left with precious little to keep her happy). It would have been easier if the gun had had a strap, if he had felt able just to push it aside and use two hands.

Eventually, in this confined, dark and shaking little area, he managed to fix one foot against the freight-car's hook, place the butt of the rifle on the platform, and lever himself into a standing position. Then he reached over, grabbed the ladder, swung a foot across, and was on his way up. He caught a glimpse inside the darkened carriage:

wooden seats, slumped and sleeping bodies, bundles everywhere.

On the roof, the world seemed a distinctly better place. The train was moving at an easy 25 m.p.h. across the vast, open bowl of the moonlit desert. Away behind – he was now sitting facing backwards, enjoying the feel of the warm wind massaging his sweaty body – the track stretched in two glistening ribbons. In the far distance, he could even see the ghostly shape of the mountains, ragged against the low-lying stars. It was really quite beautiful.

The most beautiful thing of all was the sense of freedom. Not long before he had faced the prospect of covering no more than a couple of miles an hour, in pain, until he died of thirst. Now he was being carried in ease and comfort towards a sanctuary he should reach before dawn.

He lay down on his stomach, crosswise over the carbine, on the curve of the roof, savouring the moment.

11

Tuesday 13 April

It could not last. There were a couple of stops, which set him on edge. But it was still dark, the few buildings were all single-storey, and the two or three bleary passengers who got off could not have seen him.

Sometime, there would be the border. He played with the possibilities. Stay right where he was? Risky. It might be broad daylight, or there might be lights, or observation towers. Jump off – which was possible, if he chose the right patch – and sneak across the border, out of sight of the guard post? It didn't sound too bright: he would not know exactly when to make his exit, or how far it might be to civilization, and he would be hungry, thirsty, and barefoot. Still, it was an option. He peered ahead, into the wind, determined to see the border in good time.

As it happened, events decided matters for him. It was just before 4.30 a.m., and still dark, when the door below him swung open. He heard male laughter. He tensed, but could do nothing except keep the carbine hidden beneath his body and baggy

shamma. A second later, a shadowy face poked
above the roofline. The man didn't see him at first,
for he was looking down, perhaps at someone else
below. Then, as he swung up the ladder on to the
roof, he saw Rourke, and stopped in astonishment.
At the same time Rourke recognized the uniform. It
was the scruffy guard he had glimpsed briefly just
before his journey began.

The man said something. Rourke remained silent,
at a complete loss. He didn't want to give away the
fact that he was foreign, didn't want to reveal his
gun and certainly didn't want to use it unless he
had to.

The guard began shouting at him. Rourke simply
shook his head.

Then the man was silent for a moment. Instantly
Rourke guessed what he was thinking. Hours
before there had been a fire. The train had stopped.
There had been that strange noise out in the desert.
And here was an unauthorized character on the
roof. *Shifta*! Robber!

With a yell, the guard vanished back down the
ladder. Again, Rourke could read his intentions.
He had probably been climbing on to the roof to
cool down, and maybe have a smoke. He had
been completely unprepared for the confrontation.
Now he had scurried back inside to find a weapon,
and help.

Rourke moved fast. He grabbed his rifle, stood
up and jumped the three feet on to the next car – a

small gap, but not without its dangers in a 25 m.p.h. wind. His first aim was to get as far away as possible from the guard and his mate. With luck, he would be able to slip down between the first freight-car and the engine. If he had to, he would jump off. He didn't relish the prospect. Out in the desert he would for a few seconds be a clear target, even in moonlight, and anyway they might have some way of stopping the train. Best evade them as long as possible.

As it happened, he didn't have to. They spotted him before he reached the end of the leading freight-car. Rourke, who had been casting glances behind him, saw first one, then the other, emerge on to the roof. They were carrying guns. One of them yelled at him. Possibly they hadn't yet seen he was armed. That gave him a few more seconds' grace. He flattened himself on the roof, still keeping his rifle hidden by holding it tight against his body, but slipped the safety-catch off, ready to fire if he had to.

Two coaches away, the two guards seemed uncertain what to do. One stood up, and jumped across to the next coach. His mate followed. They knelt down, as if waiting for Rourke to make a move. He did nothing.

Now number one, presumably the senior, shouted at Rourke again, gesticulating with his gun.

'No way, sunshine,' muttered Rourke, but did nothing.

Something flipped in number one. Perhaps he was too nervous to approach further, suspecting that the odd, silent *shifta* had a weapon of some kind. He raised his own weapon, but warily, probably intending to advance while keeping his intended prisoner covered.

For Rourke, the risks were too high. In those conditions – darkness, wind, shaking coach, no night-sights – there was little chance of being hit, but he didn't fancy staring down the barrel of a gun for no good reason.

Even as number one raised his gun, Rourke slid his weapon into position, aimed as well as he could, though he could not even see his sights clearly, and fired. He had great advantages – training, conviction, a firm position – and they told. The man screamed, toppled sideways, overbalanced in the wind, and rolled off the edge of the roof. He hit the ground with a thump. Rourke had a final glimpse of him rolling away sideways, then vanishing behind a bush.

Number two stood as if transfixed, his wind-blown head haloed in moonlit hair, and made no move even to raise his weapon. Rourke thought: this guy's about to crack. He fired a shot, deliberately wide. The man dropped his gun, which clattered away over the edge of the roof, and clasped his chest in a caricature gesture of imminent death, then, without a sound, leaped into the darkness. Personally, Rourke would rather have a fire-fight than make a jump like that into the unknown. Still, he made it. Rourke saw him land, somersault and roll to a standstill.

The train rumbled on. Rourke was alone with his thoughts, the darkness, the wind and the shaking carriage roof below him. It was as if nothing had happened. But he didn't like it. There was a carriage full of passengers back there. Some of them must have seen the guards leave, return, grab weapons, climb out again. They must have heard the shots, the screams, the thump of the falling body on the roof. Even if they had all decided just to sit there, somebody would probably do something at the next stop.

Right: no stop.

He turned, decisively – and there, on top of the engine, was the driver. He was standing, unsteadily, and he seemed to have only one arm. For a second, Rourke could not make sense of the sight. Then he understood: the man's other arm was raised in front of him, seemingly a part of his shadowy form. Rourke could tell the arm was raised, because as he now saw from the glint of moon on metal, it held a pistol.

As the driver fired, Rourke threw himself flat. He was icy calm, on home ground. He knew that a man with a pistol standing on shaking foundations had precious little chance of hitting anything, even in daylight. He pulled the carbine up into his shoulder. This took time. As he aimed, the man fired again.

To Rourke's surprise, the bullet zinged off the metal just by his left elbow, which was already cradling the Williams. He fired. It was a large target, and he knew he had hit his mark. This guy was made of different stuff. He crumpled, but supported himself with one hand, aimed shakily with the other, and fired again. Rourke returned fire. Lucky shot. A spray of something soft left the man's head, and he fell backwards, to lie unmoving along the top of his engine.

The train rolled on.

The problem was: no driver.

Well, thought Rourke, that's one way of ensuring we don't make the next stop. What now?

He ran along the top of the engine, to the driver. The man was not in good shape, having lost half his head. Rourke hesitated for only a moment. He would have some explaining to do anyway, and didn't fancy making things worse by arriving wherever he was going with a corpse aboard. He rolled the body sideways until it slumped off the engine.

He stood back, braced himself against the shaking and the gusting wind, and ran forward towards the cab. He noticed how sure-footed he had become. He was above the driver's cab fast and easily. It was not enclosed, like normal diesels, but half open, like a steam train, shaded from the sun, but well ventilated. Presumably the bit that he was on, from which ran an access ladder into the cab, held the fuel. At the front was the engine itself. He had put down the carbine and was about to descend the ladder when he realized why he was able to move so sure-footedly, why he had been able to hit the driver so easily. It was getting light. In the heat of battle, he simply hadn't registered the fact. He stared round. Yes, he could see over twilit grey to the horizon. Behind, no sign of mountains. He turned to look ahead – and he saw low buildings, cars, people. A station.

He scrambled down into the cab, lifting the carbine down beside him. His main aim was not to get at the controls – it would take time to work them out – but to keep out of sight.

He caught only a glimpse as they rumbled through the stop. He heard a sort of communal groan, saw hands raised. There was quite a crowd. He wondered how many the train could take, or whether perhaps they were waiting not as passengers but for the contents of the freight-cars. Whatever, they were history now. Ahead lay more desert, the border, and more trouble.

Because a runaway train tends to draw attention. Forget the fact that three Ethiopians had been scattered along the track, one of whom would be eager to tell his story. Behind him he had two bunches of disappointed people, one lot at the station, another lot riding along with him, in the rear carriage. Some of them, presumably, would have been expecting to get off. Now he had ruined their weekend. Someone would make a fuss. Up ahead, he could expect an interesting reception.

He stared at the array of throttles, levers and knobs on the dashboard. All the gauges were in Squiggly – Arabic, Amharic, something. One pointer hovered erratically around '40'. Kilometres per hour, probably. Other gauges indicated various levels and pressures, but there was no way of knowing what they measured.

One good thing: four flasks hung from hooks above him. Suddenly realizing just how much he needed water, he grabbed one and drank, feeling relief spread through him. He drank until he could drink no more, then forced himself to drink again. There was a whole day to get through, and he would need his eight pints.

It seemed to him that to make the best of a bad job he should probably stop somewhere short of the border. What then? Head off across the desert, find a shady spot, rest up, sneak over at night? Ridiculous. The heat was already building, and the landscape was as forbidding as ever. Not flat now, he noticed – the track led through hills of tortured, jagged outcrops – but equally forbidding.

He tentatively pulled a lever, hoping it might be the accelerator. The engine let out a foghorn bellow. Great. Now the whole fucking desert knew he was on his way.

He looked ahead, through a little side window, and saw it was pointless to make plans, because there, less than half a mile away, was the border. It had to be. Two flag-poles, platforms, two low buildings, a siding, another train waiting. And a barrier pole across the track.

He stared as if mesmerized, knowing there was simply nothing he could do about what was about to happen. The track was clear, no one was going to get hurt. He smiled at the thrill of it. He was living a schoolboy dream, a made-for-TV movie. What a way to leave the country! They had planned everything to be secret, and here he was on the verge of creating an international incident. The long-term impact – how he was going to stop the train, whether Djibouti would put the army on to him, how he would get back to London, whether he would get any of the cash he had been promised, what the Regiment would do about it – none of that mattered. He was living for the moment, and he loved it.

In fact, when the moment came, he hardly noticed. It would have looked good on camera, with the red and white barrier pole splintering, officials waving, street traders with food, drink and trinkets open-mouthed. But Rourke's view was limited. A mere glimpse of flying wood, a blur of buildings and people, and he was through.

Djibouti, he remembered, was a small place, hardly more than the capital and its hinterland of wilderness. It was a port. So he was already near the coast, maybe twenty, maybe fifty miles to go.

An hour at least, time enough to experiment with the controls, and find out how to stop the thing before he drove over the dockside into the sea. He would try each handle in turn, producing a series of slight responses in the engine, thus building information and experience.

'Hey!' The shout jerked him round. He was already reaching for the carbine, without even identifying where the cry had come from, when it came again. 'Hey! Do you speak English?'

Rourke paused, and looked up. There, peering into the cab, was the face of a man: young, early twenties probably, blue eyes above stubble. But it was the language that stopped Rourke dead – that and the accent. Eton, Oxford, Guards. Not a 'Rupert' – as the SAS squaddies called their officers – but certainly Rupert material.

Rourke controlled his astonishment. 'Yes,' he shouted. There was a lot of noise, what with the wind and the engine and the rattling wheels. He signalled: Get down here.

The figure nodded, and swung down the ladder. Yes, a fit bloke, dressed in wide shorts and a black T-shirt. Well, he would have to be to make the climb from the rear carriage, which was where Rourke assumed he came from.

'Terrific,' said the Rupert with a grin. 'What luck. An Ethiopian train driver who speaks English.'

'I *am* English, you prat,' Rourke replied.

The Rupert stared up and down at the local

costume and the bare feet, then back at the face.

'Good heavens. So you are. Well.' Rourke could almost hear the sound of old assumptions being dumped, and new ones slamming into place. 'Gibbs. Christopher Gibbs.'

'Hi.' Rourke paused. He wondered briefly about his mission and his supposed identity. Fuck it. That was over. Right now he needed all the help he could get. He might not tell the whole truth, but he needed to tell some of it. 'Michael Rourke. Now listen. There's a problem.'

'Ah.'

'The engine. Do you know anything about engines?'

'You're the driver,' said Gibbs. 'I just came to find out what's going on.'

Rourke's expression did not change. 'I am *not* the fucking driver,' he snapped. 'The fucking driver is dead. I blew his head off. This train is out of control, and we have to stop it.'

Gibbs had been through a number of surprises in the last minute. He seemed to take it well.

'Ah,' he said again. He registered the carbine. 'Are you in trouble?'

'A bit. I've killed at least one, maybe two, of the locals and I've hijacked a train I can't control. You could call it trouble.'

'Do you make a habit of this sort of thing?' Gibbs was clearly wary of asking outright the question that was bothering him: Are you a violent criminal on the run? Should I be frightened?

Rourke had to come up with something to reassure him, or risk losing his help. 'MI5,' he said. 'I was trying to leave the country discreetly. There was trouble. I lost a couple of friends. I had to improvise.'

'Good heavens. Well, that explains one or two things.'

Rourke liked him. Gibbs was clearly used to coping with the unusual. Rourke glanced out of the front window again, wondering how much longer they had. 'Tell me,' he said, turning back to the controls and reaching for a lever.

'Well, I was back there with Stella and the baby . . .'

'You brought a *baby* into this hole?'

'What's wrong with that? It's a regular service, you know. Besides, it's the cheapest way to Djibouti. We're picking up a boat there.'

Rourke paused, his hand on the lever. He had some adapting of his own to do. He had dropped out of civilization two days ago, and assumed that its benefits were way ahead. It was a shock to realize there were ordinary people following a regular lifestyle right there, with him.

'Anyway,' continued Gibbs, then broke off. 'Shouldn't we be doing something?'

'I'm doing it,' Rourke said. 'You talk.' What

Gibbs had to say might give him a clue about how to proceed.

Gibbs was an anthropologist, returning from a dig in the Rift. His words stirred in Rourke vague memories of what he had learned when setting up the fuel dumps. He and his family were experienced travellers, and had actually made this trip a couple of times before. Stella and baby Joe had been rocking in their seats asleep, like everyone else, when they had been disturbed by the sudden action, the back and forth of the guards and the trouble on the roof. All was darkness, of course, because the lights were down, but Gibbs had heard the gunfire, and the two men had not returned. Nothing seemed amiss, however, so he and Stella had dismissed their fears for a while, until the train rattled through the station and then crashed through the frontier. That was serious. Gibbs had asked around. This was an international trip, so among the forty-odd passengers was a scattering of foreigners: Germans, French, English-speaking Arabs, and one American, a UN aid worker. All were worried. Gibbs, the fittest and most experienced, took it upon himself to find out what was happening.

'So,' he finished. 'I'd better get back.'

'Not yet.' Rourke had tried a number of switches and levers. He knew the hooter, of course, and now, although he wasn't sure what he had tried, he knew he had not found the throttle or the brakes. But there weren't many more levers and buttons to try.

One of them would probably be an emergency stop. He didn't want that. 'Listen. I don't want to get arrested.'

'I bet.'

'I need your help.'

'Ah. How did I guess?'

'You know the place. Got any ideas?'

'Yes, as a matter of fact.'

Rourke hauled on a lever. There was a grinding noise from the wheels, and the train shuddered. He had found the brakes. But they were still under power. He released the lever again.

'Good show,' said Gibbs. 'Try this one.'

'I'm going to, OK? Just tell me about Djibouti.'

'Quite small. Taxis. A few embassies.'

'So all I need to do is hop off, get a cab, and say "British consulate",' Rourke said drily, trying another lever. The sound of the engine rose. The train began to gain speed. The throttle! He moved the lever the opposite way. The train began to slow. He wondered if there was a clutch as well. Apparently not: probably the engine simply disengaged at low revs.

'Progress,' commented Gibbs. 'Well, there's no British rep here. The Yanks do that job. You should be OK as long as you choose a spot not too far outside town. There's a sort of shanty area that might give you some cover. But you won't get much joy from a cabby dressed like that.'

Rourke grimaced.

'I've got a jacket you can borrow,' said Gibbs decisively. 'And a pair of sandals. Hang on.'

He reached for the ladder.

'One more thing,' said Rourke. 'Got any cash?'

'Enough for a cab.'

'Local currency?'

'Francs. It'll do.' Gibbs glanced out, and started to climb. 'I have to move fast.'

'Better if I stopped. You could run along the track.'

For answer, Gibbs nodded meaningfully to the west, and vanished. Following his gaze, Rourke saw a flashing blue light, then another, heading south fast. There was no doubting their purpose: as he watched, he saw the cars stop, reverse, turn, and drive off northwards. They were tracking the train.

No slowing down yet, then.

Around him, tin-roofed shacks appeared, joined by rough tracks. Steadily, as the train maintained its skaky progress, the density of dwellings increased, until the desert had become mere scars between the shacks.

Rourke waited with growing tension for Gibbs to reappear. The main road, along which the police cars were heading, began to close in on the railway, until he could hear the wail of sirens. Another couple of minutes and they would be right beside him, and any chance of a secretive getaway would be lost.

'Mike!' It was Gibbs, almost falling down beside him. 'Get that thing' – he indicated the *shamma* – 'off, and this on.' He opened out his bundle, which turned out to be a dusty, crumpled colonial-style white jacket wrapped around some sandals. 'There's a couple of hundred francs in the pocket. So's my card. I expect a drink from you some day.'

'Jesus, can I still do it?' asked Rourke, executing a high-speed change of clothes.

'Yes. The road bends away from the track up ahead, when we start going along the coast. What you have to do is scoot down to the shoreline, and lie low. You don't want the passengers to see you.'

To their right, Rourke saw a wonderful sight. The low, rocky foreshore was yards away, giving on to a ribbon of sand. And there, to the skyline, was the Red Sea. A tanker was heading away from a curve of land out past two dhows. He had been so immersed in drab desert colours and desiccating heat that to see such an immensity of blue water shocked him briefly into immobility.

'Move!' said Gibbs. 'Now!'

Rourke hit the only two levers that mattered. The engine died, the brakes seized, and the wheels locked with shrieks and groans of protest as they slid along the tracks.

'What about you?' Rourke shouted, gripping the side of the cab.

'I'll be OK. The driver was killed, the killer vanished, I found the cab empty, and stopped the train. I'll be a hero!' Gibbs grinned. 'But take this . . .' As the train squealed to a halt, he tossed the *shamma* over Rourke's shoulder. 'And that.' He pointed to the carbine. 'I don't want any evidence!'

'Thanks. Next time we meet, I'll buy.'

'You certainly will. Now go!'

Rourke grabbed the gun, leaped down, and ran as quickly as his sandals would allow to the foreshore. In five seconds, he was down, invisible to the train, among rocks.

He heard sirens, the roar of car engines, the shriek of brakes, loud voices.

He glanced round. Gibbs had been right. There was nothing on this side of the track. No one had seen him. But he couldn't risk staying there. Besides, it was the beginning of another searing day, and among those rocks he would be grilled meat in hours.

But when he moved, he could not afford to attract attention. He buried the rifle, the one remaining magazine and the *shamma* in the sand, and hauled a few rocks over the spot. One day, perhaps, after a storm, some astonished local would find them, and praise Allah for his good fortune.

He felt in the pocket of his newly acquired jacket, which was not a bad fit. No shirt, of course, but good enough for a cab ride. There was the money, two 100-franc notes, and Gibbs's card: an address in London, care of a university department, and a box number in Addis Ababa.

He lay there, feeling the sun beating down, and looked at the card. His training told him to memorize the information, and destroy the card, because to be caught with it would incriminate a colleague. On the other hand, he had no identity at all. It might, perhaps, come in useful.

He began to work his way northwards, along the foreshore, away from the train. He took care to keep low. He could hear nothing now. Gibbs was playing out his role as hero.

And who would gainsay him? Many people could vouch for the ambush out in the desert, which was obviously when the bandit had boarded; all would vouch for the rooftop fight, the fate of the two guards; a brief search would reveal the dead driver; and it was only logical that a fleeing criminal would jump off some time before the border, leaving the train to rumble on unattended, until Gibbs daringly made his climb along the roof to the cab. Perhaps he could even explain his brief return as a mission to reassure his wife and the other passengers. It could make some sort of sense, for a while at least. And certainly it would take even longer to tie up a train hijack in the desert with the disappearance of the Emperor.

A quarter of a mile from the train, he risked a peep over the rocks. Before him lay the railway track. Despite his low-profile view, he could see between the houses – larger ones now, some villas, some apartment blocks – that the road, busy with cars and pedestrians, approached it closely, then crossed it. At this point, buildings blocked his view, sweeping round to crown the peninsula from behind which he had seen the tanker emerging earlier.

He decided to risk exposure. He rose, dusted sand from his trousers and jacket, and walked towards the buildings. He followed a wire fence, and found himself on a paved road. A road sign in Arabic and French told him he was in Ave. M. Lyautey. There was a junction to his left, and just beyond it the level crossing he had seen from the beach. The railway must lead to the station, he thought, and at the station there will be cabs. He was among a mixture of apartment blocks and offices. Few people were on the streets, but about half were in loose European dress. He was a mess, but not a spectacle. No one gave him a second glance.

The station was an early-twentieth-century monument to French colonialism: built of imported stone, ornate, imposing. It was also in an uproar. Street traders blocked the entrance, men and women in Arab dress milled about among them. They had, after all, been waiting for a train that had not yet arrived, and no doubt word had already spread of violence aboard.

But the consequence was that the ramshackle

cabs baking in the heat had had no custom. Rourke went to the first in line, and said the magic words: 'American Embassy.' The driver, in flowing Arab gear, nodded in relief, for his long wait was over.

'You take francs?'

'*Des francs? Naturellement, monsieur.*'

The taxi, a 1960s Citroën, swung round and turned out on to the road by which Rourke had arrived. He had imagined himself in the centre. Apparently, not so. The cab headed south, along the road which Rourke had already seen from a distance. There was only one road. Within half a mile, there again was the level crossing, and there – easily visible, not fifty yards from the road, which was almost blocked by cars and trucks – was the train, surrounded now by most of Djibouti's police force. Rourke could even see a TV crew.

'What's happening?' he asked.

The cab driver, his English tested to the limits, shrugged: 'They say, a crazy with gun. Boum, boum, train stop.'

Rourke sank back into his seat. He hoped Gibbs would get credit. You didn't get many Ruperts like that outside the Service.

As the cab negotiated a central area neatly laid out in turn-of-the-century stonework, Rourke focused on his story. He had no identity papers or cards, so he needed an exit document and a ticket home. It would not be easy. He had to ensure he was not connected with the business on the train.

269

But in that case how did he get into the country? Lies would rapidly land him in trouble. There was no way he could say anything convincing about a spurious business, a flight, a hotel. And the truth, even if it was believed, would lead back to the train. That opened dire prospects: the Djibouti police, charges, extradition back to Addis.

The US Embassy proved to be a substantial new place, set in a compound, and well protected by a high wall. The State Department had taken advantage of its closeness with France to create a listening post in this strategic spot. The whole area was a political powder keg, with Suez to the north, Saudi Arabia and the volatile Yemen just opposite, and all the surrounding countries – Egypt, Somalia, Ethiopia, Sudan – up for grabs in the Cold War. Hence the heavy-duty iron gates, the guardroom inside, and the barbed-wired walls.

He paid the cab, and was worried to find his 200 francs cut almost in half by the transaction.

He rang a bell. A lugubrious Arab in a business suit emerged from the guard post. 'British,' Rourke explained. 'My passport was stolen.' He handed over Gibbs's card. The man vanished into his guardroom, made a phone call, and pressed a button. One of the gates swung slowly open. Rourke was in.

By the time he had crossed the courtyard, entered the embassy, stood for a few seconds to drink in the bliss of its air-conditioning, and knocked, as instructed, on the first door on the left in the hall, he had his approach ready. He had to go to the top.

The receptionist, a local girl, called her boss, the Personnel Officer. She summoned the Duty Officer, who brought in Immigration. At each stage, Rourke explained that he was an academic compromised by Soviet intelligence in Ethiopia, and that he had driven into Djibouti in a hired car. The car, together with his wallet, passport and all his possessions had just been stolen. He needed US help to repatriate him. Of course, the key to the story was the exact nature of the 'compromise by Soviet intelligence' and he refused to be drawn on this by anyone but the Ambassador himself. He suggested, with some conviction, that what he had to say was so astonishing and significant that it had to be for the ears of the top man. It took two hours to convince them. By then, Rourke, having consumed five glasses of water, was much restored.

The Ambassador was a career diplomat, in his late fifties. He was a time-server, in place to oil the wheels of diplomacy. The real power was held by the intelligence officer, a CIA man in his mid-thirties whose ostensible job was vetting passport applications.

Rourke was eventually confronted by the two of them together. To them, Rourke told the truth. It was easier that way, and he could ensure a degree of control by presenting his information in the order of his choice and by making requests at strategic moments.

First, he told of his arrival in Addis. US diplomats and intelligence sources in Addis would be able to confirm a few essential details: the flight from London, the stay at the Hilton under the assumed names, the use of the Swiss Embassy.

He told them his real name, and his real occupation, and said he was concerned to tell his parents that he was all right. He gave phone numbers. The steely young CIA man, whose name was Barrow, went to make the calls, for it was an easy way to check immediately on the truth of his statement. There was no point in any other calls. The Regiment would disown him, and Cromer would deny all knowledge.

'And now,' he said when Barrow returned. 'You might like to know the purpose of this trip.'

He enjoyed that: talking about the Emperor being still alive, Cromer's plan to kidnap him, his own expedition to dump fuel along the helicopter route south. The two men opposite were riveted.

Just before he started on the story of his escape and the Emperor's death, he got what he needed: a promise of diplomatic immunity and a booking

272

on the afternoon Air France flight to Paris, and on to London.

So then he told them the rest, all of it.

At the end, Barrow asked: 'How much did you tell Gibbs?'

'Nothing. We didn't have much time for chat.'

'So who knows the truth of all this?'

'The top Ethiopians. Cromer. That's it.'

'Fascinating. So much, yet so little.'

'What?'

'It will all, of course, remain secret.'

'Fair enough.'

'Hear me out. Clearly, your role must never be known. Mengistu is not a nice man. He would blame you for killing his golden goose. You would be a marked man for the rest of your life. And perhaps Sir Charles Cromer might not be too happy to have you around, either. Best lie low, Mr Rourke.'

Rourke made no response for a long moment. It was the first time he had really considered his own future. 'Right,' he said.

Barrow hadn't finished. The US also had an interest. If the West was to retain any influence in Ethiopia, it would not do to reveal the Ethiopian plot to keep Selassie alive after they had said he was dead. What, after all, had changed? The Emperor had been declared dead in August 1975, and his money was securely in the West. Now he really was dead, and his money was still there. In the

end, Western interests would be best served by
pretending nothing had happened.

'So you see, Mr Rourke, we hold each other
hostage. If we talk, it's political suicide. If you
talk, it's suicide for real. Do we have a deal?'

There was just one problem before he left: who
would pay?

Rourke could hardly believe what he was hearing. He was giving them the inside story of the
century, and they worried about the cost of a flight
to London.

'I know. Petty, huh? We can drive you to the
airport, but flights are something else. We have
accounts committees, and you can see why we
don't exactly want to be up front about you. So
help us. You have cash? Cards?'

'No.'

'Anyone you want to call?'

There was only one person who might, with luck,
guarantee him the cost of a plane fare.

They allowed him to call. He called the shop, for
its number was imprinted on his mind.

'Lucy?'

'Mike.' She sighed, as if he'd been a naughty boy.
'I thought I told you not to call the shop.'

'It's an emergency. Listen . . .' And he told her
where he was and what was required.

'Tell me, Mike,' she said. 'Why am I doing
this?'

'For the same reason I'm asking. I don't want

to go away again. I want you to meet me at the airport.'

There was a pause.

'I'll be there,' she said.

Epilogue

Rourke's escapade had significant consequences, some short-term and secret, some long-term and anything but secret.

News of his escape with the Emperor reached Mengistu in minutes. Within hours, the Bell's flight path had been identified, and the helicopter had been found. At first it seemed that both the Emperor and Rourke must have perished. The chances were that a weak old man and an inexperienced foreigner – there was no way of knowing that Rourke was in fact a member of the SAS – would not survive for long in the desert, without food and water. Within a few days, when the report came through of the Emperor's body being found in the desert, Mengistu revised his conclusions marginally. The odd business of a lone *shifta* hijacking a train caused him to wonder, but there was no evidence to link those events with Rourke. He had apparently vanished, to become food for the vultures.

Cromer's role in all this was realized immediately. In one way, Cromer was relieved. Things had worked out well for him, if in ways he could never have predicted. There was no need after all to renegotiate a complex contract with Selassie, no need to make secretive, expensive and politically explosive arrangements for Selassie's well-being. At a stroke, the fortune was safe. He did not even have to pay out any more to Collins, Halloran and Rourke.

Cromer naturally offered specious apologies to Mengistu for the extraordinary behaviour of his banking colleagues. Of course he denied all knowledge of their agenda. As a face-saving gesture and sign of his continuing goodwill, he at once offered a $200 million loan, which was accepted.

The public consequences of the plot were brought about by Mengistu, who was not only ruthless, but fast-thinking and astute, a true survivor. He had from the start promised a revolution, national security, and the funds to fuel both.

At first, he had put his faith in the Americans, for Moscow was committed to Ethiopia's hostile neighbour, Somalia. Despite his adherence to Marxism, he had made no immediate break with the USA. American advisers had remained. In early 1976 came the possibility of wealth from Selassie. Mengistu made more promises: with Western cooperation he would end famine, secure the borders, defeat the enemy.

Cromer's duplicity and Rourke's astonishing actions tipped the balance. In anger, and in defence of his own political position, he prepared a new pro-Soviet policy.

The change came in late 1976. Mengistu used much of Cromer's loan as a down payment on Russian arms. Moscow was amazed, and delighted to receive such an approach from a country that could dominate North-East Africa as Somalia never would. Somalia was repudiated, Ethiopia vaunted as Moscow's true friend. In early 1977, the Americans were thrown out. For the next decade, Ethiopia became the strongest Soviet satellite in Africa.

There has always been a debate about just how much difference an individual can make on events. Normally, the debate focuses on the rich and powerful. Here, however, was a case in which one ordinary man, seeking nothing but his own safety, changed the course of recent history.

SOLDIER R: SAS

DEATH ON GIBRALTAR

SOLDIER R: SAS

DEATH ON GIBRALTAR

Shaun Clarke

PRELUDE

On the evening of Thursday 7 May 1987 fifteen soldiers from G Squadron, SAS, all dressed in standard DPM windproof, tight-weave cotton trousers and olive-green cotton battle smocks with British Army boots and maroon berets, were driven in four-wheel-drive Bedford lorries from their base at Stirling Lines, Hereford, to RAF Brize Norton, Oxfordshire, where they boarded a Hercules C-130 transport plane.

The men were armed with L7A2 7.62mm general-purpose machine-guns (GPMGs), 7.62mm Heckler & Koch G3-A4K twenty-round assault rifles with LE1-100 laser sights, and 5.56mm M16 thirty-round Armalite rifles. They also had many attachments for the various weapons, including bipods, telescopic sights, night-vision aids, and M203 40mm grenade-launchers. The ubiquitous standard-issue 9mm Browning High Power hand-gun was holstered at each man's hip. Their personal kit, including ammunition, water, rations, a medical pack, and spare clothing and batteries, was packed in the square-frame Cyclops bergens on their backs. Finally, they had with them crates filled with various items of high-tech communications and surveillance equipment, including Nikon F-801 35mm SLR cameras with Davies Minimodulux hand-held image intensifiers for night photography, a PRC319 microprocessor-based tactical radio, Pace Communications Ltd Landmaster III hand-held transceivers and Radio Systems Inc. walkie-talkies.

From RAF Brize Norton, the men were flown to RAF Aldergrove in Belfast, where they were transferred with their kit to three unmarked Avis vans and then driven through the rolling green countryside to the Security Forces base built around the old mill in the village of Bessbrook. There they were united with the twenty-four SAS men already serving in Northern Ireland, making a total force of thirty-nine specially trained and experienced counter-terrorist troopers.

The next morning was spent in a draughty lecture hall in the SF base where, with the aid of maps and a scale model of the Royal Ulster Constabulary police station of Loughgall, the combined body of men were given a final briefing on the operation to come.

Early that afternoon, when the RUC had thrown a discreet cordon around the area, diverting traffic and keeping all but local people out, the SAS men, with their weapons and surveillance equipment, were transported in the rented vans to Loughgall. Small and mostly Protestant, Loughgall is surrounded by the rolling green hills and apple trees of the 'orchard country' of north

Armagh. It is some eight miles from Armagh city, and the road which leads from Armagh slopes down into the village, passing a walled copse on the right. The RUC station is almost opposite, between a row of bungalows, a former Ulster Defence Regiment barracks, the football team's clubhouse and a small telephone exchange. It is small enough to be run by a sergeant and three or four officers, and unimportant enough to be open only limited hours in the morning and afternoon, always closing completely at 7 p.m.

That day, well before the 'barracks', as the RUC station is known locally, was closed, some of the SAS men entered the building to occupy surveillance and firing positions at the rear and front, those at the front keeping well away from one particular side. While they were taking up positions inside, the rest were dividing into separate groups to set up ambushes around the building.

Two GPMG teams moved into the copse overlooking the police station, which enabled them to cover the football pitch facing it on the other side of the Armagh road. Others took up positions closer to and around the building, and behind the blast-proof wall protecting the front door.

Another team took the high ground overlooking the rear of the building. The remainder assumed positions in which they could act as cordon teams staking out the approach road in both directions.

Meanwhile, as members of the RUC's Headquarters Mobile Support Units were deployed in the vicinity, companies of UDR and British Army soldiers, as well as mobile police squads, were ready to cordon off the area after the operation.

That same afternoon a group of masked men hijacked a blue Toyota Hiace van at gunpoint from a business in Mountjoy Road, Dungannon. Sometime after five o'clock the same group hijacked a mechanical digger from a Dungannon farm, and the vehicle was driven to another farmyard about nine miles north of Loughgall.

With the SAS in position inside the RUC station, the building was locked up at the usual time. The troopers dug in around it had melted into the scenery, and apart from the sound of the wind, there was absolute silence.

Just before seven o'clock that evening, in the farmhouse north of Loughgall, close to the Armagh–Tyrone border and the Republican strongholds of Washing Bay and Coalisland, an IRA 'bucket bomb' team carefully loaded a 200lb bomb – designed to be set off by lighting a simple fuse – on to the bucket of the hijacked mechanical digger. Waiting close by, and watching them nervously, was a support

4

team consisting of two Active Service Units of the East Tyrone Brigade of the IRA. Inside their stolen van was a collection of weapons that included three Heckler & Koch G3 7.62mm assault rifles, two 5.56mm FNC rifles, an assault shotgun and a German Ruger revolver taken from one of the reserve constables shot dead during a raid at Ballygawley eighteen months earlier.

Of the three-man bucket bomb team, one was a twenty-one-year-old with five years' IRA service, including several spells of detention; another had six years in the IRA behind him and had been arrested and interrogated many times because of it; and the third had twelve years' IRA service and six years' imprisonment.

The leader of one ASU team was thirty-year-old Patrick Kelly. Though known to be almost rigidly puritanical about his family and religious faith, Kelly was the commander of East Tyrone Provisional IRA units and suspected of murdering two RUC officers. The other ASU team was led by thirty-one-year-old Jim Lynagh, a former Sinn Fein councillor with fifteen years in the IRA and various terms in prison to his name. Though Lynagh, in direct contrast to Kelly, was an extrovert, good-humoured personality, he was suspected of many killings and, though acquitted of assassinating a UDR soldier, was widely believed to have done the deed.

The rest of the ASU teams consisted of a thirty-two-year-old escaper from the Maze Prison with fifteen years' violent IRA service to his credit; a nineteen-year-old who had been in the IRA for three years and claimed that he had been threatened with assassination by the RUC; and a twenty-five-year-old who had been in the IRA for five years, had been arrested many times and was a veteran of many terrorist operations.

These eight men were hoping to repeat the success of a similar attack they had carried out eighteen months earlier at Ballygawley, when they had shot their way into the police station, killing two officers, and then blown up the building.

This time, however, as they loaded their bomb on to the digger, they were being watched by a police undercover surveillance team, Special Branch's E4A, which was transmitting reports of their movements to the SAS men located in and around Loughgall RUC station.

The five armed men accompanying the three bombers had initially come along to ensure that no RUC men would escape through the back door of the building, as they had done at Ballygawley. However, just before climbing into their unmarked van, the two team leaders, Kelly and Lynagh, appeared – at least to the distant observers of E4A – to become embroiled in some kind of argument. Though what they said is not known, the argument was later taken by the Security Forces to be a sign of a last-minute confusion that could explain why, by the time the terrorists reached Loughgall in the stolen Toyota, their original plan for covering the back of the RUC police station had been dropped and they prepared to attack only the unguarded side of the building. Ironically, by ignoring the rear of the building, they were repeating the mistake they had made eighteen months earlier.

Their plan was to ignite the fuse on the bomb, then ram the RUC station with the bomb still in the bucket of the digger. They chose the side of the building because of the protection afforded the front entrance by the blast-proof wall. As an alternative to the usual attacks with heavy mortars or RPG7 rockets, this tactic had first been attempted eighteen months earlier at Ballygawley, then again, nine months later, at the Birches, Co. Tyrone, only five miles from Loughgall. Both operations had been successful.

To avoid the Security Forces, the terrorists travelled from the farmyard to Loughgall via the narrow, winding side lanes, rather than taking the main Dungannon–Armagh road. The five-man support team were in the blue van, driven by Seamus Donnelly, with one of the team leaders, Lynagh, in the back and Kelly in the front beside the driver. The van was in the lead to enable Kelly to check that the road ahead was clear. The mechanical digger followed, driven by Declan Arthurs and with Tony Gormley and Gerard O'Callaghan 'riding shotgun', though with their weapons concealed. The bucket bomb was hidden under a pile of rubble.

While the terrorists thought they were avoiding the Security Forces, their movements were almost certainly observed at various points along the route by surveillance teams in unmarked 'Q' cars or covert observation posts.

The Toyota van passed through Loughgall village at a quarter past seven. SAS men were hiding behind the wall of the church as it drove past them, but they held their fire. They wanted the van and mechanical digger to reach the police station as this would give the SAS men inside an excuse to open fire in 'self-defence'.

At precisely 7.20 p.m., possibly trying to ascertain if anyone was still in the building, Arthurs drove the mechanical digger to and fro a few times, with Gormley and O'Callaghan now deliberately putting their weapons on view. What happened next is still in dispute.

As the terrorists all knew that the Loughgall RUC station was empty from seven o'clock every evening, their timing of the attack is surely an indication that their purpose was to destroy the building, not take lives. More importantly, it begs the question of why the ASU team leader,

Patrick Kelly, a very experienced and normally astute IRA fighter, would do what he is reported to have done.

Though believing that the police station was empty, Kelly climbed out of the cabin of the Toyota van with the driver, Donnelly, and proceeded to open fire with his assault rifle on the front of the building. Donnelly and some of the others then did the same.

Instantly, the SAS ambush party inside the building opened fire with a fearsome combination of 7.62mm Heckler & Koch G3-A4K assault rifles and 5.56mm M16 Armalites, catching the terrorists in a devastating fusillade, perforating the rear and side of the van with bullets and mowing down some of the men even before the 7.62mm GPMGs in the copse had roared into action, peppering the front of the van and catching the remaining terrorists in a deadly crossfire.

Hit several times, Kelly fell close to the cabin of the van with blood spreading out around him from a fatal head wound. Realizing what was happening, the experienced Jim Lynagh and Patrick McKearney scurried back into the van, but died in a hail of bullets that tore through its side panel. Donnelly had scrambled back into the driver's seat, but was mortally wounded in the same rain of bullets before he could move off. After ramming the mechanical digger into the side of the building, the driver, Arthurs, and another terrorist, Eugene Kelly, died as they tried in vain to take cover behind the bullet-riddled Toyota.

Even as the driver of the mechanical digger was dying in a hail of bullets, O'Callaghan was igniting the fuse of the 200lb bomb with a Zippo lighter. He then took cover beside Gormley.

The roar of the exploding bomb drowned out even the combined din of the GPMGs, assault rifles and Armalites. The spiralling dust and boiling smoke eventually settled down to reveal that the explosion had blown away most of the end of the RUC station nearest the gate, demolished the telephone exchange next door, and showered the football clubhouse with raining masonry. The mechanical digger had been blown to pieces and one of its wheels had flown about forty yards, to smash through a wooden fence and land on the football pitch. Some of the police and SAS men inside the building had been injured by the blast and flying debris.

When the bomb went off, Gormley and O'Callaghan tried to run for cover, but Gormley was cut down by heavy SAS gunfire as he emerged from behind the wall where he had taken cover. O'Callaghan was cut to pieces as he ran across the road from the badly damaged building.

But the IRA men were not the only casualties.

Because the GPMG teams hidden in the copse were targeting a building that stood close to the Armagh road, the oblique direction of fire

meant that they also fired many rounds into
the football pitch opposite and into parts of
the village, including the wall of the church
hall, where children were playing at the time.
In addition, three civilian cars were passing
between the RUC station and the church as the
battle commenced.

Driving in a white Citroën past the church and
down the hill towards the police station, Oliver
Hughes, a thirty-six-year-old father of three, and
his brother Anthony heard the thunderclap of the
massive bomb, braked to a halt immediately and
started to reverse the car. Unfortunately, both
men were in overalls similar to those worn by
the terrorists, so the SAS soldiers hidden near the
church, assuming they were terrorist reinforce-
ments, opened fire, peppering the Citroën with
bullets, killing Oliver Hughes outright and badly
wounding his brother, who took three rounds in
the back and one in the head.

Travelling in the opposite direction, up the
hill towards the church, another car, containing
a woman and her young daughter, was also
sprayed with bullets and screeched to a halt. In
this instance, before anyone was killed the commander of one of the SAS groups raced through
the hail of bullets to drag the woman and her
daughter out of the car to safety. Miraculously,
he succeeded.

The third car contained an elderly couple, Mr

and Mrs Herbert Buckley. Both jumped out of their car and threw themselves to the ground, to survive unscathed.

Another motorist, a brewery salesman, had stopped his car even closer to the main action – between the IRA's Toyota and the copse where the two GPMG crews were dug in – and looked on in stunned disbelief as a rain of GPMG bullets hit the blue van. During a lull in the firing, he jumped out of his car and ran to find shelter behind the bungalows next to the police station. He never reached them, for after being rugby-tackled by an SAS trooper, he was held in custody until his identity could be established.

When the firing ceased, all eight of the IRA terrorists were found to be dead. Within thirty minutes, even as British Gazelle reconnaissance helicopters were flying over the area and British Army troops were combing the countryside in the vain pursuit of other terrorists, the SAS men were already being lifted out.

The deaths of the eight terrorists were the worst set-back the IRA had experienced in sixty years. During their funerals the IRA made it perfectly clear that bloody retaliation could be expected. It was a threat that could not be ignored by the British government.

1

'It is the belief of our Intelligence chiefs,' the man addressed only as 'Mr Secretary' informed the top-level crisis-management team in a basement office in Whitehall on 6 November 1987, 'that the successful SAS ambush in Loughgall last May, which resulted in the deaths of eight leading IRA terrorists, will lead to an act of reprisal that's probably being planned right now.'

There was a moment's silence while the men sitting around the boardroom table took in what the Secretary was saying so gravely. This particular crisis-management team was known as COBR – it represented the Cabinet Office Briefing Room – and all those present were of considerable authority and power in various areas of national defence and security. Finally, after a lengthy silence, one of them, a saturnine, grey-haired man from British Intelligence, said: 'If that's the case, Mr Secretary, we should place both MI5 and MI6 on the alert and try to anticipate the most likely targets.'

'Calling in MI5 is one thing,' the Secretary replied, referring to the branch of the Security Service charged with overt counter-espionage. 'But before calling in MI6, would someone

13

SOLDIER R: SAS

please remind me of the reasoning behind what was obviously an exceptionally ambitious and contentious ambush.'

Everyone around the table knew just what he meant. MI6 was the secret intelligence service run by the Foreign and Commonwealth Office. As its links with the FCO were never publicly acknowledged, it was best avoided when it came to operations that might end up with a high public profile – as, for instance, the siege of the Iranian Embassy in London in May 1980 had done.

'The humiliation of the IRA,' said the leader of the Special Military Intelligence Unit (SMIU) responsible for Northern Ireland. 'That was the whole purpose of the Loughgall ambush.'

'We're constantly trying to humiliate the IRA,' the Secretary replied, 'but we don't always go to such lengths. What made Loughgall so special?'

'The assassination of the Lord Chief Justice and his wife the previous month,' the SMIU leader replied, referring to the blowing up of the judge's car by a 500lb bomb in the early hours of 25 April, when he and his wife were returning to their home in Northern Ireland after a holiday in the Republic. 'As Northern Ireland's most senior judge, he had publicly vowed to bring all terrorists to justice, so the terrorists assassinated him, not only as a warning to other like-minded judges, but as a means of profoundly

14

embarrassing the British government, which of course it did.'

'So the ambush at Loughgall was an act of revenge for the murder of the Lord Chief Justice and his wife?'

'It was actually more than that, Mr Secretary,' the SMIU man replied. 'Within hours of the assassination of the Lord Chief Justice – that same evening, in fact – a full-time member of the East Tyrone UDR was murdered by two IRA gunmen while working in the yard of his own farm. That murder was particularly brutal. After shooting him in the back with assault rifles, in full view of his wife, the two gunmen stood over him where he lay on the ground and shot him repeatedly – about nineteen times in all. The East Tyrone IRA then claimed that they had carried out the killing.'

'And that was somehow connected to the Loughgall ambush?'

'Yes, Mr Secretary. We learnt from an informer that two ASU teams from East Tyrone were planning an attack on the RUC police station at Loughgall and that some of the men involved had been responsible for all three deaths.

'Was this informer known to be reliable?'

'Yes, Mr Secretary, she was.'

'And do we have proof that some of the IRA men who died at Loughgall were involved in the assassinations as she had stated?'

'Again, the answer is yes. Ballistics tests on the Heckler & Koch G3 assault rifles and FNCs used by the IRA men at Loughgall proved that some of them were the same as those used to kill the UDR man.'

'What about the Lord Chief Justice and his wife?'

'For various reasons, including the reports of informants, we believe that the ASU teams involved in the attack at Loughgall were the same ones responsible for the deaths of the Lord Chief Justice and his wife. However, I'll admit that as yet we have no conclusive evidence to support that belief.'

'Yet you authorized the SAS ambush at the police station, killing eight IRA suspects.'

'Not suspects, Mr Secretary. All of them were proven IRA activists, most with blood on their hands – so we had no doubts on that score. That being said, I should reiterate that we certainly knew that the two ASU team leaders – Jim Lynagh and Patrick Kelly – were responsible for the death of the UDR man. So the SAS ambush was not only retaliation for that, but also our way of humiliating the IRA and cancelling out the propaganda victory they had achieved with the assassination of the Lord Chief Justice and his wife. Which is why, even knowing that they were planning to attack the Loughgall RUC station, we decided to let it run and use the attack as our

excuse for neutralizing them with the aid of the
SAS and the RUC. Thus Operation Judy was put
into motion.'

'The RUC was involved as well?'

'Of course, Mr Secretary. It was one of *their*
police stations, after all, that was the target. Also,
they knew that this was a plum opportunity to
take out some particularly valuable IRA men,
including the two ASU team leaders.'

'So the IRA gunmen were under surveillance
long before the attack took place?'

'Correct, Mr Secretary. We learnt through
Intelligence sources at the TCG . . .'

'The *what*?'

'The Tasking and Co-ordination Group. We
learnt through the TCG's Intelligence that Lynagh
and Kelly would be leading two of the ASU teams
against the police station and that they would be
heavily armed. It's true that we were aware that
their intention was not to kill but to destroy the
police station – they knew that it was normally
closed and empty by that time – but given their
general value to the IRA, as well as their direct
involvement in the murder of the UDR man and
suspected involvement in the assassination of the
Lord Chief Justice and his wife, we couldn't let
that consideration prevent us from grabbing this
golden opportunity to get rid of them once and
for all. Therefore, long before the attack, we had
them shadowed by Army surveillance experts

and the Special Branch's E4A. It was members of the latter who actually witnessed the ASU teams placing the 200lb bomb in the bucket of that mechanical digger and then driving it to the Loughgall RUC station. We believe that what happened next was completely justified on our part.'

The man known to them all only as the 'Controller' was one of the most senior officers in the SAS, rarely present at Stirling Lines, though often to be seen commuting between the SAS HQ at the Duke of York's Barracks, in Chelsea, and this basement office in Whitehall. Up to this point the Secretary had ignored him, but now, with a slight, sly smile, he brought him into the conversation.

'As I recall,' the Secretary said, 'there were certain contentious aspects to the Loughgall operation.'

'Oh, really?' the Controller replied with a steady, bland, blue-eyed gaze, looking like an ageing matinée idol in his immaculate pinstripe suit and old school tie. 'What are those?'

'For a start, there are a lot of conflicting stories as to what actually happened during that ambush. Why, for instance, would seasoned IRA terrorists open fire, at 7.20 p.m., on an RUC station widely known to keep limited hours and to close completetly at 7 p.m.? Why didn't they just bomb it and run?'

'I know what you're suggesting, Mr Secretary,

but you're wrong. Rumours that the SAS opened fire first are false. At least two of the IRA men – we believe Kelly and his driver, Donnelly – stepped down from the cabin of the Toyota and opened fire on the police station with their assault rifles.'

'Even believing it to be closed and empty?'

'Yes. It seems odd, but that's what happened. The only explanation we can come up with is that Kelly and the other ASU team leader, Jim Lynagh, had an argument as to what tactics to use. That argument probably continued in the van as the terrorists travelled from their hide in the farmyard near the border to Loughgall. Kelly became impatient or lost his temper completely and decided to terminate the argument by getting out and opening fire on the police station, using it as the signal for the other men to start the attack. We can think of no other explanation for that rather pointless action. Either that or it was an impulsive act of bravado, though the general belief is that Kelly was too experienced a man to succumb to that.'

'And it's for that very reason that there are those who refuse to believe that the IRA opened fire first. They say that Kelly was simply too experienced to have fired his assault rifle at an empty police station he intended to destroy with a bomb.'

'My men swear that the IRA opened fire first and that's in their official report.'

'But your men *were* there to set up an ambush.'

'Well, Mr Secretary, we'd been briefed by British Intelligence that the mission was to be an OP/React. In other words, an observation post able to react.'

'In other words,' the Secretary said drily, 'an ambush. Isn't that more accurate?'

'Yes, Mr Secretary, it is. An OP/React is a coded term for an ambush.'

'And we can take it from the wide variety of weapons and the extraordinary amount of ammunition used by the SAS – about a thousand bullets fired, I believe, in a couple of minutes – that the purpose of the exercise was to annihilate those men.'

'I believe the proper word is "neutralize",' the SMIU leader put in, feeling obliged to defend the operation he had helped to set up.

'My apologies,' the Secretary responded testily. 'To *neutralize* those men. Does that explain why there were ambush teams outside as well as inside the building and why some of the local townsfolk were shot up – with one actually killed – by the SAS?'

'Those were unfortunate accidents,' the Controller replied firmly, 'but they weren't caused by an unnecessary display of fire-power on our part. The GPMG assault groups positioned in the copse were placed there because it was believed at the time – erroneously, as it turned out – that the IRA bomb team would approach the police station by way of the football pitch across the road from Armagh. The reason for having other troopers hidden elsewhere, including behind the wall of the church and in the town itself, is that we had also been informed that the IRA bomb would be set off by a timer or a remote-control device. We therefore had to be prepared to shoot at any point where a terrorist, irrespective of where he was located, looked as if he was about to do a button-job.'

The Secretary looked perplexed.

'Detonating the bomb by a small, radio-control device hidden on the person and usually activated by a simple button,' the SMIU leader explained. 'Which means it can be done by a demolitions man some distance from the target. In the event, a simple fuse was used, which meant that those placing the bomb at Loughgall had to stay with it until the last moment and then personally light the fuse.'

'That explanation doesn't help us,' the Secretary said, sounding aggrieved. 'The widow of that dead man, now left with three fatherless children, is claiming compensation from our government and will doubtless get it, albeit in an out-of-court settlement.'

'That man wasn't the first, and he won't be

the last, civilian casualty in the war in Northern Ireland.' Again, the shadowy SAS Controller was being firm and not about to take the blame for an action he still deemed to have been justified. 'Sometimes these unfortunate accidents can't be avoided.'

'True enough,' the Secretary admitted with a soulful sigh. 'So, let's forget about Loughgall and concentrate on what we believe it will lead to: a bloody act of retaliation by the IRA.'

'Do you know what they're planning?' the Controller asked him.

'We have reason to believe that the target will be soft,' the SMIU man replied on behalf of the Secretary, 'and either in southern Spain or Gibraltar – the first because it has thousands of British tourists as potential victims, the second because the IRA have often publicly stated that it is a potential "soft target" and, even better from their point of view, one strongly identified with British imperialism.'

'Do you have any specific grounds for such suspicions?'

'Yes. We've just been informed by the terrorist experts from the Servicios de Información in Madrid that yesterday two well-known and experienced IRA members, Sean Savage and Daniel McCann, arrived in Spain under false names. Savage is a shadowy figure of no proven IRA affiliations, though he's been under RUC surveillance for a long time and is certainly suspected of being one of the IRA's best men. McCann is widely known as 'Mad Dan' because of his reputation as an absolutely ruthless IRA fanatic up to his elbows in blood. It's our belief that their presence in Spain, particularly as they're there under false passports, indicates some kind of IRA attack, to take place either in Spain – as I said before, because of the enormous tourist population, presently running at about a quarter of a million – or in their oft-proclaimed soft target of Gibraltar. If it's the Rock, where there are approximately fifteen hundred service personnel, then almost certainly it will be a military target.'

'Do we know where they are at the moment?' the Controller asked.

'No,' the SMIU leader replied, sounding slightly embarrassed. 'We only know that they flew from Gatwick to Málaga. Though travelling under false passports, they were recognized by the photos of criminal and political suspects held by the security people at Gatwick. However, when we were informed of their presence at Gatwick, we decided to let them fly on to Spain in order to find out what they were up to. Once in Spain, they were supposed to be tailed by the Spanish police, who unfortunately soon lost them. Right now, we only know that they hired a car at Málaga airport and headed along the N340 towards Torremolinos or somewhere further in that direction. The Spanish police are therefore combing the area between Torremolinos and Algeciras and, of course, we're checking everyone going in and out of Gibraltar. I'm sure we'll find them in good time.'

'So what happens when they're found?' the Controller asked.

'Nothing,' the SMIU man told him. 'At least not just yet. We just want to observe them and ascertain what they're planning. Should they remain in the Costa del Sol, then naturally we must be concerned for the safety of its thousands of British residents and tourists. On the other hand, if they cross the border into Gibraltar, our suspicions about the Rock as their soft target will be, if not actually confirmed, then certainly heightened.'

'What if they simply have a holiday and then fly back to Northern Ireland?' the Controller asked.

'We'll let them go, but keep them under surveillance, whether it be in the Province or somewhere else. We're convinced, however, that they're not on the Costa del Sol to get a suntan. We think they're there to gather information about a particular target – and our guess is that they'll materialize quite soon on Gib.'

'To cause damage?'

'Not now, but later,' the SMIU leader said.

'These men have entered Spain with no more than suitcases, so unless they meet up with someone, or pick up something *en route*, we have to assume that this is purely a scouting trip.'

'Given all the questions you've just asked me about the Loughgall affair,' the Controller said, smiling sardonically at the Secretary, 'can I take it that you're considering future SAS involvement?'

'Yes.' The Secretary leant across his desk to stare intently at the Controller. 'If the terrorist outrage is going to be on Spanish territory, the scenario will place enormous constraints upon us – notably in that we'll be totally dependent on the cooperation of the Spanish police and the Servicios de Información. This problem, unfortunately, will not go away if the IRA plan their outrage for the Rock, since any attack there will almost certainly have to be initiated on the Spanish side of the border, which will again make us dependent on Spanish police and Intelligence. Either way, they won't be happy with any overt British military or Intelligence presence on the scene; nor indeed with the possibility of an essentially British problem being sorted out, perhaps violently and publicly, on Spanish soil. For this reason, as with the Iranian Embassy siege, we'll be caught between making this a police matter – in this case the Spanish or Gibraltar police – or a military matter undertaken by ourselves. If it's the latter, we'll have to persuade the Spanish authorities that we can contain the matter as an anti-terrorist operation run by a small, specially trained group of men, rather than having any kind of full-scale action by the regular Army. That small group of men would have to be the SAS.'

'Quite right, too,' the Controller said.

The Secretary smiled bleakly, not happy to have handed the Controller a garland of flowers. 'While undoubtedly your SAS have proved their worth over the years, they are not the only ones to have done so: the Royal Marines, for instance, could possibly undertake the same, small-scale operation.'

'Not so well,' the Controller insisted. 'Not with a group as small as the one you'll need for this particular task.'

'Perhaps, perhaps not,' the Secretary said doubtfully. 'I have to tell you, however, that I've chosen the SAS not just because of their counter-terrorism talents but because they're experienced in working closely with the police – albeit usually the British police – and, more importantly, because the Iranian Embassy job has given them the highest profile of any of the Special Forces in this or indeed any other country.'

'Not always a good thing,' the Controller admitted, for in truth he detested the notoriety gained by the SAS through that one much-publicized operation.

'But good in this case,' the Secretary told him, 'as the Spanish authorities also know of your Regiment's reputation for counter-terrorist activities and will doubtless respond warmly to it.'

'So at what point do we step in?' the Controller asked, now glancing at the SMIU leader, who was the one who would make that decision.

'This has to remain a matter between British Intelligence and the Servicios de Información until such time as the terrorists actually make their move. Once that appears to be the case, the decision will have to be taken as to whether the Spanish police, the Gibraltar police or the SAS will be given responsibility for dealing with it. In the meantime, we want you to discuss the two possible scenarios – the Spanish mainland or Gibraltar – with your Intelligence people at SAS HQ and devise suitable options for both. When the time comes we'll call you.'

'Excellent,' the Controller said. 'Is that all?'

'Yes,' the Secretary told him.

Nodding, the Controller, the most shadowy man in the whole of the SAS hierarchy, picked up his briefcase, straightened his pinstripe suit, then marched out of the office, to be driven the short distance to the SAS HQ at the Duke of York's Barracks, where he would make his contingency plans.

A man of very strong, sure instincts, he knew already what would happen. The SAS would take over.

2

After removing his blood-smeared white smock and washing the wet blood from his hands in the sink behind the butcher's shop where he worked, Daniel McCann put on his jacket, checked the money in his wallet, then locked up and stepped into the darkening light of the late afternoon. The mean streets of Republican Belfast had not yet surrendered to night, but they looked dark and grim with their pavements wet with rain, the bricked-up windows and doorways in empty houses, and the usual police checkpoints and security fences.

Though only thirty, 'Mad Dan' looked much older, his face prematurely lined and chiselled into hard, unyielding features by his murderous history and ceaseless conflict with the hated British. In the hot, angry summer of 1969, when he was twelve, Catholic homes in his area had been burnt to the ground by Loyalist neighbours before the 'Brits' were called in to stop them, inaugurating a new era of bloody warfare between the Catholics, the Protestants and the British Army. As a consequence, Mad Dan had become a dedicated IRA veteran, going all the way with his blood-chilling enthusiasm for extortion, kneecapping and other forms of torture and, of course, assassination – not only of Brits and Irish Prods, but also of his own kind when they stood in his way, betrayed the cause, or otherwise displeased him.

Nevertheless, Mad Dan had led a charmed life. In a long career as an assassin, he had chalked up only one serious conviction – for possessing a detonator – which led to two years in the Maze. By the time he got out, having been even more thoroughly educated by his fellow-Irishmen in the prison, he was all set to become a fanatical IRA activitst with no concept of compromise.

But Mad Dan didn't just torture, maim and kill for the IRA cause; he did it because he had a lust for violence and a taste for blood. He was a mad dog.

At the very least, the RUC and British Army had Mad Dan tabbed as an enthusiastic exponent of shoot-to-kill and repeatedly hauled him out of his bed in the middle of the night to attend the detention centre at Castlereagh for an identity parade or interrogation. Yet even when they beat the hell out of him, Mad Dan spat in their faces.

He liked to walk. It was the best way to get round the city and the way least likely to attract the attention of the RUC or British Army. Now, turning into Grosvenor Road, he passed a police station and regular Army checkpoint, surrounded by high, sandbagged walls and manned by heavily armed soldiers, all wearing DPM clothing, helmets with chin straps, and standard-issue boots. Apart from the private manning the 7.62mm L4 light machine-gun, the soldiers were carrying M16 rifles and had stun and smoke grenades on their webbing. The sight of them always made Mad Dan's blood boil.

That part of Belfast looked like London after the Blitz: rows of terraced houses with their doors and windows bricked up and gardens piled high with rubble. The pavements outside the pubs and certain shops were barricaded with large concrete blocks and sandbags. The windows were caged with heavy-duty wire netting as protection against car bombs and petrol bombers.

Farther along, a soldier with an SA80 assault rifle was covering a sapper while the latter carefully checked the contents of a rubbish bin. Mad Dan was one of those who often fired rocket-propelled grenades from Russian-manufactured RPG7 short-range anti-tank weapons, mainly against police stations, army barracks and armoured personnel carriers or Saracen armoured cars. He was also one of those who had, from a safe distance, command-detonated dustbins filled with explosives. It was for these that the sapper was examining all the rubbish bins near the police station and checkpoint. Usually, when explosives were placed in dustbins, it was done during the night, which is why the sappers had to check every morning. Seeing this particular soldier at work gave Mad Dan a great deal of satisfaction.

Farther down the road, well away from the Army checkpoint, he popped in and out of a few shops and betting shops to collect the protection money required to finance his own Provisional IRA unit. He collected the money in cash, which he stuffed carelessly into his pockets. In the last port of call, a bookie's, he took the protection money from the owner, then placed a few bets and joked about coming back to collect his winnings. The owner, though despising him, was frightened of him and forced a painful smile.

After crossing the road, Mad Dan stopped just short of an RUC station which was guarded by officers wearing flak-jackets and carrying the ubiquitous 5.56mm Ruger Mini-14 assault rifle. There he turned left and circled back through the grimy streets until he was heading up the Falls Road and making friendlier calls to his IRA mates in the pubs of Springfield, Ballymurphy and Turf Lodge, where everyone looked poor and suspicious. Most noticeable were the gangs of teenagers known as 'dickers', who stood menacingly at street corners, keeping their eyes out for newcomers or anything else they felt was threatening, particularly British Army patrols.

Invariably, with the gangs there were young

people on crutches or with arms in slings, beaming with pride because they'd been knee-capped as punishment for some infraction, real or imagined, and were therefore treated as 'hard men' by their mates.

Being a kneecapping specialist, Mad Dan knew most of the dickers and kids by name. He was particularly proud of his kneecapping abilities, but, like his fellow Provisional IRA members, used various methods of punishment, according to the nature of the offence.

It was a harsh truth of Republican Belfast that you could tell the gravity of a man's offence by how he'd been punished. If he had a wound either in the fleshy part of the thigh or in the ankle, from a small .22 pistol, which doesn't shatter bone, then he was only guilty of a minor offence. For something more serious he would be shot in the back of the knee with a high-velocity rifle or pistol, which meant the artery was severed and the kneecap blown right off. Mad Dan's favourite, however, was the 'six-pack', the fate of particularly serious offenders. The victim received a bullet in each elbow, knee and ankle, which put him on crutches for a long time.

While the six-pack was reserved for 'touts', or informers, and other traitors, the less damaging, certainly less agonizing punishments were administered to car thieves, burglars, sex offenders, or anyone too openly critical of the IRA, even though they may have actually done nothing.

As one of the leading practitioners of such punishments, Mad Dan struck so much terror into his victims that when they received a visit from one of his minions, telling them that they had to report for punishment, they nearly always went of their own accord to the place selected for the kneecapping. Knowing what was going to happen to them, many tried to anaesthetize themselves beforehand by getting drunk or sedating themselves with Valium, but Mad Dan always waited for the effects to wear off before inflicting the punishment. He liked to hear them screaming.

'Sure, yer squealin' like a stuck pig,' he would say after the punishment had been dispensed. 'Stop shamin' your mother, bejasus, and act like a man!'

After a couple of pints with some IRA friends in a Republican pub in Andersonstown, Mad Dan caught a taxi to the Falls Road, the Provos' heartland and one of the deadliest killing grounds in Northern Ireland. The streets of the 'war zone', as British soldiers called it, were clogged with armoured Land Rovers and forbidding military fortresses looming against the sky. British Army barricades, topped with barbed wire and protected by machine-gun crews atop Saracen armoured cars, were blocking off the entrance to many streets, with the foot soldiers well armed and looking like Martians in their DPM uniforms, boots, webbing, camouflaged helmets and chin-protectors. The black taxis were packed with passengers too frightened to use public transport or walk. Grey-painted RUC mobiles and Saracens were passing constantly. From both kinds of vehicle, police officers were scanning the upper windows and roofs on either side of the road, looking for possible sniper positions. At the barricades, soldiers were checking everyone entering and, in many instances, taking them aside to roughly search them. As Mad Dan noted with his experienced gaze, there were British Army static observation posts with powerful cameras on the roofs of the higher buildings, recording every movement in these streets. There were also, as he knew, listening devices in the ceilings of suspected IRA buildings, as well as bugs on selected phone lines.

Small wonder that caught between the Brits and the IRA, ever vigilant in their own way, the Catholics in these streets had little privacy and were inclined to be paranoid.

Turning into a side-street off the Falls Road, Mad Dan made his way to a dismal block of flats by a patch of waste ground filled with rubbish, where mangy dogs and scruffy, dirt-smeared children were playing noisily in the gathering darkness. In fact, the block of flats looked like a prison, and all the more so because up on the high roof was a British Army OP, its powerful telescope scanning the many people who loitered along the balconies or on the ground below. One soldier was manning a 7.62mm GPMG; the others were holding M16 rifles with the barrels resting lightly on the sandbagged wall.

Grinning as he looked up at the overt OP, Mad Dan placed the thumb of his right hand on his nose, then flipped his hand left and right in ironic, insulting salute. Then he entered the pub. It was smoky, noisy and convivial inside. Seeing Patrick Tyrone sitting at one of the tables with an almost empty glass of Guinness in front of him, Mad Dan asked with a gesture if he wanted another. When Tyrone nodded, Mad Dan ordered and paid for two pints, then carried them over to Tyrone's table. Sitting down, he slid one over to Tyrone, had a long drink from his own, then wiped his lips with the back of his hand.

'Ach, sure that's good!' he said.

When Tyrone, another hard man, had responded with a thin, humourless smile, Mad Dan nodded towards the front door and said: 'I see the Brits have some OPs on the roof. Do they do any damage?'

'Aye. They're equipped with computers linked to vehicle-registration and suspect-information centres, as well as to surveillance cameras. Also, the shites' high visibility reminds us of their

36

presence and so places a quare few constraints on us. At the same time, the OPs allow members of regular Brit units and 14 Intelligence Company to observe suspects and see who their associates are. This in turn allows the shites collecting intelligence at Lisburn and Brit HQ to investigate links between meetings of individuals and our subsequent group activities. So, aye, those bastard OPs can do us lots of damage.'

'Sure, that's a hell of a mouthful, Pat.'

'Sure, it's also the truth.'

'Do those OPs have any back up?' Mad Dan asked.

'Ackaye'. Each of 'em's backed up with another consisting of two to four soldiers and located near enough to offer immediate firearms support. If that weren't enough, those two OPs are backed up by a QRF . . .'

'Sure, what's that if you'd be writin' home?'

'A Quick Reaction Force of soldiers or police, sometimes both, located at the nearest convenient SF base. And that QRF will respond immediately to a radio call for help from the OPs. So, no, they're not alone, Dan. Those Brit bastards up there have a lot of support.'

Mad Dan nodded, indicating he understood, but really he wasn't all that interested. He was there to receive specific instructions for the forthcoming evening. It was what he now lived for.

'So what is it?' he asked.

'A double hit,' Tyrone informed him. 'A bit of weedin' in the garden. Two bastards that have to be put down to put them out of their misery.'

'A decent thought,' Mad Dan said. 'Now who would they be, then?'

Tyrone had another sip of his Guinness, then took a deep breath. 'Detective Sergeants Michael Malone and Ernest Carson.'

'Two bastards, right enough,' Mad Dan said. 'Sure, that's a quare good choice. Tonight, is it?'

'Aye. They'll be in the Liverpool Bar for a meetin' from eight o'clock on. Just walk in there and do as you see fit. We've no brief other than that. Just make sure they stop breathin'.'

'Any security?'

'None. The dumb shites think they're in neutral territory, so they're there for nothin' else but a quare ol' time. Let the bastards die happy.'

'Weapon?'

'I'll give it to you outside. A 9mm Browning, removed from an SAS bastard killed back in '76. Appropriate, right?'

'Ackaye, real appropriate. Let's go get it an' then I'll be off.'

'Sure, I knew you'd say that.'

After finishing their drinks in a leisurely manner, the two men left the bar. Glancing up at the OPs and fully aware that the pub was under surveillance, Tyrone led Mad Dan along the street and up the concrete steps of the grim block of flats. He stopped on the gloomy landing, where the steps turned back in the other direction to lead up to the first balcony. There, out of sight of the spying Brits, he removed the Browning and handed it to Mad Dan, along with a fourteen-round magazine.

'That's the only ammunition you're gettin',' he said, 'because you've only got time for one round before hightailing it out of there. That also means you've no time for mistakes, so make sure you get them fucks.'

'Sure, that's no problem at all, Pat. I'll riddle the bastards and be out of there before they hit the floorboards.'

'Aye, make sure you do that.' Tyrone glanced up and down the stairs, checking that no one was coming. 'So,' he said, 'I'm goin' home for a bite. Off you go. Best of luck. I'll see you back in the bar in forty minutes.'

'I'll be there,' Mad Dan said.

As Tyrone turned away to go up the steps to his mean flat on the first floor, Mad Dan loaded the magazine into the Browning, then tucked the weapon carefully down the back of his trousers, between the belt and his shirt, hidden under the jacket but where he could reach round and pull it out quickly. He walked back down the stairs and out into the street, in full view of the OPs up above. Bold as brass, he walked alongside the waste ground as the street lights came on to illuminate the dark evening. Emerging into the busy Falls Road, he turned right and walked down the crowded pavement until he reached the nearest parked car. When he bent down to talk to the driver, he was recognized instantly.

'Sure, how did it go, Dan?'

'You know Tyrone. Eyes like cold fried eggs and yammerin' on about the Brits, but he gave me the go-ahead and the weapon.' Mad Dan checked his watch. It was five past eight. 'They'll be in the Liverpool Bar and they should be there now. So, come on, let's get goin', lad.'

When Mad Dan had slipped into the seat beside the driver, the latter said: 'Sure, would that be the Liverpool Bar on Donegall Quay?'

'Aye, that's the one. Drop me off there, keep the engine tickin' over, and get ready to hightail it out of there when I come runnin' out. Then don't stop for anything.'

'I'll be out of there like a bat out of hell. Sure, you've no need to worry, Dan.'

'Just make sure of that, boyo.'

As the car moved off, heading along the Falls Road in the direction of Divis Street, Mad Dan felt perfectly relaxed and passed the time by gazing out of the window at the hated RUC constables and British Army soldiers manning the barricaded police stations and checkpoints.

He had no need to feel concerned about the car being identified because it had been hijacked at gunpoint on a road just outside the city, and the driver warned not to report the theft until the following day. The stolen car would be abandoned shortly after the attack and, when found unattended, it would be blown up by the SF as a potential car bomb. The unfortunate owner, if outraged, at least could count himself lucky that he still had his life. To lose your car in this manner was par for the course in Northern Ireland.

It took no time at all for the driver to make his way from Divis Street down past the Clock Tower, along Queen's Square and into Donegall Quay, which ran alongside the bleak docks of the harbour, where idle cranes loomed over the water, their hooks swinging slightly in the wind blowing in from the sea. On one side the harbour walls rose out of the filthy black water, stained a dirty brown by years of salt water and the elements; on the other were ugly warehouses and Victorian buildings. Tucked between some of the latter was the Liverpool Bar, so called because the Belfast–Liverpool ferries left from the nearby Irish Sea Ferry Terminal.

The driver stopped the car in a dark alley near the pub, out of sight of the armed RUC constables and British soldiers guarding the docks at the other side of the main road. He switched his headlights off, slipped into neutral, and kept the engine ticking over quietly.

Mad Dan opened the door, clambered out of the car, hurried along the alley and turned left into Donegall Quay. There he slowed down and walked in a more leisurely manner to the front door of the Liverpool Bar, not even looking at the soldiers guarding the terminal across the road. Without hesitation, he opened the door and went inside.

Even as the door was swinging closed behind him, he saw the two well-known policemen, Detective Sergeants Michael Malone and Ernest Carson, having off-duty drinks with some fellow-officers at the bar. Wasting no time, Mad Dan reached behind him, withdrew the Browning from under his jacket, spread his legs and aimed with the two-handed grip in one quick, expert movement.

The first shots were fired before anyone knew what was happening.

Mad Dan fired the whole fourteen rounds in rapid succession, aiming first at Malone, peppering him with 9mm bullets, then swinging the pistol towards Carson, as the first victim was throwing his arms up and slamming back against the bar, knocking over glasses and bottles, which smashed on the floor.

Even before Malone had fallen, Carson was being cut down, jerking epileptically as other bullets smashed the mirrors, bottles and glasses behind the bar. The barman gasped and twisted sideways, wounded by a stray bullet, and collapsed as one of the other policemen also went down, hit by the last bullets of Mad Dan's short, savage fusillade.

Chairs and tables turned over as the customers dived for cover, men bawling, women screaming, in that enclosed, dim and smoky space. Hearing the click of an empty chamber, Mad Dan shoved the handgun back in his trousers and turned around to march resolutely, though with no overt display of urgency, through the front door, out on to the dark pavement of Donegall Quay.

Swinging shut behind him, the door deadened the sounds of screaming, bawling and hysterical sobbing from inside the bar.

The RUC constables and British soldiers guarding the terminal across the road neither heard nor saw anything unusual as Mad Dan walked at a normal pace back along the pavement and turned into the darkness of the alley a short way along.

By the time the first of the drinkers had burst out through the front door of the bar, bawling across the road for help, Mad Dan, in the hijacked car, had been raced away from the scene, back to the crowded, anonymous streets of Republican Belfast.

'Out ya get,' his driver said, screeching to a

halt in a dark and desolate Falls Road side-street.

Mad Dan and the driver clambered out of the car at the same time, then ran together out of the street and back into the lamplit, still busy Falls Road, where they parted without a word.

As the driver entered the nearest pub, where he would mingle with his mates, Mad Dan went back up the Falls Road and turned eventually into the side-street that led to the pub facing the desolate flats that had the British Army OPs on the rooftops. Though picked up by the infrared thermal imagers and personal weapons' night-sights of the men in the OPs, Mad Dan was viewed by the British observers as no more than another Paddy entering the pub for his nightly pint or two. However, once inside he went directly to the same table he had sat at an hour ago, where Tyrone was still seated, staring up with those eyes that did indeed look no more appealing than cold fried eggs.

'So how did it go?' Tyrone asked, showing little concern.

'The garden's been weeded,' Mad Dan told him. 'No problem at all.'

'Then the drink's on me,' Tyrone said. 'Sit down, Dan. Rest your itchy arse.'

Mad Dan relaxed while Tyrone went to the bar, bought two pints of Guinness and returned to the table. He handed one of the glasses to Mad

Dan, raised his own in a slightly mocking toast, then drank. Mad Dan did the same, wiping his lips with the back of his hand.

'Neutralized or semi-neutralized?' Tyrone asked.

'As cold as two hooked fish on a marble slab,' Mad Dan replied.

'Gone to meet their maker.'

'Ackaye,' Mad Dan said.

Tyrone put down his glass, licked his thin lips, then leant over the table to stare very directly at Mad Dan with his cold eyes. 'Sure, I want you to meet someone,' he said.

'Who?' Mad Dan asked.

'A kid called Sean Savage.'

3

Sean Savage loved his country. At twenty-three he was an incurable romantic who read voraciously about the history of Northern Ireland and travelled frequently across the Province by bicycle, his rucksack weighed down with books, as well as food and drink. He had done this so often that he was now considered an expert on Irish history.

With his vivid imagination Sean could almost see the island coming into existence at the end of the Ice Age, some 20,000 years ago, when the ice melted and the land rose up to fight the stormy sea. Cycling along the spectacular crags of the North Antrim coast, he would imagine it being shaped gradually over the years as the sea eroded the land on either side of the rocks, before human habitation was known. Northern Ireland's first inhabitants, he knew, were nomadic boatmen who had crossed from south-west Scotland in 7000 BC and left the debris of their passing, mostly pieces of flint axes, in the soil along the rugged coastline.

Sean was particularly intrigued by those early explorers, often wishing he had been born in that distant time, sometimes even imagining that he

had been one of them in a former life. One of
his favourite spots was the crag surmounted by
the remains of Dunlace Castle, where, sitting as
near the edge of the cliff as possible, gazing down
at the sea far below, he would imagine himself
one of those early explorers, venturing in a flimsy
coracle into the enormous cave that ran through
the rock to the land.

He was a solitary person, enjoying his own
company. Shy with girls and still living with his
parents in a terraced house in Republican West
Belfast, he filled his spare time with evening
classes on the Irish language, cycling all over
Northern Ireland, and exploring and reading
about the formation of the land and how those
early explorers from Scotland were followed by
various invaders, including the Christians, the
Vikings and, finally, the Normans, who had
marked their victories by building castles along
the coastline. The remains of those castles still
covered the land, reminding Sean that Northern
Ireland had often been invaded and was still a
country ruled by hated foreigners – namely, the
British.

Sean wanted to free his country. As he cycled
to and fro across this land steeped in myth
and legend – with 'giants, ghosts and banshees
wailing through the sea mist', as one of the
guidebooks had it – as he read his books and
explored the ancient ruins or drank in the beauty

of the Mountains of Mourne, the lunar landscape of the Giant's Causeway, or the soothing green glens of Antrim, he wanted desperately to return to the past when Ireland belonged to the Irish. Like his early hero, Sorley Boy MacDonnell, who had boldly captured Dunlace Castle from the English in 1584, Sean wanted to break out of his anonymity and achieve heroic victories.

'Sure, you're just a wee dreamer,' his friend Father Donal Murphy told him, 'wantin' what can't be had. You can't get the past back, boyo, and you'd better accept that fact.'

But Sean couldn't accept that fact. Like many of his friends, Father Murphy knew him as a reflective Irish-language enthusiast, rambler, cyclist, Gaelic footballer and cook. Still single, he neither smoked nor drank alcohol, rarely expressed political views, and was never seen at Republican functions. Not for one second, then, did the priest suspect that Sean was a highly active, dangerous member of the IRA.

The nearest Sean had come to recorded involvement in the 'Troubles' was when, in 1982, he had been arrested on the word of an unknown 'supergrass' who had denounced him as an IRA hit man. Resolute in protesting his innocence, Sean was strongly defended by many friends, including Father Murphy, who all viewed the arrest as yet another example of the British tendency to imprison innocent people on flimsy evidence. Released a month later, Sean returned to his peaceful activities and, in so doing, reinforced the conviction of most of his friends that he had been wrongfully accused.

'They're so keen to find themselves some terrorists,' Father Murphy told him, 'they don't bother with facts. Sure, they only had to run a proper check and they'd have found you were innocent.'

'Ackaye,' Sean replied. 'Sure, that's the truth, Father. They probably didn't care who they arrested – they just needed some fish to fry. We're *all* at risk that way.'

In fact, as only a few, highly placed members of the IRA knew, Sean was a dedicated freedom fighter who would go to any lengths to get the Brits out of the Province. To this end he had joined the IRA while still at school and soon became an expert 'engineer', or bomb maker, responsible for the destruction of RUC stations, British Army checkpoints, and, on more than one occasion, lorries filled with soldiers. Thus, though he seemed innocent enough, he had blood on his hands.

But he was not a 'mad dog' like Daniel McCann and took no great pleasure in killing people. Rather, he viewed his IRA bombings and, on the odd occasion, shootings, as the necessary evils of a just war and despised the more enthusiastic or brutal elements in the organization – those who did it for pleasure.

As Mad Dan McCann was one of those whom he most despised, even if only from what he had heard about him, never having met the man, he wasn't thrilled when, in early November 1987, after receiving a handwritten message from his Provisional IRA leader, Pat Tyrone, inviting him to a meeting in Tyrone's house, he turned up to find McCann there as well.

Sean had long since accepted that once in the IRA it was difficult to get beyond its reach. Like the killing of Prods and Brits, he viewed this iron embrace as another necessary evil and was therefore not surprised that the message from Tyrone was delivered to him by another Provisional IRA member, nineteen-year-old Dan Hennessy, who drove up on a Honda motor-bike to where Sean was sitting on the lower slopes of Slieve Donard, gazing down on the tranquil waters of Strangford Lough. Braking on the slope just below Sean, Hennessy propped the bike up on its stand, then swung his right leg over the saddle and walked up to Sean with a sealed envelope.

'From Pat Tyrone,' Hennessy said, not even bothering to look around him at the magnificent view. Hennessy was as thick as two planks and only in the IRA because he thought it would give him certain privileges in Belfast's underprivileged society. In fact, he would be used as cannon-fodder. As such, he would almost certainly end up either in a British prison or in a ditch with a bullet in his thick skull. It was an unfortunate truth that such scum were necessary to get the dirty work done and that most came to a bad end.

'How did you know I was here?' Sean asked as he opened the envelope.

'Tyrone sent me to your house and your mum said you'd come up here for the day. Sure, what the fuck do you do up here?'

'I read,' Sean informed him.

'You mean you beat off to porn.'

'I read books on history,' Sean said calmly, unfolding the note. 'This is a good place to read.'

'You're a bloody queer one, that's for sure.'

Sean read the note. It was short and to the point: 'Sean: Something has come up. We need to talk. I'll be home at four this afternoon. Meet me there. Yours, Pat Tyrone.' Sean folded the note, replaced it neatly in the envelope, then put the envelope in his pocket and nodded at Hennessy.

'Tell Pat I received the message,' he said.

'Ackaye,' Hennessy replied, then sped off down the slope, still oblivious to the magnificent scenery all about him.

To Sean it was clear that Hennessy loved only himself – not Ireland. He was a teenage hoodlum. Vermin. A former dicker elevated to

51

the Provisional IRA ranks and dreaming of better things. An early grave is all he'll get, he thought as he packed up his things and prepared to cycle back down the lower slopes of the mountain. And it's all he'll deserve.

Disgusted by Hennessy, Sean was reminded of him as he cycled back through the grim streets of West Belfast, where he saw the usual depressing spectacle of armed RUC constables, British Army checkpoints, Saracens patrolling the streets and, of course, the dickers, keeping their eye on the every movement of potentially traitorous Catholics, as well as the Brits and Prods. Like Hennessy, most of those ill-educated, unemployed teenagers were hoping to eventually break free from the tedium of being mere lookouts to become active IRA members and kill some Prods and Brits. As their dreams had little to do with a love of Ireland, Sean despised them as much as he did Hennessy and others like him, including Mad Dan McCann.

He was reminded of his contempt for Mad Dan when, entering Tyrone's two-up, two-down terraced house in one of the depressing little streets off the Falls Road – a strongly Republican street barricaded at both ends by the British Army – he found McCann sitting at the table with Tyrone in the cramped, gloomy living-room, both of them drinking from bottles of stout and wreathed in cigarette smoke.

'Have you come?' Tyrone asked, using that odd form of greeting peculiar to the Ulster Irish.

'Aye, sure I have,' Sean replied.

'You look fit. Been out ridin' on that bike of yours again?'

'Aye. Out Armagh way.'

'Sean rides his bicycle all over the place,' Tyrone explained to Mad Dan, who was studying the younger man with his dark, stormy eyes. 'He sits up there on the hills, all wind-blown, and reads history and studies the Irish language. He's our wee intellectual.'

'Aye, sure I've heard that right enough,' Mad Dan said. 'He's got a right brain on his head, so I've been told.'

'You've met Dan?' Tyrone asked Sean.

'No,' Sean replied. 'I've heard a lot about you,' he added, turning to McCann, but finding it difficult to meet his wild gaze.

'All good, was it?' Mad Dan asked with a leer.

'All right, like,' Sean replied carefully.

Mad Dan burst out into cackling laughter. 'Aye, I'll bet,' he said, then stopped laughing abruptly as Sean pulled up a chair at the table in the tiny living-room. The walls of the house, which belonged to Tyrone's mother, were covered with framed paintings of Jesus, the Virgin Mary and numerous saints.

A real little chapel, Sean thought, for Tyrone's

ageing mother. Certainly not for Tyrone. Indeed, when he looked at Tyrone, he knew he was looking at a hard man who had little time for religion, let alone sentiment. Like Sean, Tyrone lived for the cause, but his motives were purely political, not religious. For this reason, Sean respected him. He did not respect McCann the same way, though he certainly feared him. He thought he was an animal.

When Sean had settled in his hard-backed chair. Tyrone waved his hand at the bottles of stout on the table in front of him. 'Sure, help yerself, Sean.'

Sean shook his head from side to side. 'Naw,' he said. 'I'm all right for the moment.'

'Oh, I forgot,' Tyrone said with a grin. 'You don't drink at all.'

'Nothin' but mother's milk,' Mad Dan said. 'Sure, wouldn't that be right, boyo?'

'I just don't like drinkin',' Sean replied. 'What's the matter with that?'

'Men who don't drink can't be trusted,' Mad Dan informed him with a twisted, mocking grin. 'Sure, isn't that a fact now?'

'It's men who drink who can't be trusted,' Sean told him. 'The drink loosens their tongues.'

'And more,' Tyrone said, wiping his wet lips with the palm of his hand. 'It also makes 'em too cocky and careless – too inclined to make mistakes. You stay away from it, laddy.'

The remark offended Mad Dan, making him turn red. 'Sure, you wouldn't be accusin' me of carelessness, would you, Tyrone?'

'Not you, Dan,' Tyrone said, though he had his doubts. 'You can hold your own. I mean in general, that's all.'

Sean coughed into his clenched fist.

'He doesn't smoke either,' Tyrone explained.

'Bejasus!' Mad Dan said sarcastically. 'Sure, isn't he a right wee angel? Where's your gilded wings, boyo?'

Sean didn't bother replying; he just offered a tight smile. 'So what's up?' he asked Tyrone.

'Sure I know you like travellin', 'Tyrone replied, 'so I'd like to offer you the chance to travel a bit farther than the tourist sites of Northern Ireland.'

'What's that mean?' Sean asked in his quiet, always deadly serious manner.

Tyrone drew on his cigarette, exhaled a cloud of smoke, then leant slightly across the table, closer to Sean.

'It's to do with the massacre of our eight comrades by those SAS bastards in Loughgall last May.'

Sean knew all about that massacre and felt rage just recalling it. This was a real war in the Province, with real death and destruction, so Sean normally tried to remain objective and not let hatred motivate him or, worse, distort his judgement. Nevertheless, the shooting of eight of his comrades by a large SAS ambush team placed inside and around the RUC station at Longhgall, with a civilian driver also killed and his brother badly wounded, had filled him with an anger that could not be contained. While Sean had not personally been informed of that particular IRA raid, it was as clear as the nose on his face that the Provisional IRA teams involved had timed it to take place after the police station was closed, which meant they had not intended bodily harm, but only to blow up the empty building. The response from the SAS had therefore been out of all proportion to the size of the event – a bloody overkill that had merely confirmed for Sean and other IRA members that the SAS was an officially sanctioned assassination squad acting on behalf of the British government.

'A revenge attack,' Sean said, certain of what was coming.

'Correct.' Tyrone blew another cloud of smoke, then stared intently at Sean. 'We've been thinking about it for the past six months or so and now we're ready to do it.'

'We're going up against the SAS?'

'No. We want something bigger – to humiliate the British government and, at the same time, regain the prestige we lost when our eight comrades were butchered. We want something outrageous.'

'But not on British soil.'

Tyrone smiled in recognition of Sean's ability to read between the lines of what he was saying. 'Right. Not on British soil. We want an outrage that takes place elsewhere and, as well as shockin' the British public, embarrasses the government. That's why you're off on a trip.'

'Where?'

'We want a soft target – not a military target – and as thousands of British tourists visit the Costa del Sol every year, that seems a logical choice.'

'You're going to hit civilians?'

'Aye. That's the general idea.'

'I don't like it,' Sean told him. 'To hit innocent civilians on British soil is bad enough, but it can at least be justified in that we're attacking behind enemy lines and the civilians are innocent bystanders caught up in that war. But to go out and deliberately bomb them in another country isn't remotely the same thing. Sure, it's something that's bound to be viewed as a deliberate atrocity and, worse, one that could outrage the Spanish government even more than the British.'

'Which is precisely what we want,' Tyrone informed him. 'We want them bastard Brits to know that they can't come over here and slaughter eight of our men without expectin' rough justice. An eye for an eye, right?'

'But a civilian target on foreign soil . . .'

'Just what we're after,' Tyrone interrupted

him. 'We want the British government to know
– we want the whole damn world to know – that
the IRA is willin' to take this war to any country
where British citizens are to be found in large
numbers. We want 'em to know that we consider
no one to be innocent – not even ordinary Brits
sunnin' it up in Spain. That's one reason. The
other is that we'll involve the Spanish authorities
in this, whether or not they like it. In doin' so
we'll further embarrass the Brits and give them
cause to think twice before orderin' the slaughter
of IRA men out on missions clearly designed to
cause no fatalities. This time *we'll* be the ones to
cause a lot of fatalities – mostly innocent citizens
– while lettin' the world know exactly why we're
doing it: as an act of revenge for Loughgall.'

As Sean was digesting this, Tyrone blew
another cloud of smoke, sipped some stout, then
asked: 'Have you heard about the assassination
of Detective Sergeants Malone and Carson in the
Liverpool Bar last August?'

'Ackaye. Who hasn't?'

Tyrone nodded in the direction of the stony-
faced Mad Dan. 'Dan here did that one.' When
Sean glanced sideways, he saw the assassin
grinning with mad pride. Chilled, he had to look
away, returning his gaze to Tyrone. 'We ordered
those two killed,' Tyrone explained, 'because
they spent most evenings drinking in that pub
and watching who got off the Liverpool ferry:

our own men and the Brits. We believe they were docking our men while givin' the Brits protection when they came off the boat. We also ordered their deaths as an indication to the Brits that we wouldn't take Loughgall lyin' down. Which is exactly why you're goin' to Spain, Sean.'

'No complaints from me,' Mad Dan said. 'I could do with some sunshine.'

After glancing with distaste at Mad Dan, Sean turned back to Tyrone. 'What's our brief? Do we pick our own target?'

'You don't pick anything. You don't even carry weapons. This first trip is only for preliminary reconnaissance. You're to act like normal holiday-makers while you reconnoitre the area – right along the whole coastline, from Málaga to Algeciras – and come back with some minimun-risk targets. We'll take our pick after careful consideration, then send you back, suitably armed, to do the job.'

'What about Gibraltar?' Sean asked.

'What about it?'

'If the security isn't too tight, it could make an even better target.'

'Sure, I never even thought about that,' Tyrone said. 'Why even better?'

'Because it adds a political dimension to the otherwise bare killing of innocent tourists,' Sean told him.

'How's that, then?'

'Gibraltar's always been strongly identified with British imperialism and it's still protected by British soldiers. If we can kill a lot of those, as well as some tourists, the raid would have a certain logic to the rest of the world. In other words, outrageous though the bombing would still be – including the deaths of innocent bystanders – the military nature of the target would make it less reprehensible to those not directly involved in Anglo-Irish politics.'

Tyrone stubbed out his cigarette, then sat back in his chair, clasping his hands behind his head and grinning broadly at Sean. 'Obviously all that reading up on history hasn't gone to waste, Sean.' He turned to Mad Dan. 'What do you think, Dan?'

'I know nothin' 'bout fuckin' history, except that the Brits are over here an' killin' the Irish. You just tell me where to aim the gun an' I'll squeeze the trigger.'

'Good.' Tyrone turned back to Sean and said: 'Right, then. Include Gibraltar in your travels. If you think we can pull something successful there, then come back with the details.'

'How long are we going for?'

'A week. A seven-day return ticket from Gatwick to Málaga, travelling under false passports. Hire a car when you get to Málaga and play it by ear from there, checking into hotels where and when you want, but for never more than one night at any one place. Naturally, since both of you are almost certainly under British surveillance, you'll be given false passports to use from Gatwick onward. To complicate matters a bit more, you'll fly to London from Dublin – not from here.'

'When do we leave?' Mad Dan asked, clearly keen to get going.

'Tomorrow,' Tyrone told him. 'Come back here at seven tonight and I'll give you the false passports, train tickets to Dublin and tickets for your flight. I'll also give you enough English, Spanish and Gibraltar currency to keep you from having to change money when you're there. If you piss it away in Spanish bars, you'll come back to a six-pack.'

Mad Dan grinned in his evil manner. 'Sure, I give those,' he said. 'I don't get 'em. Who'd six-pack me?'

'Me,' Tyrone said.

The two hard men stared at each other for a few uneasy seconds, as if challenging each other, and Sean realized that Tyrone secretly shared his opinion that Mad Dan was a man who could not be trusted, even though, undeniably, he had his uses.

I'll have to keep my eye on him, Sean thought, when we get to Spain. I may have to muzzle the bastard, like the mad dog he is. This may not run too smoothly.

Eventually, turning away from Mad Dan, Tyrone asked: 'Any questions?'

'No,' Sean said. 'I'll go home right now and pack, then come back here at seven this evening to pick up what's required.'

'Me, too,' Mad Dan said. 'Though I'll have another bottle of stout before I leave.'

Wanting to talk to Tyrone about Mad Dan, whom he viewed as a dangerous partner, but realizing that it was Mad Dan who would get the chance to talk about him, Sean simply nodded, left Tyrone's place, and cycled home.

Irish mothers love their sons dearly and Sean's mother was no exception, but she may have loved him even more because he was so quiet and studious. Therefore she believed him implicitly when he told her that he was taking a break in the rural, Irish-speaking area of Galway, in the Republic, where he was going to stay in a caravan. Long accustomed to her son's impromtu cycle trips, Mrs Savage thought nothing of this latest plan, and gladly packed his suitcase that evening when he was, as she thought, out visiting Father Murphy.

When Sean returned that evening – having been to collect his false passport, Dublin train ticket, return Gatwick–Málaga air ticket, and currency from Tyrone – his suitcase was packed and a supper of cheese and tomato sandwiches was

62

laid out on the table. Sean gratefully ate the sandwiches, drank his cup of tea, kissed his mother on the cheek and went upstairs to bed.

The following morning, he left for his supposedly healthy weekend in the Gaeltacht. Travelling separately from Mad Dan, he caught the train to Dublin, flew from there to Gatwick, from where, using his false passport, he caught anothe flight to Málaga. Having flown in two hours earlier, Mad Dan met Sean at the airport.

With scarcely a word spoken between them, they went off to hire a car.

4

Nineteen seventy-six was a memorable year in Belfast. In January, after fifteen Protestants and Catholics died in sectarian revenge attacks in one week, the SAS were ordered into the 'bandit country' of south Armagh for the first time, following a spearhead battalion of six hundred British troops, and thus bringing the total Ulster garrison strength to about 15,200. In May ten people were left dead and fifty-six hurt after one of the Province's most violent weekends. In July the British Ambassador to Dublin was killed when his car was blown up by a land-mine. In August three children were killed after being hit by a car hijacked by the IRA and careering out of control after the driver had been shot by British soldiers. Those three deaths led to the launch of the Ulster Peace Movement at a rally of 20,000 Protestants and Roman Catholics. In September Britain was accused by a European Commission of 'inhuman treatment and torture' in its use of 'deep interrogation' techniques on Republican supporters. In October, the Ulster Peace Movement founders were attacked by an angry mob and the Belfast Sinn Fein vice-president was shot dead. In December the wife of the British

Ambassador murdered by the IRA the previous July joined the heads of the Church of England and the Roman Catholic Church in Britain in a 30,000-strong peace march organized and led by the co-founders of the Ulster Peace Movement.

Nineteen seventy-six was also the year in which Mairead Farrell bombed the Conway Hotel in Belfast. Ten years later, recently released after almost a decade in prison for her crime, she still dreamed about that bombing. Tossing and turning on her bed, her ravishing long, black hair twining around her pale face, she would see it as she had witnessed it at the time, as if in slow motion: the cracks zigzagging down the walls, bricks and powdered cement blowing outwards, a rain of shards of glass from the windows, then the vivid eruption of flame, boiling smoke and noise, a bass rumbling, followed by a deafening blast, as the bomb did its worst. The explosion made Mairead, then ten years younger, tremble with a mixture of pride and terror.

She had run, but she had not got very far. For even as the first of the nightmares came to haunt her, during those few nights after the deed, when she was being congratulated by her comrades and smiling gratefully to hide her dread, for she was so young at the time, the Brits, particularly those bastards in 14 Intelligence Company, were using their touts to learn who had planted the bomb. They found her, right enough, surprised to learn that the perpetrator had been a woman, and came for her with some RUC bitches to take her away.

Ten years in prison. God, yes, she had paid the price. And only last year, in that bleak September, ten years older but none the wiser – in fact more committed than ever – she had said goodbye to her comrades in the prison and accepted their parting gift of a watch inscribed 'Good luck. From your comrades in Maghaberry, September 1986', and walked out to freedom and a new life with Tom.

God, yes, God help me, Tom. My rock and my cross. Oh, please, Tom, be careful . . .

Everything was a wheel. It all went in circles. She had started as a bomber and now Tom Riley, the man she loved, was out there doing the same. Right now. Sweating somewhere. Planting a bomb. Continuing the war against the hated Brits.

Oh, be careful, my love.

In her dream she saw the exploding Conway Hotel, then Tom walking ghostlike from the flames and smoke, his body on fire, his face melting, calling out to her: 'Help me! Please help me!'

Mairead groaned aloud and awoke, clawing at the sweat-soaked sheet, then let her racing heart settle down and controlled her frantic breathing. When she had surfaced, getting her grip back on reality, she slipped out of the bed.

It was two o'clock in the afternoon. Having trouble sleeping at night, even with Tom, she often slept during the day. She had picked up this particular form of insomnia in prison.

She saw herself in the bathroom mirror. She was still beautiful. The shadows under her dark eyes only enhanced her haunted beauty; her striking long hair framed it. She knew that men found her attractive; she just couldn't feel it. Ever since the bombing, after her decade in prison, she had felt old and used up. Without Tom, when his physical presence was not there to protect her, she wanted only oblivion. She had killed, would certainly kill again, and was savaged by this knowledge. Mairead wanted oblivion.

She bathed, dressed and had an afternoon breakfast of cornflakes and milk, followed by a large cup of tea. Without Tom in it, the small, two-up, two-down terraced house seemed gloomy and unwelcoming, reminding her of her prison cell and the small room she'd had in the convent. For she was a former convent girl, God-fearing, pious, who had bombed a hotel and killed people. In prison, with others of her own kind, other politically committed women, she had not been taught the error of her ways; instead she'd picked up more terrorist skills from those with more experience than her. Mairead had once believed in God and her country; now she only believed in her country and wanted the Brits out.

And yet, although she was still in her early thirties, her belief in the fight for freedom was not enough to sustain her when the bouts of depression hit her. At such times, which now came with increasing frequency, she wanted to die.

Without Tom, she might have died.

But right now he wasn't at home. He was somewhere out there, on the streets of Belfast, intending to plant a bomb in a Protestant hotel on behalf of the IRA. Mairead, who couldn't imagine life without him, could only feel anxious.

Glancing at her watch, she saw that it would be another two hours before Tom's bomb went off. Unable to bear being alone any longer, she put on her coat and left the house, walking hurriedly along the street, past the boarded-up windows and bricked-up doorways of houses either partially destroyed in riots or vacated by their frightened Protestant owners, who had once lived here in peace with their Catholic neighbours. Gangs of unsupervised, often uncontrollable children were shouting noisily at one another in the road, which was littered with broken glass and stones from previous attacks on the soldiers. To Mairead they looked like ragged urchins from some impoverished Third World country and the street didn't look much better. This is what we've been reduced to, she thought, by these British bastards.

Reaching the end of the street, she came to

the British Army barricade at the Antrim Road,
known as 'Murder Mile' because of the many
sectarian killings that took place there. Watched
carefully by unsmiling soldiers, who searched
only those entering the street, not those leaving
it, Mairead gratefully went through the steel cage
beside the barrier and turned along the pavement
of the main road, feeling like she was getting out
of prison.

Belfast was now a city of steel-caged entrances
and barbed wire, so when Mairead reached the
fortified pub she had to pass through another
double barricade of thick steel wire extending from the roof to the pavement. This, too,
reminded her of being in prison. Once inside the
steel cage, she made her way along a bunker-like
hallway to a locked, reinforced door with a closed
viewing panel at eye-level and a bell fixed beside
it. When Mairead rang the bell, the viewing panel
slid open and a pair of eyes stared suspiciously at
her. Recognizing her, the man opened the door
and let her in.

Though the interior of the pub was depress-
ingly plain and dirty, it was crowded, smoky
and packed with people clearly enjoying themselves and the lively 'crack', or conversation,
they were sharing. Seeing that her three best
girlfriends, Maureen Tyrone, Aine Dogherty and
Josie McGee, were already gathered around a
table and drinking a fearsome mixture of vodka

and beer, Mairead bought four of the same and then carried them, expertly held between both hands, to the table.

'Sure, I wasn't thinkin' of another drink,' Josie said out of a cloud of cigarette smoke, 'but since you've bought it already . . .'

'Us wee girls just out for a quiet afternoon and now we're bein' corrupted,' Maureen said. 'You're a wicked one, Mairead.'

'Drink up and shut up,' Aine told her. 'Sure, never look a gift-horse in the mouth. Now isn't this grand, girls?'

Though her friends were all good-humoured, Mairead knew that all of them had suffered, one way or another, through the Troubles. Aine's husband, a member of the local Provisional IRA, was serving a ten-year sentence in the Maze after being caught with Semtex and an electrical detonator, leaving her with three small children to support on nothing other then what she got from the 'Buroo' – Social Security. Josie, still unmarried, had lost her father when he was 'executed' in a ditch – shot six times in the head – after being hauled out of his car by some vengeful UDA men as he was driving through south Armagh. Worst hit of all was Maureen, whose twenty-one-year-old son, Seamus, had been shot down in the street the previous year as a punishment for deserting from the 'Stickies' – the official IRA – which would probably not have happened if, as she'd begged him, he'd joined the Provos, who did not expect the same level of commitment. Now, though Maureen was as fanatical as Mairead in her determination to drive the Brits out, she hated the IRA and described them as a bunch of butchers. Sooner or later, if she didn't curb her tongue, she was likely to be picked up by the very people she was criticizing, then tied to a lamppost and tarred and feathered, irrespective of her husband's position in the organization. Rough justice was common here and these women, though secretly suffering, had razor-sharp tongues.

'So how's my wee convent girl from Andersonstown?' Maureen asked, exhaling a cloud of smoke.

'Fine,' Mairead replied, sipping her vodka and beer.

'Sure, if I felt half as bad as you look I'd be six feet under. You still have trouble sleepin'?'

'Ackaye. I wake up in the middle of the night and sleep half the day. I need some of them Valium.'

'You were cut to the bone by all them years in prison,' Josie told her. 'Your heart's been scalded by that, sure it has, and it's racin' too quickly.'

'Where's Tom?' Aine asked.

'Out,' Mairead replied.

'We gathered that,' Maureen said. 'What we

want to know is where the wee lad is when he should be in your bed.'

'He just went out,' Mairead said. 'Sure, I didn't ask where he was goin'.'

'You didn't ask because you knew,' Maureen insisted. 'Sure, we understand that. We know why you don't feel good.'

This was true. In fact, Maureen probably knew more about what Tom was doing than Mairead did. She was the wife of Patrick Tyrone and knew as much about local goings-on as anyone else in West Belfast. This was virtually confirmed when she reached across the table to pat the back of Mairead's hand, and said: 'You don't have to bother yourself, love. Sure, Tom will be right as rain. He's done jobs like this one a lot of times.'

'It doesn't matter how often you've done it. Sooner or later your number will come up and either the bastards will get you or you'll be in the soft clay. God, Maureen, I worry.'

'Sure, we all worry, girl, but that's part of the life these days. You probably worry a lot more than most because of your ten years behind bars. You paid a high price for your convictions and now your nerves are on edge. Sure, I've seen it so many times – in the men as well as in the women – and it makes my wee heart bleed. But what can you do? You live with it, that's all.'

'I'm not sure I can live with it. I've been

approached – yes, by your Pat among others – to start doin' things here an' there, but I can't work up the courage. I still back the cause – God knows, I love my country – but I have this feelin' I won't survive if I involve myself all over again. I see prison a second time around – or a premature grave – and I don't want either, thanks.'

'You're one of the best, Mairead. You know you'd be looked after.'

'Sure, bein' looked after's no help when the slightest wee thing goes wrong. You're there and somethin' goes amiss and then the Brits are all over you. After that, it's either another ten years in jail or a copper-lined coffin. That thought keeps me awake at night.'

'An' makes you sleep durin' the day,' Josie said.

'Aye, that's right.' Mairead raised her glass, waving it to and fro mockingly. 'And makes me drink this as well. Sure, I'm floatin' on clouds these days.'

'You'll survive,' Maureen told her.

'It's Tom I'm worried about. Ever since prison, I haven't seen my parents and I only step out of the house to come in here and forget myself. Tom's all I've got. Sure, he's blood and bone to me. When he's with me, when he's lyin' there beside me, I can forget all the rest of it. Only then. Only with him.'

'Sure, that's nice,' the romantically inclined Aine said.

'Ackaye, it's nice,' Mairead agreed. 'It's just that when he's not actually there, I'm hardly there myself. And when he's been called, when he's out on a job, don't I just fall to pieces?'

'That's natural.'

'No, it's not. It's not natural to think about death every time your man's away doing his bit of business.'

'It's the business he's in,' Josie told her.

'And the convent,' Maureen added. 'Sure, you were brought up in a convent, your head filled with thoughts of life an' death, God an' the devil, this life and the hereafter, so you always think about extremes and the worst that can happen. Ach, Mairead, you're a basket case.'

They all laughed, including Mairead, though she saw her life unravelling behind her in its simplicity and horror: a happy childhood, early years in the convent school, piety instead of true living, seduction through politics, outrage at the Prods and Brits in Northern Ireland, active involvement in the IRA, the bombing of that Protestant hotel in Belfast; then the ten most precious years of her life wasted in prison and, finally, release and being introduced to Tom by some IRA comrades. Tom was gentle with her. He was also an IRA assassin. He had killed many people in the past, some of them highly placed, and was willing to do so again. Nevertheless, he loved her and she had come to love him.

Mairead's love for Tom sprang out of her fear and was deepened by her knowledge of their shared commitment to the cause. They now had that and each other.

'Let's drink up and get four more,' Maureen said. 'Sure, let's all get tight.'

'I'll second that,' Mairead said.

She was just about to reach for her glass when she saw it tremble a little, the drink slopping slightly from side to side. Even as she noticed this, she felt the slight shaking of the floor beneath her, then heard the muffled blast of a distant, obviously large explosion.

Instantly nervous, she looked at her watch, then said: 'That's him. It's Tom. That must be his bomb.'

'That should give the Prods and the Brits somethin' to think about,' Maureen said, reaching over to squeeze Mairead's hand. 'And give us somethin' to celebrate at the same time. Come on, love, drink up and let me buy you another. Let's make a real day of it.'

'Ackaye,' Mairead said, finishing off her drink and handing the glass to Maureen. 'Sure, that's a grand idea.'

While Maureen was at the bar fetching four more drinks, Mairead chatted with Josie and Aine, glancing around the packed room as she did so. Through the haze of cigarette smoke she could see that some of the other customers were staring surreptitiously at her – some with frank admiration because of her long-haired, pale-faced beauty; others with curiosity and, perhaps, a touch of fear because they knew that she had spent ten years in prison for bombing a Prod hotel. The combination of notoriety and beauty would always make her a marked woman in this tight and paranoid community. Mairead should have been used to it by now, but it still made her uncomfortable.

An exuberant Maureen came reeling back out of the crowd, precariously balancing between her hands four more pints of beer topped up with vodka, splashing some on the floor and giggling hysterically. She was just placing the glasses on the table when the man guarding the door opened it and Patrick Tyrone walked in.

As Tyrone made his way urgently through the people standing up and packed tightly together in the middle of the floor, emerging ghostlike from the swirling cigarette smoke, Mairead noticed that he was not staring at his wife, Maureen, but directly at her. She then realized, with a swooping feeling of horror, that he was looking distraught.

Just about to reach out for her drink, Mairead jerked away without thinking and placed a hand on each side of her face, as if seeking protection. When Tyrone bent down slightly to place his hands consolingly on her shoulders, she heard what seemed to be a roaring inside her head. It was in fact the beating of her heart and the rushing of blood to her head. The pain came before Tyrone spoke, before the words destroyed all hope, and when finally he spoke – 'I'm so sorry, Mairead, but Tom . . .' – she burst into tears.

'Something went wrong,' Tyrone explained. 'We don't know exactly what. We only know Tom didn't manage to get away before his bomb went off. When the building went up, Tom was still inside it. I'm sorry, Mairead. He's dead.'

Mairead broke down completely, sobbing and shaking, and had to be helped out of the pub and back to her lonely house. Though her heart was still beating, though she was still alive physically, in a very real sense she died that night.

When eventually she emerged to the light of day, she was ready for anything.

5

The four-man SAS surveillance team had been in their covert OP a long time and were beginning to hate their own stench. They were in a loft that overlooked the fortified pub used constantly by hard-line members of the IRA and their Provisional IRA groups, as well as uninvolved locals, and had been there for five days, keeping watch on the movements of Patrick Tyrone and the female terrorist they knew only as Mairead. Now, in the early evening of the fifth day, they were beginning to wonder just how long they would have to stay there.

'That woman hasn't done a damn thing since getting out of prison last year,' Sergeant Bill Carruthers whispered as he studied the fortified entrance to the bar across the road through his black-painted military binoculars, 'so I don't know what those bastards in Intelligence are expecting.'

'They think that sooner or later she'll go back to her old game of bombing hotels,' Sergeant Roy Ainsworth replied. 'Particularly since she's fallen into bed with Tom Riley. We all know he's been responsible for some of the biggest IRA assassinations of recent years. She's also heavily influenced by Tyrone, and he's good at the soft push. If he pushes her gently enough in the right direction, she'll eventually make a move. When she does, she'll be dangerous.'

'My bet's on that Riley,' Corporal Mark Dymock said. Trained at the Hereford and Royal Signals establishments at Catterick and Blandford, he was fiddling with his Landmaster III hand-held transceiver. 'I've been listening to those two all week and they're a pretty hot item. So if Riley asks her to go back to work, I reckon she'll do what he says.'

'Hear, hear,' Corporal Ralph Billings said.

The four men had moved into the loft of a house occupied by a tout, Mick O'Mara, under cover of a British Army cordon-and-search sweep of the lower Falls Road, with particular emphasis on this particular street because it harboured not only the pub opposite, but also the Tyrones' house, located further along. The dawn sweep had been conducted just like the real thing, with hundreds of troops being brought into the area in Saracen armoured cars, armoured troop carriers and RUC paddy-wagons. After rumbling ominously past police stations and army barricades along the Falls Road in the early-morning darkness, the vehicles had divided into three separate columns that swept into three parallel side-streets to begin the search. Within minutes the area was surrounded and the streets were blocked off.

Pouring out of the various vehicles, some two hundred troops in DPM clothing, body armour and helmets, armed with a variety of weapons, made a great show of searching every house, after throwing their occupants temporarily out into the street and frisking the men on the pavements, in full view of their wives and kids and, in most cases, while being attacked by excited children and dickers throwing stones, bottles and other debris.

During this noisy confusion a team of Parachute Regiment troops had entered one of the houses under the pretence of searching it, but instead they had gone ahead of the SAS men up a stepladder and then 'mouseholed' along the single loft space of the terrace to O'Mara's loft, where they had deposited most of the heavier surveillance equipment. When they had come back down the ladder and were making a great show of violently searching the house – sweeping bric-à-brac off cupboards and shelves, emptying the contents of drawers on to the floor – the four-man SAS team, carrying their personal weapons and kit, were able to clamber up the ladder and crawl along to the same loft. Even as the trapdoor was being tugged shut by one of the paratroopers, the SAS men were setting up their surveillance and survival equipment. By the time the mock cordon-and-search sweep was over, they had settled in.

It had been a grim five days, but they had been rigorously trained for this kind of surveillance. Included in their personal kit were ten days' high-calorie rations, mostly chocolate and sweets because they could not use their hexamine stoves or otherwise cook or heat anything in the loft. In pouches on their belts they carried spare underwear and the usual first-aid kit; also, on the belt itself, a torch and binoculars. They carried as well extra ammunition for the only weapons they were allowed in the OP: their standard-issue 9mm Browning High Power handgun and the short 9mm Sterling MK5 sub-machine-gun with retractable butt and thirty-four-round magazine. The rest of their equipment, which had been brought in before their arrival by the paratroopers, consisted of water in plastic bottles; spare radio batteries; medical packs; extra ammunition; 35mm SLR cameras and film; tape-recorders; thermal imagers and night-vision telescopes; an advanced laser audio-surveillance transceiver; ball-points and plastic-backed notebooks; sleeping bags; packs of moisturized cloths for cleaning their faces and hands; towels; toilet paper; and sealable plastic bags for their excrement and urine.

For the past five days they had been spying on the fortified entrance to the pub through a peep-hole created by removing a slate nail in the roof and replacing it with a rubber band that allowed the slate to be raised and lowered to accommodate the naked eye, binoculars, cameras or the thermal imager. Their visual surveillance was complemented by miniature fibre-optic probes that had been placed at four o'clock in the morning in narrow holes drilled in three of the walls of the pub, both sides and rear, to pick up as much of the conversation as possible. This wasn't all that much because, although the laser system was highly advanced, the conversation of individuals was usually drowned by the general babble of the drinkers.

Nevertheless, with the aid of the hand-held thermal imager weighing only 11lb, the fibre-optic probe inserted in the wall of the pub and transmitting aural data back to the laser system in the loft, and the many photos taken with a 35mm Nikon F3HP camera, fitted with a Davies Minimodulux image intensifier, of everyone entering or leaving the pub by night or by day, they were gradually building up a comprehensive picture of the kind of activity and conversation taking place there.

From this, and from other pieces of moderately valuable information, they were able to glean the knowledge that the female IRA bomber went to the pub every afternoon and usually stayed until about six o'clock, which was, for local people, just before dinner-time.

'As regular as clockwork,' Corporal Dymock observed. 'She must like to feed her face.'

'Fried fish and spuds,' Corporal Billings replied. 'It'll be a Good Friday diet every day of the week.'

'She looks good on it,' Dymock said.

'A luscious piece,' Billings agreed.

'You could spot her a mile away with that long hair,' Sergeant Ainsworth added. 'It's really quite striking.'

'She doesn't look like she could hurt a fly,' Billings said. 'I mean, I can't imagine her bombing a bloody hotel or anything else.'

'Well, she did,' Sergeant Carruthers told him, 'and she might do so again. So shut your traps and pay attention to your work. We want to hear what she says in there.'

Though none of the recorded conversations between Mairead and her friends, usually women, revealed anything of much interest, the soldiers learnt from the banter between her and Maureen Tyrone that the former's boyfriend was planning a bombing for the near future. What they had not been able to ascertain was the exact nature and location of the target, as these had never been mentioned during the daily get-togethers between Mairead and her friends.

'You can tell from the conversations that those women know when their men are on a job,' Carruthers said, 'but I don't think they're given any details. Either that or they simply make a point of never discussing precise details with each other – certainly not in the pub. That bastard Riley's planning something, but that's about all we know. Keep listening. Keep watching. Maybe, when the pieces come together, we'll be able to suss what he's planning before he actually pulls it off.'

Apart from that glimmer of information about a possible bombing in the near future, the men in the loft could do little but endure days of dreadful discomfort and a tedium so absolute that it could only be broken by the less than exciting revelations of their visual and audio surveillance.

One day in the tiny loft was enough to make all of them feel grubby, exhausted and claustrophobic. Also, though it was freezing cold, the need to be quiet and not let O'Mara's neighbours suspect their presence had forced them to take off their boots and wear only extra layers of socks – as, indeed, they were doing with their underclothes. Nutritionally, the situation was even worse. As no food could be cooked, they were forced to subsist on dry high-calorie rations, such as biscuits, cheese, chocolate and sweets. Although they had a couple of vacuum flasks of hot tea and coffee, they had to limit themselves to one hot drink a day and, for the rest of the time, tepid water from the plastic water bottles.

As there was nowhere to wash, they could only clean themselves with moisturized cloths and freshen their teeth as best they could with chewing gum. Even worse, as the loft was not divided from the other lofts in the terrace, the corresponding space in the adjoining house had to be used as a toilet. For this purpose the men used plastic bags, which they had to seal and store carefully after use. Since they had to do this in full view of one another, they found this aspect of the OP particularly humiliating.

'We should at least be able to shit in private,' Dymock complained. 'If I'd known I'd have to do it in front of you lot, I'd never have volunteered.'

'As I recall,' Carruthers reminded him, 'you only volunteered by not refusing when I submitted your name for the detail – so don't come it with me, son.'

'You've always been so kind to me, Sarge,' said the corporal. 'Now please let me shit in peace.'

Even during the night they found no respite from the discomforts of the day. Given the lack of space, let alone floorboards – they made their way about the place by hopping from one joist to the other – they could only sleep sitting upright, against the brick walls, with a blanket wrapped around them for warmth and a cushion under the backside. They rested two at a time, one sleeping, the other just relaxing, though the second was compelled to keep a constant eye on the first in case he talked or cried out in his sleep, alerting the neighbours on either side.

'I think we should put a clothes peg on Ralph's nose,' Dymock said of his fellow-corporal, 'to stop him from snoring.'

'I don't snore,' Billings shot back.

'You snore like an elephant bellowing,' Dymock insisted, 'and it could get us all killed. That's why I have to keep waking you to prevent us from being discovered and getting our balls shot off.'

'Obviously that's why I'm so exhausted,' Billings said. 'I never get any sleep.'

Temporary escape from the claustrophobia of the loft came through communication via the hand-held transceiver, operating in the VHF/UHF frequency range, or through the UHG band on their portable radio. The men were able to do this when manning the surveillance equipment because they were equipped with Davies M135b covert microphones with standard safety-pin attachment and ear-worn receivers, positioned on the collar of the jacket, with the on-off switch taped to the wrist. One of these was tuned in to the military command network at Lisburn; the other to the surveillance network, including two Quick Reaction Force units located in two separate RUC stations nearby and prepared to rescue them should their presence in the loft be discovered by the neighbours and the information passed on to the IRA.

'If I'm hearing right,' Carruthers said, removing his receiver to scratch his ear, 'Mad Dan's had a few meetings with Tyrone over in that pub.'

'Who's Mad Dan?' Ainsworth asked him.

'He's the bastard who's widely believed to have shot Detective Sergeants Michael Malone and Ernest Carson in the Liverpool Bar on Donegall Quay. He keeps popping in there to see Tyrone. Unfortunately, like the women, they never discuss anything too specific, though both of them keep making veiled references to some job coming up.'

'Maybe they're talking about the planned bombing by Riley.'

'No. They're talking about using some other man – and they've also mentioned Mairead once or twice. I think they have plans for her.'

'With a woman who looks like that, I don't blame them.'

'No, dickhead. I mean real plans. IRA work.'

'Then let's keep listening and watching,' Ainsworth said, 'and maybe, given time, they'll have a slip of the tongue and give something away.'

'That sounds very wise, Sarge,' Billings said, 'but just how long do you think we can stay up here? We're already very low on water and our food's running out. Not to mention the fact that

we're beginning to stink the place out. We can't
stay here for ever.'

'A couple more days,' Carruthers said, 'then
we'll request that they pull us out.'

'Two more days and I'll be stark, raving mad,'
Dymock said.

'So, what's new?' Billings said. 'In fact . . .'

He cut his remark short when he and the
others heard the distinct sound of an explosion
not too far away. All of them jerked their heads
around and looked automatically at the peep-
hole, though they couldn't see anything from
where they sat.

As the echo of the explosion died away,
Carruthers exclaimed softly: 'That was a bomb!'
Then he hurried across to the peep-hole and
looked out to see a column of smoke spiralling
over the centre of Belfast, its base tinged with the
red and yellow glow of flickering flames. 'Looks
like someone's bombed a building in the centre
of town,' he said. 'In the Protestant area. That
makes it a Catholic bomb.'

He scanned the area for some time with his
black-painted military binoculars and was just
about to put them down again, thinking he
wouldn't see much more, when the front door
of a house further along the street opened and
Tyrone emerged, hurried along the pavement and
went into the pub. He was, Carruthers noticed,
unusually tense.

'Tyrone's just dashed into the pub,' the sergeant told the rest of the men, 'and he looks pretty upset. Listen carefully, Dymock.'

Unfortunately, Dymock could only hear the general babble of those inside – not specific conversation. He was informing Carruthers of this fact when the pub door opened and Mairead emerged, sobbing profoundly and being supported on either side by the Tyrones. They helped the distraught woman along the street, passing their own house and finally disappearing from view.

'Obviously Tyrone went into that pub to give some news to Mairead,' Carruthers said. 'And whatever it was, it was bad enough to reduce her to tears. I think they're taking her home now. Dymock, get on that Landmaster, contact HQ and find out what's happening.'

Dymock did so, listened intently to what he was being told, then turned the transceiver off and said: 'Wouldn't you know it? That stupid bastard Riley's been found dead in the ruins of the hotel he's just blown up. They think he mistimed it and the bomb went off before he could leave the building. So the dumb fuck blew himself up along with the hotel. That's why Mairead's crying.'

'Jesus Christ!' Carruthers hissed, then stared through the peep-hole at the pub across the road. 'That should certainly change things down there – and not for the better.'

'That's what Captain Edwards thinks,' Dymock informed him, referring to their young CO, presently located at HQ Lisburn. 'In fact, he told me to tell you that we're going to be pulled out of here immediately and have to pack up and prepare to leave. We'll be taken out under cover of another mock cordon-and-search sweep, early tomorrow.'

'That means something really urgent has come up,' Carruthers replied, turning away from the peep-hole and staring at each of the other three men in turn. 'OK, let's get to it.'

Delighted to be leaving the loft, the men started packing up their kit.

The mock cordon-and-search sweep took place the following morning, just before dawn, with the customary convoy of Saracens, armoured personnel carriers and RUC paddy-wagons pouring down the Falls Road with their headlights beaming into the morning darkness. Once they had cordoned off three parallel streets, so concealing the fact that they were really only interested in one of them, British Army, including Parachute Regiment, troops poured out noisily on to the streets. Wearing DPM clothing and helmets, but bulked out even more with ArmourShield General Purpose Vests, including ceramic contoured plates, fragmentation vests, and groin panels, they looked like invaders from outer space. They

were armed with sledgehammers, SA-8 assault
rifles, and Heckler & Koch MP5 sub-machine-
guns, the latter particularly effective for use in
confined spaces. The 'snatch' teams, there to take
prisoners, looked just as frightening in their full
riot gear, including shields and truncheons.

RUC officers trained at the SAS Counter Revolutionary Warfare Wing at Hereford, wearing
flak-jackets and carrying 5.56mm Ruger Mini-14
assault rifles, jumped out of the paddy-wagons
and surrounded their vehicles as the soldiers
and paras raced in opposite directions along
the street, hammering on doors with the butts
of their weapons and bawling for the inhabits
to come out.

At the same time, British Army snipers were
clambering on to the roofs from lightweight
aluminium assault ladders, to give cover with
Lee Enfield .303-inch sniper rifles. Wearing
earphones, they were warned of any likely trouble
spots either by officers down in the street or by
the Royal Marine Gazelle observation helicopter
that was hovering right above them, its spinning
rotors whipping up a fierce wind that blew the
rubbish in the gutters across the street.

As Carruthers glanced down through the peep-
hole he saw the soldiers roughly pushing angry
women and dazed children aside to grab their
menfolk and haul them out on to the pavement.
Other soldiers were forcing their way into the

houses to begin what would almost certainly be damaging searches of the properties. When front doors were not opened immediately on request, the soldiers with the sledgehammers smashed them open. As the male residents of the street, many still in their pyjamas, were pushed face first against the front wall of their own houses and made to spread their arms and legs for rough frisking, the women screamed abuse, the children either did the same or burst into tears, and the dickers farther along the street hurled stones, lumps of concrete, bottles and verbal abuse. Meanwhile, a line of soldiers formed a cordon of riot shields across both ends of the street, to prevent any further advance against the troops engaged in the searches.

'Right,' Carruthers said to the other SAS men. 'The street's been cordoned off and the paratroopers are on their way to give us cover. Pick up your gear and get ready to move out. Lift that trapdoor, Billings.'

The corporal was lifting the plywood trapdoor just as the first of the paras burst into the downstairs living-room, being none too gentle with the furnishings. O'Mara made a great show of protesting noisily for the benefit of any neighbours who might be watching from outside or listening through the walls.

Once the paras were inside, Billings lowered himself down through the hole and dropped on to the landing. Dymock then passed the personal kit, weapons and surveillance equipment down to him. By the time everything had been stacked on the landing around Billings, Dymock was dropping down beside him and the paras were rushing up the stairs, hammering on the walls with the butts of their Sterling sub-machine-guns to convince the people next door that their neighbour was just another victim of British brutality.

'Let's move it!' the para sergeant bawled as Carruthers and Ainsworth dropped on to the landing.

'We're all set,' Carruthers said.

Surrounded by the bulky paras, some of whom had divided the boxes of surveillance equipment between them, the SAS troopers picked up their kit and personal weapons, then let themselves be led down the stairs and out through the living-room, where the nervous O'Mara was staring at them wide-eyed, then out into the noisy street.

They barely had time to take in the two cordons of British soldiers blocking off the street before they were raced across the road, still surrounded and shielded by the well-armed paras. As they ran towards the Saracen armoured car that would take them away, armoured personnel carriers screeched to a halt and disgorged riot-control troops. Menacing in their flak-jackets, Perspex-visored helmets and reinforced leg and arm pads, they charged the crowds of men, women, teenagers and children, holding large shields up high and wildly swinging their truncheons as bottles, stones and other debris rained down on and all around them. Reaching the far side of the road, the SAS men were bundled up into the Saracen, their equipment was passed in after them, then the armoured car, with a personnel carrier front and rear, rumbled off along the street. With the Gazelle circling above, the Saracen passed through a pathway formed in the cordon of soldiers, turned into the Falls Road, then headed back for Bessbrook camp, away from the riot caused by the bogus search operation. Soon the noise of the riot was far behind them, to be replaced by the moaning of the wind over the broad, dark fields of Antrim.

Back at Bessbrook, the four men were informed that they were being returned to Hereford, for special retraining in the 'Killing House' in preparation for a forthcoming, as yet unidentified, mission.

6

Sean and Mad Dan both felt mildly uncomfortable at Málaga airport because neither had travelled outside the British Isles before, neither was used to even the relative warmth of early November in southern Spain, and neither spoke a word of Spanish. Also, they were still wearing their heavy, drab Belfast clothing – grey suit, shirt and tie, black shoes – and had felt out of place in the luggage collection area, surrounded by brightly clothed and suntanned British expatriates, most returning to Spain after holidays in Britain.

'Sure, what a bunch of ponces they were,' Mad Dan said to cover his discomfort as Sean drove them in the rented car along the N340. 'All suntanned an' wearin' their lovey-dovey rags even in November.'

'It's still warm here,' Sean replied. 'And a couple of weeks back, when those expats were just flying out to Britain for their hols, it was probably as hot as hell. So their suntans are genuine.'

'Watch that road,' Mad Dan warned him. 'Sure, these Spanish drivers are madmen. An' you're drivin' on the wrong side of the road, so you'd best be doubly careful, boyo.'

'That I will,' Sean promised. He was in fact feeling a little nervous because he had never driven on the right before and was also confused by the forest of international road signs. Startled by the sheer blueness of the sky, catching glimpses of a luminous green-blue sea between the low hills and white Moorish-style villas to his left, he was already realizing just how dreary Belfast was compared with this Mediterranean coastline. The sky, in particular, seemed so high . . . so immense that he felt disorientated. At the same time he was excited to be there, but tried to contain that, not wanting to forget just *why* he was.

'According to that girl in the car-hire office,' he said, 'Torremolinos is only about ten minutes from the airport.'

'Spoke bloody good English for a Spaniard,' Mad Dan said. 'An' had a nice set of water-wings, too.'

Offended and embarrassed by Mad Dan's remark, Sean felt himself blushing and tried to concentrate on the road, which had two lanes each way and too much traffic for comfort. He saw a sign reassuringly indicating 'Torremolinos', and said: 'It's supposed to be a small place, so we'll have one night there and then move on.'

'Sure, boyo. No problem.'

'It doesn't take long to get from Málaga to Gibraltar – a couple of hours at most, I think – so we'll probably spend the rest of our time here driving back and forth, checking and then double-checking to make sure we don't miss anything.'

'Sure, that's fine by me as well. We could have a quare good time here, boyo, even while we're workin', like. I think it's that kind of place.'

'As long as we remember that we're here to work, ' Sean said, rather primly.

'Ackaye, boyo, no sweat.'

Within minutes, before he'd had time to gain confidence in driving on the right-hand side of the road, Sean had taken a wrong turning and found himself swept along in the traffic around a bypass that brought him back to the N340 and a series of signs indicating Benalmádena-Costa, Fuengirola, Marbella, Estepona, Algeciras and Cádiz.

'Sure, where the hell are we?' Mad Dan asked, glancing anxiously from the map spread out on his lap to the sea glittering beyond the white houses on his left, and those raised on the parched hills to his right, many with swimming pools, and the mountains soaring up in a blue heat haze beyond the scattered buildings.

'It's all right,' Sean replied, trying to sound more confident than he felt. 'We've just bypassed Torremolinos by mistake, so we'll leave it until the end of the week and check it out on the way back to the airport. The next stop is Fuengi . . .'

Sean couldn't pronounce the word, so Mad Dan checked the map and said: 'Fooengirola. About another fifteen kilometres along this road, so we should be there in no time.' He raised his eyes from the map and glanced with growing enthusiasm at the sunlight beaming down over the road and the cars racing along it with apparent disregard for personal safety. As Mad Dan had little regard for his own safety, this didn't bother him much. 'Sure, isn't this some road?' he asked rhetorically.

'There's an awful lot of accidents on it, so I'm told. They even call it the Road of Death.'

'Sure, given what we're here for,' Mad Dan replied, 'that's a guare good nickname! The Road of Death!'

Finding his partner more distasteful with every passing minute, Sean concentrated even more on the busy road and was glad to see the sign for Fuengirola looming up. Now getting used to driving on the 'wrong' side of the road, he took the marked slip-road and soon found himself sweeping around towards the town, in the shadow of a mountain bleached by the sun, dotted with more white villas and bright-blue swimming pools and surmounted by what he knew from the map was the picturesque village of Mijas.

The confidence Sean had built up driving from the airport soon evaporated when he found himself in the chaotic tangle of traffic in the centre of Fuengirola, but he eventually managed to find a parking space in a relatively quiet side-street. The two men climbed out, removed their shoulder bags from the boot, and made their way into town, through the square and down to the waterfront, where they meandered along the broad seaside promenade until they came to a small hotel set back behind gardens and palm trees. Entering, they were relieved to find that the receptionist, a pretty young Spanish girl, spoke perfect English and was able to give them a single room each. Once in their rooms, they showered, changed into more suitable clothing, then went out to investigate the town. They were both relieved to find that it was packed with English-speaking residents and that most of the Spaniards working in the bars and restaurants spoke it too.

Luckily, though the November weather was relatively mild compared with the British climate, the short Spanish winter was on the way and the temperature was low enough for them to be able to wander about in a fairly relaxed way. As there were quite a few 'Irish' bars in the town, they had no trouble in striking up conversation with fellow-Irishmen and asking questions that seemed perfectly normal coming from new arrivals ostensibly on a package holiday.

From such casual conversations they soon picked up all they needed to know about potential targets for bombing, notably the hotels frequented by the British. Having ascertained the largest of these, which was located right on the Paseo Marítimo, or promenade, they wandered along to it, ordered drinks in the lounge bar, and used this as a pretext for a careful examination of the grand, seemingly always busy lobby. Sean drank only lemonade, while Mad Dan continued drinking San Miguel beer, as he had been doing all afternoon in the various Irish bars they had visited.

'Sure, the beer is really cheap here,' he said, by way of justifying his drinking. 'An' it's a quare good wee drop.'

'Just don't drink too much,' Sean advised him. 'We're both here to work.'

'Sure, I haven't forgot that, boyo. I'm taking in what I see here and sayin' this is the right spot. Biggest hotel in town, packed with people, even at this time of year, and dead easy to walk into, with no questions asked. Sure, we could get up from our chairs an' go up them stairs an' plant a bomb this minute without bein' stopped. It's all free an' easy here.'

'It's certainly a possibility,' Sean said. 'Particularly as there don't appear to be any other major targets in town.'

'Aye, that's right. There's only pubs, restaurants an' hotels, except maybe the beach. But now that summer's over, I don't recommend that, like. Not enough people.'

'I agree,' Sean said. 'This is the biggest hotel in town – not the best, but about the biggest, the most used – and we could just waltz in like we did just now and leave a bomb under this very table without it bein' noticed. Let's put it down on our list.'

'Ackaye, let's do that. Now what about dinner? I don't want any of that Spanish shite, so let's find a Brit-run place where we can read the menu.'

'Right,' Sean said.

Ignoring the many excellent Spanish restaurants along the Paseo Marítimo and the streets just off it, they had their dinner in an English-run pub most notable for the tattiness of its furnishings and the simplicity of the menu. Ordering the kind of food they were both used to – fish and chips – with another lemonade for Sean and more San Miguels for Mad Dan, they filled their bellies, then wandered idly back along the promenade towards their own little hotel. But before they reached it, Mad Dan, now the worse for wear from his long day's drinking and constantly eyeing up the sensually dressed young Spanish señoritas, insisted on going for another drink or two.

'Sure, these Spanish skirts go to the English bars,' he said, 'and spend most of the night there. We're bound to pick up somethin' an' have somethin' better to do than just sleepin' it off, like.'

'No, thanks,' Sean said. 'I'm tired and I want to go to bed. Besides, it's not our own money we're spendin', so let's be careful.'

'Bollocks, boyo. That's just shite for an' excuse. Sure, yer just a puritanical wee bugger who's frightened of the wimmen. Now, come on, let's go drinkin'.'

'I'm goin' back to take notes on this place an' then have a good sleep.'

'Sure, you do that. I'm off.'

Back at the hotel, Sean conscientiously made notes on the location and interior of the hotel picked as the most likely bombing target in Fuengirola. He also noted the fact that the town itself was family orientated, rather than singles on the loose and couples out for a good time, which would make it a more suitable target for their purposes. As for the hotel, he noted with equal diligence, it was used mostly by English-speaking residents, and, having practically no security arrangements, was easy to enter. Planting a bomb, either in the large, busy lobby bar or in a toilet upstairs, would present few problems. Few other targets in town would be so easy, but then, in propaganda terms, few would be so valuable.

Having completed his notes on Fuengirola in general and the one hotel in particular, Sean undressed and, just before going to bed, went to the window to stare across the promenade to the sea. After the claustrophobic streets of Belfast, it looked incredibly spacious, even exotic, to him. Wondering where Mad Dan was and what he was up to, and worried about his drinking and general propensity for trouble, Sean went to bed and fell into a troubled sleep.

The following morning, over breakfast in the small dining-room of their modest hotel, Sean was compelled to listen to Mad Dan's boastful talk about how he had picked up a 'bit of Spanish skirt' in one of the English pubs, gone on a lengthy pub crawl with her, and ended up in her bed. Judging by Mad Dan's appearance, it was clear to Sean that he had done nothing other than drink until the early hours, but deciding that discretion was the better part of valour, he did not voice his thoughts.

They booked out of the hotel shortly afterwards and took to the Road of Death again, heading for Marbella. The sun was already high over the Mediterranean, laying its light on the water, and Sean, a romantic in all things, even killing with reluctance, felt that he had almost found heaven and was saddened at the evil necessity of causing destruction in it.

'Beautiful,' he whispered as he drove.

'Sure, you're right there, boyo,' Mad Dan replied. 'You should've tried a bit. These Spanish tarts are as hot as green peppers. Sure I had me a grand time.'

'I was talkin' about the scenery,' Sean told him.

Mad Dan snorted with contempt, though he glanced left and right, first at the glittering Mediterranean spread out to their left, below the highway, then at the soaring slopes of the Sierra de Mijas and the clusters of white dwellings scattered about them. Though the light was dim by Mediterranean standards, it was still strong enough to affect Mad Dan's eyes, more used to the grey light of Northern Ireland and now reddened by drink.

'Sure, I always thought sunglasses were pretentious,' he said, 'but now I see the need for them. This is a quare strong light, boyo.'

'You shouldn't drink so much,' Sean said.

'Hark the herald angels sing. Sure, if that's as good as yer feelin' right now, you're not goin' to feel better later. That's what not drinkin' does for you.'

'We're here on a job,' Sean insisted.

'Aye, boyo, I know that. Just because I went out an' had me a good time, doesn't mean I've forgotten what we're here for. Sure, you should be in the Salvation Army – or in a Prod church – you're so damned puritanical, like.'

'All right, let's forget it.'

Quietly furious that he had to work with a man like Mad Dan, but accepting that his colleague had a well-earned reputation as a shoot-to-kill man, Sean drove on along the highway that skirted the sunlit coastline until they arrived at Marbella, which looked particularly sophisticated to his unworldly gaze. Finding a parking space was particularly difficult, forcing them to crawl uphill through the old part of town, through narrow streets filled with white houses, black-shawled women, noisy children, various delivery vans and other cars, then back to the bustling centre of town again, and finally out of town on the same highway, heading towards Nueva Andalucía. Frustrated, Sean used a slip-road to turn around and drive into town, this time managing to find a cramped parking place where he and Mad Dan were able to pay a gypsy parking attendant and then find a hotel that had its own car park.

After booking in, which was conducted in a mixture of broken English and their own minuscule Spanish, both feeling hot and frustrated, they returned to the parked car. They had trouble getting it out of its parking space and then got lost trying to drive back to the hotel, but eventually managed to do so.

They had breakfasted in Fuengirola at eight that morning, but it was now almost one in the afternoon, and Mad Dan said: 'Lunchtime, bejasus. An' I'm dyin' of thirst, like.'

With a sinking heart, Sean agreed to join Mad Dan for a drink in the hotel's bar. Mad Dan finished his San Miguel even before Sean had finished his Coke; but when he discovered that the beer cost almost twice as much as it had in the beach bars and pubs of Fuengirola, he insisted on having lunch elsewhere. Intimidated by the quiet elegance of the hotel, Sean was only too willing to agree, but had the sense to check his guidebook for the most popular area of Marbella.

'The Plaza de los Naranjos,' he said, hoping he was pronouncing it correctly, though realizing that Mad Dan wouldn't know if he wasn't.'

'What's that?'

'The Plaza of the Orange Trees. It's right in the centre of town, just round the corner from here. Sure, that's where most people go, so we'll check it out first.'

'Ackaye, let's do that.'

Sean felt overwhelmed by the sophistication of Marbella almost as soon as he stepped out of his hotel. Making his way to the Plaza de los Naranjos, he was struck by the elegance of the narrow, twisting streets leading off in all directions and by the many traditional shops and restaurants they passed, most of which he would have been nervous of entering, particularly with Mad Dan by his side. In the event, arriving at the square itself, he saw that it was encircled by flower-covered balconies, that the pretty white buildings had elegantly tiled, green-shrubbed patios of the most picturesque kind, and that elegantly dressed people were drinking and eating at tables out in the open, under trees laden with oranges.

'Sure, this is the place, all right, boyo,' Mad Dan said with relish. 'You set something off here and you'd blow the whole place away. Let's sit down and check it out.'

Mortified at the very idea of sitting at a table in close proximity to those suntanned, sophisticated men and women, Sean was just about to protest when Mad Dan, seeing a nearby vacant table, hurried up to it and planted himself in a chair. Seeing that it was too late to do otherwise, Sean did the same, taking the chair facing his despised companion.

'This is the life, boyo,' Mad Dan said, glancing sideways at a young lady wearing a skin-tight T-shirt, a skirt so small it looked like a pair of hot plants, and stiletto-heeled shoes. 'Now isn't that a sight for sore eyes? Sure, a man could die happy here.'

When the waiter came, Mad Dan, after an

initial communication problem exacerbated by his marked accent, ordered a beer for himself and a Coke for Sean. When the drinks came, they both slaked their thirst, Sean drinking about a quarter of his Coke and Mad Dan polishing off his beer in one long, thirsty gulp. Wiping his lips with the back of his hand, he called the waiter over and ordered another.

'A good start to the day,' he said, then glanced around the picturesque, sunlit square and added: 'Ackaye. A few pounds of Semtex and sure you'd raze this effin' place to the ground and wipe away all these Brits – them and their suntans.'

'They're not all Brits,' Sean pointed out.

'They're not working-class Irish, that's for sure, so this place would do fine.'

'Where do we leave the device?' Sean asked.

'What?' Mad Dan was obviously distracted by the suntanned legs at the next table.

'It's too open here for the leavin' of anything under a table, so where do we leave the device?'

Temporarily removing his eyes from the young woman in hot pants, Mad Dan nodded towards the restaurant that owned the outside table. 'In there. Sure these dumb effin' Spaniards wouldn't suspect a thing. You just place the device in a briefcase, take a table out here an' order a real big meal, then ask the waiter if he'd mind keepin' yer briefcase behind the bar until you've finished yer meal. Set the timer to ignite the explosive about twenty minutes later, when yer supposed to be halfway through your magnificent repast, like. Then, instead of finishin' the meal, you wait till the waiter's inside the restaurant collectin' more food, and you leave the table an' hurry away before anyone notices. When the waiter returns and sees you gone, knowin' your briefcase is behind the bar, he'll assume that you haven't gone far an' will soon be returnin'. Before the dumb bastard realizes it isn't so – like, say, five minutes from when you've pissed off – the bomb will explode. By which time you're back in yer car and harin' out of this place. Sure, it'd work a treat, wouldn't it?'

Sean sighed. 'Maybe . . . maybe not. I still think it's too problematical an' should be avoided.'

Mad Dan winked at the young woman with the long legs and received a frosty stare in return. Unperturbed, he accepted the fresh beer brought by the waiter, waited until he had departed, then took a sip and picked up the guidebook, where he had left it, opened face down, on the table. 'Sure, what about this here Marbella Club? That's filled with rich and perfumed gits who could do with a scorchin'.'

'That's the whole problem,' Sean told him, fighting hard to stay patient. 'They *are* mostly rich and perfumed – the international jet set. The club's owned by a European nobleman and not particularly British. What good would it do to blow up a club used by a bunch of rich internationals? Sure, it'd do us nothing but harm. Besides, they probably wouldn't even let us through the door.'

Mad Dan snorted at that. 'Aye, yer right there. They'd sneer at us down their long noses an' then call for the Spanish police. Right, boyo, I'll give you that. We need somethin' else.'

'Not this place,' Sean said. 'Not Marbella at all. It's too much an international jet-set place. Sure it has as many foreigners as Brits, which isn't what we're after. Given a choice between here and Fuengirola, I'd take the last any day. At least it's full of retired Brits – and they're the ones that we want.'

'Too right,' Mad Dan said.

'So let's strike Marbella off our list.'

'Aye, I agree. So what now?'

Sean looked at his watch. 'Lunch?'

'Ackaye. Sure, I thought you'd never ask. One of them late, long Spanish lunches, then a bit of a kip.'

'We'll have lunch, then a bit of a siesta, then go out and explore again. We might find something suitable.'

'Sure, I thought you said you didn't approve of this place at all.'

'I don't. But we're already booked into our hotel, so we might as well see as much as possible. Sure, you just never know.'

'Aye, right. What about eatin' here?'

'I don't like it,' Sean confessed. 'It's too fancy for me, like. Let's wander down to one of them beach bars where we can relax a lot more.'

'Aye, let's do that. That waiter's lookin' down his long nose at us and I might break it for 'im. So come on, let's pay up an' go.'

They headed for the beach and then wandered up and down it, bickering about where they should eat. In Marbella, even the beach bars looked a bit upmarket, but eventually they managed to settle on one, mainly on the grounds that it had a multilingual menu from which they could easily order. Sean washed his sardines, chips and salad down with Fanta orange, but Mad Dan, enthralled by the relatively low prices, began with a couple of whiskies, then had another four beers with his meal. Throughout, he talked, ever more drunkenly, about the hated Brits, the even worse Brits over here living off low taxes, the various possibilities they had seen so far for a truly outrageous bombing target, and the differences between him and Sean, whom he accepted as a loyal IRA comrade, but otherwise thought of as a Catholic plagued by Prod-style puritanism.

'Sure, a man who doesn't like his drink or sex has to be missin' somethin',' he explained to Sean. 'Ach, boyo, fer Christ's sake start livin'!'

But Sean didn't want to live. At least not that way. What he wanted was to complete this great

mission and find something worth bombing. He
tried explaining this to Mad Dan, placing their
task in its proper context – a necessary evil,
a wrong to make something right, random
but faultlessly planned destruction to redress
an historical injustice – but Mad Dan wasn't
listening. He was lost in the glittering sea, the
last few suntanned women on the cooling beach,
the beer and the thought of another evening in
more expat bars, even here in Marbella.

'Now why would I give a bugger if they're all
stuck-up ponces around here?' he asked Sean.
'Sure, they're no better than me when they sit
on the pot – and that bein' the common line,
boyo, I'll go and sit in their bars.'

'Yer goin' out tonight again?' Sean asked him,
unable to hide his anxiety.

'Sure, I am that. You've already said we can't
make plans for this toffee-nosed place, these bein'
international jet-setters, so what's the point in
wastin' the evening in pretendin' otherwise? We'll
move on farther along the coast tomorrow, but
in the meantime, let's make the most of the trip
and make a night of it. Come with me, boyo.'

'No, thanks,' Sean said firmly.

That evening Sean retired again to his hotel
room to write up his notes while Mad Dan
went out for a night on the Spanish tiles. He
recorded in his notes more or less what he
had told Mad Dan – that while Fuengirola

112

held possibilities, being dominated by Brits, Marbella was too international to be anything other than counterproductive. He then went to bed, read his guidebook on Spain, memorized a few more words and phrases of Spanish, then fell into a sleep in which the long legs that had so hypnotized Mad Dan mesmerized him too. He did not have a good sleep.

Mad Dan looked even worse the next morning, clearly having drunk away most of his normal sleeping hours, but insisted on boasting, over breakfast, of the great time he'd had with another ripe piece of local skirt. Desperate to avoid such conversations, which always unsettled him, and also very conscious that he had been sent here for a purpose, Sean finished his breakfast more quickly than was necessary and insisted that they get out on the road again before the traffic built up. Groaning, Mad Dan agreed.

Once back on the road in their rented car, Mad Dan, feeling the worse for drink and with his nerves on edge, twitched at every passing police car and eventually said to Sean: 'Do you think those bastards back at Málaga airport fell for our false passports?'

'Sure, how could we be drivin' all this time if they knew who we really were. If they'd sussed when we showed them the passports, they'd have sent us right back, like.'

'Ackaye, I'm sure you're right. I just wondered, you know, if maybe they had us on that list they sometimes check at passport control and, you know, had our pictures there.'

'No, I don't think so.'

'Aye, I suppose you're right, boyo. So where are we goin' now?'

'We'll be stayin' tonight in San Pedro, but first I want to check out Puerto Banus, which I was told contains a lot of boats, many of them British.'

'Sure, boats are bloody easy,' Mad Dan said, 'so we'd be right as rain there. Christ, my throat's like a rasp.'

Built along an Andalusian-style harbour village, Puerto Banus had berths for nearly a thousand boats and certainly had several hundred at anchor, ranging all the way from small motor launches to the magnificent craft of the extremely rich. The L-shaped walkway that ran around the port was lined with many boutiques and outdoor restaurants and bars, from where the customers, while sipping their chilled white wine or *vino tinto* could look on, as if at a cabaret, while bronzed deck-hands, mostly young men and women, tended to the boats or served the tables of the wealthy owners.

'Sure, isn't that a sight to make you want to bomb the place,' Mad Dan said in disgust as he sipped his ruinously expensive San Miguel at one of the outdoor tables. 'A bunch of filthy rich parasites!'

'We're not here to take revenge on the rich,' Sean quietly reminded him. 'Not unless they're British.'

'Sure there's plenty of rich Brit scum out there,' Mad Dan said with some venom. 'Let the others drown with them.'

'This place certainly has possibilities,' Sean acknowledged, though with some reluctance, 'so I'll put it down on our list. Now let's drive on to San Pedro.'

'What about lunch?' said the ever-thirsty Mad Dan.

'It's only five minutes by car to San Pedro,' Sean informed him impatiently, 'so it'll be too early for lunch when we get there.'

'I'm just thirsty,' Mad Dan explained without conviction.

Sean felt that he was quietly taking over Mad Dan, getting used to him, controlling him, and he exercised that control by ensuring that he could not have another lengthy, drunken lunch and instead took him back on the road for the drive to San Pedro Alcántara. There wasn't much to see there – the place was just too small, too unknown to make a big splash – so after a light lunch during which Sean let Mad Dan have one beer – they drove on for another fifteen kilometres to Estepona, arriving there still too early for lunch.

Once off the promenade, they found a more authentically Spanish town than Marbella, with *típico* bars, goatherds driving their herds through the narrow streets, and black-shawled older women sitting on hard-backed wooden chairs outside their front doors, chatting animatedly.

To the historically minded Sean it was incredibly romantic, the real, uncorrupted world; but it was not a suitable target for a bombing, since there weren't enough Brits – at least not enough to warrant a bombing outrage. This was still a Spanish town.

The next two days were spent driving repeatedly up and down the coast between Estepona and Algeciras, just across the bay from Morocco, with stops at Sotogrande, San Roque and Carteya, a small village whose sole point of interest – at least to Sean, if not to Mad Dan – was some Roman remains. San Roque was not much better, still being almost wholly Spanish; but Sotogrande had strong possibilities, being a luxury development with two world-famous golf courses and a polo ground.

'Plant a device in *that* place,' Mad Dan said, 'and you'd get attention all right. Sure, it'd make the press worldwide.'

'You could be right,' Sean replied.

That evening, they booked into a ramshackle hotel in the hot, dusty port of Algeciras, from where they had a magnificent view across the

bay to the Rock of Gibraltar. Sean was thrilled
to see it. From his reading of history – and he
did not read only Irish history – he knew that
the Rock was three-quarters of a mile wide,
two and three-quarter miles long, and 1396
feet high at its peak. He also knew that it had
taken its name from Gibel-Tarik, or the 'Rock
of Tarik', so named after Tarik-ibn Zeyad, the
Moorish general who had captured it in 711
when he launched his attack on Spain. Even
more romantically, it had been known by the
ancients as one of the Pillars of Hercules.

Sean was enthralled by it.

'God, I'm dry as a boot strap,' Mad Dan said,
turning away from the window of the hotel lobby.
'Does this dump have a bar?'

Early the next morning, having ensured that
Mad Dan, who'd had another night out on the
town's could not linger over breakfast, Sean
drove them both to the romantically named La
Línea de la Concepción, a decidedly unromantic
town located right on the border of Spain and
Gibraltar, and went from there across to the
mighty Rock itself. There, they found a little
England in the Mediterranean, with bilingual citizens, Spanish-speaking English 'bobbies' wearing traditional helmets, though in shirt-sleeves,
shops filled with English products, pubs with
English beer, two English cinemas, and even
the Trafalgar Cemetery, containing the graves

of some of those killed in the Battle of Trafalgar in 1805.

'This is it,' Sean said excitedly. 'This is what we've been looking for.'

'Damn right,' Mad Dan growled.

7

The 'Killing House' is the SAS's nickname for the Close Quarter Battle (CQB) building at Stirling Lines, Hereford. Initially designed and constructed for the perfecting of bodyguard skills, it had gradually come to be used for training in counter-terrorist tactics and hostage rescue.

The four men pulled out of Belfast – Sergeants Bill Carruthers and Roy Ainsworth, and Corporals Mark Dymock and Ralph Billings – were all familiar with the Killing House because, as recruits in the final stages of their rigorous Selection and Training, they had each been compelled to attend a six-week CQB shooting course there, expending some five thousand rounds per week on various exercises with personal weapons. These included rapid magazine changes, malfunction clearance drills, shooting on the move and from unconventional positions, rapid target acquisition, exact shot placement, and head shots. Nevertheless, after a few days' leave in which they visited their families, the men were sent back to the Killing House to further refine their already sharply honed skills in the use of personal weapons, notably the 9mm Browning High Power handgun.

Until 1986 the Killing House had contained a single room set up to represent the kind of place where a hostage or hostages might be held. Inside the room were live 'hostages' (SAS men) and 'terrorists' (cardboard cut-outs). To make life more difficult for the SAS rescuers, the room was often in total darkness and the rescue team had to burst in and, in less than four seconds, identify the 'hostages' and then shoot only the 'terrorists', using live ammunition. When, in 1986, this dangerous system led the death of an SAS sergeant, killed by a head shot when he moved at the wrong moment, the whole system had to be revised.

By November 1987, when the four-man SAS team led by Sergeant Carruthers arrived for their further training, the Killing House had two rooms: one containing the 'terrorists' and 'hostages', the other being the one to be attacked by the assault team. The two separate rooms were connected with a sophisticated camera system that gave a 'real time' coverage of events taking place in one room to a life-size 'wraparound' screen in the other, and vice versa. This enabled the assault team to fire at the images of terrorists projected on the walls, rather than at fellow SAS men acting as such. Special low-charge rounds were used and the walls were made of a bullet-absorbent material that prevented ricochets. The whole exercise would be videoed for debriefings afterwards.

However, when Carruthers's team arrived at the Killing House they were not given further training in hostage-rescue tactics, but in the Standard Operating Procedure known as the 'double tap'. This was a method of 'neutralizing' a terrorist at close quarters by firing in quick succession with a Browning handgun. This SOP had been devised by Major Roy Farran during World War Two. Farran taught his men what was then a rather unorthodox triangular firing posture known as the Grant-Taylor Method: legs spread and slightly bent, pistol raised in the two-handed grip.

The SOP was fully developed and used extensively during the highly dangerous 'Keeni Meeni' operations in Aden in 1964. 'Keeni Meeni' is a Swahili phrase that describes the movement of a snake in the long grass: sinuous and unseen. The same term later became a synonym in Africa – and with the slave trade in the Arabian Gulf – for undercover work. The British Army picked it up in Kenya during the Mau Mau campaign of the early 1950s, and from Kenya it travelled to the SAS in Aden. There it soon came to relate purely to the use of plain-clothes undercover work carried out in the crowded souks and bazaars of the town, when the SAS men, wearing Arab *futahs* and with faces dyed brown, either drove around in unmarked 'Q' cars to pick up terrorists alive and bring them back for questioning or engaged them in CQB and shot them using the 'double tap'.

Though the 'double tap' originally meant two shots fired in quick succession, Major Farran insisted that his men be able to put six rounds through a playing-card at fifteen yards. Eventually, when it was realized that terrorists often carried sophisticated remote detonation devices and that two shots were often insufficient to stop them before they ignited their bomb, the 'double tap', while retaining its original title, evolved into a method of delivering sustained and accurate fire – up to fourteen rounds from a Browning in under three seconds. The troops were taught always to aim at the body and to use the sustained fire-power as a way of keeping the terrorist's hands away from any weapons or remote-control button that he or she may have been carrying.

When Carruthers and his team arrived back in Hereford they were given no information about the nature of the mission they were being prepared for, other than that it would involve CQB and could be highly dangerous. Told that they would be retraining in the Killing House, they had expected to have to don Bristol body armour with high-velocity ceramic plates, S6 respirator masks, black ballistic helmets and skin-tight aviator's gloves in order to undergo Counter Revolutionary Warfare (CRW) training.

Instead, they were instructed by their young CO, Captain Mike Edwards, who had returned from Belfast to Hereford with them, to wear only jeans, a shirt and a light jacket, and to holster their Browning in the cross-draw position under the jacket.

Thus dressed, they were sent into the Killing House for days on end, to perfect their already highly developed skills at the double tap, using the 'nine-milly', as the Browning was widely known. Though they were not training for hostage-rescue work, they still had to work with 'hostages' and 'terrorists' in the form of either dummy figures bearing painted weapons and popping out from behind open doors and window frames, or images projected on the walls of the second room. The idea was to quicken the reactions of the SAS men in differentiating between a terrorist and a hostage, avoiding the shooting of the latter by mistake.

Carrying out this exercise repeatedly, hour after hour, was bad enough, but it was made even worse by the fact that once the dummy figures had been stitched with low-velocity bullets, the men then had to paste paper patches over the holes in the figures, so that the targets could be used again for exactly the same routine. This, even more than the repetitive exercise, nearly drove them all crazy.

'I feel like an interior decorator,' Dymock

complained. 'Or a kid in a nursery school. What a waste of time!'

'Stop whining and get on with the job,' Ainsworth told him. 'We haven't got all day.'

'Yes, we have,' Billings retorted. 'We've been doing this all day every day of the week for two weeks now. I'm going spare, Sarge.'

'*I'll* go spare if you don't shut your mouth,' Carruthers told him, 'and give us some peace. None of us like doing this, but it has to be done, so be quiet and get on with it.'

'Yes, boss!' both corporals piped.

For the first few weeks, Carruthers and the others completed the exercises by shouting instructions or warnings at one another as the dummy figures popped out from behind walls, opening doors or up into view in window frames. However, once their skills in this had been honed to a fine pitch, they were given Davies M135b miniature microphones, attached to a covert ear-worn receiver and two miniature radios, operated by an on–off switch taped to the wrist. With this virtually invisible means of communication, the men were able to communicate not only with each other, but with the Drill Instructors checking their activities from outside the Killing House. In the event of a real operation, however, one of each pair of radios would be tuned into the military command network, the other to the surveillance network.

'You sound like a Dalek through this earpiece,' Dymock told Billings when they were taking a break back in the sleeping quarters of the eight-legged dormitory area known as the 'spider'. 'You sound all distorted.'

'I *am* distorted,' Billings replied. 'My whole body is distorted by all that turning and twisting to get off the double taps. I feel bruised and aching all over. I think I'm misshapen.'

'If you didn't drink so much in Hereford,' Ainsworth informed him, 'you wouldn't be feeling so bruised and battered, and you wouldn't be out of shape. Now me, if I was in charge of you, I'd work you to death.'

'I think I'm dead already, Sarge.'

'You're just a limp-wristed ponce.'

'My mother would take offence at that description, Sarge, and I greatly respect her views.'

'A mother's boy,' Sergeant Ainsworth said.

'A fairy,' Sergeant Carruthers added.

'I'm a man among men,' Billings replied. 'I just don't boast about it.'

'That's because you've got nothing to boast about,' Dymock chipped in, although he instinctively sided with his mate against the NCOs in their customary exchange of bullshit.

Once equipped with the covert communications equipment, the four men were sent into a Killing House plunged into darkness, where they had no time for banter. In that almost pitch blackness, which was disorientating in itself, the dummies or projected images, popping out as if from nowhere, seemed to move even faster than usual. At times this made the men, even though seasoned troopers, forget that it was only an exercise and fire wildly, peppering the walls more than the targets. When this happened, they would nearly collapse with nervous exhaustion.

'You nearly shot *me* in there!' Carruthers bawled at Dymock. 'What the hell were you up to?'

'Sorry, Sarge, but it was so dark I just got confused and turned the wrong way. When you jumped up where the target should have been I fired automatically.'

'And nearly killed me!' Carruthers bawled.

'You shouldn't have been there,' Ainsworth told his fellow-sergeant. 'You turned the wrong way yourself and then jumped up right in front of the next target. We *all* nearly shot you!'

'That's not the point,' Carruthers said.

'What is?' Billings asked him.

'The point is to instantly judge the difference between the enemy and hostage, then shoot the right one. The fact that you bastards almost shot me just goes to show that you failed to differentiate between me and the target.'

'You shouldn't have been there,' Ainsworth insisted.

'That doesn't excuse you,' Carruthers replied. 'In a real CQB, in all the noise and confusion, men get scattered and can end up in the wrong place – but we still have to see who they are before we open fire. That's the whole bloody point of it.'

'We're just tired,' Dymock said. 'We've been doing too much of this. We've been doing it so much we've gone stale and that's the truth of the matter.'

'Freshen up,' Carruthers told him. 'And keep your bloody eyes open.'

When, after a few more weeks of this drill the men had still not been given further retraining in blasting metal locks off doors with Remington 870 pump-action shotguns or in acting as backup for each other in seizing locked rooms, they all guessed that whatever the forthcoming task, it would take place outdoors. They also guessed, from the fact that they were being trained in civilian clothing, that the mission was to be carried out in an area populated with civilians.

'Britain or overseas?' Dymock asked.

'Overseas,' Carruthers reckoned. 'And somewhere pretty warm. They're making us train in light, civilian clothing, which suggests a soft target in a warm climate.'

'What kind of soft target?' Billings asked.

'Non-military. That explains the civilian clothing. We're being prepared for a counter-terrorist mission in an area populated either entirely or largely by civilians.'

'At least it's not Belfast,' Ainsworth said. 'I've had enough of that hell-hole.'

'No, it won't be Belfast,' Carruthers told him. 'That much is certain. It's going to be overseas, somewhere warm, and where civilians gather.'

'Third World?' Ainsworth asked.

'I can't think of anywhere else where a CT mission would presently be required, so the Third World seems likely.'

'Some African shit-hole,' Dymock ventured. 'That would just be my luck. Malaria, rabies and AIDS. We've got a lot to look forward to!'

'It's time to get back to the Killing House,' Carruthers wearily reminded them.

'Lord have mercy!' Billings groaned.

'Not in the Killing House, he won't,' Dymock said.

Finally, after weeks of their tediously repetitive, nerve-racking, exhausting training, the four men were called to a briefing by the SAS Intelligence Corps, in a room in the 'Kremlin', the Operations Planning & Intelligence Wing. There they found Captain Edwards on the dais beside a senior 'green slime' officer who was, appropriately, wearing his green beret. Pinned to the board behind that unknown officer and

Captain Edwards was a large, badly frayed and extensively annotated map of the Rock of Gibraltar.

8

The cold November winds were blowing even in Spain when the shadowy SAS Controller flew in with Alan Reid, a top Intelligence operator from the RUC's undercover surveillance team, F5, for a top-secret meeting with him and Chief Inspector José de Vega of the Málaga Special Branch regarding the presence of Sean Savage and Daniel McCann on Spanish soil. The Controller had been informed of the Irishmen's arrival in Spain by Madrid's Servicios de Información, the intelligence organization that had also arranged this visit to the Málaga Special Branch.

The movements of the two IRA members from Spain to Gibraltar and back to Ireland had led, over the past few months, to intense surveillance activity and cooperation between British and Spanish police, counter-terrorist and intelligence agencies. Now, having had lengthy discussions with his fellow 'green slime' officers in the SAS HQ in the Duke of York's Barracks, London, and agreed to general tactics in the event of a possible IRA attack on the Spanish mainland, or indeed Gibraltar, it was the Controller's intention to draft a counter-strategy with Spanish Intelligence and then quietly disappear from the scene, leaving the actual job of prevention to Captain Edwards and his four-man CRW team.

'It's our belief,' the Controller said, opening the conversation over coffee in a well-guarded room in the Málaga Special Branch building, 'that the changing of the guard outside the Governor of Gibraltar's residence is the terrorists' most likely target. By this I mean the changing of the guard and band parade ceremony of the 1st Battalion of the Royal Anglian Regiment, due to take place on 8 March 1988.'

'Yes. I agree. What better target could there be in terms of outrage?' Señor de Vega replied in perfect English.

'Quite,' the Controller said, not taking the situation as casually as his pragmatic Spanish friend. 'Our first step, therefore, was to postpone the ceremony, ostensibly for refurbishment of the guardhouse. The real reason, naturally, is to give our Intelligence services more time to prepare for the arrival of the terrorists when they plan the actual bombing.'

'Very wise,' Señor de Vega said. 'But when do you think that might be?'

'We don't know,' the Controller confessed, 'but we assume that when the same men, or other known or suspected terrorists, enter this country you'll inform us immediately.'

'Naturally. It is, after all, in our own interests. We cannot have such an outrage on Spanish soil – particularly as this is a British problem.'

'I appreciate that it isn't a Spanish problem, but we cannot prevent them from coming here. They're legally entitled to do so.'

'*We* could prevent them from coming into this country on the grounds that they're listed as known or suspected terrorists.'

'That remark,' the Controller said, 'is based on the assumption that the same people will return to do the bombing. That isn't necessarily so.'

'True,' Señor de Vega acknowledged. 'But even if they send others, we will almost certainly know – as you will – if they have terrorist links with those in Belfast. Most of these people, after all, even if not proven guilty of anything, are under surveillance – by us as well as by you. Our problem, therefore, irrespective of who comes here – and my personal belief is that the group will at least include the two who have already been here – is what to do when they arrive on Spanish soil.'

'On the assumption that the target is Gibraltar – and I think we can safely assume that it is – the problem taxing the British and Gibraltarian authorities is just when they should be detained.'

'Naturally we would detain them at the airport,' Señor de Vega said, looking a little puzzled, 'and return them instantly to Britain.'

The Controller did not reply immediately,

looking a little uncomfortable. Finally, with what could have been a sigh, he said: 'Unfortunately we have a little problem with that.'

'A problem?'

'To move prematurely,' the Controller explained, obviously trying it on, 'would perhaps leave other IRA teams free to proceed with the bombing.'

'Other IRA teams?' Señor de Vega asked, even more confused by what was no more than a classic manoeuvre in the notorious repertoire of British diplomacy. 'Surely we would deal with those as they arrived – just as we would with the first group.'

At this point, Alan Reid, the softly spoken, politically adroit Intelligence operator from the RUC's undercover surveillance team, F5, coughed into his clenched fist, as if clearing his throat, and said: 'Please understand, Señor de Vega, that official Gibraltar is in a state of fear, if not actual panic, in the light of the recent events at Enniskillen.' He was referring to the bombing of 8 November, in the middle of the Remembrance Day parade in Enniskillen, in which sixty-three people had been wounded, some critically, and eleven people killed outright, including three married couples. 'Their fears,' he continued, 'have in no way been eased by the recent bomb attacks at the British headquarters of Rheindahlen in Germany and elsewhere. Official Gibraltar is frightened.'

'This is not Gibraltar,' Señor de Vega responded testily. 'This is Spain. So what is your point, Mr Reid?'

'My point, señor,' Reid replied in his soft Ulster accent, 'is that while the security people here in Spain are admirably cooperative, there's no guarantee that the Spanish courts will be willing to hand over terrorists to a government they don't really recognize.'

'You mean the government of Gibraltar.'

'Exactly. Nor will they hand the terrorists over to a UK which depends on a case of conspiracy as grounds for extradition.'

Señor de Vega, not a man to be won over by soft talk, yet understanding the need for warm relationships between Spain and Britain, thought about Reid's comments for a moment, then said: 'Naturally we're prepared to treat this affair as a perfectly legitimate surveillance of suspected international terrorists in transit through our jurisdiction.' He paused deliberately for dramatic effect, then added: 'So long as no one is likely to detonate any Semtex on Spanish territory.'

'In other words?' Reid asked.

'In other words, we must insist that any action taken against these terrorists must be taken on the Gibraltar side of the border.'

'In that case,' Mr Reid said smoothly, realizing that he was getting just what he and the Controller had wanted, 'the terrorists must be allowed into Gibraltar before any action against them is taken.'

'Exactly,' the Controller said, seeing instantly what the RUC Intelligence officer had done and so moving in to lend him support. 'The best place to arrest the terrorists will be on the road to Spain, where it crosses the Gibraltar airport runway. We can then bundle them aboard an aircraft and fly them straight back to Britain, secure in the knowledge that we've not only caught them, but done so publicly and gained ourselves a propaganda victory.'

'Which means,' said Señor de Vega, no longer confused but increasingly nervous, 'letting the terrorists pass through Málaga passport control and travel without interference from there to Gibraltar – a journey ninety per cent of which is through Spanish territory.'

A collective sigh signalled that this was, unfortunately, the case.

'We will, of course, provide you with names and photos,' Mr Reid said in a thoughtful manner, 'to ensure that you know just who you're dealing with and enable you to track them throughout their journey. Knowing exactly who they are will also enable you to intervene at any juncture where you feel they may be about to commit an offence on Spanish soil.'

'Most kind of you,' Señor de Vega said with all the dry aplomb of David Niven.

After thinking about the proposal for some time, the Spaniard, who was as politically adroit as the Ulsterman, said: 'This is all very well and good, Mr Reid, but what makes you so sure that the bombing will take place in Gibraltar and not on Spanish soil?'

Reid smiled, acknowledging that he realized he was not dealing with a fool. 'Soon after the IRA's bombing of the Remembrance Day parade at Enniskillen on 8 November,' he said, 'British signallers in Gibraltar detected a powerful radio tone transmitted on a military frequency. Though the exact source remains unclear, that transmission was traced to the Spanish mainland. As British security is presently engaged in the most secret of secret wars against terrorism – the war of electronics – this mysterious transmission naturally has them worried.'

'This I understand,' Señor de Vega replied. 'It's a well-known fact that, with the help of technology supplied by American citizens and institutions as well as revolutionary regimes such as Libya, the IRA, now the oldest terrorist group in the world, has also become the most innovative. In fact, with regard to modern technology, it is highly advanced.'

'Exactly what I'm saying,' Mr Reid concurred.

'So how does this relate to the Enniskillen atrocity?'

'The Enniskillen bomb was detonated by a

simple timer. It was, in effect, a form of targeting based on blind and indiscriminate guesswork. However, the IRA can do better than that when it so desires.'

'Meaning?'

'More precise operations,' the SAS Controller informed him at a nod from Mr Reid, 'already tended to use a bomb that exploded in response to a signal from a human observer, whether by a command wire leading to a device concealed in a culvert or hedge or – as in the assassination of Lord Mountbatten off the Irish coast in 1979, or the Lord Chief Justice of Appeal for Northern Ireland on the Irish border in 1987 – by radio signal. Indeed, hard as it is to believe, some of the IRA's signal equipment was adapted from such innocent artefacts as model aircraft.'

'I believe it,' Señor de Vega said. 'But where is this leading us?'

'Our most recent countermeasures designed to jam the bombers' systems,' the Controller confessed, 'have encountered three new problems. One is that the terrorists are known to be working to adapt American radar equipment, normally used for detecting speeding motorists, to trigger bombs, but operating on much higher frequencies – say, 10,000 megahertz and above.'

'Such as?'

'To give you an example: wallet-sized radar sensors costing about £75 and rewired for use as detonators are often concealed in target vehicles. To set off the charge, an electronic gun normally used by police in estimating a car's speed can be aimed at the target from a distance of half a mile. When the signal's detected by the radar receiver, the bomb explodes.'

'Very neat,' Señor de Vega commented drily.

'Another refinement,' Reid said, wishing to add his contribution to the seduction of the wary Spanish Intelligence officer, 'has been described by Dr Michael Scott, a lecturer in electronics at the National Institute for Higher Education in Dublin.' Ignoring Señor de Vega's raised eyebrows, he continued: 'Having noted that each side in Ireland is involved in what he described as a race to produce and counter new technology, a survival of the technologically fittest, he pointed out that a method favoured by the IRA is a hybrid device linking a mechanical clock, such as the timer from a parking meter, to an electrical contact. This prevents the radio signal from working until a certain time has passed – and it is, according to Dr Scott, an absolutely fail-safe way of stopping a signal getting through before the man with the button is ready.'

Señor de Vega sighed. 'All of this is very impressive, but it still doesn't persuade me that the target will be Gibraltar, rather than Spain.'

'The third nightmare haunting Gibraltar,' the Controller informed him, 'is that the mysterious signal intercepted shortly after the Enniskillen bombing in November was not interpreted as a means of detonating a bomb but of priming it in such a way that the next signal on the same military frequency – probably from an Army vehicle in the immediate vicinity, engaged in routine signals traffic – would cause the explosion. This means, in short, that whatever the precise design of the bomb to be planted by the IRA in Gibraltar, it is our considered opinion that it could be triggered by radio from anywhere in Spain.'

'The fact that it *could* be triggered from Spain doesn't mean that it *will* be,' said Señor de Vega, a stubborn man. 'More likely, if they wish to bomb Gibraltar, they will trigger the bomb from there.'

'No,' the Controller said firmly. 'We don't think so. According to the Royal Signals team on Gibraltar who analysed the transmissions from Spain, the signal appeared to become stronger as they drove towards the Spanish border on the landward side of the colony's airport, farthest away from the Rock. In other words, the terrorists appear to be planning to allay all suspicions regarding their presence on the Rock by planting the bomb there, then exploding it at a later time, or even date, from somewhere in Spain – most likely La Línea, right on the border, though possibly farther away.'

'What precisely are you trying to tell me?' Señor de Vega asked.

'Rightly or wrongly, we're basing our plans on three assumptions,' the Controller told him. 'One: that there's a plot to place a car bomb somewhere in Gibraltar. Two: that the bomb will be detonated by a radio or radar pulse, possibly on a military frequency. Three: that the terrorists might be able to detonate the weapon from the sanctuary of foreign territory; in this case, on the Spanish side of the Spanish–Gibraltar border. For this reason we need your help in intercepting – and possibly neutralizing – the terrorists before that bomb is exploded. Will you give it?'

'Have I a choice?' the Spaniard asked.

'No,' the Controller said.

Señor de Vega glanced from the Controller to the gently smiling RUC Intelligence officer, then raised his hands in the air as if offering a prayer.

'What is a poor man to do,' he asked, 'when he is given no choice? Yes, gentlemen, Spain will cooperate. We will keep our eye on your terrorists. Now may I offer you cognac?'

'Please do,' the Controller said.

9

The sky was hanging low and slate-grey over Belfast when, in late February 1988, Pat Tyrone paid a visit to Mairead at the small house in Andersonstown where she was then living. Not expecting him, Mairead was sitting in front of an open fire in the cramped living-room, holding in her cold hands a cup of hot tea laced with whisky.

She felt like death. She always did these days. Ever since the death of Tom, killed by his own bomb, she had felt that she had somehow lost herself and was empty inside. Mairead rarely went out now, but instead spent most of her days either lying in bed in a daze or sitting in her chair, either watching television or simply staring into the fire. She found it very hard to read; her concentration was completely gone. When she picked up a book, the words blurred before her eyes and she started thinking of Tom, seeing his face before her, practically feeling him, desperately wanting to hold him and be held by him, until reality clamped around her again and she filled up with pain. That pain was like a cancer inside her, blotting out all reasonable thought. She wanted to die and be with him.

The doorbell rang. Not hearing it at first, lost in her dead world, Mairead continued sipping her hot tea. Eventually, however, the insistent ringing pierced her consciousness. Placing the teacup on the mantelpiece, above the blazing fire, she went to open the front door. She was still wearing only her dressing-gown but she didn't care about that. Opening the door, she was surprised to find Pat Tyrone smiling at her, though his grey gaze was searching.

'Surprised to see me?' he asked her.

'Yes.'

'How have you been, Mairead?'

'Ach, all right, I suppose.'

'Maureen tells me you haven't been well.'

'Sure, I'm all right. I'm fine. I just don't go out much.'

'Aye, it must be hard for you . . . I mean Tom an' all.'

'I'm over that,' Mairead lied. 'What do you want, Pat?'

Tyrone glanced to both sides, keeping his eye on the soldiers at the checkpoints at both ends of the street, then he turned back to Mairead. 'Can I come in?'

She stared thoughtfully at him for a moment, then shrugged. 'Sure, why not?' she said. When he had stepped inside, she indicated the other chair in front of the blazing fire. 'Can I get you a cup of tea?' she asked. Tyrone shook his head, and Mairead returned to the chair she had been sitting in, asking once again as she sat down: 'So what do you want?'

'Sure, that doesn't sound too friendly,' Tyrone said teasingly.

Mairead managed a smile. 'I'm not bein' unfriendly,' she told him. 'I just want to know why you're here.'

'I'm here to see how you feel.'

'You must know how I feel. I'm not really recovered. I'll never recover. When Tom died, so did I.'

'That's melodramatic, Mairead.'

'It's a fact of life, Pat. I've lost my heart and soul, lost my strength, an ' now I just watch the days pass. I feel empty inside.'

'You need to do something.'

'You're tryin' to get me back to work.'

'Why not? It'd be better than just sittin' here, day in, day out.'

'I like sittin' here.'

'No, you don't. You just do it because you've lost the will to live, but that can't go on for ever.'

'Like to bet on it?'

'No, Mairead, I wouldn't. But we need you. And you need us. That's why I'm here. We have a job for you, and I think it would do you good to get involved. You need to force yourself out of here.'

'I want nothin' that reminds me of Tom.'

'Everything will remind you of Tom, so that's no excuse, Mairead. Sure, every time you switch on the telly, you'll see news of the Troubles and think of Tom. Every time you read about a bombin', you think about Tom. Every time you step out on that street and see a Brit soldier, you'll be thinkin' of Tom. Until you fill your life with somethin' else, you'll always think about Tom. We think about him as well; he was one of our best men. We think about him, but that doesn't stop us: we just keep on with the work. So do this job for us, Mairead – and do it for yourself. It'll get you out of this house and also take you out of yourself and help you stop all this broodin'. Believe me, it will.'

Mairead gazed into the flickering yellow flames and saw them constantly changing shape, forming figures and faces. She saw Tom there, felt the burning in her soul, and realized that though Tyrone was exploiting her, he was right in what he had said. She couldn't live this way for ever and the time had come to change things. Besides, as she really wanted to die, why not go back to work? She might find death through it.

'What's the job?' she asked.

Pleased, Tyrone told her about Gibraltar, then summarized the task: 'We've decided that the best time and place for the bombing would be the band assembly area during the changing of the guard and band parade ceremony of the 1st Battalion of the Royal Anglian Regiment, when there should be lots of tourists about. The ceremony's scheduled to take place on 8 March. That means we have time to check out the area more thoroughly than Sean and Mad Dan did. We want you to do that.'

'You want me to go to Gibraltar?'

'Aye. Via Spain. Like Sean and Mad Dan, you'll go just like a normal tourist and make your own way down to the Rock. Lots of tourists do it: they cross over to the Rock, have a good look around or do a bit of duty-free shopping, then return to Spain the same day. That's what you'll do, like. Except you'll do it more than once – at least as many times as is required to suss out the whole area and decide the best way to insert the bomb. Sure, you'll also pick up a suntan, which can't be that bad.'

Mairead actually smiled, then brushed her long hair back from her pale face. 'Who's to do the actual bombing?'

'You, Sean and Mad Dan. We think that'd be best because you're the three that are goin' to know the place and how to move around it. Will you do it?'

Mairead studied the flickering flames in the fire, seeing images, ghosts, the face of someone she'd loved. The pain that now resided in the heart of her welled up like a flood and she had to escape that. Tom had died bombing the hated Brits, so in a sense they had caused his death. Mairead hadn't really hated the Brits before – they were just the enemy – but so many of those she loved had died in the war against them and now Mairead hated them. On the other hand, the very thought of having anything to do with Mad Dan . . .

'Why Mad Dan?' she asked.

'Why not?'

'He has the reputation of being a mad dog who enjoys the killin'. I don't think I'd like that.'

'He may be that, all right, but he's also a good man to have in a tight spot and one who knows all about plantin' bombs. In fact, no matter what he's like personally, he's one of our best.'

'I'd rather go with someone else.'

'You like Sean, all right?'

'Ackaye, he's a good wee lad. Sure, I like him a lot.'

'Then let him be your comfort. He'll act as a balancer. Just stick close to him and try not to take too much notice of anything Mad Dan says – other than anything relatin' to the mission, that is. He knows his business that way. Now will you do it or not?'

Mairead thought about it for some time, gradually accepting that she needed such a job to stop her from brooding and becoming more melancholic.

'Yes,' she said, hoping to sweep the pain away with the strength of her hatred. 'I'll do it. When do I leave?'

'In a few days,' Tyrone told her. 'You'll travel under two different passports, flying Aer Lingus from Dublin to Brussels as Mary Johnston, and from there to Málaga with a stolen British passport in the name of Mrs Katherine Alison Smith. You'll be booked into a hotel in Marbella – just another tourist, like, in an upmarket area – and from there you can make a few day trips to Gibraltar, taking normal tourist buses. Once on the Rock, you can wander about at your leisure, taking in all the sights. No one'll suspect a thing, even if you take photographs, which we want you to do. We want you to reconnoitre the whole area and come back here with a game plan. So pack your suitcase, include some summery clothes, and I'll come back tomorrow with the tickets and passports. Thanks a lot, Mairead.'

'No need for thanks,' Mairead said. 'I'm doin' this for myself. I see nothin' in my future but another spell in prison or an early grave. I just hope it's the latter.'

Tyrone stood up and placed his hand on her shoulder, shaking her affectionately. 'You're just down at the moment, Mairead, but sure you'll feel better soon – when you get to Gibraltar. Apart from the sunshine, you'll feel a lot better knowing that you're doin' something for the cause. Till tomorrow, then.'

'Right.'

Mairead stayed in the chair, studying the flames, as Tyrone let himself out. Sitting there, she smiled slightly, bitterly, then sighed and nodded off.

Three days later, carrying two false passports in her shoulder bag and dressed like a smart businesswoman, Mairead caught the train from Belfast to Dublin. Not wishing to draw attention to herself, she buried her nose in a book until the train reached Dublin, where she picked up a bus to the airport. After checking in at the Aer Lingus desk, she passed through customs using the false passport in the name of Mary Johnston. No questions were asked.

Again, Mairead managed to avoid conversation by concentrating on her book while having a drink in the bar of the departure lounge. In the plane to Brussels, however, she was seated beside an English businessman who first kept glancing sideways at her, clearly smitten by her pale beauty and long, black hair, and finally, when the steward came along with the drinks trolley, ordered a white wine for himself and asked if Mairead would like a drink too.

'Sure, that would be grand,' Mairead replied, realizing that conversation was inevitable and deciding to get something out of it. 'I'll have a wee whisky, thanks.'

'Irish!' the man exclaimed softly as the drinks were being served. 'I should have known by the looks of you.'

'Oh, how?'

'That long, dark hair. The pale skin. Just something about you.'

Mairead smiled cynically, knowing he was talking shite and hadn't known she was Irish until she opened her mouth. 'Aye, I suppose so.'

'Ken Chambers,' the man said, introducing himself.

'Mary Johnston. Nice to meet you.'

'I've been to Ireland a lot,' Chambers said when the steward had served the drinks and moved on. 'North *and* south. The people on both sides are so pleasant, it's hard to believe what goes on there . . . all the bombings, the shootings, kneecappings. It hardly makes sense.'

'Nor to me,' Mairead lied, enjoying her whisky. 'It's just one of those things, like.'

'Bad to live there, is it?'

'Desperate,' Mairead said, pushing the long hair back from her face and sipping more whisky. 'But you get used to it, don't you? Like you Brits did during the Blitz. It becomes natural, like.'

'Yes, I suppose so,' Chambers said. 'Are you going to Brussels on business?'

'No,' Mairead replied. 'Just the transit lounge.

I'm on my way to Spain and got a cheap flight by going this way. I'm off to pick up a suntan.'

'Oh,' Chambers said, obviously disappointed, having imagined he was on to a good thing, 'what a pity. I know an awful lot about Brussels, I could have shown you round.'

'Too bad,' Mairead said.

Though not hiding his disappointment, Chambers remained pleasant enough and made small talk throughout the rest of the flight. When the aircraft had landed at Brussels, he waved goodbye and headed for passport control while Mairead went straight to the transit lounge. As she did not have to show her passport here and would go through Málaga airport using the other false passport, there would be no record of a Mary Johnston having disembarked at either Brussels or Málaga. Mary Johnston, in a sense, already no longer existed and Mairead would pass through Málaga under the name of Mrs Katherine Alison Smith.

The flight was uneventful. Mairead had a window seat beside a rather formal, middle-aged couple who rarely talked to each other and, in the case of the woman, who was in the middle seat, only offering the most basic, distracted pleasantries to Mairead when passing her the food tray or miniature bottles of whisky.

Mairead had three whiskies in quick succession and became pleasantly, though imperceptibly drunk. In fact, by now she was really feeling like a tourist and almost enjoying herself. It was only when she thought of her dead lover that the pain returned to torment her.

But she was thrilled to see the parched, mountainous landscape of southern Spain spread out below her, criss-crossed with snaking rivers, dotted here and there with brown-roofed, white houses, some isolated on the hillsides, others clustered together as villages and towns. Even though it was November the sun was shining over the land as brightly as during an Irish summer. She felt better already.

A fleeting moment of panic came when she had to pass through passport control, but the Spanish official scarcely glanced at the second false passport, merely noting that it was an old-fashioned British one and waving her through. The customs officers didn't even check her suitcase and soon she was outside.

As instructed by Tyrone, she took a cab to her hotel in Estepona. She thought the views along the coastline were wonderful, but she was puritanically shocked by how long the journey was and how much it cost. Nevertheless, she had been given the money to cover it, so she paid, overtipping the delighted driver, and then entered the hotel

The receptionist spoke English, which made checking in easy, and soon Mairead was sitting in a rattan chair on the balcony of her room, drinking another whisky and gazing across the road to the vast, glittering Mediterranean. It was nice to go travelling.

She had the first good night's sleep she'd had in a long time and woke the next morning feeling particularly refreshed. Dazzled by the brilliance of the light, she put on light clothing – shirt, cotton slacks and flat shoes – and went down for breakfast. She felt self-conscious in the dining-room, too aware of the fact that she was being stared at surreptitiously by the other guests. One reason was simply that she was a woman holidaying alone; the other that she was a strikingly attractive woman with long, lustrous hair.

Finishing breakfast, which was standard British fare for the tourists – bacon and eggs, toast and coffee – she went down to the lobby and checked the notice-board, where she found leaflets advertising day trips to Gibraltar. Seeing that she was still early enough to pick up the last of the trips, she bought a ticket and hurried out to the bus, which, minutes later, was trundling along the busy, scenic N340, *en route* to the Spanish–Gibraltar border at La Línea.

Once more, Mairead was thrilled by the scenery on either side of the road, which snaked sinuously between the sierras and the green-blue

Mediterranean, all under a vast azure sky with few clouds. Normally oppressed by the low, grey skies of Northern Ireland, Mairead now felt that she was spreading her wings, as free as a bird.

'Fantastic, isn't it?' the portly woman seated beside her said.

'Ackaye,' Mairead replied. 'Sure, I've never seen anything like it. My eyes hurt just to look at it.'

'Irish?'

'Wouldn't you know it?'

'Never been here before?'

'No.'

'Then it must be quite a contrast from home – I mean all of this sunshine.'

'Sure, it is, right enough.'

'Here on holiday?'

'Aye.'

'On your own?'

'Aye.'

'That makes two of us,' the Englishwoman said. 'You're all right on your own here.'

'You've come before?' Mairead asked.

'Every year,' the woman said. 'I came with my husband every year for fifteen years, but he died four years ago. I still come. I pretend he's beside me. I still love it here.'

Mairead thought about Tom and the scalding pain returned. 'I understand why you do,' she said quickly, not wanting to show her emotions. 'Sure, it's real lovely here. I might come back myself. Just look at that sea and sky!'

However, once at the border, which was a surprisingly unattractive area, she was reminded again of Belfast and her dead lover. With the brutally swift return of her grief and pain, she forced herself to think of just why she was there and disembarked from the bus on the Spanish side of the border in order to walk the rest of the way and see as much as possible.

'I know this place so well,' the woman said. 'Let me show you around.'

'Sure, that's kind of you,' Mairead told her, 'but I'd like to walk the whole way, rather than taking the bus.'

'Fine. I don't mind,' the woman said, smiling broadly. 'You always see more on foot, so we'll walk and talk.'

'Really, you don't have to.'

'Honestly, I don't mind.'

'Sure, I'd really prefer to be on my own and keep my own thoughts, like.'

'Oh, nonsense!' the woman said.

Suddenly exasperated, hardly thinking of what she was doing, Mairead shoved her face close to the other woman and whispered fiercely: 'Do I have to say it half a dozen times to make myself understood? I want to be alone, you stupid cow, so get back on that bus.'

'Well, I never . . .'

When Mairead jabbed her finger at the bus, the shocked woman beat a hasty retreat and clambered up into it. Relieved, Mairead turned away and walked towards the airport. 'Dumb bitch,' she hissed.

After crossing the runway, she walked along Winston Churchill Avenue, passing a petrol station. A short distance farther on, coming to the junction of Smith Darrien Road and Corral Road, she took the latter and walked all the way down to Main Street and the central shopping area. She didn't even have to ask to find the band assembly area, as the guards on duty were enough to tell her where she was. Once there, however, she walked around, gawping and taking photographs just like all the other tourists, but paying particular attention to what surrounded the assembly area.

The Hambros Bank, she noted, was directly opposite the assembly area, just across Line Wall Road, and the Garrison Theatre was right beside it, where the road turned back towards the border at the public car park by the High Stone Wall. That same route, Mairead soon found out after asking a few questions at a nearby pub, was also the route taken by the parade after the band of the 1st Battalion of the Royal Anglian Regiment had assembled. Just down from the bank was the Jewish Old People's Home. Behind the High Stone Wall was the Toc-H Hostel and the Bishop

Fitzgerald School. Apart from the high density of buildings around the assembly area, it was a real little corner of England packed with shoppers and tourists: men, women and children.

In terms of casualties designed to cause public outrage, it could not have been bettered.

Mairead, who had suffered the pain of loss, tried not to think of the dreadful pain she would cause to others if she set a bomb off here. The end justifies the means, she told herself.

Having taken all the photos she required, she went to the pub she had been to earlier and there, over a pint of Guinness, she made a drawing of the area, with arrows indicating how her comrades could enter the area, deposit the bomb and then leave before it exploded. She also meticulously noted the exact location of the car park where, as she would recommend, a 'blocking' car could be left for two or three days before the car bringing in the bomb took its place, just before the timed explosion.

Satisfied with her work, and noting that it was already late afternoon, Mairead walked back across the runway and boarded the bus that would take her back to Estepona.

She slept well that night and returned to Gibraltar the following day, this time to observe with other tourists the routine changing of the guard and then follow the route that would be taken by the bandsmen during the major band ceremony on 8 March.

She did this every day for the rest of the week, always taking photographs and jotting down many notes, and by the end of the week had worked out that between 130 and 145lb of Semtex, appropriately located, would devastate this densely packed area during the band ceremony, and that a retaliation highly successful in propaganda terms would thereby be realized.

By concentrating on words such as 'propaganda' and 'retaliation' she could forget words such as 'carnage'. She could thus, without feeling too much remorse, avenge Tom and all the other comrades who had died for the cause.

When she had completed her research, she phoned Pat Tyrone from the privacy of her hotel room and informed him: 'The job can be done. Sure, it should be right easy.'

'Good,' Tyrone replied. 'Then stay where you are and I'll arrange to have someone come and see you about getting enough groceries to keep you goin' until you have to come home.'

Tyrone was referring to the Irishman resident in the area who would visit her in the hotel regarding the supply of enough Semtex for the bombing.

'Fine,' Mairead replied. 'An' what about the help you promised me?' she asked, referring to Sean and Mad Dan.

'They'll fly out on 5 March. Sure, I'll fax you details of the flight and trust that you'll meet them at the airport.'

'Ackaye, I'll do that all right. It's the least I can do, like.'

'Enjoy yourself in the meantime. Do some more sightseein'. Have a good time.'

'Sure, it's nice to go travellin',' Mairead said.

'It's all part of the job,' Tyrone replied, then the line went dead.

Mairead replaced the receiver and walked on to the balcony of her room to look out at the sea, now turning grey in the dimming light of winter. Sitting down at the glass-topped table, she opened a romantic novel and started reading – simply passing the time until the Irishman arrived to negotiate the purchase of 145lb of Semtex.

Mairead had not passed through Gibraltar unobserved. Under surveillance in Belfast from the moment she had left prison in September 1986, she had been observed at every stop on the journey from Belfast to Málaga. Also, determined not to let international terrorism, Irish or otherwise, flex its muscles in Spain, the Servicios de Información in Madrid had given permission for a junior representative of the Gibraltarian Special Branch, Detective Constable Kenneth Wilby, to mount a special surveillance operation on the Spanish side of the border.

Seated in an enclosed room beside a Spanish immigration officer, Wilby was facing a screen on to which the Spaniards projected images of passport photographs and numbers taken from people crossing the border. Car registration numbers were also passed to him by the Spanish immigration officer, who was in contact by telephone with his colleagues watching the cars go through.

As both the British and Spanish authorities knew about the visit of two suspected terrorists the previous November, as well as Mairead's arrival in Málaga airport just a few days ago, Wilby had been instructed to look out for two men and a woman travelling either together, or seperately, from Ireland under false passports, but already included in the photographic files of the passport and border security officers concerned with international terrorism.

Mairead was therefore identified by Detective Constable Wilby when she crossed the border from Spain into Gibraltar. Nevertheless, when he saw her entering Gibraltar, as instructed he made no attempt to stop her. Instead, he kept checking, hoping to see the two men. When they failed to materialize, Wilby merely logged the time of Mairead's return to the border as she crossed back into Spain. He did this meticulously every day, still not interfering with her movements, because, as he had been informed, the Spanish and British authorities had jointly decided not to act until it was clear that a terrorist outrage was being prepared – which would most likely be when all three terrorists had entered Gibraltar together.

In short, they would not be stopped from entering Gibraltar, with or without their car and its possible bomb. They would, however, be stopped, either by arrest or by lethal gunshots, once they were all in Gibraltar.

10

'A bombing is definitely imminent,' the Controller said, opening the meeting of the Joint Intelligence Committee in London. 'We can now confirm that the trip of two well-known IRA members, Sean Savage and Daniel McCann, to Spain and Gibraltar, has been followed up with a separate trip by Mairead Farrell, the woman who bombed a Loyalist hotel in Belfast a decade ago, spent the next ten years in prison, and then, on her release, became intimately involved with Tom Riley, who was killed by his own bomb last year when he tried to blow up another Protestant hotel. Farrell therefore has to be treated as a known terrorist who, when she went to Spain nine days ago, visited Gibraltar five days in a row and was observed doing so by the Gibraltarian Special Branch. We can only deduce from this that the target is definitely Gibraltar.'

There was an uneasy silence for a moment, broken only when the Secretary asked: 'Whereabouts on Gibraltar?'

The Controller sighed with relief, realizing that he would now have the Secretary's fullest cooperation. 'While we can't yet be sure, we think the most likely target will be an assembly point where the band of the garrison regiment, the lst Battalion of the Royal Anglian Regiment, prepares for the ceremonial parade – the Changing of the Guard. This takes place in what's actually a public thoroughfare surrounded by buildings including houses, shops, a theatre, an old people's home and, worst of all with regard to potential casualties, a school.'

The Secretary visibly winced at the last named. 'Dreadful,' he murmured.

'Naturally,' the Controller added, 'during the Changing of the Guard the place fills up with tourists, who would also become victims of such a bomb.'

'Do we know the identities of the bomb team?'

'We don't yet know just who will arrive in Gibraltar or when,' the leader of the Special Military Intelligence Unit replied. 'But the Spanish authorities have confirmed that the two men who passed through Málaga airport under false passports last November were Sean Savage and Daniel McCann, both known terrorists under constant surveillance. Savage is twenty-three and a young man of many hobbies, including rambling, cycling, football, cooking and the Irish language. He doesn't smoke or drink and has never publicly expressed a political viewpoint. In fact, few of those who know him would believe that he's in the IRA. Nevertheless, he is. Though his IRA involvement is strictly covert, we know for a fact that he's an expert engineer, or bomb maker, responsible for more than one atrocity.'

'And McCann?' the Secretary asked.

'A thirty-year-old butcher's assistant from the Clonnard district of Belfast, known far and wide as 'Mad Dan'. Began his IRA activities at the age of twelve, in the summer of 1969, shortly after Catholic homes in his district were burnt to the ground by the Loyalists. The remarkable thing is that in the many years he's been an IRA assassin he's only been convicted once for anything major. He got two years in the Maze for possessing a detonator. As the name suggests, Mad Dan's the kind of fanatical activist who knows no compromise and implacably opposes what he sees as Britain's criminal presence in his country. The RUC regarded him as a particularly ruthless exponent of shoot-to-kill. Indeed, they hold him responsible for the murders of Detective Sergeants Michael Malone and Ernest Carson in August last year. They were off duty, taking a glass in a part of Belfast traditionally regarded as neutral ground. Having murdered Malone and Carson and wounded another police officer and a barman, McCann fled in a waiting car.'

'I take it,' the Secretary said in his dry manner, 'that you feel the world would be a better place without him.'

'I do, sir.'

'And we're absolutely sure that he and this Sean Savage were in Spain last November?'

'Absolutely. Savage told his mother that he was taking a break in Galway. Instead, he . . .'

'How do you know what he said to his mother?'

'He's been under surveillance for the past eighteen months. During a deliberately mounted cordon-and-search sweep of the area, when the residents of Savage's street were temporarily evicted from their homes, one of our surveillance teams entered his house and inserted a miniature fibre-optic probe on top of the picture-rail running around the living-room. That probe was tuned to an advanced laser audio-surveillance transceiver that picked up all conversations taking place inside the room. So we were able to record Savage telling his mother that he was taking a break in Galway when in fact he went to Dublin – we had him under visual surveillance by now – and from there flew to Málaga via Gatwick, with a driving licence, birth and baptism certificate and organ-donor card in the name of Brendan Coyne. McCann travelled separately, also with false documentation, as Robert Wilfred Reilly. The two men met at Málaga airport, hired a white Renault 5 from Avis, and then spent the next seven days travelling along the N340 from Málaga to Algeciras, and crossed at least once into Gibraltar.'

'They were observed entering Gibraltar?'

'Yes. Covertly photographed and entered in the records by the Gibraltarian Special Branch in cooperation with the Spanish police on the Spanish side of the border.'

'How long were they in Spain?'

'Seven days.'

'Did they meet anyone there?'

'They did a lot of drinking – at least McCann did – in a lot of bars, particularly Irish pubs, where doubtless they picked up information from innocent locals. They may also have had arranged meetings with fellow-terrorists, or the suppliers of explosives, but we can't be sure of this as the Spanish police lost them for long periods of time, notably during their trips along the N340.'

'And now we have this female entering the picture, following in their tracks.'

'Yes, Mr Secretary. Though a former convent school girl from Andersonstown, Mairead Farrell is a woman with particularly strong – and possibly deadly – motivation.'

'How come?'

'After leaving the convent school, she served ten years in prison, most of them in Armagh, for planting a bomb in a Loyalist hotel in Belfast in 1976. According to our informants, those ten years merely strengthened her resolve and made her a more fanatical IRA activist. Nevertheless, she appears to have ceased her political activities since getting out of prison in September 1986.'

'So why would you think of her as still being highly motivated?'

'Because last November, just before Savage and McCann arrived in Málaga, Mairead's lover and fellow-bomber, Tom Riley – a man suspected of some very important assassinations, as well as numerous bombings – blew himself up accidentally when bombing a Protestant hotel in Belfast. That same evening, a pub frequented by Provisional IRA leader Patrick Tyrone was under SAS surveillance from a loft in the house opposite and Mairead was observed entering that pub just before the explosion of the bomb that killed her lover. Shortly after the bomb went off, a visibly disturbed Tyrone entered the pub. He emerged with his wife and a sobbing Mairead Farrell. A short time later, Farrell showed up in Málaga. Though recognized instantly as a known terrorist from the photo files held by the Spanish security police at Málaga's passport control, she was travelling with a false passport in the name of Mrs Katherine Alison Smith. Also, she had flown in from Brussels via Dublin – an unnecessarily elaborate route to take and one clearly designed to make her hard to track.'

'But the Spanish police let her through without attempting to arrest her or even question her.'

'At our request, yes. We saw little point in stopping her and we really wanted to know what she was up to.'

'Gibraltar.'

'Yes. It's our belief that Patrick Tyrone used the death of Tom Riley to encourage Farrell back into the business, perhaps as an act of vengeance against the Brits. Subsequently she visited Gibraltar five days in a row. As a known bomber, we believe she's there to reconnoitre the area and plan a forthcoming attack – almost certainly near the band assembly area during the band ceremony planned for 8 March.'

'Like the first two, this woman was *definitely* observed entering Gibraltar?'

'Yes, Mr Secretary. Exactly like the other two, she was photographed and listed entering and leaving the Rock by the local Special Branch acting with the Spanish police on their side of the border.'

There was a moment's tense silence, then the SMIU leader said: 'I don't think I have to tell anyone around this table what a bomb explosion in such a densely packed area, particularly during such a ceremony, would do in terms of human and political devastation. We simply cannot let that happen.'

After another long silence, during which the men glanced uneasily at one another and the Secretary thoughtfully scratched his nose, the latter finally said: 'I agree. So what happens now?'

The Controller coughed into his clenched fist. 'We notify the Joint Operations Centre – which includes an SAS liaison officer – to dispatch an SAS Special Projects Team of a dozen men to Gibraltar, along with a number of security people of both sexes, mainly from MI5, augmented by local Special Branch personnel, to act as watchers and an armed reserve. This operation will be code-named "Flavius".'

'Was that name chosen for a particular reason?' the Secretary asked.

The Controller smiled. 'Whatever can you mean, Mr Secretary?'

'I did ancient history at Cambridge and, as I recall, Flavius was a Roman magistrate who enforced the rule of law. His role model was a Roman soldier of common background, grandson of a gladiator and a centurion, who fought his way to the top, was eventually hailed as the Emperor Vespasian in AD 69, and took over a Rome debauched by the excesses of the mad Emperor Nero. A year later, Vespasian opened the Flavian Amphitheatre, otherwise known as the Colosseum, which became the place where public duels between gladiators were held.'

Still smiling, the Controller said: 'I don't see what you're driving at. I . . .'

'Flavius's circus specialized in the type of

combat with no rules except that the winner is the man who walks away alive. Is that the game plan for Gibraltar?'

The Controller thought a moment before answering, then decided on honesty. 'The aim of the operation is arrest – arrest, disarm, defuse the bomb. But we have to bear in mind that we're going after dedicated terrorists, an Active Service Unit who're planning to explode a bomb in a crowded public place and may do so by using a remote-control device triggered by a button on their person. We have to ensure, when we tackle them, that none of them presses that button. That doesn't leave any time for indecision. So, yes, if the terrorists cannot be arrested, or if they refuse to surrender – if, in other words, it gets to a fire-fight – we will shoot to kill.'

'I understand,' the Secretary said. 'Operation Flavius is hereby authorized. You may proceed at will, gentlemen.'

The meeting was adjourned and the Controller hurried back to SAS HQ at the Duke of York's Barracks, to get in touch with his Special Projects Team and prepare them for Gibraltar.

Operation Flavius was under way.

11

Before his second trip to Spain, Sean told his mother that he was taking another holiday across the border, staying in a caravan and studying the language. But once again he took the train to Dublin and flew to Málaga, this time via Paris, with the same false papers in the name of Brendan Coyne. He arrived in Málaga at 8.50 p.m. on Friday 4 March on the same Iberia flight as 'Robert Wilfred Reilly' – actually Daniel McCann.

Mairead met both men at the airport and led them out to the white Renault 5 she had hired the day before. She had always liked Sean, who she thought was rather sensitive and killed only with reluctance, but she detested Mad Dan and fully understood why he had that nickname. McCann was a mad dog, efficient when it came to the gun, but not trustworthy otherwise. She knew why he'd been chosen for this task, but she still didn't like it.

'Sure, I've actually hired two cars,' she told them. 'The other's the same as this one – a white Renault 5. One's to take us to the Rock and be used as a blockin' car; the other's to transport the bomb the next day, driven by someone else.'

'Who?' Mad Dan asked testily.

'You're not to know that,' Mairead told him. 'Pat Tyrone was adamant about that. He said the less each of us knew the better it'd be for the movement if we were caught by the Brits.'

'Sure, isn't it quare good to know how confident he is in us?' Mad Dan said, practically sneering. 'Caught by the Brits, like.'

'Confidence breeds mistakes,' Mairead told him. 'Tyrone has it right.'

Having placed their travelling bags in the boot of the Renault, the two men clambered into the car, Sean in the back and Mad Dan beside Mairead, who was driving.

'I hate drivin' on this side of the road,' she said. 'It makes me feel really nervous.'

'Ackaye,' Sean said candidly. 'I felt exactly the same. Sure, I hardly knew my left side from my right, but I managed it somehow. You get used to it, don't you?'

'Aye, you do, but I'm still feelin' nervous.'

'So we're actually goin' to do it,' Sean said as Mairead turned out on to the N340, heading westwards into the brilliant March light with the Mediterranean glittering on the left, beyond the white houses, blue sea meeting blue sky in the horizon's heat haze.

'I don't know yet,' Mairead surprised herself by saying. 'We're goin' out to have another look at the place, but I still have my doubts.'

'That's not what you told Tyrone,' Mad Dan said. 'He said *you* said the target was perfect.'

'Aye, it is in certain ways. But I've had growing doubts about certain aspects of it an' I'm thinkin' more an' more about those. Maybe it's just bein' out here on my own. Sure, we'll know soon enough.'

'What doubts?' Sean asked.

'It's a wee area,' she said. 'Very tight an' cramped. Where we want, our target, the band assembly area where the parade takes place, there's an old people's home, a hostel used by walkers and even a school. There's a bank, always busy, an' a theatre, but it's the others I'm especially concerned about. I'm not sure we should be bombin' old people, backpackers an' children just to make a point. Particularly since few of 'em can be considered legitimate targets.'

'You're goin' soft,' Mad Dan said. 'You're a woman who's bombed a whole hotel, killin' people who just happened to be stayin' there, friend and foe alike. So what's the difference here?'

'That hotel was in Belfast. In a Loyalist area. It's fair to say that anyone stayin' there was doin' so in the full awareness of where they were stayin' and what it meant — loyalty to the Prods.'

'So?'

'So this isn't Northern Ireland. It isn't even related to it. The people livin' in that old people's home, the backpackers in the hostel and, more

172

importantly, the wee children in that school aren't the same as the people who were stayin' in that hotel I bombed, not even remotely. They're innocent in the truest sense of the word and that makes me feel bad.'

'That's shite,' Mad Dan said brutally. 'There's no such thing as an innocent person when it comes to the struggle. Sure, innocent children have died in Belfast an' we don't like it but we've learnt to accept it. That's the cud we all chew over an' over. It's the vomit we swallow.'

'That doesn't make it right,' Mairead said. 'An' even if it did, those kids were in Belfast – our own – so at least, even if it wasn't admirable, it was our own we were makin' to pay the price. This is different. This isn't in the Province. An' we're not about to blow up just a few British soldiers – or even Irish children. That's what sticks in my craw.'

'She's right,' Sean said before Mad Dan could retort, which he was just about to do. Sean had read his guidebooks on the area and he, too, had his doubts. 'Most of the people on the Rock are of Italian, Portuguese and Spanish descent. Most are Roman Catholic. We could end up killin' a few Brit soldiers an' an awful lot of the others. I'm not sure if that'll do our cause any good. In fact it could set us back ten years. Mairead has a point here.'

'Shite!' Mad Dan exploded. 'The Rock of

Gibraltar's another British Crown Colony – Christ, they've colonized everything – and that's the concept we're attackin', so let's go and do it.'

Taken aback that Mad Dan even knew a word like 'concept', Sean did not reply and instead distracted himself by gazing out of the window of the car. Having already passed through Torremolinos and Benalmádena-Costa, they were racing along the constantly curving racetrack of a highway towards Fuengirola.

'Still in Marbella?' Mad Dan asked.

'Aye,' Mairead replied. 'The other car's in the car park of my hotel and we'll talk to our demolitions man when we get there. He'll be expectin' us in the bar in an hour and so far we're on time.'

'He's Irish?'

'Ackaye.'

'Where does he get his groceries?'

'Brings it over from Morocco in a fancy boat owned by a wealthy English arms dealer. The boat's berthed in Puerto Banus and few questions are asked. The owner's been resident here for years and pisses money in all the right directions, so he has dispensations.'

'Him an' the Pope,' Mad Dan said. 'Sure, don't some have all the luck?'

'Anyway,' Mairead continued, not amused at all by Mad Dan, 'he has the stuff stacked up in his

fancy apartment in Sotogrande – the last place the
Spanish police would think of. So we just need a
date an' time.'

'I thought we had that,' Sean said.

'We have the date – the eighth – but I still
have my doubts about the target, so that has to
be sorted out.'

'You better sort it out quick, girl,' Mad Dan
said, 'or Tyrone'll be lookin' you up with his
Black an' Decker. You told him we were going
to do this job and that's what he's expectin' –
not some shite about hittin' innocent women and
children. Pat just wants results.'

Mairead sighed. 'Sure, I know that.'

She had just come off the bypass around
Fuengirola and was racing past the Playa
de Calahonda, around the high-rise apartment
blocks towering over the promenades that ran
parallel to the beaches and the sea in the afternoon's shimmering light.

'I've already booked you into the hotel,'
Mairead told them. 'No problem at all. As I'm
payin' the bill you're both booked in under my
false passport and don't have to sign in. We'll
just be there tonight. Tomorrow we'll book out
of the hotel and visit the Rock. If we decide to do
the job, we'll phone for the second car and let our
driver bring in the bomb. The blocker, this car,
will leave the parking space and let the driver in
with the bomb. He'll then leave the car, following

us back across the border. When we detonate
the bomb, which we'll do from the Spanish side,
we'll avoid Málaga entirely – they'll be checkin'
everyone at that airport – and instead drive all
the way across country to Bilbao and take the
boat from there to Southampton. With luck, we
should make it.'

She felt more confident having said it, but then
Mad Dan leant a little sideways, breathing into
her ear, to tell her in his frightening way: 'You
just said: "If we decide to do the job."'

'Aye, I . . .'

He stabbed at her shoulder with his index
finger – once, twice, three times. 'Well, I'm
tellin' you, girl, there's nothin' to decide. Tyrone
wondered about you, he had his doubts there, an'
he sent me along to make sure that there was no
backin' out. We're goin' to do it, you hear me?
Fuck the Spanish and the Portuguese. Fuck the
pensioners an' the backpackers and the so-called
innocent children. We're going to bomb the shite
out of that little England on Gibraltar an' that's
all there is to it. Now let's get to the hotel.'

Mad Dan had long been confident of his ability
to frighten people and he therefore thought it
natural that Mairead did not respond to his tirade
but merely drove on in silence until they arrived
at Marbella and the kind of hotel he would
normally not even have considered entering.
Once out of the car, however, and walking to

the bar where they were to meet the demolitions man, she stopped, turned to face him, poked her finger repeatedly in his chest as he had done to her, and whispered, as if not wanting Sean to hear: 'There *are* things to decide and I'm the one to decide them. While we're here, while we're not packing guns, you'll take orders from me. We're carryin' no weapons, McCann. We won't be picked up for that. Without a gun in your hand you're not nearly as strong as I am and don't ever forget it. Sure, I'm in charge here, Mister. I decide what's right and wrong. An' if I decide that we're not bombin' the Rock, then we *don't* bomb the Rock.'

'For God's sakes, girl, I just . . .'

'If you don't like it, leave. Explain that to Pat Tyrone. Go back an' tell him that you let a woman defeat you and then wait for his thanks. Meanwhile, whether you like it or not, I'll do what I think's right. So are you in or out, Mister?'

Mad Dan quivered with rage, opened and closed his mouth, breathed deeply, then eventually managed to control himself and whispered: 'I'm in.'

'Sure, that's a grand thing to hear. Now be careful what you say in this bar when we talk about business. This man, though he's always helped us out, is still an unknown quantity. He makes his money here – not in Northern

Ireland – and that makes him suspect. Do you understand?'

'Ackaye.'

'Let's get on, then.'

Mairead led Mad Dan and Sean into the bar, where they found a suntanned Irishman, Neil Dogherty, wearing a flowered Hawaiian-style shirt, white trousers and flip-flops, a Rolex on his wrist, with what looked like a doubled gin awash with ice cubes on the table in front of him. He had one of those ready-made smiles that only fools trust but few can resist.

'Have you come?' he said.

'Ackaye,' Mairead replied, then introduced Sean and Mad Dan by the names they had on their false passports.

'Nice to meet you,' Dogherty said.

'And you,' Sean replied.

'Grand,' Mad Dan said. 'Sure, you look like a very healthy Irishman with that tan an' all.'

'Nearly ten years here by now,' Dogherty explained when they were all seated around the table and had ordered their drinks, including another double gin for himself. 'So the suntan comes for free. As for the clothes, sure you couldn't wear them in Ireland, but they're natural here.'

'Must've cost a bob or two.'

Mairead cast a quick, nervous glance at Mad Dan, which he failed to notice.

'Enough,' the man said.

'You make a good livin' here, then.'

'Aye, it's all right.'

'Sellin' groceries to your fellow-countrymen instead of makin' a contribution.'

Now the arms dealer was looking uncomfortable. 'Sure, a man has to eat,' he said.

'Aye, don't we all?' Mad Dan replied with a sneer.

'So,' Mairead broke in. 'Can we pick up the groceries?'

'They're all ready,' Dogherty said, referring to the Semtex and detonators paid for in advance when Dogherty had met her in the same bar three days earlier. 'Sure, I've done all the shoppin'. My car's parked beside your Renault down below in the car park, so we just have to go down an' collect them.'

'Sure, that's grand,' Mairead said. 'I hate shoppin' when I don't know the language. Makes me feel a quare fool.'

'Aye,' Dogherty said with a broad grin. 'I used to feel that way myself, but my Spanish is pickin' up.'

'Must be grand to speak a foreign language,' Sean said with no trace of irony.

'Sure, it helps,' Dogherty told him. 'When in Spain, do what the Spaniards do. That law applies to everywhere.'

'Exceptin' Ireland,' Sean told him. 'In Ireland,

the Irish language is for the minority an' I think that's real criminal.'

'Sure, it is, when you think about it,' Dogherty said, 'but what can you do? The Brits robbed us of our language as well as our freedom and it's possible we'll never get it back. These are quare times indeed.'

'We'll get it back,' Mad Dan said. 'Sure, that's part of why we're here. We're not here just to get a suntan and wear fancy clothes. We're here to buy groceries that some countrymen would offer us for free because they know what we're plannin' to do will help set Ireland free.'

'Don't tell me what you're plannin',' Dogherty replied, his suntanned face flushed with anger. 'That's not part of the deal.'

'I wouldn't deal with the likes of you,' Mad Dan said, 'if I had my own way. I'd stay clear of the smell of you and your groceries. You can take that as written.'

Mairead glared at him. Apart from the possibility that he might blow this deal with his insults, you could never tell where a wall was bugged, when a man had been wired, and Mad Dan was blabbing too much for her liking.

'Sure, let's all relax,' she said.

'Sure, what else are we here for?' Mad Dan asked with a crooked, malicious grin.

'To have a holiday,' Mairead said. 'To get pissed and get a suntan. To eat all those groceries

Neil brought and wash them down with cheap wine. Sure, isn't life in Spain grand? Isn't that right, Sean?'

'Ackaye, this is a grand place to be. Sure, it's summer already. That's why I come here – for the sun. For the cheap booze and food. I've always loved it in Spain.'

'Me, too,' Mairead said. 'And talkin' about the groceries,' she added. 'Was the money enough?'

'Right as rain. You can have the change later.'

'Well, let's go an' eat.'

They all finished their drinks, then followed Dogherty out of the bar and down into the hotel's dimly lit underground car park. There, as Dogherty had stated, they found his gleaming Audi 80 parked beside their rented white Renault 5. No further transactions were necessary and when the Semtex, already packed into a bomb made by Dogherty, was passed with the detonators from the boot of the Audi into the much smaller boot of the Renault, Dogherty placed his hand on Mairead's shoulder and said: 'Thanks for the business. Sure, come back anytime.'

Mairead did not smile. 'If this lot's not to standard,' she said, 'we'll come back to find you.'

The smile froze on Dogherty's face, became a grimace of fear, then returned to the semblance of good humour. 'Sure, you've no need to worry,' he said. 'Certain people I wouldn't cross.'

'Make sure you don't.'

Shaking his head from side to side, as if saying, 'What next?', Dogherty climbed into his car and roared off, leaving the other three standing beside the white Renault in the dimly lit, concrete wilderness of the car park. They all gazed down at the boot for some time, breathing heavily, saying nothing, as if hypnotized, or possibly frightened, by what was in there.

After a long silence Mairead took a deep breath and said: 'Right. So everything's set. Tomorrow we'll take the other car over to the Rock and check the target area again. If we decide to do it – if *I* decide we do it – we'll phone the driver, who's here in the hotel, and tell him to bring this car across. If we decide not to do it – if *I* decide that – then we'll come back here, get rid of this stuff, and head back to Málaga. Now let's get back to the hotel. Right?'

'Right,' Sean said.

There was a long, uncomfortable silence before Mad Dan, trying to control himself, nodded and said: 'Right.'

With everything arranged, they all went to their separate rooms and lay down in darkness. Mairead couldn't sleep at all, Sean had dreams of death and destruction, but Mad Dan slept the sleep of a child with his thumb in his mouth, at peace with the world.

The next morning, still undecided, they drove to Gibraltar.

12

Three days before the assumed date of the attack, shortly after the arrival of the three terrorists at Málaga had been reported to British Intelligence by Madrid's ever-alert Servicios de Información, the Special Projects Team, including the SAS, were flown into Gibraltar to await the arrival of the IRA bombers. The eleven members of the team, including the four-man SAS CQB team and two Special Branch women, arrived over a period of days and finally assembled at the Rock Hotel on Friday 5 March.

Gathering in other parts of the Rock was a swarm of security people of both sexes, mainly from MI5, augmented by local Special Branch personnel, to act as watchers and as an armed reserve.

That evening, in a room in the Rock Hotel, the SAS tactical leader, Captain Mike Edwards, introduced the two MI5 women who would work with the SAS men in tackling the terrorists when they arrived. Dressed in deliberately chosen plain clothes — blouse, skirt, short jackets and flat shoes, in keeping with local styles — both women, in their early twenties, were slim, attractive, good-humoured and surprisingly tough.

'These two ladies are from MI5,' Captain Edwards said to his gathered men, 'and have been assigned as plain-clothes watchers who'll follow both the terrorists and you lot while keeping in touch with operational control via Landmasters. This is Mary Hattersley,' he continued, indicating the smaller, blonde woman. He then pointed to the taller brunette and said: 'And this is Barbara Jennings. You may address them by their first names, just as you do each other.'

'How are you?' Sergeant Carruthers asked distractedly, keen to get on with the business in hand.

'Fine, thank you,' Mary Hattersley said.

'Welcome to the SAS,' Sergeant Ainsworth said.

'Thanks, Sarge,' Barbara Jennings said.

'Good to have you aboard,' Corporal Dymock said. 'You're a sight for sore eyes.'

'I'll second that,' Corporal Billings said.

'My two corporals aren't as rakish as they sound and look,' Captain Edwards said slyly. 'They're actually both engaged to be married to very nice girls.'

'Congratulations,' Mary Hattersley said.

'Gee, thanks, Captain,' Dymock practically whined.

'Shot down in my prime,' Billings added. 'It's great to be in the SAS.'

'All right, you two,' Carruthers reprimanded

them, wanting to get on with the business at hand. 'Stop fooling around. OK, boss, the floor's all yours.'

As his four men, all wearing civilian clothes – casual jackets, open-necked shirts, jeans and trainers – broke into cheesy grins, Edwards introduced them to the ladies, pointing to each in turn as he called out their names. 'They're all brighter than they look,' he explained, 'though that may not be saying much.'

The two groups, men and women, smiled again at each other, then settled back to listen to the 'Head Shed'.

'These four men,' Captain Edwards began, addressing the ladies, 'will be split into two balanced CQB teams – by balanced, I mean one sergeant and one corporal in each team – and each of you ladies will follow one of those teams until the mission's been completed.'

'Are any other SAS men involved?' Barbara Jennings asked.

'Yes. We *do* have other SAS men on the Rock, but they'll be deployed at various points along the crossing from Spain right into Gibraltar.'

'Just who are we looking for?' Carruthers asked.

'You'll be informed in greater detail at the briefing scheduled to take place at midnight tonight. For now, I can only tell you that we're dealing with an IRA Active Service Unit that's planning to detonate a bomb here on the Rock. The purpose of the mission is to arrest them – arrest, disarm, and defuse the bomb. The people involved are all highly trained activists with considerable knowledge of both the making and use of bombs. They've also been known to have used a wide variety of personal weapons in the past and are knowledgeable about surveillance and interrogation techniques. In short, they're not back-street thugs, but highly trained, dangerous terrorists.'

'Are they under surveillance right now?' Ainsworth asked.

'Yes and no. The two men were observed arriving today by separate flights at Málaga, where they were met by a female and driven off by her in a rented white Renault 5. They're now somewhere between Málaga and the Rock.'

'You mean the Spanish police lost them,' the sergeant said contemptuously.

'Not that easy, I suspect,' Edwards replied generously, 'to keep your eye on three people driving a common type of car along the busy N340. Nevertheless, as they haven't yet shown up at the border, they're fully expected to materialize some time tomorrow, when they'll be allowed in.'

'Why not stop them there and then?'

'We have to ensure that no military action takes place on Spanish soil.'

'I'm glad to hear we're taking care not to embarrass the Spaniards,' Dymock said. 'Let's not spoil the tourist trade, eh?'

'So what are they actually here for?' Billings asked more seriously.

'The present action,' Edwards told him, 'is based on surveillance conducted on the same three when they came to Spain and Gibraltar previously – two in November, one earlier this month. For this reason we believe that they've returned to plant a bomb at the location of the Changing of the Guard and band parade ceremony, now set for 8 March, in three days' time. We also have reason to believe that they'll use a large bomb designed to kill as many soldiers as possible, as well as the civilians watching the event. That bomb will probably be detonated by remote control, almost certainly with a button control carried by at least one, and possibly all three, of the terrorists.'

'Which means that if confronted, the terrorists might instantly detonate the bomb,' Carruthers said.

'Correct. We also believe that these three extremely dangerous individuals will be armed and, if challenged, won't think twice about using their weapons.'

'So though the intention is to arrest and disarm them, and defuse the bomb, we have to bear in mind that if given enough time they'll use their weapons and probably press the button too.'

'Correct.'

'That doesn't give us any time at all to decide what to do – either shout a warning and arrest, or shoot to kill.'

Edwards sighed. 'I'm afraid not.'

'Do they plan to make the bomb here on the Rock or are they bringing it in?' asked Ainsworth.

'Based on information received from MI5, we believe that they'll arrive here by car and that the car will contain a bomb and won't be just a blocker.'

'I'm sorry,' Mary Hattersley interjected, 'but I'm not familiar with that terminology. What's a "blocker"?'

'An empty vehicle used to occupy a space that will subsequently be filled by the car containing the bomb. Usually the blocker will be driven into the nearest convenient parking space a few days before the day chosen for the bombing. Should any search be made of the cars parked in that area, the blocker will be found to be safe. Then, on the day set for the actual bombing, sometimes mere minutes before the time chosen for detonation, the blocker will be driven away and its space immediately taken up with the car containing the bomb. The driver then leaves the second car, gets well clear of the area and finally either he or another member of the ASU team detonates the bomb by remote control. That's what we believe is going to happen in this particular instance.'

'At what point do we use our weapons?' Carruthers asked.

'I repeat: the purpose of the mission is arrest, disarm and defuse the bomb. However, weapons may be used should you – and I quote from the official directive – "have reasonable grounds for believing that an act is being committed which would endanger life or lives and if there is no other way of preventing that other than with firearms". Read that as you may.'

'So if we have to shoot, we shoot to kill?' Carruthers asked.

'You neutralize, yes. These people may have a button control or hidden weapons, so you shoot and keep shooting until their hands are well away from the body.' Though the men were grinning, the women glanced uneasily at each other as Edwards studied his watch. 'It's nearly midnight,' he said. 'Time for the official briefing. Follow me, please.'

After leading them out of the room and down the stairs to the hotel car park, Edwards personally drove them in a borrowed Ford Cortina along the dark, lamplit Europa Road to the Lathbury Barracks. When they had each shown their personal identification card to the armed guard at the steel gates they were allowed to drive through to a car park filled with British Army troop lorries, jeeps, some Saracen armoured cars, a few ambulances and unmarked 'Q' cars. They clambered out of the car, which Edwards carefully locked, and marched to the solid steel door of a lift that carried them up to an ultra-secure briefing centre hidden deep within the gun galleries of the Rock itself. As Edwards knew from personal experience, these secret galleries and caverns also contained a model of a 'typical Ulster village' where soldiers, including the SAS, were trained in counter-insurgency techniques. He did not, however, impart this knowledge when he left the lift and led his six-strong team into a large hall where other elements of the Flavius force, about fifty people in all, including carefully screened members of the local police, were waiting for the briefing to commence.

Seated at the long table on the raised dais overlooking the men and women in rows of steel-framed chairs was the advisory group in charge of the briefing. Studying them, Edwards recognized some British Intelligence officers from MI5 and MI6, the chief of Gibraltar's Special Branch, the Deputy Commissioner of Gibraltar, and two Lieutenant Colonels, one from HQ Special Forces, the other from 22 SAS. This, Edwards knew, was also the team that would advise the Police Commissioner, who was nominally in charge of law enforcement.

The briefing opened with the head of Special Branch repeating the official objectives of Operation Flavius and the 'rules of engagement', including the need for 'minimum' force, which contradicted what Edwards had just told his men in private. 'In other words,' he summarized, after droning on for ten minutes to the increasingly bored, sometimes confused SAS men, 'every effort should be made to protect life, to foil the bomb attempt, to make arrests and to take custody of the prisoners. Any questions?'

'Yes, sir,' Edwards responded promptly. 'Do you now know the identities of the terrorists?'

'Yes. Daniel McCann, Sean Savage and Mairead Farrell.'

'A psychopath and a female fanatic,' Carruthers whispered to his fellow-sergeant, Ainsworth, 'with an unknown quantity in between. It doesn't look good to me, mate.'

'The three terrorists,' the head of Special Branch continued, as if to confirm what Carruthers had whispered, 'are believed to be armed and highly dangerous – so dangerous, in fact, that we can't leave this job to the local police. That's why the SAS were called in. Though the Spanish police lost track of the terrorists soon after they left Málaga, they're believed to be heading for Gibraltar in a rented white Renault 5 containing a bomb. But at this point we don't know exactly where they are. And nor do we know exactly when they plan to cross into Gibraltar.'

'There are no Spanish representatives at this briefing?' Edwards asked in disbelief.

'No.'

'So we can't ask what the Spanish authorities are doing about a large bomb being driven around one of the most densely populated tourist areas in Spain.'

'No.'

'Do the Gibraltar police know that a high-powered anti-terrorist operation is going on under their very noses?'

'Some are uninformed,' the head of Special Branch replied with a steely smile. 'Others have been deliberately misinformed for security reasons.'

'So can we take it,' the British Army Lieutenant Colonel asked, 'that the Spanish authorities – and therefore, by implication, the British authorities – may indeed have the terrorists under surveillance, but actually *want* them to enter Gibraltar in order that they can be either arrested or neutralized?'

'You may deduce from it what you like, but I simply cannot answer that question.'

'How will the terrorists be dealt with?' the Police Commissioner asked, looking worried.

The head of Special Branch nodded at the SAS Lieutenant Colonel sitting to his left, indicating that he should answer the question. 'A four-man team wearing civilian clothing and carrying radios and nine-millies – 9mm Browning High Power handguns,' the Lieutenant Colonel said, clarifying the term for those not familiar with SAS slang, 'will arrest the terrorists and allow the bomb to be defused. The other SAS men, supported by male and female watchers from MI5 and Special Branch, will be in various strategic positions from where they can track the terrorists' movements and, if necessary, lend support in a fire-fight. All will be in radio contact with an operations centre located here and commanded by Captain Edwards.'

'What about the legalities of this affair with particular regard to the laws of Gibraltar?' the Commissioner asked.

'A local policeman will be with the soldiers to act as witness and take any arrested terrorists into custody.'

'Are there any clearly defined rules for a situation such as this?' the Commissioner persisted. 'I mean in a situation where the attempted arrest could lead to a fire-fight or, even worse, to the setting off of the bomb by a button control?'

'The SOP – standard operating procedure – has been well rehearsed. Once the SAS men decide to make the arrest, they'll shout: "Stop! Police! Hands up!" If the terrorists comply, they'll be made to lie face down on the ground with arms away from the body, to ensure that they can't press the button or reach for their weapons. Should they attempt to do either before obeying the commands, the SAS will open fire. Any more questions?'

There were no more questions.

Back in the Rock Hotel in the early hours of Saturday 6 March, when the four men chosen for the assault team had gathered together for a 'Chinese parliament' – an informal discussion of tactics – with Captain Edwards, Sergeant Carruthers said bluntly: 'Now that the political and diplomatic bullshit is over, Captain, what's the real story regarding how we should tackle these murdering Paddies?'

'You heard the real story at the briefing,' Edwards replied disingenuously. 'And I'm sure you heard correctly.'

'But before the briefing, you said . . .'

'What I said was off the record, Sergeant.'

'A lot of what was said at that briefing was just rubbish kit,' Carruthers persisted. 'More dangerous to us than to the enemy. Never mind bloody minimum force! I want to know what we *really* do when push comes to shove.'

'Yes, sir, what *is* minimum force,' Dymock asked, 'in a situation like this?'

'Let's call it *reasonable* force,' Edwards told

him. 'Shooting only if absolutely necessary and no more than's required.'

'That tells us a lot, boss,' Ainsworth said. 'What's reasonable in Northern Ireland might not be reasonable here. You've already said that if we shoot, we shoot to kill. Given what we've just heard about minimum force, can we take that as read?'

Well aware of the fact that if anything went wrong he would carry the can, Edwards replied carefully: 'I believe the orders provide for the use of lethal force for the preservation of life. In other words, if you think they're going to fire or press the button, you shoot before they can do so.'

'Do we have any proof that they'll be armed as the head of Special Branch said?' asked Carruthers.

'No, Sergeant, in truth we haven't. Given their track records, we can't imagine them coming here *unarmed* – but we don't have the proof.'

'So we stand the chance of shooting unarmed people.'

'Possibly unarmed – but almost certainly carrying a button-job. I think that's the clincher.'

'So if they offer any kind of resistance,' Dymock said, 'or even refuse to put up their hands, we don't hesitate to open fire.'

'No, you don't,' Edwards said.

'In that case, how many rounds?' Carruthers asked.

'You keep firing until the terrorist is no longer a threat.'

'If we do that, we could be accused of over-kill.'

'A wounded terrorist – even mortally wounded – can still initiate the button to detonate a bomb. You must ensure that he or she doesn't get the chance to do so.'

'So even if he or she is down, we keep firing until we're absolutely sure that they've been neutralized.'

'Correct.'

'We'll only have the nine-milly?'

'Yes, only one handgun each. Each with four magazines – forty-eight shots per man. A total of 192 rounds between the four of you. The ammo, however, will be a new 9mm mix of British and French smokeless propellant. It emits less smoke and flash than traditional gunpowder.'

'And those two sexy ladies,' Dymock said. 'The MI5 watchers. What will they be doing while we're closing in on the terrorists?'

'They'll be giving us hand-jobs,' Billings said hopefully.

'To relieve the tension,' Dymock clarified.

'You two have filthy mouths,' Ainsworth said, 'and you're not concentrating, so shut up, listen and concentrate.'

'You men won't be able to take your eyes off the terrorists for a second,' Edwards explained. 'You'll have your nine-millies holstered in the cross-draw position under your jackets and you'll have to be ready to use them on the instant. This means, in effect, that you could find yourselves in a situation where you don't have time to communicate with me, even using the miniature microphones and ear-worn receivers. Those two sexy ladies, therefore – incidentally both well trained and highly efficient – will always be a short distance behind you and the terrorists, out of sight but in constant contact with the operational room, to call in a Quick Reaction Force if necessary. If, on the other hand, the QRF isn't required, but the terrorists have been neutralized, the watchers will call for a couple of Q cars to lift you out of the killing grounds before you're identified.'

'Well, *that's* a relief,' Ainsworth said.

'So what happens now?' Dymock asked, checking his watch and noting that it was nearly two in the morning of Sunday 6 March.

'Now you sleep,' Edwards told him, 'and hopefully wake refreshed tomorrow, prepared for anything.'

The Chinese parliament broke up and the CQB team retired to their beds in a British Army barracks not much different from the 'spider' back in Hereford. Given the dangerous task they had been set, they all slept surprisingly well.

13

Jolted out of their sleep by early alarm calls, the four SAS men rolled out of their beds in the Rock Hotel, showered, shaved and dressed in their civilian operational clothes, then went down to the dining-room for breakfast like normal residents, all sitting at separate tables and pretending not to know one another.

As they finished eating they left the restaurant one by one and made their way along Europa Road to the Lathbury Barracks, where, after showing their identification cards, they were admitted through the guarded steel gates. Each of them then walked to the steel lift that took them up into the network of gun galleries and caverns where the briefing centre was hidden, along with various military command centres and the mock Ulster village used for training purposes. There, in a small room containing only a rectangular wooden table with bench-style seats around the four walls, the men gathered together with Captain Edwards and the two MI5 watchers, the small, blonde-haired Mary Hattersley and the taller brunette, Barbara Jennings. Both women were dressed, as the day before, in relatively plain blouse, skirt, short jacket and flat shoes. Only

Captain Edwards was in uniform, the maroon beret with its winged-dagger SAS badge perched at a rakish angle on his head.

Behind Edwards was a cork pinboard covered with maps of the Rock of Gibraltar and photos of the three terrorists expected that day.

Four 9mm Browning High Power handguns were laid out on the table, each with a single fourteen-round magazine beside it and a leather holster with belt. At one end of the table there were two Pace Communications Ltd Landmaster III transceivers and four sets of Davies M135b covert microphones with accompanying ear-worn receivers, matching pairs of miniature radios and wrist-worn on-off switches.

'Morning, ladies and gentlemen,' Edwards said in his urbane manner. 'I trust you're all feeling bright and chirpy after a good night's sleep.' When this greeting was returned with various murmured salutations, Edwards picked up a pointer and tapped it against the photos of the three terrorists, one after the other: 'Sean Savage,' he said, tapping the head-shot of the younger man. 'Mad Dan McCann,' he said, tapping the nose of the older man. 'And this,' he continued, tapping the image of a strikingly attractive woman, 'is Mairead Farrell.'

Lowering the pointer and looking at everyone in turn, Edwards saw that even the younger men, Dymock and Billings, were listening intently and not casting flirtatious glances at Mary Hattersley and Barbara Jennings. Pleased, he raised the pointer to the board and again tapped each of the three photos.

'Study these faces well. Let them burn into your memory. Make sure that when you go out into the streets of Gibraltar, you don't mistake anyone else for these people.' Tapping the photos of the two men in turn, he said: 'These are the two who turned up in Málaga last November and paid a couple of visits to the Rock. The woman arrived a week ago, visited the Rock just about every day, and was observed yesterday afternoon greeting Savage and McCann when they arrived for the second time at Málaga airport. We still don't know where they are at this moment, but we're expecting them to turn up here sometime today. If this is the case, we must assume that they're here to do serious damage.'

'So this is the day we stop them,' Ainsworth said.

'Correct. For this purpose you four men will be divided into two-man teams. Team One will be Sergeant Carruthers and Corporal Dymock, Team Two Sergeant Ainsworth and Corporal Billings. You four have been picked because it was considered wise for each team to have a lead and a backup man – a sergeant and a corporal – and, in particular, because you're all proven experts at the double tap. And this is a CQB double-tap operation.'

'You hear that, ladies?' Dymock said with a cocky grin. 'We're the best of the best.'

'We're so thrilled just to be here,' Barbara Jennings said deadpan. 'It's an honour, believe me.'

'We believe you,' Billings said, grinning.

'Modesty becomes you,' Carruthers told the corporals. 'Now shut up and listen to the boss. This is no time for silly games.'

But he wasn't angry. He was experienced enough to know that the younger men had decided to flirt with the women in order to settle their own nerves. This was a dangerous, unpredictable operation and all of them knew it.

'Don't forget,' Edwards said, 'when you're out in the street that you'll have backup not only from these two fine ladies here, but also from armed Gibraltar policemen, other MI5 surveillance officers, and the rest of the SAS men flown in yesterday. Though keeping out of sight, they'll have you under surveillance at all times and be ready to make an urgent appearance should it be necessary.'

'When does all this start?' Ainsworth asked.

'A local Special Branch officer is working hand in glove with Spanish security on the Spanish side of the border. He's aware, as are the Spanish, that we're expecting the three terrorists today – he knows there are two men and a woman – and that they're travelling in a hired white

Renault 5. He also has the registration number, which was picked up from the Avis office in Málaga. Whether the terrorists arrive together or separately, the Special Branch officer will be able to identify them and will notify my command centre of their arrival. When he does, you'll move out and track them down, following directions transmitted to your covert receivers. When you see the terrorists, you'll attempt to get into a position where you can challenge them, giving them the chance to surrender. From that point on you must use your own initiative, bearing in mind what was said formally at the briefing and what I personally told you rather more informally.'

'That's walking a tightrope,' Carruthers said.

'I know, Sarge, and I don't like it either, but we'll have to live with it. Are there any last questions?'

All the men shook their heads.

'Good. Your weapons are on the table.' Edwards jabbed his index finger at the four handguns spread out neatly on the table. 'One nine-milly and one magazine each. That's it. That's all you get.'

As the men were loading the magazines, which made a sharp, metallic sound as they were slotted in, Edwards turned to Mary Hattersley and Barbara Jennings. 'You ladies,' he said, 'will be equipped with one Landmaster III transceiver each, tuned to this operational HQ, where I'll be in charge. Your brief is to stay well behind the CQB teams following the terrorists and to keep me informed of what's happening. Most importantly, as stated yesterday, once the terrorists are apprehended, you'll call in the transport to take them away and also the bomb-disposal team who're on stand-by here. Finally, should the CQB teams be forced to neutralize the terrorists, you'll immediately call up two Q cars to remove them before they're identified. Any questions?'

Mary Hattersley shook her head from side to side.

'No,' Barbara Jennings said.

'Good. Now pick up your transceivers and keep them with you at all times – at least from now until the mission has been completed and my men are out of town.'

As the two MI5 watchers picked up and checked their transceivers, Edwards turned back to his men and checked that they were all wearing their Brownings in the proper cross-draw position up under their jackets, around the back where they could be easily withdrawn. Satisfied, he nodded towards the miniature communications equipment still left on the table. 'One set to each man,' he said. 'Please put them on and check that they're working. They should already be tuned in to the command centre, and someone at the other end, in my HQ, is waiting to hear if they're working. Just state your rank and name.

When the man on the other end of the line responds, say: "Over and out." Now get to it, chaps.'

Already familiar with this kind of communications equipment, which they had used in the OP in Belfast when spying on Mairead Farrell and the others entering and leaving the Republican pub across the road, the men had no trouble in sorting out the various components: M135b covert microphone attached to a standard safety-pin; miniature microphones positioned in the collar of the shirt; the on-off switch taped to the wrist of the hand not used for firing the handgun; and two miniature radios hidden on the person; one tuned into the military command network, there deep within the Rock, the other to the surveillance network, including the Landmark III transceivers in the care of Mary Hattersley and Barbara Jennings.

When everything was in place, the men took turns to identify themselves through the microphones, checking that they could indeed be heard where they were supposed to be tuned to. With everything deemed to be in working order, they turned back to Edwards.

'What now?' Carruthers asked.

'Now we wait,' Edwards told him.

The local Special Branch officer, Detective Constable Wilby, on duty on the Spanish side of the border, was seated in an enclosed room beside a Spanish immigration officer, Juan Ribera. Both men were facing a screen on to which the Spaniards were projecting images of passport photographs and numbers taken from people crossing the border by foot. Also, car registration numbers were being passed to Wilby by Ribera, who was in contact by telephone with his Spanish colleagues watching the cars go through.

Aware of the fact that the white Renault 5 hired by the terrorists at Málaga airport might have been changed for another car by now, Wilby was checking the registration numbers given to him by Ribera against a list of all the available rental cars along the coast between Málaga and Algeciras – enough to give him a headache. He was also checking them against a second list of suspect registration numbers, taken from Spanish and Gilbraltarian police files of cars either stolen or known to have been used for illegal purposes.

Wilby had been instructed to look out for two men and a woman named as Savage, McCann and Farrell, but travelling under false passports, the details of which had been given to him by his superiors. Pinned to the wall in front of him, just below the window, were photographs of the three wanted persons. Wilby was in contact by personal radio with Captain Edwards in his HQ in the command centre and prepared to call him the minute the white Renault 5 or the terrorists on foot were sighted outside. He was also passing on details of passports and car registration numbers given to him by the Spaniards, where he thought they had, or may have, relevance.

He had been doing this all morning and was becoming monumentally bored, convinced that it was all a hoax, when, just before 12.30 p.m., Ribera listened to the telephone, scribbling down a number as he did so, then tore the paper out of the notebook and handed it to him.

It was a Spanish registration number.

'A white Renault 5,' Ribera told him. 'Just coming through.'

When Wilby saw the car, with an Avis sticker on it, approaching from the gates of passport control and customs, he became very excited and checked the registration number against the one he had listed for the terrorists' rented vehicle. It was the same number.

He watched as the white Renault 5 drove past him and across the runway towards Winston Churchill Avenue, which led to the central shopping area of Gibraltar, including the band assembly area. There was only one person in the vehicle: a male driver.

As instructed, Wilby did nothing to stop the car. He did, however, hurriedly telephone Captain Edwards at the operations centre.

'Mike?'

'Yes.'

'Our white Renault has just gone through and is heading for the centre of town, probably for the car park.'

'Were all three subjects in it?'

'No, only the driver – a male.'

'Right. The other two are either coming in a second car or have been dropped off on the Spanish side and will cross by foot. If they're in a car, they might be difficult to spot, but please do your best.'

Two hours later, Wilby saw two faintly familiar faces – one male and one female – emerging from the sea of people crossing by foot into Gibraltar. When he glanced down at the photos pinned to the wall beneath the window, he was able instantly to match their faces with those of Daniel McCann and Mairead Farrell. The woman he would have recognized a mile away from her pale face framed by long, dark hair.

Now even more excited, Wilby watched the man and woman as they passed his hidden room and walked on towards the runway that led to the Rock. He then picked up the telephone and dialled the command centre again.

'Mike! McCann and Farrell have just passed through on foot and are walking towards the airstrip right now.'

'Good work,' Edwards replied. 'That's all three of them in. Thanks a million, Ken.'

'My pleasure,' Wilby said.

209

Dropping the telephone, Wilby continued to watch the couple as they crossed the runway and eventually were lost to sight somewhere in the heat haze along Winston Churchill Avenue. Even when they were out of sight, he kept looking towards the Rock, expecting to hear or see something dramatic at any moment.

In fact, forty-five minutes passed before the phone rang again. When Wilby picked it up, noting that it was exactly a quarter past three, he was informed that the IRA team had been spotted on the Rock and that he could now leave and return to his own HQ there.

Delighted that things had gone so smoothly, Wilby left the concealed office, climbed on to his motor-bike and raced across the airstrip, along Winston Churchill Avenue, then into Smith Darrien Road. Bogged down in traffic in the latter thoroughfare, he slowed practically to a crawl, then had to stop altogether.

There, mere yards away, he saw Mad Dan McCann and Mairead Farrell, walking side by side and, as he watched, exchanging newspapers. Sean Savage was trailing close behind them.

Mesmerized by the sight of all three terrorists so close to him, the Special Branch man had no way of knowing that all three of them would be dead within minutes.

Mairead Farrell was dressed in a skirt and blouse, Daniel McCann was in grey trousers and a white shirt, and Sean Savage was wearing grey trousers and a sober pinstripe jacket when they descended to the basement car park of their hotel in Marbella. First they checked that the Semtex and the detonators in one of the white Renaults were still in good shape, then they climbed into the other Renault, and Sean drove them out of the garage, leaving the car containing the bomb still in its parking space.

'I still don't think this is right,' Mad Dan said as Sean joined the N340 in the direction of Gibraltar. 'We shouldn't leave that bomb-car so long in the car park. Sure, we should get it over an' done with. Set the bomb off today.'

'I don't give a damn what you think,' Mairead replied. 'I still have my doubts about this job and I want 'em resolved. So we'll drive to Gibraltar and look around one last time, then decide yes or no. If yes, we'll do the job two days from now, right in the middle of the Changin' of the Guard. You want somethin' outrageous, Dan? Then that should do the trick. Not today, not tomorrow, but the next day, when the place'll be packed with bystanders. Isn't that what you want?'

'Sure, I'm not convinced we should do it at all,' Sean told her, 'but if we do, then we should do it on Tuesday. I agree on that much.'

Sean was still feeling haunted after a night of vivid nightmares in which he'd seen the ghosts of all the dead of all the buildings he had bombed in the past: bloody, broken, scorched, stripped to the bone, howling out in a manner so dreadful that it went beyond agony. Sean was torn by what he did, which is why he was quiet about it. On the one hand he believed that a man should fight for his beliefs; on the other he had never bombed an inhabited building without suffering the torments of the damned.

Essentially religious, steeped in history and the beauty of the Irish language, Sean lived as intimately with guilt as a man could do without being destroyed by it. His silence was based on shame. He had tried to bury it, but failed. In the incandescence of his dreams he saw hell's fires waiting to claim him. He believed in his country, was willing to fight for it, but increasingly he bore the burden of guilt over those he had killed. So he had doubts about Gibraltar and was glad he was not alone.

'We should at least be armed when we go there,' Mad Dan insisted, growing ever more frustrated but still shocked by the ruthlessness shown so clearly by Mairead the previous day. 'Sure, bejasus, that place is filled with Brit soldiers and we might have to . . .'

'I've told you before and I'm telling you again,' Mairead said, glancing back over her shoulder to where Mad Dan was sitting in the rear seat. 'We're taking no guns. Those things invite trouble. There could be X-ray machines at those border posts and if there are we'd be licked before we started. So no guns, an' that's final. No guns and no bombs today.'

And maybe not even on Tuesday, she thought. Not while Mad Dan is with us.

She felt exhausted and nervous from lack of sleep, not having slept a wink the previous night. She'd tossed and turned, recalling the Conway Hotel all of ten years ago, the smoke and the fire and the ruins, with the dead and injured buried under rubble, the latter screaming for help. In order to carry out that bombing Mairead had been compelled to bury a small, secret part of herself. But once the deed had been accomplished and she'd found herself in prison, her moments of guilt and horror, which came fleetingly but often, had gradually faded away as she prided herself on the admiration of her fellow prisoners.

'Sure, you sacrificed yourself for your country,' they constantly told her. 'You're the best of the best, girl.'

Such praise had sustained her for the first few

of her ten long years, but eventually, as her first prison friends were released, she had withdrawn into herself. Eventually, as she felt herself ageing within those walls, gradually being drained dry, she had succumbed to relentless insomnia and started taking sedation to help her sleep. By the time she got out of prison, ten years older, she was a shadow of the woman she had been, albeit still beautiful.

It was her beauty that had saved her, bringing Tom Riley to her. God, yes, even now when she thought of Tom, she swelled with pride and pain. She had met him in that pub, the one she was in when he died, and the meeting of their minds, their mutual commitment to the cause, had soon led to physical affirmation and the flowering of true love. Then Tom had blown himself up and after that it had *all* blown apart: all her great hopes for the future.

Had it not been for the Prods, Tom wouldn't have died. Mairead blamed them even for that. Yes, she hated the Prods. But did she? Not really. It was the Brits she hated, for setting the Prods against the Catholics and creating a war. She knew that right enough, lived by it, killed for it; but she had always tried to remember that there were limits and that one had to abide by them. The Rock of Gibraltar could represent one of those limits and she was trying to work it out.

A bomb outrage was one thing – nasty but

necessary. But the Rock of Gibraltar was a British Crown Colony – not really British; just another colonized piece of land, ruthlessly stolen, like Northern Ireland – and as Sean had rightly said, it was filled with foreigners, including old people and children, who in no way represented Britain or even supported it. To bomb such a place, particularly where they were planning to do so – a school, a Jewish old people's home, a walkers' hostel, never mind the foreign tourists – might be something more than a bloody outrage; it would be downright wicked.

God might never forgive her.

'I feel naked going into a British Crown Colony without a gun in my belt,' Mad Dan said, glancing out of the rear window of the car as Sean turned off the N340 and headed for the border at La Línea. 'Sure, I might as well have no pants on.'

'Sure, that's a sight I'd rather not see,' Mairead said caustically, not caring if she angered him, thinking: God, no wonder I have doubts! With a vampire like this by your side, you're bound to start worrying. Him and his guns and all . . .

'Sure, I'm choosy about who I drop 'em for,' Mad Dan sneered, 'and yer not on my list.'

'Thank God for that.'

Mad Dan quivered with rage and had to fight to control himself. He was under strict instructions from Pat Tyrone to take his orders from this woman, but even though she'd bombed a Prod hotel ten years ago, he couldn't stand the sight of her. Proud in her beauty. Too proud for the likes of him. Brushing back her hair from her eyes and looking down her nose at him. Mad Dan wanted to crush her. He wanted to be in charge. That Rock was a fucking British colony and he wanted to bomb the place. Take all the bastards out. Shock the whole bloody world. Pay the British government back for the eight good men killed by the SAS at Loughgall and show them that they could never feel safe any more — anywhere.

But were they going to do it? No, they were just looking. They were going like bloody tourists to see the sights and twiddle their thumbs. This damned woman was indecisive. Sean wasn't much better. Here he was with a woman who'd bombed a hotel ten years ago — done nothing since, mind — and a kid who cycled about the countryside and studied history and Gaelic. What a pair to be stuck with! Both whimpering about what was right. Well, by God, *he'd* show 'em what was right if he got half the chance.

Mad Dan was simmering silently, boiling up inside. He'd come here to do some serious damage and this bitch could well put a stop to it. Besides which, she practically sneered at him every time she opened her mouth.

Just give me a Webley pistol, he thought,

and she'll be the first to go. Never mind the fuckin' Brits.

But he didn't have a Webley – he had nothing – so he just sat there simmering . . .

As the car drove into the ugly, ramshackle border town of La Línea, Mairead said to Sean: 'Try to find a bar or café near the border, where you can leave me and Dan to warm our bums for a couple of hours while you go on ahead in the car and find a good parkin' space.'

'Sure, why are we doin' that?' Mad Dan asked. 'We don't have any weapons or bombs, so why can't we all drive on, like?'

'I know we've had no trouble with the authorities so far – not when you two came last November; nor this trip with the three of us – but there's a quare chance the bastards are watchin' us an' bidin' their time. Sure, if Sean's been drivin' in alone an' parkin' the car – an' if it's true, as some suspect, that he's under Brit surveillance – then the police here just might check his car – and if they do, they'll find nothin'. Then, if we decide to do it, we can drive in two days later an' replace his car with the bomb-car. Can yer thick head digest that?'

'Ackaye, it can,' Mad Dan said, choking back his rage. ''Cause it isn't that thick, girl.'

'Sure, we don't need to argue among ourselves,' Sean reprimanded them with surprising firmness. 'What Mairead says makes sense to me, Dan.

She's simply suggestin' that we use this car as a blocker and I fully agree.'

'Aye, right,' Mad Dan replied, almost bursting with the desire to look down the sight of a Webley at Mairead Farrell's haughty head. 'Anything you say, like.'

'Good,' Mairead said.

Sean drew up outside a café near the La Línea gate. It was nearly 12.30 and the sun was high in the sky, making those in the car, all used to the cold of Belfast, feel hot and sweaty.

'This'll do,' Mairead said, opening the door and slipping out of the car as Mad Dan reluctantly did the same behind her. Walking around the car, she bent down to Sean's open window and said: 'Just drive on through, park as close as you can get to the band assembly area – there's a car park almost facin' it – and then go for a bit of a gander. At half past two, we'll walk across and meet you in the car park. That's exactly two hours from now. That's a reasonable enough time to discourage any connection between us if we're all bein' watched. All right?'

'Ackaye,' Sean said.

When Sean drove off, passing unchecked through the La Línea gate, Mairead and Mad Dan took a table outside the Spanish bar – it was already warm enough for that – and ordered a couple of beers, which would last them longer than coffee.

When the white Renault disappeared from view, obviously crossing the runway on its way to the centre of Gibraltar, Mairead pulled a romantic novel out of her handbag and started reading.

Mad Dan, who knew she didn't want to talk to him, simply sighed, inhaled on a cigarette and blew smoke rings.

Two hours and three beers later, at precisely 2.30, Mairead and Mad Dan entered Gibraltar on foot and met up with Sean by the car.

Even as the three terrorists were getting together, they were being observed from a short distance by the two MI5 women. When she saw the meeting being completed, Mary Hattersley gave an imperceptible hand signal to Barbara Jennings, indicating that she should do nothing, then raised her transceiver to her lips and spoke quietly into it, telling Captain Edwards, in his HQ in the command centre, that the three targets had finally met up and were standing by their hired car.

'Let's go, men!' Sergeant Carruthers snapped urgently at a signal from Edwards.

The four SAS men, still wearing civilian clothes, hurried out of the building.

15

Crossing into Gibraltar at 12.30 in the white Renault 5 after dropping off Mairead and Mad Dan, Sean was impressed by the sheer size of the Rock, which appeared to rise towards the azure sky and grow bigger as he moved closer to it. Having familiarized himself with its history, he knew that it consisted mainly of limestone and had many caves and tunnels that had been excavated for defensive purposes and were still being used by the Brits and the Gibraltarian police. Gibraltar, though steeped in both real history and mythology – it was supposed to be one of the Pillars of Hercules, after all – was now a fortified naval base and much of the town, which had been partly built on land reclaimed from the surrounding sea, was occupied by army barracks, naval establishments and hospitals. As such, no matter how romantic it seemed to Sean, it made a legitimate target.

After driving through the winding, packed streets of the central shopping area, he eventually passed between the Hambros Bank and the band assembly area. Following the road around, he passed the Jewish Old People's Home, then the Toc-H Hostel and the Bishop Fitzgerald School by the High Stone Wall. Just past the school was the entrance to the car park. Sean collected his ticket as he drove in, then parked the car.

By this time, equipped with their concealed transceivers broadcasting on a network dedicated to the operation, Mary Hattersley and Barbara Jennings were making their way down into the centre of town to locate the white Renault 5 and, with luck, its driver. Just as they were approaching Main Street, Sean was leaving the car park to wander around and have a bit of a 'gander' that might help with decisions regarding the placing of the bomb two days from now, during the band parade ceremony.

Knowing that the only place to park was the car park, Hattersley and Jennings, taking slightly different courses and a good distance apart, made their way there. While Hattersley waited outside to check the people swarming through the surrounding streets, Jennings entered and walked along the rows of cars until she saw the terrorists' car. Having confirmed that it had the same registration number as the one she had been given, she put out a general message – to Captain Edwards and to the four SAS men now hurrying down from the Lathbury Barracks – confirming that the car had been parked, but that the driver was nowhere in sight.

The four SAS men in civilian clothing immediately separated into two teams, each of which took a different direction into the centre of town.

While Jennings remained in the car park, keeping a discreet distance from the parked white Renault 5, Hattersley wandered up and down the High Stone Wall and Line Wall Road, looking for Sean Savage, whom she hoped to recognize from the photo she was carrying on her person. She had studied that picture many times and felt sure she would know him, but she still wanted the photo for confirmation. In the event, it was another hour before she finally spotted him.

Wearing a pinstripe jacket and grey slacks, he was standing beside a group of Japanese tourists close to the band assembly area, which he was carefully studying. Removing the photo from her pocket, Hattersley checked that it was indeed Savage. When she had confirmed, she notified the others on the transceiver.

'We're on our way,' Carruthers responded. 'Don't let him out of your sight. Over and out.'

Sean walked away from the band assembly area, trying to act like a normal tourist, and indeed feeling a certain regret that he could not take the cable car up the face of the mighty Rock and have a look, in particular, at the Barbary apes that roamed free up there. At the same time, Màiread looked at her watch, saw that it was just after 2 p.m., and told Mad Dan that it was time for them to leave the bar and enter Gibraltar.

'About time,' Mad Dan growled.

Placing her book in her bag, Mairead pushed her chair back, then stood up and walked with Mad Dan to the La Línea gate. The officer at passport control barely glanced at their false passports, apparently noting only the fact that they were British. Within minutes they were walking across the runway and heading for town.

They were unaware of the fact that they had been identified by the staff of passport control and their presence in Gibraltar made known, by phone and radio, to Edwards, his four SAS men and the MI5 watchers.

It was exactly 2.30.

By this time, Sean had wandered back to the car park, as arranged, and was already waiting by the white Renault when the others showed up.

'Everything all right so far?' Mairead asked him.

'Ackaye. Sure, I'm just another tourist. There's so many people here, we'll just be tourists in the crowd. No problem at all.'

'Let's take another look,' Mairead said.

It was 2.50 when the three terrorists walked out of the car park and headed for the Alameda Gardens, a short distance away. They were being followed at a discreet distance by Hattersley and Jennings, who were transmitting a running commentary on the trio's movements to the two-man SAS teams.

As a result, the SAS teams were also tracking the three terrorists and waiting for an opportune moment to challenge them, preferably well away from the central shopping area, crowded mainly with tourists.

'Sure, this place is a piece of piss,' Mad Dan said as he and the others rested in the shade of the Alameda Gardens. 'As Sean said, there's so many people runnin' about we'll just be thought of as other bloody tourists.'

'It's busy enough, all right,' Mairead said. 'For such a small place, there's certainly a lot goin' on, like.'

'An' in two days' time,' Mad Dan reminded her, 'when the actual Changin' of the Guard's goin' on, there's goin' to be even more people. This place'll be like an anthill.'

Sean, still romantically inclined and recalling what he'd read about the place, pointed up the face of the mighty Rock, above the tiers of houses perched precariously above the old defensive walls, to where it became a series of sheer, inaccessible cliffs and sand slopes surmounted by sun-scorched shrubs and trees.

'Do you want the Brits out of here completely?' he asked with a sly smile.

224

'Sure, I want them out of *everywhere*,' Mairead replied.

Sean pointed up to where the cable car was climbing the cliff face. 'Up there are the Barbary apes. It's said that if the apes ever leave Gibraltar, then the Brits will lose it. So why not, instead of bombing during the ceremony on Tuesday, go up there instead with a couple of sub-machine-guns and blast all the apes to kingdom come. When you've killed the last ape, the Brits will be finished here for good. No apes, no Brits.'

Mairead chuckled. 'Ackaye, it sounds good in theory, but not quite what we're after.'

'So we do it?' Mad Dan asked anxiously. 'We bomb the shites as planned?'

'Aye, I suppose we'll do it,' Mairead told him. 'I have my doubts because of the school and the old people's home, but we've done worse in the past, I suppose. You're right – there are no innocents in war – and we didn't come all this way for nothin'. We have to finish what we started. There's not really a choice now.'

'On Tuesday?' Mad Dan asked, looking relieved.

'Aye, on Tuesday. We'll leave the car we've come in today as a blocker and take a bus back to Marbella. On Tuesday morning, we'll come back here in the bomb-car. At the La Línea gate, Sean will get out of the bomb-car an' walk from there to the blocker in the car park. We'll give him fifteen minutes, then follow him in the bomb-car. At a time to be decided between us, but when the Changin' of the Guard has begun, we'll drive up behind the parked blocker and then Sean, when he sees us right behind him, will drive off and leave us the space. Sean will stop in his car just before leavin' the car park. When we've parked the bomb-car, we'll get out, lock it, and join Sean in the other car. Sean will then drive us back across the airport and back into Spain. The bomb-car will be set to explode about ten minutes after we've exited Gibraltar by the La Línea gate and are well on the way back to Marbella. We should be fairly safe then, and from there we'll drive across Spain to Bilbao. Then we take the boat back to Britain and head on home with no bother.'

'Perfect,' Mad Dan said, pleased at last.

'Aye, right,' Sean said. 'Now let's make our way back to the border.'

They returned to the square forty minutes later, at 3.25, to once again look at the car, checking its position in the crowded car park. Then they turned away, left the car park, and headed north, back to the border.

Sitting in his HQ in the command centre deep within the Rock, Captain Edwards was informed by Mary Hattersley, still out in the streets, of the movements of the three terrorists.

'They're studying the Renault,' she had said

over the transceiver. 'There are some kids nearby
. . . McCann is looking thoughtfully at the car
. . . Now he's speaking to the other two . . .
Farrell seems to be amused . . . Now they're all
moving off, out of the car park. They have smiles
on their faces . . . Yes, definitely: they're leaving
the car in the car park and heading back to the
border on foot. They've just gone out of sight.'

Learning this, Edwards instantly assumed that
the Renault had been left there as a blocker or
a bomb-car and that, either way, it and the
terrorists themselves had to be dealt with before
the latter left the Rock.

'In that case,' said the Police Commissioner,
who had been in the crowded command centre
since morning and appeared to be excited and
nervous at the same time, 'we must formally pass
the situation to the Army and let your men get on
with it.'

'Good,' Edwards said. 'The other surveillance
teams aren't expecting to go into action for
another thirty-six hours, but I'm going to deploy
them right now, to put a ring of steel around the
terrorists. We'll also have that car checked out.'

'Very wise,' the Commissioner said.

While the Commissioner was preparing to
sign the relevant documentation, transferring
authority for the operation from his own men
to the Army, Edwards contacted his two SAS
teams to fill them in on the situation.

'Good,' Carruthers replied on hearing that the Army was soon going to be in charge. 'We were beginning to feel a bit hamstrung, waiting for the police to act. This should make it much easier.'

'Exactly,' Edwards said. 'Now keep on the terrorists' tail, don't let them out of your sight, but do nothing until I can confirm that we're formally in charge.'

'Make sure you do it before they cross the border,' Carruthers said. 'And that won't be long, boss.'

'I will, Sarge. Don't worry.'

When Edwards conveyed the same information to his MI5 watchers, they were less enthusiastic about the transfer of authority.

'These last-minute changes aren't helpful,' Hattersley said, 'at such a crucial phase of the operation. They could cause some confusion.'

'There's nothing to be confused about,' Edwards reassured her. 'Very soon we'll be in sole command, and once I've confirmed that, you can move the men in with all possible speed. Meanwhile, please keep me informed of their movements.'

'Will do,' Hattersley said.

'What's happening right now?'

'Team One is following them past the Garrison Theatre and I'm only a short way behind them. Team Two has disappeared up ahead of them, hoping to box the terrorists in.'

'Excellent,' Edwards said. 'Over and out.'

As Edwards cut Hattersley off, he saw that the Commissioner was in heated discussion with someone on the telephone. When the Commissioner had hung up, he turned to face Edwards, mopped sweat from his flushed face with a handkerchief, and said nervously: 'I've changed my mind, Captain. I'm resuming control again. I want another identity check of the three suspects before making any kind of decision regarding what we should do.'

'With all due respect, Commissioner,' Edwards replied, practically grinding his teeth, 'the identity of those three terrorists has already been checked by the security officers at both borders and independently by two MI5 watchers. There's simply no doubt about who they are and . . .'

'We have to be . . .'

'. . . and we have to move in on them before they cross back into Spain. And time's running out, Commissioner.'

The Commissioner kept mopping sweat from his face and glancing anxiously about him, as if looking for help from an invisible ally.

'The car,' he said. 'Perhaps we should at least . . .'

'It's being checked out this very minute by one of the three regular Army officers on my team, a lieutenant from the Royal Army Ordnance

Corps.' Edwards checked his watch. 'He should be calling through any second now.'

As the Commissioner was nodding his agreement, a call came through from Hattersley.

'What's happening?' she asked.

'I thought you'd tell *me* that,' Edwards snapped.

'I mean about the transfer of authority. The terrorists are halfway to the border and it's not a long walk. If you want to challenge them, you'll have to do it soon. Time's running out.'

'A slight delay,' Edwards replied, trying to sound calmer than he felt. 'The Commissioner's resumed control for now and is waiting to hear from Lieutenant Raleigh regarding the Renault left in the car park.'

'We haven't time for that, sir.'

'The call should be coming through any second now. I think we . . .' The call was indeed coming through on the receiver held open especially for it. 'That's it,' Edwards said. 'I'll get back to you in a couple of minutes. Over and out.'

Cutting Hattersley off, Edwards picked up the other receiver and said: 'HQ. Flavius. Captain Edwards speaking.'

'Lieutenant Raleigh here, sir. I've visually inspected the white Renault 5 . . .'

'And?' Edwards interjected impatiently.

'I suspect it's a car bomb.'

'Not just a blocker?'

'No.'

'If you've only visually inspected it . . .'

'I'm not allowed to break into it.'

'Fine. If you've only visually inspected it, what makes you think it's the car bomb and not just a blocker?'

'It's a fairly new Renault, but the aerial placed centrally on the roof is old and rusty. That makes me think it may not be the original aerial and therefore that the car's been tampered with.'

'You think the aerial could be part of a remote-control detonator?'

'It's a distinct possibility, Captain.'

'Thanks. Over and out.'

Edwards cut Raleigh off and turned back to the sweating Commissioner.

'I heard him,' the Commissioner said.

'So what's your decision, Commissioner? Time's of the essence now.'

'Where are the terrorists right now?'

'Still walking north towards the border. They'll soon be in Winston Ch.... ....enue. After that, there's only the runway, ... anish border.'

The Commissioner wiped his face yet again and licked his dry lips. 'If you think there's a bomb in that car and sign a declaration saying so, we could arrest all three terrorists on suspicion of conspiracy to murder.'

'I'll sign,' Edwards said.

'No need,' the Commissioner replied with a

sheepish grin. 'Just checking. I wanted to be sure you're convinced. All right, let's proceed.' He turned back to the desk behind him, leant over it, withdrew a pen from his breast pocket, and signed the document that had been lying there for hours. When he had signed, he handed a copy to Edwards. 'You're now formally in charge of Operation Flavius,' he informed Edwards. 'The best of luck, Captain.'

Shoving the document carelessly into a pocket in his tunic, the exultant Edwards grabbed the radio microphone and sent out his instructions to all concerned.

'Intercept and apprehend!' he ordered. 'Intercept and apprehend!'

16

Even as Mary Hattersley was whispering into her radio to summon the two SAS CQB teams, the three terrorists were walking through the suburban sprawl where Smith Darrien Road runs into Winston Churchill Avenue, the north–south dual carriageway leading to the runway and, beyond it, the border.

'The parked Renault is believed to be a bomb-car,' Mary whispered into the transceiver. 'Repeat: a bomb-car. The target subjects might therefore be armed and carrying button-jobs. Situation alert. Intercept and apprehend. Intercept and apprehend with caution.'

'Message received,' Sergeant Carruthers of Team Two said. 'Over and out.'

'Message received,' Sergeant Ainsworth of Team One said also. 'Over and out.'

Having converged at Rodney House, at the junction of Smith Darrien Road and Corral Road, both teams conferred urgently before separating once more and moving north again in pursuit of the terrorists.

'If the Renault 5 in the car park *is* a bomb-car, not a blocker,' Carruthers said, 'then either one or all of the terrorists will be carrying a button-job and all of them are almost certainly armed. That means we have to approach them with caution – and I mean *extreme* caution. We have to formally challenge them, but be prepared to fire if they make any quick move that suggests they're either going to detonate the bomb or withdraw their weapons. The aim is to intercept and apprehend, but we have to be prepared to neutralize them with all possible speed. OK, let's go.'

Shortly after entering Winston Churchill Avenue, when they were at the petrol station opposite the six-storey Lugana Estate apartment complex, the terrorists stopped and started talking to one another. As they were talking, both SAS teams took up positions on the same side of the avenue, but some yards south, spaced well apart and loitering like ordinary citizens. Though they could clearly see the terrorists, they couldn't hear what they were saying, but assumed that they had stopped merely for a rest and a chat in the sun.

'What's the problem?' Sean asked.

'I've just had a thought,' Mairead replied. 'I think we're makin' a mistake here. As I said before, we might be under surveillance an' if we are then they'll know that parked car's ours. Also, if they checked us as we came across the border, they'll know that Sean drove in an' we . . .' – she nodded to indicate Mad Dan – 'came in together on foot a couple of hours later. They might be wonderin', then, about why we're all leavin' together an' put two and two together the wrong way, mistakin' that blocker for a bomb-car. If they do, either they'll close the car park for a demolitions search of the blocker or they'll arrest us at the border as we try to cross back into Spain.'

'Aye, you're right there,' Mad Dan conceded. 'So what should we do?'

'I think we should leave the way we came in,' Mairead told him. 'You and me together on foot; Sean travelling separately in the car. Then, to be sure, once back in Marbella we change the car for another – not a Renault 5 – and bring it back late tomorrow afternoon and park it as another blocker. Also, that way, the blocker will only be in the car park for one night and part of the mornin' before we explode the bomb. What do you think?'

'I agree,' Sean said.

'Aye, me too,' Mad Dan agreed.

'Right, Sean, you get goin',' Mairead said, 'back to the car park. Meanwhile, me and Dan'll go on and cross into Spain. You can pick us up at the bar we were in before, just beyond the La Línea gate, and the three of us can then drive back to Marbella as planned previously.'

'Right,' Sean said, turning immediately and walking back the way the three of them had come, towards the centre of town, while Mairead and Mad Dan started away from the petrol station, again intending to head north towards the border.

As Sean moved away from the other two, Ainsworth and Billings moved out from the side to the centre of the pavement. Unconcerned, Sean kept walking towards them, then skirted around the sergeant, his shoulder lightly bumping him as he passed.

Ainsworth had been fully prepared to shout the challenge and then summon the police by radio while covering the three terrorists with his drawn Browning. Now, however, with the group breaking up to go in two directions, one of them actually brushing past him, he experienced a momentary confusion that threw him off balance.

He's going to detonate the bomb-car, he thought as the terrorist passed him and headed on down the avenue.

When Ainsworth jerked around, however, starting to reach behind him for his handgun, he first caught a glimpse of Billings's equally confused face, then saw that Carruthers and Dymock had stepped out of the side of the pavement and were already hurrying down the avenue to catch up with Savage.

'Go after McCann and Farrell,' he heard the voice of Carruthers saying tinnily in his covert microphone. 'Intercept and apprehend.'

'Let's go,' Ainsworth said to Billings, knowing he had also heard the instruction. '*Now!*'

Never a gentleman, Mad Dan was walking along the inside of the pavement, away from the road, close to the low wall flanking the petrol station. Mairead walked on his left, nearer the gutter, frequently brushing her hair away from her eyes when the wind made it whip around her pale, haunted face.

Suddenly, as if by instinct, Mad Dan looked back over his shoulder – directly at the two SAS men. He was smiling.

That smile on the lips of a man known to have killed many people and reported to be mad sent a chill combination of fear and revulsion through Ainsworth.

Mad Dan's wild eyes fixed him. They looked directly at each other. Then, as if his killer's instincts had told him that something was wrong – that these two men coming up behind him were not ordinary civilians – Mad Dan stopped smiling and stiffened into animal alertness.

Reacting instinctively, Ainsworth went for his Browning. As he did so, Mad Dan's right arm moved across the front of his body and the SAS man, thinking he was going for the button-job, about to detonate the bomb, dropped into the 'double tap' firing position and took aim, holding the pistol in both hands.

The weapon was already loaded. One round

was in the breech and the firing pin was cocked. A quick flick of the thumb released the safety-catch and then Ainsworth squeezed the trigger.

The first round went into Mad Dan's back as his arm was still moving across the front of his body. He jerked violently, flung his hands above his shoulders, then staggered drunkenly sideways, already collapsing.

As the sound of the shot rang out, probably even before she had seen that Mad Dan was hit, Mairead grabbed for the bag under her arm. Assuming that she was reaching for a button control or weapon, Ainsworth aimed at her and fired. He kept firing at the rate of one shot approximately every second and a half, turning the Browning on Mad Dan a second time as he continued firing.

Even before Mad Dan had fallen to the ground, he took one shot to the body and two to the head, with his skull smashed open.

A police siren wailed.

Hearing it, Ainsworth raised both hands, still gripping the pistol, and shouted: 'Police!'

Hearing that single, bawled word, Billings also opened fire, putting seven bullets into Mairead and Mad Dan even as they were falling.

As Mairead twisted to the ground with blood pouring from her face and back, Billings shot her again because he could not see her hands and feared she still might press the button control. Only when she had flopped on to the pavement with her hands away from her body – thus away from a weapon or the button control – did Billings ease his finger off the trigger.

Behind Ainsworth and Billings, Hattersley, at the sound of the first shot, had already called up one of the police cars that had been following the hunted and the hunters alike from a discreet distance. This accounted for the siren that had been heard in the distance and was growing · rapidly louder as the car approached the killing ground.

Seeing no movement from either terrorist, Ainsworth, covered carefully by Billings, the latter still aiming his Browning in the two-handed position, ran forward and knelt down to examine the two motionless terrorists. The woman, he saw immediately, had been shot four times in the face and also in the back, with blood spreading out from under her, all around her. Both terrorists were dead.

'Good riddance,' Ainsworth murmured as he straightened up, gave the 'All clear' signal to Billings, and waited for the police car.

Within seconds, the car had pulled up to spirit the two SAS men away from the scene of the shooting.

As the first bullets were hitting the two terrorists, Sean Savage was 120 yards away; walking in the opposite direction, along Corral Road, towards the Landport Gate. He was unaware that he was being tailed by Carruthers and Dymock, who in turn were being followed by the other MI5 watcher, Barbara Jennings.

When Sean heard the shooting and the police siren, he spun around and saw the two men following him. They raced up to him, guns already drawn as part of the intercept-and-apprehend SOP.

'Stop!' Carruthers bawled. 'Police! Get down! Hands above your head! Stay still!'

Shocked, Sean ignored the bawled instructions and instead reached down instinctively to his jacket pocket, forgetting that he did not have a pistol and dropping into the CQB stance that he had learnt with the IRA. Seeing that movement, Carruthers didn't think twice about opening fire.

Only fifteen yards away, Jennings turned her head aside, not wanting to see the rest of what was happening. She heard a wailing police siren, a buzzing from her earpiece, and, above the buzzing, more gunshots. Nevertheless, she managed to put through a call for another police car.

Carruthers carried on firing as the terrorists's body spiralled down, hitting him four times in the chest and twice in the head. At the same time, a woman walking towards the Landport Gate accidentally got between Dymock and the falling terrorist. With his free arm, Dymock pushed the woman aside, then, with his other hand, drew his pistol and fired nine shots.

He fired the first round and carried on firing, very rapidly, into Sean's body as the terrorist was shuddering violently and falling away to the ground. The last two rounds were aimed at his head when it was mere inches away from the ground, just before his skull cracked against the pavement and his body went limp.

Dymock kept on firing until the terrorist was absolutely still and his hands were well away from his body. Then, as Dymock kept Carruthers covered, the latter ran forward and checked that the IRA men was well and truly dead. Seeing that his body was riddled with bullets, his head had been virtually pulverised, and he appeared to be losing blood from every pore, Carruthers knew that he was dead.

Within seconds, a second wailing police car stopped by the two SAS men and they jumped into the back and were driven away.

Ten minutes later all four SAS men handed their weapons and unused ammunition to the Gibraltar police, then went to report to Edwards, who congratulated them on a job well done and reassured them that if the killings were queried, he would stand strongly behind them.

'Not that there *will* be queries,' he added. 'Clearly you did what you had to do.'

In fact, before being flown back to England the two SAS teams learnt that no bomb had been found in the Renault and that none of the terrorists had been armed.

POSTSCRIPT

Operation Flavius became the most contentious in the history of the SAS, with the men involved being described as an officially sanctioned 'special assassination squad' and 'an unholy priesthood of violence'. The outrage was only compounded by the fact that the terrorists had not been armed and no bomb was found in the parked Renault 5. And nor was the SAS helped by the fact that many of the official watchers professed to have seen nothing while civilian witnesses not only came forward with detailed statements but, in more than one instance, insisted that the SAS had shot their victims without provocation and in the back while they were unaware or while they were spread out on the ground.

Mairead Farrell had been shot four times in the face and three times in the back, dying of two wounds in the heart and one in the liver, though other bullets had also broken her back. At least sixteen bullets had been shot into Sean Savage and he had suffered a total of twenty-nine injuries, including those shot into his head from above, either just before he hit the ground or as he actually lay on it. Daniel McCann had been hit by a similar number of bullets, both front and rear.

At the inquest conducted in September 1988 the four SAS troopers defended the killings by saying that although they had been given orders to arrest the terrorists, they were also given permission to use their weapons 'if those using them had reasonable grounds for believing that an act was being committed or about to be committed which would endanger life or lives and if there was no other way of preventing that other than with firearms'.

Certain Spanish officials expressed a sense of betrayal at the killing of the terrorists. One claimed that the British informed him that the terrorists had died in a 'shoot-out', which clearly was not true. The same official complained that by killing all the terrorists, instead of only one or two, the SAS had left the Spanish authorities in the uncomfortable position of having no one to question regarding the location of the car bomb.

However, the notion that the Spanish police may not have been informed about the anti-terrorist operation, may have been misinformed, and may have been seriously outraged by it was placed in serious doubt when, in March the following year, twenty-two Spanish police officers received citations for their part in the surveillance operation preceding the killings.

The death of the three terrorists resulted in questions being asked about the amount of control exercised over the SAS, about whether or not they had a licence to kill, and about whether or not the British government, specifically Prime Minister Margaret Thatcher, had ordered them to kill the terrorists rather than capture them.

The debate raged throughout the following months and was not extinguished by the inquest's verdict in September 1988 that the three had been lawfully killed.

The SAS were vindicated somewhat by the official announcement that the Spanish police had found the IRA's car bomb in an underground car park in Marbella, a location only thirty miles from Gibraltar and one which the terrorists would have had to pass through *en route* to the Rock. The car bomb contained 143lb of Semtex explosive and an unattached timing device set for 1120 hours, which is exactly when the Changing of the Guard ceremony on Gibraltar took place.

The implication, therefore, is that the white Renault 5 parked near the assembly point on Gibraltar on 6 March was indeed a 'blocker' and that the original estimate of a bombing planned for 8 March was correct.

Nevertheless, while this news raised the possibility that the terrorists intended leaving the 'blocker' in the car park in Gibraltar until they returned on 8 March with the bomb-car, there are those who still insist that the car bomb found in the car park in Marbella was a fiction created by the Spanish and British authorities to save them embarrassment.

The truth may never be known.

Though the operation resulted in the 'neutralization' of a highly dangerous IRA Active Service Unit, whether intended or not, the publicity surrounding the affair was deemed negative from the Regiment's point of view as it prefers to work covertly, well away from the attention of the media.

In June 1994 the European Commission of Human Rights decided that the SAS soldiers involved in the Gibraltar killings did not use unnecessary force in violation of the European human rights conventions. Eleven members of the Commission found in favour of the British government, but six dissented. At the time of writing, the European Court of Human Rights has yet to make its final decision regarding the matter.

SOLDIER S: SAS

THE SAMARKAND HIJACK

SOLDIER S: SAS

THE SAMARKAND HIJACK

David Monnery

PROLOGUE

Bradford, England, 14 March 1979

It was a Wednesday evening, and Martin could hear the *Coronation Street* theme music through the wall. His mother was in the back room ready to watch, but he had not been allowed to join her, allegedly because he had homework to finish. The real reason, though, was that there was a sex scandal going on; one of the characters was sleeping with another's wife, or something like that. His mother didn't like any of her children watching such things, and certainly not Martin, who at twelve was the youngest of the three.

He continued drawing the blue border around the coastline of England with the felt-tip pen. He liked drawing maps, and he was good at it, both as a copyist and from memory. England, though, was always something of a challenge: it was so easy to make the fat peninsulas too thin and vice versa.

The coastline was finished, and he stopped for a moment. It was dark outside now, so he walked over to draw the curtains across the front windows. The sound of raucous laughter floated down the street; it was probably the youths with the motor bikes who habitually gathered outside the fish and chip shop. Thinking about the latter made Martin feel hungry, even though he'd only had supper an hour or so earlier. His father, brother and sister would be getting chips on their way home from the game, like they always did, but by the time they came through the front door the only thing left would be the smell on their hands.

It was no fun being the youngest. Still, next season he would be able to go with them to the evening games. His father had promised.

Martin stood by the table for a moment, wondering whether to ask his mother again whether he could watch TV with her. But she would only say no, and anyway he didn't really want to – it was not being allowed that was so annoying.

He sat back down with his map, and started putting in red dots where all the First Division teams played. He had just put in the one for Norwich when there was a knock on the front door.

He hesitated in the doorway to the hall, but there was no sign of his mother coming out. It was probably only one of those political canvassers in any case, and Martin enjoyed telling them what he had once heard his father say: 'A secret ballot should be just that!'

He walked towards the door, noticing the shadow through the leaded glass, and pulled it open.

Almost immediately a foot pushed it back, and Martin himself was propelled backwards into the hall. He had a momentary glimpse of a helmeted figure silhouetted against the starry sky, before something flew over his head and exploded into flames in the hall behind him.

It all happened so fast. 'Burn, you Paki bastards!' The words seemed to echo down the street as the attacker scrambled back down the path and disappeared into the darkness. Martin turned to find a sheet of flame where his mother's wall hangings from home had been, and fire already spreading up the carpeted stairway. Then a sudden draught fanned the flames and he heard her scream.

He started forward, but the heat from the flames threw him back, the smell of singed hair in his nostrils. His mind told him his mother could get out of the window into the back garden, while his heart told him she needed him. But now the flames were forcing him back towards the front door, and he knew that to try to run through them would be suicide.

He backed into the front garden, and then spun round and raced next door, where he banged the polished iron knocker like a madman.

'What the blazes . . . ?' Mr Castle said as he opened the door.

'There's a fire!' Martin screamed at him. 'Our house is on fire! Mum's inside!'

Mr Castle advanced two steps down the path and saw the light from the flames dancing in the porch. 'I'll ring 999,' he said, and disappeared back inside, leaving Martin in a paroxysm of indecision.

Then inspiration struck. He ran back out to the street, past their house and the other neighbour's, to where the passage ran through to the allotments. At the end of his own garden he clambered over the rickety fence and ran to the back of the burning house. The kitchen door was closed, and so was the back room window. Inside there was nothing but fire.

In later years, the rest of the evening would come to seem like a blurred sequence of images – the sirens of the fire engines, the people gathered in the street, his father, brother and sister coming home, the policemen with their bored expressions and stupid questions. But that moment alone in the darkened garden would never lose its sharpness, with the windows full of flames and the dreadful truth they told.

1

They were standing on a dry, broken slope. There were no fragments of masonry to be seen, no shards of tile or pottery, but the configuration of the land, the angular ditches and the flattened hillocks all suggested human occupation.

'This was the southern end of the original Afrasiab,' Nasruddin Salih told the tour party, 'which became Maracanda and eventually Samarkand. It was razed to the ground in 1220 by the army of Genghis Khan. Only a quarter of the population, about a hundred thousand people, survived. It was another one and a half centuries before Tamerlane revived the city and made it the centre of his empire. These buildings here' – Nasruddin indicated the line of domed mausoleums which gracefully climbed the desolate hillside – 'were probably the finest architectural achievement of Tamerlane's time.'

'Bloody incredible,' Mike Copley murmured, holding up his exposure meter.

It was, Jamie Docherty thought. The blue domes rose out of the yellow-brown hill like articles of faith, like offerings to God which the donors knew were too beautiful to be refused.

' "Shah-i-Zinda" means "The Living King",' Nasruddin was explaining. 'This complex was built by Tamerlane to honour Qutham ibn Abbas, who was a cousin of the Prophet Muhammad, and one of the men most responsible for bringing Islam to this area. He was praying in a shady spot on this hill when a group of Zoroastrians attacked and beheaded him.

4

Qutham finished his prayer' – Nasruddin acknowledged the laughter with a slight smile – 'picked up his head and jumped into a nearby well. He has lived there ever since, ready to defend Islam against its enemies.'

The guide smiled again, but there was something else in his expression, something which Docherty had noticed several times that morning. The British-born Pakistani had been with them since their departure from Heathrow six days before, and for the first few days of the tour had seemed all affability. But over the last twenty-four hours he had seemed increasingly under some sort of strain.

The tour party was moving away, down the path which led to the Shah-i-Zinda's entrance gate. As usual, Charles Ogley was talking to – or rather at – Nasruddin. Probably telling the guide he'd made yet another historical mistake, Docherty thought sourly. The lecturer from Leeds seemed unable to last an hour without correcting someone about something. His lecturer wife Elizabeth was the most frequent recipient of such helpfulness, but seemed to thrive on it, using it to feed some reservoir of bitterness within her soul. They were not an attractive couple, Docherty had decided before the tour's first day had ended. Fortunately they were the only two members of the party for whom he felt any dislike.

He banished the Ogleys from his mind, and focused his attention on the magical panorama laid out before him.

'I think you take photographs with your eyes,' his wife said, taking an arm and breaking into his reverie.

'Aye,' Docherty agreed. 'It saves on film.'

Isabel smiled at the idea, and for the hundredth time felt pleased that they had come on this trip. She was enjoying it enormously herself, particularly since phoning the children and setting her mind at rest the night before. And he was loving it.

They caught up with the rest of the party at the foot of the hill, and waited by the archway which marked the entrance to the complex of buildings while Nasruddin arranged their collective ticket with the man in the booth. Then, their guide in the lead, the party started climbing the thirty-six steps which led up past one double-domed mausoleum towards the entrance gate of another.

'This is called the "Stairway to Heaven",' Nasruddin said. 'Pilgrims count each step, and if they lose count they have to start again at the bottom. Otherwise they won't go to heaven.'

'I wonder if this is where Led Zeppelin got the song title from,' Mike Copley mused out loud.

'Idiot,' his wife Sharon said.

At the top of the stairway they passed through an archway and into the sunken alley which ran along between the mausoleums. Here the restoration work seemed to be only just beginning, and the domes were bare of tiles, the walls patchy, with swathes of mosaic giving way to expanses of underlying buff-coloured brick. At the end of the alley they gathered around the intricately carved elm door of Qutham's shrine, and Nasruddin pointed out where the craftsman had signed his name and written the year, 1405. Inside, the Muslim saint's multi-tiered cenotaph was a riot of floral and geometric design.

Docherty stood staring at it for several minutes, wondering why he always felt so moved by Islamic architecture. He had first fallen in love with the domes and mosaics in Oman, where he had served with the SAS during the latter years of the Dhofar rebellion. A near-fluency in Arabic had been one legacy of that experience, and in succeeding years he had managed to visit Morocco and Egypt. His final mission for the SAS, undertaken in the first weeks of the previous year, had taken him to Bosnia, and the wanton destruction of the country's Islamic heritage had been one of several reasons offered by that war for giving up on the human race altogether.

Not to worry, he thought. After all, Qutham was down there in his well taking care of business.

He looked up to find that, once again, the tour party had left him behind. Docherty smiled to himself and walked back out into the shadowed courtyard, from where he could see the rest of the party strolling away down the sunken alley. Isabel, her black hair shining in the sun above the bright red dress, was talking to Sam Jennings. The silver-haired American didn't walk that gracefully, but at seventy-five his mind was as young as anyone's in the tour party. Both Docherty and Isabel had taken a liking to him and his wife Alice from the first day.

Their small bus was waiting for them outside the entrance. It had six double seats on one side, six single on the other, and a four-person seat at the back. Despite there being only fourteen in the party – fifteen counting Nasruddin – the four Bradford Pakistanis usually sat in a tightly bunched row on the rear seat, as if fearful of being contaminated by their infidel companions. This time though, one of the two boys – Imran, he thought – was sitting with Sarah Holcroft. Or Sarah Jones, to use the name she had adopted for this trip.

Docherty wondered if Imran had recognised her as the British Foreign Minister's daughter. He hadn't himself, though the girl had made no attempt to disguise her appearance, and her picture had been in the papers often enough. Isabel had, and so, if their behaviour was anything to go by, had both the Copleys and the Ogleys.

Brenda Walker, the social worker who usually sat with Sarah, was now sitting directly behind her. Docherty had his suspicions about Brenda, and very much doubted whether she was the social worker she claimed to be. He had come into fairly frequent contact with the intelligence services during his years in the army, and thought he knew an official minder when he saw one. But he hadn't said anything to anyone else, not even Isabel. He might be wrong, and in any case, why spoil the generally good atmosphere that existed within the touring party? He wasn't even sure whether Sarah herself was aware of her room-mate's real identity.

'Enjoying yourself?' Isabel asked, leaning forward from her seat directly behind his, and putting her chin on his shoulder.

'Never better,' he said. 'We seem to go from one wonder of the world to another.'

The driver started the bus, and they were soon driving back through the old city, up Tashkent Street and past the ruined Bibi Khanum mosque and the Registan assemblage of *madrasahs*, or Muslim colleges, both of which they had visited the previous afternoon. It was almost half-past twelve when they reached the cool lobby of the Hotel Samarkand. 'Lunch will be in five minutes,' Nasruddin told them, 'and we shall be leaving for Shakhrisabz at one-thirty.'

While Isabel went up to their room Docherty bought a stamp and postcard from the post office on the ground floor and then took another look at the Afghan carpets in the hotel shop. They weren't quite attractive enough

8

to overcome his lifetime's hatred of having something
to carry.

In the largely empty dining-room fourteen places had
been set on either side of a single long table. The four
Bradford Pakistanis had already claimed the four seats
at one end: as usual they were keeping as separate as
civility allowed. The two older men flashed polite smiles
at Docherty as he sat down in the middle of the other
empty places.

On the first day he had made an effort to talk to them,
and discovered that the two older men were brothers,
the two younger ones their respective sons. Zahid was
the family name, and the elder brother, Ali Zahid, was
a priest, a mullah, attached to a mosque in Bradford.
The younger brother, Nawaz, was a businessman of
unspecified type, which perhaps accounted for the
greater proportion of grey in his hair.

Ali's son Imran and Nawaz's son Javid were both
about seventeen. Unlike their fathers they wore Western
dress and spoke primarily in Yorkshire-accented English,
at least with each other and the other members of the
party. Both were strikingly good-looking, and the uneasy
blend of respect and rebelliousness which characterized
their relationship with their fathers reminded Docherty
of his childhood in working-class Glasgow, way back in
the fifties.

The two academics were the next to arrive, and
took opposing seats at the other end of the table
from the Zahids, without acknowledging either their
or Docherty's presence. The Ogleys had really fallen
on hard times, Docherty thought. They had probably
expected a party full of fellow academics, or at the very
least fellow-members of the middle class. Instead they
had found four Pakistanis, a Glaswegian ex-soldier and

his Argentinian wife, a builder and his wife, and a bluntly spoken female social worker with a northern accent. Their only class allies turned out to be a cabinet minister's daughter known for her sex and drug escapades, and two elderly Americans who, it soon transpired, were veterans of the peace movement. The Ogleys, not surprisingly, had developed a bunker mentality by day two of the Central Asian Tours 'Blue Domes' package holiday.

Isabel came in next, now wearing a white T-shirt and baggy trousers. She was accompanied by Brenda Walker and Sarah Holcroft. The first had changed into a dress for the first time, and her attractively pugnacious face seemed somehow softened by the experience. The second had swept back her blonde hair, and fastened it with an elasticated circle of blue velvet at the nape of her neck. Even next to Isabel she looked lovely, Docherty thought. On grounds of political prejudice he had been more than ready to dislike a Tory cabinet minister's daughter, but instead had found himself grudgingly taking a liking to the girl. And with a father like hers, Docherty supposed, anyone would need a few years of letting off steam.

The two Americans arrived at the same time as the soup. Sam Jennings was a retired doctor from a college town in upstate New York, and his wife Alice had had her hands full for thirty-five years raising their eleven children. The couple now had twenty-six grandchildren, and a continuing hunger for life which Docherty found wonderful. He had met a lot of Americans over the years, but these were definitely the nicest: they seemed to reflect the America of the movies – warm, generous, idealistic – rather than the real thing.

As usual, the Copleys were the last to arrive. Sharon had changed into a green backless dress, but Mike was still wearing the long shorts and baseball hat which made

THE SAMARKAND HIJACK

him look like an American in search of a barbecue. With his designer stubble head, goatee beard, stud earrings and permanently attached camera, he had not immediately endeared himself to Docherty, but here too first impressions had proved a worthless guide. The builder might seem like an English yobbo who had strayed abroad by accident, but he had a smile and a kind word for everyone, and of all the party he was the most at ease when it came to talking with the locals, be they wizened women or street urchins. He had a wide-eyed approach to the world which was not that common among men in their late thirties. And he was funny too.

For most of the time his wife seemed content to exist in his shadow. Isabel had talked with her about their respective children, and thought her nice enough, but Sharon Copley, unlike her husband, had rarely volunteered any opinions in Docherty's hearing. The only thing he knew for certain about her was that she had brought three suitcases on the trip, which seemed more than a trifle excessive.

After announcing an hour's break for lunch, Nasruddin Salih had slipped back out of the hotel, turned left outside the doors and walked swiftly up the narrow street towards the roundabout which marked the northern end of Maxim Gorky Boulevard. A couple of hundred metres down the wide avenue, in the twenty-metre-wide strip of park which ran between its two lanes, he reached the bank of four public telephones.

The two at either end were in use, one by a blonde Russian woman in jeans and T-shirt, the other by an Uzbek man in a white shirt and a *tyubeteyka* embroidered skullcap. In the adjoining children's play area two Tajik children were contesting possession

11

of a ball with their volume controls set on maximum.

Nasruddin walked a few more metres past the telephones and sat down on a convenient bench to wait. He was sweating profusely, he realized, and maybe not just from the heat. Still, it was hot, and more than once that morning he had envied Mike Copley his ridiculous shorts.

The Uzbek had finished his call. Nasruddin got up and walked swiftly across to the available phone. The Russian woman was telling someone about an experience the night before, alternating breathless revelations with peals of laughter. These people had no sense of shame, Nasruddin thought.

He dialled the first number.

Talib answered almost instantly. 'Yes?' the Uzbek asked.

'There are no problems,' Nasruddin told him.

'God be praised,' Talib said, and hung up.

Nasruddin heard footsteps behind him, and turned, slower than his nerves wished. It was only the Tajik boy's father, come to collect their ball, which had rolled to within a few feet of the telephones. Nasruddin smiled at him, waited until the man had retrieved the ball, and then turned back to dial the other number. The Russian woman was now facing in his direction, nipples pressing against the tight T-shirt, still absorbed in her conversation.

He dialled and turn away from her. This time the phone rang several times before it was picked up, each ring heightening Nasruddin's nervousness.

'Sayriddin?' he asked, struggling to keep the anger out of his voice.

'*Assalamu alaikam*, Nasruddin . . .'

12

'Yes, yes. You are ready? You know what to do?' Though if he didn't by this time, then God would surely abandon them . . .

'Of course. I deliver the message this evening, one hour after I hear from Talib. On Thursday morning I check *Voice of the People*. If there is nothing there I try again the next day. When I see it, then I call you at the number you gave me.'

'Good. God be with you.'

'And you, brother.'

Nasruddin hung up, and noticed that the Russian woman had gone. In her place was a young Uzbek, no more than seventeen by the look of him. He was wearing a sharp suit with three pens prominent in the top pocket. It sounded as if he was trying to sell someone a second-hand tractor.

Nasruddin looked at his watch. It was still only ten to one – time to get back to the hotel and have some lunch. But he didn't feel hungry. Nor did he fancy small talk with the members of the party.

He sat down again on the bench, and watched the world go by. The uneasy blend of Asian and European which was Samarkand still felt nothing like home to him, even though one side of his family had roots in the town which went back almost a century. A great-great-grandfather had originally come as a trader, encouraged by the bloody peace the English had imposed on Afghanistan in the late nineteenth century. Nasruddin's side of the family had come to England instead, much later, in the mid 1950s. He himself had been born in Bradford in 1966, heard about his relatives in far-off Samarkand as a young adolescent, and had determined even then to visit them if ever the chance arose.

13

And here he was.

Two Uzbek women were walking towards him, both clothed head to foot in the Muslim *paranca*, eyes glinting behind the horsehair mesh which covered their faces. There was something so graceful about them, something so beautiful. Nasruddin turned his eyes away, and found himself remembering the pictures in *Playboy* which he and the others had studied so intently in the toilets at school. He watched the two women walking away, their bodies swaying in the loose black garments. When English friends had argued with him about such things he had never felt certain in his heart of the rightness of his views. But at this moment he did.

Not that it mattered. He had always been certain that the other way, the Western way, the obsession with sex, could never work. It had brought only grief in its wake – broken families, prostitution, rape, sexual abuse, AIDS . . . the list was endless. Whatever God expected of humanity, it was not that. In the words of one of his favourite songs as a teenager, that was the road to nowhere.

And whatever befell him and the others over the next few days, he had no doubt that they were on the right road.

He made his way slowly back to the hotel, arriving in time to supervise the boarding of the tour bus for the two-hour ride to Shakhrisabz. He watched with amusement as they all claimed the same places they had occupied that morning and the previous afternoon, and idly wondered what would happen to anyone daring enough to claim someone else's.

Now that the dice were cast he felt, somewhat to his surprise and much to his relief, rather less nervous than he had.

Docherty also registered the guide's change of mood, but let it slip from his mind as the views unfolding through the bus window claimed more and more of his attention. They were soon out of Samarkand, driving down a straight, metalled road between cherry orchards. Groups of men were gathered in the shade, often seated on the bed-like platforms called *kravats*.

'Do you think they're waiting for the cherries to ripen? Docherty asked Isabel.

'I doubt it,' she said. 'The women probably do all the picking.'

'Aye, but someone has to supervise them,' Docherty argued.

She pinched the back of his neck.

The orchards soon disappeared, giving way to parched fields of grain. As the road slowly rose towards the mountains they could see the valley of the Zerafshan behind them, a receding strip of vegetation running from east to west in a yellow-brown sea, the domes of Samarkand like blue map pins in the green swathe.

'What do you know about Shakhrisabz?' Isabel asked.

'Not a lot,' Docherty said. 'It was Tamerlane's home town – that's about all.'

'There's the ruins of his palace,' Mike Copley volunteered, open guide book in his lap. 'It says the only thing left is part of the entrance arch, but that that's awesome enough.'

'The son of a bitch didn't do anything by halves,' Sam Jennings commented. 'I was reading in this' – he held up the paperback biography – 'about his war with the Ottoman Turks. Do you want to hear the story?' he asked, with the boyish enthusiasm which seemed to make light of his years.

'Go on, educate us,' Copley told him.

'Well, the Ottoman Turks' leader Bayazid was just about to take Constantinople when a messenger from Tamerlane arrives on horseback. The message, basically, says that Tamerlane is the ruler of the world, and he wants Bayazid to recognize the fact. Bayazid has heard of Tamerlane, but thinks he's just another upstart warlord. His guys, on the other hand, are the military flavour of the month. The whole of Europe's wetting itself in anticipation, so he can hardly believe some desert bandit's going to give him any trouble. He sends back a message telling Tamerlane to go procreate himself.

'A few weeks later the news arrives that Tamerlane's army is halfway across Turkey. Bayazid's cheesed, but realizes he has to take time out to deal with the upstart, and he leads his two hundred thousand crack troops across Anatolia to meet Tamerlane. When the armies are a few miles apart the Turks get themselves in formation and wait. At which point Tamerlane's army hits them from every conceivable side. A few hours later Bayazid is on his way to Samarkand in a cage. And the Turkish conquest of Constantinople gets put back fifty years, which probably saves the rest of Europe from Islam.'

The American smiled in pleasure at his story.

'I think it's a shame the way someone like Tamerlane gets glorified,' his wife said. 'In Samarkand he's becoming the new Lenin – there are statues everywhere. The man turned cities into mountains of skulls, for God's sake. He can't be the only hero the Uzbeks have in their past.'

'He wasn't an Uzbek,' Charles Ogley said, his irritable voice floating back from the front seat. 'None of the Uzbeks' heroes are. Nawaii, Naqshband, Avicenna. The

16

Uzbeks didn't get here until the end of the fifteenth century.'

Docherty, Mike Copley and Sam Jennings exchanged glances.

'So who was here before them, Professor?' Copley asked.

'Mostly other Turkic peoples, some Mongols, probably a few Arabs, even some Chinese. A mixture.'

'Maybe countries should learn to do without heroes,' Sarah Holcroft said, almost defiantly.

'Sounds good to me,' Alice Jennings said.

Ogley's grunt didn't sound like agreement.

There were few signs of vegetation now, and fewer signs of farming. A lone donkey tied to a roadside fence brayed at them as they went past. The mountains rose like a wall in front of the bus.

The next hour offered a ride to remember, as the bus clambered up one side of the mountain range to the six-thousand-foot Tashtakaracha Pass, and then gingerly wound its way down the other. On their left were tantalizing glimpses of higher snow-capped ranges.

'China's on the other side of that lot,' Copley observed.

They arrived at Shakhrisabz soon after three-thirty. 'The name means "green city",' Nasruddin told them, and it did seem beautifully luxuriant after the desert and bare mountains. The bus deposited them in a car park, which turned out to occupy only a small part of the site of Tamerlane's intended home away from home, the Ak Saray Palace. It would have been bigger than Hampden Park, Docherty decided.

As Copley's book had said, all that remained of the edifice was a section of wall and archway. The latter, covered in blue, white and gold mosaics, loomed forty metres into the blue sky. Awesome was the word.

The other sights – another blue-domed mosque, a couple of mausoleums, a covered market – all paled in comparison. At around five-thirty, with the light beginning to take on a golden tinge, they stopped for a drink at the Ak Saray café. 'We'll leave for Samarkand in twenty minutes,' Nasruddin said, before disappearing back outside.

The tourists sipped their mint tea and watched the sun sliding down over the western desert horizon. As the jagged-edged tower of Tamerlane's gateway darkened against the yellow sky Docherty felt at peace with the world.

He smiled across the table at Isabel. Twelve years now, he thought, twelve years of the sort of happiness he hadn't expected to find anywhere, let alone behind enemy lines in Argentina during the Falklands War.

It was an incredible story. At the beginning of the war Isabel, an exiled opponent of the Junta living in London, had agreed to return home as a spy, her love of country outweighed by hatred of its political masters. Docherty had been the leader of one of the two SAS patrols dropped on the mainland to monitor take-offs from the Argentinian airfields, and the two of them had ended up escaping together across the Andes into Chile, already lovers and more than halfway to being in love. Since then they'd married and had two children, Ricardo and Marie, who were spending these ten days with Docherty's elder sister in Glasgow.

Isabel had made and mostly abandoned a career in compiling and writing travel guides, while Docherty had stayed on in the SAS until the early winter of 1992. Pulled out of retirement for the Bosnian mission a month later,

18

his second goodbye to the Regiment in January 1993 had been final. Now, eighteen months later, the couple were preparing to move to Chile, where she had the offer of a job.

Chile, of course, was a long way from anywhere, and they had decided to undertake this Central Asian trip while they still could. It hadn't been cheap, but it wasn't that expensive either, considering the distances involved. The collapse of the Soviet Union had presumably opened the way for young entrepreneurs to compete in this market. Men like Nasruddin, Docherty thought, and idly wondered where their tour operator and guide had got to.

Nasruddin had crossed the road to the car park, and walked across to where two cars, a Volga and a rusting Soviet-made Fiat, were parked side by side under a large mulberry tree. There was no one in the cars, but behind them, in the circle of shade offered by the tree, six men were sitting cross-legged in a rough circle. Four of them were dressed modern Uzbek-style in cotton shirts, cotton trousers and embroidered skullcaps, but the other two were wearing the more traditional ankle-length robes and turbans.

As Nasruddin appeared the men's faces jerked guiltily towards him, as if they were a bunch of schoolboys caught playing cards behind the bicycle sheds. Recognition eased the faces somewhat, but the tension in the group was still palpable.

'Everything is going as expected,' Nasruddin told them, squatting down and looking across the circle at Talib Khamidov. His cousin gave him a tight smile in return, which did little to soften the lines of his hawkish face.

'They all came?' Akbar Makhamov asked anxiously,

19

'the Americans too?' Despite Nasruddin's assurances the others had feared that the two septuagenarians would sit out the side-trip to Shakhrisabz.

'Yes. I told you they would come.'

'God is with us,' Makhamov muttered. The bearded Tajik was the other third of the group's unofficial ruling triumvirate. He came from a rich Samarkand family, and like many such youths in the Muslim world, had not been disowned by his father for demonstrating a youthful excess of religious zeal. His family had not objected to his studying in Iran for several years, and on his return in 1992 Akbar had been given the prodigal son treatment. Over the last year, however, his father's patience had begun wearing a little thin, though nothing like as thin as it would have done had he known the family money was being spent on second-hand AK47s and walkie-talkies for a mass kidnapping.

'Everyone knows their duties?' Nasruddin asked, looking round the circle.

They all did.

'God be with us,' Nasruddin murmured, getting to his feet. He caught Talib's eyes once more, and took strength from the determination that he saw there.

He walked back to the tour bus, and found the driver behind his wheel, smoking a cigarette and reading one of the newly popular 'romantic' graphic novels. Nasruddin was angered by both activities, but managed to restrain himself from sounding it.

'I told you not to smoke in the bus,' he said mildly.

Muran gave him one contemptuous glance, and tossed the cigarette out through his window.

'We'll be picking up two more passengers on the way back,' he told the driver. 'A couple of cousins of mine.

20

Just on the other side of Kitab. I'll tell you when we get there.'

Muran shrugged his agreement.

Nasruddin started back for the café, looking at his watch. It was almost six o'clock. As he approached the tables the Fiat drove out of the car park and turned up the road towards Samarkand, leaving a cloud of dust hanging above the crossroads.

The group was ready to go, and he shepherded them back across the car park and into the bus, wondering as he did so which of them might make trouble when the time came. The ex-soldier and the builder looked tough enough, but neither seemed the sort to panic and do something stupid. Ogley was too fond of himself to take a risk, and the American was too old. Though neither he nor his wife, Nasruddin both thought and hoped, seemed the type to drop dead with shock.

Muran started up the bus, and Nasruddin sat down in the front folding seat. Once out on the road he sat staring ahead, half listening to the murmur of conversation behind him, trying to keep calm. He could feel a palpitation in his upper arm, and his heart seemed to be beating loud enough for everyone in the bus to hear.

He glanced sideways at the driver. There was a good chance the man would take the hundred American dollars and make himself scarce. But even if Muran went to the authorities, it wouldn't matter much.

Nasruddin took a deep breath. Only ten minutes more, he told himself. It was almost dark now, and the fields to left and right were black against the sky's vestigial light. Ahead of them the bus's headlamps laid a moving carpet of light on the asphalt road. In the wing mirror he had occasional glimpses of the lights of the following car.

21

They entered the small town of Kitab, and passed families sitting outside their houses enjoying the evening breeze. In the centre a bustling café spilled its light across the road, and the smell of pilaff floated through the bus.

Nasruddin concentrated on the road ahead as they drove out through the northern edge of the town. A hundred metres past the last house he saw the figures waiting by the side of the road.

'Just up here,' he told Muran.

Docherty's head had begun to drop the moment they started the return journey, but the jerk of the bus as it came to a halt woke him up. His eyes opened to see two men climbing aboard, each with a Kalashnikov AK47 cradled in his arms. A pistol had also appeared in Nasruddin's hand.

The three men seemed to get caught up in one another's movements in the confined space at the front of the bus, but this almost farcical confusion was only momentary, and all three guns were squarely pointed in the passengers' direction before anyone had time to react.

A variety of noises emanated from the passengers, ranging from cries of alarm through gasps of surprise to a voice murmuring 'shit', which Docherty recognized as his own.

2

A stunned silence had settled on the tour party.

'Mr and Mrs Ogley,' Nasruddin said politely, 'please move to the empty seats in the back.'

The academics stared at him for a moment, as if unable to take in the instruction. Nasruddin nodded at them, like a teacher trying to encourage a child, and they responded with alacrity, moving back down the aisle of the bus as if their lives depended on it. Elizabeth sat down next to Brenda Walker, while Charles took the single seat across the aisle from her.

Docherty was examining the two men holding the assault rifles. Both were in their late twenties or early thirties, and both, to judge by the slight body movements each kept making, were more than a little nervous. One wore a thin, dark-grey jacket over a white collarless shirt, an Uzbek four-sided cap and black trousers. His hair was of medium length and he was clean-shaven. Dark, sunken eyes peered out from either side of a hooked nose. His companion was dressed in a black shirt and black trousers, and wore nothing on his head. His hair was shorter, his Mongoloid face decorated with a neat beard and moustache.

'I don't suppose I need to tell you all that you have been taken hostage,' Nasruddin begun. Then, as if realizing that he was still talking to them like a tour guide, the voice hardened. 'You will probably remain in captivity for several days. Provided you obey our orders quickly and without question, no harm will come to any of you . . .'

There was something decidedly unreal about being taken hostage in Central Asia by a Pakistani with a Yorkshire accent, Docherty thought.

'We do not wish to harm anyone,' Nasruddin said, 'but we will not hesitate to take any action that is necessary for the success of this operation.' He looked at his captive audience, conscious of the giant step he had taken but somehow unable to take it in. It felt more like a movie than real life, and for a second he wondered if he was dreaming it all.

'Can I ask a question?' Mike Copley asked.

'Yes,' Nasruddin said, unable to think of a good reason for saying no.

'Who are you people, and what do you want?'

'We belong to an organization called The Trumpet of God, and we have certain demands to make of the Uzbekistan government.'

'Which are?'

Nasruddin smiled. 'No more questions,' he said.

'Can we talk to each other?' Mike Copley asked.

The bearded hijacker spoke sharply to Nasruddin – in Tajik, Docherty thought, though he wasn't sure. Their guide smiled and said something reassuring back. Docherty guessed that neither of the new arrivals spoke English.

'You can talk to the people next to you,' Nasruddin announced, deciding that conversation would do no harm, and that enforcing silence might be interpreted as a sign of weakness. 'But no meetings,' he added. He turned to Talib and Akbar, and explained his decision in Uzbek.

'So what shall we talk about?' Isabel asked Docherty in Spanish. She sounded calm enough, but he could hear the edge of tension beneath the matter-of-fact surface.

'Some ground rules,' he said in the same language. The two of them were used to conversing in her mother tongue, and at home often found themselves slipping between Spanish and English without thinking about it.

'OK,' she agreed. 'Number one – you don't try playing the hero. You're retired.'

'Agreed. Number two – don't you try arguing politics with them. These don't strike me as the kind of lads who like being out-pointed by women.'

'That doesn't make them very unusual,' she said, putting her eyes to the window. 'Where do you think they're taking us?'

'Somewhere remote.' Docherty was watching Nasruddin out of the corner of his eye, thinking that he would never have suspected the man of pulling a stunt like this. He suddenly remembered something his friend Liam had said the last time he'd seen him, that the more desperate the times, the harder it was to recognize desperation.

He turned his attention back to his wife's question. They seemed to be travelling mostly uphill, and the road was nowhere near as smooth as they were used to. He tried to remember the map of Central Asia he had examined before the trip, but the details had slipped from his mind. There were mountains to the east of the desert, and Chinese desert to the east of the mountains. Which wasn't very helpful.

He thought about leaning across the aisle and asking to borrow Mike Copley's guide book, but decided that would only draw attention to its existence and his own curiosity. Better to wait until they reached their destination, wherever that might be.

He turned round to look at Isabel, and found her

angrily wiping away a tear. 'I was just thinking about the children,' she said defiantly.

He took her hand and grasped it tightly. 'It's going to work out OK,' he said. 'We're going to grow old together.'

She smiled in spite of herself. 'I hope so.'

Diq Sayriddin plucked a group of sour cherries from the branch above the *kravat*, and shared them out between the juice-stained hands of his friends. 'I have to go inside for a while,' he told them.

It was fifty-five minutes since he had received the call from Shakhrisabz at the public telephone in Registan Street. Nasruddin had expected him to make his own call from there, but somehow the place seemed too exposed. He had decided to use his initiative instead.

Sayriddin passed through the family house and out the back, climbed over the wall and walked swiftly down the alley which led to Tashkent Street. His father, as always, was sitting outside the shop in the shade, more interested in talking with the other shopkeepers than worrying about prospective customers. Sayriddin slipped round the side of the building and let himself in through the back door.

The whole building was empty – no one stayed indoors at this hour of the day – and the office was more or less soundproof, but just to be on the safe side he wedged the door shut with a heavy roll of carpet. Exactly an hour had now gone by since the call from Talib – it was time to make his own.

He pulled the piece of paper with the number, name and message typed on it from his back pocket, smoothed it out and placed it on the desk beside the telephone. He felt more excited than nervous, but perhaps they were the same thing.

After listening for several seconds to make sure he was alone, he picked up the receiver and dialled the Tashkent number. It rang once, twice, three times . . .

'Hello,' an irritable voice said.

'I must speak with Colonel Muratov,' Sayriddin said. His voice didn't sound as nervous as he had expected it would.

'This is Muratov. Who are you?'

'I have a message for you . . .' Sayriddin began.

'Who are you?' Muratov repeated.

'I cannot say. I have a message, that is all. It is important,' he added, fearful that the National Security Service chief would hang up.

There was a moment's silence at the other end, followed by what sounded like a woman speaking angrily.

'What is this message?' Muratov asked, almost sarcastically.

'The Trumpet of God group . . .' Sayriddin began reading.

'The what?!'

'The Trumpet of God group has seized a party of Western tourists in Samarkand,' Sayriddin said, the words tumbling out in a single breath. 'They were with the "Blue Domes" tour, staying at the Hotel Samarkand. There are twelve English and two Americans among the hostages . . .'

Muratov listened, wondering whether this was a hoax, or simply one of his own men winding him up. Or maybe even one of the Russians who had been jettisoned when the KGB became the NSS. It didn't sound like a Russian though, or a hoax.

'Who the fuck are The Trumpet of God?' he asked belligerently.

'I cannot answer questions,' Sayriddin said. 'There is only the message.'

'OK, give me the message,' Muratov said. Who did the bastard think he was – Muhammad?

'There are eight men and six women,' Sayriddin continued. 'All will be released unharmed if our demands are met. These will be relayed to you, on this number, at eleven o'clock tomorrow morning. Finally, The Trumpet of God does not wish this matter publicized. Nor, it believes, will the government. News of a tourist hijacking will do damage to the country's tourist industry, and probably result in the cancellation of the Anglo-American development deal' – Sayriddin stumbled over this phrase and repeated it – 'the Anglo-American development deal . . . which is due to be signed by the various Foreign Ministers this coming Saturday . . .'

Whoever the bastards were, Muratov thought, they were certainly well informed. And the man at the other end of the line was probably exactly what he claimed to be, just a messenger.

'Is that all clear?' Sayriddin asked.

'Yes,' Muratov agreed. 'How did you get my private number?' he asked innocently. His answer was the click of disconnection.

In the office of the carpet shop Sayriddin was also wondering how Nasruddin had got hold of such a number. But his second cousin was a resourceful man.

He placed the roll of carpet back up against the wall, and let himself out through the back door.

In the apartment on what had, until recently, been Leningrad Street, Bakhtar Muratov sat for a moment

28

on the side of the bed, replaying in his mind what he had just heard. He was a tall man for an Uzbek, broadly built with dark eyes under greying hair, and a mat of darker hair across his chest and abdomen. He was naked.

His latest girlfriend had also been undressed when the phone first rang, but now she emerged from the adjoining bathroom wearing tights and high-heeled shoes.

'I'm going,' she said, as if expecting him to demand that she stay.

'Good,' he said, not even bothering to look round. 'I have business to deal with.'

'When will I see you again?' she asked.

He turned his head to look at her. 'I'll call you,' he said. Why did he always lust after women whose tits were bigger than their brains? he asked himself. 'Now get dressed,' he told her, and reached for his discarded clothes.

Once she had left he walked downstairs, and out along the temporarily nameless street to the NSS building a hundred metres further down. The socialist slogan above the door was still in place, either because no one dared take it down or because it was so much a part of the façade that no one else noticed it any more.

Muratov walked quickly up the stairs to his office on the first floor and closed the door behind him. He looked up the number of the Samarkand bureau chief and dialled it, then sat back, his eyes on the picture of Yakov Peters which hung on the wall he was facing.

'Samarkand NSS,' a voice answered.

'This is Muratov in Tashkent. I want to speak to Colonel Zhakidov.'

'He has gone home, sir.'

'When?'

29

'About ten minutes ago,' the Samarkand man said tentatively.

The bastard took the afternoon off, Muratov guessed. 'I want him to call me at this number' – he read it out slowly – 'within the next half hour.'

He hung up the phone and locked eyes with the portrait on the wall once more. Yakov Peters had been Dzerzhinsky's number two in Leningrad during the revolution, just as idealistic, and just as ruthless. Lenin had sent him to Tashkent in 1921 to solidify the Bolsheviks' control of Central Asia, and he had done so, from this very office.

If Peters had been alive today, Muratov thought, he too would have found himself a big fish in a suddenly shrunken pond. And an even less friendly one than Muratov's own. Peters had been a Lett, and from all the reports it seemed as if the KGB in Latvia had actually been dissolved and had not simply acquired a new mask, as was the case in Uzbekistan.

Muratov opened one of the drawers of his desk and reached in for the bottle of *canyak* brandy which he kept for such moments. After pouring a generous portion into the glass and taking his first medicinal gulp the NSS chief gave some serious thought to the hijack message for the first time. If it was genuine – and for some reason he felt that it was – then it also represented a new phenomenon – hijackers who didn't want publicity. Their name obviously suggested some strain of Islamic fundamentalism, but could just as easily be a cover for men who wanted money and lots of it. Which it was would no doubt become clear when the demands arrived on the following morning.

Muratov walked across to the open window, glass

in hand. The dim yellow lights on the unnamed street below were hardly cheerful.

The telephone rang, and he took three quick strides to pick it up. 'Hamza?' he asked. The two men had known each other a long time. Four years earlier they had been indicted together on corruption charges for their part in the Great Cotton Production Scam, which had seen Moscow paying Uzbekistan for a lot of non-existent cotton. The break-up of the Soviet Union had almost made them Uzbek national heroes.

'Yes, Bakhtar, what can I do for you?'

The Samarkand man sounded in a good mood, Muratov thought. Not to mention sleepy. He had probably gone home for an afternoon tumble with his new wife, whom rumour claimed was half her husband's age and gorgeous to boot.

'I've just had a call,' Muratov told him, and recited the alleged hijackers' message word for word.

'You want me to check it out?'

'Immediately.'

'Of course. Will you be in your office?'

'Either here or at the apartment.' He gave Zhakidov the latter's number. 'And make sure whoever you assign can keep their mouth shut. If this is genuine we don't want any news getting out, at least not until we know who we're dealing with and why.'

Nurhan Ismatulayeva studied herself in the mirror. She had tried her hair in three different ways now, but all of them seemed wrong in one way or another. She let the luxuriant black mane simply drop around her face, and stared at herself in exasperation.

The red dress seemed wrong too, now that she thought about it. It was short by Uzbek standards, far too short.

If she had been going out with an Uzbek this would have been fine – he would have seen it as the statement of independence from male Islamic culture which it was intended to be. But she was going out with a Russian, and he was likely to see the dress as nothing more than a come-on. His fingers would be slithering up her thigh before the first course arrived.

She buried her nose in her hands, and stared into her own dark eyes. Why was she even going out with the creep? Because, she answered herself, she scared Islamic men to death. And since the pool of available Russians was shrinking with the exodus from Central Asia her choice was growing more and more limited.

There was always the vibrator her friend Tursanay had brought home from France.

She stared sternly at herself. Was that what her grandmother had fought for in the 1920s? Was that why she'd pursued the career she had?

She was getting things out of proportion, she told herself. This was a dinner date, not a life crisis. If he didn't like her hair down, tough luck. If he put his hand up her dress, then she'd break a bottle over his head. Always assuming she wasn't too drunk to care.

That decided, she picked up her bag and decided to ring for a taxi – most men seemed to find her official car intimidating.

The phone rang before she could reach it.

'Nurhan?' the familiar voice asked.

'Yes, comrade,' she said instinctively, and heard the suppressed amusement in his voice as he told her to report in at once. 'Hell,' she said after hanging up, but without much conviction. She hadn't really wanted to go out with the creep anyway, and after-hours summonses from Zhakidov weren't exactly commonplace.

She called her prospective date at his home, but the line was engaged. Too bad, she thought, and walked out to the balcony and down to the street. Her car was parked in the alley beside the house, and seemed to be covered in children. As she approached they leapt off and scurried into the darkness with melodramatic shrieks of alarm. Nurhan smiled and climbed into the driver's seat. Of the two Samarkands which sat side by side – the labyrinthine old Uzbek city and the neat colonial-style Russian one – she had always loved the former and loathed the latter. One was alive, the other dead. And the fact that she had more in common with the people who lived in the Russian city couldn't change that basic truth.

As she started up the car she suddenly realized that her dress was hardly the appropriate uniform for an NSS major in command of an Anti-Terrorist Unit. What the hell – Zhakidov had said 'now'. She pressed a black-stockinged leg down on the accelerator.

It took no more than ten minutes to reach the old KGB building in Uzbekistan Street. There was a light burning in Zhakidov's second-floor office, but the rest of the building seemed to be in darkness.

She parked outside the front door and climbed out of the car. As she crossed the pavement a taxi pulled up and disgorged Major Marat Rashidov, commander of the largely theoretical Foreign Business and Tourist Protection Unit. Rashidov had been a friend of Zhakidov's for a long time, and those in the know said he had been given this unit for old times' sake. The bottle was supposed to be his real vocation.

'My God, is it an office party?' he asked, looking at her dress.

She smiled. 'Not unless it's a surprise.' There was something about Marat she had always liked, though

33

she was damned if she knew what it was. At least he was sober. In fact, his brown eyes seemed remarkably alert.

Maybe he had moved on to drugs, she thought sourly. There were enough around these days, now that the roads to Afghanistan and Pakistan were relatively open.

The two of them walked up to Hamza Zhakidov's office, and found the bureau chief sitting, feet on desk, blowing smoke rings at the ceiling, his bald head shining like a billiard-ball under the overhead light. He too gave Nurhan's dress a second glance, but restricted any comment to a momentary lifting of his bushy eyebrows.

'We may have a hijack on our hands,' he said without preamble. 'Someone phoned the office in Tashkent claiming that a party of tourists has been abducted here in Samarkand . . .'

'Have they?' Marat asked.

'That's what you're going to find out. It's supposedly the "Blue Domes" tour . . .'

'Central Asian Tours – it's an English firm,' Marat interrupted, glad he had thought to do some homework on his way over in the taxi. 'They do a ten-day tour taking in Tashkent, Bukhara and Khiva as well as here. They use the Hotel Samarkand.'

Zhakidov looked suitably impressed.

'Has the hotel been contacted?' Nurhan asked.

'No. Tashkent's orders are for maximum discretion. The hijackers . . . well, you might as well read it for yourselves.' He passed over the transcription he had taken from Muratov over the phone.

Nurhan and Marat bent over it together, she momentarily distracted by the minty smell on his breath, he by the perfume she was wearing.

34

'Publicity-shy terrorists,' she muttered. 'That's unusual.'

'The tourists are probably all sitting in the Samarkand's candlelit bar, wondering when the electricity will come back on,' Zhakidov said. 'But just go over there and check it out.'

'And if by some remote chance they really are missing?' Marat asked, getting to his feet.

'Then we start looking for them,' Nurhan told him.

Zhakidov listened to their feet disappearing down the stairs and lit another cigarette. He supposed it was rather unkind of him, but he couldn't help thinking a hijacked busload of tourists would make everyone's life a bit more interesting.

Her Majesty's Ambassador in Uzbekistan lay in the bath, his heels perched either side of the taps, a three-day-old copy of the *Independent* held just above the lukewarm water, an iced G&T within reach of his left hand. Reaching it without dipping a corner of the newspaper into the water was a knack gathered over the last few weeks, as the early-evening bath had gradually acquired the status of a ritual. The long days spent baking in the oven which served as his temporary office had required nothing less.

The British Embassy to Uzbekistan had only opened early the preceding year, and James Pearson-Jones had been given the ambassadorial appointment at the young age of thirty-two. His initial enthusiasm had not waned in the succeeding eighteen months, for post-Soviet Uzbekistan was such a Pandora's Box that it could hardly fail to be continually fascinating. It was 'the mullahs versus MTV' as an Italian colleague had put it at one of their unofficial EU lunches, adding that he wouldn't like to bet on the outcome.

35

'God save us from both,' had been a French diplomat's comment.

Pearson-Jones smiled at the memory. His money was on the West and MTV – from what he could see the average Uzbek was much more interested in money than God. And the trade and aid deals to be signed over the coming weekend would put more money within their reach.

His thoughts turned to the arrangements for putting up the junior minister and various business VIPs. He had been tempted to place them all in the Hotel Uzbekistan, where his own office was, just to give the minister an insight into what life was like in Central Asian temperatures while a hotel's air-conditioning was – allegedly, at least – in the process of being overhauled. But he had relented, and booked everyone into the Tashkent, which had the added advantage of being cheaper. After all, no one had said anything about increasing his budget to cover the upcoming binge.

There was a knock on the outside door.

He ignored it, and started rereading the cricket page. Cricket, he had to admit, was one very good reason for being in England during the summer. That and . . .

The knocker knocked again.

'Coming,' he shouted wearily. He climbed out of the bath, reached for his dressing-gown and downed the last of the G&T, then walked through to the main room of the suite and opened the door. It was his red-headed secretary, the delicious but apparently unavailable Janice. He had tried, but these days a man couldn't try too hard or someone would start yelling sexual harassment.

She wasn't here for his body this time either.

'There's been no call from Samarkand,' she said. 'I thought you ought to know.'

He looked at his watch, and found only an empty wrist. 'What time is it?'

'Eight-thirty. She should have called in at seven.'

'What were they doing today?'

'The Shah-i-Zinda this morning, and Shakhrisabz this afternoon.'

'That must be it then. It's a long drive – the bus probably broke down on the way back. Or something like that.'

'Probably. I just thought you should know.' She started for the door.

'Wait a minute,' Pearson-Jones said. There might be no brownie points for being too careful, but the Foreign Office sure as hell deducted them for not being careful enough. 'Maybe we should check it out. We have the number of the hotel?'

'It's in the office.'

'Can you get it? We'll ring from here.'

He got dressed while Janice descended a floor to the embassy office, thinking that he'd never heard her mention a boyfriend. Still, she handled the post, and for all he knew there were a dozen letters a day from England that arrived reeking of Brut.

Dressed, he poured himself another G&T, and took it out on the concrete balcony. In the forecourt below a couple of early drunks seemed to be teaching each other the tango.

Janice knocked again, and he went to let her in. 'You do the talking,' he said, 'your Uzbek is better than mine.'

Nurhan Ismatulayeva and Marat Rashidov arrived at the Hotel Samarkand some five minutes after leaving the NSS building. The coffee shop in the lobby was full of local youths, all of whom looked like bad imitations of Western rock stars. The hotel restaurant was almost empty, but one long table had been set and not used, presumably for a tour party.

Nurhan showed the receptionist her credentials, and got a scowl in return. One of these days, she thought, it would be nice to have a job which encouraged people to smile at her. Maybe she could join the state circus as a clown.

'The Central Asian Tours group,' she said. 'Are they in the hotel?'

The receptionist shook his head, his eyes apparently fixed on her black-clad lower thighs.

'Do you know where they are?'

He shook his head again.

'Look, friend,' Marat said cheerfully, 'let's have a little co-operation here.'

Reluctantly turning his attention to the male member of the duo, the receptionist gave him a pitying look. 'They're not back yet – that's all I know.'

'From where?' Nurhan asked patiently.

'I don't know. This is a hotel, not a travel agency.' Seeing the look on Marat's face, he added: 'You could try the notice-board in the lounge – they sometimes put the itineraries up there.'

Marat went to look.

'Which rooms are they in?' Nurhan asked.

He sighed and opened the register book. 'Three-o-four to 310.'

'Keys,' she said, holding out her hand.

'All of them?'

'All of them.'

He passed them over, just as Marat returned. 'Nothing,' the NSS man said.

38

They walked up the four flights of stairs to the third floor, and let themselves into the first room. Two open suitcases half-full of neatly folded clothes lay up against a wall. If the group had been hijacked it was without a change of underwear. A novel – *A Suitable Boy* – lay on the bedside table. Inside the front cover 'Elizabeth Ogley, May 1994' had been inscribed.

They had been through three of the seven rooms before Marat found what they were looking for. Inside another paperback – *Eastern Approaches* by Fitzroy Maclean – the folded piece of paper used as a bookmark yielded a handwritten copy of the tour itinerary. A trip to Shakhrisabz had been scheduled for that afternoon.

'That's it then,' Marat said. 'That road across the mountains is terrible. They've had a puncture, or driven into a ravine or something.'

Nurhan looked at the itinerary. 'Bit of a coincidence,' she said, 'that the only time they go off on a jaunt into the countryside we get a call to say they've been hijacked.'

'For someone in the know that would be the best time for a hoax,' he suggested, but with rather less confidence.

'I think it's for real,' she said, walking across to the window. A car was drawing up down below, not a tour bus. This would be her first real chance to prove herself, she thought.

'We'd better call Zhakidov,' Marat said.

They went back downstairs to the desk, and found the receptionist had disappeared. Nurhan used his phone to call in.

'You'd better drive over to Shakhrisabz,' Zhakidov said. 'If you meet them on the way, fine. If you don't, then find out if they ever got there.'

Nurhan was not pleased. 'Why can't we just phone our office there?' she wanted to know.

'Discretion, remember?'

'It's a nice ride,' Marat added for good measure. And besides, he thought, it would remove him from temptation for a few hours.

Another phone suddenly started ringing in the office behind the counter.

'Maybe it's them,' Marat suggested. 'Maybe someone got taken ill and they had to find a doctor in Shakhrisabz.'

'Maybe,' Nurhan agreed. She moved towards the office's open door just as the receptionist re-emerged from wherever it was that he had been skulking.

'I'll answer that,' he said indignantly.

'If it's anything to do with the Central Asian Tours party I want to speak to them,' Nurhan said.

'OK, OK,' the receptionist said, picking up the receiver. 'Yes,' he said, in answer to some question, glancing across at Nurhan and Marat. 'Wait a moment,' he told the caller, 'the police want to speak to you.' He held out the phone for Nurhan. 'Who is that?' she asked.

'I am calling from the British Embassy in Tashkent,' a female voice said in reasonable Uzbek. 'I wish to talk to someone staying at the hotel. Brenda Walker.'

Nurhan cursed under her breath. 'The group has not returned from their trip yet,' she said.

'Do you know why they're late?' the woman asked.

'No. A problem with their bus, most likely. Do you wish to leave a message?'

'Why are the police involved?' the woman asked.

'We just want to talk to the tour operators,' Nurhan improvised. 'Is there no message?'

'No, I'll try again in an hour or so.'

Nurhan put the phone down. 'Why did you say "police", you idiot?' she asked the receptionist.

He shrugged. 'You didn't tell me not to.'

She looked at him. 'The woman will be calling back. You will tell her the same thing I told her – that you don't know why the tour group has not returned, but it's probably that their bus has broken down. Is that clear?'

'Of course.'

'Then don't fuck up,' Marat warned him. 'Or our next meeting will not be as convivial as this one has been. Now what sort of bus are they in?'

'A small one. Green and white.'

The two NSS officers headed out through the glass doors in the direction of their car, oblivious to the disdainful finger being raised to their retreating backs.

Four hundred kilometres to the north-east Janice Wood was trying to explain the tone of the policewoman's voice to James Pearson-Jones. 'I'm sure she was lying, or at least not telling the whole truth. Something's happened.'

Pearson-Jones sighed, thought for a moment, and muttered 'shit' with some vehemence. 'We'd better call London,' he said.

'And bring Simon in?' she asked. Simon Kennedy was ostensibly Pearson-Jones's number two at the embassy, with a portfolio of responsibilities which included that of military attaché. He was also MI6's representative in Central Asia.

'Yes, bring him in,' Pearson-Jones agreed. 'I'll go down to the office and make the call.'

3

In London it was nearly four in the afternoon, and the tall patrician figure of Alan Holcroft had just arrived back at the Foreign Office from the House of Commons. Prime Minister's Question Time had been its usual farcical waste of time, and Holcroft had sat on the front bench wondering why they didn't put a cock-fighting arena by the dispatch box, and give the two sides some real blood to cheer about. He was quite willing to agree that the occasion was a useful theoretical demonstration of democracy in action, but could see no reason why anyone with real work to do should have to sit through the damn thing twice a week.

And as Foreign Minister he had plenty of work to do. The rest of the world seemed even more of a mess than usual. The Americans had found something new to panic them – North Korea, this time – but at least for the moment they seemed to have dropped the idea of invading Haiti. Russia was still collapsing, the Brussels bureaucracy its usual irritating self, and the French as difficult as ever. Bosnia continued on its bloody way, despite losing top spot in the genocide league to Rwanda. And then there was the Middle East . . . If this was the New World Order, Holcroft thought, then he would hate to see chaos.

On his desk he found a memo waiting for him. The two British hostages held by the Khmer Rouge in Cambodia were getting a full-page write-up in tomorrow morning's *Independent*, and it was expected that the Labour MP championing their cause would be seeking a government response the following afternoon.

Holcroft sighed. What did they expect – a gunboat? That the government would send the hostage-takers to bed without any supper? The honest answer would be to say that Her Majesty's Government had no influence whatsoever on the Khmer Rouge, and to admit in addition that it had more important things to worry about than a couple of British citizens who had been stupid enough to travel in a country that was clearly unsafe. As far as Holcroft was concerned they were like transatlantic rowers or potholers – he had no objection to them taking risks, but every objection to their using taxpayers' time and money to pull themselves out of jams of their own making.

None of which he could say at the dispatch box. He settled down to read through the memo, confident that the author would have supplied him with either a more acceptable reason for doing nothing or a convincing explanation of how much he was already doing.

Holcroft was nearly halfway through the three-page memo when there was a sharp rap on his door. He looked at his watch – there was still at least forty minutes left of the one hour without interruption which he demanded each day. 'Come,' he snapped.

It was his Parliamentary Private Secretary, Michael Allsworth. 'Sorry to interrupt you,' the intruder said, 'but the embassy in Tashkent has been on the line.'

Holcroft felt the familiar mixture of anger and frustration seize him by the throat. 'What in God's name has she done now?' he demanded.

'No, it's nothing like that ... it's ... well ...' Allsworth took a seat. 'It all seems a bit iffy, Minister. The gist of it is that the tour party your daughter is with seems to have disappeared. Or at least not returned to the hotel in Samarkand when it should have. As you know, the agent assigned to your daughter is supposed to report in each day at seven local time. Today she hasn't. But we have no actual reason to suspect foul play . . .'

'No *actual* reason?'

'Well, when the embassy tried to contact her at the hotel they were asked to speak to the police, which they found a bit odd.'

'Was there no reason given for the tour party not being there?'

'Just lateness. And that may be . . .'

'What's the time there now?' Holcroft wanted to know.

'About ten o'clock in Samarkand, eleven in Tashkent.'

'And they were due back when?'

'For dinner at eight o'clock.'

'So it's only two hours. That doesn't seem much.'

'No, it's just . . .'

'The police business. I understand.' Holcroft considered for a moment. The familiar thought of how much easier life would be, both for him and his wife, without their youngest daughter flitted across his mind, and for once induced a slight sense of shame. Rather more to his surprise, Holcroft also felt a tinge of panic. 'If they're not simply late, then what are the possibilities?' he asked Allsworth.

'An accident of some sort, a simple hold-up, a political hijack.'

Holcroft wondered which would be worst. 'So what do you suggest?' he asked.

'Get the intelligence boys working on it, just in case. After all, they've already got someone with the party, and MI6 have another man in Tashkent. MI5 or Special

Branch can do any spadework that needs doing this end. The tour company operates out of Bradford,' he added, in response to Holcroft's raised eyebrow.

'Of course.' Sarah had told him as much when she'd announced this ridiculous jaunt. That was how he had managed to arrange the accompanying minder. 'Right,' he told Allsworth. 'Do that. And call me if any news comes in. I'll be at home.'

The secretary disappeared, leaving Holcroft with a sinking sensation in his stomach. 'They're just late,' he murmured to himself, but it didn't sound convincing. He wondered what, if anything, he was going to tell his wife Phyllis.

Marat Rashidov watched Nurhan's thighs shift as she changed gears and had a fleeting memory of being excited by his ex-wife in similar circumstances. 'What were you planning this evening?' he asked.

She didn't answer for a moment, being absorbed in circumnavigating a goat which had strayed into the middle of the road, and now seemed transfixed by the car's headlights. 'What did you say?' she asked, once they were past the belligerent-looking animal.

He repeated the question.

She smiled to herself. 'Just a dinner date,' she said.

'Who was the lucky man?' he asked.

She laughed. 'Mind your own business,' she retorted. 'What did you have planned?'

He grunted. 'Nothing much.' Another evening staring at the walls and wondering who he was staying sober for. He glanced across at Nurhan, whose black hair was now gathered at the nape of her neck and held by an elastic band she had found in one of the tourists' rooms. Marat had known of her for a long time, occasionally run into her when their professional duties overlapped, but he had no real idea of who she was. Rumour had it that she'd screwed her way to the position she currently held, but in the predominantly male world of the Samarkand NSS such an explanation of her success was almost inevitable. Marat doubted it was true. She didn't seem like the scheming sort. Or the sort who wanted to be beholden to anyone for anything.

'How did you get into this work?' he asked.

'It's in the family blood,' she said. 'My grandmother was in the Chekas during the Revolution.'

'Tell me about her,' Marat said.

She glanced across at him. 'It's ancient history,' she said. 'Why would you be interested?'

'It's going to be a long ride,' he said. 'Humour me.'

She shrugged. 'She was my mother's mother. Her name was Rahima Asankulova. She was the wife of one of the first Uzbek Bolsheviks, a very young wife. Of course he treated her like any Uzbek husband treated his wife in those days, and in 1921, when she was only about nineteen – she never knew exactly which year she was born in – she ran away to Moscow, to the headquarters of the Party women's organization, the Zhenotdel. There was a big fuss, but six months later she came back as a Zhenotdel worker, one of the first in Central Asia. You know what they went through?'

'I imagine they weren't too popular.'

'That's an understatement if ever I heard one. They campaigned against the veil, and for an end to the selling of brides, and in favour of education for women . . . the usual. Some were stoned to death, some were thrown down wells, one woman was actually chopped up. All these murders were committed by fellow family members, of course.'

46

Glancing to his left, Marat could see her staring angrily ahead.

'And your grandmother?'

'She survived until the thirties, then died giving birth in one of Stalin's prisons.'

'To your mother?'

'No, she was born in 1928. She worked for the Party too, though not for the KGB. She was a union representative for the Tashkent textile workers. She's retired now, but she still lives in Tashkent . . .'

She broke off as two headlights appeared round a bend in the mountain road.

'It's a lorry,' Marat said, rummaging in his pockets. A hand emerged holding a tube of mints. He offered her one.

She took it, wondering if she had been wrong earlier in assuming that the mint on his breath had been a cover for the smell of alcohol.

'I've just given up smoking,' he said, as if in answer to her unspoken question.

'Good idea,' she said.

He rearranged himself in the seat and asked her why she had joined the KGB.

She was silent for a few moments. 'I think the main reason was that I couldn't think of an alternative,' she said eventually.

'You're joking . . .'

'No. I got accepted at Moscow University, and could hardly believe my luck. I really wanted to get out of Tashkent. To get out of Central Asia, full stop.'

'Why? You're Uzbek . . .'

'An Uzbek woman. I don't expect any Uzbek man to understand . . . but for anyone brought up the way I was there's not many chances of fulfilment in this culture.'

'So why did you come back?'

'I missed the place.' She laughed. 'But that's only part of the story. I don't know how you feel about what's happened in the last few years . . .'

'Ambivalent, I suppose.'

'That sounds about right. I hated it in Moscow – it was so obvious there that the system only worked for a few people at the top. Back here it was different. Oh, I know it was far from perfect, and every time I turn on the TV now there seems to be some new horror story about what's been done to the environment, but . . . well, look at the place compared to what it was before the Revolution. We have education for everyone, and health care . . .'

'I saw what this place must have been like before the Revolution,' Marat said. 'In Afghanistan.'

'Exactly,' she said. 'I guess I wanted to preserve some of what had been achieved.'

'And the KGB seemed the best place?'

'One of the best. Advances in things like women's rights are enshrined in the state law. Which is what we're supposed to protect, among other things.'

'You're not too worried about the other things?'

'If you mean locking up fundamentalists, no I'm not. They're not interested in democracy.'

'What would you do if they came to power?'

'Leave, I expect. What would you do?' Islamic Republics were alcohol-free zones, after all.

'Probably the same. Though I've no idea where I'd go. America maybe, if there was a way to get in.'

'If they declared an Islamic Republic here I expect the West would bend over backwards to take in political refugees.'

He grunted with amusement. 'Maybe I should be

48

voting for the bastards. If we ever get another vote, that is. As our beloved President is so fond of pointing out: "Do not destroy your old house until you have build another." '

'Makes sense to me,' Nurhan observed.

'Maybe. But only if people are allowed to start work on the new house. Bakalev is putting anyone who tries in prison.'

She looked at him. 'You've given up hope, have you?'

He smiled. 'Let's just say I'm not expecting too much from the next few years.' He put his hands in his pockets to conceal the fact that the left hand had begun to shake. Looking out of the Volga's window at the mountains and star-filled sky he had the sudden conviction that the ancient Greeks had got it wrong – Orion was holding a bottle opener, not a sword.

Simon Kennedy had left Tashkent about half an hour after Nurhan and Marat's departure from Samarkand. The main road between the two cities wasn't bad, and he reckoned he would be in Samarkand not much later than two in the morning. He didn't expect there would be a great deal he could do before daylight, but at least he would be on the spot.

Driving, in any case, was something he always enjoyed, especially at night. He had done quite a lot of it lately, usually with Janice, who seemed much more happy indulging her sexual appetite in some desert lay-by than in either of their rooms at the Hotel Uzbekistan. Kennedy wasn't complaining, though he did sometimes wonder what the local police would make of it if the two of them were ever caught in the act.

Janice had a brain, though, and he was inclined

to trust her judgement in this business with Sarah Holcroft. There probably was something funny going on in Samarkand. Either way, he supposed he would know by morning.

The tour bus had been travelling for slightly more than three hours when it finally reached its destination. Its occupants had seen no other vehicles during the journey, and passed not a single light, either beside the road or off in the distance. They could have been driving across the moon.

'Please stay in your seats,' Nasruddin said.

'Until the plane has come to a complete stop,' Docherty added under his breath. He wondered if there had ever been such a courteous hijack as this one.

'The women will leave the bus first,' Nasruddin told them. 'They will have separate quarters from the men.' There was a muted wail of fright from Elizabeth Ogley at this news.

'There is no cause for alarm,' Nasruddin said, almost indignantly. 'On the contrary – such an arrangement is in accord with Islamic tradition.'

And will make it harder for any rescue operation, Docherty thought. He wondered what sort of 'quarters' were awaiting them outside in the darkness.

'The women will now leave the bus,' Nasruddin announced.

For a moment no one moved, as if in instinctive mutiny against the demand. Alice Jennings was the first to stand up. She leaned over to kiss Sam on the forehead, murmured something to him, and started down the aisle, head high. Docherty didn't see the look she gave Nasruddin, but their former guide looked as if he had been slapped.

One by one the others followed. Sarah Holcroft and Sharon Copley both looked frightened, Elizabeth Ogley close to panic. Brenda Walker showed no emotion, encouraging Docherty to believe that she was indeed what he had suspected. With any luck she would have the same training as he had in dealing with hostage situations.

Isabel was last, her face stern as she disappeared down the steps at the front of the bus. Docherty prayed to any possible gods that might be up there that he would see her again.

Nasruddin disappeared, leaving just the clean-shaven man with them. The AK47 was held loosely, but its barrel was pointed right down the aisle between them. There was no sign of carelessness, and the previous hint of nervousness had given way to a watchful confidence. This man has seen military action, Docherty thought.

Several minutes went by. The men didn't speak, but their shared glances were eloquent enough. What a fucking mess, Copley's expression said. This can't have happened to me, was written all over Ogley's face. The Zahid men were trying to hide their anxiety behind stoical exteriors and failing. Their sons, like Sam Jennings, could not conceal the absurd sense of excitement which was bubbling up through the fear.

'Talib,' a voice said from outside, causing the clean-shaven man to prick up his ears. Words in a foreign language followed.

Talib gestured with his left hand for the men to follow him, and retreated down the steps. Docherty stood up quickly, intending to position himself at the head of the procession, but then thought better of the idea. A time might come for him to assume some sort of command responsibility, but it hadn't arrived yet.

They filed off the bus, stepping down on to a gravel surface. Ahead of them was a long, one-storey building with dim lights showing in two of the windows. Two men with automatic rifles stood on either side of the twenty-metre path which led to the front door, channelling their passage. Another two waited by the door. Since Nasruddin was not among them, this raised the number of the hijackers to at least seven.

While making this simple calculation, Docherty was also taking in the panoramic sweep of countryside to either side. Though moonless, the clear sky offered enough illumination to make out the jumble of slopes which receded into the distance. The lodge had been built at the back of a wide shelf, at the upper end of a deep valley. Behind the building a bare rock-face rose almost sheer, while from its front the folds of the valley stretched away into the darkness. In the few seconds he had left before reaching the door Docherty searched for and found the North Star, low in the sky away to his left. The building faced west.

Not that it mattered. They seemed to be a long way from civilization. In more ways than one.

The interior of the building, though, exceeded all his expectations. It seemed to have been decorated and furnished to a higher standard than most of the Central Asian hotels they had stayed in, which perhaps wasn't saying much. Docherty had a glimpse of a large living-room with bear rug and open hearth, before passing down a long corridor full of closed doors. At the end they were ushered into a dormitory room. It was reasonably large, about four metres by six, with two-tier bunks on three of its four walls. Otherwise the room was empty, save for the cheap rug which covered most of the floor. Docherty was still wondering what the place was when he heard a bolt slam shut on the outside of the door. And then another.

He looked round at his fellow-captives. The two elder Zahids had begun talking animatedly in Urdu, with their sons looking on anxiously. They suddenly looked no older than adolescents, Docherty thought.

Ogley was sitting on one of the bunks with his head in his hands, Copley pacing up and down. 'Where do you think the women have been taken?' the builder asked nobody in particular.

'A room like this one,' Docherty said.

Copley looked at him with worried eyes. 'You don't think they'll . . .'

'No I don't,' Docherty said shortly. A year ago there would have been more inner certainty behind the denial, but the mission to Bosnia had shaken his sense of how much evil was loose in the world. 'If they're Islamic fundamentalists then we can expect some sort of moral code,' he added, with more conviction than he felt. But one of the worst things that could happen here would be for the men to sit around imagining what was being done to their wives. If they were to get out of this alive then they all had to remain rational and reasonably focused. Fear and anger led in the opposite direction.

'How do you know they are Islamic fundamentalists?' Ogley asked.

Docherty shrugged. 'The Trumpet of God doesn't sound like a bunch of communists. What else could they be?' He turned to the Pakistani contingent. 'Mr Zahid,' he said, addressing the elder brother, 'have you heard of these people?'

The mullah shook his head dismissively. 'They must be Shiites,' he said angrily. 'Lunatics from Iran. That is all I can think.'

'Hey, look,' Copley said from behind Docherty.

There was another door in the fourth wall. Copley tried the handle and it opened to reveal a bathroom and toilet. Admittedly the former comprised just a tap and the latter just a hole in the floor, but a full bucket of water was standing by one wall.

'I think we must be on a Magical Mystery Tour,' Copley said. He at least seemed to be recovering his composure.

'I wonder which of us is the Walrus,' Docherty murmured.

'Will you two stop gibbering,' Ogley snapped behind them. 'We've been kidnapped, for God's sake.'

'Tell us something we don't know, Professor,' Copley said drily. 'You know,' he went on, 'I wouldn't have believed it, but I actually feel hungry.'

'So do I,' Sam Jennings agreed. 'Do you guys mind if I take one of the bottom bunks?' The Zahid fathers had already laid claim to two of the four.

'Go ahead,' Docherty said, wondering what the place was normally used for. Maybe it was a youth hostel. Or a barracks for border guards.

He noticed Ogley sitting with his head between his hands, sighed, and went over to him. 'Are you OK, Professor?' he asked.

'I am not a professor,' Ogley said. 'And what do you care anyway?'

Docherty chose his words carefully. 'I care because experience has taught me that in a hole like this people need to pull together. I want to be alive a month from now, not a name in an obituary column.'

Ogley looked at him sideways, rather like a schoolboy who wasn't sure if he was being kidded. 'So do I,' he agreed slowly.

'Good. Now is that the bunk you want?'

* * *

The women's room was a mirror image of the men's, situated at the opposite end of the lodge. Once the bolts had clanged shut behind them, Isabel went round checking all the more obvious hiding-places for listening devices. She wasn't expecting to find any, but it was better to be safe than sorry.

Once she was reasonably certain there weren't any, she asked her five companions for a conference. Both Elizabeth Ogley and Sharon Copley seemed close to hysteria, and Isabel thought developing a sense of solidarity could only help.

She also had something vital to ask. 'Sarah,' she began quietly, 'no one's mentioned it, but I think we all know who you are – or maybe I should say we all know who your father is . . .'

'I don't,' Alice Jennings said, surprise on her face.

'He's the British Foreign Minister,' Sarah Holcroft said.

'Oh boy,' Alice said softly.

'The point is, do they know?' Isabel asked, jerking her head in the direction of the door.

Sarah looked surprised. 'I . . . I don't know,' she said.

'Did Nasruddin ever say anything to indicate he knew?'

'No. At least, I can't remember . . . But he must have known, mustn't he?' A hint of a wry smile crossed her lips. 'He did live in England.'

Alice Jennings snorted. 'They're always doing polls in America that show eighty per cent of Americans don't know who the President is.'

'Nasruddin seems a serious young man,' Isabel said. 'The type who would read the *Guardian* rather than the *Mirror*. And your picture would have appeared in the tabloids, not the qualities.'

'What are you getting at?' Brenda Walker wanted to know. She had been eyeing Isabel with suspicion ever since their arrival.

'It's simple. Maybe they don't know who Sarah is. In which case we have to be damn careful not to let them find out.'

'They must know,' Elizabeth Ogley said, 'or why would they have hijacked us?'

'That would be a coincidence,' Alice Jennings agreed.

'They happen,' Isabel said. 'They may have hijacked us for no more reason than that we're British. Most of us, anyway.'

'But what difference will it make whether they know or not?' Elizabeth Ogley asked.

'Their demands will be higher if they think they have someone important,' Isabel said. 'And the lower they stay the better our chances of getting out of this.'

'You seem to know a lot about this type of thing,' Brenda Walker interjected.

Isabel was about to say that her husband had a lot of experience in these situations, but stopped herself in time. There didn't seem any point in letting Docherty's SAS background out of the bag. 'I do have some experience of this kind of thing,' she said. 'From the other side.'

'You don't mean you were a hijacker?' Alice Jennings asked with a laugh.

'I was involved in two kidnappings, nearly twenty years ago now, in Argentina. In England you had protest demonstrations, in Argentina things got a little more serious,' she added, trying to make light of it. The other women all looked dumbstruck, with the notable exception of Brenda Walker.

She already knew, Isabel realized. Hence the suspicion. Ms Walker must have some secrets of her own.

In fact, Brenda Walker had spent the last five minutes wondering whether to come clean about her own role, and deciding that she had no option. As a social worker her advice in this situation would be ignored; as an intelligence agent it would not.

'I also have a confession to make,' she began.

'My God,' Alice Jennings gasped. 'Is no one who they seem to be on this trip?'

'I am,' Sharon Copley said, with a noise that sounded half laugh, half sob.

They all laughed, and then there was a moment of silence as they realized what they had done.

'I work for the government,' Brenda Walker said quietly. 'My job was, well, it was to make sure Sarah didn't cause the government any embarrassment while she was abroad.' She looked across at Sarah. 'I've enjoyed your company,' she said simply.

'Christ!' was all Sarah could say.

'She was just doing her job,' Isabel said. It looked as if imbuing this group with a sense of solidarity was going to be an uphill task.

But Sarah sighed and gave Brenda a rueful smile. 'I've been enjoying your company too,' she said.

Sir Christopher Hanson, the head of MI6, poured himself a small glass of port and sipped at it, allowing the sweetness to smooth away his sense of irritation. Another twelve hours and he would have been on his way to Heathrow to begin a fortnight's holiday in St Lucia. At any moment now his wife would be receiving the news that he wouldn't be coming, and he was half expecting her cry of rage to be audible above the ten miles of rush-hour snarl-ups which separated them.

But one of his men – or woman on loan, to be precise – was apparently in a life-threatening situation, and he would not have felt happy deserting the helm at such a moment. Brenda Walker's file was supposedly on its way from MI5 Records, though it seemed a long time arriving. He was about to make further enquiries when an apologetic courier appeared in his open doorway.

Hanson took the discs and went to turn on his computer terminal, feeling, as usual, nostalgic for the bulging file of mostly illegible reports which had once served the same purpose. There was something real about paper and ink, something substantial.

Still, the new system was ten times as efficient, not to mention a damn sight easier to store. He accessed Brenda Walker's file and skimmed through it. The computerized portrait told him she had short dark hair and a face, which wasn't very much. Even in this brave new world there had to be a photograph somewhere, surely.

Hanson smiled, remembering one subordinate's tongue-in-cheek suggestion that they rename MI6 Rent-a-Bond.

Brenda Walker's personal details contained no surprises, unless you counted her working-class background and comprehensive education, but these days that was almost par for the course among MI5's foot-soldiers. She had done a lot of escort work with the royals, had a short stint with the embassy in Australia, and had then taken a specialist training course in immigration law. She had been working in that area for only a few weeks when given the job 'minding' the Holcroft girl, apparently because the previous candidate had abruptly fallen ill.

Was that suspicious? Hanson doubted it.

He printed out the file and then switched discs. The new one contained not only the 'paperwork' from her current assignment, but also the preliminary vetting reports on the tour group concerned and the other members of the party.

He went through the latter, his mouth opening with surprise when he read the information on Jamie Docherty and his wife Isabel. An SAS veteran and an ex-terrorist! Put them together with Brenda Walker, and that made three of the fourteen tourists who had first-hand experience of dealing, from one side or the other, with such volatile situations. If the party had indeed been hijacked, then that had to be some sort of record.

Assuming for the moment that they had been, one big question remained: whether or not the hijackers were aware of the fact that they had netted the Foreign Minister's daughter.

4

Isabel lay on the bunk, considering the irony of her situation. She wondered how many people in the world had personally experienced a hijack and kidnapping as both perpetrator and victim. She might well be the first.

Her thoughts went back to Córdoba in 1974, and the beginning of the war she and her comrades had been crazy enough to launch against the Argentinian military. The first man they had kidnapped had been a local glass manufacturer notorious both for his high living and for the low wages he paid his employees. They had kept him for three days in an apartment not two hundred metres from the city's central police station, blindfolded but otherwise not ill-treated. His family had paid the requested ransom – $60,000 worth of food and clothing for the city's poor. They had watched the man's wife hand out the packages on TV, and then let him go.

Two weeks later they had done it again. This time the victim was a member of the family which had ruled over the city for most of the century, their wealth amassed through land ownership, banking and several manufacturing businesses. The ransom demanded had been correspondingly higher – $1,000,000 in gift packages for poor schoolchildren, plus the reinstatement of 250 workers who had recently been locked out of the family's construction business.

The ransom had been paid, but the experience had not been so pleasurable the second time round. The victim had turned out to be almost likeable, and on several occasions the proximity of police teams scouring the city had made it seem likely that he would have to be killed. In the event this had not happened, but the probability had been enough to sow doubt and dissension through her guerrilla unit. It had made them look more closely at themselves and each other, and in some cases they hadn't liked what they had seen.

And now here she was among the victims. She wondered how Nasruddin and his comrades were getting on with each other. Maybe it was a crazy thing to think, but from the little she had witnessed The Trumpet of God didn't seem to be having much fun. So far, she hadn't seen a single smile on any of their faces. At the beginning of their war against the Junta, her group, the ERP, had treated it all like a mad adventure.

Though later, to be sure, there had been nothing to laugh about, only torture and death.

She had been lucky to survive, her body scarred but intact, her soul missing in action for many years thereafter. She wondered if Nasruddin and his friends believed in what they were doing as strongly as she and her friends had done, and whether they would still be alive in twenty years, and able to look back on what had happened the previous evening.

She wondered if she would be, or if her luck had finally run out. She thought about Docherty and hoped she hadn't held him for the last time.

In the men's room the light had abruptly gone out shortly after eleven o'clock.

'I guess that means it's bedtime,' Copley sighed.

'Aye,' Docherty said, remembering rooms like this in Highland youth hostels. In his early teens he and his friend Doug had spent many a weekend hitchhiking around from hostel to hostel, partly for the sheer joy of free movement, partly to get out of Glasgow and the parental orbit. After lights out they would talk in whispers and giggles until an older boy managed to shut them up.

He clambered up on to the bunk above Ogley, wondering if any of them would manage to sleep that night. He felt pretty strung out himself, and guessed that the others, none of whom had his previous experience of life-threatening situations, would spend most of the night listening to their hearts beating wildly inside their ribcages.

'The last time I was in a place like this,' Sam Jennings said, his soft drawl floating out of the dark, 'it was a police station in Mississippi. Back in the Civil Rights days, in the early sixties. We were helping to get black voters registered, which wasn't very popular with the local authorities. They arrested about twenty of us, though I can't remember what charges they dreamed up – it was something like walking on the grass with shoes on. Anyway, we were put in a cell a lot like this, except that the police dog pound was right outside, and every so often a dog's face would appear at the window, growling fit to bust and slavering something awful. We all started singing "We Shall Overcome", but I tell you, I don't think any of us felt too confident about it that night. I was scared.' There was a pause. 'I'm scared now,' he added.

'So am I,' one of the Zahid boys said, eliciting what sounded like a comforting sentence in Urdu from his father.

'What do you think, Jamie?' Copley asked Docherty. 'You must have seen some hairy situations in the army.'

'We're at the mercy of people we know nothing about,'

Docherty said, 'and that's always scary. But I don't think they're madmen. I don't think they'll harm us for fun, or without what they would consider good reason. We mustn't give them any reason to act in anger – in fact, we should do everything we can to make ourselves human to them. In situations like this people are harder to k . . . harder to harm if you know them.'

A silence of several moments was broken by Copley. 'I wonder how the women are getting on.'

'Probably better than us,' Docherty said. He knew that women always found it easier to share their feelings, and in adversity that was a useful thing to do. Still, he was worried about Isabel. Though twenty years had passed since her nightmare incarceration in the Naval Mechanical School outside Buenos Aires, being imprisoned once more was bound to give the dreadful memories new life, no matter how different the circumstances might be.

For the first time since the men with the AK47s had climbed aboard the bus, Docherty felt anger welling inside him. Anger at the bastards who were holding them, anger at a world in which such happenings had become so commonplace, anger at himself for being so helpless to save her.

He lay on his back looking into the darkness above his head, willing himself back to the state of mind he would need for all their sakes.

The thought crept in unbidden that he would willingly sacrifice all the others if only she could walk away unscathed.

It was almost twenty past eleven when Nurhan Ismatulayeva and Marat Rashidov drove down Sholkoviput Street and into the mostly sleeping town of Shakhrisabz. The soaring remnant of Tamerlane's palace loomed out of the darkness on their right, and Nurhan brought the Volga to a halt opposite the entrance to the car park.

The chain-link gate was closed, and no lights were visible beyond them.

'Do you know this town?' she asked Marat.

'Not well.' He stared past her at the palace complex. 'There must be a caretaker somewhere around.'

'Yeah,' she agreed, and reached for the door handle.

They walked across to the gate, and found it attached by nothing more than a cheap padlock. Marat lifted himself up and over, breathing a bit heavily, and raised a hand to help her down. She ignored it, and then felt a bit churlish for doing so.

'I don't think much of their security,' she said, checking anxiously to see if her best nylons had been laddered. Tursanay had brought them back from Paris with the vibrator.

'They probably think thieves would have a hard job sneaking out of the country with this thing,' Marat said drily, looking up at the ruined entrance.

'There's always vandalism,' she said tartly. 'It's been getting worse and worse in Samarkand. There's graffiti everywhere.'

'True,' Marat agreed. 'Maybe we do need an Islamic Republic after all. Bring back some discipline, eh?'

She ignored him. The nylons seemed to have survived intact.

'We could cut off the artists' hands,' he went on, warming to his theme.

'Are you finished?' she asked.

'Sure,' he said, thinking how sexy she looked, standing there in a darkened car park with a short party dress on, hands on hips and eyes flashing. 'The museum building seems the best bet,' he added helpfully. 'It's that one over there.'

'What are we standing here for then?' she asked, turning on her heel and starting off across the pock-marked asphalt surface.

After knocking at two doors they found the caretaker, a man somewhere between middle and old age, asleep on a *kravat* in the trees behind the building. His eyes opened slowly from slumber, widened quickly at the sight of Nurhan standing over him, and then narrowed once more at the sight of her NSS identification.

'They were just small pieces,' he said. 'No bigger than this,' he added, bending his forefinger inside his thumb to indicate just how small.

'What are you talking about?' Nurhan asked him sternly.

He blinked up at her, opened his mouth and then closed it again.

'Pieces of pottery or tile,' Marat said wearily. 'Our friend here has been selling them to the tourists.' He shook his head.

'That's not why we're here,' he said, 'though I may come back to find out if you're still doing it. We're looking for the tour party who were here this afternoon.'

The man blinked again. 'There were three here this afternoon,' he said.

'This one came in a small green and white bus.'

'Ah, the last one. Is there a reward for this information?' he asked hopefully.

'There's a heavy penalty for selling state property,' Marat reminded him.

'Yes, yes. What do you want to know? I see them go into the museum, and I see them go out. The last time I see them they are sitting outside the café across the street.'

'When was that?' Nurhan asked.

The man shrugged. 'It was growing dark. Maybe six o'clock.'

'You didn't see the bus leave?'

'No.'

Nurhan looked at Marat. 'The café?'

He nodded, and turned to the caretaker. 'Cut out the sideline,' he told him, 'or you'll be out of a job.'

They walked back round the building and across the vast space towards the gate, with Nurhan wishing they had brought along the caretaker and his key. She doubted whether her nylons would survive another climb.

Still, there was a simple answer to that. She turned away from Marat, lifted the dress, unhooked the French suspenders and pulled down the nylons. 'They cost a fortune,' she muttered in explanation.

He said nothing, but this time failed to offer her a helping hand.

Human beings are ridiculous, she thought, climbing down to the road.

'That's the café,' Marat said, indicating a dark shape some fifty metres up the road. They left the car where it was and walked up. It was a one-storey building set back from the road, with a yard full of metal tables and chairs strewn beneath the large plum tree in its front yard.

The proprietor finally appeared in answer to their knocking, rubbing the sleep from his eyes. 'I was working out the back,' he said, 'but my wife will answer your questions.' He disappeared to fetch her.

'Working out the back,' Nurhan repeated to herself sarcastically. The man had probably been sitting around talking to his friends while his wife ran the place for him.

She appeared at the door, a diminutive woman with quick eyes and an aura of efficiency about her. She remembered serving the group in question, but had not actually seen them leave. For that they would need to talk to her son, who was responsible for selling the tickets at the gate. She disappeared in search of him.

'I think I'll go back and break a pot over that caretaker's head,' Marat muttered, as they waited once more on the café veranda.

This time, though, it was worth it. The son had seen the bus drive out of the park, and seen it turn right on to the Samarkand road. 'And the car left right behind it,' he added.

'Which car?' Nurhan asked.

The boy described the black Volga, and the rusty black Fiat which had spent most of the afternoon alongside it. He had assumed they must be waiting for something. The Fiat had left just before the bus. He thought that each car had contained two or three men, but he couldn't be more precise than that. During the afternoon the men had sat down together under the trees behind the two cars, but it was over a hundred metres from the gate, so he had not been able to see them very clearly. Most were wearing Western dress, but at least one man was wearing a traditional robe.

'You didn't catch the number of either car?'

No, he had not.

They thanked him and started back towards their own vehicle.

'We've got a hijack on our hands,' Marat said. It felt strange saying it – hijackings were things that happened

67

somewhere else. Still, this one should keep him busy for the next few days.

'We should talk to Zhakidov,' Nurhan said, opening the door and reaching for the radio receiver. Despite the intervening mountains the signal was loud and clear. She waited while the duty operator went to fetch Zhakidov, then told him what they had discovered. 'There's no indication of where they went,' she said. In fact, as she suddenly realized, the hijackers could have left Shakhrisabz at six and got back to Samarkand before she and Marat had left. She suggested as much to Zhakidov.

'It's possible, I suppose,' he said doubtfully. 'You two had better stay in Shakhrisabz tonight, and start trying to pick up the trail at first light.'

'At the hotel?' Nurhan asked hopefully.

'At tourist prices? You must be joking,' Zhakidov said. 'It's only about five hours till dawn. Just pretend you're on a stake-out.'

'Thanks a lot,' Nurhan said under her breath.

'And keep me up to date,' Zhakidov was saying.

'Will do,' she started to say, but he had already cut the connection.

'I take it we're not sleeping between clean white sheets tonight,' Marat said.

'You got that right,' she told him, reaching over into the back seat for the rug. 'You're in your bed right now. At dawn we're supposed to find the hijackers.'

'And rescue the tourists?'

'If we're in the mood.' She let her seat back with rather more suddenness than she intended, and almost knocked the breath out of herself.

He looked down at her with a grin. 'I don't suppose I get to share the rug,' he said.

She smiled sweetly up at him. 'You got that right too.'

Nasruddin Salih was sitting in the large living-room, his foot resting on the bear's head, a bottle of lemonade in his hand. Talib Khamidov was slumped in another chair, his AK47 within easy reach, while the bearded Akbar Makhamov was almost perched on the edge of the large leather sofa, as if fearful of being contaminated by such decadence. Of the other four members of the group, Farkhot and Sabir were on guard outside the hostage's rooms, Shukrat and Chunar out front of the lodge, some fifty metres down the approach track.

The hunting lodge itself had been built and half finished under the last government of the Uzbek State Socialist Republic, and had been intended for the use of both the local Party bigwigs and any visiting cronies from Moscow. Though the same people were still in power in Tashkent and Samarkand, they had become rather more discreet about enjoying the perks of office, and the lodge had not been used for over two years. Nasruddin had been able to date the abandonment of privilege with some accuracy – among the pile of pornographic magazines found in one of the furnished bedrooms the most recent issue had been that of August 1992. Akbar had burnt the magazines out on the hillside, along with the mass-produced portrait of Red Army Marshal Frunze which had held pride of place above the hearth.

'Two of us should sleep,' Nasruddin said, though without much conviction. A day of anxious waiting had given way to that sense of liberation which came with an irrevocable leap into the unknown. He had started a new life that day, and the adrenalin was still pumping through his veins in celebration.

'Have we no decisions to take?' Akbar asked. Neither Nasruddin's manic calm nor Talib's stoicism seemed to have rubbed off on the Tajik.

'I don't think so,' Nasruddin said. 'Everything has gone exactly as we hoped.'

'God willing,' Talib murmured.

'What about the hostages?' Akbar asked. 'Do we have anything to fear from them. The soldier, for example.'

'I don't think so,' Nasruddin said. He had liked the Dochertys – they were the only members of the party who had not treated him differently because of his race. The Americans, being liberals of the old school, had overcompensated.

'I think it might be better to keep him separate from the others,' suggested Akbar.

'Then we would have to guard him separately as well. The fact that his wife is here will keep him from doing anything foolish.'

'Should we not discuss what we intend to do if our demands are not met?' Akbar asked.

Nasruddin considered. A tendency to talk too much was one of the perils of shared leadership, but it was a relatively harmless one. And in one way Akbar was right: the more eventualities they had mentally prepared themselves for, the easier it would be to take difficult on-the-spot decisions.

But at that moment he did not want to consider the possibility of such a setback. Today marked the end of his fifteen-year struggle to find a way of fighting back, and he wanted to let his heart revel in the moment. In the morning he could apply his mind to the practicalities once more.

'I think tomorrow will be soon enough for that,' he said, looking at Talib.

His cousin took the hint. 'And let us hope that God spares us from such a choice,' he said softly.

In Talib's sunken eyes Nasruddin caught an unwelcome premonition of pain both given and endured.

President Yegor Bakalev had had a premonition of disaster the moment he heard Bakhtar Muratov's voice on the other end of the line. Just when things were going so well, and the West was ready to put some serious money into the Uzbek economy, this had to happen.

It wasn't just the money, but what it represented. If the West invested in the future of a secular Uzbekistan, then he would have a powerful ally against the fundamentalists. On the one hand an improving economy would give the people less desire for change, while on the other there would be no serious criticism of the way he dealt with the Islamic dissidents. The Americans and the British knew what democracy had served up in Iran, and they weren't about to make the same mistake again. The bleeding-heart organizations like Amnesty International might complain, but they complained about everybody. The people who mattered would turn a blind eye in the interests of stability. On his last visit to London, Bakalev and the British Prime Minister had been united in the belief that a prosperous Uzbekistan would keep the fundamentalists at bay throughout Central Asia.

And now this, just four days before the deals were due to be signed. Maybe a miracle would happen, and they could keep the matter quiet for those four days. Maybe it could be resolved in such a way that confidence in his country and government would even be increased.

Maybe camels would fly. The chances of keeping this business off the world's TV screens seemed remote. He wondered who these people were and what they wanted. He hoped they were foreigners, and preferably Iranians. He hoped they would ask for something utterly ludicrous, and thereby brand themselves as lunatics. After all, every country had its share of them, and no one would expect Uzbekistan to be any different.

*   *   *

In England it was still only seven o'clock, and Detective Sergeant Dave Medwin was one of the many whose plans for the evening had been interrupted by the disappearance of a bus in far-off Samarkand. His had included taking Ben to see the comedy movie *Mrs Doubtfire*, but the call from Special Branch Central in London had put an end to that. Maureen had not been pleased. He wondered how long it would be before she gave him another opportunity to spend a whole evening with their twelve-year-old son.

His own people in London had hardly spoken to him before handing over the phone to an MI5 smoothie. The man had given him his instructions in triplicate, and then faxed the relevant papers to the Leeds office.

Now he was on his way to Bradford, and the registered office of Central Asian Tours Ltd in Westfield Street. At least the rush hour was over. And once he was finished with this errand he could see if Lynn fancied a drink in the Dog & Biscuit.

He found the office in question occupying the top half of a two-storey building, above a newsagent's, in a street mostly populated by Asian fabric shops. There were no lights showing upstairs, and the newsagent's was in the process of closing.

Medwin showed the man his warrant card, and said

he would like to ask a couple of questions about the business upstairs.

'They are closed,' the man said.

'For how long?'

The Asian looked at his watch. 'Three hours?' He shrugged. 'I didn't see the girl leave today.'

'But she was there today?'

'Oh yes. Of a certainty.' He grinned. 'She is not so light on her feet, you know.'

Medwin went back to his car. If Pinar Ishaq Khan had been there that day, it seemed unlikely she was involved in any major villainy that was under way in Samarkand. Wherever the hell that was. And it also meant she had a key to the office. The MI5 man had told him to make as few waves as possible, and breaking into the office across the road might well generate some, at least in daylight. He looked up the secretary's address in the vetting report which had been faxed to him, found out where it was in the *A–Z*, and started up the car.

She lived with her mother in a rather nice old house on the outskirts of Bradford. It was the older woman, looking rather worried, who showed him in. She, as Medwin had already learnt from the vetting report, taught in an elementary school in the centre of the city. Her son Imtiaz lived with his wife in Leeds.

Medwin waited while Pinar was summoned from the depths of the house, idly noting that the *Guardian* on the table was open at the women's page. This was not a traditional family.

Pinar, despite the newsagent's unflattering comment, was only slightly plumper than average, and had a face which made Medwin think of princesses in the *Arabian Nights*. He told her there was probably nothing to worry about, but that there was a chance the current 'Blue

Domes' tour party had run into trouble. They were still waiting for details from Samarkand.

She looked stunned.

'I have to ask you a few questions,' he went on.

She looked at him blankly, and then nodded.

'Was there anything unusual about this particular tour?'

'No. Well, this was the only one which Mr Salih escorted personally. The Jordan/Syria and Pakistan tours are escorted by local employees. But . . .'

'I meant this particular group of people,' Medwin said. 'You do handle the bookings?'

'Most of them.' She thought. 'I can't remember,' she said at last. 'I'm taking bookings almost all the time – the next five trips are already fully booked.'

Medwin handed her his copy of the list. 'Does this help?' he asked.

She studied it. 'There's one thing I remember,' she said. 'The Jenningses. Mr Salih was pleased we had some Americans at last. They were the first we'd ever had book with us.'

Medwin wondered whether it was worth giving the office the once-over, and decided not. If it was still functioning as normal, he found it hard to imagine finding anything relevant, and Pinar looked intelligent enough to ask if he had a warrant, which he did not.

He thanked her for her help, went back to the car, and consulted his street guide again. Nasruddin Salih's home was not far from the office, back towards the centre of the city.

He reached it in twenty minutes, a small terraced house in a dead-end street. After parking the car a hundred metres or so away he checked round the back, and found a path running along between a playing field and

74

the back entrances. There was still too much daylight for a surreptitious forced entry, so he went looking for a pub.

An hour and two pints later he was walking back towards Salih's house. Reaching it, he counted the houses to the end and then walked down the back path, counting them off in reverse. A couple of lights showed and a dog barked, but the neighbourhood seemed almost deserted.

The back door presented no problem to his customized piece of plastic. He took a few seconds to let his eyes grow used to the darkness, then walked through the kitchen to the living-room and pulled the curtains before taking out the torch he had brought from his glove compartment. The room looked incredibly tidy, as if Salih had been expecting guests. Maybe he had been expecting a visit from someone like me, Medwin thought.

He went slowly through the house, touching as little as possible. There was no sign of a woman's presence, and no sex magazines either. There was no alcohol.

There were a lot of bookshelves, both downstairs and up, most of them full of books about religion and politics. An incongruous group of books about railways caught Medwin's attention. He took one down and fingered through it. It was full of pictures of British Rail diesel locomotives, photographed in and around Leeds. Inside the front cover the name Martin Salih had been written.

Did Nasruddin have a son? he wondered. There had been no mention of it in the vetting report. And anyway the diesels were mostly painted the old blue colour – the book had to be fifteen years old.

He tried some of the political books, all of which had the name Nasruddin Salih inscribed inside their front covers. It was a mystery, Medwin thought, but probably not a relevant one.

It was ten minutes later that he found the photograph album, and recognized Nasruddin as one of the children in the family group pictures. There he stood, his face fifteen years younger but otherwise strikingly similar, next to a brother and sister, and behind his seated mother and father. Martin, Sheila, David, Ma and Pa, the caption read.

Medwin stared at the photograph for several seconds before inspiration struck. He picked up the telephone, called West Yorkshire Police Headquarters, and asked for the Records Department. Once connected, he asked for Rose or Mary. Rose was there. 'I need a name checked out,' he told her.

'How thrilling,' she said.

'Martin Salih,' he said patiently. 'S-a-l-i-h.'

'Your wish is my command.'

He could hear her fingers on the keyboard. 'One arrest,' she said eventually. 'Vandalism,' she added. 'He went on a window-breaking spree in the middle of Bradford. He was only thirteen. Got put on probation.' There was a silence lasting several moments, followed by a muted 'wow'.

'What is it?' Medwin asked.

'The poor little bugger had his reasons. His mother had just been killed in an arson attack. Somebody tossed a fire-bomb through their front door, and the house burned down with her in it. She was probably too afraid to come out.'

Medwin sighed. 'Thanks, Rose,' he said. 'I'll see you around.'

'Make sure you remember your wallet next time.'

Medwin smiled and sat back on Nasruddin's sofa. His

parents must have done what many immigrant parents did, and given their children English names in an attempt to smooth their passage in an adopted country. At some point after his mother's death, unable to bear the shame of an English name, Martin had rechristened himself Nasruddin. And the violence in his past had slipped between the cracks of the vetting procedure.

If there had indeed been a hijacking in Samarkand, it seemed more than possible that Nasruddin Salih had been one of its perpetrators.

5

Nurhan Ismatulayeva woke to find the new day's light filtering through the window above her head. The Volga's dashboard clock said it was six-fifteen. In the adjoining seat Marat was snoring gently. His face looked a lot younger in sleep, she decided, much more at peace. He probably wasn't much older than she was.

She reached forward for the door handle, eased open the door, and levered herself out into the dawn air. It was quite cold, and she reached back in for the rug to wrap around herself. Across the road the sun suddenly alighted on the very top of the ruined entrance gate, like a match catching fire. The birds were singing up a storm in the trees.

She stood there for a moment, savouring the scene, remembering mornings like this at the family dacha in the Tien Shan foothills north of Tashkent, and then started walking slowly across the park, her thoughts turning to who the hijackers might be, and what they might want. They might be nothing more than bandits, but she thought it much more likely that they would prove to be Islamic terrorists of one sort or another. She hoped so. If anything could set back the rise of Islam as a political force in Uzbekistan it was a bunch of psychopathic loonies masquerading as the children of Allah.

She should be back in Samarkand, she thought, where the decisions would be taken about who was to handle the potential hostage situation. By rights it should be her, but her male superiors would probably need reminding of that. She strode back to the car, pulled her seat back up and poked her colleague in the stomach.

He opened one eye, and didn't like what he saw. 'I thought you had gone for coffee,' he said.

She turned the key in the ignition. 'We can grab a cup at the bus station in Kitab,' she said, sliding the gear lever into first and bumping the car back on to the road, as he struggled to get his seat into the upright position.

'Hey, what's the hurry?' he asked.

'Why don't you call Samarkand and find out if there's any news,' she suggested.

'They'd have called us.'

'We might not have heard them over your snoring,' she said brutally.

He grimaced. 'I can't have been snoring that much – I was only asleep for about five minutes. You don't have anything for a headache, do you?'

'There's some pills in my bag.'

He reached into the back seat for it, and looked inside for the pills.

'A small brown bottle,' she said.

'Got it.' He had just noticed the pack of condoms she carried. A woman of the nineties, he thought, and wondered how happy she was behind the beautiful mask. He used thumb and forefinger to place two pills at the back of his throat, and swallowed.

'Are there any roads off this one before Kitab?' she asked him.

'Not that I know of.'

'Where would you go if you had just hijacked a tourist bus in Shakhrisabz?'

He thought for a minute. 'That would depend on what I wanted,' he said at last. 'If I wanted the maximum publicity splash I suppose I'd drive back to Samarkand

and take over one of the tourist sights – one of the
Registan *madrasahs*, maybe.'

'If they're Muslims wouldn't that be like defiling holy
ground or something?' She should know something like
that, she told herself. She should know more about Islam
if she was serious about fighting it.

Marat didn't know either. 'Maybe Tamerlane's mausoleum then,' he suggested. 'The whole world's heard
of him.'

'And it would be difficult to use force without damaging the building,' she thought out loud.

He reached for his first mint of the day. 'There's one
problem with all this,' he said. 'If they wanted to make
their stand in Samarkand then why go to all the bother
of taking them hostage in Shakhrisabz. Whatever they
did, they could have done it just as well before they left
the city. Or at least a few miles outside.'

'And if they're not in Samarkand?'

'Simple choice,' he said. 'They either turned left for the
desert or right for the mountains. In the desert they'd be
easy to find, but it would be hard to sneak up on them.
In the mountains vice versa.'

'It would be easier to stay alive in the mountains,' she
suggested.

The first houses of Kitab slipped by, and a minute
later Nurhan brought the Volga to a halt beside the
crossroads at the centre of the small town. Even at this
hour there were quite a few people on the streets, and the
cafés were already doing a roaring business in morning
glasses of tea. Marat and Nurhan walked across to the
nearest establishment and ordered coffee. Sitting down,
she became conscious of the angry looks she was getting
from the men occupying the *kravats*. Short red dresses
obviously weren't too popular in Kitab.

Marat had noticed too. 'I could tell them I've arrested you for prostitution,' he said, and wished he hadn't. The look she flashed him was mostly of rage, but if he was any judge of women there was also an element of hurt.

Of course, his ex-wife had always told him he wasn't. 'Sorry,' he said instinctively.

She gave him another look, more pitying this time, which he didn't find much of an improvement. 'But I shouldn't stray off on your own,' he added, looking round.

'I won't.'

He drained the last of his coffee. 'Let's start asking questions then.'

They began with the staff, moved on to the clientele, and then went through the same process at the establishment across the street. Half an hour and many sullen silences later they had found four witnesses to the passage of the bus the previous evening. All of them had seen it go straight across the crossroads, on to the road which led back to Samarkand.

They went back to the Volga, and Nurhan steered the car slowly out of town, past the bus station and a mosque under construction. She kept an eye on the alleys to the left as Marat scoured those to the right. There was no sign of a bus.

They emerged from the town alongside the river which had created it, now no more than a trickle of water between sun-baked stones.

'How many turn-offs do you reckon there are between here and home?' Marat asked.

'I don't remember any proper roads,' she replied. 'But it's a long time since I did this journey in daylight.'

The fields soon petered out, as the road climbed steadily into the dry hills. After two or three kilometres it was joined by a dusty track from the east. One or more vehicles turning right had left tyre tracks on the bend.

'Let's try it,' Marat suggested.

She gave him a withering look. 'There's thousands of square kilometres of wilderness out there, and I'd rather explore it with a map and some proper supplies. We could drive around all day without seeing anyone. Or of course, if we were really lucky, we could meet up with half a dozen heavily armed terrorists.'

He smiled. 'Point taken. But let's drive up it for a mile or so – just to get a sense of the lay of the land.'

Looking at him, she realized he was serious. 'All right,' she agreed reluctantly, and started the car up the surprisingly smooth track.

Half a mile later they came to an unmarked forking of the ways. Ahead of them the yellow hills rose into grey mountains, and the mountains into distant snow-covered peaks beneath a deep-blue sky. It was as beautiful as it was daunting.

'This is a job for a helicopter,' she said.

'I guess you're right,' he conceded.

Docherty's first thought on waking was to wonder why he was sleeping alone. Then realization dawned. He lay motionless for a moment, grateful that he had at least managed to get some sleep. Light was filtering in through the cracks in the boarded-up window. He looked at his watch and found that it was twenty past six.

Someone was in the bathroom, and since everyone else was visible from where he lay, it could only be Ogley. Docherty poked his head over the edge of the top bunk and confirmed as much.

He wondered if the children knew what had happened. He couldn't imagine his sister would tell them, but kids had a way of knowing something was wrong without being told. Docherty rubbed his eyes and decided he'd rather be doing something than lying there thinking.

He went to take a daylight look at the room's only window. Somewhat to his surprise, it slid open. Beyond the glass there was a mosquito screen, and beyond that planks had been nailed across the aperture. It wouldn't take much effort to break out, but it would be hard to do it quietly. The real problems would begin once they were outside. Even without any idea of where they were, one or two of them might be able to escape across the mountain wilderness, but not fourteen.

Still, he thought, it would serve as an escape hatch in an emergency. He turned away from the window and almost walked into the elder of the two Zahid brothers.

'Can you see the sun?' the man asked. 'Or any shadows?'

'I don't think . . .' Docherty began, and then noticed the rolled-up prayer mat Ali Zahid was holding in his hand. 'But the window faces east,' he said. 'I noticed the North Star when we got off the bus last night,' he added in explanation, just as the sound of cursing came from the bathroom. Ogley's voice sounded almost hysterical.

Docherty and Ali Zahid exchanged glances, and the Scot strode across to the door. He tried to open it, but Ogley had wedged his sweater between door and floor, and he had to push hard to open up a six-inch gap. Through it, he saw Ogley scrambling on a flooded floor without his trousers on, apparently trying to wipe himself with what remained of the fast-disappearing water. The bucket lay on its side. 'Get out!' Ogley shouted at him. It was almost a sob.

Docherty closed the door. Behind him Ali Zahid had laid out his mat, and was now prostrating himself in the general direction of Mecca. It had to be ironic for a Muslim priest like Zahid, the Scot thought, being hijacked by people of his own faith who claimed to be holier than he was. In his own case it would be akin to being held hostage by a bunch of Celtic's skinhead supporters.

'What have you got to smile about?' Copley asked him. 'There's no breakfast, no newspaper, and there probably won't even be a morning post.'

'You haven't heard the worst of it – the professor's just spilt our entire water supply.'

'Shit, he hasn't.'

'But I think we're going to have to be kind to him. This room isn't big enough to accommodate someone having a nervous breakdown.'

'Well, I don't suppose he can help it. And I guess we're all going to be prone to the odd fart of alarm. I was just lying there thinking about Sharon and the kids. I think she only comes on these jaunts to keep me company. Maybe next year we'll go to Majorca.'

'And you'll probably get mugged by a gang of Spanish teenagers.'

'Yeah, right.' He looked at Docherty almost as if he was seeking reassurance. 'You've never been in a spot like this before, have you?'

'Nope. But I suppose I've been in physical danger enough times to know that getting excited only gets in the way. And I guess it becomes second nature after a while.'

'Well, I'm glad you're here even if you're not.'

'Thanks,' Docherty said wryly, just as Ogley reappeared. The lecturer walked between them without saying anything, and threw himself on to his bunk.

'Is all the water gone?' Docherty asked, trying to keep any note of accusation out of his voice.

'You shouldn't have walked in like that,' Ogley said in a shaky voice. 'If we don't respect each other's privacy then we become animals like them.'

'Sorry. I thought you needed help. Now, is the water all gone?'

'Yes. It was an accident. I couldn't . . .'

'OK. We'll get some more.' Docherty went through to the bathroom, where Ogley's incontinence was much in evidence, both in the air and on the ground. He collected the bucket and took it back through to the door which led to the corridor. He rapped once, and was about to do so again when the wooden hatch was pulled back to reveal two eyes.

Docherty held up the water bucket.

The hatch slammed shut, and the seconds turned into a minute. Docherty was just coming to the conclusion that they had had their answer when the hatch opened again. 'Leave bucket by door and stand back,' a voice said in English. Docherty did as he was told, and the door slowly opened inwards to reveal a man holding an AK47 aimed straight into the room. The man's eyes darted from right to left and back again, and then he nodded, whereupon a second man appeared with a new bucket of water, and exchanged it for the empty one. He pulled the door shut behind him, and the familiar clang of bolts followed.

Docherty took the bucket to the bathroom door and then turned round. 'I think you've got some cleaning up to do,' he told Ogley.

The lecturer opened his mouth to reply, but the look on Docherty's face obviously made him think better of whatever it was he intended to say. Yet he made no move to do as he was asked.

'Like you said, we have to have respect for each other,'

Docherty pointed out, as gently as he could. Ogley was going to clean up his own shit if the Scot had to force him, but it would be a hundred times better if the man realized that here and now – maybe for the first time in his life – he had the responsibilities which went with membership of a group of equals.

For several seconds the two men looked at each other, and then it was Ogley who looked away, climbed out of his bunk, and carried the water through into the bathroom.

Thirty metres away, at the northern end of the lodge, the women's day began with a crisis. Sharon Copley had woken sometime before dawn, and rather than wake anyone else, had allowed her anxiety to build, right up to the point where an asthma attack seemed imminent. She told Isabel and Alice Jennings as much between wheezing breaths. Her inhaler was in the bag which she had left on the bus.

Alice went immediately to the door and started beating out a tattoo on it. When no one appeared she simply upped the violence of her assault, her face a study in wrathful indignation. Isabel was torn between admiration and a fear that the old woman would pay for such temerity.

Eventually one of the hijackers' faces appeared at the hatch. It took several minutes of mime to explain the situation, whereupon the face disappeared. Another minute later, with Sharon's inability to suck in breath worsening by the second, the man called Talib appeared, and raised one finger to indicate that one of the women should accompany him.

Isabel looked round, saw no one else was keen to volunteer, and put herself forward.

'Go to bus?' she asked.

The man nodded, and gestured her to walk in front of him. She retraced their steps of the night before, down the corridor which ran the length of the building from north to south. On the right were guest rooms and the large lounge with the bearskin rug; on the left what seemed to be store rooms. One wall was lined with skis.

The sun had not yet risen above the mountain behind the lodge, and the valley stretching out in front of her was still cast in shadow. It was a beautiful morning, and she felt buoyed up by it in spite of everything.

On the bus she quickly found Sharon's bag, and checked that the inhaler was inside it. Through the window she could see Talib waiting for her, his eyes seemingly fixed on the valley below. He had a sad face, she thought. And an intelligent one. These were not a bunch of mindless maniacs. But was that good or bad?

She stepped back down to the ground, and he stepped politely aside to let her pass. A minute later she was back in their room, handing over the inhaler to Sharon. For the next few minutes it was all smiles, as Sharon recovered her breath and they all shared in their small victory over adversity. But soon the basic truth of their situation reasserted itself, and Isabel found herself wondering what she could do to counter the creeping fear that seemed to be infecting them all, herself included.

They all expressed it in different ways, of course. Elizabeth Ogley talked too much and too bitterly, and often only to herself. Alice Jennings was finding it easier to be angry than admit to herself how worried she was about her husband. Sarah Holcroft seemed to be slowly sinking into a sea of self-pity, and Brenda Walker had lost all her brisk certainty of the evening before.

As for herself, Isabel seemed unable to counter the

feeling – the ridiculous feeling – that she was paying for the transgressions in her past. Maybe her unconscious was still mired in the Catholicism of her childhood; maybe it even remembered every word of the homilies she had sat through in the small wooden church which overlooked the Beagle Channel.

She lay on her bunk drifting through the conscious memories – the joy of leaving the heavy air of the church and emerging into a landscape of sea and sky which seemed to go on for ever.

It felt wonderful and wrong at the same time. She levered herself up into a sitting position and started applying her mind to the problem of how to lift the collective spirits of six terrified women.

Simon Kennedy had arrived in Samarkand at half-past two in the morning. He had not seen a single soul on the streets as he drove across town towards the missing tourists' hotel – even the drunks had bedded down for the night. The hotel was no livelier. After parking his car, rather against his better judgement, on the street outside, Kennedy had almost needed to knock the doors down in order to raise the night receptionist. Once a room had been grudgingly found for him, the MI6 man set about determining the whereabouts of the Central Asian Tours party.

The receptionist's token resistance had collapsed at the sight of a ten-dollar bill. The tour party, he said, had not yet returned from Shakhrisabz. A vehicle breakdown was doubtless the cause, and there was no need for concern – his brother worked at the tourist hotel in Shakhrisabz, and it was excellent. When asked by Kennedy about the involvement of the police, the man had denied all knowledge of any such thing.

Kennedy had phoned the lack of news to Tashkent and gone to bed, wondering if he had just driven four hundred kilometres for nothing.

He was woken four hours later by the clamour of a pneumatic drill, and almost fell out of bed in his haste to reach the window. His car was still in one piece, but major roadworks seemed to have started all around it. Kennedy dressed hurriedly, waited three minutes for a lift that never came, and ran down the six flights of stairs to the ground floor. Ignoring the ironic jeers of the Uzbek workmen, he extricated his car from under the shadow of a bulldozer, and drove it through into the hotel's now-open car park. In the lobby he checked that the keys to the Central Asian Tours party's rooms were still hanging on their nails behind the reception desk. They were. And according to the sign on the dining-room door breakfast was about to be served.

Twenty minutes later it arrived in all its neo-Soviet glory. Various cold meats with bread, jam from distant Russia, ersatz coffee courtesy of Nescafé. The only genuine Central Asian touch was a delicious glass of *lassi*, which almost made up for the rest. Kennedy was sitting with his second cup of appalling coffee, daydreaming about fresh Danish pastries and cappuccino, when a blonde woman walked past and took a seat at the table furthest away from him. He smiled hopefully in her direction, and she smiled back, but neither of them said anything.

He had the vague feeling he had seen her before, but he couldn't for the life of him remember where, and he found it hard to admit he would have forgotten anyone quite so striking. Her hair was cut fairly short – it was called an urchin cut, he thought – and she had a pixie-ish face, with a perfect small nose and mouth beneath blue eyes. There was nothing pixie-ish about her body though: she was at least five foot nine, with long legs and pronounced hips and breasts. Classic English upper class, Kennedy thought. She'd probably played hockey at Roedean.

For all he knew she was a German or a Swede. Probably waiting for her husband to finish his morning crap and join her. Slow crappers, the Germans, but thorough.

He had things to do, like find out if a busload of Brits had really been hijacked. He got up, gave her one last glance and found she was smiling across at him.

Maybe she didn't have a husband, he thought. If she was still here that evening he would have to find out.

Annabel Silcott had a better memory for faces than Simon Kennedy. She had seen him the previous week at a party in Tashkent, and though they had not been introduced, their semi-drunken Russian host had included Kennedy in the witty thumbnail sketches of other guests which he had treated her to. 'He's a paradox,' the host had said. 'Intelligence without it.'

So what, she idly wondered, was an Intelligence man doing in Samarkand? Probably nothing, but if by any chance he was gainfully employed, then the nature of that employment was bound to be more interesting than her current project, which was writing an article on 'Women under Islam around the World' for one of the Sunday tabloid colour supplements back home.

It was not an assignment she was enjoying. All her editor really wanted were horror stories of women oppressed by the dreadful Muslims, preferably with elements of romance and bondage thrown in. A sort of modern-day sheikhs-and-harems piece, but written in a balanced, multicultural style. She had to be careful to point out how fulfilling some of these women found sexual slavery.

Annabel didn't much like the way Muslim men, by and large, treated their women, but then she didn't much like the way tabloid editors treated them either. The main problem, though, was that there was nothing new to say. She could find some juicy stories – or make them up if all else failed – but no one was going to take any notice, or at least not for any more time than it took this week's paper to become next week's cat litter. This was not the way for her to become the next Kate Adie.

Something to do with Intelligence work might be. Serious news, not news as soap opera. She remembered that the British and Americans were signing some sort of trade deal in Tashkent over the coming weekend. Maybe there had been an assassination threat, or something like that.

In which case, why would Kennedy be here in Samarkand? It couldn't be that. In fact, he was probably on holiday, and she was just indulging in wishful thinking.

But she would make a few enquiries, just the same.

Nurhan and Marat arrived back in Samarkand around eight-thirty. They had counted thirty-seven turn-offs between Kitab and the intersection with the Pendzhikent road just outside the city. Twenty had led east, seventeen west. None had been metalled. They had encountered only four people on the trip across the mountains, and though two of them had seen the bus heading south the previous afternoon none had seen it return.

'How about a bath before we report in,' Marat suggested.

'Why not?' she agreed. The chance to change into something more suitable would be worth any slight delay in re-establishing their claim to lead this investigation.

She dropped him outside his apartment building – a grey Russian block on what used to be Engels Street – and drove back across to her flat in the Old Town. The water supply was acting up again, but she managed to bathe herself in two inches' worth, and then selected a pair of loose-fitting black trousers and a kaftan-style blouse to wear. The latter was loose enough for her to carry the SIG-Sauer P226 automatic concealed in the small of her back.

Marat was waiting by the kerb when she returned to pick him up, wearing what she hoped was another white shirt – it looked crumpled enough to be the old one – and dark-blue trousers.

'How long have you lived here?' she asked.

'About two years. Since I separated from my wife,' he added, as if that provided a more accurate dating.

'Where's she?'

He looked at her with a wry smile. 'You do enjoy asking questions, don't you?'

She shrugged. 'I'm just curious. You don't have to answer.'

'She and the children are in an apartment on Mirshazapova. An expensive apartment.'

'I didn't know you had children.' They were approaching the NSS building.

'I'm not sure I do any more,' he said, reaching for the door handle.

They found Hamza Zhakidov in the position they had left him, sitting behind his desk. The tiredness in his face and the still made-up camp-bed against one wall suggested he had spent all night at the office. Or maybe he had been home to the delectable Susha, Marat thought cynically.

They told him what they had discovered – or rather not discovered – since calling in from Shakhrisabz.

'So what's your guess?' Zhakidov asked them.

'The mountains,' they said almost as one voice.

'We need to take a helicopter up there and have a look,' Nurhan argued.

Zhakidov looked at her doubtfully. 'Have you any idea where to start looking?'

'We'll do some research first,' Marat said. 'Have a look at the map and see what the possibilities are. Then work out a search plan to cover the most likely places.'

Zhakidov nodded. 'OK, do it. But make sure you keep in contact.' He looked at his watch. 'In about seventy-five minutes we should be hearing from the terrorists.'

6

According to Docherty's watch it was almost nine o'clock. The atmosphere in the men's room was better than it had been two hours earlier, largely, he suspected, for the simple reason that they had been fed. It had not exactly been a feast, but it was better than Docherty had expected – the bread was only slightly stale, the tea highly refreshing, and he had always liked his yoghurt on the sour side anyway. Whoever the terrorists were, there was nothing sadistic in the way they were treating their hostages.

And everyone had managed to use the bathroom, showing exemplary restraint in the amount of water they used.

That was the good news. The bad news was that Sam Jennings seemed to be having trouble with his heart. Docherty knew that the sheer stress of such situations tended to create particular medical problems, and that the cardiovascular system was one of the main areas at risk. The respiratory system, as he unwisely told Mike Copley, was another. Sharon was apparently prone to asthma attacks.

Sam Jennings himself said there was nothing to worry about. 'Who's the doctor here?' he asked indignantly. 'I'm going to outlive these bastards if it's the last thing I do.'

Docherty hoped it wouldn't be, and not just for Sam Jennings's sake. For one thing, a doctor was always useful to have around. For another, there was no telling how the hijackers would react to the death

94

of one of their hostages. They would, after all, be blamed for it.

In the meantime, Copley had been pacing up and down the room for several minutes. He had started off making jokes about Colditz and *Porridge*, and was always ready with a grin, but left to its own devices his face settled into the grim mask it was wearing now. Some people used humour to keep them going, Docherty thought, while others used emotionalism. He preferred the former – it was kinder on the others involved.

The initial shock was wearing off, he realized. Now everyone was getting a bit restless. Maybe this was the time for him to give his version of the Counter Revolutionary Warfare Wing lecture on hostage situations and how to survive them. Always assuming he could remember any of it.

Flexibility, adaptability . . .

At that moment the sliding panel on the door jerked back. 'Stand back,' the familiar voice said, and almost immediately the door opened inwards. 'Exercise time,' the man with the AK47 said, gesturing with the gun for them to leave the room.

Everyone looked at Docherty, who said: 'Let's go.' If the hijackers wanted to shoot them, they could do so a lot more easily where they were.

The man with the gun pointed him back down the corridor they had used the previous evening, and the eight males walked in single file towards the centre of the lodge, where they took the right turn, which led to the front entrance. Docherty tried repressing his hope that the women might already be outside, but the sense of disappointment could hardly have been more acute when he discovered they were not.

Instead there was only the natural beauty of the

mountains that rose up behind the lodge and reached out on either side to enclose it. By daylight it was clear that the lodge stood at the head of a west-facing valley, almost a bay, that was gouged from the side of the range. Ahead of him wooded mountainsides sloped away into brown foothills, which in turn tumbled down to a distant yellow-brown plain.

It was a beautiful place for a prison, he thought.

No one had told them where they could walk, but the four armed men positioned on the corners of the rectangular space in front of the lodge seemed to offer a pretty good clue. Docherty recognized the man who had answered to the name Talib on the bus, and walked slowly towards him, making sure that both his hands were visible to the hijacker. He stopped when still five metres away.

'Can I ask a question?' he said.

The man looked at him impatiently. 'No speak English,' he said shortly.

'Do any of the others speak English?' Docherty asked, pointing at each of the other three men in turn.

'No speak English,' Talib said again. He seemed almost amused, Docherty thought. Maybe he did speak English.

It was more than frustrating, almost like a slap in the face. It made him feel impotent, and reminded him of the way he had always felt as a young man, when girlfriends retreated into silence in the middle of a fight.

He turned away from Talib, so as not to show the angry frustration he was feeling. The man who had let them out of the room, and who at least knew the words 'stand back' and 'exercise', was nowhere to be seen. Nor was Nasruddin, whose English was as good as his own. Probably better, if you liked the BBC version.

This was policy, Docherty realized. Someone had done their homework on hostage situations, and decided on a policy of minimal communication between hostage-takers and hostages. That was depressing enough in itself, since often the communication between the two was instrumental in saving the latter's lives. But it was also depressing in what it said about the prospects for a successful negotiation to end this business. These men did not seem likely to fold, and presumably the Uzbek government would have little more reason to make concessions. Not unless the British government was putting pressure on them, and everyone knew their policy on giving in to terrorism.

Except, he suddenly realized, that this time one of their own was caught up in the net. A cynic would expect that to make a difference. He supposed he should hope it wouldn't, but to hell with that – they needed all the help they could get.

A cynic might also think that the Zahids were prostrating themselves on the ground as a way of demonstrating their Islamic credentials. Or maybe they were praying for a rescue mission.

It suddenly occurred to Docherty that with Sarah Holcroft among the hostages his old regiment might be brought into this. Now there was a thought . . . He started scouring the horizon for suitable places to put an observation point. The SAS could hardly be here yet, but by this time tomorrow . . .

He noticed for the first time that the others were just standing idly around, and walked across to join them. 'We should be keeping moving,' he urged them. 'There's no way of knowing how long it'll be before they let us out again.'

'You should write a book,' Ogley said sarcastically,

but he accompanied the other three as they began circumnavigating the available space.

Docherty asked the American how he was.

'I've been better,' Sam said, 'but I'll be OK.'

'What did you ask the guard?' Copley asked.

'I asked if I could ask a question. The answer was no. He said he didn't speak English, but I think they've decided to keep contact to a minimum.'

'Why?' Copley wanted to know.

'Ever heard of the Stockholm Syndrome?' Docherty asked. 'Well, it was named after something that happened in Sweden, oh, about twenty years ago now. A man tried to hold up a bank, but the police arrived too quickly for him to get away, so he gathered together about half a dozen hostages and holed up in the bank's vault. They were there for six days. And during that time a bond developed between the man and his hostages. A practical bond which seemed completely crazy to those who weren't directly involved. They stood guard for him when he slept, and protected him with their bodies when he surrendered, just in case the police were feeling trigger-happy. One of the women hostages fell in love with him, and married him later in prison.

'I guess it's easier to see why he co-operated with them than the other way round. In some ways they were in the same sort of situation as a pet would be towards its owner – utterly dependent – and some psychologists reckon people do regress when they feel that powerless . . .'

'Jesus, are we going to start getting up on our hind legs and begging for dog biscuits?'

'Probably. I guess the other side of the equation is the important one for us to worry about. The hostage-taker in Stockholm ended up being unable to harm his hostages for the simple reason that they had become real human beings to him.'

'And you think that's what these people are trying to avoid?'

Docherty shrugged. 'Maybe. On the other hand they could just be rotten linguists. But any chance we get to talk, we should. Even the odd smile will help.'

Nurhan and Marat stood shoulder to shoulder over the 1:250,000 scale map of Kashkadar'inskaya Oblast, studying the mosaic of unmade tracks in the areas to either side of the Samarkand–Shakhrisabz road.

'There's nothing up there,' Marat muttered.

'What did you expect – a new housing estate? There's a hell of a lot of caves.'

'OK, so where do we start? This map doesn't seem to have a symbol for caves large enough to hide a bus in.'

She sighed. 'Christ knows.'

'Well, I vote for following that first track outside Kitab. It was the only one on that side of the mountain with definite tyre marks.'

'The other tracks weren't so dusty. But OK, it's as good a place as any.'

Marat looked for it on the map. 'It's not marked,' he decided. 'Unless this is it,' he added, pointing out a track which wound its way up a steep valley and abruptly ended. 'But there's no sign of the fork we came to.'

'These maps are hopeless,' she said. 'In the old days all they cared about were the border areas. They got them right.'

'It's all we've got,' he said, rolling it up. 'Let's go.'

It took them fifteen minutes to reach the airport, where the Ka-26 helicopter was waiting for them, the contra-rotating rotors hanging limp above the squat fuselage. Its blond Russian pilot was morosely smoking a cigarette on the cab running board of a fuel tanker nearby. Marat showed him their destination.

'What are we looking for?' the pilot asked.

'A bus,' Nurhan said shortly.

'There are plenty of those in the city.'

'Ha ha. Let's get moving.'

The pilot grinned and ushered them aboard. Almost instantly, it seemed, they were rising swiftly into the sky, Samarkand laid out in its bowl beneath them, the blue domes sparsely scattered across the brown city, like cornflowers in a desert.

After their walk in the mountain air the room seemed almost unbearably stuffy. 'I'm sticking to my shirt already,' Copley complained, 'and it's not even ten o'clock. I think hijackers should be obliged to provide fresh underwear on a daily basis.'

'They could put it in the Geneva Convention,' Sam Jennings agreed. The American seemed better, Docherty thought. The colour in his cheeks was back to normal.

'It's a serious point though,' the Scot said. 'In these conditions we're not going to be able to stay as clean as we'd like, but it is important we keep ourselves as clean as we can.' He stopped, thinking that he sounded like a preacher. Everyone was looking at him, including the Zahids. Docherty found them harder to read than the others, particularly the two older men. The young men seemed to have bounced back from the initial shock with typical adolescent bravado.

'I've done courses in how to deal with situations like this,' Docherty went on, 'though mostly from the point of view of those outside the situation. Still, I picked up a few tips on the way which might come in useful. So . . .'

'Enlighten us, Doc,' Copley said with a grin.

Docherty grinned back. 'Most of it's common sense. The basic thing is to keep active and keep flexible, both mentally and physically. We have to keep ourselves as together as we can. That means eating whatever food they give us, whether it tastes like what we're used to or not. It means wiping our arses whichever way we can, and not freaking out at the absence of toilet paper. It means accepting that we're not going to get a nice hot bath each day, and not using that fact as an excuse to get slovenly. We're in a situation where we're denied all respect from the rest of the world, so we have to get it from ourselves and each other.

'The same thing goes for our minds. We have to keep them active, one way or another. For a start, how many books do we have?'

'One guide book,' Copley said.

'A biography of Tamerlane,' Sam Jennings volunteered.

'Nothing,' Ogley admitted.

'A Koran,' Ali Zahid said with a smile. 'But in Urdu, I'm afraid.'

'Last year's *Wisden*,' Javid said.

'OK. So by the end of this we should all be experts in something. How about paper and pens. I have one ballpoint.'

There were three others, one of which had already succumbed to the heat.

'We can play word games,' Docherty said. 'We can make a draught-board and pieces. We can argue about which footballers or cricketers are the best who ever played. We can write tortured poetry. Anything is better than sitting around wondering what's happening in the world outside. Our chances of influencing the authorities are non-existent, and our chances of influencing this lot outside are not much better. But even given that, like I said before, we shouldn't miss any chance we get of making human contact with these men. Though it's wise to keep in mind the old saw about not discussing religion or politics.'

He paused for a moment. 'I don't want to scare anyone, but just remember that even a split second's hesitation – that split second most people seem to need before they can open fire on someone they know – might save your life in the event of a rescue attempt . . .'

'What are the chances of one?' Sam Jennings asked.

Docherty shrugged. 'Most situations like this end in either the terrorists' surrender or an attack by the authorities. If it comes to the second, then remember, get down on the floor and stay there. In these situations more hostages have been killed by the authorities than by their captors, and nearly always because they've stood up when they shouldn't.'

'We should try and tell the women,' Copley said.

'They should already know,' Docherty said. 'I think Brenda Walker works for Intelligence, so . . .'

'Looking after Sarah Holcroft,' Ogley said. 'That makes sense.'

'Well, it never occurred to me,' Copley admitted. 'She seemed kind of nice.'

In the women's room things had slowly improved over the last few hours. Isabel, with help from Brenda Walker, had bullied the others into talking with each other. They were not the most homogeneous of groups, in age, class or interests, but once started, the conversation, like a ball on a downhill slope, had just kept rolling.

Sarah Holcroft, rather nervously for someone with her

tabloid reputation, had suggested that the four married women tell the story of how they met their husbands, and before anyone could object Alice Jennings had launched into the tale of how she had met Sam nearly sixty years earlier, in New York's Central Park. She had slipped when getting off her horse on the famous old carousel, and he had grandly come forward, parting the crowd with the words 'Make way – I'm a doctor.' In matter of fact he had only just entered medical school, but her ankle had only been slightly sprained, and they had even managed to go out dancing the same night.

Sharon's account of meeting Mike was not quite so romantic. They had met when Sharon was asked to sing with a Coventry-based punk band called The Hump. Mike was the drummer. 'He had a Mohican then,' Sharon said, 'and I thought what a dipstick! I still do sometimes. Anyway, we sort of started talking to each other a lot about my boyfriends and his girlfriends, and then one day we just started kissing each other. Just like that. It was weird. But nice.'

Isabel had half expected Elizabeth Ogley to decline to take part in this sharing of personal histories, but the lecturer seemed more than willing. 'It was a very sixties meeting,' she said drily. 'A party in Ladbroke Grove in the summer of '68. I was lying stoned out of my mind on one of the beds upstairs listening to a Cream record coming through the floor. This guy was sitting on the floor with his back to the bed telling me about the demonstration he had been on that day, and how 'Ho, Ho, Ho Chi Minh' was a modern mantra. I must have fallen asleep because the next thing I knew he was on the bed beside me with his hand inside my bra. And the next thing after that he was pulling himself out, apologizing for coming too soon, and promising that he would do better next time.' Elizabeth grimaced. 'So it started with a lie,' she said matter-of-factly. Then her face softened momentarily. 'But it hasn't been all bad,' she said.

'Your turn, Isabel' Sarah said.

Isabel hadn't been sure whether this group was ready for her story, which she sometimes had trouble believing herself. She knew the disclosure of her career as a political kidnapper had shocked the others, and she wasn't at all sure whether she wanted to re-underline the extraordinariness of her younger life. But then again, it was a good story, and as far as the other women in the room were concerned, she'd at least been on the side of the angels that time round.

So she had told the story of her meeting with Docherty, of how she, an Argentinian exile in London, had agreed to work for MI6 in Argentina during the Falklands War, and how Docherty, himself leading a British unit behind enemy lines on the Argentinian mainland, had come to the hotel in Rio Gallegos to warn her that her cover might have been blown. Together they had escaped the country, hiking their way across the southern Andes into neutral Chile.

'You have had an exciting life,' Alice Jennings said, and the looks on the faces of the other women expressed much the same thought.

'The last twelve years it's just been bringing up the kids,' Isabel said.

'I thought they were all great stories,' Sarah Holcroft said, with a brusqueness which seemed to hide more than a trace of wistfulness. 'Have you ever been married?' she asked Brenda Walker.

'No,' was the answer, and there was sadness here too, Isabel thought. Both of these young women had been unlucky with men, she decided. Either with fathers or lovers or both.

* * *

Bakhtar Muratov noticed that the President was staring at the Georgia O'Keeffe print, an enormous red flower which seemed to be reaching out to suck him in. He had bought it in New York several years earlier, and the print had occupied pride of place on his living-room wall ever since. He had fallen in love with the original at first sight, without really knowing why until a fellow gallery visitor had explained the implicit sexuality. This visitor had then taken him back to her Lower East Side apartment for a coffee and twenty-four hours of the explicit version, entangling the print with memories of such pleasure that Muratov felt good whenever he looked at it.

The President was not impressed. 'I could have painted this,' he muttered.

Muratov scowled at Bakalev's back and looked at his watch again. It was one minute to eleven. He had the feeling that – Uzbekistan Telephone willing – the call would come on time.

It did.

Muratov switched on the tape and picked up the receiver, holding up a finger to indicate the need for Bakalev to remain silent. The President's presence in the room was the last thing he wanted the hijackers to know. 'Muratov,' he said.

'Good morning, Colonel,' a voice said. It was not the same man Muratov had spoken to the day before – both the tone and the accent were different. 'My name is Nasruddin Salih. I am the spokesman for The Trumpet of God.'

'Then speak,' Muratov said.

Nasruddin ignored the sarcasm. 'Have you verified what you were told yesterday?' he asked.

'The tour party is missing.'

'It is here with us.'

'And where are you?'

'In the Fan Mountains. I am sure you will work out the exact location soon enough.'

There was amusement in the bastard's voice, Muratov thought. It was the first time he could remember one of these Islamic zealots having a sense of humour.

'These are our demands,' Nasruddin told him abruptly. 'Our organization's programme is to be printed in full in tomorrow morning's *Voice of the People*. And the following men are to be released from your prisons – Muhammad Khotali, Timur Lukmanov, Akhmadzhon Pulatov and Erkin Saliq.'

Muratov waited several seconds, expecting more.

At the other end of the line, Nasruddin had been diverted by the sound of an approaching helicopter and the sudden appearance of Talib to tell him about it.

'Visitors,' the Uzbek said. 'In an army helicopter. But they're only looking, I think. It's only a Ka-26. There can't be many people up there.'

But they would have seen the bus, Nasruddin knew. It didn't matter a great deal – he had never expected that their location would remain undetected for very long.

'Colonel Muratov,' Nasruddin said. 'It seems you have discovered where we are . . .'

'What?'

'There is an army helicopter in the sky above us. Since we have the means of shooting it down, I suggest you recall it to base immediately. I will call you again in ten minutes.'

Muratov rubbed his eyes, and dialled a new number.

In the Ka-26 Nurhan and Marat were staring down at the lodge nestled at the top of the valley. The bus was sitting outside like a trophy, and three armed men were staring up at them as they hovered some two hundred metres above.

'It's not marked on the map,' Marat was saying. But then the approach road had not been marked either.

The pilot was more interested in the visible guns. 'Can we go now?' he asked anxiously.

'No,' Nurhan ordered. She had taken about a dozen photographs so far of the building and the surrounding area, but wanted more close-ups. Through the zoom lens she could see a man emerge from the lodge's front door with what looked distinctly like a shoulder-held missile launcher.

'What's that?' she asked Marat calmly, passing him the camera.

'It's a fucking Stinger,' he said. 'Get the hell out of here,' he told the pilot.

Nurhan carried on taking pictures until the lodge was out of sight. A few seconds later Zhakidov's voice came through on the radio, advising their immediate withdrawal.

'Happy?' Muratov asked Nasruddin.

'I have no desire to needlessly take human life,' Nasruddin retorted.

'I hope not,' Muratov said. 'Shall we get back to your demands?'

'You have heard them. You will find a copy of our programme in the Hotel Samarkand safe, where I deposited it under my own name yesterday. Once it has been printed in the newspaper – and we shall know if it has or has not – the four released prisoners are to be brought here by helicopter – an Mi-8. They, ourselves and the hostages will then fly across the border to Tajikistan. You will announce that the prisoners have been granted exile, and we shall release the hostages. By then the deal with the Western governments will have been signed, and no one will be very interested in such a benign act of terrorism. I am sure you will come up with a half-convincing explanation for it all – an anti-terrorist exercise which went wrong, perhaps.'

Muratov raised an eyebrow. 'That will be easier if the hostages are all alive and in good health,' he said.

'They are.'

'You understand that I cannot say yes or no to you myself?'

'Yes, but I am sure you will have no difficulty in reaching the President.'

Muratov smiled to himself, looking across at Bakalev's angry face. 'How can I reach you with a reply?'

'I will ring you at three p.m. In the meantime the hostages' well-being depends on your behaviour. We do not wish to see anyone within a mile of here, either on the ground or in the air. Is that clear?'

'Perfectly. I . . .' Muratov began, but the call had been disconnected. He stared at the phone for several seconds, before replacing the receiver. It was the first time he had ever talked to a hijacker, but even so he had the distinct impression that Nasruddin was not typical of the species.

'Well?' Bakalev asked him.

Muratov told him the hijackers' demands, and how they were supposed to be met, adding that he was surprised they hadn't asked for more.

The President looked at him. 'These are not insignificant demands,' he said sarcastically. 'Khotali has been a thorn in our side for years, and I like him where he is. And how do we explain our sudden decision to print these lunatics' programme?'

Muratov thought for a moment. 'The second wouldn't be too much of a problem. We could print it as the first of a series – every mad group's manifesto that we can find. Though of course we won't say that it's part of a series until the second one is printed, by which time the hostages will have been released.' He smiled. 'And you'll get extra credit from the West for your determination to support democracy.'

Bakalev grunted. 'Are they that stupid? Maybe they are.' He exhaled noisily. 'But ... you now what Khomeini did from exile ...'

'Khotali's not in the same class.' And if that many people in Uzbekistan supported the clerical zealot, Muratov thought, then he and Bakalev were both wasting their time anyway.

'So you think we should just give them what they're asking for?' Bakalev said. He had begun to pace up and down.

'It looks better than the alternative. We need the Western deal and we need tourism. If The Trumpet of God' – Muratov curled the words derisively on his tongue – 'starts killing these tourists then we can say goodbye to about a quarter of our foreign-currency earnings for the next few years.'

'The deal would probably still go though,' Bakalev replied. 'After all, the English and Americans are not in it for charity – they want it as much as we do.'

'They want it, we need it.'

'Yes, yes ... wait a minute,' Bakalev said, stopping in his tracks. 'Once the hostages are released, what's to stop them telling the newspapers? Our tourism income will be affected anyway.'

'It will be damaged much more if people are seen to die. If everyone is rescued then we can use it as proof of how efficient our police are, how safe this country is.' Muratov paused, wondering whether he really believed what he had just said. 'The only alternative,' he added sardonically, 'would be to kill the tourists ourselves after their release by the terrorists.'

Bakalev stopped once more. 'Or we could kill them all now,' he said softly. 'We know where they are, don't we?'

'They're in the new hunting lodge.'

The President looked surprised, and then almost indignant. 'The bastards,' he said, and then shrugged resignedly. 'Well, there was no way we were ever going to be able to use it again. And it's certainly a long way from anywhere. What's to stop us launching an air strike? Who will know? We can say their bus went over a cliff and exploded.'

7

After putting the phone down Nasruddin sat there for several seconds, feeling his heart thumping like a steam hammer. He had never imagined that it would feel like that – the exhilaration of talking on equal terms to someone who was probably the second most powerful figure in the country. He had told the man to get his helicopter away and he had done so, just like that.

And yet, having experienced the feeling, he knew where it came from. Any sociologist could write reams on the sense of powerlessness endemic in oppressed minority cultures, and his personal history had accentuated that sense.

My mother is dead, went the forgotten voice inside his mind, and I can't bring her back.

'Well?' Akbar asked explosively.

'You heard what I told him. He will put our demands to the President.'

'The son of Satan was probably sitting there beside him,' Talib said. 'I wonder how they found us so quickly.'

Nasruddin shrugged. 'Guesswork, perhaps. Once they worked out we were in the mountains then the choices were limited.' He still seemed to be shaking inside from the experience.

'How did he sound?' Akbar asked.

'The way you would expect – clever, condescending, sarcastic.'

'You got no sense of what they will do?'

'None. They will not know themselves yet. They must

111

weigh the costs of acceptance against those of rejection. And we must wait four hours.'

It sounded like eternity. Nasruddin was conscious of the dizzy sense of power slipping away, and in its place a growing awareness of the hard choices that might yet be forced upon them.

'Do you think it was one of ours?' Copley asked.

'If it didn't land I think we can assume it was,' Docherty said. Whoever 'ours' might be in this context. He hadn't said anything to the others, but the old Soviet Union had not been slow to take on terrorists in situations like this, often with scant regard for the hostages concerned. Sometimes it had worked: one group of Lebanese Shiites who had kidnapped four Soviet diplomats had been sent a finger from one of their relatives, and had hastily released their captives. Sometimes it had not, and a hostage's chances of survival had come down to how adept or lucky they were when it came to dodging the bullets of both terrorists and authorities.

Of course, there was always the hope that the new Uzbekistan had not inherited such KGB propensities, but somehow Docherty didn't feel optimistic. He still felt their best chance rested on Sarah Holcroft's involvement drawing in help from home.

'It didn't seem to be moving,' Sam Jennings was saying.

'No,' Docherty agreed. The helicopter had been hovering. And presumably watching.

'Well, it's gone now,' Copley said.

'At least they know we're here,' added Ogley, as if a weight had been lifted from his mind.

'They always knew we were somewhere,' the American said unhelpfully.

112

This is just the beginning, Docherty thought. Despite his own pep talk he felt almost consumed by powerlessness. They didn't know what the hijackers wanted, or whether it could be granted, or what the authorities were planning. They were the ones at risk, and they were the ones who knew the least.

When the sound of the helicopter had faded into the distance, the women had drawn much the same conclusions as the men.

'They know where we are,' Elizabeth Ogley said, unaware that her husband was saying much the thing thirty metres away.

'But what does that mean?' Sharon wanted to know. 'Isabel?'

Isabel pulled herself out of her reverie. During the flying visit her mind had gone back twenty years, to the room in Córdoba where they had held the industrialist whose name she had long since forgotten. There had been no helicopter whirring above them, but she remembered the sound of sirens on the streets outside, and the strange blend of thrill and fear which they had evoked in her and her comrades. She wondered if Nasruddin and the others had watched the helicopter with the same intense emotions, and found herself feeling almost sorry for them.

'Isabel?' Sharon repeated.

'I don't know,' Isabel replied. 'But it can't be bad news.' Docherty would know, she thought, and felt the fear of loss wash through her mind once more.

Simon Kennedy wiped his brow and stared across the car park at the Ak Saray Museum. Maybe there would be someone over there he could question about the missing tourists.

It had taken only one and a half hours to reach Shakhrisabz on the mountain road, but it had still been cool when he started out, and the wind blowing behind the moving car all the way had not prepared him for the heat of the day. And he had forgotten his hat. As he approached the museum, the patch of shade under the overhanging acacia looked positively paradisal.

The *kravat* which occupied this space was home to an ageing Uzbek. Throwing English reticence to the winds, Kennedy took a seat without being asked and wiped his brow again. 'Do you speak Russian?' he asked, without much hope.

'*Da*,' the man said.

Kennedy explained about the missing tourist party. The Uzbek said he had information, and unselfconsciously extended his palm. The MI6 man gave him a five-thousand-rouble note, thinking that he would claim it back on expenses under the heading 'greedy peasant'. The old man told him about his visit from the police the night before, and then pulled several pieces of mosaic tile from somewhere within the robe he was wearing. 'Only a dollar each,' he said in Russian. 'Genuine fifteenth-century.'

Kennedy walked back across the car park, wondering how long it would be before someone noticed that the tiles on the gateway were growing fewer day by day. It was probably his imagination, but the boy on the gate seemed to smile knowingly at him.

The café across the street was just opening, and he went in search of coffee and an interpreter. The former was available, if almost undrinkable, and he had to wait over half an hour before a customer arrived who spoke both Russian and Uzbek. The man initially looked at Kennedy as if he was mad, but was persuaded to humour him by the sight of a five-thousand-rouble note. They walked across the street to interview the boy on the gate, who told Kennedy, through the bewildered interpreter, the same story he had told the NSS man and woman the night before, and generously added that he had seen the two of them head off in the same direction as the bus soon after first light that morning.

All of which seemed pretty decisive, Kennedy thought, once more ensconced behind the wheel of his car. He suddenly remembered the black Volga he had seen parked on the side of the road on the other side of the mountains. A rather striking-looking woman in a short red dress had been talking to two men, one of whom had been dressed in Western clothes, the other not. They must have been the police in question, he realized, though there had been no reason to think so at the time. The KGB had never been noted for its fashion sense.

Like the two of them, he could see no reason for lingering in Shakhrisabz once he had reported in. 'The Mystery of the Disappearing Bus,' he murmured to himself. What would Poirot make of it? he wondered, and wished he hadn't. His staff college instructor's remark – that he would make the perfect Hastings – had not yet ceased to rankle.

Still, even Hastings could probably put two and two together. Kennedy had no direct evidence that the bus had been hijacked, but the circumstantial facts – the disappearance, the security police interest, the cars which left with the bus – seemed conclusive enough. He told Janice as much when he finally managed to get through to Tashkent from the Shakhrisabz post office. Five minutes later she was walking through to see Pearson-Jones in the adjoining room. He listened, sighed, and asked her to connect him with London once more.

There were only three men gathered around the table in the Cabinet Office – the Prime Minister, Alan Holcroft and Sir Christopher Hanson. All three looked decidedly bleary-eyed. The last-named had just finished briefing his political masters on what had happened over the previous eighteen hours, beginning with Brenda Walker's failure to check in and ending with Kennedy's report from Shakhrisabz. He stressed that most of what they knew was educated guesswork, but added that in his opinion they were dealing with a real hijack.

'All right,' the Prime Minister said quietly, 'the first question has to be: why have the Uzbek authorities not contacted us?'

'Two possibilities,' Hanson said precisely. 'One, they don't yet know about the hijack. Two, they have reasons of their own for keeping silent. The first seems possible but unlikely. I don't know of any reason they might have for keeping silent.'

'I do,' Holcroft said. 'The trade deal is due to be signed this weekend. They may think this counts as bad publicity.'

'Really?' the Prime Minister said, as if he found it hard to believe. 'All right, assuming that is the case, what are we to do with our knowledge.'

'There is another question,' Hanson interjected. 'Why have the hijackers not publicized the abduction?'

'Perhaps the Uzbek government is keeping a tight lid on all the channels of information,' Holcroft suggested. It felt strange talking so logically about the problem when his own daughter was involved. For most of a sleepless night his brain had assaulted him with pictures of Sarah at every conceivable stage of her childhood and youth.

'Perhaps,' Hanson agreed, 'but usually hijackers work this sort of thing out in advance. The last thing they want is to pull off a stunt like this and have no one know about it.'

'So what is the answer?' the PM asked petulantly.

Hanson shrugged. 'I don't know. The third question, of course, is whether they know that one of their captives is the Foreign Minister's daughter.'

'You think it's possible that they don't?' Holcroft exclaimed in surprise. It had to be better if they didn't know, he thought. And then again . . . she would have more value as his daughter, and therefore be less likely to be harmed. If one hostage was selected for killing, he thought, remembering the *Achille Lauro*, then they would be less likely to choose her if they knew who she was.

'It does seem unlikely,' Hanson was saying, 'and something of a coincidence, but until we know for certain . . .'

'So what are we to do?' the PM asked Hanson.

'Well, the first thing we need to know is what the hijackers want and whom they want it from. If, for example, they do know that they have the Foreign Minister's daughter, then their demands will almost certainly be levelled at us rather than the government of Uzbekistan. If they don't know, then it's a different matter.'

'But what if the demands are levelled at us, but the Uzbeks are not passing them on?' Holcroft asked, thoroughly alarmed.

'A good question,' Hanson agreed.

'We have to inform the Uzbek government that we are aware of the situation,' Holcroft said, trying to keep a pleading tone out of his voice.

'Knowing that we know may reduce their anxiety,' Hanson agreed. And prevent them from charging in with guns blazing, he thought to himself.

'All right,' the PM agreed. 'I had better talk to President What's-his-name.' He picked up the nearest internal phone and asked his private secretary to get hold of an interpreter and the relevant number.

The ensuing silence was broken by Holcroft. 'Prime Minister,' he said formally, 'we could offer the Uzbeks help in dealing with a hostage situation. We do have the best people in the world in that department.'

'We'll see, Alan,' the PM said coolly. 'Let's wait until we know more about the situation.'

A long ten minutes went by before the interpreter arrived from elsewhere in the Whitehall labyrinth. The private secretary then started the laborious task of linking them, through Moscow, with Tashkent.

The call from London reached President Bakalev's office just as he returned from his meeting with Bakhtar Muratov. The moment he was told the British Prime Minister wished to talk with him the President realized the cat was out of the bag. While the interpreters wished each other good morning he congratulated himself on allowing Muratov to talk him out of ordering the air strike.

Then he picked up the waiting receiver. 'Mr Prime Minister,' he said, realizing he had forgotten the man's name.

'Mr President,' came the eventual reply. Probably the Englishman had forgotten his too. 'We have reason to believe,' Balalev's translator passed on, 'that a group of our British citizens has been the subject of a terrorist kidnapping in your country. In Samarkand, to be precise.'

'That is correct,' Bakalev agreed. 'We have only just been informed of this ourselves,' he lied. How the hell had the English already found out? he wondered. And what would they want now they knew?

'Do you have a list of those taken hostage?' the Prime Minister asked.

'No, only the numbers of men and women . . .' He was about to add 'and their nationality', but thought better of it. Maybe no one else knew that Americans were involved.

In London, the PM, Holcroft and Hanson shared glances. It seemed that the Uzbeks were unaware of Sarah Holcroft's presence among the hostages. 'We can supply you with a list,' the PM told Bakalev.

'Thank you.'

'Do you know who these terrorists are?'

'They call themselves The Trumpet of God. They are religious fanatics.'

'Have they told you what they want in exchange for the hostages' release?'

'We received their demands half an hour ago. They wish to have their programme printed in our state newspaper, and they are demanding the release of four other zealots from prison.'

There was a slight pause as the Prime Minister sought out the most sensitive phrasing. 'This is clearly an internal matter for the government of Uzbekistan,' he said eventually, 'but I am sure you will understand, Mr President, that the safety of British citizens is a matter of great importance to us, wherever they may be in the world.'

'Of course,' Bakalev agreed. 'But I am fully aware of British policy as regards such situations – "no surrender to terrorism". Were those not the words of your illustrious predecessor?'

'Yes, yes, they were,' the PM agreed. 'And as a general

rule we hold to that policy very firmly. But there can be exceptions, special circumstances to consider ... It is not for the British to dictate the government of Uzbekistan's response. I can only say that the British government would consider it a most friendly act, and I would consider it a personal favour, if the government of Uzbekistan could do its best to secure the peaceful release of these hostages.'

The translation of this last sentence ushered in a lengthy silence. In London, Holcroft gave the PM a grateful glance. In Tashkent, President Bakalev wondered if he had really heard what he thought he had heard.

'I would naturally like to help,' he began cautiously, 'but conceding these demands could be very costly for my country. As you must be aware, a semblance of political stability has been hard to achieve for many of the newly independent states in this region, and to be seen to give ground to the Islamic fundamentalists would be profoundly destabilizing. And an increase in political problems will of course exacerbate our existing economic difficulties. As I said, I personally would be happy to offer assistance, but I must think first of my country and the people who elected me.'

Hanson rolled his eyes at the ceiling. Holcroft found he was clenching his fist. The PM bit the bullet. 'I realize that no price can be put on such things,' he began, 'but I think it would be possible for the British government to offer compensation for any problems which arose as a result of this situation.'

Bakalev smiled to himself. 'I think $200 million would be a reasonable sum.'

'I will need to discuss such an arrangement with my colleagues,' the PM said.

'Of course.'

'If we can keep this line open then I will talk to you again in fifteen minutes.'

'Very well.'

The PM signalled his secretary to cut off the extensions, and looked round at Holcroft and Hanson.

'It's a lot less per person than we paid out for the Falkland Islanders,' Hanson said drily.

'It's a drop in the bucket,' the PM said. 'And in any case, as long as it's tied to development deals this country won't be any the poorer. The only problem will be hiding the transaction in the public accounts.'

'There's always a way,' Hanson said cynically. 'And in any case, who could object to expenditure aimed at saving lives?'

'The people who say we should never give in to terrorism?' Holcroft asked wearily.

'Nobody cares who runs Uzbekistan,' Hanson insisted. 'It could just as well be the Muslim loonies in government, the communists doing the hijackings. We worry too much about these small countries. They're basically irrelevant to how we do in the world.'

'Maybe,' the PM said. 'But in any case, no one has made any demands of the British government, so there's no way we can be giving in to terrorism.' He looked thoughtful for a moment. 'But just in case – I think your earlier suggestion was a good one, Alan.' He nodded, as if agreeing with himself.

In Tashkent, President Bakalev had been smoking a cigarette, unable to believe his luck. Perhaps next time, he thought ironically, his own people could do the kidnapping and cut out the middlemen.

He wondered why the British government was so concerned about the fate of these fourteen hostages.

Maybe there was an election coming up – after what had happened to Jimmy Carter in the USA no one wanted to face one with a hostage crisis under way.

Bakalev sighed with satisfaction, blowing smoke at the fan spinning round above his head. 'They're on again,' an aide called to him from the open door.

The Prime Minister wasted no time. 'The sum you suggested is acceptable,' he began. 'It will of course be in the form of development grants, with half the sum tied to the purchase of British products.'

Bakalev grimaced, but concurred. 'And the deal already agreed will be signed here this weekend, as arranged?'

'Yes. But there are two further conditions. First, we expect to be consulted at all levels throughout the duration of the hostage crisis. After we two have finished speaking I would like your operational commander to get in touch with our embassy, so that a British liaison officer can be attached to his team.'

'Is this really necessary?' Bakalev asked. 'The situation should be resolved by this time tomorrow, and the hostages on their way home.'

'I hope you are right,' the PM agreed. 'But there is no way we can be sure. The second condition is that you accept help from us in dealing with the hostage situation. I intend no disrespect to your country, Mr President, when I say that the British Army has more experience of dealing with such situations than anyone . . .'

'How many men?' Bakalev asked bluntly.

'Two,' the PM said, picking a figure out of the air. 'They will serve only in a consultative capacity, of course.'

'Of course,' Bakalev said, wrinkling his nose. After all, what difference could it make? By the end of the week these two soldiers and all the hostages would be back in England, leaving behind a richer Uzbekistan and a more popular President.

'Are these two conditions acceptable?' the Englishman was asking.

'They are,' Bakalev said.

8

On his way to see the President, Muratov realized how relieved he was that the English had suddenly intervened. The idea of taking out the hostages and hijackers in one explosive swoop had certainly had an appealing simplicity to it, but over the years experience had taught him that such schemes had a habit of rebounding on their architects. And, he had to admit, while fourteen innocent deaths might represent no more than an average week's murder toll in a large American city, it still seemed an excessively large burden to put on one's conscience.

Muratov wondered whether he was succumbing to the new religious mania. This is where seventy years of enforced secularism leads a culture, he thought. Right down the throats of the hungry mullahs.

He found the President smoking a cigarette and gazing happily out of the large picture window at the opera house across the square. Bakalev lost no time in filling him in on all the delightful details.

'Two hundred million dollars, plus the trade deal,' he gushed, 'and all for letting a few madmen out of prison and printing some idiotic religious drivel. If the whole business gets out we can say we conceded to the demands on humanitarian grounds, and because the British asked us to.'

'What interests me is why they asked us to,' Muratov said, mostly to himself.

'Who knows? Maybe they have an election coming up and don't want any bad publicity. It's not as if they're giving up anything, is it?'

'Except $200 million.'

Bakalev shrugged. 'It's hardly anything to them. I probably should have asked for more.'

You probably should, Muratov thought. 'So I just tell the hijackers we accept their demands?' he said.

'Yes. Arrange the prison releases and the printing of their programme. Ah, I almost forgot – the British did insist on sending two experts in hostage situations to help us. They will arrive early tomorrow. Until then they want one of their embassy staff to liaise with your people.'

'What's the point? If we're giving the hijackers what they want . . .'

'That's what I said. They claim they want people here in case something goes wrong, or the hijackers change their minds. Whatever.'

'Our people are going to love this.'

Bakalev smiled. 'And I had an idea,' he said. 'That Ismatulayeva woman is in charge of the Anti-Terrorist Unit, right? Her mother was always a pain in the arse. Anyway, put her in charge of this operation, responsible directly to you. If anything does go wrong, then having a woman in charge will be good publicity for us in the West.'

Muratov frowned but said nothing.

'And I've been wondering,' Bakalev continued, 'should we contact the Americans? Do you think they would pay another $200 million for their two hostages?'

'No,' Muratov said. He still wasn't at all sure why the British had suddenly become so terrorist-friendly. Until he did understand their reasons – or lack of them – it felt better not to further complicate matters. He told Bakalev so.

The President was in too good a mood to argue with him.

*   *   *

Nurhan and Marat drove back into town from the airport in silence. Her mind was fully engaged with the problems posed for her unit by the terrorists' location, while his was still recovering from the sudden recognition of the Stinger on the man's shoulder. The last time he had seen one had been eight years earlier, on a two-helicopter patrol in Afghanistan. A split second after visual identification the missile had been fired, turning one of the helicopters into an instant ball of flame. This explosion had sent Marat's helicopter into a spin which the pilot was still struggling to right when the ground intervened. Marat had spent one month in a field hospital and several more in a convalescent unit in Tashkent. He had never enjoyed a helicopter flight since.

They arrived back at the NSS HQ for the second time that day shortly before noon. The temperature was in the low thirties and still rising, but all the shady parking spaces had been taken. They left the Volga to bake and walked into the cool of the building.

Zhakidov's office was the only one with an air-conditioner, an ancient machine which, according to the manufacturer's plate, had been made in Springfield, Massachusetts, and had somehow contrived to spend its working life in the service of the KGB, deep in the heart of Asia. To judge from the noises which emanated from it, that life was almost over. The machine seemed to gulp rather than simply ingest electricity, because every now and then the noise would suddenly rise to a tumult and every light-bulb in the building would momentarily flicker and dim.

The air in the office, though, was almost cold, and Zhakidov was actually wearing his jacket. He gestured them into chairs with a wave of his hand and carried on

126

writing something into some sort of ledger. He looked vaguely pissed off, Marat thought, and wondered if the new young wife was proving more trouble than she was worth.

'Do you know what that place is?' Zhakidov asked abruptly.

'No idea,' Nurhan answered, assuming he meant the lodge where the terrorists were holed up.

'It's Bakalev's personal hunting lodge. Or at least it was intended to be. It was built a few years ago, for the Party bosses. Gorbachev was going to be the first invited guest to spend a weekend there.'

'Surprise surprise,' Marat murmured. Lately he had begun to wonder whether the Party leadership had done anything other than feather its own nest during the final thirty years of Soviet rule.

'But he was too busy dismantling the country,' Zhakidov went on. 'Anyway, it was only used once or twice, and it hasn't been used at all since the break-up.'

'Too embarrassing,' Marat murmured. He wondered if Zhakidov had ever made use of the facilities, and decided to risk asking. They would need a first-hand description of the place from somebody.

But Zhakidov had never been invited.

'What's been decided?' Nurhan interjected. Zhakidov had let them know what the terrorists were demanding during the return helicopter flight, and she had assumed that Bakalev's answer would be a cross between outright refusal and delaying tactics. Then it would be up to her to dream up a workable rescue attempt while the terrorists were stalled in negotiations.

Zhakidov punctured the balloon.

'What!?' she exclaimed angrily. 'We're just going to let them get away with it? Why?'

Zhakidov simply shrugged, which infuriated her even more.

'What's the point of setting up an anti-terrorist unit and then not using it the first time it's needed?' she demanded to know.

'You won't be idle,' Zhakidov told her calmly. 'The agreement may break down, the terrorists may change their minds, who knows? Make contingency plans. Get your people in position and ready to go if the need arises. And be prepared for visitors.' He told her about the embassy official and the experts flying out from Britain.

She exploded a second time. 'You mean I'm going to have two Englishmen leaning over my shoulder?'

'Maximum co-operation,' Zhakidov said.

Marat remembered reading about the Iranian Embassy siege in London. 'Are they from the SAS?' he asked.

'I wasn't told,' Zhakidov said.

'What difference does it make?' Nurhan said automatically, though a small voice at the back of her mind admitted to an interest in meeting them if they were. Several of the hostage-release operations she had studied had involved the SAS.

'There's one other thing,' Zhakidov told her. 'You have been given command of the situation on the ground. From now on you will report directly to Colonel Muratov in Tashkent. Is that understood?'

'Yes, sir,' Nurhan said. She felt elation at the implicit promotion, but it was tinged with annoyance at the emptiness of the context – she was being placed in command of a surrender to terrorism, after all – and sorry for the implied slight to her immediate boss. She didn't exactly like Zhakidov, but she had always respected his professionalism.

'Congratulations,' Marat said drily. 'Who am I supposed to take orders from?'

'You're still mine,' Zhakidov said. 'And I want you to track down any contacts Nasruddin Salih has in the city. His tours have been coming here for several months, and he must have been here before that to set things up. He may even have relations here. Find out. I'm assuming,' he added to Nurhan, with an air of slightly mocking deference, 'that the more we know about these people the better.'

'Yes, sir,' she agreed.

It was almost two o'clock when the three men gathered again in the lodge's living-room. Talib had taken his first few hours of sleep since their arrival, and was still rubbing the tiredness out of his eyes.

'Any sign of the enemy?' he asked the others.

'None,' Akbar said, almost smugly.

'If they're not out there now they soon will be,' Talib said. 'If Bakalev rejects our demands we shall have to start making it more difficult for any watchers. I told you what happened at Djibouti.'

They remembered. All four terrorists had been taken out simultaneously by accurate long-range fire. It was a sobering thought.

'And they may have thermal imaging,' Talib went on remorselessly. 'We must keep at least some of our men close enough to the hostages to confuse the picture.'

Nasruddin glanced across at Akbar and realized why Talib was bringing this up now. The Tajik was getting overconfident, and needed reminding that some of the futures beckoning them were decidedly less rosy than others.

129

'If we have calculated correctly,' Akbar said, 'then our demands will be accepted . . .'

'God willing,' Talib murmured.

'But we have to consider rejection,' Nasruddin insisted reluctantly. What with Akbar's optimism and his cousin's fatalism he sometimes felt compelled to shoulder the burden of all their doubts.

'We will have a simple choice,' Talib said. 'To abandon the game or to up the stakes.'

'How do you mean?' Nasruddin asked softly. In their discussions and arguments prior to setting this operation in motion they had always skirted around this point. All three men had voiced their theoretical willingness to face a martyr's death, but on the subject of killing there had been a unanimous silence.

Talib broke it. 'We will have to kill one of the hostages.' He looked at each man in turn. 'I have questioned myself on this matter, and prayed for clear guidance. None has been given to me. But if, on balance, it seems that we can only achieve our goals by doing so, then I do not see how we can shrink from it. In the end, God will decide if we were clear-sighted or blind.'

'How would we choose which hostage to kill?' Akbar wanted to know.

'We can worry about that if and when it becomes necessary,' Nasruddin told him bluntly. He had struggled with his own conscience, and, like his cousin, had found it hard to reach a clear decision. Being with the tour party for almost a week, getting to know them as people, had, as expected, strengthened his doubts. But seventeen hours had passed since he had last set eyes on them, and already their reality as human beings was fading. 'I think we have no choice but to countenance such a step,' Nasruddin said slowly, 'but until . . .'

'We all hope it will not be necessary,' Talib interrupted. 'There is no joy in killing.'

' "You shall not kill any man whom God has forbidden you to kill, except for a just cause," ' Akbar quoted from the Koran. 'And ours is a just cause.'

'That is for God to decide,' Talib reminded him.

Lieutenant-Colonel Barney Davies, Commanding Officer 22 SAS, had rarely been more surprised. He had met the Foreign Minister before – several times in fact – but had never expected to have the man stride into his own office at the Regiment's Stirling Lines barracks on the outskirts of Hereford. Nor, in all their previous meetings, had he ever thought of Alan Holcroft as anything other than utterly certain of himself. An arrogant bastard, through and through.

But not today. The Foreign Minister looked almost shell-shocked. Maybe the man had found God. Or caught AIDS off a rent boy, like that politician in *Prime Suspect*, which Davies had watched on video a few evenings before.

Or maybe not. Holcroft sat down, looked round the office, abruptly stood up again, and asked if the CO would take a walk outside with him.

'Across the parade ground?' Davies asked.

'Anywhere where we won't be heard,' Holcroft said.

Davies raised an eyebrow but said nothing. He led the way out of the building, noting in passing Holcroft's chauffeur leaning against the ministerial limousine. His opinion of politicians, never high, had not really recovered from his first run-in with Holcroft five years earlier, during and after the Colombian mission. The man had not only personally intervened to make sure that no public recognition was given to the two SAS troopers

131

whose lives had been lost, but neither had he offered any private recognition of their sacrifice. Like countless soldiers before them, those two men had deserved better of their political masters.

Davies smiled to himself, remembering Trooper Eddie Wilshaw's utterly insubordinate face.

'This is a delicate matter, Lieutenant-Colonel,' Holcroft began. He stopped, as if collecting his thoughts. 'I will be as concise as I can. A British tourist party has been hijacked, kidnapped – whatever the right word is – in Uzbekistan. That's one of the successor states of the Soviet Union . . .'

'I know where it is,' Davies said coldly, keeping to himself that this knowledge was a fairly recent thing, stemming as it did from the secret mission to Kazakhstan undertaken by the SAS the previous year. They had lost three men on that one. He hoped to God this was not going to be a rerun.

'Good,' Holcroft was saying. 'Well . . .' He quickly went through what was known of the events of the past twenty-four hours, concluding with a mostly uncensored blow-by-blow account of the Prime Minister's conversation with President Bakalev.

'I see,' Davies said when he was finished, though he still didn't understand why they were discussing it all in the middle of a parade ground on a decidedly cool summer day. So the government was leaning on the Uzbeks to give the local opposition some breathing space, and getting some hostages released in the process. He had no argument with that.

Holcroft took a deep breath. 'There's one other thing,' he said. 'My daughter is one of the hostages.'

'Oh.' Suddenly the whole business made more sense. 'I'm sorry about that,' Davies murmured.

'But the kidnappers don't know who she is,' Holcroft went on. 'And of course it's important that they don't find out. Which is why I'm here in person. At this moment only the Prime Minister, myself and Christopher Hanson are aware of the full situation. And now yourself, of course. I'm relying utterly on your discretion – and those of the two men who are chosen to go.'

'You can take that for granted,' Davies said coolly.

For a moment Holcroft looked decidedly human. 'I know,' he said. 'But . . . this is hard for me. And my wife, of course.' He managed a smile. 'Look, I won't take up any more of your valuable time. Hanson has all the information about the hijack you will need . . . he already has a man out there. And Special Branch is covering the Bradford end.'

They had retraced their steps almost to the limousine. 'Ah, by the way,' Holcroft said suddenly. 'I forgot – one of your old boys is one of the hostages. James Docherty? Does that name ring a bell?'

'He led the team we sent into Bosnia last year,' Davies said dully. He couldn't believe it.

'Ah yes, a good man,' Holcroft said. They had reached the limousine. 'Keep me informed,' he added as he climbed inside.

'Of course.' Davies watched the car glide out of sight. Docherty! The man seemed destined for adventures, even when he no longer wanted them. Only eighteen months earlier Davies had coaxed him out of retirement to undertake the mission in Bosnia, and the Scot had come back with the bitterness woven a little more tightly through his smile. Davies knew all too well that you could send a soldier to war once too often, particularly a soldier who refused to close his conscience down for the duration.

In any case, Docherty had retired for good after that one, and Davies had heard nothing of what he was doing until now. The card he had received the previous Christmas from Glasgow, though very welcome, had been lamentably devoid of information.

Davies wondered whether Docherty's wife and children were also among the hostages. He walked back towards his office, stopping to ask his aide to find and summon Major Jimmy Bourne, the long-time commander of the Regiment's Counter Revolutionary Warfare Wing. Once behind his desk he called a number in Whitehall, and asked to be called back on a secure line. Then he ordered tea and a rock cake from the mess.

The call came first. Hanson gave him a brief verbal update, faxed the relevant information, and said he would call again in half an hour to see if there were any questions. The tea arrived when Davies was still on the first page. In his relief at finding that Docherty's children weren't on the list of hostages he bit with inadvisable vigour on the rock cake, causing a chain reaction of vibrating fillings.

A rap on the door was followed by Bourne, who was carrying his own mug of tea. 'Good morning, boss,' he said, eyeing the rock cake with distrust.

'Trouble,' Davies began, and went through what Holcroft had told him from start to finish, before handing over the reports from Hanson.

'Two men,' Bourne murmured to himself when he had finished reading. 'May I?' he asked, reaching for Davies's computer keyboard.

'Be my guest,' Davies said. He hated the damn thing. 'I think they should be relatively senior men,' he decided. 'We need to pull out all the stops on this one. No,' he said, seeing Bourne's expression, 'I don't like thinking

134

that way either, but the bastards have us by the throat these days. And I don't mean the hijackers,' he added, somewhat superfluously.

'Well, I don't think there'll be a wide choice anyway,' Bourne said. 'They'll have to be Russian-speakers . . .'

'We're not out of Uzbek-speakers, are we?'

'Surprisingly, yes.' Bourne had the personnel of G Squadron on screen – this was the squadron currently on twenty-four-hour standby in case of terrorist incidents. He shook his head. 'I think we should send a couple of my lads,' he said.

'No objection from me,' Davies said, watching Bourne's two index fingers flashing to and fro on the keyboard.

'OK, then. Rob Brierley for one. He teaches the "Hostage Situation" course, and he's one of the three Russian-speakers. The other two are Terry Stoneham and Nick Houghton.' He paused a moment. 'I'd go with Stoneham, mostly because he gets on well with Brierley.'

'Fine. Brief 'em and kit 'em up. I'll get started on the transport arrangements.'

Terry Stoneham couldn't believe it. 'You're kidding me, right?' he asked his brother.

'Wish I was,' Mike Stoneham said. He was phoning from the cinema he managed in the West End.

'Tell me again,' Terry demanded.

'We've been fined half a million quid, banned from the FA Cup, and had twelve points deducted before we start next season in the League.'

'We start with minus twelve points!?'

'Right.'

'We'd be better off relegated. At least there'd be something to play for.'

'There still is – survival.'

'But the management's different now, the owner's different. How can they be blamed for what the fuckers before them did? And why should the fans suffer? Why should I suffer, for fuck's sake – I didn't do anything wrong.'

'Yeah. Anyway, I just thought you'd like to hear the bad news from your brother, and not a total stranger.'

'Ha-bloody-ha.' He still couldn't believe it. They'd only escaped relegation by four points last season, and now they'd be starting off with a twelve-point handicap.

'How are you otherwise?' Mike asked.

'Fuck knows. OK, I suppose . . .' He knew it was only football, but somehow he hadn't needed this.

'Have you seen the baby yet?'

'Yeah, once.'

There was a few moments' silence at both ends of the line.

'Why don't you come up to town for the weekend?' Mike suggested.

'Maybe. Don't worry about me, OK? I'm all right. Really.'

'OK, we're here if you feel like a laugh.'

'I know. Thanks.' He put down the phone, and slumped back on to the sofa. The clock on the mantelpiece said he had another hour before teaching his 'Hearts and Minds' class to the latest bunch of insolent newly badged bastards.

'Only football' – he could remember Jane aping the words sarcastically. He thought about the baby, their son. The boy didn't even have a name yet, or at least not as far as he knew. Maybe she and her boyfriend had come up with one.

Terry thought about the boyfriend. Don his name was, but he would always be 'the boyfriend'. Was the guy really willing to take on someone else's kid and be a proper father to it? Jane obviously thought so, but it seemed a lot to ask. Terry wasn't at all sure he could do it if the situation was reversed.

Maybe Don could. He didn't seem such a bad bloke, much as Terry had wanted him to be. And if he was prepared to be the boy's father then maybe Terry should just back out of the situation, pretend he hadn't got a son. That was what Jane had asked him to think about. That was obviously what she wanted. It would be easier, no doubt about it. But was it right? He was buggered if he knew. In fact, when it came down to it, he didn't really know what he felt about it all. When he'd seen the baby, the little face and all the little limbs, he hadn't really felt any connection with himself. But maybe men didn't, at least not straight off.

He sighed and looked round the one-room flat. It still felt cramped, even after five months. He thought about all the work he'd put into their house, and felt the familiar anger well up inside him. I didn't deserve this, he thought, and felt instantly ashamed of feeling so sorry for himself.

It was time to get moving. He got to his feet, walked through into the tiny bathroom, and picked up the reusable razor which Jane had foisted on him as ecologically correct. He studied his face in the mirror, the blue eyes beneath the short, straw-coloured hair. 'And Tottenham didn't deserve it either,' he told his reflection.

The door broke open with a crash, and the room suddenly filled with smoke. The leading members of the rescue team burst into view, looking like *Star Wars* rejects in their flame-retardant hoods and respirators.

The red dots from the aiming-point projectors on their MP5s searched and found the two terrorists standing by the wall to the left. They opened fire, killing them before their guns were even half raised into the firing position.

The terrorist by the hostages had his arm round one of their necks, and was in the act of pulling the man towards him when the tell-tale red dot appeared just above his waist.

Good, Brierley thought, very good.

But there was still the terrorist behind the door. His SMG had reached the firing position, and was spewing bullets around the smoke-filled room. One hostage went down, and another, before one of the rescuers pumped upwards of fifty bullets through his torso.

'OK,' Brierley shouted, and everything came to a halt. 'That was better. Far from perfect, but better.'

But it was a good thing the room on the screen was really two. Ever since an NCO playing hostage had been tragically killed by rescuers in a similar exercise, the Stirling Lines 'Killing House' had been a very different place. Now those playing the hostages and terrorists occupied one room while the rescuers attacked another, with cameras and wraparound wall screens giving each group the illusion that they were all in the same room. Both sides were able to riddle the bullet-absorbent walls, while their instructors kept score on film.

The system worked so well that American Special Forces had copied the idea lock, stock and wraparound screen. And it offered the sort of training that a few years before had only been possible at enormous risk to life and limb.

Brierley waited for the participants to file in through the door for debriefing. On this particular morning he was feeling more than usually pleased with life. He enjoyed his teaching work, despite originally expecting not to. He had a whole weekend of flying coming up, and Margie had finally accepted that he wasn't going to give her the sort of commitment she wanted. He supposed it was kind of sad that they couldn't go on the way they had started – like friends who enjoyed sex together – but the way things had been going lately her decision to stop seeing him was also something of a relief. When all was said and done they just didn't want the same thing, and all the resulting hassles had taken a lot of the fun out of being together.

It was better to be single. Even most of the happy couples he knew told him so.

Watching the group of young men now taking their seats in front of him, he wondered how many of them had been stupid enough to replace their mothers with a wife.

'Two hostages were killed,' he began. 'The first question is why.'

'Because they stood up,' one man said.

'They weren't *trying* to get shot,' Brierley began, before his attention was captured by the adjutant who had appeared in the doorway.

'Major Bourne wants to see you immediately,' the man said.

Brierley acknowledged the message with a wave and handed the class over to a fellow-instructor. Two minutes later he was walking into Bourne's office. Terry Stoneham was already sitting in one of the two chairs facing the CRW boss's desk.

'Right,' Bourne began the moment Brierley sat down,

'you two are leaving today for the middle of nowhere.' He turned the opened atlas around, placed it in front of them, and jabbed a finger at the map. 'Samarkand. Ever heard of it?'

'It was on the old Silk Road,' Brierley said.

Bourne tried not to look impressed. 'It was also in the Soviet Union until a couple of years ago. Now it's in Uzbekistan. Lots of tourists go there apparently, though I have no idea why. Lots of monuments, I suppose.'

'The Registan is supposed to be one of the finest pieces of Muslim architecture in the world,' Brierley told him. 'There was a documentary about it on the TV a few weeks ago,' he added. 'They've run out of money for the restoration work since the Russians pulled out.'

'Are we taking them the Regimental savings, boss?' Stoneham asked with a straight face.

'There aren't any. Fourteen of these tourists – all but two of them Brits – have been hijacked, and you two are being sent out as advisers to the Uzbek authorities.'

'Who are the hijackers?' Brierley asked.

Bourne shrugged. 'They call themselves The Trumpet of God . . .'

'Fundies,' Stoneham murmured.

'Probably.'

'What do they want?'

'Publicity and some friends out of jail. The government has agreed, and it should all be over by eleven a.m. their time tomorrow. Samarkand is five hours ahead of us, by the way.'

'I don't understand, boss,' Stoneham said. 'We're flying all that way just to watch a handover? They don't need advice on how to cave in, do they?'

'You're flying all that way at the taxpayers' expense just in case,' Bourne said. 'And the reason you're going, just between us, is that one of the hostages happens to be the Foreign Minister's daughter.'

'Not Sarah Le Bonk?'

Bourne smiled wryly. 'The very same.'

Stoneham's eyes narrowed. 'Excuse me for saying so, boss, but . . . are you saying that we're only going out there because her dad's got clout? If so, it stinks.'

'It does,' Bourne agreed. 'But we do what we're told. And in this instance we do it knowing that Alan Holcroft will have an important voice in whether we get the funding we need over the next few years.'

Stoneham said nothing, but the expression on his face was lucid enough.

'There are also a couple of good reasons for going,' Bourne said mildly. 'First off, the other thirteen will get the same luxury treatment from Her Majesty's Government as Miss Holcroft. And by the way, from what we can gather the hijackers haven't twigged who she is.'

'That's a bit of luck.'

'Looks like it. Second, one of those thirteen also happens to be one of our old boys. Jamie Docherty. I trust you agree he deserves our best shot.'

'Of course, boss. Why didn't you tell us that first?'

'Do either of you know him, personally I mean?' Bourne asked.

Neither did, but both knew of his reputation. 'I wonder if he's enjoying captivity with Sarah Le Bonk,' Stoneham wondered out loud.

'I doubt it,' Bourne said drily. 'His wife is with him.'

'Oh Jesus.'

'Exactly.'

'When do we leave?' Brierley asked.

Bourne was about to say he didn't know when his

phone rang. He jotted down the times on his notepad and put back the receiver.

'We're in luck,' he told them. 'Uzbekistan Airways flies direct to Tashkent three nights a week, and this is one of the nights. Twenty hundred hours from Heathrow, arriving 0730 their time in Tashkent. The locals will fly you down to Samarkand from there.' He looked at his watch. 'That gives us more than nine hours to get you kitted up and on to the plane.'

'More than enough,' Brierley said. 'What sort of set-up is it? I mean, where are the hostages being held?'

'In a hunting lodge up in the mountains, that's all we know at the moment.'

Brierley grimaced. 'It would be nice to have an idea of the terrain. Still . . . I take it our equipment will be cleared through customs at Heathrow?'

'If it isn't we can always hijack the plane,' Stoneham observed. 'We have the expertise.'

9

In Leeds a slight rain had just begun to fall, and Detective Sergeant Dave Medwin was able to savour the cooling drops on his face as he walked across the police station car park. This sense of relaxation was short-lived – he had barely poked his head through the front doors of the building when the duty officer barked out that London had been calling him every five minutes for the last half an hour.

'Bloody Londoners think they're the only people with a rush hour,' Medwin snarled back, and walked slowly upstairs. He had only downed three and a half pints on the previous evening, so it could hardly be the alcohol to blame for another semi-sleepless night. Maybe he was allergic to something. Celibacy, perhaps.

The phone was ringing as he entered his office. It was London, telling him to mount a full-scale investigation of Nasruddin Salih. They wanted personal history, psychological profile, estimates of intelligence. They wanted any evidence of who his contacts might be in Central Asia. They wanted anything he could find. The local CID had been instructed to issue him with any search warrants he required, but had not been told anything. Nor would they be. Complete discretion was still required, right up to the point where it might hamper the investigation. If that point was reached, then Medwin should call London for fresh instructions.

He sat there for a few moments trying to focus his mind, before reminding himself that such a difficult process required coffee. He walked down the hall, inserted his coins, and kept his thumb jammed on the extra sugar button as the machine coughed up its usual 'fresh-brewed' monstrosity. Back in the office he started with the obvious, calling British Telecom to check on Nasruddin's long-distance phone calls over the last few years, both from home and the office. There were none from the former, and all the latter were apparently to hotels. He took the numbers down anyway.

He then called Records and asked them to send up copies of both Nasruddin's personal file and the incident report on the arson attack. While he waited for these to arrive he called the local probation service, and found out that Nasruddin's officer had recently retired to Ilkley. He took down the address and decided against the hassle of demanding a copy of their file. He could do that song and dance later, if and when it proved necessary.

The copies arrived from the basement. He read through the arson incident report, and found nothing much more than Rose had told him the previous evening. The father and two elder children had been watching a Leeds game at Elland Road, and young Martin had gone to answer a knock on the front door. A youth in a crash helmet had thrown the Molotov cocktail over his head, and it had smashed on the living-room door jamb, setting both the hall carpet and wall hangings ablaze. His mother had apparently been trapped in the downstairs back room, on the other side of the flames from Martin. By the time the fire engines arrived most of the house had been consumed or blackened, but the spray-painted words 'Paki scum' were still visible on the front gate.

Medwin sighed and picked up Nasruddin's personal file. There was nothing much new here either – the boy had just gone berserk one evening, smashing windows in what seemed to be a paroxysm of grief. God only knew why they had put him on probation. If someone had done that to his family, Medwin thought, he would have gone and killed somebody.

He locked the two copies in his desk and walked down to the car park. The rain was still falling gently, almost like a lawn sprinkler. Once in the car, he turned on the local radio station, and spent most of the next half hour wondering why pop music sounded so much the same these days. Was he just too old to hear whatever subtleties it might contain? No, he didn't think he was. Lynn's fourteen-year-old son spent half his time listening to Hendrix and Dylan. The music really had been better twenty-five years ago.

He drove to Bradford and parked outside the newsagent's in Westfield Street, found the travel agency was open for business, and walked upstairs to find Pinar Ishaq Khan sitting and looking industrious behind her desk.

'Do you have more news?' she asked immediately.

'No, I'm afraid not.' With her lustrous hair and beautiful skin colour Pinar looked even better than she had the evening before. Even the faint shadow-line on the upper lip, which Medwin usually found a little off-putting, seemed part of her attractiveness.

'I tried to ring Samarkand a little while ago,' she said, 'but there's a problem with the line.'

I bet there is, Medwin thought. 'I have to take a look through the office,' he said, hoping she wouldn't want to see his authorization.

'Shouldn't you have a search warrant?' she asked politely.

He reluctantly retrieved the paper from his inside pocket and passed it over. She examined it with interest. 'This is serious, isn't it?' she said.

145

He shrugged and began methodically working his way through Nasruddin's desk.

'Can't you tell me any more?' she asked.

'No,' he said. There was nothing in the desk, and, as it turned out, nothing in the office. At the end of twenty minutes Medwin knew a bit more about travel agenting but nothing new about Nasruddin. 'Have you got a phone number for his sister, brother or father?' he asked Pinar.

'No,' she said.

'Do you know where they live?'

'Sheila lives in Bradford, I think. He didn't . . . he doesn't talk about his family much.'

'OK, thanks for your co-operation.'

'Should I just carry on?' she asked, as he made for the stairs. Medwin stopped and thought about it. He could hardly say no without giving her more of an explanation. 'You might as well,' he said. 'When I hear anything definite I'll let you know.'

She smiled without much conviction.

His next stop was Nasruddin Salih's local police station, where he picked up a constable to stand guard during his second search of the hijack leader's house. It was an easier job in daylight, but as on the previous evening he was close to conceding defeat when he finally found what he was looking for. Having failed to discover either an address book or a hoard of letters, he lifted a large, unmarked volume from a shelf, only to have several empty envelopes fall out to the floor. The volume was a stamp album, and two of the envelopes bore return addresses in Samarkand.

After the meeting with Zhakidov, Nurhan used the phone in her own office to call the city's army barracks, where the twelve men in her unit had been on alert since earlier that morning. The Anti-Terrorist Unit was in fact considerably less grand than it sounded. Nurhan was its only permanent member; those under her command were regular army soldiers who had been given special training in anti-terrorist situations, and placed on permanent standby should one such arise.

She filled in the ranking NCO Sergeant Abalov on what they were up against, and went through the list of what would be needed in the field, both for daily survival and completion of the task in hand. Most of what they required would be stored at the barracks, and if it wasn't then there was little likelihood of their finding it anywhere in Uzbekistan. Night-sights and goggles unfortunately fell in the latter category, as did stun grenades. Nurhan told the sergeant to gather together what he could and get the men to the airport, where she would meet them in an hour.

She then unrolled the map they had taken to the mountains, weighed it down at the corners on her desk, and studied it once more. During their flight that morning Marat had drawn in both the unmarked road and the lodge where it ended, high up the steep-sided valley. The terrorist leader had forbidden anyone to approach within two kilometres, so she drew a rough circle centred on the lodge with the appropriate radius. There were only a couple of points outside this circle from which the lodge and its approach road could be kept under long-range observation – in most directions visual contact was lost in considerably less than the specified distance.

There was only the one approach road, so if anyone wished to reach or leave the lodge in a vehicle that was the way they had to go. On foot the options were more numerous, in fact almost infinite for anyone fit enough to cope with the broken terrain. The border with Tajikistan was about sixty kilometres away to the east, perhaps two days' journey for a group of determined young men. With the hostages it would be more problematic. And probably impossible for the two American septuagenarians.

She sighed and stared straight ahead for a moment. It was all academic anyway, since the terrorists' demands had been granted. Still, it would be good practice for the next time, and maybe by then she would have political masters with backbones.

Nurhan decided she would put three men in each of the observation points, and spread the other six, in pairs, in a rough semicircular cordon to the east of the lodge. When darkness fell two men from each observation post could begin scouting out the land immediately in front of the lodge, to see if a surprise approach was possible from that direction. They could also pinpoint any guards the hijackers had posted on the road, and ascertain how easy their silent removal would be, before a direct approach at speed up the road itself.

The lodge itself was another matter. She needed more information, either through talking to people who had been there or through tracking down the architectural plans. Both options probably involved treading on sensitive toes. She seemed to remember that the Chairman of State Construction had been one of the big names in the last of the Soviet-era corruption trials.

She looked at her watch, and decided that the lodge could wait; it was more important to get the unit out into the mountains before nightfall. Downstairs she made a dozen photocopies of the relevant portion of the map, and then headed out for the car. As expected, it felt like climbing into an oven. In America, someone had told her, you could even get cars with air-conditioners.

At the airport the twelve men were still sitting in the lorry that had brought them from the barracks. A few of them managed a welcoming smile but most maintained the distance she had come to expect from them. She thought they had been disabused of any notion that she was incapable of running the unit, but the fact remained that they weren't used to taking orders from women in general, and generally uncomfortable with a woman who was so aggressively modern by Uzbek standards. And then there was the additional psychological complication of her sexual attractiveness. Wanting to fuck one's infidel boss was probably a hard thing to live with. Sometimes Nurhan almost felt sorry for them.

She took the austere Sergeant Abalov aside and swiftly briefed him on the entire situation. As usual he absorbed the information in silence, with the minimum of questioning. Fifteen minutes later she watched two Ka-26 helicopters carry the twelve men and their equipment off into the eastern sky.

After their meeting with Zhakidov had broken up, Marat had also felt more than a twinge of disappointment. The last eighteen hours had been among the most diverting of his NSS career – there had even been fifteen-minute stretches when he had forgotten he wanted a drink. And he had been finding Nurhan's company more than a little enjoyable.

He remembered the look on her face when Zhakidov had said she was in charge, and smiled to himself. She was so transparent in some ways. But, he had to admit, they would have to go a long way to find someone better able to run such a unit. And next time around maybe she really would get the chance to show all the men how good she was.

Marat reminded himself that, for the moment, they were pretending that the terrorists would still be in Uzbekistan this time tomorrow. He picked up the phone, called Immigration Control in Tashkent, and asked the woman who answered to check the arrivals and departures of Nasruddin Salih. Once armed with a list of dates, he phoned round all the major hotels in Samarkand and got them to check their registers against it. Over the previous two years the terrorist leader had stayed three nights in every month at the Hotel Samarkand, presumably as part of his own tour group. Before that none of the major hotels had any record of a stay, although the list from Immigration showed that he had been making regular visits to Uzbekistan for at least two years more.

Marat drew the obvious conclusion – Nasruddin had stayed either at one of the small hotels or in a private home.

He laboriously worked his way through the former to no avail. He then tried checking through the phone book for the name Salih, also in vain. Finally, he went through the old Soviet electoral register for the city, and drew a blank for the third time.

Marat checked his drawers for cigarettes and was pleased to find there weren't any. He leaned back in his chair and yawned, just as a tall blond man in obviously foreign clothes appeared in his doorway. 'Major Marat Rashidov?' the man asked.

'That's me.'

'Simon Kennedy,' the man said, walking forward with hand outstretched. 'From the British Embassy,' he added in Russian. 'I am told you can take me to Major Ismatulayeva.'

Marat shook the proffered hand. 'I don't know where she is at the moment,' he said in the same language, realizing with some surprise how long it had been since he had spoken Russian. A sign of the times. 'But you can either wait here, or I can tell her you called in. She can reach you at your hotel?'

Kennedy frowned. He had been warned that the NSS might give him the runaround, and told to be brutal if they did. 'She must be in touch with this building,' he said.

Marat scratched the back of his neck. 'I'll see,' he said, and picked up the phone to ask the operations room where she was. From the expression on the Englishman's face Marat guessed he didn't understand Uzbek. As he waited for the operations room to find her he suddenly had a brilliant idea.

The voice on the other end told him Nurhan had just left the airport and was on her way back to the office. He replaced the receiver and smiled at Kennedy. 'She'll be back in about twenty minutes,' he said.

'Then I'll wait here, if that's all right . . .'

'Of course. Mr Kennedy, I understand we are to share . . . I think "pool" is the English word, yes? To pool all the information we have?'

'So they tell me,' Kennedy said breezily.

'Good.' He told the Englishman that he was trying to find out where Nasruddin Salih had stayed on his earlier visits to Samarkand. 'I presume your police have searched his house in England. Can you find out whether they have discovered anything which might help me – an address book, perhaps, or letters?'

Kennedy considered, and could see no harm in it. In

fact it might win him the Uzbeks' trust. 'I'll do what I can,' he said, and gestured towards the phone with a questioning look.

Marat pushed it towards him.

Kennedy dialled the Tashkent number, and Janice answered. He passed on Marat's request and the number he was on. 'They'll phone here direct from England if they have anything,' he said.

Marat smiled at him.

'Now if you can give me a rundown of what's been happening,' Kennedy said.

Marat wondered whether Nurhan would consider that her job, and decided that she would probably have more important demands on her time. He went through the official version of the story so far, which carefully omitted any governmental knowledge of the hijack prior to that morning. Kennedy, who knew better after his fact-finding trip to Shakhrisabz, chose to let sleeping dogs and NSS agents lie. As far as he could tell, the only thing they knew which he had not was the exact location of the hostages.

Marat was just describing the lie of the land around the mountain lodge when the call arrived from London. He handed the phone to Kennedy and watched him write down two names and addresses on the piece of paper he pushed his way.

'These . . .' Kennedy started to say once his call was over, but the phone rang again. It was the operations room telling Marat that Nurhan had returned. He pocketed the piece of paper, and walked Kennedy down a floor just in time to intercept her on the way back out again.

She shook Kennedy's hand distractedly, and just about noticed a large-boned Englishman with an arrogant red face and straw-like blond hair cut short at the back and sides. At the same time he was confirming the impression gained at a glance from his car that morning. The revealing red dress was unfortunately gone, but even in the baggy black blouse she looked much sexier than a Soviet policewoman was supposed to.

'Marat, can you . . . ? she pleaded, but to no avail.

'Mr Kennedy wants to see the lodge,' Marat said. 'And I have a lead,' he added, moving towards the stairs. 'I'll see you later.'

Annabel Silcott's eyes roamed round the courtyard, noting the grey-brown walls, the dresses drying on the line, the broom with its fan of twig bristles leaning against a balustrade, and the pomegranate tree under whose shade they were sitting. A moment ago a small boy had stuck his head round the edge of the open doorway in front of her, dark eyes full of curiosity. He had probably never seen a blonde goddess before, she thought.

Reluctantly she refocused her attention on the woman she was interviewing. Jenah, the senior wife of Samarkand's head imam, was putting the case for Islam as the best thing that had happened to women since sliced bread. 'Adam and Eve equally guilty,' Annabel had written in her notebook – apparently Islam didn't share the Christian penchant for loading all the blame on poor old Eve and her seductive wiles. Nor were Muslim women's prayers – their link to God – mediated through men, as they were in the Catholic Church. And women had control over their own possessions – they could conduct business without their husband's consent.

So why are you stuck in this courtyard, Annabel wanted to ask, and only able to go out dressed up like the Invisible Man in drag?

But she didn't ask it. Jenah seemed so content with her lot, sitting there in her beautiful courtyard, wearing her gorgeously coloured, flowing silk *atlas*. And why shouldn't she be? The imam no doubt had a bob or two stashed away, so his wife would hardly be wanting for any of the necessities of life. In fact her worries were probably as few and far between as they seemed to be.

Thinking about her friends in London, most of whom had dysfunctional relationships with their partners, their own bodies, their jobs and – if they could afford it – their therapists, Annabel had no difficulty understanding the attraction of a life like Jenah's. In fact this woman was a much better advert for Islam than the hotshot liberal she had interviewed earlier had been for secularism. That particular woman had spent the first half of the interview talking about how wonderful it was that Uzbek women were coming out of the dark ages, and the second half complaining about how hard it was to get decent cosmetics in Samarkand.

I'm too young to be this jaded, Annabel thought.

The interview over, she decided to brave the heat and walk back up Tashkent Street to the hotel. Eyes followed her every step, and what were probably ribald comments floated past her ears. She ignored it all, stopping occasionally to look at the rugs hanging outside the carpet emporiums, and feeling her appetite respond to the smell of skewered meat being barbecued on the braziers.

The sun was halfway down in the western sky, but it was still hot, and the shade offered by the Bibi Khanum mosque was too much to pass by. She paid a few kopeks at the small office and walked in under the huge ruined arch. The interior courtyard seemed almost the size of a football pitch; at its far end a group of Western tourists were having something explained to them. Annabel sat down in a shady corner and stared up at the half-restored dome filling half the sky above.

She didn't want to write this story. It had seemed like a good idea at the time: a vital contemporary theme – she had said so in her original submission – and lots of free travel to exotic places, all on expenses. She had already been to Egypt and Saudi, with India and Indonesia still to come. Most people would give their eye-teeth for a job like this, she thought. She felt bored by it, bored by its predictability, its sleazy opportunism, its utter inconsequentiality. Filling newspapers and magazines these days was like painting the Forth Bridge. No one had anything new to say, so it was just a matter of endless recycling. There would be an article on 'Women under Islam' in some magazine or other every three months, all saying much the same thing with different pictures. What was the point?

Earning a living – that was the point.

She walked out of the mosque and continued up Tashkent Street to the Registan, where she turned right towards her hotel. The man from British Intelligence intruded on her consciousness. What was he doing in Samarkand? Come to that, what did any of them do anywhere these days, now that the Cold War was over and the old enemy laid low? Who were the new enemies? Drug smugglers and terrorists, probably. It could be either around here.

At the hotel she took her key from the receptionist, turned away and then, on a whim, turned back. 'The Englishman who is staying here on his own,' she said.

'Mr Kennedy?'

She described him.

'It is Mr Kennedy.'

'Can you tell me about him?' she asked. 'I will pay for information.'

The receptionist looked around, satisfied himself that they were alone, and leaned forward confidentially. 'How much?'

'That depends on the information. Can you tell me why he is in Samarkand?'

'Yes.'

'Ten dollars.'

'Twenty.'

She smiled. 'All right.'

He waited for her to produce it from the purse tied around her waist. 'He is looking for the tourists.'

'Which tourists?' she asked, more sharply than she intended.

'The ones who do not come back from Shakhrisabz.'

Bakhtar Muratov lay full length on the sofa in his apartment, reading a copy of The Trumpet of God's manifesto. The original, which had been faxed from Samarkand an hour before, was now *en route* to *Voice of the People*. God knew what they would think of the order to publish it. Muratov supposed they were lucky the editor still did what he was told, as was no longer the case in some of the neighbouring ex-Soviet republics.

He had to admit that whoever had written the manifesto knew what he was doing. It was not couched in terms only likely to stir the already faithful, and it didn't claim that Islam would solve all the people's earthly woes. It simply put forward, with some coherence, the argument that an Islamic Republic would provide a better moral, political and economic framework for the people of Uzbekistan. Though a distinct whiff of puritanism seemed to seep out between the words, there was little in the words themselves that most Uzbeks would object to.

It was a more dangerous document than he had expected, Muratov decided. But it was too late to worry about that now.

And maybe releasing Khotali and his acolytes would actually help to undo the damage. Khotali had never shown this much subtlety.

The timer on his VCR said two fifty-nine. Muratov levered himself into a sitting position and reached for a cigarette.

In the hunting lodge nearly six hundred and fifty kilometres to the south Nasruddin Salih was watching the second hand on his watch cover the last minute before three o'clock, his hand poised over the telephone. He supposed they should be grateful that the Party leaders had wasted so much of the people's money stringing a fifty-kilometre line across the mountains for their personal convenience, though they could always have communicated by radio. Still, Nasruddin preferred using technology he was familiar with.

He dialled the number.

Muratov let the phone ring twice, and then picked up.

'Good afternoon,' Nasruddin said.

'Good afternoon.'

'What is your answer?' the Englishman asked, his voice sounding more nervous than he would have liked.

Muratov allowed a few seconds of silence, just for the hell of it. 'We have accepted your demands,' he announced coldly.

'The prisoners are being released, and our programme printed in full in *Voice of the People*?'

'Yes'

'I am glad,' Nasruddin said. And he was. Another day and it would be over. As long as Muratov was not lying to him.

'The prisoners will arrive at the specified time in the helicopter you requested,' Muratov added.

The NSS chief sounded almost indifferent, Nasruddin thought, as if none of it mattered. It felt suspicious, somehow. 'We have heard your helicopters this afternoon . . .'

'None has approached within the two kilometres you specified.'

'Perhaps. I will just tell you again that if anyone, whether on foot or in the air, attempts to get any closer then one of the hostages will pay the price. Am I making myself clear?'

'Very.'

'It would serve no purpose for anyone to be hurt when we have already reached an agreement.'

'I understand.'

Nasruddin put the phone down, a huge smile spreading across his face. 'They agreed,' he told the others. 'No questions, no time-wasting, no demands to speak to one of the hostages. They just agreed. Our manifesto will be in the paper tomorrow morning, and the Imam Khotali will be here at eleven o'clock in the morning.'

'And the others?'

'All of them. They agreed,' he repeated, as if unwilling to believe it.

'Maybe they are saving the time-wasting for later,' Talib suggested pessimistically.

'Maybe we asked for too little,' Akbar retorted. When they had been planning the operation he had consistently argued for increasing their demands.

'Maybe it worked out exactly as we planned it would,'

Nasruddin argued. 'If they have no idea what a great man the Imam Khotali is, then they are bound to think exile will be just another prison for him.' He smiled. 'They cannot see the threat. Whereas losing out on development deals and tourist revenue – they know what a collapsing economy will do to their popularity.'

Talib let a rare smile cross his lips. 'It just seems too easy, somehow,' he said.

'You overestimate them,' Akbar said. 'What are they? Just a few communists clinging to power, that's all.'

That angered Talib. 'I fought them in Afghanistan, remember? And the power they are clinging to is real enough. We must stay alert, particularly tonight but tomorrow as well. The helicopter could be booby-trapped . . .'

'With their pilot flying it?' Nasruddin asked.

Talib gave him a look which told him not to be so naïve. 'And expect there to be "unavoidable delays". They are bound to test us at some point. I'm only surprised that they haven't already.'

His cousin might be right, and Nasruddin was more than prepared to act as if he was, but neither he nor Akbar had heard Muratov's voice. There had been more than a trace of repressed anger in the tone, as if the NSS boss was bitterly resenting every word he was forced to utter.

Nasruddin was convinced they had got it right. He and the others might be outlaws everywhere but Iran for the next few years, but during their exile there seemed every chance that Central Asia would fall to a resurgent Islam for only the second time in thirteen hundred years.

10

Brierley and Stoneham spent the last hour of the morning deciding what to take and the early afternoon gathering it all together. Their role was to be purely advisory, so equipping themselves fully for a combat role was obviously out of the question, but both men knew enough SAS history to realize that 'advisory' could be pretty loosely defined. Sometimes a teacher just had to show his pupils how something should be done.

For personal armament they agreed on a well-tested combination – a Browning High Power 9mm handgun and the silenced MP5SD variant of the Heckler & Koch sub-machine-gun. The latter had been specially fitted with laser guidance to pick out targets in darkened rooms. They also decided to take one Remington 870 pump-action shotgun. Men in purely advisory roles weren't usually given the task of blasting open doors, but who knew what might happen in a crisis?

By the same token they packed two sets of GPV 25 body armour, pouches for the spare ammo, stun and CS gas grenades, two AC100 helmets, and a pair of respirators fitted with CT100 Davies communications gear. Working on the assumption that the Uzbek authorities would lack such equipment, and that their hosts might be grateful to receive some, Stoneham added three more helmet-respirator combinations to the pile. 'It's like kids in the park,' he explained. 'If you turn up with a better ball then they tend to let you join the game.'

To Brierley's insistence on their including two abseiling

harnesses Stoneham retorted: 'Why not? We can hang outside the windows offering advice.'

Clothing was more of a problem. Uniforms were not to be worn, in case some local bright spark started wondering out loud what the SAS were doing in Central Asia. 'Dress like tourists,' Bourne had told them. But how did tourists dress?

'Camera, dark glasses and a straw hat,' was Brierley's suggestion.

'You'll cause a sensation. I'm wearing clothes. I take it it's hot in Samarkand at this time of the year.'

'Very. Which reminds me – mosquito repellent. And I assume we're not going to need any jabs for this one.'

Stoneham shrugged. 'Doesn't look like it. The whole business seems a bit iffy, if you ask me.'

'I'm glad I didn't.'

'*The Crow*,' Javid Zahid said, grinning at his cousin.

'Never heard of it,' Copley said.

'I have,' Ogley said surprisingly.

It was almost three-thirty, and seven of the eight male hostages were almost an hour into a game dreamed up by Copley. The first person had to think up a film beginning with A, the second one beginning with B, and so on. When Z was reached the next person started again with A, and anyone failing to come up with a title had a point deducted. X, they soon realized, had to be omitted.

Docherty and Nawaz Zahid were tied for last place. Ali Zahid had had the sense not to play.

The panel on the door abruptly swung back, a piece of paper was pushed through and the panel swung shut. The paper floated slowly to the ground.

They all looked at it. 'And I said we wouldn't get any post,' Copley said wonderingly.

Docherty walked over and picked it up. 'The government of Uzbekistan has agreed to our demands,' he read. 'Providing everything goes according to plan you will all be released around noon tomorrow. The Trumpet of God.'

There was a short silence, which Sam Jennings broke. 'Sounds good to me,' he drawled.

'It sounds bloody fantastic,' Copley agreed, then noticed the look on Docherty's face. 'What's the matter, Doc?'

'Nothing.' It just seemed too good to be true. You're frightened of hope, he told himself.

'You don't look happy,' Copley insisted. 'Don't you think this is kosher?'

They were all looking at him, Docherty realized. Whether he liked it or not he'd been elected guru of this particular bunch of hostages. 'They've no reason to lie to us,' he said, choosing his words carefully. 'But the authorities may have reason to lie to them. I think this may be good news, but I don't think we should let ourselves get too carried away.'

'You think the authorities are going to attack?' Javid asked.

'I don't know. We don't know what these people asked for. Maybe it was a price the government didn't mind paying.'

'We will know tomorrow,' Ali Zahid said, making one of his rare pronouncements.

'Aye, that we will.'

It was a pleasant, well-shaded dead-end street on the northern outskirts of the city. On one side of the road an irrigation channel carried water to the cotton fields stretching out across the plain. On the other, behind a line of cherry trees, sat a row of relatively new houses.

Marat walked up to the door of number eight, and rapped loudly. The uniformed militiaman beside him sucked his teeth and shifted from foot to foot as if he needed a toilet.

An adolescent Indian boy opened the door and looked up at him enquiringly.

'Please get your father,' Marat said, stepping forward into the archway that led through to the courtyard.

The boy disappeared through a doorway into the house. Soon several voices could be heard in conversation, and a minute or so later a man appeared through the doorway. He was about thirty-five, with hair thinning on top and gold-rimmed spectacles. He was used to deference, Marat decided.

'How can I help you?' he asked confidently.

'Are you Mahmoud Ali Shahdov?'

'Yes.'

Marat showed him identification, and asked the man if he knew Nasruddin Salih.

'He is my cousin. Why do you want to know?' he asked, suddenly looking worried. 'Has there been an accident?'

'No,' Marat said, thinking furiously. In his haste to interview Shahdov he had forgotten that no public mention could be made of the hijacking. Yet no serious questioning would be possible without revealing at least some notion of what Nasruddin was involved in. He realized that he had no alternative.

'Mr Shahdov, I must ask you to come with us to police headquarters. There are a number of questions we need to ask about your cousin's business . . .'

A little of the man's self-assurance ebbed visibly

away. 'The tour company. There is nothing wrong there, surely . . .'

'If you would come with us . . .'

'But can't . . .'

The uniformed man moved his hand to the butt of his holstered gun, as if he was following the script of a bad movie.

It worked.

'Of course. I will happily help you to clear up any misunderstanding. May I tell my wife? . . .' He waited for permission.

'Yes.'

A couple of minutes later the Volga was on its way back into the city, the Indian sitting nervously in the back seat. At the NSS building Marat led him down to the basement, where the cells and interrogation rooms were. Nowadays they were more often empty than not, but on each of his rare visits to this nether region Marat had thought he could smell the legacy of fear. Terrible things had been done in this basement, particularly during Stalin's reign of terror.

The Indian seemed to sense it too. He had not said a word since entering the Volga, and all his previous confidence seemed to have vanished. Maybe there was something wrong with his business, Marat thought.

'What business are you in, Mr Shahdov?' he asked.

'Import and export,' the Indian said. 'Mostly from Pakistan,' he added as an afterthought.

Marat ushered him into one of the interview rooms. It had no windows, one desk and two chairs. The lighting was provided by one glaring fluorescent tube.

Shahdov took the seat in front of the desk without waiting to be told. Marat sat down opposite him. 'Your cousin, along with several other men, has hijacked a busload of Western tourists. I would like you to tell me everything there is to know about Nasruddin Salih, starting with the first time you laid eyes on him.'

The rain had cleared away in Bradford, leaving the sun struggling to break through. Dave Medwin's next port of call was the local comprehensive, which all three Salih children had attended. He searched in vain for a legitimate parking space and settled for leaving the car smack in front of the main entrance.

The headmaster's secretary wondered out loud whether he had time for an interview, but then discovered a 'window of opportunity' five minutes hence. Medwin tried hard not to show too much gratitude. He didn't expect much out of this visit – from what he had gathered at his son's school, these days headmasters rarely even knew their pupils by name. Still, the school should at least have academic records.

Despite Medwin's fears, the headmaster turned out to be one of those ageing teachers of the old school who had somehow refrained from quitting the system in disgust over government mismanagement. He had taught Martin Salih history, both in the boy's second and fifth years at the school, and remembered him well.

'Partly of course because of the tragedy,' he admitted. 'It had a marked effect on his schoolwork, as you can imagine. Before it happened, he was one of the best pupils in his year. After it, well, he struggled. Not through any lack of intelligence, mind you. He was bright. He even worked. And he passed a couple of A levels, I think. But the will to excel was gone, the sense that it was worth it. I often used to wonder whether he would shake it all off one day, you know, rise like a phoenix from the ashes. I take it he hasn't, or at least not in one of those ways that society finds acceptable.'

'No, I don't think so,' Medwin admitted. He found himself liking this man. 'I'm afraid I can't tell you anything . . .'

'I'll probably read it in the papers, will I?'

'Maybe. Can I ask you . . .' He paused for a moment. 'This may sound crude, but when I'm trying to put a personality to a name I've often found it useful to differentiate between three types of intelligence. The first one is intellectual – you know, an ability to juggle ideas. Abstract thinking, I suppose you could call it. The second one is practical – knowing how to get something done efficiently. And the third is something like wisdom, which I guess you could define as knowing what's worth doing. Now when you say Martin Salih was intelligent, which of these did you mean?'

The headmaster smiled at him. 'He was intellectually bright, or at least as much as an adolescent boy can be. Let's face it, none of us know very much about anything at that age. But he certainly wasn't a dreamer – he was very organized as I remember. As for wisdom, well, I think I'm too young for that.'

Medwin thanked him and walked back down to find his car being scrutinized by a caretaker. 'You can't park there,' the man said.

'I know,' Medwin said, and climbed back in behind the wheel.

It wasn't even noon by the dashboard clock, but he was already feeling hungry. After the probation officer, he told himself – there were several nice pubs in Ilkley.

The trip across the moors, along a narrow, madly winding road which seemed to bring out the worst in his fellow-drivers, took a hair-raising half an hour.

Finding the probation officer's house took another fifteen minutes, thanks to some idiot constable giving him the wrong directions. He walked up the path to the door, rang the chimes, and stood admiring the roses in the front garden.

Norma Cummings opened the door. She had to be over sixty, but didn't look it. He explained why he was there, and she seemed to think about it before inviting him through the house and out into an equally attractive back garden. 'Take that one,' she said, indicating the blue deck-chair, 'the other one's not too sturdy.'

He sat down and waited for her to speak, but she seemed more interested in staring into space. 'Martin Salih,' he reminded her.

'I know,' she said. 'Well, I remember him, of course. I remember most of the younger ones. What exactly do you want to know?'

'Anything you remember.'

She seemed to find that amusing for a moment. 'He was a sensible boy,' she said at last. 'He knew that breaking windows was no answer to anything. He was simply angry, and with good reason. The police never caught the ones who killed his mother.' She looked at Medwin, almost as if seeing him for the first time. 'He did everything that was required of him while he was seeing me. But who knows where an anger like that can take someone?' she asked.

'Do you think he could kill someone?'

She made an exasperated noise. 'I met him when he was thirteen or fourteen. What is he now, about thirty?'

'Twenty-eight.'

She shrugged. 'And in any case, I don't think there are many people on this planet who are incapable of killing someone, provided they think they have a good enough reason. My late husband killed four Germans in the war – four that he knew about, that is. And he had no crisis of conscience about it.' She looked at him again. 'I know – I'm not helping. You want to know what Martin Salih is capable of, and I don't know. I don't expect he does either. All that distinguished him from other boys his age was his anger. Maybe he got over it. But then I suppose the fact that you're here asking me about him means that he didn't.'

'Will you have dinner with me?' Kennedy asked, as they waited at the side door of the airport building for the security people to let them in.

He was standing too close to her again. All afternoon he had either been brushing up against her breasts or staring at them.

'I'm busy this evening,' Nurhan said curtly, thinking that his mother had a lot to answer for.

'Tomorrow maybe.'

'Maybe.' Tomorrow she'd have two more oversexed Englishmen to deal with.

It had been a frustrating last couple of hours. Extracting the architectural plans of the hunting lodge from State Construction had been like trying to drag blood out of stone. She had finally been given a copy, but only after being given the runaround through several departments, with Kennedy following her around like a sex-mad puppy. She had half expected him to straddle a desk leg and start pumping.

Then Muratov had run her to earth with fresh instructions. There were to be no attempts to penetrate the terrorists' self-proclaimed security perimeter that night

– her unit was simply to stand by, where it was, in case the situation changed.

She had taken another helicopter ride out to the mountains – with Kennedy almost pinning her to the door – and climbed up the steep path to where Sergeant Abalov and two other men were keeping the lodge under observation. The NCO had shared her disappointment at the ban on taking a closer look that night. All fourteen hostages, he told her, had been brought out for exercise shortly before she arrived, the women first, and then the men.

Both she and Kennedy had examined the lodge through the binoculars, but there had been nothing new to see. She had guessed the hostages were being held in the communal sleeping quarters situated at both ends of the building's rear. Reaching one of these rooms would be difficult enough, let alone reaching both simultaneously. She had decided to work out a plan that evening. It might not be put into practice, but she could ask for the English experts' opinion of it when they arrived. And once the terrorists had flown away she could examine the lodge, and compare the reality to the plans. It would be an interesting exercise.

All she had to do first was get rid of Mr 'Call me Simon' Kennedy.

'Do you want to be dropped at your hotel?' she asked, as they walked across to the car.

'Oh, yes, I suppose so. Sure you won't change your mind about dinner?' he asked, with what she supposed was intended as a winning smile.

'Sorry, no,' she said, wondering why she found him such a turn-off. He was good-looking, probably clever. She had no reason to think he was unkind.

She felt his gaze on her thighs as she changed gear.

169

That was it, she thought. The man had no sense of her reality as another person. He had no idea that she noticed his stares, much less that she found them offensive. He probably knew she was a sentient being, but only because he could imagine her writhing in pleasure at his touch. She shuddered.

'Gets cool in the evenings, doesn't it?' he said conversationally.

She spent the next ten minutes concentrating on wending her way through the rush-hour traffic. At the Hotel Samarkand he climbed reluctantly out of the car.

'Your office at seven-thirty?' he reiterated.

'Right.'

'It would be easier if you stayed the night and drove me,' he said.

She smiled at him. 'Try tying an alarm clock to your cock,' she suggested, and pulled away in the car.

It probably wasn't what Zhakidov had meant by maximum co-operation, but at least she hadn't arrested the bastard for sexual harassment.

Back at the NSS offices the Operations Room had no messages from Muratov in Tashkent, but Nurhan found one from Marat on her desk. He was behind his own desk upstairs.

'What have you done with the Englishman?' he asked.

'Less than he deserved.'

'Uh-huh. Well, I need your say-so on an arrest warrant.'

'Whose?'

'One of Nasruddin's cousins. He's in a cell downstairs.'

'What has he done?'

'Nothing, as far as I can tell. But now he knows about the hijack, so I figure we can't afford to let him out until it's all over.'

'I suppose you had a good reason for telling him?'

'I had to give information to get some.'

'And what did you get?'

'The names of the two other Trumpet of God leaders. Talib Khamidov and Akbar Makhamov. Khamidov is another cousin, by the way.'

She grimaced. 'Nice family. Where did you get the first cousin's name from?'

'Our English friends. Do you fancy a drink?'

'What about these men – Khamidov and . . .'

'Makhamov. I've got the uniforms at work trying to find addresses, but with orders only to observe. I assume discretion is still more important than digging for new information, given that the deal is going through tomorrow?'

She agreed, feeling impressed.

'So how about the drink?' he asked.

'A short one.'

They walked downstairs together, and he waited while she countersigned the unfortunate Shahdov in for the night. Out on the pavement the streetlights were glowing against the fast-dimming sky. 'Where to?' she asked.

'I know a café not far from here,' he said. 'We can walk.'

He led the way, zigzagging through several blocks of the old Russian section to the edge of the Uzbek town. Halfway down a small dark side-street the barely lit façade of a small family restaurant suddenly appeared. The front room was empty save for two old men playing draughts, but the terrace at the back, which looked across the stony bed of a stream, was more populated.

Most of the clientele seemed to know Marat. 'Do you want to eat?' he asked her.

She suddenly realized she felt hungry. They ordered shashliks, and she asked for a glass of red wine. He settled for Coca-Cola.

'Have you stopped drinking?' she asked bluntly.

'It looks like it,' he said. 'Feels like it too.'

'Any particular reason? For the timing I mean.'

He grimaced. 'I think I finally realized one life was over, and it didn't seem like a very good habit to carry over into the next one.' He gave her a faint smile. 'Who knows? Maybe I'm punishing my wife. She spent years complaining about my drinking, so what better way to pay her back than pack it in the moment I'm living somewhere else.'

'Do you want her back?' Nurhan asked.

'No. We'd run our course and a bit more besides. I guess I'd like to have a better feeling about it all. That's the trouble when it all goes sour – the sourness eats up the past as well as the present.'

'I know what you mean,' she said, just as the food arrived. It tasted as good as it looked. 'How long has this place been here?' she asked him.

'Only a couple of months. I found it by accident one night.'

She took another mouthful, thinking that he wasn't what she had expected. Most men weren't, but usually it was more of a disappointment than a nice surprise. And he wasn't that bad looking, she thought. Maybe a bit overweight, but . . .

She pulled on the mental brakes. The man was a married alcoholic, for God's sake, and she was hardly the mothering kind. They were two colleagues sharing a meal in the middle of a joint operation. A good meal.

When the owner came to offer coffee she declined. 'I've got things to do,' she claimed. 'No, you stay,' she told Marat, 'I can find my own way back.'

And she did, occupying her mind with the tactics of a direct assault on the hunting lodge. Some sort of diversion at the front, she thought, while a dozen men abseiled down the sheer slope behind the lodge and mounted simultaneous assaults on the two side doors. They would need sledgehammers.

Back at the office she checked that no message had arrived from Muratov, and then called him. He told her that the printing presses were rolling out The Trumpet of God's programme, and that the four Islamic extremists were in a holding cell at Tashkent airport. They would be flown down to Samarkand the following morning.

Nurhan then spoke to Sergeant Abalov, who told her there had been no significant developments. The hostages and their takers were still in the lodge. Everything seemed to be going according to plan.

Which reminded her. She told Abalov to call her on the radio if anything remotely out of the ordinary occurred, and took the architectural plans of the lodge home with her. Once there, she spread them out on the only table, took a notepad and pen and started jotting down a timetable for an assault. One diversion tactic that occurred to her was for a telephone conversation to be in progress at the time.

That started her thinking about the wisdom of leaving the phone line open in the first place. She had mentioned her doubts to Zhakidov earlier that day, but his response had been to ask how else they were going to communicate with the terrorists. Which sounded like common sense.

The line was being tapped, of course, so there was no possibility of the terrorists using it to organize anything without the NSS knowing.

She walked out on to her veranda, and leaned on the balcony rail overlooking the still far from sleepy street, thinking that if the government thought they could come to some sort of compromise with the new Islamists then they were making a big mistake. There was no room for compromise between male gods and a society based, theoretically at least, on equal rights for women.

To pretend otherwise, she thought, staring at the slim cream crescent which had just cleared the rim of the southern mountains, was – in the words of the old Uzbek proverb – to throw seeds at the moon.

11

After consuming a pint and a Cornish pasty in one of Ilkley's ungentrified pubs, Dave Medwin drove back across the moors towards Bradford. It had turned into a beautiful day, with fluffy white clouds floating serenely across the blue sky.

He wasn't looking forward to interviewing the sister. Her family seemed to have suffered enough without all this. The whole business was like a wound that refused to heal.

Maybe if they had caught the bastard responsible it would have been different. Maybe not. He would be in his early thirties by this time, probably a father infecting his kids with the virus of hatred.

Medwin swerved to avoid an oncoming car that was straddling the centre of the road, and only just restrained himself from turning in pursuit and throwing the book at the bastard. But there seemed to be enough anger going around without him adding to it.

It was shortly after two-thirty when he reached the sister's house, a well-kept semi in a neat suburban street. Medwin sat in the car for a moment drinking in the air of contented conformism, and wondered for the thousandth time how he could both envy and despise the same thing.

He recognized the face of the woman who answered his knock from the photograph he had seen in Martin's flat. 'Sheila Salih?' he asked formally.

'Yes,' she said doubtfully. 'I am Sheila Majid now.'

175

Medwin showed her his ID, and asked if he could talk to her inside.

'What about?' she asked.

'Your brother Martin.'

'Has something happened to him?'

'He's in good health,' Medwin said noncommittally.

A shadow fell across her face, and she stepped aside to let him in. 'It's not very tidy,' she said.

It wasn't. The first downstairs room looked like a tornado had passed through, or maybe just a bunch of children. The second was festooned with adult mess – papers, mostly. It had that 'lived in', family look, Medwin thought.

She offered him a seat at the kitchen table, and sat down opposite him. Over her shoulder he could see a riotous garden sloping down towards an abandoned railway line.

'What has Martin done?' she asked.

He came straight to the point. 'It looks as though he has been involved in hijacking a bus full of tourists in Central Asia.'

She stared at him in disbelief for a moment, then sighed and looked down at the table.

He waited for her to say something, to ask for details.

'You know what happened to our mother?' she said at last.

'Yes.'

'The man was never caught,' she said, echoing Medwin's thoughts on the drive over. 'Not that catching him would have brought Mum back, but it would have been something, like a line drawn underneath it . . . you know what I mean? Like some sort of place to start again.' She looked straight at him, her dark eyes dulled by resignation. 'As it was, well, we all carry it. David has always buried himself in business, and ... well, I suppose I bury myself in my family. Martin found religion, but he was the youngest. And I thought ...' Her voice faded away, as if she was listening to another one inside her head. 'He was there,' she said at last. 'He opened the door.' She smiled faintly. 'We thought that he was coming out of it – building up his business.' Her eyes widened. 'Oh, but he couldn't have been planning ... what exactly has happened?' she asked.

Medwin told her most of what he knew, omitting only Sarah Holcroft's presence in the tourist party. 'The more we know about Martin, the better chance there is that the authorities out there can resolve things peacefully,' he said.

'Why?' she asked, as if it had suddenly occurred to her that this conversation constituted a betrayal of her brother.

'In negotiations like this it's important that people don't misunderstand each other,' he explained. 'For everyone's sake.'

She absorbed this, and seemed to find it made sense. But she didn't see what she could tell him. 'He's an honest man,' she said. 'If he says something, he means it.'

Medwin forbore from pointing out that the hostages had good reason to doubt such an assessment of Nasruddin's character. 'Is your brother a desperate man?' he asked, thinking as he did so what a ridiculous question it was. 'Do you think he wants martyrdom?'

She shook her head. 'I don't know. Part of him, maybe. But ... you should see him with the children. He loves them so much. Especially Meyra.' She shook her head.

'Do you think he could kill someone?'

Her eyes widened again, but only for a second. 'I don't know,' she said quietly.

In Samarkand, Kennedy was still chortling over Nurhan's farewell remark as he came down the hotel stairs in search of a belated dinner. He held no grudges over either the fact or the manner of her rejection, having long since accepted that some women found him attractive and some did not. Since he had yet to discover a better way of ascertaining which was which than simply asking, he took it for granted that every now and then a woman would say no. Luckily there had always been enough who said yes to provide him with ample compensation. Spotting the blonde woman from breakfast across the dining-room, he immediately began to wonder which category she fell into.

Annabel Silcott had been waiting almost two hours for him to appear, and the second of two coffees was only beginning its work of cancelling out the bottle of Georgian wine she had worked her way through. Still, here he was, and as far as she could work out no one else was likely to unravel the mystery of the missing tourists for her. There was nothing in the papers here, and nothing in the papers at home either, as she had verified at great length and expense by calling up an old and not very bright school friend. An offer of more money had failed to elicit more information from the receptionist. Kennedy was her last chance.

She waved an invitation for him to join her. He needed no second bidding. As in the morning, he was convinced he had seen her somewhere before, but couldn't remember when or where.

'Simon,' she said, having bolstered her shaky memory of his name by checking with the receptionist.

'Er, hi,' he said.

'Don't be embarrassed,' she said. 'We only met for a few seconds in Tashkent – at the Brunanskys', remember? I'm Annabel Chambers.'

So that was where. Though he still couldn't remember ever having spoken to her.

'You're with the embassy, right?'

He nodded.

'And I'm with UNERO,' she reminded him. 'The United Nations Equal Rights Organization. I'm here on a fact-finding tour, almost literally. Not so much gathering statistics as gathering the different statistical bases which different countries use, so that we can start making useful comparisons.' She smiled. 'Sorry, you probably don't need to know all this.'

'Not at all.' Kennedy smiled. 'UNERO does a great job.'

This was news to Annabel, who had spent part of the last two hours inventing it. Having once ruled out the possibility of approaching Kennedy in a journalistic role, she had decided that a little subtlety would be required. She had chosen to bank on him being one of those chauvinists who couldn't resist the chance to make a play for a feminist. And he was young enough and good-looking enough to spend a night with, if that seemed worthwhile or necessary.

His dinner arrived, and she accepted his offer of more wine. They talked about travel in general, Central Asia in particular, what a hole England was becoming, why Phil Collins was better off without Genesis, the problems of the New World Order. He was kind of sweet, she decided. Not someone you'd want to spend your life with, but fun for a few hours.

'What are you doing in Samarkand?' she asked, about an hour into their relationship.

'Just checking out a few trade possibilities. Nothing interesting. Do you fancy another drink upstairs? I've got some whisky in my room.'

'I've already had enough,' she said suggestively, 'but I'll come and watch you drink.'

They went up in the lift, somehow slipped an arm round each other in the corridor, and were twining tongues the moment his door was closed behind them. Feeling his cock swelling against her belly she undid his belt, pulled down the zip and lifted it free of his boxer shorts.

Kneeling down she ran her tongue lightly up the back, and then abruptly took it into her mouth. For a minute or more she had him moaning with pleasure, only ceasing the tongue massage when she suddenly felt him swelling even more.

'Oh, don't stop,' he said breathlessly. Janice wasn't half as good at this.

'If I don't stop, you won't have anything left to give,' she murmured, standing up and turning her back on him. 'The zip,' she said.

The dress fell to the floor, swiftly followed by her bra and panties. She lay back on the bed, arms above her head and legs bent. 'It's your turn, now.'

He kissed her breasts and stomach before obliging, using his own tongue on her clitoris with rather more delicacy than she had expected.

Soon she was stopping him, and asking if he had . . .

He pulled a condom out of nowhere like a conjuror with his rabbit, slipped it on with more ease than any other man she had ever known, and then lay on his back for her to climb astride him. As she eased herself to and fro with mounting pleasure, a voice in the back of her mind reminded her that this was just a bonus. She was here for a story.

They came together, just like in the manuals, and lay side by side in silence for a few moments. 'That was good,' he said, with a self-satisfied smile.

'Mmmm,' she agreed, managing to keep the surprise out of her voice. It was a long time since she had enjoyed sex anything like as much.

'We must do it again sometime. Like in the next half an hour.'

She snuggled closer. 'OK. But you have to tell me a story in the meantime. Have you seen any excitement since you came here?'

'No, not really.'

She decided to take the plunge. 'What about the disappearing tourists?' she asked casually.

He stiffened. 'What disappearing tourists?'

'Don't you know? Maybe it's not true, then. There's a rumour going round the town that some foreign tourists have simply gone missing or something. I must admit, when I saw you this morning – knowing you were from the embassy – I thought that must be why you were in Samarkand . . .'

He sighed and then smiled. 'I don't suppose it matters if you know,' he said. After all, the deal had been struck, and the hostages would be free by noon. 'A bunch of tourists were hijacked yesterday, but it's all been sorted out. The Uzbek government agreed to the demands and they're being released in the morning.'

'Who were they? Where are they? What were the demands?'

He told her.

'Lucky for the hostages it wasn't the British government in charge,' she said.

He grunted, muttered 'maybe', and hoisted himself up on one side. 'I'm ready,' he murmured, cupping one breast in his hand and leaning down to kiss the other.

Her body felt ready too, but her mind was not so easy to put on hold this time around. The grunt and the sardonic 'maybe' seemed to hint at deeper concealments, though what they might be she couldn't begin to imagine. Later, Annabel told herself, letting him in and crossing her legs behind his back.

This time they took a longer and slower route to the same lovely destination. Afterwards she lay there thinking how amazing it was that she could have such perfect sex with someone she didn't care a jot about. Amazing and somehow sad, she decided, because it meant that true love was just what she had always feared it was – a convenient lie.

She was about to share this revelation with her bed partner when he began to snore.

Instead she turned her mind to what he had confided to her. That grunt had been so . . . so definite. She should search the room, she decided. He wasn't going to wake up, and in any case what could he do if he caught her?

As it happened she didn't need to search very far. His jacket was lying on the floor on her side of the bed, and she managed to reach it without falling out. There was a notebook in the inside pocket, and just about enough light coming in through the window to examine it by. Half expecting to see 'Simon Kennedy, Secret Agent' written inside the front cover, she opened it up.

The first thing she found was a list of CDs, presumably ones he wanted to buy. The second was a list of armaments, together with numbers followed by question marks. Looking through it, the notebook seemed a dizzying mixture of the mundane and the stuff of which espionage thrillers were made. Had he really jotted down possible arms sales in a Ryman notebook? She supposed he had, and could think of no real reason why not. It just seemed ludicrous.

She reached the last used page. On it, the letters NSS had been written, followed by an address and Samarkand phone number, and underneath this the name Nurhan Ismatulayeva in capital letters. The word 'superwoman' had been doodled to one side.

Beneath this was what looked like an out-of-town phone number.

Lastly, he had written 'Tashkent arrive 0630, Samarkand around 0800.'

Annabel slid out from under the sheet, walked round the bed to where she had dropped her bag, and extracted a pen. With one eye on the sleeping Kennedy she copied out the address, phone numbers and times into her own notebook. She then retraced her steps, replaced his notebook and walked across to the open window. Outside on the balcony she leaned against the balustrade and looked out across the darkened city towards the silhouetted line of mountains. Maybe the tourists were out there somewhere, she thought.

For some reason she suddenly felt the need to fight back tears. It had to be that time of the month, she thought.

In one of the finished guest rooms Nasruddin Salih lay in the gloom on the double bed, fingers intertwined behind his head, staring at the faintly lit ceiling. He was thinking about the others, how they had all come together, how a plot born one evening of an idle conversation beneath a cherry tree had grown, so effortlessly and logically, into events which would change the lives of so many people.

Talib had been on one of his rare visits to the house of his uncle in the northern outskirts of Samarkand, and Nasruddin, staying with these far-flung members of his family while he organized the arrangements for his agency's planned tour programme, had met him for the first time. He had heard a lot about him, of course. Talib had disappeared on active duty in Afghanistan, and for several years no more had been heard of him. Then the break-up of the Soviet Union had made it possible for many Uzbek deserters to return home, and he had been one of them. He brought with him the wife and children he had acquired in Peshawar, and a stern new faith which made many in his extended family uncomfortable.

Nasruddin was not one of them. Though their lives up to that point could hardly have been more different, each had grasped hold of a purified Islam to pull them through when all else had failed. Almost from the first moment both knew that, whatever their differences in upbringing or culture or tastes, they were brothers of the soul.

The day of that first meeting had been important for another reason: Muhammad Khotali – whom both men had come to greatly admire over the preceding months – had finally been arrested by the government authorities. Nasruddin, Talib and Akbar Makhamov, who was there as a friend of Nasruddin's cousin's family, had discussed the case as the sun went down, and wondered out loud what they could do about it.

Akbar had an answer ready for them – direct action. He had spent several years in Iran as a religious student, and during that time had taken a basic training course in the use of weaponry and explosives. There was no point in trying to work within the system, he said – you could not expect justice from men who had no fear of God.

The three men had discussed possibilities, at first tentatively, and then with increasing seriousness. At one point in that evening's conversation they had all looked at each other, as if each man needed to be reassured that the other two were as serious as he was.

The preparations had taken nearly two years, but not because of any intervening difficulties. Everything had fallen into place with unerring certainty. Akbar had provided ideas, money and a meeting place, Talib the contacts necessary for buying weapons and the four other members of the unit. Nasruddin had offered up the victims.

It had all dovetailed so beautifully, he thought, lying there on the bed. As if it was meant to work. As if God knew that their hearts were pure and their aim true.

Bourne drove the two CRW instructors to Brize Norton, and from there a chopper took them south-east to RAF Northolt, where another car was ready to ferry them across the last few miles. At Heathrow a young man from Airport Security took them through a maze of empty corridors to a room overlooking the runways. They just had time to watch a Virgin Airbus lumber up and away before the door opened to admit a tall, dark-haired man in a navy pinstripe suit.

'Hanson,' he announced. 'Foreign Office,' he lied blithely. 'I'm here to fill in any gaps in your knowledge that you think need filling.'

Brierley and Stoneham took the invitation at face value, and pumped the MI6 chief for details of the hostage situation. He didn't seem to know much more than Bourne had, but promised that they would be fully briefed the moment they reached Tashkent by a member of the embassy staff. They would of course be liaising directly with the local security forces in Samarkand.

'Who are they?' Brierley wanted to know. 'Police or army?'

'A bit of both, really. Strictly speaking it's the old state KGB with a new name – the National Security Service they call themselves now, the NSS. Their Anti-Terrorist Unit are running the operation. With a woman in charge, I'm told.' His voice expressed mild disapproval.

Stoneham, remembering Rosa Klebb in *From Russia with Love*, was inclined to agree.

'I have a list of the hostages,' Hanson told them, reaching into his briefcase, 'with whatever information we've been able to gather about each of them.' He passed it over to Brierley. 'You'll notice that Sarah Holcroft's name has been changed to Sheila Hancock . . .'

'The actress?' Stoneham asked.

Hanson looked blank.

'The actress Sheila Hancock,' Stoneham repeated.

'I was unaware there was anyone famous by that name,' Hanson admitted. 'Is she very well known?'

'No, not very.'

'Well, in that case . . . the name was changed in case this list fell into the wrong hands, of course.'

'Meaning whose?'

'In the final resort, anybody's.'

'But surely the Uzbek authorities must have a record of visitors in their country?'

Hanson spreads his hands. 'Maybe not. I must admit to finding it hard to believe that no one has put two and two together, but . . .'

'Let's hope there's not a branch of the Sheila Hancock Fan Club in Uzbekistan,' Stoneham murmured.

'Indeed. You'll also find information on the terrorist leader – at least we assume he's the leader. That investigation is still ongoing, so you can expect updates while you are in Uzbekistan. Any other questions?'

Brierley could think of none.

'As far as Her Majesty's Government is concerned,' Hanson said carefully, 'your primary mission is exactly what we have agreed with the Uzbek President – a matter of sharing the expertise your regiment has gathered over the years in dealing with these situations. There is however a secondary mission here, as I'm sure you have already realized. If the hijackers become aware of Miss Holcroft's identity then they will presumably begin pressing their demands on us rather than the Uzbeks. In that instance the safety of Miss Holcroft will become a matter of national interest, and it may become necessary for you to take a more active part in the proceedings, perhaps even to the extent of acting without the sanction of your hosts.' He looked at the two SAS men, as if willing them to accept this in silence.

'Are you telling us that we should see the other hostages as second-class citizens?' Stoneham asked abruptly.

'No. Only that the hijackers will consider Miss Holcroft a first-class bargaining counter.'

Brierley and Stoneham exchanged glances. Suddenly it had all got a bit complicated.

It was nearly eight when Barney Davies got home. As usual the darkened house depressed him, and he went around turning on lights before pouring himself a whisky and making the choice between several equally uninviting microwave meals. Once the food was heating he put on a Miles Davis album and sat back to enjoy his drink.

Miles had hardly broken sweat when the thought occurred to Davies that he should ring Alan Holcroft. He didn't like the man, but he did know what it was like to worry about one's kids. And it would be hard to find a more worrying situation than having one taken hostage.

He dialled the first of the numbers he had been given, announced himself, and was told the Foreign Minister had gone home. He dialled the other number and the phone had hardly started ringing when Holcroft picked it up.

'I just thought I'd let you know that our men are on their way,' Davies said. 'They'll be in Samarkand around two a.m. our time, breakfast time there.'

'Thank you, I appreciate it,' Holcroft said.

He sounded terrible, Davies thought. 'There's no more news?'

'No. They should be freed sometime tomorrow morning – at around five a.m. GMT.'

'I hope it all goes OK,' Davies said.

'Thank you.' Holcroft put down the phone and stood beside it for a moment.

'News?' his wife asked anxiously from the doorway.

He shook his head.

'Are you sure we shouldn't be going out there?' she asked.

'It would look strange. Might even jog someone's memory and get Sarah recognized.'

She nodded, as much in resignation as agreement. Both of them stood there in silence, unknowingly sharing the same questions.

How was it possible to care this much about a daughter they had often wished would simply disappear from their lives? And what did such a level of self-deception say about who they were, both as parents and as human beings?

12

Uzbekistan Airways' Wednesday evening flight to Tashkent left Heathrow on time, and was soon travelling east at thirty thousand feet above the north European plain. Brierley and Stoneham had boarded the aircraft before any of the regular passengers, having avoided the usual trek through passport control and the X-ray machines. Their lethally loaded bergens had been stowed separately in the luggage bay.

The plane had turned out to be only half full. There was one tour group of academic-looking Brits, but most of the other passengers looked like they were on their way home, suitably loaded with duty-free purchases from the no longer forbidden West.

After dinner each SAS man grabbed a row of four seats and laid himself out horizontally. Rob Brierley tried his usual remedy for sleep, visualizing the waves sweeping in over the pebbles of the Brighton beach he had lived by as a boy. But he was pumping too much adrenalin, and instead of slipping into unconsciousness he found himself thinking about his late father.

Gerald Brierley had spent his entire adult life commuting to a solicitor's office in London. Day after day throughout his childhood Rob had watched him leave in the morning and return in the evening, and on three or four occasions he had seen his father's face reflect a lack of fulfilment in life that could hardly have been sadder. It was to avoid such a fate that Rob, against both his parents' wishes, had joined the army.

It was one of the three decisions he had never

regretted. The others had been to try for the SAS and to stay single.

In the seats behind him, Terry Stoneham was also having trouble getting to sleep. It wasn't the possibility of action ahead which was keeping him awake, but the troubling direction his life seemed to be taking. Lately he had come to realize how happy his life had always been, and how rare such uncomplicated happiness was. He had taken for granted what most people never had – a really happy childhood, good friends, an enjoyable job. Getting married to Jane and starting a family had been more of the same happiness, right up to the moment when she had told him about the boyfriend. The thought of them doing it together had been almost unbearable in itself, and he still didn't know how he had managed not to hit her, even though she was five months pregnant with his child. But the gradually dawning fear that maybe he had been equally blind in all sorts of other ways was even harder to take. His faith in himself had been shaken. Still was.

It was good to be getting away from it all for a few days. He tried switching his problems off, and started mulling over the penalties inflicted on his football team. It was all too fucking predictable, the way the game was run. Such a beautiful game, run by such ugly people. He started imagining himself on the pitch at White Hart Lane, the last minutes against Arsenal in a championship decider, Anderton on the ball, a deep cross, Sheringham nodding it back, and there was Stoneham smashing an unbelievable scissors kick past Seaman into the top corner . . .

There was light in the sky when he woke up, and his mouth was dry enough to tame a swamp. His grandad had always produced this phrase when he had a hangover, to the general mystification of all present. Stoneham leaned forward over the seat in front and found Brierley looking up at him. 'Another twenty minutes,' the older man said. 'I won't ask if you slept well – I could hear you doing it.'

'Gentlemen,' a steward said behind them, almost in a stage whisper. 'We'll disembark you immediately we land.'

He was as good as his word. A few seconds after the rear wheels of the Airbus hit the runway the steward was back, and ushering them past passengers who seemed uncertain whether or not they ought to feel indignant. The moment the plane stopped the door was opened, and a mobile stairway pushed towards it. On the tarmac two uniformed men and a redhead in dark glasses and white dress were waiting for them.

'Janice Wood,' she said, shaking each man by the hand. 'I'm the embassy secretary. 'These are the local NSS,' she explained. 'They don't speak English,' she added, as more hands were shaken. 'They're just here to make sure you don't do anything naughty between getting off one plane and getting on the other. It's OK to ignore them.'

The two SAS men's bergens were trundling down the mobile luggage chute. Once they had been reclaimed the three Britons were put in the back of a jeep-like vehicle, with one of the NSS officers chauffeuring them several hundred metres across the tarmac to where a small propeller plane was already warming up.

Janice told the NSS men 'two minutes' in Russian, and turned to the SAS men. 'There are no new developments,' she informed them. 'The released prisoners are supposed to reach the hijackers at eleven, and then the whole ensemble will fly on into Tajikistan, where the hostages are supposed to be released. Simon Kennedy will meet your plane in Samarkand, and he'll probably have the NSS operational commander with him. Her name is Nurhan Ismatulayeva, and she's the head of the Anti-Terrorist Unit. According to Kennedy she's a bit full of herself, but that probably just means she rejected him. OK?'

Stoneham smiled. Brierley didn't. 'What about the hostage situation?' he asked. 'What exactly has been done?'

'What do you mean?'

'Have they established that the leader can deliver what he says he can? Has the situation on the ground been contained? Have all the means of access been controlled? That sort of thing.'

'Sorry,' she said. 'No one's told me any of that. Simon will know.'

The NSS man was beckoning. The SAS men manoeuvred themselves and the bergens aboard the six-seater and strapped themselves in. The pilot, who looked about eighteen, took one look round at them, grinned inanely, and set the plane in motion. Within minutes Tashkent was spread out beneath them in the early-morning light. It looked more modern than either had expected.

'Where are you off to so early in the morning?' Diq Sayriddin's wife asked, as she watched him pull up his trousers and button his shirt. 'Business,' he said curtly, noticing how her nipples peeked over the rim of the sheet.

'What business?' she asked suspiciously, sitting up so abruptly that her large breasts wobbled violently.

'My own,' he said, turning away. Maybe he should insist she wore something in bed, he thought, or at least remember to put something on after he had satisfied his carnal desires.

Sayriddin made his way out through the house, past a disdainful stare from his father's wife, and into the street, where he turned left in the direction of the Bibi Khanum mosque. In the old market-place in front of the ruined mosque he found the kiosk already open, and several men sitting on the nearby seats reading their newspapers.

There was no excited discussion going on, and Sayriddin's heart sank – the government must have refused to print the manifesto. He bought a copy of *Voice of the People* nevertheless, found a place to sit that was as far from his fellow-readers as possible, and started thumbing through the thin pages.

And suddenly there it was – a full page of small type. Looking up to make sure no one was watching him, he extracted his own copy of the manifesto from his jacket pocket and started comparing the two.

They were the same. Exactly the same. He looked up to see if there were any signs of surprise among the other readers, and noticed two of them talking excitedly about something. It had to be the manifesto. This was the beginning, Sayriddin thought, and he was here to witness it. And he was a part of what was making it all possible.

He walked back past the kiosk and up Tashkent Street towards the public phone which Nasruddin had stipulated he use for both calls. This time he intended to obey – there was every chance they were tapping the line, and he didn't want this call traced back to the carpet shop.

At the phone he stopped and looked around before putting the money in. There were a few people on their way to work, but little traffic as yet, and no one seemed to be watching him. He inserted the coins, dialled the number and waited.

'Yes?' the familiar voice said.

'It's me,' Sayriddin said. 'It's in the newspaper. All of it. Word for word. A whole page.'

Nasruddin hung up, leaving Sayriddin with more than a slight sense of anticlimax, and turned to tell Talib and Akbar the good news.

Talib allowed himself one of his rare smiles. 'If all else fails then at least we have told the people,' he said.

'It will not fail,' Akbar said excitedly. 'We have won. Why would they print our words if they mean to renege on the deal? They have simply surrendered, that is all. They are weaker than we thought. We should have asked for more.'

The flight south, mostly across grey-brown desert, took little more than an hour, and it was not quite eight when the two SAS men had their first view of Samarkand's blue domes. Once more there was a reception committee of three, and it wasn't hard to pick out which of the men was English. Simon Kennedy, to both Brierley and Stoneham, looked like an identikit public school product, from the wave of hair dropping over one eyebrow to the boyish grin.

The woman, Stoneham thought, looked like she had just sat down on something pointed. The other man had the slightest of ironic smiles, but otherwise looked vaguely bored.

Which was not far from the truth. Marat's interest in the art of dealing with hostage situations was a purely practical one, and since the only such situation available would soon be history, he would rather have been getting on with tracking down the identities of all the hostage-takers. But Nurhan had asked him to accompany her, mostly, he suspected, to avoid having to cope alone with her breast-fixated Englishman. She had told him about Kennedy's staring, and Marat had been curious to observe the phenomenon in action. But so far Kennedy seemed to be ignoring her, lost in some reverie of his own.

Nurhan watched the new arrivals step down from the plane with a mixture of apprehension, irritation and curiosity. They certainly didn't look like their fellow-countryman, though exactly where the difference lay was hard to pinpoint. Maybe it was just that they had other things on their mind than sex.

'Tell them we are going first to my office,' she instructed Kennedy.

'We both speak Russian,' Brierley interjected. 'Though not perfectly,' he added.

She smiled at them, and Stoneham instantly changed his mind about her. 'Good,' she said. 'But it is a foreign language for me, also. So we are even.'

She introduced herself and Marat, and led them across to a large black car. The bergens fitted into the roomy boot, and the three Englishmen shared the back seat. Nurhan drove.

'Have you been here before?' she asked as they swung on to a four-lane highway.

'No,' both replied at once.

'Well, once the situation is cleared up you must see the sights. And I would like to talk with you about the business we are both in, if there is time.'

'Of course,' Brierley said. It all sounded thoroughly wrapped up, he thought. Which, no doubt, he should find a cause for rejoicing. But that was like expecting firemen to wish there were never any fires – fine in theory, but anyone with expertise could hardly help wanting the chance to demonstrate it in practice.

Through the window he noticed what looked like a field full of levelled ruins, and beyond that a sloping line of buildings, some with blue domes.

'That's the Shah-i-Zinda,' Marat explained. 'They are mausoleums from the time of Tamerlane.'

Once more the male hostages were led out through the lodge to the improvised exercise yard. This was the third time they had been brought out, and the fourth would hopefully be the last. The scenery was stunning, but then the view from Colditz had probably been impressive too.

Docherty had to admit that, as jails went, this had been a pretty luxurious one. The beds were comfortable, the food, though restricted to soup, bread and tea, had been both tasty and nutritious. A new set of clothes would have been great, but the guards always seemed prepared to bring more water. It was how an Englishman would do a hijacking, Docherty decided – politely, courteously, as if it wasn't really happening. But then of course Nasruddin was an Englishman, and he seemed to be in charge.

The other male hostages seemed to be bearing up well. Though the general upbeat cheerfulness couldn't quite conceal the underlying anxiety, everyone was trying, even Ogley. The previous evening had been a long one, despite the draughts tournament. Imran Zahid had won with ease.

This morning there had been a general reluctance to talk, as if each man was busy gathering the strength to cope with potential disappointment. Even now, all eight of them were shuffling around the space in front of the lodge in silence.

In a couple of hours, Docherty thought, things would change. Either it would be all smiles, or the situation would start to deteriorate. The hostages, after all, would not be the only disappointed ones if the deal fell through. Their captors would have to start making tough decisions.

Docherty looked down the valley, thinking that there had to be men out there now, watching them through binoculars or telescopic sights. Someone out there would be working on a plan of how to storm the lodge, and Docherty didn't envy him. The hijackers had chosen well – the site would be a bastard to approach unobserved. It would have to be after dark, but even then . . . There had been a new moon the night before, and a clear sky. Anyone trying to scale the cliff behind the lodge would be a sitting target to anyone at the front. Snipers would have to take the guards out first with silenced rifles.

And then the hostages would have to do whatever needed doing to keep them alive. That might be to hug the floor, or it might be to try to disarm whoever came to kill them. There was no way of knowing until the time came.

He needed some sort of weapon, no matter how crude. On the next circuit he went down on one knee, and as he pretended to tie his shoe managed to pocket a smooth, round stone. It wasn't much, but Docherty hadn't lasted twenty years in the SAS without working out that the difference between life and death was often measured in inches. And when it came down to it, aiming a gun had to be easier if stones weren't flying past your head.

The two SAS men were a very different proposition from Kennedy, Nurhan thought, as she sipped her black coffee and watched them work their way steadily through breakfast. There was a sense of self-containment about them both, almost a glow of self-assurance. It might be all front, of course, and she would probably never know the truth of the matter, but they certainly gave an impression of men who knew exactly who they were and what they were doing.

Sitting across from her, Terry Stoneham was thinking that the SAS had taken him to some pretty weird places, and that the old KGB canteen in Samarkand had to qualify as one of the weirdest. The room itself was unremarkable – they could have been in England but for the slowly whirring fans overhead and the unfortunate lack of Weetabix– but the combination of cruelties which it represented had to be unique. Breakfast courtesy of Tamerlane and Stalin!

He had to admit that Major Ismatulayeva didn't look much like Rosa Klebb, but there was no way of knowing whether she had a retractable poison blade concealed in the toecap of her shoe.

'So shall I fill you in on what's been happening?' Simon Kennedy asked in English.

'I think the Major is probably the best person to bring us up to date,' Brierley said diplomatically in Russian. He had taken an instant aversion to the MI6 man, and wasn't making much of an effort to disguise the fact.

Nurhan smiled and did as Brierley asked, tracing the crisis through from the first telephone message to the present, and, to the Englishman's surprise, openly expressing anger at her government's capitulation to the terrorists' demands. Of course, he realized, she probably didn't know how much pressure London had exerted on Tashkent. From her point of view, the government's reaction must have seemed nothing short of spineless.

'How were communications established at the beginning? I mean, who contacted who, and how?'

She told him about the first call from someone in Samarkand.

'I wonder why,' he asked himself out loud.

'To keep us guessing,' Marat volunteered.

'Did it?' Stoneham asked.

'Oh yes. It was about sixteen hours before we found them.'

'Interesting,' Brierley murmured. They must have known that they would be found, and that staying undetected, even for sixteen hours, would not make a great deal of difference. Nasruddin Salih – assuming he was the terrorist leader – was obviously a man who took any slight edge that the situation offered. Brierley thought about the new information from Bradford which the woman had passed on to them in Tashkent. A map-drawer. Precision. Care. 'The telephone line,' he asked, 'is it still open? To the rest of the system, I mean.'

'Yes, it is,' Nurhan said. 'They said they needed independent confirmation that their programme had been printed in the newspaper. We offered to deliver . . .'

'But they realized you could have doctored a copy.'

'Exactly. So one of their supporters phoned them this morning, from a public phone in the city.'

'It might be wise to cut it off now.'

'I suggested it, but my boss decided that it wasn't worth taking any action which could be considered hostile.'

Brierley nodded. 'Fair enough.'

'So, what do you think?' Kennedy asked them, with the air of someone who had just consulted a fortune-teller.

Brierley smiled. 'Not a lot, yet. There are obviously two separate problems in situations like this – how to conduct the negotiation and how to rescue the hostages when the negotiations break down. In this instance there haven't really been any negotiations to conduct – not yet anyway. And to evaluate the rescue option we need an on-site inspection.'

'When you're finished, the helicopter's in the car park behind the building,' Nurhan told him.

Brierley and Stoneham both gulped down the rest of their tea and got to their feet. 'Lead on,' Brierley said.

She did. As the pilot started up the engine and the three Englishmen climbed aboard, she shared a few words with Marat, who raised a hand in farewell and walked back into the building. Both Brierley and Stoneham found themselves wishing that it was Kennedy they were leaving behind.

The flight took less than half an hour, but packed a lot of scenery into the available time. Views of the city gave way to wider vistas of the green Zerafshan valley, and these to desert before the land crumpled and climbed beneath them into a wilderness of mountains.

The helicopter landed in a flat clearing about the size of a tennis court. Two lorries stood to one side, and several young soldiers were sitting in the shade their awnings offered. A dirt road wound up from the valley below, skirted the clearing and climbed out of sight around a protruding ridge some hundred metres further up.

'Some of my unit,' Nurhan explained, gesturing towards the lorry. 'They're on an eight-hours-on four-hours-off duty cycle.'

They looked fit enough, Brierley thought.

Nurhan led the SAS men up the steep path towards one of the observation points, talking into her walkie-talkie in Uzbek as she did so. Sergeant Abalov met them, and they all squatted in a circle as he brought her up to date. She translated into Russian for the SAS men. Both the men and the women hostages had been allowed their half hour of exercise, the latter having been taken back in not much more than twenty minutes before. Nothing unusual had occurred – the two terrorists standing sentry on the road were still there, and were relieved, one at a time, every three hours. The other five remained indoors, except at exercise time, when one would stand guard in front of the lodge.

The observation point was fifty metres further on. Abalov led the way, with Nurhan and the two SAS men following the Uzbek down a rocky gully. At its end the path ducked through a narrow gap between two huge boulders, and a few metres further on came to an abrupt halt behind what looked like a pile of flat rocks some local giant had arranged in a spare moment. Between the second and third from the ground a natural slit some three inches high and four feet wide presented a fine view of the valley's upper reaches.

Some two kilometres away Brierley could see the long, low building, its back up against the cliff wall at the valley's head. Looking through the binoculars, he could make out more details of the structure itself, but nothing of what might be going on inside. They would have to get a good deal nearer than this, Brierley thought. He turned his attention to the intervening space below, which offered a veritable labyrinth of cross-cutting ridges, crevasses and jumbled rocks. There was plenty of cover, he thought, but it was all a long way below the altitude of the lodge. To get near enough for a proper eyeful they would have to practically push their noses up against the front windows.

As Stoneham took his turn with the binoculars, Brierley looked at Nurhan's copy of the architectural drawings and asked her about the building. She told him its history in a tone which suggested she would rather not entertain questions. It occurred to Brierley for the first time that someone like this – an ex-KGB, Uzbek, apparently intelligent woman – might be having an interesting time making sense of where her loyalties lay in post-Soviet Uzbekistan.

13

After Kennedy had left the room, presumably to meet whoever was arriving at 'around 0800', Annabel Silcott had started going through the rest of his belongings. She found nothing, which at least went a little way to restoring her faith in British Intelligence. Back in her own room she ran as deep a bath as the hotel's plumbing would allow and lay in the water wondering what to do next. Basically, she only had two things to work with: the address with the phone number and the phone number without the address. First she would have to find out who or what the NSS was. It sounded vaguely educational.

She was rummaging through her suitcase, trying to decide what to put on over her underwear, when she suddenly remembered that in Kennedy's story the tour party had been hijacked in the middle of a day trip. So where was their luggage? Still somewhere in the hotel, was the first answer that came to mind.

She put on baggy black trousers and a black T-shirt and went downstairs, hoping against hope that the same receptionist would be on duty. He was, albeit surrounded by an incoming tour group. After extracting all the cash from her money belt in the toilet, she browsed in the souvenir shop in the lobby until the new party had all been dealt with, then walked over and came straight to the point. 'I'll give you a hundred dollars to let me see the missing tourists' luggage,' she said.

He wasn't slow on the uptake. He turned, picked a key off the rack, and placed it on the counter. '*Two* hundred in dollar bills,' he said. 'And if the police ask I shall say you must have stolen the key.'

She counted out four of her five fifty-dollar bills and took the key. He pocketed the notes and said: 'Second floor.'

She walked up and found the room without difficulty. On the outside it looked like any other of the twelve doors leading off the corridor, but the room inside looked more like a left luggage office. Belongings had been gathered in neat piles, and atop each one sat a passport. Annabel went through the names one by one, and then the photographs inside. Inside the one bearing the name Sarah Jones she found the face of Sarah Holcroft.

When the women were let out for their half hour's exercise Isabel found Sarah walking by her side. This wasn't a great surprise – she had the feeling that the young woman had been wanting to talk to her for some time, and there were certainly no chances of a private conversation in their room.

For a few minutes they talked about their situation, and Isabel, struck by how level-headed Sarah seemed, realized that she too had been half expecting the degenerate airhead that the tabloids had presented to the world. Being Isabel, she took the bull by the horns, and asked Sarah if the newspapers had made it *all* up.

'I'm afraid not,' was the rueful answer. 'I did a lot of stupid things, and I didn't make much effort to do them in private. In fact' – she smiled – 'I probably did them in public on purpose. But on the other hand, if

I had slept with as many men as the papers said, I would never have been off my back.' She laughed, but there was a brittle edge to it. 'I've slept with about fifty men,' she suddenly confided. 'Do you think that's a lot?'

Yes, Isabel wanted to say, but who was she to judge? She and her friends might have been revolutionaries but they had also been pretty puritanical with it. There had been none of that 'free love' so popular in the northern hemisphere's sixties. Sarah had probably been sexually active for about eight years, so fifty lovers equalled about one every couple of months. Put that way . . .

'No,' she said, 'but it doesn't sound much like a recipe for happiness either.'

'It isn't, but I guess happiness wasn't what I was looking for then. I don't know. Did you read the orgy story last year?'

Isabel admitted she had.

'That was partly true. It was a party, and we all got very high, and I ended up in bed with two men. That wasn't a recipe for happiness either, but it was fun. And it didn't do anyone any harm. The press . . . I mean, it's all double standards. Men are always fantasizing about going to bed with more than one woman.' She sighed. 'But you're right – it's fun but it gets pretty empty after a while.'

This wasn't a stupid woman, Isabel thought. A damaged one perhaps, but not beyond repair. 'So what are you going to do with the rest of your life?' she asked.

'Something positive. I've given up drugs, and I've decided to be more choosy when it comes to men. You know, I think I was afraid to say no before, as if somehow I didn't have the right to. Does that sound crazy?'

'No, it doesn't. It sounds like you had a really low opinion of yourself.'

'I did. I still do, but maybe not so much, and I have found something I really want to do. You know, in London there's all sorts of fabric shops these days – Chinese, Indian, Turkish, Latin-American, hundreds of them, all specializing in one culture. Well, I had the idea for a shop selling fabrics from all around the world, just the best from each place, you know.'

'Sounds great.'

'But that's not all. I want to get local co-operatives to supply the shop, so that the women who actually make them share in the profits. I don't want it to be just a money-making thing – we have enough of that in my family already. But that's where Brenda and I were the other day in Tashkent, when the rest of you were at the History Museum – we went to see these people whose names I'd been given. And they were really interested.'

Her eyes were shining now, and she was looking at Isabel with a need for reassurance which was almost heart-breaking.

'It sounds fantastic,' Isabel said.

After watching the helicopter drift away across the old city Marat had climbed into his car and driven out to the airport. The plane from Tashkent had arrived half an hour earlier, and the four released prisoners were being held in an ordinary office in the airport's administration building.

It was almost half-past ten. Marat gave the order for

them to be taken to the transport helicopter which was waiting on the tarmac nearby, and watched as they filed out of the building, blinking in the sunlight. Muhammad Khotali was the second in line, a tall man in traditional clerical garb, with deep-set eyes under bushy black eyebrows. Marat had seen him in person only once, through a one-way window at the post-arrest interrogation, some two years before. He had been reluctantly impressed at the time, without really knowing why. There was something about those eyes, the intelligence that filled them and the honesty they seemed to promise, even when the mouth was spouting Stone Age nonsense. The man had charisma, all right. In dangerous quantities.

Marat followed the four men across to the helicopter, and watched them received into its cavernous belly. Uzbekistan's new flag had recently been painted on the machine's sides, but the two pilots were both Russian. Marat recognized the senior of the two from his time in Afghanistan.

'Hey, Marat,' the man said with a smile. 'I don't think much of the cargo you've given us.'

Marat grimaced. 'Join the club,' he said drily. 'You're clear about what you have to do?'

'Land outside the lodge, pick up the bad guys and their hostages and take them where they want to go.'

'That's about it.'

'So I can't just drop these four out at six hundred metres?'

Marat sighed. 'Not this trip.' He looked at his watch. 'You'd better get going. We don't want them getting nervous.'

'If you'll step out of the way . . .'

Marat did so. As the giant helicopter strained its way into the air, he called Nurhan on the radio link to say it was on its way. Then he stood watching it dwindle into the south-eastern sky, before walking back across the tarmac towards his car. Tonight they would have to play host to the SAS men, he thought, but maybe tomorrow she would have dinner with him again.

Isabel could remember that last morning in Córdoba with the glass manufacturer. The deal had been struck, but he had grown more terrified as the hour agreed for his release had approached. As they left him there, still blindfolded, for the authorities to find, he had been sobbing with fright.

Now she understood why. The anticipation of release was a good feeling, a safe feeling, but the actuality represented a plunge back into the unknown.

It was almost a quarter to eleven, and it was hard not to simply lie there listening for an approaching helicopter. Instead, she heard the distant ringing of a telephone. That puzzled her for a moment, but she supposed there had to be some means of contact between the hijackers and the authorities, and searching her memory she could see the line of telephone poles which led away down the mountain road.

'Yes?' a male voice asked.

'Hello, who is that?' Annabel asked.

'Who are you?' Nasruddin answered in English. He shrugged at Talib to show that he didn't know who it was.

She found his accent both strange and familiar. 'My name is Silcott. I'm a journalist. If you are who I think you are I would like an interview . . .'

'I think you have a wrong number,' Nasruddin said. It sounded ridiculous, but it was the first of several things that came into his mind. The second was that talking to a journalist would constitute a breach of their agreement with Muratov. The third was to wonder whether that mattered.

'Surely you can only benefit from publicity,' Annabel insisted. His answering in English had been the giveaway. These had to be the people.

Nasruddin didn't offer a reply, mainly because he couldn't decide on what it should be.

'Are you in contact with the British government?' she asked, taking his silence as assent.

'No,' he said automatically.

'No?' she echoed, astonished. Why would the kidnappers of the Foreign Minister's daughter not be in contact with the British government?

'You are holding Sarah Holcroft?' she asked.

Nasruddin almost dropped the phone. He had known all along that Sarah Jones's face was familiar, and now he knew why.

'Are you intending to ask a ransom?' Annabel asked. The man at the other end sounded educated enough, but he didn't seem to have much idea of what he was doing.

Nasruddin put the phone down, and instinctively took it off the hook. The motion reminded him of that evening years before, when the phone calls had poured in after his mother's death, half of them offering sympathy, half expressing regret that the whole family hadn't burned with her.

'What is it?' Talib asked.

'It's . . .' Nasruddin's mind was racing ahead. This changed everything. 'The women hostages, the younger blonde girl,' he said. 'You remember her?'

Talib nodded.

'She is the daughter of the British Foreign Minister . . .'

Talib looked astonished. 'But how?'

'She's travelling under a different name. The girl's famous in Britain, or at least she used to be.'

'Why didn't you recognize her?'

'I don't know. I did think I'd seen her face before but . . . well, she has a reputation for drugs and promiscuity, and this girl didn't seem like that.' Nasruddin ran a hand through his hair. 'I still find it hard to believe.'

'It explains a lot,' Talib said.

'What do you mean?'

'Why they have been so accommodating. The British have been leaning on our government.'

Nasruddin thought about it. 'Or bribing them,' he suggested.

'Probably both. The question is, what do we do with this new knowledge?'

'Yes.'

The two men looked at each other, each knowing what the other was thinking. It was Talib who voiced it. 'We can ask for anything,' he said.

It was four minutes to eleven when Nurhan and the two SAS men saw the helicopter, and almost two minutes later before they heard the asthmatic scrape of its rotor blades echoing up the valley. The craft flew almost directly in front of them, before climbing to a hovering position above the improvised landing site in front of the lodge. Then slowly it settled to the ground.

The watchers waited for the hostages to be led out.

One minute passed, and another, and suddenly the door opened and what looked like a group of four males was hurried across the space and into the helicopter. The watchers' eyes returned to the door, expecting the next batch, but before anyone else could emerge the craft was lifting off and climbing rapidly into the sky.

'What the fuck?' Stoneham said quietly.

'What indeed,' Brierley agreed, just as a call came in on Nurhan's radio. They watched her eyes narrow and her lips purse as she listened, and knew the news wasn't good.

'That was my boss,' she explained. 'The bastards have reneged on the deal. They're releasing the four Muslim hostages, but not the others. Apparently they've found out that one of the women is the daughter of the British Foreign Minister. I take it you already knew that.'

'Yes, but . . .'

'It's all right,' she said. 'It doesn't take a genius to work out why your government didn't want anyone to know.'

'Did they say anything else?' Brierley asked.

'No. Only that they'll present a new set of demands sometime later.'

'They probably still can't believe their luck,' Stoneham said.

'Probably. Anyway, we're back to square one,' Brierley said. 'And while we're waiting for Chummy and his friends to work out what they want, I think we might as well start making some plans. Under your authority, of course, Major.'

'Of course,' she agreed drily. 'Exactly what do you have in mind?'

Bakhtar Muratov's conversation with Nasruddin had been not much longer than Nurhan's précis suggested. The terrorist leader had begun by announcing he was cancelling the prisoners-for-hostages exchange. He had been deceived, he said, as to the true identity of one of their captives. Nevertheless he would release four of them, along with the 'illegally imprisoned' four Islamic leaders.

When Muratov had expressed ignorance as to the deception, Nasruddin had not believed him. 'If you did not know the girl was the British Foreign Minister's daughter, then why did you accept our demands so easily?' he asked scornfully.

Because we were bribed to do so, Muratov thought, but didn't say so out loud. No wonder the British government had been so keen to abandon its own principles.

Nasruddin had moved on to practicalities. 'Our new demands will be addressed to both the Uzbek and British governments,' he said. 'I will talk to both you and the British Ambassador on this line at six o'clock this evening.'

And that had been that. Bakalev was not going to be pleased, Muratov thought, as he strolled the short distance that separated his flat from the President's office.

He was right. Bakalev's face grew harder and harder as Muratov told him what had happened, until the NSS boss had visions of it cracking under the stress. In actuality, the President uttered one explosive 'fuck!' and slumped back down into his Swedish desk chair.

There followed several moments of uncomfortable silence.

'How did they find out?' Bakalev asked eventually.

'We don't know.'

'Fuck,' the President said again, more quietly this time. 'So we print their ludicrous programme . . . Have you got any reports yet on how it was received?'

'Not yet.'

'I want to see them as soon as you get them.' He slumped even further into the seat, and massaged his chin. 'It certainly explains why the British were so generous,' he said sarcastically. 'A ransom for a princess,' he muttered.

Muratov said nothing.

'You say they're busy dreaming up new demands. What else can they ask for? How many more zealots do we have in prison?'

'Maybe two hundred. But none worth feeding. We can give them all away without losing any sleep.'

'OK,' Bakalev agreed. 'What else?'

Muratov shrugged. 'Money. More manifestos. A TV show. Your resignation . . .'

Bakalev grunted. 'When I quit it'll be because I want to.' He looked at Muratov. 'And anyway, I think we've offered these bastards more than enough already.'

'The English may offer us more.'

'It wouldn't be worth it. There's a limit to how much damage you can cover up with money.'

He was probably right, Muratov thought. Any more concessions and it would be hard to avoid getting stuck with a fatal reputation for weakness. 'They'll have demands on themselves to think about,' he said. 'And I can't see them being able to concede very much given their stated policy on terrorism.'

'You mean, up until now they could let us do all the conceding?'

'Of course. But now it may well be different. If the new demands can be met in private, then that's one thing. But if they're the sort which involves publicity then they'll have to live up to their own principles . . .'

214

'Are the terrorists still saying they don't want publicity?' Bakalev interjected.

'They didn't say one way or the other. They may not have made up their minds yet. It's hard to say . . .'

'Cut them off,' Bakalev decided abruptly. 'Tell them the line's down, or someone acted without authority. Just keep a two-way line open between us and them. Whatever. And get hold of the British Ambassador. Be nice to him. I don't want the British to think we're being anything less than completely co-operative. Give their two military experts a free hand. If it becomes necessary for us to go in, I want the British in there with us, whether they like it or not. If there's a fuck-up they can take the blame, at least as far as the world is concerned. Maybe we can even get them to believe it.'

'It might put the trade deal in jeopardy.'

'I know, but that's too bad. I still want it, but not if it's going to cost me the country.'

Back at the NSS HQ Marat found a message on his desk. He left the building again and drove a few hundred metres down Tamerlane Prospekt to the telephone exchange. In a small basement room he found the two-man unit whose job it was to monitor the hijackers' phone line.

'Listen to this, boss,' one of the men said, and flicked a switch on the reel-to-reel tape recorder.

'Yes?' asked a voice, which Marat instantly recognized as the terrorist leader's.

'Hello, who is that?' an unfamiliar woman's voice asked in English.

'Who are you?' Nasruddin Salih answered in the same language.

'My name is Silcott. I'm a journalist . . .'

215

Marat listened to the rest of the conversation, noting the shock in Nasruddin's voice when he learnt of the female hostage's real identity. Then he phoned the NSS operations room and asked them to check the journalist's name against the hotel register.

She had been staying at the Hotel Samarkand for two nights.

He was there five minutes later, asking the receptionist if she was in. The man looked vaguely worried by the question, but his answer was definite enough. She had gone out.

'Any idea where?'

'No. Maybe she went to meet the Englishman,' he added, half-consciously trying to divert attention away from himself.

'Which Englishman?' Marat asked patiently.

'Mr Kennedy.' The receptionist managed a leer. 'They got quite friendly last night,' he offered by way of explanation.

Great, Marat thought. The man really was as big a fool as he looked. And since he was up in the mountains with Nurhan the journalist could hardly be with him. So where the fuck was she? And who else was she busy telling?

After putting down the phone Annabel Silcott had been momentarily appalled by what she had done. But there was no way to take it back, and no use in crying over spilt secrets. And in any case, the whole business was ridiculous. She should never have been able to pick up a phone and ring a terrorist group holding hostages – the authorities needed their heads examining for letting something like that happen.

She sat down on a convenient bench, and watched

the morning traffic go by. It all seemed so ordinary, so mundane.

What was she to do? This was the biggest story that had ever come her way, and there must be some way for her to make use of it. But how? She could ring the story in to any of the British dailies on the phone right in front of her, but that wouldn't do much for her reputation. Samarkand would instantly fill up with competing journalists from all over the place, and she would be just one more of them, dutifully taking down whatever the official spokesman chose to tell them.

There had to be some way of keeping the story to herself. Maybe she should wait, keep in touch with what was happening through Kennedy. If the authorities managed to keep the lid on right up to the end, then that would be the time for her to produce her investigative masterwork. Blow the whole thing wide open without risking any lives.

That was the way to go. Feeling pleased with herself, and even vaguely proud of letting her better nature win out over the demands of instant gratification, she walked briskly back to the hotel, hoping that Kennedy had returned.

She was crossing the lobby when a man blocked her way.

'You will come with me,' Marat said, showing her his ID.

'But . . .'

'You are under arrest.'

To say it had been a disappointment was definitely an understatement, Docherty thought to himself. They had been informed in writing by Nasruddin of an unspecified deceit on the part of the authorities, and The Trumpet of

God's consequent decision to release only the four Muslim prisoners. The four Zahids had been understandably relieved, but also unmistakably embarrassed by their good fortune. Ali said he would pray for them, and Nawaz promised to bombard the British government with demands for action. The two teenagers earnestly shook hands with those they were leaving behind, and Javid offered to leave them his *Wisden*.

That had been nearly three hours ago, Docherty thought, looking at his watch. For most of that time he, Mike Copley, Sam Jennings and Charles Ogley had been immersed in their own gloomy thoughts. Somehow, there didn't seem much worth saying.

It was the not knowing that was hardest. Not knowing what was happening out there, not only as regards their own situation, but in the world at large. Docherty had never been addicted to news, and in fact enjoyed few things more than isolating himself in some beautiful spot – the Hebrides came to mind, or Chiapas in Mexico – and just letting time flow by. By choice, that was. What a difference it made when someone did the choosing for you. Then being cut off began to seem . . . well, like the prison it was. You were trapped inside yourself, and being human was about making contact with others . . .

Anything could be happening out there. Another Chernobyl, a cure for AIDS. Celtic might have signed a player who lived on the same planet as McStay.

His reverie was interrupted by the swelling drone of a helicopter. Judging from the noise it was the same one. A big transport chopper. A 'Hip' probably, if he remembered his NATO code-names correctly.

'They suddenly realized they left us behind,' Copley said, but the joke was in the words rather than his tone.

All four of them were probably hoping the same thing, Docherty thought – that any moment now the door would open and someone would tell them that it was all over, and that they were on their way home.

But no footsteps sounded, and no one came for them. The sound of the rotors died, ushering back the silence.

Some three kilometres from the lodge Nurhan and the three Englishmen extricated themselves from the convenient area of shade they had discovered beneath a north-facing overhang and walked back down the path towards the checkpoint on the approach road. On the helicopter's return a few minutes earlier one of the two pilots had been taken out and pointed in their general direction.

They arrived at the checkpoint just as he loomed into view round the bend, walking briskly towards them.

His news proved neither better nor worse than expected. He and his co-pilot had dropped off their passengers on the other side of the Tajik border, and then one of the hijackers had flown the helicopter back. 'He watched us all the way on the outward flight,' the pilot said, 'and then took the controls himself on the return leg. He had obviously flown helicopters before, but probably nothing as big as an Mi-8.'

'That means they're mobile,' Brierley observed. 'We should think about destroying that helicopter,' he added.

'They're keeping my co-pilot on board.'

'Fuck.'

Shortly afterwards Muratov came through with confirmation of the co-pilot's whereabouts courtesy of

Nasruddin himself. The NSS boss also OK'd the after-dark reconnaissance for which Nurhan had requested permission.

'So how many?' she asked the SAS men.

'Just the two of us,' Brierley said, surprised. 'More than that would only add to the noise.'

'That makes sense,' she agreed. 'But this is a joint operation, so one of the two will be me.'

Brierley and Stoneham looked at each other. 'We've worked together before,' Brierley said. 'I don't want . . .'

'You don't want to wonder out loud what a liability a woman might be,' she said, 'but you're thinking it. Well, maybe I won't live up to your standards. Maybe you won't match up to mine. But this is my operation. Either I go with one of you two, or I go with one of my own men. I'd rather it was one of you two,' she added diplomatically, feeling a pang of disloyalty as she did so.

Brierley and Stoneham shared another look. 'I'll toss you for it, boss,' Stoneham said.

'Forget it,' Brierley said. 'Privilege of rank.'

'Shit,' Stoneham said.

'When do you think would be the optimum time?' Nurhan asked, wondering if she was taking her instructions to be nice too far. 'Around ten o'clock? There were still some lights burning at that time last night.'

'Earlier,' Brierley suggested. 'They won't be expecting anything soon after dark. And if it looks good we could even give the politicos the option of going in before dawn.'

They agreed on eight o'clock, and settled down to wait. Over the next few hours they were interrupted only once, by a radio message in Uzbek which first made Nurhan angry and then amused. But despite questioning looks from the three Englishmen she kept the news about Silcott and Kennedy to herself. Muratov was apparently *en route* from Tashkent to a new operational HQ in the Samarkand NSS building, and bringing the British Ambassador with him. The latter would no doubt be dealing with Kennedy in person.

Around four o'clock the call came through to say Pearson-Jones had arrived. He wanted to see Kennedy immediately, and requested that Brierley accompany the MI6 man back into town. Having been thrust into the role of negotiating for the British government, the Ambassador thought it wise to avail himself of the expert adviser who had been sent from England. A crash course was duly expected over dinner that evening.

'Looks like I'll have to fill in for you on the easy job then, boss,' Stoneham observed casually.

'Yes, I suppose you will, you little fucker,' Brierley admitted, without a great deal of grace.

14

Sabir put the glass of tea down on the polished surface of the long table, and Nasruddin absent-mindedly moved it on to one of the place-mats which depicted Soviet beauty spots. Noticing what he had done, he smiled wryly to himself. It was obviously OK to hijack a bus-load of tourists, but not to leave a ring on Bakalev's table.

'Where is Talib?' Akbar asked, almost angrily.

'He'll be here in a minute.' The Tajik was obviously feeling the tension, and Nasruddin could understand why. He felt nervous and uncertain himself, unsure of his own judgement. One part of his mind — perhaps the most rational part — was telling him that they had accomplished everything they had intended, and that now was the time to cut and run. Another part, which often seemed no less reasonable, was pointing out how much more they could extract from the situation now that Sarah Holcroft's identity was known to them. A third, almost incoherent, voice was crying out that here at last was his chance to make the bastards pay for everything.

All three voices were his, Nasruddin thought, just as Talib entered the room. He watched his cousin sit down opposite Akbar, carefully put two heaped spoonfuls of sugar into his tea and stir. Even doing something as ordinary as this, there was a stillness, a centredness, about his cousin which Nasruddin continued to find impressive. Sometimes he wondered why Talib deferred to him, what such a man could find to respect in a man like himself. Cleverness was the only thing that ever came to mind.

Well, they certainly needed clarity of thought now. Nasruddin set out to prove himself worthy.

'We are here to assess the options open to us,' he said formally, 'and to choose between them. But first I think we should discuss what response we should make to their action in cutting our access to the outside world. If any.'

'We could demand its reinstatement,' Akbar said.

'Only by threatening to kill a hostage,' Nasruddin argued. 'And I think they might call our bluff.'

'Would it be a bluff?'

'I don't know,' Nasruddin admitted. 'It seems to me that killing a hostage for such an unimportant reason would be seen as a sign of weakness.'

'It would,' Talib agreed. 'Especially if we have no need of such access. And that will depend on which of the possible paths we take from this place.'

'Then let us discuss that,' Nasruddin said, looking first at Talib, then at Akbar.

The latter spoke first. 'God has given us this woman,' he said, 'and we must use the gift wisely.'

'How?' Nasruddin asked brusquely.

Akbar was not disconcerted. 'We are agreed that the British must have bribed the regime to accept our demands?'

The other two nodded.

'That shows how far they are prepared to go to save this woman,' Akbar continued. 'I think we must find out how much they are prepared to pay us.'

There was a short silence, which Talib broke. 'No,' he said slowly, and looked straight at Akbar. 'I agree that God has blessed us with a gift, but not to use in this way.' He turned to include Nasruddin. 'What more do we need that they can give us? Our leader is free,' he said,

223

his mind going back to their short exchange of words in the helicopter, the awe he had felt in Muhammad Khotali's presence. 'But not enough of the people will hear of his release. The papers and the television will not report it, and they will not print the speeches he will make in exile. The regime will not allow his books to be published, or his cassettes to be sold in our markets. He will be a leader and a guide to those who know him and love him, but these will be few' – Talib smiled at them both – 'unless we bring him to them.'

'How do we do that?' Akbar wanted to know.

'It is simple. We turn this hostage-taking into a public seminar. In the name of the Imam we demand all those things which we know to be right, both from the British and the godless regime in Tashkent. It will not matter that such demands cannot be met – for a week or more we will fill the air with truth and light. I do not believe that Bakalev and his cronies can survive such an onslaught.'

The other two looked at him, the eyes burning in their sockets above the hooked nose.

'It is good,' Akbar said.

'And after the week?' Nasruddin asked. 'Won't a public defeat undermine what we have achieved?'

'Martyrdom is never a defeat,' Akbar said.

'I am ready to die,' Talib agreed, 'but while God has work for me here on earth I am also ready to live. After a week we can accept a compromise, release the hostages in the cause of mercy, and accept safe passage across the border, where the Imam will be waiting to welcome us. And our people will be talking only of things that matter once more, not wallowing in the corruption of the West.'

'I am for it,' Akbar said. His eyes were also shining at the prospect.

Nasruddin understood why. Though his rational self found flaws in Talib's programme, they seemed almost insignificant when compared with the potential harvest of souls. 'What are our demands to be?' he asked.

The appointment by telephone with Tashkent was still almost an hour away when Sir Christopher Hanson was admitted to the Prime Minister's Downing Street study. He found the PM working his way through the pile of briefings that had been prepared with the afternoon's education debate in mind, and not too unhappy to be interrupted. If the new matter in hand had been anything else, Hanson reckoned, he would probably have thrown the briefings in the air and let out a wild whoop.

Or maybe not. This Prime Minister was not noted for his spontaneity. In fact, Hanson couldn't remember a single PM who had been, except perhaps for Harold Wilson, and he'd only used it as a means of keeping other people off balance.

'There's no fresh information,' Hanson said. 'The lid is still on, at least for the moment.'

The PM ran a hand through his sparse hair. 'But for how much longer?' he asked rhetorically. 'And now that we're in the firing line, what are the Uzbeks going to do? Can we rely on them to carry on being discreet?'

On their continued discretion, Hanson mentally corrected him. The PM's way with words tended to falter under stress. 'There doesn't seem to be any profit to them in going public,' the Intelligence chief replied.

'Well, that's something, I suppose.' The PM scratched his head this time. 'But the moment it goes public we have to play it by the book,' he said. 'Her book,' he added as an afterthought.

Hanson nodded.

225

'Terrorism cannot be seen to pay,' the PM said, as if he was trying to convince himself. Or perhaps he was just rehearsing for the TV cameras.

'How is Alan Holcroft going to take it?' Hanson asked.

'God knows. How would you?' The PM looked at his watch. 'He'll be here any minute. Perhaps I should have excluded him – it seems almost cruel to ask a man to share in decisions which could kill his daughter.'

'But just as cruel to shut him out of a say in such decisions.'

'I know.'

Almost on cue, there was a rap on the door, followed swiftly by the appearance of the Foreign Minister. 'Any news?' he asked at once.

'No,' Hanson said. In one way Holcroft's face looked the same as ever, but in some subtle way it also seemed to have collapsed. There were now two faces visible, Hanson decided: it was as if the human face was pressing up against the inside of the official mask.

The PM waited until the Foreign Minister was seated, and then told him what he had just told Hanson, that in the event of the hijack becoming public knowledge it would not be possible to deviate from official government policy.

'I realize that,' Holcroft said tightly. He had just left an hysterical wife at home, and, had he but known it, every instinct in his body was urging him to go down on his knees and beg. But he had survived a lifetime in politics by severing the connections between brain and soul, and now all he could hear was the beating of blood in his temples and the mad racing of his heart.

The three men sat there waiting for the call.

It came through punctually, at 1400 hours GMT, and

the laborious business of holding a conversation through translators began once more.

President Bakalev seemed determined from the outset to placate those whom he was addressing. There was no mention of the British having concealed Sarah Holcroft's identity from him, or of the fact that it had been a British journalist who had let the cat out of the bag. Instead there were expressions of gratitude for the men who had been sent, and confident predictions that the business could still be contained and resolved outside the spotlight of publicity. They would all know more in the morning when the terrorists passed on their new demands, but in the meantime joint planning was under way in case decisive action proved necessary. He sincerely hoped that such co-operation between the two countries would continue, though of course in less harrowing circumstances.

The PM kept his own remarks to a minimum. After the call was over he let out a deep breath and shared a look of resignation with the other two. All they could do was wait.

They had been given no exercise that afternoon, and no reason why not. Perhaps the presence of the helicopter outside had something to do with it, but Isabel couldn't see why. It seemed more likely that the terrorists were feeling less generous since the breakdown of their deal with the authorities.

The women had been given a pretty good idea of what the alleged deceit had been. Twice that morning, eyes had appeared in the door hatch, and scanned the room before settling on the face of Sarah Holcroft. If they hadn't known before, they knew now.

Isabel put herself in the hijackers' position, something

she found alarmingly easy to do. With their new knowledge they would make new demands, and these would be either accepted or rejected. If it was the latter, then the hijackers faced their moment of truth – could they kill someone in cold blood?

Of course, they might have killed someone already. She had always thought that if something happened to Docherty or the children she would know it, but maybe she was just fooling herself. Francisco had been dead for days before she found out for certain.

'We ought to do something,' Brenda Walker said, her face suddenly looming over the rim of Isabel's upper bunk. 'Play a game or something.'

She was right, Isabel thought. They were all drifting off on their own. Like paper boats on a lake. She remembered a moment in the previous week, and her daughter catching her in mid-reverie. 'You're staring at *nothing*, Mama,' Marie had said.

'Good beer?' James Pearson-Jones asked.

He and Brierley were sitting on the balcony adjoining the former's recently taken room at the Hotel Samarkand, watching the last embers of the sunset fade in the western sky. The Ambassador was nursing his second G&T, and Brierley was into his second bottle of a surprisingly fine beer.

'Not bad at all,' the SAS man said.

'Probably German in origin,' Pearson-Jones said. 'During the First World War there were several camps for German POWs in this area. Then there was the revolution in Moscow, and Russia pulled out of the war, and of course all the POWs had to be released. Only problem was, they couldn't get home. Russia was in chaos, with civil war and famine breaking out all over, so the Germans had to wait several years before they could leave. In the meantime, being Germans, several of them started breweries.'

'Interesting,' Brierley observed politely. And he supposed it was, though considerably less so than reconnaissance jaunts with beautiful majors. That bastard Stoneham! Still, at least he hadn't been sent back to London with his tail between his legs, like that idiot Kennedy. 'What's happened to the woman journalist?' he asked.

'She's still locked up,' Pearson-Jones said. He grunted. 'If I had my way they'd throw away the key.'

'Her and the rest of the media,' Brierley said sourly.

'All right, let's run through it once more,' the Ambassador said, perhaps sensing something of Brierley's mood. 'I'll go over the points, and you can correct me if I'm wrong.'

'Right,' Brierley agreed, with more enthusiasm than he felt.

'Negotiating points,' Pearson-Jones began, holding up a fist to raise fingers from. 'One, try to keep the enemy in detail-coping mode. Overload him with decisions that don't really matter.'

One finger shot up. 'Two, always ask open-ended questions, ones that can't be answered just yes or no. Three, use their own rhetoric against them when possible. So if they keep going on about God, stress what a nice guy God was, and maybe they should try a bit harder to live up to him.' He smiled at Brierley, who smiled back.

'But?'

'But four, avoid ideological confrontation. In fact don't talk about God or sex or politics if you're afraid you might enrage the enemy by doing so. This is a thin line, isn't it?'

'Very. What's five?'

'Play down the importance of the hostages. Let the enemy know that they are not the *only* factor you are taking into consideration. There are limits as to how far you can or will go to save their lives.' A thumb joined the four raised fingers. 'Christ, this is depressing.'

'I know. Six?'

'Try and divide the hostages into groups, so that you can ask for their release bit by bit. The children first, for example. And then the women.'

'One more.'

Pearson-Jones searched the sky. 'Don't tell me . . . I know, avoid completely negative responses. Even if he says he wants a night with the Queen tell him you'll see what you can do.'

Brierley grinned. 'You can tell him it's unlikely she'll be in the mood, but don't slam the door entirely. Now the three general points.'

The fingers came back down again. 'Right. One, if they set deadlines try and talk through them . . .' He stopped. 'Who are we trying to get off the hook by doing that – them or us?'

'Both.'

'Hmmm, I see. Right. Two, make sure that their access to the outside world is as much under our control as possible. Pity that wasn't done two days ago. But it is under our control now, isn't it?'

'Not completely. They could be talking to supporters by radio.'

'Yes, I suppose they could. Oh. Three, manipulate their environment . . . I'm still not clear about this.'

'You don't really need to be. It's just that in the past

people have found that shutting off water, electricity, things like that, can wear down the terrorists' morale. One hostage-taker in the States actually surrendered rather than crap in front of his hostages, after the authorities cut off access to the toilet they were all using.'

Pearson-Jones sipped at his G&T. 'Sounds a bit like a two-edged sword,' he observed. 'Surely there's just as much chance of provoking a violent reaction.'

'Good point. You do have to play that one by ear.'

Pearson-Jones beamed, like a little schoolboy with a gold star.

Brierley looked at his watch. Stoneham and the Major would probably be on their way by now.

A hand on his shoulder woke Stoneham from his few hours of catch-up sleep. For a few seconds the strange surroundings disoriented him, but then he remembered he was in one of the locals' lorries. He stretched and groaned at the stiffness, and lay where he was for a few more moments, remembering the thoughts which had been spinning around in his head for what seemed like eternity as he tried to get to sleep. Bloody Jane! Even five thousand miles away she was still ruining his day. He had to talk to her, really talk to her, find out what had gone wrong.

He couldn't do that halfway up a mountain in the middle of Asia.

Work, he told himself. Concentrate on the here and now.

He edged himself the short distance to the open back of the vehicle, and found Major Ismatulayeva there waiting for him, dressed in what looked like a black boiler suit, her usually severe face looking softer in the pale light.

Work, he told himself again. 'Time to go?' he asked.

'It soon will be,' Nurhan said. She felt nervous. It was all very well insisting on taking at least an equal part in this operation – national and gender pride demanded no less – but she didn't want to end up making a fool of herself. Five years ago she would have seen no reason to worry, but over the last tumultuous few years the inferiority of just about all things Soviet had become painfully obvious. Specialist training might well turn out to be another case in point. She had done courses with the Spetsnaz special forces which had stretched her to the physical and mental limit, but who knew what these wretched English supermen could do?

'Make-up?' Stoneham asked her. He took a small canvas bag from his bergen, removed a handful of tubes from the bag, set up a mirror, and began spreading a dark cream across his face. 'It's not Helena Rubinstein,' he added.

'I'll use the mirror after you,' she said. 'Let's get some things straight. Like what we want to achieve from this.'

'Who's in which room, accurate ident on weaponry, access points,' Stoneham rattled off. 'Maybe an astrology chart for each terrorist, if we can manage it.' He daubed an artistic streak of lighter cream across the dark background. 'But the one thing we have to know before we go busting in there with a full team is where the hostages are being held. Even if that's the only thing we find out, then this little jaunt will still have been well worth taking. Your turn,' he said, stepping away from the mirror.

Nurhan stepped up to it, smelling the cream before applying it. In the good old Soviet days they had been told to find any dirt that was available. 'We've got another problem,' she said. 'They've turned on the searchlight under the helicopter, and they must have placed a mirror directly underneath it, because the whole area seems flooded with light.'

'Shit,' Stoneham said in English.

She understood the tone. 'Exactly,' she said in Russian. 'There's no way we can go in from behind – the whole rock-face is lit up.'

'Wait a minute,' he said. 'If most of the light is being reflected upwards then the ground must be in some sort of shadow, even if it's not actually dark.'

'Maybe,' she agreed. 'There's no way to tell from here.' She turned to face him. 'How do I look?' she asked.

'Like Catwoman in *Batman Two*,' he told her. 'But I don't suppose that's reached Samarkand yet.'

'It has,' she said coldly. 'Now what about signals?'

They decided on a basic selection of hand signals, and agreed that sub-machine-guns, while decidedly useful when it came to a fire-fight, might well get in the way if silent climbing became necessary. They settled for silenced automatics, in his case a Browning High Power, in hers the German SIG-Sauer P226. Both would carry walkie-talkies, for reporting in to Sergeant Abalov if necessary, and for talking to each other if they had occasion to separate.

They walked to the head of the path they intended descending and checked out the ambient light. The new moon had just risen above the mountain in front of them, but the valley below remained deep in shadow. Stoneham didn't think they needed the Passive Night Goggles, but just to be sure he donned them. The world turned greener but no clearer. He took them off again.

She smiled for no reason apparent to Stoneham, displaying white teeth in a blackened face.

'Don't do that too often,' he warned her.

'Do what?'

'Smile. Your teeth can reflect the light,' he explained.

'I'll try not to find anything amusing,' she said drily. 'Are you ready?'

He nodded, and she turned to start down the path. It looked no more than two hundred metres in a straight line to the bottom of the valley, but it was more like four by the winding path. By the time they were halfway down it seemed to Stoneham as if the rest of the world had been left behind: there were only the jagged rocks silhouetted against the star-strewn sky and a silence which was eerily complete. He felt his senses shifting into some sort of overdrive, and the familiar, almost glee-like intoxication with pure danger.

And even in the gloom he could see that she had a nicer bum than Rob Brierley.

He smiled to himself, saw Jane in his mind's eye, and felt a sudden wave of sadness wash over him. It wasn't a painful sadness though; it felt almost like an acceptance of the fact that she was gone.

They reached the bottom of the valley, where a thin swathe of dry pebbles marked the rainy season stream-bed. They could no longer see the lodge – only the aura of light which shone in the air above it. Nor could they be seen, except in the unlikely event that the terrorists had thermal-imaging equipment. Stoneham was guessing that the trick with the searchlight offered evidence that they did not.

Nurhan led off again, keeping as close to the winding stream-bed as the terrain allowed. The ground under their feet was sometimes bare rock, sometimes sandy soil with clumps of scrub-like vegetation. Visibility was often reduced by the rocks which tumbled down on either side, and which the stream-bed squeezed its twisting way between. Progress of any sort, let alone the silent progress required, was often difficult, and as they slowly climbed the valley each became more conscious of the road above and to their right, and the sentries whom they knew were watching it.

Every now and then they would stop and listen. On the first two occasions they could hear nothing but the faintest of breezes brushing against stone; on the third they heard distant voices floating down from at least fifteen metres above them. They couldn't make out any of the words, though it seemed to Nurhan that the language was Farsi.

They continued, finding that they needed to exercise ever-greater care not to dislodge loose stones on the steepening slope. The hunting lodge was only about two hundred metres away, but still visible only as a balloon of light beyond the rim of the shelf on which it sat. The last stretch was more of a climb than a walk, but at least they could tackle it in almost total darkness. As they neared the top Nurhan had the sudden memory of stepping out from the wings and on to the lighted stage for a school ballet performance.

She moved her eyes over the edge, and was almost blinded by the light. It took several seconds to make out the front of the lodge, the steep wall of rock behind the building and the shallower slopes on either side – all bathed in the reflected glow. In the foreground the bulbous shape of the transport helicopter stood in stark silhouette.

Nurhan beckoned Stoneham forward to join her, thinking what a brilliant idea it had been to mirror the searchlight. Not perfect though: the Englishman had been right – the ground wasn't in darkness, but with everything else so brightly lit a distant watcher would have a hard time picking out any movement across it. And there certainly didn't seem to be any close watchers in attendance.

Stoneham had reached the same conclusions. He raised his eyebrows at Nurhan, who hesitated for only a second before nodding her agreement. He carefully dragged his body over the rim and started moving, ever so slowly on his stomach, across the open ground towards the side of the house. She followed, thinking that someone was bound to spot them, and after ten of the thirty metres wanted to ask Stoneham if he could try speeding things up a little. She couldn't remember ever feeling more vulnerable; it was, she imagined, rather the way an ant must feel in the middle of a pavement.

But no shouts of alarm, no deadly bursts of gunfire, erupted in their direction. After what seemed hours, but was in fact slightly less than eight minutes, they reached the corner of the lodge and passed into deeper shadow. There they slowly got to their feet.

If they had only brought another four men, Nurhan thought, they could have ended this tonight. But then again, it might have been harder to get six soldiers here undetected than two. And they still didn't know where the hostages were.

But so far it had been easy, she told herself, just as the sound of footsteps inside the lodge spun both their heads round. The side door was only a few metres away, and the footsteps seemed to be heading their way. Stoneham gestured with his head and ran swiftly towards and past the door, with Nurhan at his heels. As the door opened outwards both of them pulled the silenced automatics from their belt holsters, sucked in breath and held it.

The door closed again to reveal a man walking away, an AK47 held loosely in his right hand. He disappeared around the corner of the house, chewing a hunk of bread.

Stoneham signalled for her to stay put and padded after the man. When he reached the corner of the lodge he stopped and slowly edged an eye around it. A minute later he was back beside her, drawing a diagram in the sandy soil with the end of his knife. A rectangle marked the lodge, a cross superimposed on a circle the transport helicopter, a thumb-mark the man who had just come out. He had taken up position covering the space they had just crossed, and was effectively blocking their way home.

Maybe that was his normal post, Nurhan thought, as Stoneham erased his drawing. In which case they had been extremely lucky to get this far.

But they had, and there was no point in wasting the trip. She started off towards the back of the lodge, turning another corner to find a long, narrow gap, about two metres wide, between the rock-face and the building. About four metres down they came to a window that had been thoroughly boarded up, with adjoining wooden planks nailed into the outside frame. Only the thinnest strips of light could be seen between them.

No noise was coming from the room beyond. They waited for about three minutes, hearing nothing, and were about to give up when a woman's voice suddenly broke the silence. It was faint, as if heard through more than one room. 'The water's almost gone,' it sounded like to Stoneham.

'This must be the toilet they're using,' he whispered.

'Should we try to talk to them?' she whispered back.

He shook his head. For one thing, they would need to almost shout to make themselves heard. For another, there was no way of being certain the hostages didn't have terrorist company. 'It's too risky,' he murmured.

She nodded, having reached much the same conclusion, and led off again down the back of the lodge, ducking to pass beneath several unbarred windows. At the far end they found another one lit and barred. Here male voices were dimly audible in two accents – American and Glaswegian. Docherty was still alive!

Stoneham gave Nurhan a thumbs up. They had got the info they most needed.

Now they had to get it home.

They slipped gingerly past the end door and approached the front corner of the lodge. Once more Stoneham put his eye round the edge of the building. The bread-eater was sitting about fifteen metres away, in a patch of shadow cast by the tour bus, his attention apparently fixed on the valley beyond. Their way in offered no way out.

They waited five minutes, and another five, hoping for some change in the situation. Taking the terrorist out with their silenced automatics would be easy enough, but the consequences of doing so were likely to rebound on others. There had to be a better than even chance that the other terrorists would take their revenge on one or more of the hostages.

The minutes ticked by. At this rate, she thought, they would still be here when the sun came up. There was no way up the rock-face behind the lodge, and crossing the slope in front of them would place them in plain view of the watcher. And there was always the chance that one or more terrorists would emerge from the door just behind them, trapping them between guns. Nurhan felt the beads of sweat running down her back.

Suddenly a door banged. The one at the front of the

lodge. Two men exchanged a few words in Farsi, and then, just as Stoneham was about to risk another look, a man crossed their line of sight, headed out on to the road, an SMG draped over his shoulder. A minute later he disappeared from sight around the first bend, and Stoneham edged forward to check out the bread-eater.

He was no longer in his original position, and Stoneham searched the shadows for him in vain. Had he heard the front door shut again as the man walked away up the road, or was that just wishful thinking?

'I think he's gone,' he whispered to Nurhan. 'And we probably won't get a better chance.'

'Right,' she said. Anything was better than more waiting.

He checked the situation once more. 'We'll just run, OK?'

'OK.'

The syllables were hardly out of her mouth and he was gone. She sprung into motion, following his spurt across the open space, swerving past the bus, under the Mi-8's tail rotor, expecting any moment to feel bullets crashing into her body, or at the very least to hear cries of discovery. The Englishman vaulted over the rim of the steep slope leading down to the valley, and Nurhan followed, leaping into dark nothingness, and landing almost on top of him. They both lay there, breathing heavily, listening for any other sounds.

A door banged quietly, and then nothing. The man had come back out, Stoneham guessed. This had been their lucky night.

She made a downward gesture, and they started working their way laboriously down the slope. An hour later they were back at the main observation point, where Sergeant Abalov had witnessed their race across the front of the lodge. Hot tea was waiting for them.

'We need some sort of diversion at the front,' Stoneham said, examining the plan of the lodge with the help of a torch, 'and two teams ready to knock down those side doors. Unless the guards are in with the hostages – which seems unlikely – we should have no trouble getting them all out alive.'

'And how do we get the teams there?' she asked.

'Down the rock-face at the back.'

Nurhan smiled to herself. She had reached the same conclusions as the man from the famous SAS.

Nasruddin lay on the bed unable to sleep, his mind whirring. Tomorrow they would be famous, he thought. Even if Bakalev managed to censor the Uzbek papers, still the world's press would carry The Trumpet of God into homes across the planet. There would be pictures on television, recitals of their demands, and people would begin to wonder why it was that men had to do such things for truth to be heard.

He supposed his sister and brother would read the news in their morning papers, his brother on his way to work at the Wakefield business he ran, his sister at the breakfast table after the kids had gone to school. He knew that they would not understand why, but he hoped that somewhere, deep down in their hearts, they would accept that he was following the dictates of his own.

Though sometimes it was hard to share his grief, he knew that they too had lost a mother to the flames, a father to a broken heart.

He shook off the memories, and embraced the future once more. Their demands would set the whole world talking, and Britain in particular. Islam had been abused for so long in his adopted country, but the tide was turning, had perhaps already turned.

"'But they shall know the Truth,'" he murmured to himself, ' "before long they shall know it . . . the Trumpet shall be sounded." '

15

The four male hostages were all woken by the rap of the hatch sliding back on the door. 'You leave in five minutes,' a voice said, and slid the hatch shut once more.

It was five forty-five and still dark outside. The men scrambled into sitting positions and stared at each other. Where were they going? The room they had occupied for the past sixty hours suddenly seemed more like home than it had before.

'Better get ready,' Docherty said, thinking it was almost amusing that they had been given five minutes' notice. The phrase 'gentlemen terrorists' came to mind, like an echo of the 'gentlemen crooks' who had peopled the thirties thrillers he had read and loved as a boy.

The four men had time to dress, have a piss and gather together their few belongings before the door swung open to reveal the familiar armed figure gesturing them out. Docherty smiled at him and led the way along the corridor which led to the outside world. Another terrorist was momentarily silhouetted in the front doorway, but stepped aside to usher them through. The large transport helicopter they had heard the day before was perched on the flat shelf in front of the building, its rotor blades reaching out across the void beyond, a bright light directly beneath its belly. The side doors were open.

As they walked towards them a man in uniform was brought out and led off on a diagonal path towards the ill-fated tour bus. He glanced across at the hostages but said nothing.

Approaching the helicopter, Docherty noticed a definite lightening of the sky above the mountain crest. The sun would soon be up. For the moment though it was still decidedly cool, and the dark interior of the chopper at least offered shelter from the wind.

The door slammed shut behind them, and the four men sat down on the floor, backs against the inside walls, and waited fearfully for the sound of rotors starting up.

Silence continued to reign, and as the minutes went by their hopes began to rise. Then the doors swung open again, and the face of Alice Jennings appeared in the space.

'Well, give me a hand,' she said.

Copley and Docherty helped her aboard, their eyes hungrily seeking out their own wives as they did so. Sharon Copley collapsed into her husband's arms with almost a sob of relief, and Isabel buried her head in Docherty's shoulder, murmuring '*A Dios gracias.*'

'How are you doing?' he asked, lifting her chin with a finger and looking into her eyes.

'OK, I guess.'

He shook his head. 'Some tour, this.'

Stoneham and Brierley were woken by one of Nurhan's men with a message to join her immediately at the observation point. They scrambled out of the lorry into the pre-dawn air and fumbled with the laces on their rubber-soled boots. 'It's probably just me she wants,' Stoneham mused. 'It was the recon. She spent the night trying to forget me, and found she couldn't.'

'No one could,' Brierley agreed.

They made their way swiftly up the winding path, down the gully to the OP, and squeezed in alongside Sergeant Abalov and Nurhan. The first thing they noticed was the sound of the helicopter rotors turning; the second was the glow of the dawn above the mountain behind the lodge.

'The hostages are on board,' Nurhan told them. 'The women were brought out about ten minutes ago; the men five minutes before that.'

'What about the terrorists?' Brierley began to ask her, but at that moment two things happened. First, the whirr of the rotors abruptly went up a gear, and the Mi-8 lifted itself ponderously into the air. Second, Nurhan had to take an incoming radio call from Muratov.

'They're on their way to Samarkand,' she told the two SAS men as the helicopter glided past them on its way down the valley. 'They called Muratov to demand that the sky over the city be cleared of traffic.'

'Where in Samarkand?' Brierley asked.

'They didn't say.'

In the crisis room on the second floor of the NSS HQ, Bakhtar Muratov and James Pearson-Jones were both slumped in their seats, as if KO'd by the latest message from the hijackers. Marat got up, left the room and walked down the corridor to his own office. Samarkand, he murmured to himself, as if it were a word he'd never heard before. They would be here in half an hour, or even less. But where?

Think, he ordered himself. There had to be a reason for leaving their mountain fortress. Had cutting their phone contact with the outside world forced them to make the move? Was it publicity they wanted? Were they headed for one of the tourist spots?

His mind flicked through the possibilities. Being an atheist, he wasn't too sure how Muslims felt about using holy ground for political purposes, but he couldn't imagine them risking the destruction of mosques and *madrasahs*. In any case, the Registan didn't seem a promising place to sustain a siege. Nor did the Bibi Khanum mosque. There were no suitable spaces for a landing anywhere near the Shah-i-Zinda. Which left the Ulug Bek observatory and the Gur Emir, Tamerlane's mausoleum . . .

Marat recalled something Nasruddin's cousin had said during one of their interrogation sessions, about how much Nasruddin had loved the story of the inauspicious tomb-opening in 1941. And then he remembered suggesting Tamerlane's mausoleum himself, during the dawn conversation with Nurhan in Shakhrisabz.

He looked at his watch. Fifteen minutes had already gone by. There would be no time for concealing troops or anything like that, so what . . .?

He spun on one heel and raced out of the office, taking the wide stairway down to the ground floor three steps at a time. Still running, he headed down a corridor which led to the operations room where the surveillance equipment was stored.

'Bugs,' he told the officer in charge breathlessly.

'How many do you want?'

'Just a few. But quickly.'

The man gave him a strange look and disappeared into a maze of cabinets. The seconds ticked by.

The duty officer ambled back. 'These do?' he asked.

Marat took one look, grabbed the small box of listening devices, and stuffed them roughly into his jacket pocket as he headed back down the corridor. On his way through the front doors he slowed sufficiently to examine his watch again. He had between ten and fifteen minutes, depending on how fast they were flying the damned machine.

The Gur Emir was three minutes away by car, but even at this early hour the traffic was already building and his car was a block away in the wrong direction. He decided he could get there on foot in under ten.

Marat started running, cutting across the wide boulevard and down the first side-street which ran in the general direction of the distant blue dome. It had to be less than two kilometres away, he thought, and tried to remember how long it had been since he had run anything like that distance.

The first few hundred metres seemed surprisingly easy, and Marat was congratulating himself on being in such good shape when his breath began to grow laboured and his calf and thigh muscles started showing signs of seizing up. He pushed himself across another street, dimly aware that a passing motorist was throwing abuse in his direction, and promised himself a second visit to the NSS gym. He thanked his lucky stars he had stopped smoking.

The dome grew slowly nearer, disappeared from view, and then, just as his legs were telling him that they could go no further, suddenly appeared only a hundred metres or so away, at the end of a cul-de-sac. He jogged towards it, clambered over the ornate stone wall which surrounded the complex, and almost stumbled through a side gate into the courtyard.

His watch told him he had run out of time. His mind tried to work out where to place the devices. Put yourself in Nasruddin Salih's place, Marat told himself. Where would you put the hostages? Where would you make your HQ? There were only two obvious sites for the latter. Marat started striding towards the administrative office and felt his left thigh seize up with cramp. He rubbed it a couple of times and hobbled on, trying to ignore the pain.

The door was locked but one of the small windows had been left on a latch, slightly ajar. He reached his hand through with the self-adhesive bug and managed to clamp it above the internal window frame. There was no way of knowing how visible it was from inside the room.

The main chamber of the mausoleum was next, and here he fixed a bug beneath the rim of Tamerlane's cenotaph. The old man would have approved, Marat thought, and limped back outside.

In the eastern sky a large dot was growing even larger. Marat scurried as best he could down the courtyard and across the stretch of grass in front of the mausoleum. With the drone of the helicopter now loud in his ears, he expended what felt like his final reserves of energy in almost falling over the wall, and managed to drag himself upright behind a convenient tree.

The helicopter came down out of the still-lightening sky, and settled on the barely adequate expanse of grass in front of the Gur Emir. Chunar, who had been selected to bear word of the operation to their supporters in the city, hurried towards the rear of the complex and disappeared into the adjoining maze of streets, several days' worth of communiqués stuffed inside his jacket pocket.

Talib, meanwhile, had left two men guarding the hostages, ordered another to carry their supplies into the building, and gone off himself in search of the site's caretaker. While the latter was nervously explaining which key was which on the jangling chain at his belt, Nasruddin and Akbar walked through into the courtyard. Above them the ribbed cantaloup dome seemed to almost float above the octagonal mausoleum. Nasruddin felt a sudden pang of unfocused regret.

'Come, we must hurry,' Talib said, arriving at his shoulder.

The three men walked swiftly across to the door of the administrative office, which Talib opened with the appropriate key. Nasruddin went straight for the telephone, taking the list of news-agency numbers from his pocket as he did so.

Meanwhile the hostages had been ordered out of the helicopter at gunpoint, and ushered in through the towering gateway. Several of them recognized where they were, having walked down to view the outside of the building on the evening of their arrival four days earlier. This time they had their guide with them, Docherty thought wryly.

Across the courtyard they filed, and into the octagonal chamber where the world's largest slab of jade served as Tamerlane's cenotaph. The actual graves were in the crypt below, where tourists were not allowed to go.

Hostages were. The ten men and women were ordered down a stone stairway into the company of Tamerlane's bones, with only each other and a single electric light-bulb to keep them company.

President Bakalev was woken by the bedside phone, and instantly knew something had gone wrong. He grabbed for the receiver, scattering pills and almost knocking over the glass of water. His wife groaned and turned over.

Muratov's report exceeded the President's most pessimistic expectations. The zealots had taken over Tamerlane's mausoleum! In the middle of Samarkand! How the hell could they keep a siege in the centre of the country's second city quiet?

They couldn't, as Muratov soon made clear. The first couple of foreign journalists had already been on the phone to the local government press office.

'Don't give them anything,' was Bakalev's instinctual response.

'We'll have to give them *something*,' Muratov said.

'Just the basics then – a bunch of armed madmen have taken some hostages and occupied the Gur Emir. Stress what an insult this is – profaning the tomb of the Father of Uzbekistan.'

'Understood,' Muratov said drily.

Another question occurred to Bakalev. 'How the hell did foreign journalists get wind of this?' he asked belligerently.

Muratov had hoped to avoid that one. 'The terrorists had about half an hour's use of the phone in the Gur Emir's administrative office before anyone thought to cut it off,' he said.

Bakalev looked at his bedroom ceiling and then closed his eyes. 'They no longer have access to the outside world?'

'No. Only a direct line to us.'

'Well, that's something.' Maybe the situation could still be contained, at least for a while.

'And we have listening devices in the Gur Emir,' Muratov added. He had been saving this good news until last.

'Have you heard anything?' Bakalev asked sharply.

'Not yet – we've only just set up the reception equipment.'

'Anything else I should know?'

'I don't think so. We should be hearing their new demands soon.'

'I can hardly wait.'

*   *   *

In London it was almost two in the morning, but Sir Christopher Hanson had only been sleeping a short while when the call from Pearson-Jones in Samarkand was patched through to him. He listened, with a sinking sensation in his stomach, to the same news with which Muratov had woken President Bakalev.

After replacing the receiver he lay back for a moment, before abruptly swinging his legs over the side of the bed and sitting up. This was going to be one of those nights, he thought. When the demands were released he would have to wake up the Prime Minister. And probably Alan Holcroft, though he didn't suppose the Foreign Minister was finding it easy to sleep these days.

He put on his dressing-gown, walked across to the window, and looked out through the gap between the curtains. A light rain was falling on the Kensington street and a couple were walking, almost dancing, arm in arm along the opposite pavement. They stopped to look in a skip and then walked happily on, oblivious to the rain, to ageing men watching them from windows, to terrorists in fabled Samarkand.

Lucky buggers, Hanson thought.

'I think it's time to tell them we mean business,' Talib said, letting himself into the Gur Emir's office. 'There's about two hundred soldiers out there, and one of them may take it into his head to be a hero.'

Nasruddin nodded, and read one last time through the list of demands they had decided on the previous evening. Then he picked up the phone and waited for the enemy to answer.

'Yes?' Muratov said, almost immediately.

'*Assalamu alaikam*, Colonel,' Nasruddin said cheerfully. He had come to enjoy these conversations, he thought. He didn't think he wanted to know why.

'Is the British Ambassador there with you?'

'I am,' Pearson-Jones said tightly.

'The first thing I must tell you both,' Nasruddin began, 'is that the hostages are being held in the crypt below the mausoleum chamber, and that if any attempt is made to rescue them – or if any action whatsoever is taken against us – then one of our men is stationed by the doorway, ready to throw a grenade down the stairs.' He allowed a slight pause before asking: 'Is that clear?'

'Very,' Muratov said quietly.

'We shall consider the stone wall that surrounds the site the border between our respective territories,' Nasruddin said. 'Any attempt on your part to cross that line will be considered the opening move of a rescue attempt, and we shall take the appropriate action. Understood?'

'Yes.'

'It is written that "Whoever fights for the cause of God, whether he dies or triumphs, We shall richly reward him".' Nasruddin allowed himself a theatrical pause before adding: 'So you see, we have nothing to lose here on earth.'

'If you say so.'

'I do. I shall now read the list of our demands.'

He cleared his throat.

'One, we demand the immediate release of all political prisoners in Uzbekistan. I have a list here of two hundred and seven men and women, which can be handed to one of your men at the gate.

'Two, we demand an extension of the current British blasphemy laws to cover Islam and other major religions.

251

'Three, we demand the cancellation of the trade deal about to be signed between the governments of Uzbekistan and Britain. The people of Uzbekistan will not be sold into a world of empty pleasures and materialism.

'Four, we demand payment by the British government of 500 million dollars to the Islamic Green Cross as reparation for its part in the massacre of half a million Iraqi citizens during the Gulf War.

'Those are the demands. In addition, we are prepared to exchange the hostage Sarah Holcroft for the British author Salman Rushdie.

'Copies of this communiqué will be circulated throughout this city and Tashkent during the rest of the day.'

Oh shit, Muratov thought.

'We expect a clear response by this time tomorrow,' Nasruddin concluded. 'Do you have any questions?'

Not really, Muratov thought. These were not demands that anyone with a shred of intelligence would expect to be conceded. The bastard hadn't even give them a real deadline – he just wanted a 'clear response'. No, this was a media circus in the making, a week or more of publicity for the fucking Trumpet of God.

'Mr Salih,' Pearson-Jones was saying, 'I will convey your demands in good faith to my government in London. I can even sympathize with some of them, though not of course with your methods. I am assuming you intend to release all the hostages if and when your demands are met. Might I suggest that you show good faith by releasing the two oldest hostages, both of whom must be in some danger from such a stressful situation.'

'You can suggest it,' Nasruddin said, 'but there will

be no release of any hostages until all our demands are met in full. I assure you Mr and Mrs Jennings are in good health.'

There was silence at both ends of the line.

Nasruddin put down the phone and looked at Talib and Akbar. 'So far so good,' he said.

'Did they sound surprised?' Akbar asked.

'Not really. Neither of them said anything until the British Ambassador tried to start bargaining. They are already playing for time.'

Talib grunted. 'Of course. We know our demands are not going to be met. But time is not on their side. The question is: do they believe we will kill the hostages if they try anything?'

'And what if they don't?' Nasruddin said. 'They cannot take the chance that we are bluffing.'

'They will try to find out whether we are or not. Probably not today, but tomorrow, or the day after. One of their soldiers might stray accidentally across the wall, or they'll cut the phone line again, or the electricity. They'll keep pushing. They won't break our rules too blatantly but they'll try to bend them.'

'We have already decided what to do in that situation,' Akbar said. 'We must make it hard for them to find an excuse.'

'And we can always choose to ignore any minor transgressions,' Nasruddin interjected. He sat back in the chair, hands behind his head. 'And in any case,' he said with a smile, 'they'll be too busy dealing with the public outcry at their own actions. Tomorrow our second communiqué will be released, and everyone will find out how the Uzbek government was promised English gold in exchange for the Imam, and how the British government was willing to abandon all its principles just because the daughter of a minister was involved.'

'That is all very well,' Talib said, 'but there still may come a moment when we are forced to choose between killing a hostage or surrendering the initiative. If they are not going to meet our demands, they will probably have to try something else.'

'We shall just have to be vigilant,' Akbar said. 'What else can we do?'

After listening in with the others to the terrorists' conversation, Muratov left the operations van and walked the kilometre or so back to his temporary office in the NSS building. They had been given a day to formulate a 'clear response' to the demands, and Muratov was in no great hurry to hear Bakalev's appreciation of the situation. Or lack of it.

What he wasn't ready for was the violence of the President's temper. 'If this is allowed to go on for days,' Bakalev half shouted, 'there's no way we can keep it quiet. We shall end up looking indecisive, stupid, opportunistic, inept ... you name it. Even if we manage to kill all the bastards the damage will have been done.'

'So what do you want us to do?' Muratov asked, finding a gap in the tirade.

'God knows. What I'd *like* is for you to find a way of ending this before tomorrow morning. If the whole business lasts less than twenty-four hours then it'll be forgotten just as quickly. The world press won't have time to descend on us. CNN won't have time to get their cameras here.'

Muratov examined the back of his own hand. 'And the hostages?' he asked.

'It'll look better if they're rescued,' Bakalev said. 'Or at least some of them. But first we need a good reason for going in, even if we have to invent one.'

'I'll see what I can do,' Muratov said.

'Good,' Bakalev said, and hung up.

Muratov sat at the desk for several minutes, leaning back in the chair, hands behind his head, eyes shut. Then suddenly they opened, and his lips twisted into a cynical smile. He picked up the phone again, and asked the operations room to put him through to the mobile incident room. 'I want copies of all the listening tapes sent over here,' he told Nurhan.

'So we start from scratch,' Stoneham had said, once the van doors had closed behind Muratov and Pearson-Jones. 'Tell us what's over there. What's the place called for a start?'

'The Gur Emir,' Nurhan said. 'It means Grave of the King. Tamerlane is buried in the crypt with his son Ulug Bek and about six others.' She passed across the floor plan which the Ancient Monuments department had sent over. 'The crypt is under the octagonal chamber, and there's only one entrance.'

'Great,' Brierley said sarcastically.

As the two Englishmen examined the diagram Nurhan went through a mental checklist. Two battalions of regular troops were holding the perimeter, and it had been made clear to their commanders that no one was to even lean on the stone wall, much less cross it. Men from her own unit were currently seeking out the best available vantage-points in the area surrounding the mausoleum complex. These would be used for general observation, but also be available for the half-dozen snipers who had been placed on standby. Two more members of her unit were sitting at the other end of the van with headphones on, listening to and recording the terrorists' conversation.

That had been a brilliant idea of Marat's, she thought, and wondered where he had got to. He had been in the van five minutes earlier.

She stretched her arms in the air. There was no more she could do, other than make contingency plans for a last-resort assault. And that, she guessed, would be days away – now that the terrorists were contained the bargaining would start in earnest. There would be no point in putting the hostages' lives at risk through action, unless it became apparent that they were more at risk through inaction.

There was even the building to consider. The ministries of both tourism and ancient monuments had already expressed their concern at what gunfire might do to the green alabaster tiling and blue-gold geometric panels. Blowing in the latticed windows was out of the question.

And who knew what Tamerlane would think of it all? The words 'If I am roused from my grave the earth will tremble' were allegedly written on the underside of his tombstone, and the last time anyone had tried to take a peek had been 21 June 1941. The Germans had invaded the Soviet Union the following day. A grenade exploding in his crypt might cause an earthquake. Or a nuclear war somewhere.

Her brain was addled, Nurhan thought, and for good reason – the past seventy-two hours had been decidedly light on sleep. She yawned, just as Marat reappeared with four steaming glasses of tea balanced in a cardboard box.

'And he remembered the sugar,' Stoneham said happily.

Brierley took his glass and placed it on the floor beside the floor plan. 'I think it's time we got to work,' he said.

16

Morning turned to afternoon, and the temperature kept rising as the sun started on its downward track. In the NSS building a retired sixty-eight-year-old Russian by the name of Alexander Kustamov was working on the tapes Muratov had given him, a nostalgic smile fixed almost permanently on his face. Two storeys above, Muratov was finishing a liquid lunch, and feeling a little sorry for himself. This was not why he had joined the Communist Party all those years ago.

In London the Prime Minister was watching Sir Christopher Hanson eat an early take-away breakfast of croissants and coffee, and trying in vain to prepare himself mentally for the days that lay ahead. The prospect of an extended hostage crisis, with Her Majesty's Government a distant and largely impotent bystander, was bad enough in itself. The news that the hijackers intended publicizing Britain's attempt to buy them off for Sarah Holcroft's sake was nothing short of catastrophic. The newspapers, the opposition, the goddam BBC – they would all have a field day. Except that it would go on for weeks. His chances of surviving it all were virtually non-existent.

In the mobile incident room in Akhunbabaeva Street Brierley and Marat were trying to work out the likely location of the six terrorists they suspected were inside the Gur Emir. It had been seven, but the appearance of fly-posters around the city announcing the terrorists' demands suggested that at least one of the original seven had flown the coop immediately after their early-morning arrival.

Brierley and Marat didn't have much solid information to go on – the layout of the mausoleum complex made visual sightings hard to come by, and the thick walls of its construction had defeated the thermal image intensifiers. Basically, the two men were building their suppositions on educated guesswork, the little information offered by the two listening devices, and common sense.

Their partners of the last couple of days had both been given a few hours to catch up on their sleep, Nurhan at home, Stoneham in the British Ambassador's suite at the Hotel Samarkand. Both had gone out like lights the moment their heads hit the pillow.

In the mausoleum crypt the ten hostages were slowly adjusting to the sudden turn of events. All four couples were still feeling the relief of reunion, but the drastic down-turn in their living conditions, and the definite feeling that the stakes had been dramatically raised, made for an increase in stress levels which each individual expressed in his or her own way. There wasn't much talking as the afternoon wore on, and the little that there was was mostly confined between partners. Neither the knowledge of what lay above them, nor the tombs which filled their prison, were conducive to optimism.

The doctored tape was brought to Muratov's temporary office in the NSS building soon after three in the afternoon. He sent down for a cassette recorder and sat there wondering about the ethics of what they were about to do. There weren't any, he decided. The situation in Central Asia had gone beyond ethics: now it was a simple choice between Us and Them, between a difficult future and a swift regression to the Middle

Ages. These men had to be defeated, and quickly. If that defeat also involved the death of the British hostages it was unfortunate, but not much more.

The recorder arrived. He inserted the tape, listened to the footfalls of the courier recede down the stairs, and pressed the play button.

It began with the voice of the man named Nasruddin, whom Muratov assumed to be the terrorists' leader. 'And what if they are just playing for time?' he asked.

'We have already decided what to do in that situation,' another man said. The voice was deeper, the accent probably that of a Tajik.

'Of course,' a third, rougher voice said. 'If our demands are not met by the day after tomorrow we will kill the hostages.'

'What else can we do?' the second voice agreed.

That was all there was. Muratov played it through again. It was an excellent piece of work – even though he was listening for the joins he couldn't tell where they were.

Of course it was too short, but he supposed this was only the centrepiece. More could be added to pad it out.

It wouldn't stand proper testing, but that didn't matter. There would be no court of law involved, only the press. After a couple of people had heard it then the tape could get conveniently lost or destroyed. Or even stolen by Islamic zealots in an attempt to save the reputations of the dead terrorists.

He reached for the phone.

It rang three times before the President answered it himself, sounding decidedly sleepy. Muratov explained what had been done, and then played the tape to Bakalev over the phone.

'It's brilliant,' was the President's response.

Muratov said nothing. He wanted instructions, not a blind Presidential eye.

'What's the situation like in the city?' Bakalev asked instead.

Muratov told him about the fly-posters which had begun to appear all over the old city. 'And there's a big crowd around the area we cordoned off,' he added.

'An angry crowd?'

'Not particularly. I'd say it was one of those crowds which doesn't really know its own mind yet. It could turn nasty, could turn into a street party.'

There was another pause, and Muratov could almost hear the wheels going round in Bakalev's mind. The revelations due out the next day, the sense of a populace slowly focusing its anger, the chance to end it all.

'Order your people in,' Bakalev said.

'This moment?'

'Use your discretion. But before dawn tomorrow. I will talk to the British Prime Minister, and tell him we have no choice. And send me a copy of the full tape the moment it's finished. With any luck we won't need to use it.'

Muratov listened to the click of disconnection, and turned off the recording instrument attached to his phone. He wondered how Major Ismatulayeva would like her new orders.

'Good morning, Mr President,' the Prime Minister responded dully. In London it was shortly after eleven in the morning, one of his teeth had just started aching, and another call from the President of Uzbekistan was the last thing he felt in need of. He wished he'd never heard of the damn place.

'Mr Prime Minister, we have received information

261

which suggests that the hostages are in imminent danger. Of course, I would not take such a crucial decision without consulting you, but from what we now know I feel certain that decisive action must be taken within the next twelve hours. Such action will involve an element of risk for the hostages, but we feel that doing nothing involves a much greater risk.'

'What is the nature of this information, Mr President?' the PM asked, hope rising in his throat. Could this be the miracle he had been praying for?

'As you probably know from your people here, the terrorists are under audio-surveillance. We have a tape of them saying that they intend to kill at least some of the hostages tomorrow if their demands are not met.'

There has to be a God, the PM thought. The matter was being taken out of his hands, and the blame for any subsequent disaster would stick to someone else.

'The experience of your men will help to minimize the risk,' Bakalev was saying.

This brought the PM back to earth, but only for a moment. He couldn't be held responsible for the proficiency of the SAS, and in any case the SAS themselves could hardly be blamed for any failure if they were operating under overall Uzbek control. They were all off the hook. 'I understand, Mr President,' he said. 'If, in your judgement, immediate action represents our best hope of saving lives, then we must take such action.'

'I am glad we see eye to eye,' Bakalev said. 'I would be grateful if you could immediately inform your people in Samarkand of your decision. I will inform mine. Let us hope for a happy outcome.'

'I agree, and thank you.' The PM put the phone down and, conscious of Hanson's eyes on him, managed to repress a smile of triumph. 'They want to go in,' he said shortly.

'Why? When?'

'Within the next twelve hours. As to why – they have found out that the terrorists intend killing hostages from tomorrow.'

'Found out? How?' Hanson asked suspiciously.

'Audio-surveillance. They have a tape.'

I bet they do, Hanson thought. He hadn't spent most of his life fighting the KGB without knowing what they were capable of. And MI6 had manufactured a few fake tapes of its own down the years.

'I think my toothache's gone,' the PM said suddenly.

Hanson looked at him. There were only two groups of people, he realized, who had ever had an interest in prolonging this business – the hijackers and the hostages. And both were expendable.

The name Simon Kennedy flickered across Hanson's mind, and he found himself hoping that the SAS had sent better men to Uzbekistan than he had.

Muratov and Pearson-Jones arrived at the mobile incident room together, shortly after four-thirty in the afternoon. They found Nurhan, Marat and the two Englishmen considering the aftermath of a simulated rescue bid, with black, blue and red pieces of folded card representing the hijackers, hostages and rescuers. None of the black pieces were still upright, but neither were four of the blue ones.

'Comrades,' Muratov began, inadvertently slipping into historic usage, 'our governments have taken a decision. You will mount a rescue operation tonight.'

Eight eyes opened wide with surprise. Nurhan was the first to react vocally. 'What!? Why? I don't understand.

263

Every expert in the world agrees that such situations should be played long.' She looked at Muratov, more bewildered than angry.

'Those are your orders, Major,' Muratov said lightly. 'The whys are in the political realm.'

That was not what she wanted to hear. 'If you think . . .' she began.

Brierley cut her off in the same language. 'These are British lives at stake,' he told Pearson-Jones. 'Does London really support this?'

'Yes,' Pearson-Jones said quietly, not looking Brierley in the eye. 'It has been decided that a speedy end to the crisis will be in everyone's interest.'

Brierley indicated the fallen blue figures on the table. 'I don't think the hostages would agree with you,' he said coldly.

'If you want to help them,' Pearson-Jones said in English, 'then I suggest you stop worrying about why and start thinking about how.'

Brierley waved an arm angrily, but said nothing more.

Nurhan wasn't finished. 'If I'm to lead my men into a situation like this then I think an explanation is in order,' she said quietly.

'I can't give you one,' Muratov told her. 'It's not in my control.' He was wondering how she and Marat would react if and when the faked tape had to be used. Angrily at first, no doubt. But she would understand the need. They were all on the same side in the end.

She bowed her head. If someone had to lead her unit in, then she would rather it was her.

'Who dares wins,' Stoneham muttered.

* * *

'I've been in some strange places in my time,' Docherty observed, 'but this really takes the biscuit.'

He had an arm round Isabel's shoulder as they sat against one of the tombs in the dimly lit crypt. It was decidedly cool now, though not at all damp. The other eight hostages were scattered round the room, like children playing hide-and-seek in a graveyard.

He wondered if anyone was coming to find them.

Across the crypt someone was softly crying – Sharon Copley, it sounded like. Docherty could just about hear the murmur of her husband's voice as he tried to comfort her.

'I could do with a pint of Guinness,' Isabel said softly.

'Aye. With spring-onion-flavoured crisps. Outside on a summer evening. That pub we found on Mull that was miles from anywhere.'

'Where Marie threw the dart into the German tourist's leg.'

'That's the one.'

She looked up at him with a smile. 'I want you to know how much I love you,' she said.

It was rapidly growing dark now, and the dome of the Gur Emir was a deepening silhouette against the western sky. Brierley and Stoneham stood looking at it from the other side of Akhunbabaeva Street, imagining the ten hostages gathered in the crypt below ground level.

'If we could only find some way to give them advance warning,' Brierley murmured. 'It obviously can't be visual, so it has to be sound of some sort . . .'

'Eleven gunshots,' Stoneham suggested, not very seriously.

'Brilliant. First off, they'd have no reason for counting

them, or at least not until it was too late. Second, they'd have no reason to think it was a message at all, let alone one aimed at them. Third, even if all that's pure pessimism on my part, and they're all happily counting up to eleven and saying, "Hey, that means there's a rescue coming in at eleven o'clock tonight", what makes you think the hijackers wouldn't have come to exactly the same conclusion?'

Stoneham grinned at him. 'No one can rubbish an idea like you can,' he said with mock admiration.

'Well, think of a better one. It has to be something they'll know is aimed at them.'

'And something they will recognize but the hijackers won't.'

'Right,' Brierley agreed, 'so what separates them?'

'They're foreigners,' Stoneham said, only half in jest. 'Different cultural references. I bet none of the hijackers would know who Arthur Daley was . . .'

'Or recognize the *Coronation Street* theme music,' Brierley mused.

'Except for Salih,' Stoneham reminded him. 'In most ways he's as British as we are.'

'Shit, yes.'

The two men stood in silence for a few moments, watching the orange sky turn yellow-green behind the mausoleum.

'I've got an idea,' Stoneham said eventually.

'I hope it's better than the last one.'

Stoneham ignored that. 'You ever see the film *Rio Bravo*?' he asked.

'Probably.'

'Well, John Wayne and Dean Martin and the others are holed up in this town with a prisoner, and the prisoner's brother has the town surrounded, and there's this slow

Mexican music playing in the distance and John Wayne says it's getting on his nerves and why haven't they heard from the chief bad guy. And Ricky Nelson looks up at him and says something like "He's talking to us now." Turns out the music is some sort of death march, which means no quarter will be given when the time comes.'

'You think we should try scaring this bunch to death?'

'No, you idiot. I'm saying we should use music. That's culture-specific, isn't it?'

'Not really. You can hear Michael Jackson anywhere.'

'Make it even more specific then. How old is Docherty? What sort of music does he like?'

'He's about forty-five. If he likes rock, then it would probably be the sixties stuff he grew up with . . .'

'That would be perfect. Salih is almost twenty years younger, so the chances are he wouldn't recognize it.'

'Sounds good. But what sort of song has the word "eleven" in it?'

'God knows. But . . .' Stoneham's face lit up. 'I've got it. Remember the song "In the Midnight Hour"?' He sung the first line softly – ' "Gonna wait till the midnight hour . . ." We can put the op back an hour.'

'Maybe,' Brierley agreed, grinning in spite of himself. 'But what if Docherty's an opera freak and Salih's got a huge collection of American soul records back in Bradford. And how the hell do we find a copy of the record in Samarkand, or are you planning to sing it at the top of your voice?'

'Don't quibble,' Stoneham said. 'These are all mountable obstacles, as my grandad used to say whenever my grandma let him watch *Charlie's Angels.*'

*   *   *

It was early in the afternoon when the call came through to Dave Medwin. He heard the request, and asked for an explanation, but none was forthcoming. Salih's sister was the best bet, he decided, and reached for the phone.

'Is there any more news?' she asked, after he'd identified himself.

'Not that I know of,' he told her.

'Then what . . .'

'This may sound like a daft question,' Medwin said, 'but can you tell me what Martin's musical tastes are? And were.'

In Hereford, meanwhile, Barney Davies was phoning round the men who had seen serious service with Docherty. He eventually got what he wanted from Razor Wilkinson.

The Londoner's old Platoon Commander was apparently more than a little partial to Motown. 'You know what Scots are like – if they don't have a strong beat they lose concentration when they're dancing, and they fall over,' Razor told the Regimental CO, before it occurred to him that the original request for information was somewhat unusual. He found it even more upsetting when Barney Davies refused to tell him anything more.

In London, MI6 had dispatched a secretary to Denmark Street in a taxi, and her fifteen-minute search through several shops finally turned up sheet music for both 'In the Midnight Hour' and – another Stoneham contribution – Gladys Knight & The Pips' 'Midnight Train to Georgia'. These were then faxed via the British Embassy in Tashkent to the NSS building in Samarkand, where a young Uzbek music student was waiting with his tenor saxophone.

* * *

Darkness had fallen in the world outside, but to those entombed in the crypt the coming of night showed only on their watches. The single bare light-bulb gave off its meagre glow, aided and abetted by the light filtering down through the open doorway at the top of the steps.

The atmosphere was better than it had been a couple of hours earlier, offering new confirmation of the old adage that, given enough time, it was possible to get used to just about anything. All ten of them had played the alphabet film game, and had followed it up with a biographical Twenty Questions. Alice Jennings had survived her twenty as Amelia Earhart, but Mike Copley's Tamerlane had just fallen at the third. It was in the middle of Brenda Walker's 'dead, female and not English' that Sharon Copley first noticed the sound of distant music.

Once she had picked it up, the others strained to do the same. Some could, some couldn't – it was very faint. Docherty suggested they move around the crypt in search of the best reception, and they all did so, feeling rather silly, like adults playing a children's game.

But it worked. For some strange reason the acoustics were best in the unlikeliest of positions – deep inside the alcove behind the stone steps. It was a single instrument that was being played, a brass instrument of some sort. And the tune was one that Docherty, both Copleys and Elizabeth Ogley recognized immediately: 'In the Midnight Hour'.

Only Docherty and Sharon Copley recognized the succeeding 'Midnight Train to Georgia'.

'Midnight,' the Scot said softly, excitement in his voice. The other nine faces all looked his way, as if they were waiting for his instructions. In the yellow light each face seemed to reflect a different blend of fears, hopes and anxieties.

The saxophonist now seemed to be improvising, and for a few moments Docherty wondered if it was only an enormous coincidence. But then the player reprised the opening line of 'Midnight Hour', before striking out on his own once more.

'Gonna wait till the midnight hour ...' It was no coincidence. There was a bunch of lunatics from Hereford out there.

Upstairs, all the doors in the octagonal chamber were closed, and the music was only slightly more audible. Nasruddin, sitting in one of the cushions they had brought in from the adjoining chambers of the *madrasah*, thought at first it might be a signal of some sort, and got to his feet to listen more closely.

Minutes went by and nothing happened, except that the musician seemed increasingly uncertain of what he was playing. It had to be a music student who lived in one of the houses behind the Gur Emir, Nasruddin decided, busy practising vaguely familiar Western tunes on his Western instrument. He probably wanted a job in one of the hotel bands, and dreamed of appearing on one of the new pop music TV shows.

He had liked such music once himself, Nasruddin thought. The Jam, the Clash, Talking Heads. He remembered getting his mother to listen to the Sex Pistols' 'God Save the Queen'. She had been outraged.

He leaned up against the enormous jade slab which marked the spot above Tamerlane's grave in the crypt below, and looked up at the ceiling, which seemed to sparkle like faint silver stars in the dim light. This is paradise, he thought, as seen from death's entrance door.

The other five men were also in the chamber – Shukrat and Akbar standing sentry by the north and south doors respectively, while Sabir and Farkhot slept on beds of cushions by the wall between the north and east doors. Across the chamber from them, Talib was squatting beside the top of the steps which led down to the crypt, AK47 in one hand, grenade in the other, an open Koran between his knees. Nasruddin didn't see how Talib could read in such light, but then his cousin seemed to know most of the suras by heart in any case.

In the mobile incident room, once the plan of assault had been agreed, the evening seemed to crawl by. It had been argued by Brierley, and somewhat reluctantly conceded by Nurhan, that using the entire Anti-Terrorist Unit would be counter-productive. There were only a limited number of entrances to the mausoleum, and it would be easier to reach them in silence with five men than twenty. For much the same reason, it had been decided that, with the exception of the sector including their point of ingress, the cordon of regular troops deployed around the mausoleum complex would be given no advance information of the rescue bid. The Unit's two sniper posts would be in constant touch with the assault party in case the need for covering fire arose, but most of those in the vicinity would only know something was happening when the first shots rang out.

The figure of five had originally been suggested by Nurhan, mainly on the grounds that the members of her unit should at least outnumber Englishmen when it came to operations in Samarkand. She got her ways as regards the number, but Marat's insistence on being one of the five – 'I'm head of the Tourist Protection Unit, and if this isn't tourist protection then I don't know what is' – meant that only Sergeant Abalov could be included from the Unit.

The composition of the team once settled, the one woman and four men had gone over the plan twice. Once certain they knew what was expected of themselves and each other, they had driven the incident room around the other side of the complex and settled down to wait, mostly in silence, for the appointed hour to arrive. Brierley's thoughts were only of the operation to come, but Stoneham couldn't keep images of Jane and his unnamed son from occupying his mind. Nurhan occasionally caught Marat looking at her, and wondered whether she would risk going out with him. He was finding that daydreaming about making love to her was one of the better ways of coping without a drink.

At eleven-fifteen they started on their final preparations, and at exactly eleven-thirty they filed out of the mobile incident room and into the street. It was a clear night, with the stars dazzling in the sky above, and a yellow crescent moon only recently emerged from behind the mountains. The two SAS men were carrying Heckler & Koch MP5SD sub-machine-guns, the three Uzbeks Kalashnikov AK74s, the upgraded version of the AK47. The two MP5s had aiming point projectors fixed above the barrels, the three Soviet weapons a more primitive but equally effective torch.

The two SAS men were carrying spare magazines for the MP5s in pouches on their left hips, and one spare magazine for the holstered High Powers on their right wrists. Brierley also carried the Remington 870 shotgun, Abalov the rope ladder. All five of them were wearing body armour and communications helmets, and carrying stun grenades, CS gas grenades and gas respirators.

At eleven-forty they reached the low stone wall which

had been declared inviolate by the terrorists, and halted for something like five minutes, scanning the moonlit ground in front of them with both the naked eye and nightscopes. Nothing was moving. The terrorists, as expected, were all inside the complex walls.

Brierley led the way across the wall, closely followed by Nurhan, and the five of them walked swiftly across the short, yellowed grass towards the four-metre wall which surrounded the courtyard. Stoneham got down on his haunches for Brierley to climb aboard his shoulders, then straightened himself out to lift the senior man up the wall. With his eyes only an inch or so beneath the top, Brierley took a deep breath and heaved himself up on to the top of the wall. A few bits of stonework fell down the far face and landed with a pattering sound on the stonework below.

Brierley didn't move for a full minute, his ears straining for any sound in the courtyard below. There was none, and he slowly moved himself into a position from which he could verify with his eyes what his ears had already told him, that nothing was moving in the courtyard beneath him but the branches of the trees away to his right. Slightly to his left, some twenty metres away, the south door to the mausoleum chamber was closed.

So far so good.

He beckoned for Nurhan to join him. Stoneham did the honours once more, and Brierley helped her up on to the wall beside him. Abalov then sent one end of the ten-metre rope ladder spinning up towards them, rather like a fisherman casting his tackle. Brierley lowered half the ladder down the inner face of the wall, checked that Abalov and Stoneham were ready to take his weight, and swiftly descended to the ground. Nurhan followed him. The two of them held the ladder for Stoneham to climb up the other side, and then Marat and Abalov took the strain as he climbed down into the courtyard.

Brierley looked at his watch, and raised four fingers to show the others it was four minutes to midnight. While Marat and Abalov worked their way around to the entrances which opened off the corridors from the north and east doors, the other three squatted down in the shadows beneath the wall and put on their respirators. They looked, Stoneham thought, like Dr Who's Cybermen.

At exactly one minute to midnight they rose together, Brierley and Nurhan heading for the east door, while Stoneham, still wishing he had a more active role, made for the side door which constituted the terrorists' last possible escape hatch. As they walked stealthily across the courtyard the sound of loud talking, even shouting, could be heard from inside the mausoleum chamber.

Nasruddin heard it too. He had only left the octagonal chamber a few minutes before, having passed through the north door and into the adjoining administrative office in search of a pencil to copy down a particularly beautiful line from the Koran's 'Night Journey' sura. He walked back through, and found everything as normal.

'They wanted more water,' Talib explained from his position at the top of the steps. 'Akbar has gone down.'

Nasruddin nodded and checked his watch. It was midnight. He looked up suddenly, his mind racing with the words 'Gonna wait till the midnight hour . . .' That was the song.

It had been a signal.

Ten metres away, on the other side of the south door, Nurhan stood to one side, wondering what the Ancient Monuments people would say if they could see what Brierley was aiming the Remington at.

The gun boomed once, twice, and the hingeless door tottered for a second before Brierley shoved it aside. He and Nurhan flattened themselves against the edges of the frame, hurling stun and CS gas grenades through the opening as they did so. A dazzling light flashed out across the courtyard as the thunder sounded.

In the crypt the first blast of the shotgun jerked Akbar's head around, and Docherty launched himself across the three-metre space between them, hitting the Tajik with the concentrated force of an American linebacker in full motion. The AK47 went off, scattering bullets across the ceiling, and then flew out of the terrorist's hand as he hit the floor. Docherty landed on Akbar's chest with a force which probably broke several ribs, and a horrible wheezing noise erupted from the man's throat.

Nurhan and Brierley had stepped through the doorway, the siting-lights on their SMGs searching for targets. A man came into view directly across the chamber, coughing and spluttering. Two concentrated bursts slammed him against the far door.

On the wall to the right one man was halfway to his feet, another trying to bury himself in his hands. Both died instantly, their blood splattered across the onyx marble panels which lined the wall behind them.

Nurhan's torch beam moved right, just in time to catch a door closing behind someone. Brierley's moved left, and the lighted red dot from his aiming point projector alighted on a man's face. He pulled the trigger just as the face dropped from sight down the steps leading to the crypt.

Docherty looked up to see Talib bumping his way down the first few steps, took in the grenade in the terrorist's hand, the eyes that still seemed to burn in the bloody shattered face, and lunged for Akbar's AK47. As the Scot turned, his fingers reaching for the unfamiliar trigger, Talib, his broken face a study in demented concentration, drew the pin from the grenade, and stared around in triumph. Docherty fired, ripping the man's chest apart, and with a last loud sigh Talib crumpled forward on the steps, the hand that still held the grenade crushed beneath him.

A few seconds later it exploded, showering the crypt with a martyr's flesh.

Nasruddin had instinctively pulled the door shut behind him as he stepped back into the passageway. It was over, he thought, and that was cause for sadness, but somehow he felt a sense of relief.

He stood in the corridor for only a second, and then calmly opened the door of the chamber opposite the administrative office. He walked across it, and waited for a moment by the door leading out into the courtyard. The only sounds he could hear were coming from the corridor he had left behind.

Nasruddin pulled back the bolts and opened the door on to the night.

A man in a helmet was silhouetted against the stars, as he had been all those years before.

Nasruddin had no weapon, but it would have made no difference if he had. His limbs were frozen in the shock of recognition, and his finger on a trigger would have needed a thousand times the time it took for Stoneham's MP5 to blow his life away.